My City, My Home

Published by Sampad South Asian Arts & Heritage
c/o Midlands Arts Centre, Cannon Hill Park,
Birmingham, B12 9QH

www.sampad.org.uk
Registered charity no 1088995

First Edition 2021

This selection and edition – Sampad South Asian Arts & Heritage
2021

ISBN 978-0-9565416-7-3

Cover design by Buzby Bywater and Dave Walsh Creative

Formatted and printed by Beamreach www.beamreachuk.co.uk

My City, My Home

Edited by:

Partha Mandal

Zarah Alam

Anne Cockitt

Natasha Uzair

Mohammad Farooque

Sampad

south asian arts & heritage

Awards for winning writers sponsored by:

Mian & Co Solicitors

Dr Padmesh Gupta

Dr Sugat Raymahasay

Transforming Narratives

Transforming Narratives is a ground-breaking project that supports creative and cultural practitioners and organisations in Birmingham to engage in exchange with artists and organisations in cities in Pakistan and Bangladesh.

We offer a range of platforms for new artistic voices, exchanging narratives around contemporary lived experience across the three countries.

Transforming Narratives aims to build meaningful and enduring relationships between the cultural sectors in Birmingham, Pakistan and Bangladesh, for now and the future.

It is managed by Culture Central, supported by Arts Council England and delivered in collaboration with The British Council.

www.transformingnarratives.com

Sampad

Sampad is a dynamic development agency connecting people and communities with British Asian arts and heritage. Based in Birmingham, it plays a significant role regionally, nationally and beyond in breaking down barriers, raising critical issues, amplifying unheard voices and celebrating creative talent.

Within the *Sakshi* (meaning witness) strand of programming Sampad aims to establish dialogue, develop and nurture skills and build up trust with women in South Asian communities. Believing in the arts as an influential vehicle for provoking and catalysing change, Sampad has a firm track record of using the arts to address meaningful and pertinent issues in today's world; *Anon* (with WNO - 2014), an opera echoing the universal voice of exploited women; No Bond so Strong (for Bedlam festival) a life affirming show about motherhood among others.

Continuing over 30 years Sampad looks forward to working within a strong and thriving cultural sector with south Asian arts and Heritage at its most exciting, inclusive, progressive and innovative best.

www.sampad.org.uk

Support received from:

BRITISH COUNCIL

Supported using public funding by
ARTS COUNCIL
ENGLAND

TRANSFORMING NARRATIVES
BANGLADESH | BIRMINGHAM | PAKISTAN

Birmingham
City Council

Introduction

The theme *My City My Home* has strong personal resonance with me in the same way that it connected with many women who responded to our call for this writing competition.

The conundrum for many women to meet expectations from others and follow their fate to destinations known and unknown, to create a nest with love and care inspired the idea for this project. We posed these provocations - *Where is home? Where do I belong? What are my memories? What are my dreams? Is this city mine? Do I love my city? Does the city embrace me? Have I made a home? Who is telling my story? What memories can we make for the future? Who are the faces of our cities? Where is the soul of the cities? In its people or the buildings? Who is in the dialogue? What do we want to celebrate?*

It was greatly rewarding to receive writings from the many unheard voices of women who shared their emotions, ambitions, joys, dreams, disappointments, resentment and pain. Their words resonate with each other towards a place of strength, identity and belonging. We connect in their personal journeys and treasured memories and it is a delight to be able to share them with you. As the world is reeling under the impact of a pandemic *My City My Home* illuminates the possibilities of uniting women across nations to express poignantly that they do have the power of words that can make a difference in our societies, now and in the future.

I am grateful to everyone who became a part of this project and helped us through challenges of producing a multilingual writing competition.

We would not have been able to achieve this without our amazing team of Project Associates in Bangladesh, Pakistan, and Birmingham. Together we were able to reach, enthuse and support communities and individuals to write in their own choice of language with confidence. It was extremely important to recognise and value the diversity of languages as a critical part of our culture and identity. Accordingly, Bangla, Urdu, and English sit side by side in this publication.

Happy reading !!

Piali Ray, OBE
Director
Sampad South Asian Arts & Heritage

Adjudicators

Rukhsana Ahmad

https://www.rukhsanaahmad.com/
Agent: Diana Tyler at MBA Literary Agents

Rukhsana has written and adapted plays for the stage and BBC Radio, achieving distinction in both. Credits include: *Wide Sargasso Sea*, finalist, The Writers Guild Award for Best Radio Adaptation and *Song for a Sanctuary* Finalist, CRE award for best original radio drama. Adaptations for the BBC include: Salman Rushdie's *Midnights' Children*, Nadeem Aslam's *Maps for Lost Lovers* and Molly Keane's *The Far Pavilions*. Her stage play, *River on Fire*, was a finalist for Susan Smith Blackburn Award. Other plays: *Mistaken: Annie Besant in India, Letting Go,* and *Homing Birds* Fiction: *The Hope Chest* and *The Gatekeeper's Wife and other stories*. Translations: *We Sinful Women,* a collection of contemporary Urdu feminist poetry and *The One Who Did Not Ask,* by Altaf Fatima.

Rukhsana is a co-founder of Kali Theatre Company and SADAA. She has served on various panels at the Arts Council of England and The Writers' Guild of Great Britain. She was the Royal Literary Fund Fellow at Queen Mary's, University of London and is currently comitted to the RLF's Social Sector projects: *Tall Stories* for Room to Heal and Reading Round.

Trisha Bhattacharjee

Trisha is a Bangladeshi background theatre artiste, musician and singer, worked in a non-profit theatre group, named 'theatrEX Bangladesh'. She is living in the UK since 2017 and exploring her artistic skills with various UK-Bangladeshi arts and community organisations in London, Birmingham, Manchester and Glasgow.

Trisha is an experienced school teacher and music performer in theatre. Her performance credits including acting of over 5 plays, music and percussion of over 10 plays, conducting workshops with school children, theatre groups and arts & community organisations of over 25 in Bangladesh, India, England, Scotland and the US.

Sudip Chakroborthy

Sudhip teaches at the Department of Theatre and Performance at the University of Dhaka and currently studying PhD at Goldsmiths, University of London. He has published in the many peer reviewed journals and co-authored a research book on the 'Traditional Games of Bangladesh' that was published by UNESCO and Tencent. His papers presented in the seminars titled 'Women in the traditional theatre of Bangladesh' at the National Academy of Fine and Performing Arts Bangladesh, 'Memory and identity' at Queen Mary, University of London, at the TaPRA conference at University of Oxford, and at the 'Iran International University Theatre Festival' at Tehran University. He is actively involved with numerous national and international theatre creations, workshops, seminars and festivals including India, Bhutan, South Korea, Iran, France, England, Scotland,

Wales, US and Canada. Sudip's directorial plays have been showcased at 'Tin Forest' during Glasgow Commonwealth Games 2014, at 8th Theatre Olympics in Delhi, and so on. Sudip has contributed to the workshops and masterclasses for the UK Bangladeshi diaspora community theatre-makers in co-operation with the London Borough of Tower Hamlets since 2013.

Leesa Gazi

Leesa is a British Bangladeshi writer, actor, award-winning filmmaker, and Joint Artistic Director of an arts company Komola Collective. She was the script-writer and performer of Culturepot Global's 'Six Seasons' and 'A Golden Age' at the Southbank Centre. Gazi collaborated as the Cultural co-ordinator and a voice artist for Akram Khan's 'Desh' and 'Chotto Desh'.

Gazi is the concept developer, co-writer and performer of the theatre production Birangona: Women of War with her company, which she later developed into the documentary film Rising Silence. The film directed by Gazi sheds light on the lives of rape survivors in the aftermath of the Liberation War of Bangladesh which has won multiple international awards.

The English translation of her Bengali novel, 'Rourob' entitled 'Hellfire' tr. Shabnam Nadiya was published in September 2020 by Westland Books. She is currently working on her feature film 'Barir Naam Shahana' - 'A House named Shahana'.

Justina Hart
www.justinahart.com @justinahart_

Justina is an award-winning poet, multi-disciplinary writer and performer, whose poems have been shortlisted for the Poetry School's national pamphlet competition and widely anthologized. Most recently, she won first prize in the long poem category of the Second Light poetry competition (2020) and was shortlisted in the Wolves Lit Fest poetry competition (2021). She has written creative pieces for institutions as diverse as the Woodland Trust, the V&A Museum of Childhood and the number 73 Routemaster bus.

In 2018 Justina received a British Council/Arts Council Artists' International Development Fund Award to take her poem sequence about past climate change, *Doggerland Rising* (commissioned by Durham University, Arts Council England, and arts/ecological charity TippingPoint) to new audiences, writers and literature professionals in Australia, where she was also invited to read alongside the New Zealand poet laureate. In the UK Justina has performed her work at the Hay Festival, Durham Book Festival, Birmingham Literature Festival and Free Word in London.

After a career as an arts, education and travel journalist and commissioning editor for national newspapers and international online organisations, she now runs her own creative writing programmes and reviews for poetry magazines. From 2016 to 2020 she co-organised showcase events for emerging regional writers - fellow alumni of Writing West Midlands' career development scheme, Room 204 - as part of the Birmingham Literature Festival. Justina grew up in Birmingham and lives and writes aboard a former working Black Country narrowboat dating from the early 1800s, which is moored outside Lichfield, Staffordshire.

Irna Qureshi

Irna is an ethnographer and writer, often using oral testimony to build narratives linking personal stories to broader social themes. This includes documenting the development of Britain's South Asian diaspora heritage in a series of exhibitions and books including The Grand Trunk Road: From Delhi to the Khyber Pass. She has also written about the history of Indian cinema and curated several exhibitions on this theme for the British Film Institute and National Media Museum. Her personal essays have appeared in Critical Muslim, South Asian Popular Culture, The Guardian's Northerner Blog, Huffington Post and New Statesman. Irna's writing on the notions of love and marriage has included documenting her own experience, as well as gathering oral testimony from 3 generations of British Muslim women, which were retold in the form of a radio play and as a theatre show which she performed. With her upcoming work, Irna steps back in time to the early 1900s to retrace migration journeys from her ancestral village in Pakistan to cities in Britain.

Project Associates

Thanks to our Associate Partners for promoting the competition, organising writing workshops and reaching out to people through their organisations and contacts

Lubna Marium, Artistic Director, Shadhona
www.shadhona.org
Jyoti Sinha, General Secretary of Manipuri Theatre & Cultural officer, Bangladesh Shilpakala Academy
Sharmila Banerjee, Director, Nritya Nandan, Dancer and Choreographer, Bangladesh
Shazia Omar www.shaziaomar.com   YouTube.com/ShazzyOm
Alina Chaudhry, Vice President, Rastay Arts, Pakistan
Natasha Uzair, Half Full Studios www.halffullstudio.com
Sheema Kermani   www.tehrik-e-niswan.org.pk
Fateha Begum, Producer and Facilitator
Polly Wright, The Hearth Centre, Birmingham

Acknowledgements

Sampad would like to thank the following for their help:

Murad Khan, PURBANAT CIC
Kam Bola, Wellbeing & Engagement Coach, acp Wellbeing Hub
Shabana Shaheen, acp Wellbeing Hub
Mohammad Farooque (Urdu Editing)
Additional printing by Mithu Dass / Go Graphic India

Workshop leaders

Abul Momen, journalist, writer and litterateur
Nari Kalam Joddha, women's writing group
Selina Hossain, Bangladeshi Novelist
Maleka Begum, renowned women activist, writer and professor of Sociology and Gender Studies
Prof. Firdous Azim, Women's Activist, writer and Professor of English Department at BRAC University
Qurratul Ain Tahmina, writer and Senior Journalist of The Daily Prothom Alo
Samina Nazir, eminent writer and playwright
Kulsoom Aftab, writer and playwright
Irfan Ahmed Urfi, writer and poet
Wersha Bharadwa, journalist and writer
Abda Khan, writer

Overall winning entries

English language:

Ilika Chakravarty Mandal, Birmingham, UK
Famous Yellow Sweater

Bangla Language:

Shahana Yasmin / সাহানা ইয়াসমিন, Dhaka, Bangladesh
এক 'কিছুই করে না' মেয়ের গল্প

Urdu language:

Nadia Umer   نادیہ عمر   Lahore, Pakistan
Dil Kay Shehar   دل کے شہر

Disclaimer

We have tried our best to represent the three languages appropriately but the process of transferring writings from online entries to the publication has been challenging. Please bear with us and read with kindness if we have made any errors.

The ownership of each writing is with the author.

Book Contents

Contents

(English Entries)

English Entries

Sarah Fazli, Karachi, Pakistan.

Pakistan's global happiness indices improved this year, when compared to previous years. This year has been difficult for Karachi – where all the odds are against us. Being based in Karachi, I wrote (from my heart) what it means to be a true Karachiite – despite the negativity we face on a very regular basis.

Conflicted Happiness

As a Karachiite, I know most of our celebrations tend to be loud and marked by firecrackers and occasional fireworks displays. Retail outlets commemorate events with nationwide sales, showing consumerism at its best. Rallies, parades, and 'juloos' are seen during Rabi-ul-Awwal and Muharram. 14th August is a national holiday, patriotic embellishments become all the rage and the media airs special transmissions. Sindh Cultural Day is a newer event celebrated every December since 2009. People adorn traditional Topi and Ajrak and play songs, dance, and attend celebratory events. A friend of mine, based in Australia, recently mentioned that Eid is best in Karachi; having left several years ago, she claimed that nothing compares to 'Karachi Eid'. This past Eid-ul-Azha, a part of me wanted to re-live the memories she mentioned: henna application on my hands, snacks from Flamingo, and obligatory prayers on Eid morning.

Each celebration boasts unparalleled celebration: where a part of me wonders if New York celebrates the 4th of July with such fervour or if New Year in London can compare to celebrations in Karachi? 2020 was a rainy year and looking at post monsoonal footage on Instagram combined with COVID-19 related 'issues', another part of me wondered just how much more of Karachi's resilience would be tested.

As I write, I know COVID-19 restrictions were eased just before August 14th, enabling life to slowly start resuming normalcy. That is when headlines read that Karachiites spent PKR 25 billion on Independence Day alone. And in a sense, that is when I realised: Karachi hasn't given up on its happy, conflicted freedom. It wants more.

Question: Are there just more people in Karachi? Is our celebration spirit a little stronger than that of other cities? Or are such celebratory displays somehow aligned with our everyday modus operandi?

I'm often described as the cat – which curiosity somehow missed. Living in Karachi, 2020 so far has made me question how Pakistanis are ranked as South Asia's happiest people. It seems off – because happiness is not electricity load-shedding, roadside mugging, and random lawlessness. Happiness is not the rains that kill basic infrastructure. Happiness doesn't expose basic living insecurity: a reality for many of our masses. And happiness does not witness these things.

And this is where COVID-19 held my hand, taking me back to basics. In all honesty, I am sure COVID-19 reminded a lot of us about the things that truly matter.

Following social distancing protocols, Zoom calls allow us to connect with family and elongated phone calls replaced texts. We still run into and socialize with neighbours – whilst ensuring that all requisite physical distancing measures are maintained.

Ironically, a constant pleasantry includes, 'how are you doing?' It was this one pleasantry that made me realise that Karachiites are truly a happy people if we just ask and allow them to let their guards down and engage in conversation. Interestingly, everyone

3

had a story. One family experienced their first true Eid-ul-Azha this year when they bought their own sacrificial goats after years of struggling financially. Somebody's sacrificial animals perished in the rains. Another family had lost somebody to illness. But their lives went on. Each shared jokes and stories about kids and jobs and asked how I had been keeping. These are happy people, I realised: affirming that people are not all bad – if we give them a chance.

This made me wonder how many Karachiites find peace despite the odds, who learn to trust despite injustice, and who maintain faith despite insecurity. They say you can find God if you try. Likewise, I believe that if I tried, I would be able to find those Karachiites who helped pushed Pakistan's global happiness Indices to the top of our region.

Sana Hafeez Taimur, Islamabad, Pakistan

Scientific studies have shown that it is not only genetics but also our environment that moulds us into who we are. Places we belong to not only contribute towards our personality building but also inspire us to achieve bigger and better things. Being born to a scientist and an educationist, critical thinking came naturally to me and it only helped that, growing up, I connected with two cities that I called my hometowns.

Contradiction nurtures the need to think and contemplate. My two divergent experiences, of an aged historic city in contrast to a new-born modern city, helped me to become a keen observer capable of understanding perspectives from both sides of a story. This polarity of environment has seeped into my subconscious and resonates well with this eternal conflict of thought process. This, in turn, generates my perfectionist trait, which is an important asset in my professional field as an architect.

Witnessing the transformation of a shrub forest into vibrant urban environment was spectacle enough for anyone to be inspired to create. The inspiration, therefore, first translated into painting and eventually into a longing to be part of a process that can create human habitats that evolve to become complex yet beautiful urban systems. This would have not been possible without my connection to these two very different cities.

Evolution of cities is a natural process that cities, planned or unplanned, experience. These changes often take away the nostalgic connection from the previous generations who experience a sense of loss even if the changes are positive and desirable. This overwhelming sentiment is felt because people feel detached from the key mental benchmarks that those places represent in their mental habitat. One way to restore those connections is to document places exactly as one remembers them.

For me, this written piece is about preserving those points of reference that I can revisit to regain myself whenever life throws a curveball and tries to throw me off balance. Capturing my places in a memory book of words acts as my anchor that keeps me from drifting away from the path that I set out to travel as an inspired young woman with big dreams and hopes. It also helps me to stay true to myself, fighting the societal pressures that forever are at play to mould women to its will.

A Tale of Two Cities

Chua-chu chua-chu calls the old washerman, stumping clothes on a rock at the riverbank, as the first light touches the misty waters, and a grey haze covers the whole scene. Like a water painting, a stroke of orange light starts to bleed into the horizon and a hint of the railway bridge starts to appear in the background. The majestic crisscross iron bars of the bridge seem to hang delicately in the quiet misty morning air. Soon the morning train comes whistling loudly through the bridge and wakes up the sleeping city. The dozing sun suddenly remembers to shine more brilliantly, and as the rays fall on the *Darya Walli Masjid*, its mirror-laden facade sparkles with brilliance as if it's competing with the sun. The atmosphere is flooded with light and sounds of all kinds, breaking the spell of weightlessness. Now the bridge sits heavily on its piers as many cycles and tangas start to crowd it. The silent flow of river is now filled with bathers splashing noisily with their *shalwars* ballooning in the water. These are the scenes that the historic riverside city of Jhelum has woken up to for decade upon decade.

Behind the famed mosque starts a row of houses lining the road that runs along the bank. From here, many smaller streets pierce into the city maze. The maze that is topped with towering pigeon cages, uniquely sculpted water tanks, and the countless minarets competing to reach further into the sky. For every street must house mosques, each associated with the respective school of thought, determined to proclaim their supremacy over the other.

Fridays in the city become very interesting as clerks from these mosques transform *Jumma* sermons into actual debates right over the loudspeakers. These topics, often quite trivial, become the talk of the town for the coming week, uniting the community in its own divisive way. The general population, having been exposed to critical thinking all their lives, are exceptionally aware and invested in political and religious identities. This subsequently results in the patronage of even more mosques and, as a result, the city has come to be rightly known as city of mosques.

Amid this web of narrow streets, bazars, and mosques, the main Civil Lines Road cuts through like a sharp knife. Asserting its colonial past, the road boorishly jeopardizes the natural scheme of the rustic city fabric. All along this central nave are buildings nestled in the past of particular eras, narrating the stories of the century they belonged to. In the middle of this panorama lays a beautiful Sikh period mansion. Most of my childhood holidays were spent here. It was not less than an enchanting fairyland castle to my young eyes. The colourful tiled floor, the beautifully crafted wooden ceilings, the exposed electric wiring with vintage switchboards, the dimly lit rooms with multicoloured defused light streaming in through dusty stained-glass windows, the mysterious mezzanine floor with stores and rooms at different levels and, above all, the old grape vine in the courtyard. It had crept everywhere, even at some points broken indoors through the ventilators.

The Jhelum city, like that tangled branches of my grandmother's grape vine, has a character of a labyrinth. Here, at every turn, a surprise is hidden. The city is like a living organism, with moods and feelings. It's happy on Eid day when its streets and bazaars become carnivals. And it's sad when someone from its close-knit community dies as the same street becomes a place for funeral prayers. I have seen it angry the day two religious groups fought, and I have seen it enthusiastic during the election days.

Jhelum was a wonderland for me, something peculiar because, you see, this story is not only about my ancestral town, but also about my hometown Islamabad. In the wake of neo modernism, the contrasting clean straight design, and natural beauty, Islamabad had created a strange balance of sterility and spontaneity, much like an elegant dance between nature's rebellion and human interventive tameness.

The wilderness surrounding and even infiltrating the city was an experience very foreign to inhabitants of the traditional city dwellers of the country. To what was considered its charm by the nature-loving populous of the city appeared wasteland-ish to the outsiders, hence the city was nicknamed 'city of the dead' by the ones who misunderstood its allure. What added to this stance was the fact that any social scene or cultural identity that would develop, still needed at least a decade or two before becoming apparent. Regardless that the earliest settlers of Islamabad were older retired folks finding solace in the serenity of a picturesque environment, the fact was that the city's actual first generation was still in school. The majority of early inhabitants also belonged to middle- and upper-middle class families, associated with government services. These, unlike the people enjoying their retirement, were much younger and still building up their families. Therefore, the real-life of the city was budding in the playgrounds and streets during kids' free hours.

As the eighties were turning into the nineties, I was growing up in the newly developed capital city of Islamabad. A city that had an appearance of a chessboard compared to the eccentric nature of historic Jhelum. What I didn't realise at the time was that it was not Jhelum that was distinctive, but it was I who was actually experiencing something exceptional in Islamabad. Roving around the quiet capital as I imagined high risen buildings on the shrubby plots along the broad avenues, I could hardly appreciate the unique privilege I had to witness the birth of my own city. As I grew and understood its dramatic transformation from a planned network of plots and roads into full-scale city, it captured my imagination and inspired me to become an architect. An architect who can create something as magnificent as a building, a building that makes nowhere a place.

Farina Kokab, Birmingham, UK

I have always been interested in reflecting on our experiences of living in a country whilst maintaining such deep connections to our background and our roots. I was inspired by the title 'My City My Home' because I always felt I had multiple options for what I considered to be my city or my home, and how I perceived them. For example, my city and home could be very Pakistani, or they could be very English – it depends on what time of the day or even which year it was! It's such a unique experience growing up like this and our reflections are rich and provide, in a sense, a study of what it means to be alive amidst all this chaos – physical, emotional, spiritual, and such.

Twin Cities, Twin Auras, Twin Vibes

I can trace my roots back to the sister cities of Rawalpindi and Islamabad, much like I can trace the lines on the palm of my hand,

These lines have been here since my beginning, and some would argue even before that,

But I didn't grow up in those sister cities, I grew up in Birmingham.

Birmingham may not have had a twin city like *Pindi* and Islamabad, but for me, it has a sister spirit,

Two sides of the same coin,

The British and the Pakistani.

I grew up immersed in culture,

But from two very different perspectives –

The British, at school, in museums, on the roads and city centres with fish and chips, teatime, playing hopscotch and listening to B*Witched as we decorated our first Christmas tree,

The Pakistani, at home, in the local shops around Alum Rock and Washwood Heath, the smell of samosas on Eid day, sparkling and bejewelled outfits glistening in the Autumn sun outside clothing stores and renting videos of Punjabi stage shows.

I never felt alone in my city, because if one sister wasn't speaking to me, I knew the other was,

If I wasn't watching Big Brother, then I knew there was a *saas-bahu* drama waiting for me on StarPlus,

If I wasn't picking my new summer dresses, I knew I was picking a *lehenga* for my cousin's wedding in Pakistan.

I have lived two very different lives simultaneously, and I've tried to weave their narrative into one,

But that felt like forcing two spirits to conjoin themselves, and I respect each one of them for who they are.

I continue to discover that these distinctions I felt reside within me, live harmoniously alongside each other,

That these two spaces that occupied my city occupied my mind as well

But they no longer fight for a single territory,

They have grown out of their borders,

I no longer contain them or resign them to certain aspects of my life,

I no longer search or yearn for labels to define my experiences.

I catch myself infusing *Masala chai* into my tiramisu,

I breathe in the intoxicating fumes of the *oud* incense, but let out a sigh of relief weighted loftily by the bergamot scents in the country gardens and discover they're now fused together in high-end scents,

I drape myself in cashmere blends and veil my head in chiffon dupattas.

English isn't just for work,

Mehndi isn't just for weddings.

These sisters might quibble and argue

But as they've matured

So, have I.

They've learnt they're stronger together than they were apart.

There's so much more to it than just being Pakistani or British.

Birmingham might not have a twin city, but for someone like me, she has a sister who is always around for a chai or a tea.

Antara Islam, Dhaka, Bangladesh

I had once seen a woman with one hand full of bags and another clutching the arm of a child, while carrying an infant at her waist, getting onto a running bus. It was a feat that I felt I had to tell everyone about.

Us vs. the City

It amazes me that
every day during monsoon
thousands of women in Dhaka
have to shuffle through
mud-smeared slippery streets teeming with people
and hurl themselves at the oncoming traffic
with their bags clutched in one hand
and their kids on the other
just to get back home in one piece.
All I did was carry a bag full of books from Nilkhet
to Dhaka College in the rain
and yet
I feel like I've won against this city for the day.

Antara Islam, Dhaka, Bangladesh

A rickshaw puller restored my faith in humanity with his simple act of kindness. Ordinary people leave the most extraordinary impression in our lives sometimes.

Headlights in the Rain

The rain started to pour down hard after I got on the rickshaw this evening. The rickshaw wallah had forgotten to bring along his plastic sheet today, so we were both soaking in the rain for the first fifteen minutes of our ride. Then he pulled us over to the side of the road and bought another sheet of plastic with his own money.

He said, '*Apa apne eibhabe bhijtesen amaro khub kharap lagtese. Eta toh shudhu amar pesha na, eta amar kortobbo.*' (Miss, I felt terrible seeing you get drenched. This isn't just my profession, it's also my duty.)

By this time, it had become so cold outside that I could feel the heat radiating off the headlights as the cars passed us by. He was shivering and his trembles shook the whole rickshaw. But he still kept a steady hold over the handle and peddled away. He brought me home safe and sound, even refusing when I insisted on paying him extra for his troubles.

It doesn't take much to honour somebody. The young girls I teach at a local Madrasa often help people with directions and feed beggars in their homes. Their respect for human dignity is manifested in acts of kindness. But as they will grow older, they can easily forgo these traits. For they are living in a world full of grown-ups who, instead of compassion, use social status as a metric of how people ought to be treated.

The rickshaw wallah touched me with his sincerity in a way no other human in Dhaka ever did. I wish I could display him in an art gallery as an embodiment of the extent of generosity we are all capable of. But like the warmth of passing headlights on a cold rainy night, his presence in my life had been fleeting.

Anika Anjum, Dhaka, Bangladesh

It's my failure to speak up that keeps the writer in me alive.

This poem reflects the realisation of my adulthood which, as a child, I could hardly think about. I used to believe joys and contentment are the only truth of life. Little did I see the darker shades of life among which I pass through almost every day now. Such harshness makes me desire to turn the wheels of time and go back to the times when I could inhale peace.

I have seen inhumanity, disrespect, and cruelty in the eyes of people. The dust in their mind binds me within four walls and I dread to step out. It urges me to carry a sense of awareness in my little backpack whenever I need to walk around those evils. In every step, I get to realise that an unknown force will never spare me to spread my wings and fly under the vast sky.

Among the Lives

Busy markets in the holy month,
the narrow street with a May Flower Tree,
also the little jamboree are places
Father used to take me.

Walking down through the crowds,
putting my little fingers in a fist,
he showed me the colours of life
of which bliss was the gist.

The city lights kept me mesmerised,
nodding off in an arch.
A smiling moon travelled along
even in my journey to the dark.

The life has been lost somehow,
somewhere, with the springing up of age.
Sneaky mind peeps into the memories
leaving me behind in the cage.

Something strange is out there,
that makes Father shield his dear.
The moon doesn't seem so cheerful now,
always hiding from shame and fear.

Why didn't I see, as a child,
the filth in people's eyes?
Lips remain sealed, a thousand words
burying down deep, heavy cries.

Bring my old city back –
here's an appeal to anyone who hears.
I wish to die embracing the laughs
without getting scared of tears.

Fatima Neguib, Lahore, Pakistan

The terms 'My City' and 'My Home' inspired me to write about the obstacles faced by an 'ordinary', poverty-stricken girl in Pakistan who has the desire to take her family out of poverty, helplessness, and 'lowliness' with her hard work and determination.

My Humble Origins

I was eight years old at the time and loved immensely by my parents. I was their only born. They were both wage earners from the city of Lahore, my father was a daily wage labourer who broke bricks in the sweltering heat of the sun every day to earn a meagre wage, while my mother cleaned the houses of the rich; their combined earnings gave me three meals a day but no school. At the end of each month, my mother's purse would run out of money and the gravy was bound to become watery. When gas in the cylinder ran out, which was mostly the case; we would collect firewood to get through. Collecting and bringing firewood and water from the well were jobs for the whole family; together we could carry greater quantities. Our house was actually a makeshift tent which I always thought would be blown away in a storm, but I was at peace with life and did not sense anything missing. I enjoyed listening to my father's radio, advertisements were what we mostly heard, advertisements of TVs and other luxury items, with news in between, and the rare visits we made to different parts of the city were looked forward to.

'I have always wanted to give her at least something made of gold, even if only bangles, but I don't know how I'll be able to save that much till she comes of age,' said my mother to my father.

'Don't worry, we'll think of something. I can always get a loan from my master or something like that,' consoled my father.

At that age I didn't worry about my father having to get a loan; it was too far ahead to contemplate. I turned nine, and things didn't really change a lot, but once I got closer to ten, I started feeling left out of things I saw around me.

It was a Sunday, and I accompanied my mother to clean a house she had missed cleaning on Saturday owing to extreme exhaustion. Normally, I would not go with my mother to the houses she cleaned, but today was different. I had decided to help her, as I was feeling sorry for her; she had to do so much so that I could sleep on a full stomach. I had to walk a great deal to get there, and upon arrival, I began noticing the grandeur of their house and became fixated on the comfortable life they were living – a fridge, a TV, beds, tables, chairs, sofas, and carpets – the list was endless. As I scrubbed the floor, I couldn't help but feel hurt, I had eavesdropped and become aware of the fact that my mother's entire salary amounted to the value of a single, everyday dress those women wore.

When we returned home, I said to my mum, 'These people have everything they wish for – ample money for a car, while we have to sit on my father's bicycle to go out anywhere. They have servants to clean, cook, and drive for them, and we are dependent on them for the money they give us.'

My mother replied, 'When you are older you will understand that God has made every human equal, and because God has decided not to give us what he has given them, it does not matter; they have other problems of their own.' I turned mum. Then one day I asked the ultimate question, 'Can't I go to school?'

There was silence in the tent.

My mother and father looked at each other for a while, and then my father replied, 'Of course my love, we can and will send you to school.'

After a while, when they thought I was asleep, they started arguing, 'How do you expect to pay the fees; the money for school uniform and books?' My mother asked bitterly.

'I'll think of something,' retorted my father. 'May I ask what it is that you'll think of?' retaliated my mother.

'I'll say yes to my master. Just yesterday, he was asking me if I would like to go to his house to live with him and run errands for him. He said that I could earn much more that way,' responded my father.

'What about us?' my mother asked, her voice breaking.

'He said he does not have the space for all of us as he already has a live-in cook with his family and can't keep another one.' answered my father.

My heart skipped a beat, but I wanted to go to school at any cost, saying to myself, 'I will get them out of poverty by getting educated.'

Though I saw my father seldom, the moment I did meet him, I would give him a hug and say, 'Thank you for all this.' Nevertheless, as days without him turned into weeks, I started pining for him.

It had been two weeks since I last heard from my father; concerned, my mother and I went to the nearest neighbour who had a mobile we could call from, but no one answered. A week later, out of the blue, they brought his body in a van, claiming that he had died of a heart attack. It all happened so quick, that it was only after he was buried that I released my emotions and embraced my mother and cried. I could not be with him anymore and did not want this to be true.

Years passed by, and I finally finished school. My mother had kept working all these years, and now I was persuading her to leave work, but she would say, 'Let me make sure you pass through college, then I will do as you say.'

I finally graduated from college and found a clerk's job, but all along I remember my father's words with a few tears, 'Don't worry, we'll think of something. I can always get a loan from my master or something like that.'

Asma Parveen Iftikhar, Birmingham, UK

*I was inspired by an event that happened a long time ago –
someone close to me left home and didn't return for eighteen years.
When they did come back to their family, they said they were
confused about their identity and felt they didn't fit in even though
they outwardly got on. They were full of regret for having wasted
precious time away only because of insecurities they harboured
based on their worldview.*

*I'd like my writing to change the narrative, I'd like to write
about hope and reunions, of second chances and reconciliations,
with oneself and with ones loved ones.*

Phone Call from Home

I toss onto my left side; my gaze falls on the prayer mat neatly
folded on the bedside drawer. It is a gift from Mum. When
unfolded, it is maroon and black with an image of a mosque on it.
Cream coloured tassels adorn the edges. It's a little worn, a little
tattered. It's been used by my mother. I have never unfolded it
since the day I placed it on the drawer two years ago. She wanted
me to have it because she hoped it would remind me to pray
my *salah* – my five daily prayers. I haven't prayed in ten years.
I don't know what the urge to pray feels like anymore. I prayed
the day Dad died. Then I stopped praying. That day I stood on
my prayer mat and held my hands over my chest. I bent and
touched my knees. I prostrated to Allah. I felt nothing. I prayed
because Dad taught me to pray. He expected it. Then he died
and there were no expectations.

The phone rings. It's Mum.

'When are you coming home?' *Home*, she says.

But what's home? Home is here in Canary Wharf. Home is

there where Mum lives, Birmingham. Dirty, smelly, rubbish-filled Birmingham. Colourful, familiar, lively Birmingham.

Or is it Gujar Khan? Pakistan.

Home is none of these. Home is all of these.

But I am restless.

'I can't,' I say before she's even had a chance to beg. I don't like it when she begs me to come home. I hate it when Mum begs for anything.

'He's asking for you, Aisha. He misses you.' She says bleakly. Her voice is hopeless. She already knows I won't come home but she's asking for her son's sake. My disabled brother. Not for herself.

'Please explain it to him,' I say indifferently. But I'm not really indifferent to her. I'm indifferent to myself, to my feelings, indifferent to my life which has slipped away like an ice cube from my hands.

She sighs and, in her sighs, I hear a million protests.

The call ends. Just like that.

I throw the duvet back and stand at the window. The street is empty. Most of the city lights are off, except for the occasional yellow glow from a window here or there. It sleeps, like a tamed dragon. During the day, you'd never be able to tell that this city could be silenced, but even in the silence you can hear its secrets, even in the silence, you can hear the whimpers of the lonely souls that become lost in its carnival-like clamour during the day. Only in a city like this can the stillness of the night and the din of the day show no dichotomy.

The phone rings again.

It's my brother. He can string a few sentences together before he gets confused before he forgets who he's talking to.

He snorts, giggles. I smile despite myself. My brother has a way of making me smile. He reminds me of home, of the smell of our cosy little living room in Alum Rock, of the musty blue

23

carpet and lavender Haze air freshener. His voice reminds me of monkey nuts that Dad shelled for both of us and the fight that ensued to see who'd get the peanut.

'I was about to call you, bro.' I lie.

'When are you coming, bro?' I smile despite myself at the way he mimics me.

Never, I want to shout. He babbles and the phone goes dead.

Never. But that would be a betrayal and betrayals don't go down too well in my family. Loyalty is everything for a Pakistani.

Dad said *don't leave home* and I said to him, *but you left Pakistan.*

That was different, he said.

No, it wasn't, I said.

I had to work.

So do I.

I had to provide for my family.

I will provide too.

But London? He protested.

Yes, London.

You'll lose yourself, there. It will suck you in. You will forget who you are.

No way, Dad. You're exaggerating.

I won. Dad died.

Dad died. I lost.

But maybe he was right. I haven't been home for three years, it's only two hours' drive away, but it could be on the other side of the world, like Gujar Khan, and I've been able to stay away. If they would just stop judging me then I could go back. But they will not stop judging and I will not go back, and my mother and brother will suffer. It's always the family that suffers; it's never the ones who judge. *They won.*

My thoughts are interrupted by someone singing in the apartment above. No, not singing. Someone is reading the Qur'an. It's a man's voice and he's reading loudly. I've never heard him before.

24

He has a beautiful, deep, full-throated voice. The gentle melody in his recitation sends shivers all over my body and, strangely, his style of reading reminds me of Pakistan – of my grandfather's recitation, of the hazy glow over the cornfields of Gujar Khan, of the dew sitting on the leathery citrus leaves in the courtyard of my childhood home. But then my mind goes blank, and the sound takes over. Now it reminds me of nothing, of a blankness that is suffocating because it has no memories attached to it. Then silence.

I miss Mum, I miss my brother, I miss Dad. I need to go home. I will not let them win. I will go back and face them, their judgements, their snide remarks, their cruelty and hypocrisy and I will kiss my mother's hands and hug my brother tightly because home is where family is. *Dad said that.*

Erin Shore Gilbey, Birmingham, UK

Although I have some Black Country heritage, I moved to Birmingham in 2017 without any particular affection for or expectations of the city or the area. Over the course of three years, I fell in love with the city from my Thai boxing gym in an old garage in West Heath to the fairy-tale Highbury Park, to the allure of the jewellery quarter, to the revolution of Digbeth. For a long time, I couldn't quite put my finger on what it was that made this ex-industrial smudge in the middle of the country my home. After a conversation with my grandma, who grew up in the Black Country and visited Birmingham occasionally, where she described to me the glittering shop windows of Birmingham City Centre at Christmas, I realised what it is. I found a home in Birmingham because of a sense of potential – of possibility.

The city is always changing and moving, and, with every movement, a space is left behind for someone new to make their mark. The glittering Christmas windows for me are filled with opportunities to make art and become a part of the story of an ever-changing city. I wrote 'Sliding Puzzle' this year as I move from being a student in the city to becoming a working artist. I take comfort in the fact that my big leap of faith in starting an arts career in the year of a global pandemic is only a small moving fragment in the unstoppable whirlwind of change that takes place in my city every day. Birmingham's motto 'Forward' is fitting – although on the day-to-day the city's changes may feel like infuriating steps backwards or in circles, ultimately, we are moving forward towards a utopia that is always tantalizingly just out of reach. I wrote 'Sliding Puzzle' to encapsulate this image of an ever-changing city that draws you into its wonderful incompleteness.

Sliding Puzzle

I found Birmingham at the bottom of a party bag in the mid-2000s. You could slide its squares around to create a picture. Each time a square was moved, creating a new gap (*you can't get through there – they're doing up that bit outside the library* or *the Christmas Market's on at New Street* or *there's road works on the A48*), the anticipation of a perfect picture grew. I sat silently in the back of the car, chewing my chapped lip as I watched the pieces move beneath my sticky thumbs. I didn't like the final picture because there was still a gap where I could slide the pieces again and so I kept moving them left, right, forward, backward, forward, forward, creating transient and improbable stories.

When it fades beneath my busy thumbs, I paint new pictures over the grubby plastic. Then I return it to the pocket of my favourite raincoat, and I rearrange it again, addicted to its incomplete beauty.

Reem Arshad Khan, Islamabad, Pakistan

I thought about the connection between my city and my home, and I realised that the two have always been very different for me. My city has never felt like my home, and I have never felt a true feeling of belonging here. I wanted to create vivid images in the minds of my readers to show them what I see when I look at my city, why I see that, and why I feel fearful of my city and its people. My work is primarily based on my memories. The scenes I witnessed unfolding before me whilst buying vegetables and naan on the street with my father, and the polluted streets and stares I felt upon me when we went out to walk every night. Those were some of the few times I actually experienced what my city is like, what its roads look like, what its air smells like, and I wanted to incorporate all of that in my poem.

My City

A city is a place full of peach-coloured buildings and soft, crushed people,
   Their juices flowing down into the earth, polluting the roads littered with floating plastic birds and crushed chicken bones,
   Wet dirt and spit travelling with you like childhood friends,
   I suppose they are, in a way.
   You take your shoes off at the door and try to wash off the curdled custard air that touched your skin,
   Sweat and dirt and desperation mixed with a suppressed boiling anger,
   You look at their wrinkled, inflated faces,
   Like a puri swells up when it's thrown in hot oil,
   And your skin crawls with the black solid weight of their stares.
   Black like sunflower seeds that don't bloom,

28

Your sidewalks are surrounded by marijuana and poppy plants grown in the wild,

Watered by the monsoons and piss, some of it animal, most of it human,

And you try to look at the sky for a second to admire the tenacity of those milky pearls above,

Shining and persevering,

Despite the broken plasticine people roaming below,

But there's too much noise.

Every shop you walk into you feel exposed and jumpy,

My city and its offspring of resentment and lust.

Is it really my city?

These roads with broken glass and juice boxes littered on them,

It's all I know,

Sipping mango juice while a woman screams on the TV,

Another bomb gone off, another missing person, another beaten girl,

Pass the packet of Lay's please, I love this flavour.

We never played on the street,

Nor in the park,

Again, the stares were too much,

Like crawling ants on your skin, biting away as your body writhes underneath them,

Safety is a concept alien to us.

There is laughter and chaos and wonderful things blooming here each spring,

We have festivals and we sing and dance and love,

But we do so in secret.

The world outside this brown, faded gate is scary and rough,

People walking on the street scare you, they've always scared you,

You look at them and you see another headline, another cup of acid hidden beneath those rose-coloured shirts,

They're reckless and fearless, and generous
With their anger,
And they feel unknown to you.
They say you hate your own flesh and blood but it's not loathing,
They mistake your fear for loathing,
Outside these walls, it feels like you're an orange in someone's hands, about to be peeled and silently eaten,
And your 'flesh and blood' will think nothing of it as your sweet juice hits the pavement below.
The lines on your people's faces remind you of lines in your school's bathroom stalls,
Where your friend's brother was forced to drop his food on the floor and eat it,
Where his bottle was filled with tap water every day,
Alien things and alien feelings,
These people, this city, that crushed those unlike herself just as her children crush those below them.
I trust no one but the sun shining down in conical gold apathy,
I sleep nowhere but near my mother's arms,
Shoes at the door, body poised for flight.
They say my city is safe and beautiful,
A melting pot of cultures and leaping, joyful lives,
Why, then, do I walk with vigilance in my own home?
In my bathroom, why do my hands shake while I take off my clothes to wash away this grime?
'You have experienced nothing of great loss or devastation,'
But a little bit each day is enough to make me tired.

Madhumita Dasgupta, Birmingham, UK

My mother's fascinating life inspired me. She was uprooted from her home at a very early age during the division of India, depriving her of all childhood dreams and aspirations. The words 'my city' and 'my home' are very ambiguous to her. This is a story that many women from the sub-continent will be able to relate to.

Home

My name is Renu. I was born as the only daughter of my father, in a very small town called Pirojpur in Bangladesh. With many brothers, male cousins, and uncles, I lived a very protected and safe life. My favourite uncle was a pharmacist, and my father was the headmaster of the school that my siblings and I attended. With no understanding of what lay beyond Pirojpur, we always felt that we had more than enough. I still have memories of dancing in the rain, muddying my bare feet, and throwing stones at ripe mangos hanging in the trees. These are moments that I wouldn't trade for anything.

I lived happily within my bubble for many years until the riot began. We started to hear talk of the division of our beloved country by religion. Our notions of the future, our sense of peace, and our faith were stolen in one big sweep. We began to fear losing not only our earthly belongings but also our honour. My father became very anxious about his sixteen-year-old daughter in those uncertain and tumultuous times, and so he arranged for me to leave the country soon and move to India.

This was my home. How could I leave behind the place where I played with my friends, sang with birds, and danced with the waves of the river Kaliganga? Will I not miss the bickering at the dining table? Or how about the gossip of our neighbours? Or even the pranks of my younger cousins? I must have cried all day thinking of all the things that create the different shades of life in Pirojpur. I fought tooth and nail, I negotiated, I did everything I could, but my efforts were futile. I was left on a train, alone, crossing a border tainted with blood. The Indo-Pak border was one of the most dangerous places where many people lost their lives trying to cross the border. It was heavily patrolled by Pakistani soldiers armed with guns. My fate ultimately brought me to Calcutta after crossing the border one night all by myself.

I settled well in Calcutta, in one of my wealthy relative's house. My aunt was very keen to get me married as soon as possible. With my father's permission, I got married to a man who was ten years older than me. His name was Sudhir. He was very kind and caring. He nurtured me in his own way to be able to live alongside the Calcuttans and their sophisticated lifestyle. I had private tutors for learning English, Art, and Painting and, of course, Singing. Without me knowing exactly when, I became very used to the Calcutta lifestyle. I grew to love my life with Sudhir and my son, Sunil. This was my home.

My story did not end there, unfortunately. I had to move again. The wind blew me to New York next. My husband passed away and left me under the strong wing of my able son, Sunil. He has grown into a successful young man, working with the Wall Street's finest. He gave me no option of living alone in Calcutta and so I had to follow him to America. Once again, I was taken from one home and moved to another. I did not utter a word of protest and I hid my tears from my son. I guess that he thought this was the best option for him to look after his mother. We live now with Susan, my daughter-in-law, Sunil, and my grandchildren. I guess now this three-bedroomed flat in Manhattan is my home. I belong to this city now.

I see the same sky, the same clouds, occasional birds chirping and beckoning trees as I saw them in Bangladesh or India. I still wear my cotton sarees, I still enjoy my daal with rice, and I still chant the same mantras at dusk and dawn. Why is it not the same?

What makes a home, a home? Do I have a home where I actually belong? I grew up in my father's home, I blossomed in my husband's home, and now I spend my days in my son's home.

I overheard Susan making her future plans recently. She was suggesting that once my grandchildren go to university, they should start thinking of moving me somewhere that I can live comfortably and happily, perhaps the reputable old home down the road. After eighty years of my sheltered life, I will finally be free. I am waiting for yet another home to call my own.

Abeda Begum, Birmingham, UK

*What inspired me was growing up in the city which I call home.
My memories of childhood and adolescence helped inspire my
poem.*

*I thought of all the positive support around me and remembered
the words of my parents who are my biggest inspiration.*

Growing Up

Be the best you, that you can be
Inspirational to others, that was taught to me.
Remember your roots, don't forget where you came from
My parents would say when I returned from school prom.
Islam is my religion, it teaches you to be kind,
Neighbours from different faith share the same mind.
Good is within us all no matter the religion,
Honour your surroundings, don't make bad decisions.
Amazing is my city, Birmingham will always be
Museums, art galleries and canal boats are some of the popular
things to see.

I grew up on the streets, it is where I play,
Friends of all ages and they made my day.
Climbing trees and rooftops and pranking the neighbour
Whilst Mum and Dad grafted all day and night doing labour.

Sewing, sewing, sewing on the sewing machine,
Making clothes of all kinds for every being,
They were the real machines – non-stop and on the go,
Then they taught me to sew, as they grew old and too slow.

It was all their hard work that gave me passion,
A hobby, an interest, an eye for fashion,
A skill that I am grateful for and I will always cherish
To remind me of how hard my parents worked, an age of elegance
that has forever perished.

The city is safe (or so they say)
Be careful who you trust, you may go astray,
Follow your culture be true to yourself.
What is my culture when I think of myself?

Birmingham is my culture, my home, and my city,
A mixed bag of skittles that represent diversity.
I am Bangladeshi, my best friend is from Lahore,
There are many different cultures in Birmingham, and you are
all welcome to explore.

Aysha Islam, Birmingham, UK

I enjoy writing and reflecting, so it was easy for me to write about something that I felt comfortable discussing.

Having lived in Birmingham, I feel that everything that I have achieved is because of what this city has offered me. However, it's important to acknowledge that I once belonged to another country where I still have good memories and love and cherish just as much as I do Birmingham.

Home is Where the Heart Is!

I am a Bangladeshi woman and I have lived in the UK for half a century! Birmingham is where we settled when I came with my mum and four brothers in 1970, to join my dad... it was an amazing journey, leaving one country and beginning a new chapter in a new environment. Of course, none of these would have been possible had it not been for my mum, who gave my dad an ultimatum – *return home to help raise our children or let us join you in England*. Hence, I wish to submit this piece of narrative in memory of two important people, my mum and dad. Certainly, they were strong and determined characters, they had our best interest at heart and for that reason alone, I feel my mum secured our futures.

I was young so was not at all phased by the journey. When we stayed overnight in Karachi, I was wide-eyed with amazement when looking out of the hotel window, at the hustle and bustle of busy city life. Moreover, my recollection of the journey home from Heathrow to Birmingham was also remarkable. Whilst looking out of the window, I gazed in wonder at the greenery, open fields, and neat countryside – truly magnificent.

Living in Birmingham has been extremely comfortable. There were many immigrant families already settled when we arrived, so fitting into the community was not difficult. However, the only barrier that I had to overcome was to be able to communicate in English. There was steady progress in this department as my dad enrolled us very swiftly in our local primary school. I remember the extra English language support we had in schools and my dad also engaged a tutor for home tuition. I still have a couple of my primary school reports and know that I was a very diligent and keen learner. I feel immensely proud that I did quite well and picked up the English language fairly quickly. The best of my school days has to be my time in my secondary school. I have many happy memories of the good times I had, my achievements, and the life-long friendship I have maintained to this day. Apart from the academic successes, I feel that being voted the Deputy Head Girl was quite an achievement, especially when I arrived eight years previously, not really knowing any English words, apart from 'Hello,' maybe.

I have no regrets about getting married at the age of seventeen, not finishing my A-levels, due to my dad being unwell – these are the sacrifices we made in those days. Of course, I had passion and dreams that were unfulfilled, such as wanting to do further higher education and take up a career. Not really knowing what I wanted to pursue, I chose to go into social work as it was the only course I could do part-time. Juggling family life, child-rearing, and a host of other duties, I managed to complete my studies and take up a post as an Educational Social Worker for Birmingham City Council. I enjoyed this role enormously as it enabled me to help schools, children, and families, working to improve attendance or to advocate on their behalf to find school places etc.

I feel that living in Birmingham has given me the stability I needed to feel secure. I watched how Birmingham has developed over the last fifty years, it's cleaner, there are more affordable housing and there are schools providing excellent education to diverse communities. Certainly, the Bullring facelift has attracted a lot of attention, and shopping and the eateries are drawing in the crowds. I enjoy going shopping and there is a huge choice of places to stop for tea, coffee, or lunch/dinner. I feel very much at home here. I owe the successes that I have had to living in a city that I feel safe in and have family and friends to share my life with. I know that when I was once in Bangladesh over the Christmas holiday, I missed seeing the Christmas decorations, and even the cold, wintery weather! But it was nice to see that there was the odd Christmas tree or decoration in parts of Sylhet, where there were Christian churches or missionaries living there... of course, Christmas in the heat was vastly different.

When I visit Bangladesh, I love going back to my childhood and retracing family roots, so I think that how we feel and what we love is all relative. As long as one is happy, healthy, and secure in their relationships, one can enjoy life and live life to the fullest, that is my personal view. I know too well, though, that life would have been quite different had I not lived in a place like Birmingham. I have worked hard, my children are all successful adults in decent jobs, and they are happy, hence I feel truly blessed... Birmingham has given me the opportunities to thrive and make something of my life... so it's fitting to say that 'home is where the heart is.'

Tamanna Abdul-Karim, Birmingham, UK

The memories of my childhood in Nechells, Birmingham, intertwined with the memories my siblings and parents had in Sylhet, Bangladesh.

My City. My Home.

My city. My home. But where is that?

Swirls of smoke canvas the air like veins pumping heaviness, a clouded heaviness, through the skies. Darkness hung like a stained velvet curtain, closing in. But with it came a certain softness, the promise of something more, the feeling of warmth. Whilst darkness held down its heavy hand, the city secretly sighed: despair tinged with the hope of something better.

Shards of broken glass, damaged fences, and scattered childhoods lay strewn across the concrete playground. Faded yellow lines marked out spaces and territories, created space and divisions in equal measure.

Despite the destruction that presented itself in the everyday litter of lives, there was an orchestra of laughs that pierced the shadows, thus allowing streams of multi-coloured rainbow light to fall graciously into the air. Like dancers, the children glided, tiptoeing through their childhoods, armed together in a sense of true uniformity. Poverty may well have painted across their faces, but there was a magic in their eyes, a spirit of relentless and utter joy. These spirits refused to surrender to the tyrant clouds, nor did they stay within their faded lines; they rejoiced in their unique harmony and pieced together the broken shards to mirror their innocence. They played and played oh so freely. The train tracks became their garden and the green triangular space in the communal area, their little heaven, the mutual sanctuary. This is where the dramas unfolded: the initiations, the games upon games upon games, and the laughter of victory tinted with the silent tears of a lost game or a broken friendship.

But this joy wasn't just saved only for the children. Women congregated in kitchens all across the street, peeling, grating, binding, and frying. Their hands were filled with the bursts of colour from the array of spices, the weight of the garden-grown vegetables, from courgettes to pumpkins, and the golden bangles of their own youth from another land. Their quiet talent erupted like magic as they folded samosas, dropped pakoras in the sizzling oil or rolled out dainty delicacies. Sometimes it was spiced omelette and homemade chips, fried chicken wings, or deep-fried potato scallops. Regardless, they would be devoured within minutes. Not always by the women themselves, but their communal children and the men, their husbands, who gathered to have the spirit of sport root them, fixating their tired eyes to the screen. Bearded old men sat upon the floor discussing the routes through their new worlds, navigating from one land to another, one culture to another. If it wasn't the sport they were hooked on, it was the news, as it blared out current affairs – politics and health. The nuances not always understood, but between them and their broken English, they could each decipher some meaning and then piece it together like a patchwork blanket, a nakshi kantha.

Summer nights were nothing short of magic. The sun came down shyly, but there was no holding down the children. They could function without sleep for another game, and then another, and then one more. The raucous sound of the shuttlecock against the racket as it flew powerfully over the worn-out net, filled the evening sky. Games of Ludo, Snakes and Ladders were played in all the verandas and porches as the ladies sang, talked, and recited majestically. Every smile, every connection, every piece of magic between the souls of the city pushed away the darkness of poverty that lurked in the background.

Trees swayed, heavy with jackfruit, mangos, and starfruit. Smell of citrus filled the air but fought against the smokiness of the factories that were determined to make their mark on the skyline. The hill into the city was a mantle to a beautiful cherry tree from which the cherries were often crushed into a chutney: green chillies, coriander, and lemon juice. Vibrantly rich saris hung out on makeshift washing lines across concrete spaces, next to hard, worn-out denim and corduroy. Trains roared passed but the train in the park, pungent with urine, stood still in time and place to allow little hands and feet to climb, hide and soak up the stench into their memories. The rickety rickshaws reluctantly pulled one family in and another out in a continuous transition of joy. Both the trains and the rickshaws became a symbol of childhood – the promise of endless play.

Like the bangles and babies, the lungis and the laughter, nothing in this city stood still. There was movement, always. There was no option to be still, everyone grafted hard: providing, cooking, teaching, playing, being. In this sanctuary, to move was to create waves of change and progress, to move was to dream, and to move was to make a difference. A foot each in each culture, this place bridged the gap and offered a reminder of a home once lost. Poverty ruled the pockets, but the communal spirit made the place and its people rich. This was a village in a city – a hidden gem – a reminder that we create our own little worlds.

Pracheta Ahana Alam, Dhaka, Bangladesh

*I was inspired by the dirt and the grime my city is known for,
which was twice voted the worst city in the world to live. I grew
up in Dhaka so the terms 'My City and My Home' were easy
for me to write about.*

When in Dhaka

I live in Dhaka. I live in sin. Sloth is God's lesser sin, so I live
in filth. My childhood home is in one of the relatively cleaner
parts of the city, but I have floated in shit-strewn Uttara floods.
I swam to school once. Then my father, middle-aged, carried me
on his shoulder to take my Literature exam. They sent me home
because I smelled too bad. I was very prepared for it because it
was the only exam I wanted to sit. But the rain came heavily that
day when I decided to leave the safety of the leathery innards of
my car. When I decided to float into the arms of sloth, and thus,
the arms of sin.

But to be honest, my only sin in this city is that I am a girl and
I want to exist in it.

If sloth is the lesser sin, what is the greater? Sloth is the
materialist's sin, of owning more than it can take care of, of
housing more people than it can feed. Sloth is greed and greed
is lust and lust is vanity and… you get it. There is no greater or
lesser, only sin. Sin is born of mankind, sin is born of excess, so
know that every dense square mile of Dhaka's population is of
the thickest sin. Sin is stories, in putrefying sloth and heinous
lust. What is a story without fighting sin? Here you can toe
between the line of the darkest grey and pitch black. Sin is grime.
Dhaka is grime. Dhaka is sin.

Dhaka is body, soul, sin, grime, crime, and an endless sense of not enough time. Dhaka is djinns, pimps, and catty aunties. Dhaka is Gulshan, Dhaka is Jigatola, Dhaka is exactly how it is defined on a map but filled to brim and overflowing from the glass with sin, with no sense of time.
Dhaka is divine. Dhaka is mine.

Ilika Chakravarty Mandal, Birmingham, UK

I read and enjoy books, but over time, I somehow lost the power of putting my thoughts into words. The years after school went towards higher education, academic writing, work, marriage, miscarriage, motherhood, moving cities and continents – the joy of writing taking a complete backseat.

The topic My City, My Home connected to my persona and identity. Having moved from a small town in the lap of the Himalayas to Darjeeling-Kolkata-Delhi-Mumbai-Peterborough, Birmingham-London, and to Birmingham again, I felt I had so much to say. I lived, adjusted, made friends, made home, and often questioned myself whether I felt entrapped or rootless or enjoyed the journey across countries and continents? What was home? Which was home?

Considering the present times, where I have been unable to travel to meet my ageing parents for so long, I decided to write a letter. This would make it more personal by adding my experiences and connecting my home and city. And, last but not the least, I have a yellow sweater knit by my mum and I am a diehard Leonard Cohen fan.

Famous Yellow Sweater

It's four in the morning, the end of December
I'm writing you now just to see if you're better
New York is cold, but I like where I'm living....
Leonard Cohen

Dear Ma,

Five thousand and eighteen miles lie between us – Birmingham and Dhaka – of land, water, and civilisation. I would love for you to be present on the same strip of earth and time zone as me, now

44

separated by the crippling uncertainty of departure. You know, I consider myself a proud citizen of both worlds in my nature. A part of me loves Birmingham's heavenly Bird's Custard, the other relishes your Bengali *payesh*. I breathe the aroma of finest Sunday roasts and puff pastry here and flatbread and traditional spices in home cooking. I soak all the languages I hear, I speak the Queen's English, yet dream in Bangla.

This beautiful duality of contrasts, rather commonplace in Birmingham (a time-wrapped Jewellery Quarter Museum juxtaposed with the contemporary Think Tank), I strive to discover by learning to love the people in this city, my home. The contrasts between Bangladesh and Birmingham are stark, if not glaring. Yet, no matter what food I eat, clothes I wear, culture or religion I practice, my conscience abides, and my soul remains constant in this algorithm of variables.

Ma, do you remember the sweater you gifted me in Dhaka, knitted intricately in mustard yellow yarn forming ornate curlicues twisting around and beneath my body, like a lattice of maternal protection? To me, Birmingham is like this sweater. Beyond aesthetics, I feel an unquenched attachment and affection, entwined in wool, a knotted mesh binding our shared heritage. You have seen pictures depicting life here. Images convey a thousand words; a monologue is a natural close, I want the words to never stop counting.

Beorma-ing-ham is where the Beorma made home and nonchalant bulls roamed down a cobbled Roman road; the now tarmacked Icknield Street which people of all shades walk today. A stagnant bronze bull stands fixed in a grimace at the Bull Ring – a blast from the past, and hotspot for tourists and residents. Beside it, silver metal discs of the Selfridges building reflecting on its orbs, translate to your hands running across the static fuzz on my sweater's circular patterns. Its colour on my skin feels like tropical sunshine ripening Bengal's golden paddy and Midland's rye.

My sweater's serpentine embroidery is symbolic of our paths crossing, if not geographically, then in dreams when frogs croak in romance to dancing monsoon raindrops on banana leaves and to your mouth-watering jaggery drenched coconut balls. So many happy memories! Climbing guava and mango trees, winter picnics over Ludo, afternoons savouring bitter-sweet oranges with black salt, Sunday radio dramas over mutton curry, and watching countless fireflies, their glow incomparable to a million city lights.

Running fingers on the phone screen, twisting random routes of the Spaghetti Junction's spreading arteries or Birmingham's canals, more than Venice, I am reminded of Bengal's countless rivers draining alluvial plains. Landlocked in the Heart of England, the Rea is our only consolation, unlike Dhaka's fuller Buriganga where steamers ply peacefully. But I believe the rivers sprawling between geographical boundaries and alien climes enmesh in their waters our cultures and language, their circling ripples uniting water hyacinths and spring daffodils in one beautiful bouquet.

Many believe that in Birmingham we are stoic, stiff upper-lipped, unacquainted with next-door neighbours – separation enhanced by detached houses and sequestered flats. When I see my city, housing diverse migrants arriving with hope in this melting pot of identity and place tied by social glue, I disbelieve such preconceived notions. Birmingham has been destroyed by fire and plagues as Dhaka has from riots and partition; yet risen like a phoenix, keeping people's tales alive, defining, and helping them to survive.

Be it food or occasion, Birmingham holds a bit of Bengal. The few Bengali shops catering for the Bengali community here may not compare with the colourful, bustling markets of Bangladesh, but they feed me the best fish (*hilsa* and *chingri*), drumsticks, gourds, areca nuts, betel leaves and allow me to practice my Bangla! My corner shop stocks Asian spices. An

English shopkeeper in the Farmer's Market gets me fresh, free-range duck eggs to cook my soul food *deem er jhol* to your timeless recipe. The Balti Triangle serves the steaming *samosas* and sweet *jilipis* in Eid and Diwali, pubs, and the best fish and chips.

On misty winter mornings, sitting at home, monastic silence is broken by a distant train's whistle dissolving in the air, I hold your sweater to hear the cuckoo's song back home. Although for you nothing can quieten Dhaka's inescapable sounds – street vendors, honking traffic, rickshaws. It has been long since I held your hands Ma, with memory-lined skin, those wrinkled fingers knitting what I carried to the 'Workshop of the World,' its industrial heritage delivering nothing as special. Outworn and old-fashioned, joked by friends as the 'famous yellow sweater' (after Cohen's *Famous Blue Raincoat*), but always esteemed for its craftsmanship.

I can see you read my letter, adjusting your Gandhian spectacles, arthritic knees tired from chores, eyes heavy from midday siesta, yet smiling conceivably in recognition of our strong roots, which no cyclone can uproot. Before I left Dhaka after marriage, you said *'Maniye nibi, kemon?'* (Try to adjust). I lived by your advice. Birmingham became home, helping me grow and sustain in adaptation, not change, in commonality, not divisions. It matters little where I live or belong. I can traipse from one home to another, interpret situations to perspectives varied yet similar. I feel at home in Birmingham, and I carry Dhaka in my heart. Home is where the heart is.

Before I end, one last thing – I will not let my sweater and myself form a rift, like the partition you witnessed. That will never happen; surely, not a second time. On homecoming, when I bend to touch your feet for the customary *pronam,* I shall wear with pride my famous yellow sweater, and carry your favourite melt-in-the-mouth Cadbury chocolates, my city's best gift to the world.

Your loving daughter.

Namira Hossain, Dhaka, Bangladesh

I wanted to focus on a memory that happened in my city and home rather than focusing on the place itself. But when I thought about 'My City My Home', very specific images came to mind which I described in my poem.

Chains of Smoke

It was the year of baggy pants and stolen kisses,
When lessons came from blackboards filled with chalk scribbles.
Days were defined by the space inside pencil-drawn lines,
Faded memories of notes exchanged in classrooms left behind.

I was riding on a chariot of privilege pulled by the blood and
sweat of poverty,
Painted with faces, in contrasting colours of fantasy.
With faces painted in hopes of gaining popularity – emulating
ideals of beauty – the cover girls of glossy magazines.
The dust was rising up from the concrete,
Sparking in the sun, filtered sepia by the afternoon heat of
summer.

Drivers were honking their impatience – at traffic cops, beggars,
peddlers, and pedestrians.
There were no rules at this intersection, no respect or right of
way,
No signs to guide me through the chaos, no lights to turn green
or red.
The wheels kept turning round and round, like hands of clocks,
Every second, to your last breath – counting down.

I am still haunted by the moment the White Rabbit appeared,
As fate beckoned me to jump right in, down the hole in the
ground.
He said to me, 'Come on, just give it a try. Everybody does it,
it will be fine, don't be shy – it's only this one time.'
'I really don't want to, but that logic does seem to make sense.
And if I say no, they'll all think I'm a bit dense. It's only this
one time,' I lied to myself, 'the repercussions can't be all that
intense.'

So many rules I had broken already that day, having stolen
away like a thief,
Vanished into thin air,
without a thought or a care
But Karma would bring no relief.
A curse of Murphy's law, to pry the truth from my jaws –
Freedom came at a cost – a price that I would come to pay.

Can't get back the time lost because of what happened, on that
fateful day.
Unaware of this unpleasant surprise,
I was welcomed home by the glare in her eyes and the stern
look on my mother's face.
'Where were you?' she asked. 'I thought you had class.'
And just like that, my carefully prepared lie fell flat.
Broke no ice or 'No cigar,' as they say.
'You silly girl, haven't I told you before? When you tell a lie,
Mother always knows. Every step you take, wherever you go.
You can't escape, I'm your shadow.'

Too stubborn and defiant to fall for her bluff,
I stuck to my story and to my guns.
There's no way she could have found out that I had taken one
puff.
She looked straight at me, and all that she said, was 'let's
confirm your story.'
A rabbit in the headlights –
My heart filled with dread.
She picked up the phone and made a few calls –
Piecing together the truth that was to become my downfall.

A crossing of paths – a coincidence supreme
Or mother's intuition that worked on the same team
And all my best-laid plans and my elaborate schemes
Had just come apart, right at the seams,
As my grandmother had been parked, right on the scene
Where I had my very first taste of nicotine.

'That boy is bad news. Trust me I know. Why else did you
smoke, you never wanted to before.'
'It was only this one time,' was my weak protest. 'It's only this
one time,' I promised myself.

Little did I know, I had built my cage,
Mounting pressure to fit in had set the stage
For self-restraint to fly out the shelf.
What happened next isn't too hard to guess –
Played once with fire to be burnt to ashes.
An ashtray full of dreams was the price I had to pay.
'It's only this one time,' I wish I had not lied to myself
that day.

Shagufe Hossain, Dhaka, Bangladesh

I have a habit of running. Having grown up in different places, I struggled with a sense of belonging. And because I never felt like I belonged, never felt truly safe, I ran from one end of the world to another. I used to equate the sense of familiarity that people often associate with safety as a threat. So, every time I found myself becoming familiar, with a person or a place, it would activate a fight or flight response and I would run. But I wouldn't call it running. I would call it 'being on an adventure'. Until recently when, while one afternoon on recovery from a heartbreak, I realised I was home. But home, to my surprise, wasn't a place. It was a moment in time. A moment where I surrendered to the moment itself. This poem is an ode to that moment.

Walking Cities

i am making a habit
of walking souls
instead of cities
now
instead of taking on neighbourhoods, or cities or countries
unexplored
i sit with myself
in a familiar pub
at the corner of a known street
and let a sparkling drink
swirl on my tongue
i taste the difference
in temperature
as it warms in my mouth
the tingle on my tongue
as it fizzles out
like unkept promises
i look at the bottle

catching sunlight
glistening with sweat
like fresh morning dew
under a pink afternoon sky
lit with love
waiting for love to see
waiting for love to choose
i could choose
to run
into the arms
of temporary comfort
the shadow of loneliness
closely following at my heels
from one city
to another
to another
an other
could spend an entire lifetime
looking to belong
i could choose
to run
away
deny
instead
i am making a habit
of picking a place
like a wound
and stripping it bare to the very depths of its soul
i touch taste smell feel
i look at it from every angle
picking it apart
until it comes undone
thread by thread
so i can see all of its colours
i am done walking cities
i now walk souls
so show me all your colours.

Rujiya Sultana, Birmingham, UK

The reflections I see trigger moments from where I come from to where I am now. It's these that I have been able to grasp and put into words. The similarities from where I come from to where I am now gives me such pleasure to speak about my tales of growing up, being nurtured. Life has surprisingly guided me to find that once again to where I reside now. Memories come flooding in when I think back to where I was and where I am now.

My City My Home

This life has been somewhat of a marathon I didn't expect to run. A race to meet people's expectations of a good life led me in the direction of this beautiful and blessed city of Birmingham.

An interesting timeline that began at the roots of my mother country of Bangladesh.

In a small village, I was the eldest born child. My birth unfolded a new generation. My grandad, Dada dearest, nicknamed me 'the moon', said I was shiny like the crescent, and I've certainly had a light to pave my path since.

I remember children gathered to play with me and to get to know me, loving my company. Dressed in warm weather clothes, dancing around pretending and inventing tools to play with. Making tea in little pots with sticks and vessels. Chasing insects and falling in water, so playful so innocent. Watching how elders went about their days so attentively – they lived well. The sun beamed on our happy times. I was raised like a leader of a pack. I was raised to comply, whether I liked it or not. What others thought was important, so I had to set good habits and morals and uphold a good reputation.

Living amongst a family of three generations, I loved that my great grandparents were still around. I was blessed. I loved growing up with so many around me. Those were days of the British fathers who worked hard to provide for their families back home. Dad was British since he was fourteen, which meant I first saw him when I come to England in 1984. I felt valuable time was lost in my early years without him, but a sacrifice needed to be made for survival, or so I was told. My brave mother married him at nineteen and didn't see him till she was twenty-one when he returned to whisk us off to the UK. We settled in Lincolnshire. I grew up in a society of many white faces. It was very challenging trying to fit in with peers here, and adopting their styles, their speech, their hair. I tried to do the best I could in a role where I had nobody to lead by example. I was labelled a coconut but that didn't stop me, I took it well as it pointed to my diversity. I tried everything, from netball to hockey. I did what I could to help and please my parents and spent a good thirty years doing what would have been expected of me. My life took me on a journey, from a small town to a big city.

See, I've been lost for so long and now finally feel grounded again. As unsettling as it may seem, it was not that hard for me. The closeness of villagers from where I was born is felt through the many faces, I come across here in Birmingham. Friends are made so naturally and calling them sisters is done so easily. My neighbours have become my family. The key is to treat them like royalty. Such characters live on my doorstep. It feels like I've known them for an eternity.

The years spent here in Birmingham have given me such happiness and made me feel whole. Having access to a variety of cultures, foods and celebrations makes it a colourful place to be part of. I've been able to use my PT skills and do charity work. I've been part of projects and achievements – it's been great! I've come to learn that opportunities are not given but made. In such a short time I have seen, heard, and done so much.

I no longer have to tame my desires or desert my expressions because Birmingham has brought out the best in me. Finally, I feel as free as the children from my village, the best part is that I'm no longer tied down by expectations. I'm free like the kind of kids that run around content and satisfied with what they have – they are happy. I smile at every opportunity, and I am grateful for all that I have endured in my journey to live and reside in this home of Birmingham. The journey has had its ups and downs but that's what's moulded me, prepared me and guided me. This home is all I have ever needed and my personal stamp on it gives me such satisfaction. I'm surrounded by love and laughter; this city is my destiny. My city and my home is Birmingham. Yes, it's now away from my mum and dad's branches but it is close to my deepest roots.

Ishrat Hamid Ghani Lindblad, Stockholm, Sweden

What inspired me? While writing I was inspired by many memories of living in a number of different cities and also by the realisation that, in the present globalised world, so many of us are experiencing a similar feeling of belonging to very different worlds from the ones where we were born or grew up. The terms 'My City, My Home' immediately triggered an emotional response in me. I feel very strongly attached to India, Pakistan, England, and Sweden. At the same time as I long painfully to be in each one of these places, I feel very grateful for the enriching experience of feeling at home in such different cities and cultures.

From Home to Home

Where do I belong? *That* is the question? For me, the partition of British India meant I lost half of my heritage. Close relatives, on both my paternal and maternal sides, chose different halves of our suddenly divided land. My father was from Kashmir – a country which itself symbolises the question: where does *it* belong?

I was born in Lucknow in pre-partition India, and my father lost his home in that city when he chose to live in Pakistan. He also lost our beloved ancestral home in Srinagar, where we used to spend all our summer holidays, and which is full of precious childhood memories for me. Suddenly, in the summer of 1947, my mother was packing away all our things and we realised we had to cut short our vacation. We bade a hasty farewell in Lucknow to the relatives and friends who had chosen to stay on in India, while we caught the train to Pakistan. On the 15th of August, I awoke to the sound of festive music being played below my bedroom window. When I wondered what all the noise was about, my parents told me they were celebrating Independence, and that Pakistan was now our home.

My father was a railway officer, which meant that he was

frequently transferred from one city to another. Thus, we lived in a number of different cities, and I liked to joke that I had spent more of my childhood travelling in a railway saloon than in any home! It didn't take long before we had to move from Karachi to the railway headquarters in Lahore, and the house we lived in was swarmed with refugees and my mother ran a soup kitchen in our garden. Gradually, we began to feel at home in this house along the canal banks. It was time to go to school as both my parents believed firmly in the importance of education, and so my elder sister and I were admitted to the Convent of Jesus and Mary Catholic school. I felt a great deal of affection for the nuns who taught us and developed a passion for reading, especially Enid Blyton's books about Saint Clare's Boarding School. My elder sister and I would imagine going to an English boarding school where we could enjoy midnight feasts and meet people like the O'Sullivan twins! Unexpectedly, our fantasies were realised in 1953, when my father happened to be posted to Rawalpindi, and the government decided our school must switch from the British system to the National Matriculation one. My elder sister, who had just a year left to complete the Senior Cambridge exam, was absolutely appalled. How could she be forced to study in Urdu which she had never been taught and to replace the study of British history and Geography with Indian and Islamic history? A dear English friend of my father's, from the days of the British Raj, came up with the perfect solution: he could help us to gain admission to the boarding school where his own daughters were studying in Bournemouth, and he and his family would look after us during the holidays. No sooner said than done! When my father told my sister and me that my mother would fly with us to England for the summer holidays and then admit us to a British boarding school we were thrilled beyond words!

Arriving in England in June 1953, felt magical. It was Queen Elizabeth's coronation year, and the streets of London were decorated with triumphal arches everywhere. We couldn't believe that a big city could be kept so clean, have such beautiful parks, and that one of them had a clear blue river running through it that people were happily rowing canoes upon! When our mother decided to take us on a tour of the Lake District, I experienced a true moment of epiphany. The poetry of Wordsworth and Coleridge, which I had been studying for so many years in Pakistan, had always puzzled me. How could they idealise nature as they did, when I had been taught to look out for all the dangers that lurked in nature: snakes, scorpions, storms, and floods? Looking at the peaceful natural beauty around me, I suddenly understood what they were so lyrical about. Yes, this is where I wanted to be, this island which I had only read about, but where I already felt at home!

Then, just two years later, I had finished school, and had to leave this 'home', and return to a new one in Mayo Gardens, Lahore. There, I began my higher education at Kinnaird College for Women. Another place I learned to love, and which opened a world full of exciting possibilities for me and where I made some close friends who would remain true to me for decades ahead. Living with beloved my parents in Lahore is where I became ME!

Even so, within a few years, we were travelling again. As fate would have it, on a ship bound homewards, I met my true love. When I told my parents I had met a Swedish doctor who had asked me to marry him, my father asked me if I hadn't read enough English literature to know what happened to shipboard romances! My mother wondered how I could even think of settling in a country to which I had never been. Nevertheless, when I finally arrived to live in Stockholm, I was completely overwhelmed by the love my new family showered upon me.

My mother-in-law told me: 'I had three sons, but my only daughter married an American and lives in America—so now *you* are my daughter!'

It was as her son's wife, that I realised it is not the *place* that matters but the *person*. I could move from home to home, but as the well-known saying goes: 'Home is where the heart is' and mine is his forever!

Bassama Tanvir, Lahore, Pakistan

The theme 'My City, My Home' inspired me to observe how women were treated in my area and how they dealt with it. I made a great effort to completely understand a woman's understanding of her surroundings. A woman's place was my inspiration behind this piece.

A Cow, Her Shepherd, and Her Owner

I had seen how a shepherd took care of his cattle. He was with them since their birth. He fed them. He bathed them. He protected them. And when he saw that his cattle were old enough to give birth and produce milk, he would sell them to their prospective owners. After separating each heifer from another, he usually forgot about them. He wasn't curious to learn how their owners were treating his cattle—whether they were slaughtering them or gently patting their backs.

I was also a part of my shepherd's cattle. Mostly, he would gently stroke my back and feed me with his hands. On bad days, when I refused to eat, he would beat me with a wooden stick. But generally, I was happy to be with him. I never thought I was going to leave him but one day he sold me off to a wealthy man. My friends had told me how some of them were lucky enough to be sold to a kind owner and some were sold to men who were only happy when they gave birth or produced milk. I had my apprehensions. But I was lucky because my wealthy man was kind. I had adjusted easily in his house, in his life. Now my life was going to be spent in a routine for which I had been prepared. I had been told that it took some time to understand your owner's routine but once you got to know it, life was bliss. Every heifer should learn to judge what her owner demanded from her. There would be times in a heifer's life when she might want to break away from this life, some bad eggs might refer to this life as *mundane*. These were just tests. We should not pay heed to such satanic ideas. But that was not what was written in my fate. My owner suddenly died, bringing disruption to my monotonous life. I wasn't even allowed to completely hate the routine of my life.

After my man's death, no one in his house wanted to keep me. I was sent back to my shepherd. But this time, I brought back four calves with me. My shepherd wasn't too happy to have me back. He could only afford his cattle and I was bringing back four extra calves. Maybe it was due to an old affiliation that he took me in anyway. My shepherd and his wife kept me inside the house, out of every potential owner's sight, for four months and ten days. In those four months and ten days, I listened to his wife complaining about various things – from how my shepherd wasn't gentle towards her or how I was a strain on their budget. But I noticed one thing: her protests were always silent, unheard, or a murmur. She never said any of this to my shepherd. It was always we who were at the receiving end of her complaints. Her displaced anger didn't make any sense. Why couldn't she tell my shepherd how tired she was? It was as if my shepherd played the role of an owner towards her. In a way, he was her owner. Perhaps a woman was trained from a young age to become a perfect wife. Maybe a woman was taught how her life was only divided between her parent's house and her husband's house. There was no house of her own. Possibly, a woman was told how she had to obey her husband and give him children and give him the things he desired, day and night; keeping her head low and only taking what her husband gave her, never demanding anything extra, never raising her voice in front of him and silently eating the millet he brought for her. She was his little cow. I never dared say anything like that to my shepherd's wife. She would have found it insulting, being compared to a cow, because she was a human too. Humans had their pride, but I wanted to know was how much of a human she felt and how much of a woman every day?

I heard my shepherd wanted to sell me to a new owner. But was there any man wealthy enough to take me with my four calves? I was a beautiful heifer once, but now I was a cow. Why did my value decrease as soon as I become a mother? My owner would want me to eventually bring calves into the world to benefit him in his business. So why didn't he want to buy me with my four children beforehand? I didn't like seeing the apprehensive faces of my shepherd and his wife. I didn't like hearing their silent complaints or seeing worried wrinkles form around their eyes. If it were up to me, I would try to make myself useful in ways other than producing milk and giving birth. But it wasn't up to me. If it were up to me, I would never want to come back and burden my shepherd like that. But it wasn't up to me. It wasn't up to me because I was never asked what I wanted. I was never asked because I was only told what to do. I was only told because I was only taught to obey.

That was how our lives were usually. We came into existence and, from the time since our first breath, we were prepared to be sold to our owners, our men. Sometimes, we would ask our shepherd's wife why we couldn't only want to exist. Why was it necessary for us to be sold off to our owners? To this, she would always say, 'You are not bulls. You are heifers. This is not America. This is Pakistan. This is how a heifer lives here.'

Sarbjit Pall, Oldbury, UK

I was inspired to write my poem with it being this time of year – Christmas. I have many memories of Birmingham around Christmas time as I lived and worked in the city for many years. I have not been back to where my memories were created, but they still are very fresh in my head. I saw this opportunity at the right time as I felt I could easily put how I felt in writing. I have been following Sampad and the work they do for many years now. I am really happy to take part in this competition.

The Brummie in Me

I suppose there will always be a 'Brummie' in me, even though it has been years
Since I left this colourful city and her memories of dare, mischief, and memories you will hear.
A nervous me sat in my first job interview in a new crisp white shirt, going with the flow.
The stern-looking one in the panel said proudly, 'We have the largest Council outside of Europe, did you know?'
Weeks later, a letter arrives sporting a Birmingham City Council letter headed paper!
I got the job! I was introduced to an empty dusty desk and an abundance of knowledge for years to come.-

Twenty-something, strutting my stuff in Carvela heels along Colmore Row,
After work gossip, a 'curry in a hurry' and cappuccinos on the go,
Passing and thanking one of my favourite places, which is Birmingham Cathedral,

Where I once sat. I would feel solace, send a prayer to many
and lose the outside world's upheaval.
Always ready to attend the 'Carols in the Community'
lunchtime service,
To sing along with Christian carols and grab a mince pie from
the person serving.

See you on the last Friday of the month, without fail!
Let's go up 'town' and find something to wear in the sale.
For it is the Bollywood night at Club DV8 – isn't that the venue for
gays?!
Oh, you must try it – who cares if anyone sees you or what the
Auntyji's will say!
The hours we spent dancing and laughing at the Custard
Factory disco nights,
We were victim to aching heels and sore throats the next day
alright!

Meet me by the ramp, I'll hop on the number 78,
The Midland Metro has broken down again and there still is no
update!
It is Christmas, listen to the steel drum's sweet sound along the High
Street,
We can get to the Jewellery Quarter in no time, to that small café for a
cuppa and a sugary treat.
Then back to browsing freely in the Oasis market and a stroll in
the Pallasades,
To pass that poor version of the Santa Claus grotto, that never
quite made the grade.

Four giggly youth sitting third row at Pebble Mill Studios,
I've bagged four tickets to watch the filming of Network East and we
might feature on video!

And how can I forget the 'hungama' at the Birmingham REP when queuing to watch a play called 'Behzeti',
What was all the fuss about? Cannot wait to watch the play and see!
So much to join in with, Chinese New Year and Birmingham Pride,
Who said there is nothing to do around here, and that romance had died?

I can still smell the damp sitting in my nostrils when visiting the Handsworth indoor market,
I am five years old, waiting anxiously to have my ears pierced from the Indian lady fumbling with my earlobes, finding her target.
£3.50 for the job done and sparkly red studs,
After that, I nagged my mother to give me 25p to buy a branch of catkin Pussy Willow buds.
The Rag Market, another one of my favs! Where my posher friends would not be seen dead in, going there was only for the brave!
This is Birmingham and all that she gave.

So, fast forward, double that twenty-something wants to visit these haunts again,
Where do I start, as some are no more, and everything seems to have changed?
Can I still take that shortcut over Victoria Square to Broad Street by foot?
Or shall I risk negotiating the new routes and one-way systems or shall I simply stay put?
You see, I will have two sprogs in tow,
And a husband who is not in the know
About the Brummie in Me and all I have to show.

Rama Rani Joshi, Birmingham, UK

I have been writing more about my life as I get older in the form of short stories and poems. This title inspired me to reflect on the period time when I first arrived in Birmingham which I learnt to adopt as my home. Recently I have had three books published of poems and short stories.

My City, My Home: Birmingham

Nearly half a century ago, I arrived in Birmingham with my husband as a newly married bride. I was full of apprehension, expectations, and terribly homesick. I arrived on a dull grey January evening, wearing a bright colourful sari.

My husband had spent two years in the UK before going to India to get married. It was an arranged marriage. He had not painted a rosy image of life here but had assured me that there were opportunities for work and further education.

I had grown up in Shimla, a hill station, where my father was a government employee. Later we had moved to Le Corbusier's planned city – Chandigarh.

I had read countless novels by writers in English, including novels by Thomas Hardy, Charles Dickens, and Jane Austen to name a few. I did not know anything about Birmingham, which I learnt later, was the city of a thousand trades. The things in my favour were my previous education and my hopes of going to university for a postgraduate degree in English. I had told myself that I was going to be here for 2-3 years.

Did all this prepare me for the stark reality of cold, dark days and nights ahead? Despite all my mental preparation, homesickness affected me badly. I shed countless tears – all the time telling my family in India that life here was wonderful. I would write about my visit to big department stores where I had gone to buy

65

'imported' lipsticks. I saw no sense in making them feel upset.

I stayed initially with my in-laws in an inner-city area where they had been living for some years. They were desperate to go back and did not think much of life here. The people around me, where I lived, were villagers from India and Pakistan who hardly spoke any English. I used to wonder how they had managed to come here.

It took me some time to realise that the work in the factories and foundries, where so many of them worked, did not require much English. Some of them had their own houses, drove cars, ran shops, and were helping other members of their extended family to come and work here. Soon I was full of admiration for them and their achievements. I learnt so much from them about life in this country. It also made me see my problems in perspective. What was I complaining about?

There was no job waiting for us and we had to struggle to find suitable openings. My husband soon realised that we needed to get out of the house and meet people. But how? The area where we lived, had a community centre and we came to know that there was a vacancy to cover the office on Saturdays, from 10 am to 7 pm. The pay for that would be two pounds and fifty pence. We accepted this because our motive was to meet people.

And what a godsend that turned out to be. We met countless people there who came for help and advice. In reality, we were the people who were getting help and advice. The other benefit was that we met people from different nationalities and backgrounds.

The people who walked through those doors did not only come for advice; some of them came to volunteer their time and services. Quite a few of them became our friends and went out of the way to help us – for instance, by making us aware of job opportunities and imparting knowledge of this country. Some of them invited us to their homes and there were opportunities to share food from different countries.

I remember how happy I was to learn about the different libraries and parks in Birmingham. I feel pleased to say that the varied cultural activities at the Midland Arts Centre have benefited me and my family over the years.

Of course, what helped me was that I was genuinely curious and asked endless questions. It took me a long time to realise that asking some of those questions was not the 'done' thing here, but I am glad that I was ignorant of this protocol initially. I learnt so much. I should also say that I, on my part, was also willing to answer questions. I remember that questions about arranged marriages and the caste system in India came up a lot.

People have asked me whether I encountered any racism and was I aware of it. Initially, I was not aware of it, and I thought that people behaved like that due to ignorance. I believed that because I was in a new country, it was up to me to make more of an effort. Once they get to know me, I would think, people would behave differently – and very often they did. I know now that the problem of racism is a lot more complex.

Life did not suddenly become easy, but after a period of time, we both had jobs. I enrolled in a part-time postgraduate course at Birmingham University, we bought our first two-up, two-down house and had our first child. But all this took a good three to four years.

When I look back, I can truthfully say that living away from India, a country I never wanted to leave, has taught me so much. It has opened my eyes to a whole new world of people and ideas. It has benefited me socially and increased my understanding of the world we live in. I feel a part of the community where I live.

Yes, Birmingham is my home, as it has been for so many years. After I visit India, I feel so relieved to return to Birmingham, my adopted homeland. As a result of my involvement in the community, I was appointed the first Black/Asian Justice of Peace to serve as a magistrate in Birmingham. I worked in this position for thirty-six years and guess what? I continued to wear saris throughout my working life.

Jacky Hotchin, Birmingham, UK

This was originally written after my reading/ writing group had read Toni Morrison's Jazz, in which the city seems to be a character in its own right, and strongly supported by its music. I wanted to use that idea as a starting point for an exploration of my own city. The eponymous 'Fairy' was inspired by a Black Sabbath song. I've woven in references to other Birmingham musicians and appropriated James's 'Sit Down' from Manchester because it seemed to fit. It is my favourite song and being proud of your own tunes doesn't mean you can't welcome others.

I hoped to convey something of Birmingham's vibrancy, diversity, and feistiness, and also how change, contrast, and contradiction are inherent in the nature of cities in general and, specifically, of this city.

I'm not native to Birmingham, but I have lived here longer than anywhere else. Sometimes, if asked where I'm from, I am unsure how to respond; I don't feel that there's any place where I have 'roots'. I'm not 'from' Birmingham, but it has become 'My City and My Home' and I belong here more than anywhere else.

Fairy in Boots

I am the Fairy in Boots, and this is my city. I was young before the mounds were burnt, before the Beormingas settled, before Domesday. Twenty shillings! How I laughed. Through Battle and Blitz, gunfire and bomb blast, devilry and anarchy, dancing in the flames, I was young. I am forever young because this is my city, and I am the fairy in boots.

I am in the middle of everywhere. Come to me and go wherever you like.

Follow bright painted lines to the big red post-box for opulent dreams. Resist the silver-blue lure of the sinuous cyborg. Disenchantment lurks within. Up the escalator to be sure you're never knowingly undersold. Down the High Street for trusty knickers and sensible shirts.

My hollering markets fizz and buzz. Fine silk, fresh fish, cheap fruit and sweets, and sparkly cartoon socks.

And those who seek will find my secret enclaves for illicit indulgence of their most miscreant desires.

Listen. My city is full of noise. Preacher men and flower sellers. Repent. Turn to Allah. Jesus will save you. Last few bunches – five for a pound. Bless you, bab. Tara a bit. End times approach. A nocturne breaks free from the Symphony Hall. Sirens howl blue.

A street corner rapper beats a rhythmic vernacular. Passing conversation in a myriad of diverse tongues.

Sit astride my bull. Run your hands across his angry sculpted rump. A quickening in your belly, a chill in your fingertips, the taste of slaughter on your tongue. Pose for a selfie.

Here in my landlocked city, there are sea sharks, green turtles, and a colony of bemused penguins. My spirit has sailed the world. Beware. The piranhas snap. Step back. Sail away. Say goodbye.

My cathedral rests in a green plaza peopled by stout pigeons. Share your meal deal with them. Sit on the bench by that girl with blue hair and purple lipstick. Breathe deep the skunky musk she blows out. Go in and light a candle. Hope that God exists.

Slide onto a sofa in the backstreet cinema where once I sat alongside pinstriped men and excited boys to watch topless girls. Today it's upmarket quirky, black and white with subtitles. Text the bar for a cocktail or a bowl of jellybeans or a glass of red, red wine.

Wonder at my pagoda. Mr Wing Yip built that for me, to say thank you. Thank you for having us, thank you for welcoming us. My pleasure. Thank you, Wing Yips, for soy sauce and roasted seaweed, for Loo Choo, and Mee Goreng, and sweet Nian Gao.

Brave the sour subway beneath my pagoda. Pull your sleeping bag tight around your neck. Hope for some eye contact, some loose change for a hot drink, half a chocolate bar guiltily retrieved from the bottom of a briefcase. If you hadn't seen such riches you could cope with being poor.

Sit down, James Dobbs. Sit down, Jon Wilks. Sit down next to me. Brummagen has altered so but set aside your grief and woe. I still have Snobs. I still have rogues. I still have grime and adult shops. I'm not so clean and not so safe. I'm not so far from what you know. Let all your melancholy go.

I am the Fairy in Boots. Put down your net. You can't catch me or pin me down. I beat my wings; I rise up high. I stamp my feet. I change my shape. I love this city. I hate this city. I am this city.

Cara-Louise Scott, Birmingham, UK

The prompt made me think about what the difference is between a city and a home and how, as a university student, I feel as though I have two homes. I wanted to demonstrate how I felt living in a new place in which I had admired for so long and dreamt about living in, Birmingham, and also the way in which a city and home can feel to an individual.

My City, My Home: Birmingham

Are they the same place or do they completely
contrast one another because
my city is not my home, yet
my home is not my city,

but this city is supposed to be my home.
My new home.

Birmingham.

The place sounds foreign on my lips
but familiar in my heart,
it is the place where I want to be,
the place I
chose
for myself.

The second city,
a place that feels like a less chaotic London,
but still so vibrant
and full of opportunities,
a diverse multitude of being,
so much to see,
so much to do.

At least I have three years here,

to explore
the wondrous sights that cascade outside my flat window.
Well, there are just trees in my vision,
but they just show
how natural this city is.

Winterbourne Gardens, Cannon Hill Park,
the lake on the Vale,
the green of my campus.

Its beauty astounds me.

Old Joe, in all its glory
stands proudly.
A momentous point.
A focal point
for our eyes
surrounded by the new and the old
buildings,

a foundation for our
learning,
a place for our
yearning
for more.

And in its centre
stands the bull –
always dressed up.
Like us.

Selfies are taken and
strangers are mistaking
us for tourists.

But this is our city now.

We laugh and we stumble,
drink pumping through our veins,
the canal paves our way and
the library fascinates me.
I have never seen a library so
Funky,
So eloquent.

The lights guide us toward the eye,
It reminds me of a snake,
Grand Central –
How can a station be so big?

We nearly missed our train
but it's okay
because we were all sat
together
in our city.

It may never be like this again.

This shall just become a
memory
much like now,
as I sit on the grass
in front of old joe
writing poetry with
words spilling on the page,
on the white empty canvas,
like graffiti on a wall

and this –
this is when I feel as though
everything I've ever wanted
is here
in front of me

and these dreams
are no longer dreams,
and this city
is no longer just my city.

It is my home.

Sabahat Jahan, Dhaka, Bangladesh

As a single mother, I wear many hats – some by choice and others by necessity. Somewhere, buried beneath an avalanche of responsibilities, there is a woman – or someone who was once only a woman. What a luxury that appears to be now: to be able to be a living, feeling, breathing woman who is ablaze with hunger and dreams and longings. I wish to return, not so much to a physical place like a childhood home or a street or even a country, but to that feeling of freedom, of hope, when everything seemed possible, and no illusions had been shattered. Perhaps that is home?

Time Travel

I woke up this morning to find
two decades had passed
(since last night):
I was a mother, a father, a daughter, a son
and a million nameless things.

People had died, places had changed,
homes had shattered –
some repaired, some beyond repair –
and the dust from collapsed lives floated in the
murky air.

I woke up this morning to find
two decades had passed.
(since last night)

Sabahat Jahan, Dhaka, Bangladesh

As I've grown older, I have come to think of home, not so much as a physical space, but rather as a feeling. Often, it's a feeling of belonging; sometimes, it's a feeling of loss, longing, and nostalgia. This poem speaks to the fluidity and to the multiple definitions of home, and how they can change and shift over time.

Shapeshifter

In the many faces you now wear
It's often hard to recognise the you that's real –

The one who waited for hours on the steps of my
crumbling building
Only to catch a glimpse of me venturing onto the balcony
to dry the clothes in the burning summer heat,

The you who ran to get me a rickshaw in the rain
While I waited in the comfort of the building's shade,

The you who drove an hour each way to sneak in and kiss
me
While my parents were away at a farewell do,

The you who wrote letter upon letter and handed them
to sisters, cousins, friends, and neighbours,
Hoping that somehow they would reach me,

The you who cut his hair short or grew it long
Depending on what I preferred,

The you who wouldn't fall asleep until dreams descended
on my heavy lids,

The you who defied faith and family, religion and rituals
To follow your reckless heart,

The you who scattered petals on our wedding bed and
bought mismatched curtains
For our first anniversary,

*Where's the you who would turn off the lights as soon as I said I
was sleepy?*

I guess time robs us of many things,
Including the people we once were.

Marisha Aziz, Chittagong, Bangladesh

I focused on the idea that the city that is one's birthplace is not always their home. Rather, home is more of a collection of ideas and feelings attached to a location, and this may be somewhere far from one's birthplace. Through my work, I tried to detail one woman's journey of discovering this idea about herself and her true home.

A New Home

The chilly breeze whipped a few strands of her hair into Selina's face as she scanned the road for an empty rickshaw. The incessant rain had only stopped an hour ago, so there were few vehicles to be seen. In her eyes, Sylhet was always at its finest after a good bit of rain. The air always felt cleaner, the leaves on every tree vibrant, rejuvenated by the downpour. Even the gloomy sky added to the beauty. Yet it did nothing to lift Selina's mood today.

She gave up on finding a rickshaw with a sigh. Selina had to stock up on some groceries, and her destination wasn't too far, so she set off at a brisk pace.

As she walked, she struggled to shake away the irritation gnawing at the back of her skull. The cause of her worries was quite simple, really. She had been out late with a few friends the night before, and once she'd gotten back to her dorm, she'd pulled her phone out to let her mother know she had returned, as she always did. Only this time, in her haste to assure her anxious mother, she typed out 'I'm home' and hit send. It was only when her mother had replied, 'What? You're here?! What?' when she had realised her error.

It was only a two-word text, but it carried more weight than any ordinary paragraph. Selina had been living in Sylhet for only two years. Chittagong was where she had been born, where she had spent the majority of her life. How could she dismiss eighteen years' worth of memories with just two words?

She soon came up to the familiar shop front and entered. The place appeared to be empty of people, yet the room still felt crowded, thanks to the stacks of everyday objects piled against the walls. Selina cast her eyes around the department store, attempting to find the items on her list amongst the haphazard mess.

'Ah, Selina apa, how are you?'

A man had popped up from behind the desk on the very corner of the store. Selina's face immediately broke into a smile.

'Alhamdulillah, bhaiya, I'm good, how are you?'

They exchanged pleasantries before he snatched the list from her hands, immediately setting out to hunt down the items on it. It always amused Selina that she was on first-name terms with the owner of this shop. Had anyone at any of the big superstores back home ever asked her about her day, or her studies? Had she bothered to ask them, either?

Once she'd collected the necessities, she waved goodbye before stepping back out onto the sidewalk. The afternoon sun was peeking out from behind the curtain of clouds, casting weak rays of light onto the road ahead. The groceries had been her only errand, but she didn't feel like returning to her room just then. Instead, she walked on towards the intersection ahead, craving a cup of steaming tea from the stall in front of the Kazi Nazrul Auditorium.

The street widened as the intersection loomed nearer. Gradually, the silence in the air was replaced by a medley of sounds. Water splashed outside a fruit shop. Vendors announced the prices of their wares. At the open bazaar right before the intersection, a riot of colours bloomed against the dull brown backdrop of the road. Fresh vegetables lured pedestrians into haggling prices with the salesmen.

At the auditorium gate, though, the scenes carried a stark difference. Food carts lined the sidewalk, their eclectic menus giving rise to a heady aroma in the air. People were flocking to the food carts, their voices mingling together to create a cacophony of noise, but it didn't bother Selina as much as noisy crowds had before. She deftly avoided the clusters of people and made her way towards her favourite stall and, once there, she spotted Zarin and Ali, two of her friends from college, sipping on their glasses of tea and engrossed in a serious discussion.

'They can't just spring an exam routine on us like this!' Zarin exclaimed, a few drops of tea spilling over her cup in her indignation.

'Well, they just did,' Selina chimed in. Her friends whipped their heads around.

'What brings you here?' Zarin asked, looping her free arm through Selina's.

'Mama!' Ali motioned to the man behind the tea stall for another cup of *gur-er chaa*.

The conversation resumed, moving from upcoming exams to recent campus gossip. Selina stood there, letting her friends' words wash over her like a soothing balm as the cup of tea warmed her fingers. Even after two years, Selina still felt surprised at the ease with which she could slip into conversations, the blind certainty with which she could refer to these people as her friends.

She cast her gaze around the place, taking in the sky streaked with shades of pink and purple as sunset approached, the great tree on the opposite side of the intersection, gently swaying in the breeze. The city bustled all around her, unaware of all it had given her. She had made and lost friends at this place. There were days she had laughed her heart out, and also days where she had cried more tears than she had thought possible. Days she had been elated, intimidated, nervous, confident, heartbroken, lovesick, restless, at peace — all witnessed by the same Sylhet sky, which seemed to have just as many moods as her. If she were to be truly honest with herself, she had lived, truly lived, far more in these two years than she ever had during her eighteen years at Chittagong.

The one tie she had thought she had to Chittagong was her family, yet she knew they would be a part of her regardless of her location. But home — home seemed to have dug its roots into the last place she had expected it to.

Zehra Nawab, Karachi, Pakistan

As a journalist and as someone very fond of engaging with history found in books and those passed down through conversations with elders, I wrote my story in the backdrop of the British Raj in the Subcontinent. The story is based in Karachi, in the city I grew up in, a city that is my home and my muse. The dynamic between the colonisers and the colonised has always fascinated me. I took this opportunity to explore a scene and an interaction that is based on true facts and locations, but I have explored them through a human lens, imagining some of the emotions, sights, the pains, and the joys.

Vermillion

The day starts for the poor long before it does for the rich, for the ruled long before it does for the rulers, for the sun long before it does for the moon, for the Indians long before it does for the British.

It is a dewy morning in 1937, Sukena makes her way from the servant quarters to the main grounds of the palatial residence. The drifting clouds slice through the soft yellow rays reflecting off of the magnificent yellow limestone structure that Memsahab[1] Anne calls her humble abode. Her husband, Lancelot Graham had been made Governor of the province of Sindh in British-ruled India, a little under a year ago. As Sukena's brother readies the horses in the stables for the Governor's morning ride, she runs past him, hurrying indoors to supervise the domestic staff as they prepare breakfast. Keeping Victorian traditions alive in a land oceans away from Great Britain, the Englishmen and women do not start their day without a hefty morning meal.

---

1 Memsahab: A respectful term used by non-whites in British-ruled India to address the British women from the ruling elite.

Today's selection made by Sukena includes an array of Anglo-Indian concoctions and, since this is Karachi, the city by the sea, the menu includes a lot of fish. Outside Memsahab's room, the punkah-wallah[2] shift is ending, and the next manual fan-operator is taking his place. The pulley attached to the ceiling flap-fan makes a swift exchange of hands.

Sukena stands outside the door, tidying her hair quickly and bending low to rotate the doorknob that is at knee level, a clever design to ensure a bow-down by whoever enters the room. There is still half an hour till Memsahab Anne has to be awakened; Sukena opens her almirah to take out the long white summer gown with red painted daisies. And to match... the red shoes, of course. As she takes these into the dressing room, Sukena glances over her shoulder to ensure the muffled snores can still be heard. She takes off her kohlapuri[3] chappals to slip her small brown feet into the glistening red square heels. She marvels at her reflection: tall, regal, moneyed.

The early morning service, from the Holy Trinity Cathedral, wisps into the room as does the spiritual longings and chatter of the myna bird. Memsahab slowly begins to awaken.

***

Anne Graham has ruby-coloured rouge on her lips that she softly wipes with her handkerchief after finishing breakfast. The turbaned servant clears the table as she expresses a desire to have an oil head massage before her Sunday bath.

'I was planning on getting the almond oil pressed and delivered before waking you up today, but I ran late, Memsahab. I shall

---

2 Punkah-walla: The manual operator of the large swinging cloth fan suspended from the ceiling.

3 Kohlapuri: South Asian handcrafted leather slippers/ footwear.

just go and get it for you from the Empress Market. You enjoy the morning newspaper.' Sukena hurries out of the dining room, 'I will be back before you finish the front page!' she chirps.

As Sukena prepares the horse carriage with the help of her brother, Memsahab Anne approaches the stables accompanied by a male servant holding an umbrella over her head. She has in one hand a small, embroidered purse and in the other the newspaper.

'I want to come along for some fresh air,' she says.

The coachman takes the reins as the two women get seated in the carriage covered with a folding top. The horse saunters towards the market.

***

Once the almond oil is bought, Sukena buys a rose from a nearby stall and, with the day's purchases in the jute bag, the two women exit the Empress Market. While the coachman helps Memsahab into the carriage, Sukena runs to the southern corner of the building to place the rose on a small pile of flowers, petals, and incense sticks. Memsahab, watching her from afar, enquires about it once Sukena returns.

After some probing, Sukena says, 'The flowers are for the martyrs, a way to tell them they are not forgotten, that they are still mourned.'

As the horse carriage moves forward, the grand limestone structure and the magnificent clock tower of the Empress Market, built on the ashes of a mutiny, fade into the background.

The Mutiny of 1857 according to the British, the War of Independence according to the Indians. Sukena's mind drifts into the abyss of memories, her grandmother's voice reverberating through her mind. She would often speak about the year 1857, the year when Indian princely states and native soldiers from the British army rebelled against the gora sahab's[1] oppressive policies. The uprising across various parts of the Subcontinent was an unsuccessful one, and the agitators were duly punished.

In Karachi, those who were not hanged or sent via the port to the KalaPani[2] prison, were tied to the mouths of cannons and blown to smithereens on a large flat tract of land in the city centre. It was a message to anybody who dared risk rebelling again. Sukena's grandmother often recalled that, in the subsequent weeks, the massacre ground would be strewn with rose petals by the locals — the scarlet of the petals signifying the blood of the freedom fighters.

Fearing the space would become a permanent memorial to the martyrs, the British decided to build a monument on the site dedicated to Queen Victoria, Empress of India. And so, in 1858, the Empress Market was built on the ground hallowed by the blood of martyrs. The same grounds now inundated by vendors and buyers; a history rewritten; a history forgotten.

Sukena's great-grandfather was amongst those massacred on this site. Her grandmother referred to that day as 'when smoke rose from the ground in anger; the day the air above the bloodied earth felt dense' — to their family, it still does.

Perhaps this enslavement is in their blood, tied to their fate, Sukena thinks to herself. All the while helping cool Memsahab with a hand fan as they ride back to the Governor's House.

---

1   Gora sahab: A term used by non-whites in British-ruled India to refer to a white British man.
2   Kala Pani: A colonial prison in the Andaman and Nicobar Islands in India. A prison for political prisoners, mutineers, and those of grave threat to British rule in the Indian Subcontinent.

Sumeera Wahid, Abbottabad, Khyber Pakhtoon Khwa (KPK), Pakistan

The title of this competition was my inspiration. When I read it, I felt a surge of emotions building up in my heart. For a long time, I had wanted to pen down my feelings about what I had been through after Osama bin Laden was caught from Abbottabad. Leaving the political impact of the event aside, I wanted to voice the feelings that were felt by the common people.

The human mind is amazing at forgetting negative experiences and remembering the things which make us happy. However, this particular incident stayed with me for a long time. I still remember that, at that time, I had felt myself fast-tracking through all the stages of grief in one brief moment. The denial, anger, and bargaining all melted into one amalgam of emotions shaking the core of my soul. Hundreds of fellow Abbottonians felt the same surreal emotions that were very nascent for the peace-loving citizens of this town. When I read the title of the competition, 'My City, My Home', I could actually feel all those memories coming back and I decided there and then to write.

Misunderstood

The rattling of the windowpanes was so vehement that it woke me from deep sleep!

Instantly I got up, as memories of the terrible earthquake of October 2005 flashed through my mind. My heart was throbbing hard. Barefooted, I ran out of my room.

'Mummy, Mummy!'

Frantically, I folded my stretched arms around my daughter.

'It's a helicopter! I saw it from my room!' she screamed.

'It couldn't be my dear! Must have been thunder!' I tried to reason.

'But I saw it!'

Before we could agree on what caused the noise, another rattle seared through the night sky, mocking my naivety as we stared into each other's eyes. This time I, too, saw an extremely low flying helicopter, lurking through the darkness of the chilling night. Perhaps some military exercises were in progress. In less than twenty minutes, we heard a loud explosion, and then the sounds of a distant ambulance reverberated through the otherwise quiet night.

All kinds of thoughts crossed my mind. This was not an ordinary night!

Soon after, everything went back to normal. Puzzled by what it was all about, we had no choice but to catch up with our broken sleep.

Surprisingly when I opened my eyes again, I had almost forgotten the night's episode. The golden glow of the spring Abbottabad sun welcomed me. From my window, I could see the endless greens of the beautiful valley. Mother Nature was bestowing upon me her magical wonders in the magical landscape of Abbottabad. What a romantic feast for the eyes!

It didn't take us long to realise that last night was not a nightmare, but a stark reality. The press from all over was pouring out the story of US SEAL helicopters seeking to end the mystery of Osama bin Laden! Suddenly we were the centre of the world. I was shaken to the core of my soul. Surely not in my peaceful town? My home? Am I just having a bad dream?

Days passed but the dejection that had invaded me lingered on. I was hurt because this was not the true face of my city. I truly felt the urgency to do something that showed the world the real Abbottabad!

I was born, brought up, and married in Abbottabad. This was not just any place that I had chosen to live, rather it was the place that had given me respect as a woman and recognition for my work as a teacher. To be honest, it had given me all the best things in my life. My family, friends, and teachers, all the people I loved, were given to me by my city Abbottabad. It provided shelter to my immigrant father after the partition of the Sub-Continent. My grooming took place at the world-renowned Burn Hall, which was founded by highly dedicated missionaries after the creation of Pakistan. I found my life companion, my dear husband, in Abbottabad, and I gave birth to my beautiful children in Abbottabad. It was my home.

The people of Abbottabad feel proud of their city being the most peaceful city in the whole country. We can brag endlessly about our city having high literacy rates. We can tell stories about the best residential schools and the best teachers in the whole country hailing from Abbottabad.

Our charming city keeps us entranced for hours by the beauty of its evergreen pine forests that cover all the surrounding mountains of the Lesser Himalayas. Its dreamy Chinar Road is one of nature's greatest gift. Each season, the mesmerising beauty of its green and yellow and red and orange leaves casts a spell on us. Since its creation in 1853 by the British Raj ruler, Maj James Abbott, it has been famous for its snow-capped lofty mountains, its sparkling water streams, its clear blue skies, its walking tracks on Shimla Hill, its hospitable people who co-exist in exemplary religious harmony, its low crime rate, its delicious kebabs, and its central location for tourists and mountaineers travelling North in search of adventure and solace.

The speculative eyes of the world were unbearable. How could our city become famous overnight for all the wrong reasons? The love, safety, and comfort that I had always associated with my home and my city were suddenly being questioned by the media. Didn't they know the great resilience that we showed during the terrible earthquake in October 2005? Didn't they know that poets like Iqbal and Faraz and James Abbott had borne witness to the galore and bounties of this city? Why had they overlooked the reality that it was a place which attracted artists from all over the world to capture its shades on their canvases in each of the four seasons?

Time passed as one season melted into the other. The melodies of summer remained unheard. The rustling of the autumn leaves couldn't move the strings of love in the hearts of the people of Abbottabad, and when winter set in, the melancholy of the desolated souls with the expanse of the frost became a visible reality. It appeared as if an emptiness had engulfed the whole city.

It so happened that one cold February morning the chirping of a robin in the balcony of my room interrupted my gloom. I looked at my empty hands and felt time slipping away like sand. The robin kept chirping as if calling me to itself. A golden ray of the early morning sun was peeping through a slit in the curtain. I pulled the curtain apart. The little bird flew away but only to find a spot on the branch of a nearby pink magnolia that was all covered in flower buds, all ready to bloom in a day or two. My heart skipped a beat as I realised that spring was in the air again. The shadows were moving back, and the golden sun was ready to bathe everything with its mellow intensity.

It was a new day in my Abbottabad!

Solmaz Regi, Karachi, Pakistan

Despite the current conditions of my city, I call myself an optimist.

My City, My Home

The title 'My City, My Home' sounds very claiming to me. It's almost as if someone is forcing the idea on us. Or they want to make believe a thought very alien to the residents of Karachi. The thought is pretty scary for me! I live in Karachi, the city often numbered amongst the top twenty unsafe and most populated cities of the world. With this comes both good and bad.

For the residents of Karachi, the relativity is low. We are used to building our extreme homes and spaces safe with double locks and security cameras; the Elite hire security agencies to protect them. It is very common for us to block our balconies, lock all ways to the rooftop. Putting up grill bars on glass windows is the one I hate most; it robs the entire beauty of looking outside and feeling the city sky. We build barriers as much as possible to keep ourselves safe from the City. Yes, we are not free! We are caged inside our homes to be safe and separate from the city itself. My city! And the comma in the title is very meaningful.

The thought of low fence gardens, open porches, roadside playgrounds, no bar windows, and a life free of locks and guards, runs in anxiety through our thoughts. As much as it sounds normal to the rest of the world, it is an almost impossible thing to achieve, as reality, here in Karachi.

Our previously famous Mayor had to run a campaign with the slogan 'I Own Karachi.' This thought was new to everyone. Many were happy, for it was actually happening. Many related. We all started with thinking out our priorities. Yes, we want a clean, safe, modern, and organised city with all the possible 'greats' in the world. After all, we are amongst the largest cities in the world, so we need to get to the best title too.

This was our metropolitan dream coming to reality. Humans crave to be hopeful; they want to have faith in better days, better homes, and better cities. It felt like our dream was making sense. We want to own our city like our home.

We want to keep it safe, but from who? Who is the owner of this land? Trouble starts right then and there.

Karachiites are mostly outsiders. The land was developed as a hub and port trade centre and, in a span of one hundred years, it has become the largest of them all. Everyone belongs to somewhere else. Everyone has migrated. The closest to home are the people sharing the province. Yet we don't relate to them, we obviously don't trust them with the city that we claim to be our home. The ethnicities, the religion, the migrations, our histories, they all break us apart. Where is the solution to this all?

I'm a woman who has to walk the streets alone. I'm independent and liberal. I have my family's support for independent living and, no, I don't want to leave my city. Emotionally it is an attachment, an ownership we all feel towards it. Being a Karachiite is rather cool here. But in reality, does me being here or not being here actually matter? Am I safe here the way I am at my home? Do I feel free like I do when I walk the corridor of my home? If I have to face any of the common accidents that Karachiites come across, will I be helped or saved?

The city is bursting with street crime, rape cases, murders, and kidnapping – many of this is not even reported on official counts. The main reason remains the lack of justice served. This all is, thanks to the lack of police vigilance, bribe culture, corrupt systems, and divided political interests that make justice-seeking very complicated. I really don't want to be saying all this, but fact and wishful thinking should be kept as separate entities.

A large population of our city engages in social work, of all kinds. It varies from women's rights to orphanages, to feeding the poor, to taking up cases of the street dancing transgender and what not. This is our coping mechanism.

We are forced to help ourselves under any circumstances because we know for a fact that no one is coming to help. There are no law implementations. There is no quick justice. So we have evolved to keep safe, play safe, put our guards up, not trust strangers, and keep our boundaries well-guarded.

Coming from all of this, and thinking of 'My City, My Home' is scary. Because we are not kids anymore, this is not fiction. Our world doesn't end in the green park with swings and butterflies. The city is vast, thriving, and dangerous, but the mafias exist and also thrive.

Despite, a lot of material opportunities and good happenings for businesses, we keep our circles closed. We stay in our business only. We cannot mingle with people from all walks of life. We certainly keep the boundary between 'My City' and 'My Home.'

Yes, we do want to open up, and I like we're in a dream city. I work towards that with whatever means I have, in hopes of making a city more like a home. It's actually not the system or them, it's all of us! We are all in this together. I make it safe for my neighbour and he takes it forward. This is the way we want to live here. As much as it sounds ambitious, I believe we have started, as self-realisation is the first step. I see the good unfolding, but the pace is slow.

I am hopeful for the days where I'd calmly say 'My city, my home' with a smile, without having to compare the two in anyway. I am hopeful for the days when I walk the streets of downtown like it's my own garden. I am hopeful for 'My City' to be truly 'My Home.'

Salsabil Alam, Chittagong, Bangladesh

I came from a spiritual and superstitious city called Chittagong which is a 2000-year-old city. My city is very green and has a plethora of verdant hillsides and beaches. My hometown is famous for its seafood and mosques. I never go to mosques, but I hear the sound of the azaan. I think a lot of people in my hometown work in garment factories, as there is a myriad of garment factories. People in my hometown speak with a kind of Chittagonian dialect. My city always makes me feel special because I was born and grew up in this city. For the past two years, I make frequent visits to Singapore for my lupus treatment. So when I travel to the airport, I can see the beauty of my whole city. It makes me feel alive and inspires me to do something for my city, especially for the destitute workers. I always think about how low-income Bangladeshi workers deal with lupus. After I complete my bachelor's degree, I will contact several NGOs and hospitals. With the help of them, I will commence a lupus awareness program and provide free medications and treatment for destitute workers and folks. I am sure that I can start this program because my city my home always inspires me.

The Endless Journey of My Spiritual City

The spiritual sound of the azaan brings my consciousness back to the real, harsh world. Every time I wake up, I don't know what I am alive for; but the first ray of morning sun forces me to get up from my warm cosy bed.

As I put my warm feet on the cold floor, a burst of chill hits my body, but the melodious whistle of the winter birds makes me forget about the instant chill and piques my curiosity towards the balcony. The crispy cold and the mist-ridden morning make the Kazim Ali High School more appealing. I have grown up seeing this 168-year-old high school: one of the oldest and most renowned high schools in Chittagong, founded by the British government.

As I walk towards the dining room, the smell of brewing tea fills me with ecstasy. However, life becomes a living hell when the medicine catches my attention. After I was diagnosed with the lifelong genetic disease known as lupus two years back, I have not been able to enjoy my scrumptious breakfast because the Lucifer inside my head never lets me forget that I have to take my medicine immediately after my breakfast. As a repercussion, I forget what breakfast tastes like.

The background sound of the kitchen brings my attention towards my mother, who says to me, 'Eat your breakfast as soon as possible or we will be late for the flight to Singapore.'

Many people travel to Singapore during the festival time to enjoy their holidays. However, I travel to Singapore every six months only for treatment purposes. The saddest part of my life is that I never get time to travel to Singapore's interesting and unique places.

While struggling to put my suitcase inside the car's trunk, the driver uncle said to me 'Let me help you.'

My mother says in an irritating voice, 'Why do you have to carry that luggage? Let them do it.'

I say to her in a sarcastic voice, 'Okay, next time just feed me food like a toddler.'

While the driver is struggling to get out from the narrow road, my eyes fix on Masjid-e-Siraj-ud-Daulah. It has 17th-century architectural design and multiple domes painted in a kaleidoscope of colours which always amazes me.

As the car passes through the Chittagong college road, food vendors catch my attention – selling panipuri, chotpoti, dhup pitha, and malai tea on the footpath. I crave to eat those mouth-watering snacks, but the lost soul inside my head says to me that the physician warned me not to eat those yummy poisons.

Where do I take this sorrow? Sometimes I opine that my sorrow will not fill the Pacific Ocean. While in the traffic jam, I am struck by the angelic smile of a young woman crossing the Tiger Pass, a place where mountains and trees surround this evergreen road. This makes me forget about my sorrow. Whenever I see the two statues of a tiger at the Tiger Pass, my strength comes back immediately and I say to myself, 'You were born to fight'.

Long ago in this location, a myriad of tigers was spotted and thus the inspired the name. The car is passing along the EPZ, the hub of garment industries, I wonder how low-income Bangladeshi women deal with lupus. Once I tried to put myself in the shoes – one of those of a garment worker who has lupus and has to do work in a sordid, small junction of a monstrous factory where she can barely afford the basic treatment for the disease with her 'peanuts pay'. It might be hard for her to survive, let alone to think about the basic medication for her lupus. Does she curse her poverty and frown at me? Does she carry the ill-feelings that God unfavoured her by bringing upon her rotten luck and that she was abandoned both by money and a sound health?

I look at my mother and say to her, 'Mum, thank you for everything.'

Mother asks me rather cautiously 'What happened? Is everything okay?'

'Everything is okay. Just chill Mum!'

'This journey never makes me chill,' she says callously.

Then the cacophonous sound of cargo ships which are sailing in the Bay catch my attention. This beach of my city is famous for its savoury food, stunning sunrises, and beautiful sunsets. It whizzes me back to Cox's Bazar and I wonder how Chittagong is blessed with the world's longest beach, founded by Captain Cox in 1798. Its golden sand, foamy waters, green and low hills make this beach exceptional. My memory flitted to and fro. Although for the past two years, due to my lupus, I couldn't visit Cox's Bazaar, I wonder why its melodious sound of waves is ringing my ear now.

Sometimes I think that my dream is as big as that beach and I promise to myself one thing: that after I complete my bachelor's degree, I will contact several NGOs and hospitals. With the help of them, I will commence a lupus awareness program and provide free medications and treatment for destitute workers and folks. Recently I've realised that this city is the reason for who I am today and a plethora of things about the city bring me joy. Many cultural activities, museums, architectural heritage, and its glorious history make a city unique, but this city is alive because of its narrow lanes, crowded streets, and unruly traffic. It is not a big city, yet it bears the recognition of the commercial capital of Bangladesh which boasts the busiest seaport in the Bay of Bengal and keeps my country moving.

Suddenly I hear a roaring sound above. The sign of the airport on the roadside makes me alert that it is now time to deal with the luggage.

Mahabuba Rahman, Sylhet, Bangladesh

During the pandemic I couldn't stay alone at my own house because I am not married, and my parents live in another city. I had to travel from place to place only because I am not supposed to live alone. I then questioned whether I am really independent and established. I could relate myself to all the women around the world who are still manless and are considered helpless. This sudden thought inspired me to write a short prose or an autobiography.

To All the Women Who Do Not Have a Place of Their Own

I am from a small town in Bangladesh. I feel like I know every tree, every building, every season of the city. I was born at our home, my father's house if I have to be specific. I didn't know how it felt to live in rental houses. We never had to shift from one place to another. My childhood is full of memories of our home. I'm a proud 90's kid. We didn't have ips or a generator. During a power cut, we never got annoyed, rather we used to feel immense joy as there wouldn't be any studying for some time! We all would go to our roof with a mat and pillows and would gossip and sing together. Thus, our precious time used to pass.

Then, unfortunately, I grew up. I had to move to another city for my studies and after finishing my education I joined an office. After having my own income source, I decided to rent my own place. In Bangladesh, unmarried girls hardly ever get any space of their own. I had to show my parents to the owner to convince them for a space of my own.

I've been working for almost two years till now, having my own place, but surprisingly no one believes that! The first thing new people I meet ask me is 'Does your husband work here?' or 'Are you still living with your parents?' Why is it difficult to believe that I can have my own place too?

So, I asked my mum, 'What's wrong with the people? Why can't they accept an independent established woman? Why does she always have to live under someone's guidance?'.

My mum replied that, according to the beliefs of this society, all women are supposed to be men's property. Men will look after them, take care of them. Women are considered weak, both mentally and physically. They are not supposed to have their own place because they are supposed to live under someone else's supervision; a man's supervision.

Luckily, my father guided me enough to take good care of myself and the people around me. So, I continued to stay alone, at my own place, proving that I can guide myself.

Every day I maintain my office work and household. I socialise with neighbors and colleagues. I shop and cook for myself and the most important thing I do is keep myself happy. This is a letter to all the 'manless' women who are made to believe that they are weak, unable to manage themselves, and cannot have their own living place. Just believe that you are strong enough to create your own place, your own identity in the society, and do not believe anything else.

Saima Kamal, Karachi, Pakistan

My City, My Home: This theme was inspiring especially in this pandemic because I became more aware of my own surroundings and how we cannot escape what we know as home. We have to accept it with all its warts and learn to appreciate it in all its glory.

She Forgives

The ocean caresses her knees,
She dips her hair,
Just the ends,
And tastes it on the tip of her tongue.
She is sullen today,
Battered and bruised,
Bereft and bedraggled.
Her mood's no longer in her control,
How did she come to be this way?
My city Karachi!

She sashayed through the market,
Every eye on her curves,
Smiling coquettishly at all.
Her hair down to her waist,
Stars twinkling in each strand,
The moon beckoned to play.
She gave him no attention at all
For her heart only beat
With the love of the sea,
My city Karachi!

They cornered her one day,
They took away her green garb,
Their nails etched grooves across her sultry form.
She was sold for parts to the highest bidder,
No one came to her rescue
As she wailed for her life
They watched, her children, with apathetic eyes,
As they carried their mother to the grave
And even then, she yearned for her love,
The ocean, that never left her sight.

He crashed and tumbled,
He roared and raved,
He wanted her back in his arms.
It took every ounce of his mighty waves
To drag her back from harm,
And with the tenderness of a broken heart
He gathered her, and bathed her,
And caressed her wounds,
Until she sat back up again,
She yawned and stretched,
Her wounds forgotten,
She gathered her children in her arms,
They promised her attention and love
And she believed them,
Although she knew they would forget.
The ocean looked at her with love,
He knew that he would need to be here,
She needed a safe haven.
That is the tale
Of my city Karachi!

Saima Kamal, Karachi, Pakistan

The Female Jogger

She pulls her sneakers on. 'Self-care' was the term they were using in the pandemic. She simply picked it up to prove to herself that life had not stopped. Running was her tether to life. The aching muscles kept her alive and her growing fitness helped her stay motivated to get out of bed.

She had never truly appreciated the glory of her city until the lockdown. Until she was forbidden to go out and had the yearning to do just that. She began her jog after she had trekked down from the sixth floor of her apartment and turned into a lonesome lane that led her towards the main sea-facing promenade.

The 'lonesome lane' was the true challenge. There were three human forms, huddled together, their faces alight with the spark that lit the silver filament, equivalent to the rocket ship that takes astronauts into space. Here, the rocket was the chemical they ignited between them and inhaled. This morning, one of them was doubled over and retching into the gutter that ran alongside their living quarters. She averted her eyes and held her breath. She was reminded of how they tend to do that for everything in Karachi. If there is a garbage dump, they avert their eyes and hold their breath; when stuck in a road jam, vehicles spewing their toxins into the air, they need to live on, they avert their eyes and hold their breath; a heart-wrenching incident of child molestation and they avert their eyes and hold their collective breath till it becomes a distant memory.

She drowned it all out, jamming in her earphones and pushing the dial to max. She ran parallel to the Arabian Sea, and it became a soothing presence in her peripheral vision, father holding the hand of his child taking his toddling steps. No amount of prying eyes mattered once she was attuned to the rhythm of her legs.

There was that gentleman with his dog, always looking as though he would let go of the leash anytime because he just couldn't control his pet any longer. He reminds her of Karachi's daily challenges. The city dwellers are pulled in every direction as they try to manoeuvre around the pitfalls that are a metropolitan life. Survival in the city is no less than taking a huge, excited pet, on a leash that seems insufficient to keep it under check.

The lady holding one nostril at a time seems to be conserving oxygen for the rest of them. She watches her move into her usual Tae Kwan Do style arm movements. It is almost mesmerising, watching her go from extensions to bicep curls to reaching towards the sky trying to catch something imaginary from the air. She imagines her fellow citizens trying to make something special of the drudgery of everyday life. Being cogs in a mammoth wheel is not a palatable thought for any conscientious mind.

In a few minutes, she started to feel the exhilarating rush of cyclists passing her by. Their graceful, bent heads and their colourful garb propelled her to run faster. There was cockiness in the arrogant pedalling of their bikes, as though they could pedal their way out of any scrape. She realises how much of the essence of her beloved city is symbolised by this energetic troupe.

We are an arrogant lot of people, learning to work around every hurdle, finding loopholes and pushing past our own limits to be able to cycle past what is thrown at us.

Her walk back from the endpoint always makes her unstrap her phone from her arm and take a few pictures. The first few rays of the sleepy sun, the seashell – how did it come all the way to the pavement? Perhaps dropped by a collector. The waves were like a child's first stretch after being woken from slumber.

Having captured the glorious morning she turns into the lonesome lane only to find that her usual 'companions' are missing. Strange how she had first been uneasy due to their presence and now was finding the lane even more daunting in their absence. As she reaches halfway inside the lane, she hears the roar of a motorcycle, and it comes to an unnervingly close stop. The next few seconds are a burden that all women have felt, all over the world. It happens over and over and over again. She could be a woman in a burqa in a crowded market in Bangladesh. She might be wearing the skimpiest shorts in the middle of Birmingham, or she could be a female jogger in Karachi, she has been the target of this malice.

The motorcyclist has taken his penis into his hand in full view of her and anyone else who might be nearby and is in the process of masturbating vigorously while looking in her direction. She is frozen because no one ever expects this kind of violation.

Why did I wear this T-shirt? What will I tell my son and husband? They will be so embarrassed. They will not let me out. Were her first thoughts. The first thoughts of a 45-year-old, independent, educated woman.

'This is my city too. I have as much right to be out here, enjoying myself, as you do. I am not a teenager any longer and I will not back down. I will not bow my head and let you go about your 'business.''

She remembers the phone in her hands and simply points it at him. She relishes the haste with which he tucks himself inside his shalwar and kicks his vehicle into action. The phone camera is not even on. Her hands are shaking too much for her to be able to do that. It is her turn to 'enjoy' herself as she watches him almost topple under his bike as he makes a U-turn and makes his exit.

Mariam Hassan Naqvi, Lahore, Pakistan

The life of interior Lahore (old Lahore) is very close to my heart. The rich traditions, culture, and lives of the locals have been drastically suffered by the politicisation of religion and the state. While writing this piece, the topic 'my city my home' clearly revolves around these fragments of old Lahore's traditions and the nostalgia of a resident.

Story of a Bluebird

Bol, ke labh aazaad hain tere

People were chanting Faiz's ghazal in a disoriented chorus. The walls of Lahore's Pak Tea House were drenched in tea, cigarettes, and the sweat of progressive students. The orchestra of mall road's traffic was a piece of background music, making the air more melodious. Some fashionable ladies were laughing like free birds about some inside joke, and among all the voices, the sound of their giggles was the favourite melody for Sohni. Despite bearing Ammu's aggression every day, she manages to elope for an hour to hear the sound of their laughter, to see the wrinkles around their lips when they talk passionately about politics, and especially to watch the bluebirds in their eyes.

Qari Sahib of their Mohalla told her about those bluebirds in the eyes of modern women of the city which makes them blind to see the difference between morality and wrong deeds. According to Qari Sahib, these bluebirds will gradually turn into the huge vultures of the black playground behind Victoria School where people throw Sadqah's meat. After turning their disguise, these vultures will scratch the flesh and eyes out of these indecent women. Sohni became scared of them, and she never went back to the black ground to grab the leftover meat even after having Ammu's fragile slaps.

She felt pity for the butter-like silky skin of these women, unlike Ammu. She suddenly recalled the freckles on her mother's skin and blemishes around her fleshless cheeks. Sometimes she wonders if the vultures of the black ground have eaten the flesh of her mother too, but occasionally Ammu looks pretty whenever she wears her best hot pink dress of jammawar. She also applies the smudged drains of her only lipstick by the tip of her finger. Those are the happiest days for Sohni because on such bright evenings random chachas, including Phuphi, Majida's very old husband, visits Ammu with sweets and chicken. These are the only days when they feed themselves fully. But Ammu never allows Sohni to meet them. After such visits, Ammu becomes more aggressive and protective. Sohni also finds scars on her mother's body after each visit as if she is secretly visiting the black playground of vultures to grab some meat.

The black ground was full of pigeons and flowers when Abbu was alive. Sohni vaguely remembers the fragmented memories of her father in their crumpled little old home which was soaked in the warmth of love. Abbu used to bring jasmine flowers from the Victoria School's garden every day for Ammu and she would wear them in her ears. Back then there were also bluebirds living in Ammu's eyes.

Abbu was a kite maker and the festival of Basant was like the event of Eid for them. Months before the event, their small house started smelling like the ointments of dyes and both Ammu and Abbu used to prepare different sizes of kites in vibrant colours. All rooftops of the interior Lahore would get booked by foreigners. The skin of the blue sky would look like the colours of the rainbow. After every Basant, there was a family ritual of a picnic to Manto park, a movie of Dilip Kumar at King Cinema, and afterward her parent's long sitting session on an empty bench with a cup of tea from Lakshami chowk. In the meanwhile, Sohni always got the task of counting stars while Abu and Ammu would listen to Mehdi Hassan's, Aj Janay ki zidd na karo.

It was one of those fine days when they were returning home. A crowd appeared around their home with sticks and burners and rushed towards Abbu while chanting *gustakh* and *paleed*. Ammu clutched Sohni's hand tightly and they grabbed Abbu from his thin grayish hair. She saw Phuphi Majeeda's husband and Qari Sahib with the crowd kicking the fragile face of her father. He had a dispute with him last night when Abbu asked him to pay money for his purchase of kites. After that day Abbu never came home but Qari Sahib visited them with other respectable elders including Phuphi Majeeda's husband and he asked Ammu to recite *Kalima*. They also took away the big book of the Bible and pictures of Mother Mary, but Ammu still hides another Bible under the rack of the Quran.

Ammu and Sohni started making kites afterward until the ban by the government on Basant and kite flying. They never went for a picnic at the cinema because Qari Sahib told them it's forbidden in religion to watch indecent movies. Songs of Noor Jahan were also declared kafir. Sohni and Ammu were left with nothing that belongs to Abbu now.

The bluebirds in Sohni's heart always lured her to celebrate these infidels. She yearns to fly kites and dive into the ocean-like sky. She dreams about dancing like a peacock on the beat of Nazia Hassan's songs and she wants to embrace the bluebirds shrieking the ghazal of Faiz in her chest; *Bol k lab azad hein tere, bol, bol, bol. Bol* Sohni! she came consciousness from the heavy slap of Qari Sahib's scaly hands. He was asking her about the last lesson. Sohni suddenly started singing,

> Khulne lage quflon ke dahaane
> Phailaa har ek zanjeer ka daaman

Qari Sahib gave a strong kick on her back, *Kanjari!* he exclaimed. She started sobbing when he ordered that Sohni would stay here late until she memorises the whole lesson on one foot.

Black vultures were spreading around the ground behind Victoria School, the Moazan was giving the Azaan of Isha from Masjid Wazir Khan, and Ammu was roaming hysterically on the streets of Lahore looking for Sohni. Suddenly she saw a black vulture on her roof with blood on his jaws and a dead little bluebird in his claws. Faraway somebody in Pak tea house was singing:

> Bol, yeh thodaa waqt bahut hai
> Jism-o-zubaan ki maut se pehle
> Bol, ke sach zindaa hai ab tak
> Bol, jo kuch kehnaa hai keh-le!

Nubaha Tahannum, Chattogram, Bangladesh

Being a Bangladeshi, I see many young girls and women being married off. But some of them are confident and brave enough to stop child marriage – they run away from their old town and make a new town their own home, own city.

Divergent

A young woman, aged nineteen, is walking confidently through the aisle between the sewing machines.

Years ago, in the small village of Puthimari, Panchagarh people knew a shy, timid girl named Sumi. She was always attracted to education and was thus very studious. But her luck was not in her favour. Living in a family of seven and having a farmer father made her dreams shatter at the age of thirteen when she was just a student of Class 5. She was forced to get married which we term as 'Child Marriage' to a man sixteen years older than her.

Sumi was diffident at that age but the day before the wedding she somehow managed to leave all the bad memories in her house and escape to one of her closest teacher's houses. She did not know what she had just done after reaching the teacher's house. But she was suddenly proud of herself. The teacher let her stay in her house for two days and stayed silent for those days.

But as they both knew the storm would come in a very short period, the teacher helped her to travel around 656 km and reach Chattogram, a new place for her. The teacher let Sumi stay in one of their relative's houses, which was quite a safe place to stay for some days. Sumi now is burdened with more responsibilities and knows what life actually is. With the help of the relative Sumi finds a job, a place to stay, and food to survive the starvation.

She is now a garment worker. Incidents changed her into a different person, a totally different Sumi, not the one that the villagers knew. Years pass by and she only thinks about how she came to this position, the responsibilities, the stability, and whatnot.

Now she is nineteen, walking confidently, boldly through the aisle between the sewing machines. Her big dreams to study more do not let her sleep, and she now thinks she can fulfil her dream one day.

Opshori Nondona Khan, Dhaka, Bangladesh

Durga is the goddess of womanhood and power according to Hinduism. But also, Durga Puja is one of the biggest festivals in Bengali culture. Bangladesh has always been an open-minded country and we believe in the spirit of happiness through the festival no matter what religion we belong to. Festivals are for everybody. Though I'm from a different religion, I always felt my Bengali root during Durga Puja. When I was a young girl, I used to go to visit Old Dhaka during Durga Puja, holding my dad's hand and the colours, lights, and the festive atmosphere gave me a different kind of courage and power inside. Durga Puja feels like home to me. But a few days ago, one of my close friends was sharing her horrible experience of Durga Puja – about how she was sexually assaulted and how it changed her perspective of her favourite festival. Her experience shocked me into silence, and for a while I didn't know what to say. All I was thinking about was the girls like her who have experienced this. The city which celebrates the goddess of womanhood with such devotion, will they celebrate 'us women' the same way? That's how 'My City and My Home' inspired me to write my poem.

Durga of My City

I'm Durga,
Goddess of womanhood,
Goddess of power
Hence I was named.
People worship me
With extreme devotion.
Welcoming Maa Durga,
My city

Was full of lights and joys.
Durga puja
My source of courage,
Discovered a unique inner energy.
Since I was named after her,
Goddess inside me,
I expected people to see
I was wrong –
They saw me as a mere weak girl,
I was only ten,
Screaming for help
Which I didn't get.
They gave demon looks
Their –
Dreadful evil laughs,
Bloody red eyes,
Disgusting hands,
Coming for me…
Took me and tore my clothes…
I couldn't even cry.
City lights and concretes
Witnessing the blues
Silent sighs,
Unseen tears,
Lifeless glances,
Of several Durgas.
They worshipped Maa Durga,
Her power and grace,
Yet treated this Durga with –
Their inner demons
Maa Durga defeated monsters,
However, this little Durga couldn't.

Madeeha Noor, Lahore, Pakistan

I left (ran away from), my country of birth, Pakistan, after forty one years in 2019 with two children in search of, what I had told myself at that time, a new place to heal, a new place to lay down my roots, to call home. I've lived a lifetime since, a year in isolation as it has been for most of us and have come to understand a simple truth: for us, the outliers, the rebels, vagabonds of the heart, the only true journey ever to be set upon is the one that leads back to ourselves. It is only when we find the courage to begin that, keeping our demons and fears by our side, broken, scarred, and chipped, that we truly begin to heal. When we do, we discover that 'home' is not a geographical location or a boundary to be 'found' – we carry it in us, in little buds of spring, in our hearts.

In Foreign Land

I don't know what happy endings look like.

I don't know.

I know what yellow looks like on a rain-wet day and the dance of the trees.

I know what happy looks like: my daughter skipping to the swings or a boat, not a sound but the chirp of a *mayna*.

I know what love looks like: a strand of hair tucked behind the ear, silver bangles, music turned up loud on the stereo, a breathlessness before opening the door, two cups out, a fire lit.

I know what wonder looks like: a life that holds your hands in its tiny fist, eyes that look for your voice, only yours, a body that seeks warmth, a blanket to sleep in before then awakening, dreams clinging in dewdrops to the lashes, laughter like chocolate, your name a honeysuckle, rich with summer, 'Mama.'

I know what an island looks like: two friends, the smell of coffee, time flickering in bursts of cinnamon, 'hey, hold my hand, I cannot seem to go on.' How the waves and the storm recede as they tuck the pain quietly under cushions and coasters until you can feel your legs again, your heart again a steady rhythm

Happy endings, though, I don't know much of.

I know of the glass slippers of course, and forests where nobody ever truly gets lost, and castles built to save us from ourselves, and sunsets. I know how we spend lifetimes running after them, blistered and scratched, searching for miracles in 8pms and parking lots, chasing them through corridors marble-poured, through the planets and stars, this year is the metamorphosis, you will find finally what you're looking for. Is this what you want to hear?

I know you understand the romance of bridges and the strangers one meets in black and white mists, and the thrill of take-offs, and clouds, and unknown destinations, and the possibility that you can be anyone, brand new, full, of adventures and stories.

I know you understand that it is easier to break silences than to build them. I know how you write to erase them, back into nothing, no place that can pull you in, choke them with words until all you are is a daily column critiqued by the world, but listen,

Breathe. Nobody understands any of this, I promise. We are just trying, each of us, to make it home before the dark, and even if there is no one waiting for the doorbell to ring, there is still you who was brave enough, not as afraid enough, to have made this journey. That matters. It matters.

Happy endings, though, I don't know much of.

Madeeha Noor, Lahore, Pakistan

Home, for many decades, has been a place of deep unhappiness for me – Pakistan is not an easy place to live in for a woman, especially one that does not fit into a preordained box of what one should look like or behave like. 2020 brought a crumbling of many such edifices in our personal and socio-political canvases and with it came a new beginning of sorts – of what love looks like, of what a family is, a shared connection, and of the truest meaning of 'home' – I have come to discover since that 'home' is what we build in ourselves, acknowledging all we have been, the choices that we have made, the loss and the scars and once we find the courage to lay them to rest, the demons and the past, a different blueprint of 'home' is born, one sown in geographies of the heart.

The Tower

I'm going to write my fears into a story and brick them into a tower – it feels like the most logical thing to do since I am running out of places to hide it in.

Drawers are full, flowerbed choking, rooftop swollen spaces under my bed have already been long occupied by ghosts which have taken to singing lullabies instead – nobody is scared of those particular scars anymore, and frankly, their tales have become trite – how many hours can one spend, anyway, being spooked to sleep by ancient bones?

On the ground floor of the tower is longing – on the left a powder room with three oblong mirrors, each a reflection of the years I've spent running towards distant lands of vague, undefined happiness –

I have not arrived yet.

In the room on the right, next to the TV cabinet, is loss. I've arranged it into a geometry of tablemats so I can keep track, see in a glance what has been taken, in which angular proportions and how much.

Up ahead is the stairway, a spiral of solid birch wood. It will last you a lifetime, he had said. I've lost many since but, who is counting?

It opens onto a landing whitewashed in song – there are a few framed photographs of my daughter's artwork from when she was little, before she was 'diagnosed'

Splitchy splotchy green grey fields flow into the sky that flow into the field that flow into a daisy – I see all this where you might see a blotch because I am looking for her and you, for art. I get that.

In the study behind the bamboo are yesterdays –

Afternoons hang in curtains of light by the sofa, and on the walls, silence.

I go there for conversations sometimes folded in red and white rugs on the floor and listen, listen, isn't that the sea swishing around in the corner?

All the books I have ever owned since I was seventeen, croweaters, beloved, Tower of Babel, home – all line the shelf in a rhapsody, dust-like, spine a pathway, scribble a moment inked in black – I remember more of me through words than in fact – strange – paragraphs line my hands, apostrophe breath, my skin a universe, secret codes unlocking journeys of the heart.

Beyond the window dreams a rooftop in cymbals flutes and a star

Keep this,

a teardrop, a rose, a ticket stub

Here I'll sketch you the sky

'Would you like to come home now?'

Jennifer Cousins, Birmingham, UK

Birmingham has been my city and my home for all my adult life. I am a white European woman and I share Birmingham with women from a wide range of ethnic backgrounds. We may look different from each other, and communicate only through gestures, but women share one unique thing: their connection with babies.

Our City, Our Home

Her breasts, heavy and milk-laden were demanding that she should feed the baby. But was this possible in such a public place? Was it allowed? Rodica sat quietly on the cold bench, absent-mindedly rocking the pram, watching her three-year-old happily going from sandpit to rocking horse to climbing frame. She was copying the other children, making cautious little attempts to co-operate and be friendly, necessarily without words: universal child behaviour, whatever the language or culture. Rodica caught the child's eye and gave a little wave of encouragement.

But now the baby was looking up at her from the cumbersome charity pram and beginning to whimper with hunger. There were corresponding spikes of pain from her urgent breasts: she really needed to feed him, for both their sakes. The other parents, mostly mothers, were dutifully pushing delighted toddlers on the swings and chatting; an elderly Asian woman was sitting relaxed on a bench. Rodica watched them: would they mind if she rolled up her tee-shirt and tucked the infant into her waiting breasts? How strange it was not to know the rules of this unfamiliar country.

***

Farida sat watching the children on the swings and sighed. So long ago, all that, and such precious memories. The little gestures and squabbles and screeches of delight, so like her own sons' all those years ago, recognisable across time and continents. She felt tears coming, and shifted position on the bench, unaware that her faded rust-coloured dupatta trailed in the accumulation of bronzed leaves at her feet, so it was difficult to see where the leaves ended and the material began. She seemed to grow out of the earth, the landscape. And what an alien landscape this had once seemed! With her husband and little ones, she had arrived here after the concrete monster had drowned their village, when the life they had built together was lost; their homeland left far away across ocean and mountains. So strange, so misty this new, kindly, country had seemed: in place of the noisy brightness of purple and red and turquoise she was used to, here the colours were muted and gentle (the browns and greens – so many greens!). And now her own autumn: husband gone, children flown, career over.

But now a toddler in the sandpit was crying – sand in her eyes from an unfortunate push from a small companion. Farida looked around for the parent and saw a young woman about to respond, hampered by a bulky pram she was trying to manoeuvre out of the way. Farida signalled to the mother, smiling, and, rising a little stiffly, she retrieved her leafy dupatta and picked her way across the sand to reassure the wailing toddler and return her to maternal safety. Farida smiled again shyly as she did so, and pointed at the vacant place on the seat:
'May I?' she asked.

***

Rodica nodded her thanks and moved a little to make room; the toddler, quickly recovered, wriggled away, and re-joined her new friends. Now the baby began to fret and grizzle and Rodica lifted him apologetically from the pram, beginning to panic. She still could not guess the rules, nor what was expected in this baffling new situation. She took courage:

'Please,' she began. 'Please, it is good to feed baby here? Or no?'

Timidly she indicated her leaking breasts, now staining her tee-shirt. Farida looked momentarily perplexed, then smiled a wide smile.

'Of course!' she said, and, nodding encouragement, shifted slightly on the bench so the baby could be adjusted into place. Rodica almost cried with relief as the baby latched on, nuzzling into her warmth.

'My babies are big now,' Farida said.

Rodica looked puzzled and shook her head. Smiling, Farida pointed at the baby and then to her own chest. Then she raised her hand high in the air, laughing, indicating with no need for words.

'These are my babies now!'

Rodica understood and smiled.

Darin Khair Husain, Dhaka, Bangladesh

The topic of 'My City My Home' has been something I often reflect on quite a bit, which is why I had a lot to say on the matter. This competition was a great opportunity to put my thoughts on paper, to truly express my experiences and opinions.

My City

As a sixteen-year-old Bangladeshi girl, when I imagine what my ideal city looks like, it's a modern city with a futuristic environment. Bangladesh is an emerging nation that has shown major economic growth with an annual GDP of 8.2%. Despite Bangladesh's economic improvements, there is room for more in regard to social norms, points of interest, safeguarding biodiversity, and tackling the ongoing environmental issues. The economic growth in Bangladesh doesn't mean much if it doesn't bring prosperity to its citizens. Home isn't what a built environment *looks* like, it is what it *feels* like. To me, a perfect city would be one that brings me joy and makes me feel safe and included.

Firstly, my city has unfortunately struggled to promote community bonding. Studies have emerged that state that social cohesion helps communities cope with difficulty and can increase an individual's happiness rapidly. However social cohesion is difficult when individuals only have exposure to people with the same financial status quo. I've had the privilege to travel to several different countries from a young age. When visiting Thailand and England, the countries I visit most frequently, I mostly remain in the most populous cities. Despite not holding citizenship, I feel a sense of belonging. This is due to the many events that the two cities, Bangkok and London, uphold such as

119

concerts and carnivals. This makes outsiders feel like more than visiting tourists. In these events, there are individuals of different financial statuses and cultural backgrounds. Unfortunately, in Dhaka, we lack economic diversity – it feels as though the upper class and lower class are a part of two separate worlds. Giving every citizen, ex-pats, and tourists public events to attend in conjunction would create a very joyful and inclusive experience.

Furthermore, one large issue that makes me feel like my city has serious room for improvement is the overwhelming amount of gender exclusion displayed towards women in our community. My experience alone as a sixteen-year-old girl can evidence the toxic mindsets that men acquire, normalised by South Asian societies. Recently, I have been jogging on the streets of Baridhara daily. I have frequently been catcalled by men, including the police officers and guards. It would go as far as cars speeding up behind me and my friends, to the path we would be walking on, and they would stare at us in an inappropriate way. This happened to me numerous times just this week.

In spite of facing street harassment myself, I often reflect on my privilege. Coming from a family with open views on principal concepts like education that ultimately shapes one's future, I understand how fortunate I am to be able to learn about basic etiquettes. I also understand that the underprivileged or minorities don't always have this opportunity. I was oblivious in thinking that as a sixteen-year-old girl, I should feel safe walking on the streets of residential areas in broad daylight.

Despite my several attempts to forget, I can recall one memory from my early years, from the age of ten: I was getting my eyes checked alongside my mother. After my check-up, the doctor attempted to converse with me, and he kept fondling my arm. Even being ten years old, I understood that an eye doctor touching me was not normal and attempted to cease him from grazing my arm. I persistently pulled my arm away from him and consistently yelled at him to stop. Every time I removed my arm, he would tenaciously grip my arm even tighter than before until my indefatigable screams finally caught the attention of my mother.

She stood up instantaneously and yelled 'Let's go!' and 'What do you think you're doing to my daughter?'

After my mother yelled at him, right before I could even have the courage to stand up, he touched my arm, again and said 'What's wrong? We are just talking.'

It broke my heart, so much so that I remember this story six years later. I want to live in a city where it is safe to visit a doctor, where it is safe for my mum to visit a doctor. A city where it is safe for every woman to go everywhere at any time.

All in all, Dhaka is a beautiful city with a lot of potential, and there are always ways to improve on just about everything. Dhaka is improving at a vast pace, and it is slowly becoming my generation's responsibility to build a more desirable environment. A city goes way beyond its appearance, it is about creating an environment in which everyone feels as though they are a part of a community. An environment that treats everyone as equals. An environment that my generation would thrive in. As a proud Bangladeshi, I would like to see my city, Dhaka, flourish.

Nabila Hussain, Birmingham, UK

I have many fond memories of growing up in Birmingham. When growing up I had to face many obstacles that sometimes made me feel chained and alone. Growing up for me, as a Pakistani girl, surrounded by culture and family with outdated views, I want the readers to feel and see through my eyes.

My City, My Nostalgia

Bright lights, beautiful city, iconic buildings, Selfridges, mesmerising structures, St Philips historic Cathedral, awe-inspiring architecture, Aston Villa ground, just to mention a few. There's many more. Beautiful people and the ethereal lakes and bistros of Brindley Place.

Colours so bright, sparkling everywhere you go. The amazing canals and river running throughout the city. All so serene and welcoming. Inviting you to get lost, forget your troubles, watch the water flow, as the boats go by on the canals in Brindley Place. Taking your thoughts and troubles along with it as you get lost in the sound and sights of it all.

So many different people, so many backgrounds, races, gender, cultures from all over the world.

As a child, Birmingham, to me, was all this and more.

As I grew older, the weight of troubles and worries grew with me, changing my view of this incredible city to something much more sinister. It felt like it was becoming a large dark cloud, looming over my head and shoulders, like a shadow that's dark and menacing. My disquietude spread out like the branches of a tree, covering me with an immense feeling of claustrophobia and dread.

Being a Pakistani girl meant growing up in a culture that was oppressive and restrictive for me. Watching my friends looking forward to their dreams and ambitions and knowing I would never be able to follow mine. My life and everything around me started to feel and look gloomy and isolating.

Birmingham started to look the way I felt. Now, where once I saw lights and sparkles before, suddenly they became dull and murky.

Instead, I started seeing tall buildings covered in scaffoldings everywhere I looked, which felt like the invisible shackles I felt all around me, tugging and pulling me down as if I could no longer move forward, as if I was held in place by scaffolding put up around me.

The mirage of the sparking beautiful city had faded and now I could see the full picture; the corruption that fills the city creating starving children, drug abuse, and poverty. How the elite live in luxury whilst the poor are struggling to even survive; all of this happening in that same charming city I saw growing up.

As a young adult, Birmingham to me was all this and more.

In full adulthood, my life became different: fighting against my oppressors and all the restrictions bounding me down. To look and find different dreams and aspirations I fought for made me stand tall and strong like all these buildings improved by the scaffolding holding them up, making them new and strong in different ways. The more I stood strong, the more I improved in new different ways.

In full adulthood being aware of all this, the good and the bad, the bright and the dull, the safe and the scary, I still feel a huge sense of nostalgia when looking and being in Birmingham, the city that taught me so much, which made me the strong woman I am today, even with all the oppressive and restrictive obligations of my Pakistani culture. It was Birmingham that gave me the strength and courage to be myself and fight for what I believed in. Birmingham will always be a part of me.

As an adult, this is how I feel and see Birmingham.

Shanjida Hossain, Dhaka, Bangladesh

I have been living in Dhaka for almost half my life and trust me when I say this, this city is filled with unique stories – ecstatic, mysterious, comedy, tragic, grief-ridden, violent – name it and it is there.

So, I pondered upon which genre of my city I related to the most, and every time my mind associated with the tragedy, grief, and violence aspects. The anti-rape protests also played a major role in generating my storyline. This is one of the many things I love about my city – the sense of unity and collective action people take whenever society gets hit by yet another disgrace of humanity.

In spite of this, no one can deny the crimes that take place every moment in buses, alleys, main roads, and even inside houses. One of the horrifying news that traumatised me significantly was that of a girl whose father died during COVID-19. She always wore a burqa, covering her face. Her mother left her alone at night to collect the dead body of her father from the hospital. A few neighbours, knowing very well about the situation of their household, broke into their house and raped the girl. The so-called pious people of society were tongue-tied as there was no way to victim-blame based on the girl's dress. Surprisingly, these people still found ways to find fault in a woman in this situation, asking why the girl's mother left her alone so late at night. Sometimes, no, most of the time, I feel ashamed to be a human in my city.

As a development journalist in the leading financial daily paper of this country, I also had the opportunity to interact with women facing domestic violence, sexual harassment at work, and roadside eve-teasing to name a few. So, one day, I decided to write my storyline showcasing the collection of individual stories and news I got to learn about women all over Dhaka and representing my city under the light of gender-based violence, highlighting how the women in this city never really possess a secure home despite having families. One thing that is common in all these stories is women, including mothers, suppressing other women's voices. The 'Mother' in my story is not just a maternal figure but also all the women – in not only in my city but also in every society – who have justified staying quiet for centuries.

Never a Mother

Ma pours a concoction of coconut and jasmine oil on my scalp, massaging with a hint of aggression. I am twenty-one years old – apparently too old to smile. There is a charming government official, eight years older than me, full of maturity. He sent me a proposal through Khalamoni. He has a package of fifty-thousand-taka, health insurance, government-subsidised quarters, name it.

I refused.

Ma says, applying a little more pressure on my scalp, 'You will understand when you become a Mother.'

But I don't want to be a Mother. My mind automatically drifts to the days after Abbu's death, when my paternal cousin called me to a corner and started caressing my face. I shoved his hand away and ran to Ma. She pinched my mouth shut. Instead of berating my cousin, she held my hand and dragged me to our microbus in the middle of the night, assuring me that we were on our way to freedom. For the next three years, I felt a prisoner in my own mind.

I don't want to be a Mother who would make promises she can never keep to her daughter. I don't want to impose on her that her genital is the first thing to get weaponised during a war, turning her against, yet turned against by, the people she calls her own. I don't want to make her feel that she is as strong as the fragility of her femininity.

When Nanumoni kicked us out of her house, Ma took my promise to remind her of Nanumoni's behaviour towards us if she ever forgets about it in the future. The following summer, when

I refused to go to Nanumoni's house for Eid, Ma said I won't ever get happiness in life for my disrespectful behavior. My heart constricted with panic, quivered with terror. So, before Ma's sigh reached Allah, I convinced my heart to go – because didn't Allah say that no one can escape from a Mother's curse?

Why doesn't my life bloom with happiness then?

I don't want to be a Mother who would forget to water the flowers in her veranda, sucking their colour out, making them feel so worthless that they fear facing the sun. I don't want to forget telling my daughter to forgive herself first before forgiving the world.

Right before my high school exams, I needed to stay up late to study. So Nanumoni said I would not get breakfast anymore because my sleep habits were unwomanly. I thought it was just a love-packed scolding from Nanumoni because she worried so much about my health. But for the next two years, I did not get a single breakfast. Ma told me to tolerate my hunger until I become an officer one day. So I requested the pangs in my stomach to sleep. However, years later, when Nanumoni visited our own house, Ma cooked Nanumoni's favorite *Mishti kumra bhaji* and *Ruti* for breakfast, but, painfully, forgot how much I hated *Mishti kumra*.

I don't want to be a Mother who would tell her daughter to compromise between her dreams and body, who would become so habituated to her daughter's suffering that she stops loving herself. I don't want to be a Mother who would become a slave to the Jannah beneath her Mother's feet to a point where I forget to give my daughter the Jannah she deserves.

As my shoes step on the preceding day's footmarks on the muddy Satmasjid road every day, I realise how similar, yet different, the world around me is. The ever-present kaleidoscopic rickshaws. The puddle of water that never dries. The sparsely scattered trees. The group of boys who hang out in the Tong every evening. *Wafting aroma of puris and shingaras*. This is my Dhaka – the place that holds me together, but where I could never find my Home.

126

One day, I told Ma about the time I fell down on the ground when a boy whistled, followed by the time when one of the boys grabbed my dupatta on a stormy night. And instead of hugging me tightly, she told me that I was at fault for not telling her before, that I was shameless for having too many opinions – for having opinions in the first place. Instead of helping me take the first step the next morning, she showed me another road to our house so that the boys didn't pester me anymore, but she never tells me which road I should take to reach my Home.

When people tell her to remarry, saying how a single Mother in Dhaka can never protect her female child from the gazes of lecherous men, my back bends, shoulders weigh down, heart sinks with shame – for belonging to a gender that becomes a burden without a father.

I am afraid of becoming a Mother who would never be enough for her daughter.

I am afraid of judging my very own flesh.

So not a Mother; never a Mother.

When I tell all these to Ma, she scoffs, applies even more pressure on my scalp, and asks, 'Do you even know what it means to be a Mother?'

I remain speechless for five minutes. I think about the traumatic night where I promised myself that my younger sister would get an education even if I didn't. I rewind the days where I just lived on water throughout the day to save enough money for taking Ma to hospital. I think about the time I picked my younger sister up from school.

And for the first time in what seems like decades, my heart feels a little lighter, my smile dares to linger a little longer, and as my mind replays how I positioned my body like a shield, between my sister and the man, who was about to touch her, my head rises with full confidence and I say, 'I do.'

Because in my city, even a six-month-old girl knows what being a Mother is.

Kam Bola, Birmingham, UK

I work for a charity and I became interested when I saw the brief and was promoting it. I enjoy writing but have never really had the time or space to focus on it as much as I would like to. The lockdowns have given me time and space to put my energy into things I enjoy. So here's something that shares my experiences and tells an informal story of Brum.

My City, My Home

Birmingham, a vibrant city full of people, interesting places, and some cool green spaces

Birmingham, a city made up of a mix of old architecture and anew

Once an old town, now a city, money invested to make it modern and pretty

Birmingham New Street, once an old and tired railway station. Its' name's been changed to Grand Central, it's like we're living under the shadow of New York's Station!

A place bustling with buses old and a few new, young people sitting on the top decks smoking and hustling

Trams taking over, young people sitting under the metro stops, yet the old folks still prefer the bus and wait at the bus stop

A mixture of generations, colours, and races, going out and about frequenting places

The second-largest city of the nation and women represent 51%.

I'm a woman from the southwest of the city and it's a place that's really pretty

I have worked in inner-city places most of my life: educating, empowering, and inspiring

For ten years it felt like I was doing time behind bars, a role that challenged my delicate soul and made me tough enough to understand that some men make mistakes and don't know how to recuperate.

The Green was a huge part of my employed life - crime and a lack of education creates a barrier, and no amount of money and politics is going to correct a man who is fighting a constant battle with his own life.

As a mother of boys, I have seen with my own eyes, and experience has shown me that we must raise our children with love and patience so that they grow wise enough to be able to understand life and control their fate

Birmingham, a place well renowned for gangsters and crime, each man a Peaky Blinder of his time

Hidden meetings and secrets under the arches of the railways, they don't mind doing the stretch

A generation of young people experimenting with drugs, some turn into thugs and lose their minds engage in knife crime, listening to drill and grime.

A generation caught in a trap, going around acting all big but with no substance or education. They need to break the cycle and raise their vibes for a better, healthier, and happier new generation.

Clean air zones introduced in the city, but it's okay to light up a zoot and contaminate the air, really is that fair?

Birmingham, also known as Brum, before it was crowned a city, people from down south thought it was pretty shitty!

Over time and with money, the city has turned into a place some may say is as sweet as honey.

Museums, art galleries, the Library, and food places and fewer car park spaces

Grand hotels and afternoon tea, fancy spas and gyms, cars parked outside with fancy trims

Birmingham City, a host for sports events, Velo and Half Marathons to name some, and soon the Commonwealth

Music concerts, operas, and theatres a place to escape when life gets dim

Birmingham, my city, my home, a place that celebrates many faiths and life to the fullest

After all, we are one race

Brum in my eyes is the capital of culture

Birmingham canals, lakes and the reservoir, it's really splendid to get out in nature

Birmingham universities and colleges supporting education and inspiring a new generation

Birmingham healthcare and super hospitals serving the people of the city and beyond

Consultants and doctors from across the globe, they deserve to be adorned in golden robes

Good mental health is in itself, the real wealth

People forget to look after their heads and sometimes lose it to long term meds

Birmingham is my city, my home, and it truly deserves its very own diamond crown

I'm a queen of my home and bearing the weight of my crown makes me strong and vulnerable, and yet sometimes I still frown from the responsibilities of being a wife and a mum.

Just like the city has changed over time, my life as a mum and a wife evolves and moves with the times, learning lessons and reflecting on the challenges and experiences I encounter

A positive spirit, and in the face of adversity, my faith, my soul and my feet remain rooted in the ground, how I have grown from a humble and loving upbringing, trust the process, and always have hope

How the place has matured, and the population grown. Once a small dot on the map, a place full of good energy and good people from across the globe gathered in a place they now like to call home

Indian, Pakistani, Bangladeshi, Sri Lankan, European, African, South American, Canadian, Jamaican, Chinese, Irish, Welsh, and Scottish to name a few that live in Brum, each with a story of their own

Birmingham is a place with space for every race

Birmingham is a city full of hope

Birmingham is a city that's pretty dope

Birmingham is a city of sheer delight

And if you lived here, you would know I was right!

Magdalen Tamsin Gorringe, Birmingham, UK

I wrote this poem inspired by thinking about the two stretches of time I have lived in Birmingham: now, and when I was six years old, what I remember, what stands out, what I cherish about my city – and what makes a place feel like home.

Birmingham: 1979, 2019

I remember the trees.
My hand in my dad's on the way down to school.
I always loved those cheap, cheesy crisps at break time.

Forty years later, I returned.
My hand in my sons' on their way to school.
And still loving the trees.

I don't go to New Street if I can help it –
I map my city by its green –
Picnickers in Cannon Hill Park,
Dog walkers in Highbury,
Children paddling in the Rea.

And its people.
A lifetime ago, my neighbour's parents' parents
were in Italy. Mafia connections, she thinks
(though that may be just to thrill me).
Now she greets me across the fence
pegging clothes out in my garden.
'Alright bab?' she asks.
And I feel suddenly at home.

Magdalen Tamsin Gorringe, Birmingham, UK

As with my earlier entry, I was inspired by thinking of the two different stretches of time I have spent in Birmingham. For this piece, I reflected on how dance has been important to me during both time periods, and on how the journey in between my times in Birmingham has meant that the dance styles marking each period are very different. This piece also meditates on a rather grumpy throwaway comment made as a friend and I were dancing bharatanatyam outside the city's Gas Hall. I can't be sure of the intention of the comment, but it certainly got me thinking about what might make someone or something 'Brummie' and about who 'belongs'.

Brummie

I have learned my city through dancing. Weaving a reel through shoppers on New Street. Treading the two-step-pause of a protest march past Selfridges.

Six years old – shining in a red tutu. My grandma put my hair up in a bun. Later, gazing up at the stage, *The Nutcracker*. I remember mainly the mice.

We left Birmingham on an Air India plane, walls woven with pictures. My brother and I sobbed at the unknown. Two kind strangers promised us India as home. We went to see the pilot in his cockpit. It was a different time.

Two countries and five cities later, I returned to Brum, ballet swapped for bharatanatyam, red tutu for blue silk sari. Dancing bharatanatyam to Abba outside the city's Gas Hall, giddy in velvet flares.

'So very British,' someone mumbled. 'Very Brummie.'

Days later, I climbed up to the Toposcope in the Lickey Hills (built, I suppose, thanks to cocoa from West Africa). I watched the city stretched out before me. The QE like an oversized liner in a suburban sea. The university, Old Joe, the green glint of the Serbian orthodox church.

And I saw, through time, great waves of people, going and coming, coming and going, a ceaseless dance of return and retreat, the city, generous to embrace and as ready to let go. By barge and train, coach and plane, by cart and on foot, people, travelling. From hill and valley, they came along the canals and across the oceans, going back, back to the warriors in boats from Norway, Germany, Imperial Rome, then back, back... still further back.

What would be 'very Brummie?' I wondered and found no answer, but the wind, the wind dancing to a rhyme that spoke of everywhere and nowhere and sped, laughing, on its way to other worlds.

Rusafa Hussain, Dhaka, Bangladesh

When I was writing the piece, I had to really look inward and pinpoint what exactly made this city so magical to me. I've lived in Dhaka for twenty-two years, and despite all the good and the bad, this city has me completely enamoured, as if I'm partaking in a turbulent love affair. I hope I managed to somewhat convey my emotions and the feelings that are associated with my home, and I hope I managed to do this city some kind of justice through my writing.

Hope

Within the breast of the city, and the breasts of its people, hope is a sparking fluid igniting dreams across a landscape of burdensome ails and ancient grievances. The citizens of Dhaka are sufferers, the lines and grooves etched onto their faces, painting a portrait of perfect grief. The citizens of Dhaka are dreamers, their heartbeats spelling out inner desires, as their black and brown pupils invitingly sparkle in faith of better days. This is a city of senses, of a tenderness so potent it sinks into the greying cement — into the fine river of cracks cutting through concrete. This city — an unnatural machine, a preservation of traditions, a city of seasons, of pollution, a backdrop for weddings and funerals alike — it is one too many contradictions coexisting within the bodies of the children it raised.

Dhaka's stifling cityscape, the malls, the overhead bridges, old crumbling brick buildings, and dingy restaurants births unequivocal yearnings yet to be understood. There is a quiet tenacity echoing in the howls of the winds that carries everyone's voiceless aspirations towards the skies, feeding and condensing the clouds until the cascading rain washes away the sorrows of the people.

Underneath the filth and plastic of Dhaka, there lies the honeyed scents of Dahlias-Tulips-Daffodils that homeowners carefully bloom. There is loss and there is romance, there is the collective experience: of labourers and bankers, lawyers, and rickshaw-pullers, all striving towards a private dream. Everyone in Dhaka nurses this resilient hope, this secret prayer that sinks into the marrows, and slips between the cracks of bones.

The true sound of the city is not the unceasing cacophony of car horns, television screens, megaphones, rather it is the silent, deeper melody that lay at the core of the souls living in Dhaka. It is a mother humming softly as she prepares Eid desserts during the new-moon night, a grandmother whispering fables of beasts and lairs of earthly jinn under the heavy winter comforters, school friends gossiping as they drink coconut milk by the roadside in scorching sunlight, the resounding crack of the cork in a late-night badminton duel against cousins, and laughter rising as a family gathers around the steaming cups of cha set on the table as twilight engulfs the city in a pink-orange hue.

Dhaka encapsulates a treasure trove of these beloved, cherished stories. Stories of families, of friendships, of companionship, stories spinning silver threads connecting the unlikeliest of people, stories inked into invisible scrolls that memorialise the hardship and the hope that emerges in spite of pain. These undying embers of hope, acting as a tangent between reality and reverie, stirs the sweet nectar of song, and like the healing hands of a saint, remedies the wounds of the city.

Zoha Jan Tagi, Islamabad, Pakistan

I was born and brought up in the capital of Pakistan after my parents moved here for a better livelihood. For the most part of my life, I have struggled with claiming my hometown, divided between two identities; one which I got from my parents and one I own. This was an attempt to claim the place I truly consider my home. It felt like an exercise to mark my own territory in the face of my own uncertainty. I truly felt proud of the poem for depicting all my emotions aligned with the landscape of Islamabad as well as the way I perceive the city. Most importantly, it articulates the idea of making history rather than claiming it and the fissures in concrete history. It is an ode to my city and an oath of locating my identity in it, despite all odds.

History, No More

This city gives, gives, and gives but we always take it for granted.

Spring sprouts like a miracle that we witness every year,
Autumn spreads all around the space as though it finally found its home.
This city gives, gives, and gives but never owns.

This city is so fast for most people that time slips through their hands in the blink of an eye
Yet it stops for you, early in the morning and welcomes you
With leaves slow dancing to birds humming in the background.
This city is all skyscrapers and urban life for most people,
Coffee cups brimming with the urgency of meetings,

Shoelaces entangled in the fear of what will be tomorrow,

Goals too high to reach, and hills hiding behind the skyscrapers weaving false promises.

But for you it's the homemade out of footsteps of familiar shapes,

Every turn specks of memories,

Every road unfolds a story,

Every signboard smiles at you as it tries to remember your name.

This city belongs to no one but

There is no other place in the world that you would belong to.

This city speaks of earthquakes and bomb blasts

But deep down inside it speaks of survival.

There was a time when you'd see how the sky turned from red to green

To the darkest shade of blue during the summer nights,

Now it only wears the light and dark, and often is engulfed in the darkest shade of black.

This city is scared of responsibilities, yet it is responsible for all that you are,

For how you talk and how you walk,

For how your dreams always begin with seasons of spring and fall,

For how you appear so calm even when there are fires of rage burning inside of you,

For how you climb at the rooftop at midnight to gaze at that one star that dares

To shine among all the city lights and see yourself in it.

Bad news is that this city possesses no history,

Good news is that you have it in your hands to create it.

Zoha Jan Tagi, Islamabad, Pakistan

The recent changes in the environment on account of the global pandemic outbreak have most significantly shaped my relationship with the place I live in. This short story was an attempt to let out all that I have felt in the recent months. There has been less action and more thought, so the story is styled in a modernist stream of consciousness manner. It would have been nearly impossible to shape my fluid and troubled thoughts into words, but this is an attempt to put those thoughts to rest. I have spent the last few months pondering and strolling on the rooftop as my only past-time.

The terms 'My City, My Home' invoked in me the need to articulate how the things around me have changed recently in the background of all the significant changes I have witnessed living in the city I call my home. Islamabad has a lot of tragedies in its memory store; however, the natural landscape of Islamabad is the same as it was twenty years ago and that provides hope for getting through the pandemic as we have faced the past atrocities. I have also touched upon the inimical behaviour of the society towards women. This piece is perhaps my most spontaneous and expressive one.

The Margalla Miracle

It's March 13th, 2020. The world will never be the same again, they announce on the microphone. 'Stay safe, stay home', reads the biggest billboard in the city. She chuckled in her cab after making a quick trip to the grocery store, the future lay as uncertain as a woman walking on the streets of a metropolitan city in this part of the world, as they eloquently term it, like an 'unsafe treasure box' *Khuli Tijori,* her mother would often remind her. In circumstances like these, you must stock on groceries to better equip yourself for a future lockdown or a shortage, as you cover up as much as you can to stay safe from the virus. The cab driver was looking at her through the rear-view mirror. She took out a mask from her grocery bag and fastened it on her face to save her from the virus and the gaze that was hovering over her like a monster inside the car.

The best and worst thing about being looked at and about being preyed upon is that you can never be too sure; be it an invisible virus or a six-foot bulky man sitting in the front seat, and you must be completely sure before letting others know what just happened to you, so they can distance themselves from you. A woman who is known for shouting or slapping any man who tries to approach her inappropriately will be feared. A song here, a scrap of paper there, these are the common signs of being an object of desire, or potential attack, if you will. For as long as she had lived in this city, the city of tall buildings engulfed in hills where the fate of the whole country is often decided, men had dominated the buildings and the streets. Now it seemed like an invisible virus of hardly the size of a bean had won over everyone, including the towering men, in deciding who goes out and when. She had always hated being told not to go out once the sun set:

'Beta, we trust you, but not the society, and the men who are out there,' her father would often remind her while making her cancel yet another trip with friends.

We trust you but not the virus out there which is waiting to prance at you the second you step out, she thought while gazing at the pine trees lining the roadside.

She had always loved how the trees and the hills were still the most prominent part of Islamabad, despite the emerging traffic and skyscrapers. Anything else almost did not matter when you set your eyes on the Margallas reaching out to the sky among all the lush greens. It was like a sigh of relief in a city of capitalist dreams and diplomatic promises. She had always wanted to walk on the roadside, trek up to the hills without a man of the house, without any strings attached to safety. In brief moments of recognition like these, she felt like this place was her home. It always had been, despite brimming with cars and motorbikes and now the metro-bus, it's as familiar as it was during her Eid holidays back in the day when not more than five cars would appear on the scene. You can burn a home, but you can never relocate it. She once heard a story of a pigeon-house being bombed in a war zone after the owner let them free. The pigeons still came back to the rubble every day to find their home.

It was December 25th, the end of the year and the festive season, except the air did not speak of festivity, but conformity to the cold and the looming fear now fading behind the fog. The cars of the road were plenty and not a single soul was walking – December is too cold for a stroll in Islamabad, both for men and women. She went out to take a break from staring at the walls all day, and from her books. Walking to the nearby market felt like reclaiming her space that never was. She thought about how this city had grown with her, had become more vulnerable and resilient at the same time. It was the 27th of December when a popular female politician had been shot and she was in the Markaz. All people were huddled in front of the TV screen, whispering their fears and muffled sobs.

'There might be a curfew, we would not be able to step out, an elderly man exclaimed.

Curfew, she tried to remember the word so she could tell her friends about it.

'Would they shoot us if we step out?' my friend asked after she broke the hot news from the mouth of an elderly man she barely saw.

'They might,' she replied mindlessly, while looking over the receding cars from the window, the same window which crackled when a bomb blast was heard for the first time. She stood at the same window with her cup of coffee while fearing the invisible invader which was, without a sound or a shape, looming over their heads now.

Years from now, this event would also go down under the chapter of resilience.

It was a global pandemic and equaliser that highlighted the ugliest of the inequalities prevalent all around the world.

Then it became normal once again to climb up the rooftops and look at the sun falling into the ebbs of the Margallas. Home is the place where you can be the most vulnerable and yet are the most resilient, looking for little things to give you hope to hold on to. Not much has changed, the sky is the same shade of purple just before the sunset and the perpetrators are walking on the road with masks on and eyes to the ground. She had just learned how to endure it all and never take home for granted.

Nida Malik Hussain, London, UK

*The term 'My City, My Home' inspired me to really reflect on
the journey of my life and share my experiences.*

My City, My Home

Where are you from? Who knew that the conventional way
of being acquainted would become a predicament for me? For
the first ten years of my life, home for me was Chiangmai,
Thailand. My parents were restaurant owners, and we were the
only Pakistani family in the city at that time. Living on top of
a restaurant had its own perks. My elder sister, the twins, and I
would ring the intercom and order anything we wanted at any
time. It was more than a child could ever dream of. Walking
around the streets was exciting, the fruit was exquisite, the
music captivating, and the people were absolutely lovely. I knew
that I had the perfect home and lived in the most beautiful city.

One day, Mum said that we were moving to Pakistan. The
first feeling I felt could be described as a pinch in my stomach
that led on to tremendous excitement as we jumped up and
down saying, 'We'll see our cousins!'

The only resource we had was a huge hard-cover book about
Pakistan that we would flip over, amazed by the country's
splendour. My favourite page was a picture of a fabulously
decorated colourful truck and a group of schoolgirls with
hennaed hands, wearing glass bangles. Little did we know
that this move would change our lives forever. The move was
exciting, and we settled in Lahore. I liked Lahore more than
Karachi, as it looked much greener and had the mountains
close by, the energy felt familiar, felt like Chiangmai.

My first memory of the city was being almost traumatised by a beggar who pushed his face against the window and asked for money in the most horrific way. I quickly looked to the other side to find a donkey cart driver, whipping the donkey as though all of the problems in his life were its fault. I felt the struggle, the pain, and the helplessness around me and knew that this wasn't going to be an easy ride. Dad invested his nest egg in some land that he wanted to build our house on, which was illegally occupied by the infamous 'Qabza group' at the time. I saw it slowly taking over his zest for life.

Mum became the bread earner of the family which led to many more problems in their relationship. I saw the same struggle, the pain, and the helplessness in their eyes. It felt like life had just stopped for us, but I found solace in being with my siblings as we desperately held on to each other for reassurance. We soldiered on, moved from house to house with big smiles on our faces, hoping that things would come around. We travelled in rusty old cars, whatever we could afford, without any complaints. We saw our dreams being shattered but funnily we were still happy, because we had each other.

When I turned twenty-five, I was approached by a family with a marriage proposal. They seemed like nice people, so my parents agreed. It was an arranged marriage; another step I was taking that would change my whole view of life. After my marriage, I moved to Luton, UK. Everything that was promised was a lie, he didn't have a flat of his own, he didn't have a job, and he wasn't a decent human being. My abusive marriage lasted nine months.

My mother said, 'You've tried everything to make this work, now it's time to come back home,' but I couldn't go back broken and frail.

I had seen the ugliness of life too closely and needed time to heal and process everything. I had no choice but to become strong and needed it to make me, not break me. I became independent, got a job, and lived with my dear friend in her council flat. Feeling all that pain but being away from my family taught me so much about myself. My horizons broadened, I wanted to see more and that's when I found London.

I loved all the monumental sites but, more than anything, I loved how ethnically diverse it was. I formed beautiful friendships with kind-hearted people who showed me love and appreciation, it felt like home. After two years I said my goodbyes and marched back to Pakistan holding my head up high. Being back with the tabooed word 'divorce' was interesting. I saw pity, judgment, and fear on many faces, but my family helped me through it. I was living the way I wanted, and with their support, I was doing my best to just be me. I found myself disliking confinement more than ever, so what better time to explore the picturesque valleys of Khyber Pakhtunkhwa, surreal plateaus of Gilgit Baltistan, and the dense mountain ranges of Kashmir.

Seven years had passed, and my parents needed me to believe in marriage again. My father found a match for me and after a lot of shilly shally, I finally agreed to meet. But this time round I didn't leave any loose ends, I spent time getting to know him and finally felt that I had found a companion. We were married and moved to where he lived, in London.

It's funny how life begins, takes you on a roller coaster, and gives you a different aspect on its every bend. I feel like all of my experiences were necessary, like it was a course of action that had to be taken for me to be where I am today and who I am today. I turned forty last month, am a mother of two wonderful children, and have a husband who is first my friend. We love travelling and experiencing new countries and cultures. When someone asks me where I'm from, I like to say, I'm a citizen of the world, my city is the state of mind I'm in and my home is where my loved ones are.

Lovely Home, Dhaka, Bangladesh

The grief and sorrows of women followed by present social evaluation of the role of women, and violence towards women, have taken an unbearable turn. I let my pen speak in favour of them.

Pen, the Power

I need a pen,
Whether it is blue or black,
I need to write
The present and past
Which will help the future
To know itself.

I need a pen,
Whether it is pink or red,
I need it for bread!
It writes for those
Who are the deprived citizens.

I need a pen,
Whether it is green or brown,
I need it for writing,
For the hidden stories
Which a woman bears in her brain
Though it makes her pain!

At last I have a pen
It is black,
As life is like white paper
The black pen writes on it.
It always writes about its pain
And through it love is gained!

Jarin Subah, Chittagong, Bangladesh

The deprived transgender community and their struggle to lead a normal life inspired me. I want to be their voice and speak up for them. I hope Sampad will help me achieve that goal.

Hijras

Bangladesh, an overpopulated country with immense bravery. People from all castes, religions, races and genders live under this sky with huge hopes. Some become famous while some wait for their time to come. Because we know that if you suppress us, hide us, ignore us, we will gleam even more. Nobel laureate Dr. Muhammad Yunus is the glory of Bangladesh. But do you know that people like Ananya Banik exist in Bangladesh too? Unsurprisingly you don't.

Ananya Banik is a brave transgender who lives openly as a hijra with pride. Usually, hijras are persons who are born a boy but later identify as female or neither of the genders. In short, they are the third gender. Let's read out her part of the struggle.

Ananya was an exceptional sixteen-year-old. Her struggle was real. She fought for the rights of the transgender community and came to this honourable position. Yet many of us don't know her. Like other South-Asian families, Ananya was also rejected by the people who surrounded her. She loved dressing up and felt the necessity to prove her thoughts and feelings.

'A female was dominant in my body and mind,' implored Ananya.

People started denying her existence. Her mother was her only support but after her father's death, her brothers disowned her.

She wiped her tears at the struggle. She left home at the age of sixteen and fought for the rights of people like her.

Bangladesh has more than 15,000 hijras and sadly, they are the most marginalised group despite being officially recognised as third gender.

In a society like ours, transgender people aren't given jobs easily. They live in slums and face difficult circumstances. They beg and they try entertaining passengers in order to collect money. They are misused in different sectors for personal gains. How long? How long are they going to be suppressed like this? They are humans too and they have the equal right to live like all others. Ananya fought alone for her rights. Huge support grabs more attention. If we stand together, all the transgender community will be able to have a perfect family, acceptable job, and equal status.

Ananya: a fighter, a warrior, and a proud citizen of Bangladesh. She didn't have the comfort of family. Her home rejected her, but her city accepted her wholeheartedly. She had the opportunity to highlight her talents. She performed classical South-Indian dance, sang Bangla Folk songs, represented her community on national television and worked with a non-government organisation to uphold their dignity.

So, I come from a city and a home where Hijras aren't considered as a burden but rather treated with pride. My city, my home, belongs to heroes of this kind. Ananya dreams of a society where even a single transgender won't be discriminated against. Some parts of the world don't give due respect to them. As black lives matter, women rights matter, privilege for transgenders matter too.

Tehmeena Malik, Lahore, Pakistan

I sometimes write for myself but never get to share it. When I heard about this competition, I wanted others, especially the ones who do not know about my city Lahore, to see it through my eyes and feel what I feel. Thank you for this opportunity.

Lahore is Lahore

My relationship with Lahore started back in 1991 when I arrived in Lahore with my husband and my four children. We had been residing in Chiangmai, Thailand for nine years, running a restaurant. Previous to that, I had lived in Karachi and grew up in England. Being Punjabis by birth, it seemed like the right place to bring up our children so that they become familiar with their roots.

I had my reservations about settling in Lahore because whatever I had heard or known about this city was said to 'not be my cup of tea'. Twenty-nine years later I am smiling as I say that I wouldn't at all be embarrassed to admit that I was way off the mark, and over the years I have learnt to love this quirky city called Lahore. Over the years my relationship, my bond with this city has become stronger. Lahore is not just a city – it's a pulsating entity with its strengths and weaknesses, its beauty and ugliness, its kindness and wickedness and most of all its ability to share the laughter and grief of its inhabitants with equal fervour and passion.

Lahore is the second-largest city in Pakistan and capital of the Punjab Province. Its existence can be traced to around 5000 B.C. Originally a Hindu stronghold, it has seen and borne the reigns of many heroes and villains from the Hindu Maharajas to the Mughal Emperors, the Afghani Chieftains, the Sikh Rajas, and the British Colonial masters. Today, as it stands, it boasts the conquest of the negativity and animosity and the ravages of various wars upon its land.

The city is a wide spectrum of the lifestyles of the very diversified peoples who have resided here over the centuries of its existence. The interior Lahore, (a much smaller area as compared to the present city) houses many ancient architectures, such as the Lahore Fort, the Shalimar Gardens, the Badshahi Mosque and Chawburji. The Lahore Fort and Shalimar Gardens are both UNESCO world heritage sites. The Lawrence Gardens and Aitchison College, and many such sites, remind us that even the negativity of colonisation can leave some beautiful memories of people who loved this land and made it their home.

In 1947 when India gained independence, so did the Muslims, and Pakistan came into being. Lahore at that time was the host to the historic declaration of India's independence and to the resolution calling for a separate state for Muslims. A monument called Minar-e-Pakistan stands tall at the site of the meeting. Lahore warmly welcomed most of the refugees from India and gave them shelter until they moved on to other cities.

From the richest to the poorest, the most educated to the most illiterate, Lahore treats its inhabitants and visitors alike, showing its warmth in its hospitality. Today it is a socially liberal, progressive, cosmopolitan city of Pakistan. It is often referred to as the 'Heart of Pakistan.' Not only has it preserved its colourful, vibrant past but has continued to flourish as the major publishing centre, and home to many leading universities. It is also the breeding ground for many academicians, poets, writers, Sufi saints, lawyers, doctors, actors, musicians, and sports stars, some known worldwide.

Although there are many local stars in the Pakistani sky, there are some that are recognised internationally who I am proud to say shared Lahore with me, calling it their home. Sir Henry Lawrence, Sir John Lawrence, John Lockwood Kipling, Sir Ganga Ram, Rudyard Kipling, Allama Iqbal, A. R. Chughtai, Faiz Ahmed Faiz, Dr. Abdus Salam (the Nobel Prize winner), Sadequain, Bapsi Sidhwa, Imran Khan, Waseem Akram and the list goes on. Since

1947 many presidents, prime ministers of the world, the kings and queens of the Islamic world and even Queen Elizabeth II have made Lahore an important stop-over in their visits to Pakistan.

A city is the body and the citizens its soul. The soul of this city is full of life and whoever lives here or visits it cannot but praise its nurturing customs. Just as any other place in the world, it has many faults and weaknesses in its infrastructure or lack of civic sense, but Pakistan is only seventy-three years old – a toddler in the lead of nations, therefore a lot can be overlooked, when you feel the positivity emanating from the people.

This city, throbbing with activity, is famous as it openly celebrates its traditional culture with the newly acquired Valentine's Day and New Year. Lahoris are by nature fun-loving and 'foodies'. Our entertainment starts with food and culminates with food. The hundreds of restaurants and food stalls all over the city are ample proof of our love of eating and feeding others. Even the very elite malls, cinemas, theatres, and parks are incomplete without the culinary layout to suit an array of palates.

Some may refer to Lahoris as 'laid back' but I prefer to call them 'chilled out'. The extreme -2 Celsius winter nights or the 44 Celsius summer afternoons are not an obstacle in the routine activities. Come rain, come shine, Lahore with its gutsy persona faces all. Even COVID-19 has not been able to dissuade its spirited soul.

So much to say, so much more to explain, but the rules confine me to end the story of my relationship with Lahore. It is a place that has shared, like a friend, my initial struggle to blend in and find a livelihood: my immense joy at the weddings of my four children, the wonder at the birth of my grandchildren, the tears and heartache at the loss of my loved ones, and the hope and prayers for the betterment of humanity all over the world. Yes, today I can shout out confidently that Lahore is Lahore – My City, My Home.

Muhesena Nasiha Syeda, Dhaka, Bangladesh

Home is a place that offers warmth, affection, and acceptance. For me, my home resided in my grandparents who were always there to shower me with their love. Ever since they passed away, I have been feeling like a part of me is lost forever. My home will never be complete without their presence. Unfortunately, it is the memories that act like my shelter and remind me of how empathetic they were and how love is the only truth that exists on the face of Earth. Love is the only feeling that sets us apart from robots. The warmth that I feel every time I think about my grandparents or the place they lived in, is what truly inspired me to write this. Hearing someone going to Barishal makes me yearn to pack my bags and go there. Based on this feeling of running to Barishal to be surrounded by the memories that they made inside that house, I poured out my heart into this writing.

A Lost Soul

Does your heart ache at the thought of not being able to return home because it no longer exists? My soul gets crushed to pieces every time I am reminded of my haven. My heart is engraved with the town of Barishal city, the place that never fails to welcome me with warmth and a sense of familiarity. Growing up in Dhaka felt like a nine-to-five office job, while visiting Barishal felt like returning home after years of battle. Despite being miles away, the sense of belonging was eternal whenever I inhaled the scent of my city.

As I strolled through the walkway, my heart skipped a beat as if falling in love with the house all over again. I spared a glance at the spider web on the wooden door before sitting on the concrete bench, which was right outside the domicile.

'Why does my wandering soul keep stumbling upon this place to look for myself?' I asked under my breath.

Closing my eyes, I paid attention to the sound of the birds chirping and the leaves rustling in the trees. Little did I expect to be hit by a wave of cherished memories and strong emotions. I witnessed my nine-year-old self impatiently sitting on the sofa. My eager eyes were looking at my grandfather who was opening a packet of chips for me. As soon as he handed me the packet, I ran to the kitchen to watch my grandmother cook mouth-watering dishes for lunch. At the sight of me eating right before lunch, instead of lashing out at me, she gave me a serene smile. I let out a grin and my eyes twinkled at her. She extended her arms to welcome me for a gentle hug but when I tried to reach out the scenery shifted to the dark night where I stood in front of her cold body with tears rolling down my eyes. I shifted my gaze to look at my grandfather who sat there grieving the loss of his dear wife. When I attempted to step forward, the setting changed again and this time I was standing outside the ICU where he was declared dead an hour ago.

Hot tears were streaming down my face by then and I forcibly pulled myself out from going down memory lane. Wiping my face with the ends of my sleeve, I got up to look around the city only to realise I do not know the roads well. I chuckled at the irony of fate and the city for fooling me to think that this city was mine when I do not even know it properly.

I ended up walking to the soul of the city – the graveyard where my two most beloved people lay in the harsh cold ground. I smiled at how even death failed at keeping them apart. My mind was reminded of the respect they showed, their compassion, kindness, and love for their family made them absolutely perfect for each other. Unfortunately, after sixty-five years of togetherness, my grandmother left the love of her life alone in this harsh world. The void that I saw in my grandfather's eyes then was like the silence that haunts a graveyard.

My intention to visit my hometown was not to grieve over their death again after all these years but it was to help myself look for a new home. But how can I possibly do that when a part of my soul will linger in this city forever?

Ambling my way out of the graveyard, I looked around to imagine the affection this city offered my grandparents to make them start their family here. Like the brightly coloured leaves descending down from the trees, my mind will come to this place to coat the city with warmth as a sign of celebrating eternal adoration right before the winter visits with its cruelty to immobilise people's hearts.

Esha Aurora, Dhaka, Bangladesh

I have been thinking lately of how my city, my home has become a lost city, a lost home, and how that change gradually took place, and what took the place of my city, my home. While thinking about writing this essay, I was inspired to look deeper into why I have been having these feelings. What is it exactly that has been bothering me? How do I fit into that narrative, or do even fit in anymore?

A Dream That Never Was

She can't sleep. Every morning at 5 am. Every afternoon at 1 pm. Every evening at 5 pm, and then again at 7 pm. Each night filled with anxiety, 'Will I get a full night's rest?', 'Should I wait till it's over and then go to sleep?', 'Will a sleeping pill help to get through it all?'

There are microphones downstairs, they are also mounted on the roof of the building across the street, six more in one square block. For five times a day, they compete to be the loudest, longest call to prayer in what once used to be a quiet middle-class residential area.

She once asked them to turn it down, but men dressed in Saudi Arabian garb came to break down the door for hurting their 'religious sentiments.' That's her country's unofficial blasphemy law for you and me. Her city, once a cherished secular dream is now crawling with holier than thou fundamentalists, hell-bent on a theocracy. They will impose their will onto everyone and slit your throat if you beg to differ.

Her home was once a sanctuary. For years, it was calm, children of all genders rode their bikes down the street. They wore whatever they wanted and played with whomever they wanted. Nobody told them to play with just boys or just girls. Nobody grabbed the vulnerable kid and indoctrinated them slowly. Nobody said, 'go pray.' Nobody morally policed them. Now these people are gone. Where? Nobody knows, some of them suddenly began to don all the symbolisms of Wahhabism while the others have just left. Leaving behind a vacuum to be filled with the dubiously rich whose easiest path to respectability is religion. The louder the better.

Her city no longer feels like home. Perhaps it never was. It was an idea of a home; a dream she was sold when she was young of a diverse, accepting, intellectual culture. Everyone celebrated each other's events. Now the haram brigade has moved in, making memes (it's the 21st century after all) about not wishing 'Merry Christmas' and how going to Pujas will strip people of their faith. There are people morally policing, proactively indoctrinating, canvassing the streets every day, saying things that will easily land anyone else in jail.

Yet, movies, books, articles, songs, anything with an iota of criticism of the state machinery are deemed provocative and will be used to prosecute their makers. But not the hardliner saying women should not be educated beyond grade 5 or that their place is at home being a second-class citizen – only alive to be an empty vessel of passage for a man's desire and unpaid labour. This messaging, it seems, is completely fine. That toxicity is even allowed to be broadcast on hydraulic microphones at all hours of the day.

Her home, her city, the one she remembers smelled of desert marigolds (bailey flowers) in winter. It's a bittersweet nostalgic smell. A smell that takes her back to many winters spent on the roof rubbed down with olive oil in the sun while her grandmother stood guard. It's a smell of Pahela Boishakh, women clad in colourful saris, their arms glistening with glass bangles, singing Tagore songs at the break of dawn at Ramna Park.

This home, like a mythical beast, no longer exists, and neither does the city she knew. An ocean of change, of intolerance, has washed over it and with it has taken all her hopes of it ever realising its true potential.

Her home makes her anxious, she can't sleep. Her city makes her angry. It is a physical manifestation of crabs in a bucket (with skull caps). Her country no longer makes sense. There are Chanel bags traveling down the same streets where people making less than $5 a day literally live in (sometimes still inside garbage bins).

Nothing about her home feels like home. Nothing about her city feels like home. This city no longer belongs to her. This city, in perpetual flux, has now been delivered to someone else, a different thought, a different culture. It smells different, it tastes different, it speaks different, it's even taken the language and turned it on its head. The bhais have now become vais.[1]

---

1 The word 'bhai' means brother in Bangla which over the past few years have become colloquially spelt as 'vai'

Huma Bibi Khan, Gloucester, UK

I was inspired by the journey taken by many Pakistani women to the UK after marriage and the sense of longing they must have felt for home. However, over time, home changes as humans are creatures of habit and familiarity.

Home

December 1985.
Birmingham, England.

From the airport to her new home
strips of amber
provided by the passing streetlamps
illuminate her henna-stained hands.
Her husband and his cousin talk in the front seat
but she is lost in the patterns
that her sister only painted a few days ago.
So this is England, she thinks.

Later that night,
she undresses and peaks out of the window
at a row of houses jumbled together
just like the one she looks out from.

From her suitcase she extracts
her mother's scarf and wraps it around her.
She dreams of home, of fields and space.

April 2020
Islamabad, Pakistan.

The virus has delayed her journey back home.
She longs for cuddles with her grandchildren,
Dairy Milk,
The Bullring,
Barbara from next door's apple pie
and the cosiness of small houses.
Home.

Reba Khatun, Birmingham, UK

The brief 'My City, My Home' inspired me to write about how Birmingham became my home. People are constantly asking me 'Where's home?' When I reply the answer isn't satisfactory and they keep asking. Even after forty years, I'm still asked the same question. When will they stop asking? Will my daughters still be asked the same thing when they're forty years old? I hope not. I hope we've learnt to get along better with everyone by then.

Although there are many differences between Britain and Bangladesh the one similarity that stays with me is the rain! So what better subject for a poem than the weather? It's what we love to talk about in Britain apparently and funnily enough it's a good subject for small talk on international phone calls.

Rain, Rain, Go Away

Pitter, patter. The sound of raindrops trickling down the double-glazing
Puddles forming everywhere, umbrellas turning inside out

Incessant drumming of downpour, hammering on the corrugated tin roofs
Sylheti rice fields overflow, flooding roads and villages

Rain seeps into collars and down backs, into shoes, soaking socks
Sending a cold shiver down your spine and a craving for hot delicious soup

Dirt roads turn into muddy streams, sucking your Bata sandals down
Boats are needed to cross the flooded roads

Peel off wet clothes, drop into a pile,
Dry yourself off with a fluffy towel and slip into dry clothes

Hang up the wet clothes on a clothesline in the veranda
It'll take a day to dry in the monsoon

Run a hot bath that fills the room with clouds of steam
Submerge yourself in bubbles with the aroma of lavender and rose

Grab a bar of soap and head to the fushkuni
Lather up your body and wash it off amongst the fish

Fill the silence with the television or your phone
Grab some food from the fridge or cupboard

Family milling around in every room: aunties, uncles, cousins and
grandparents
Subdue the hunger with a glass of water collected earlier from the
tubewell

Switch on the kettle, grab a mug, teabag and the biscuits
Add a spoonful of sugar and dollop of milk

Boil the water in a handi over an open flame, pour into a jug
Add loose tea leaves, plenty of sugar and a sprinkle of Dano milk
powder

Sweet hot tea glides down your throat
Bangladesh and Britain, maybe not so different after all

Reba Khatun, Birmingham, UK

I was born in Britain, grew up in Birmingham, currently live in Birmingham but Birmingham is my home because I love it. I've glimpsed London, Wales and Bangladesh but there's no place like home.

London boasts the underground, but Birmingham buses are good enough to travel all over to places like Small Heath, Sparkhill, Digbeth, West Bromwich, and the City Centre.

I wanted to write about what Birmingham means to me, my happy memories of it and sad.

The Oxford Dictionary Definition of 'Home'

The Oxford Dictionary definition of home is 'the place where one lives permanently, especially as a member of a family or household'. Well, the first part could apply to a prison, boarding school or even an orphanage but that doesn't make them a home. A better explanation of home would be the second half of the definition because wherever my family are, home is there with them. They do say 'home is where the heart is' and that's definitely true. Birmingham has been the home of my family ever since I was a little girl.

My dad was born in Bangladesh and lived there until he came to work in the foundries in Britain in the late 1970s. He settled in Birmingham and called my mum over to join him. Home was a two-bedroom terraced house with flowery wallpaper, swirly carpet, polystyrene tiled ceilings, and a garden swing. Our house was home to five siblings and our parents. As kids, we played out the front with our neighbours and explored the local area. Our dad took us to the park and relatives' houses at the weekends and holidays. Once a month we would catch the 74 bus and go to the city centre where we'd spend the day window shopping. Lunch would be fish and chips from the Bullring market followed by buying fruit and vegetables from the outdoor markets. If we caught the 74 bus in the opposite direction it would take us to the wonderful Dudley Zoo. So Birmingham was the perfect place to grow up until my dad passed away when I was just thirteen. His body was flown to Bangladesh like many elderly Bengalis that die here but when my sister died twelve years later, she was buried in Handsworth Cemetery.

My earliest memory of Birmingham is school and the library. Unfortunately for me, school wasn't the best years of my life. I was bullied relentlessly in primary school, but the school library saved me, literally. It was the place I took sanctuary in, away from the bullies. It was crammed with lovely books into which I could disappear and find solace in for a bit.

Our house was not short of books. My parents took us to Handsworth Library every Saturday. Afterwards, we'd go over to the laundrette and read the books while my dad put the wash cycle on. We'd walk down Soho Road to get home and see an assortment of cultures and their effect on the surroundings: the Bangladeshi fish shops, Pakistani greengrocers, Indian sweet centres, Halal butchers, Afro-Caribbean hair salons and bakery, gurdwaras, churches and house-converted mosques. Walking down Soho Road didn't make you feel different, it made you feel as if you belonged. My best friend was a mixed-race girl who joined my school during the academic year. Our best neighbours were Jamaican on one side and Indian on the other. We would be in and out of each other's houses all day long.

There are tainted memories of Birmingham amongst the good, the ones where racist people shouted obscenities at us in the street; people in authority spoke down to us presuming we couldn't speak a word of English. And when they discovered my English was fine, it was followed with 'your English is very good, where are you from?' and when they weren't happy with my answer that I'm from Britain they asked 'But where are you really from? Where's home?'

And that's the million-dollar question, where's home? Is it Bangladesh, my parent's birthplace? If home is your birthplace, then Bangladesh is not mine as I wasn't born there. I've been a few times and love aspects of it – the greenery, deserts, hospitality of the people, family, but even there I'm an outsider. We stick out like a sore thumb, and they call people like me 'Londonees'. Even the beggars beg for British currency from us.

Home doesn't have to be my birthplace or the country where my parents migrated to/from. It's the place where I belong, or should I say, where I feel I belong the most. Birmingham is where my parents put down their roots, where I've put down roots. Birmingham is where my dad and sister died, where I gave birth to both of my beautiful daughters. Birmingham is where I went to school, college, got my first job. Birmingham is where I spent weekends in the precious libraries, visiting the beautiful parks, the Sea Life centre, and the farm with the one pony. So the next time a racist shouts 'Go back home' to me in the street I might reply with 'Yes thanks, I am already home.'

Nazifa Afsin, Dhaka, Bangladesh

While writing this literary piece, I was more inspired by the words 'my home' and 'womanhood' than the word 'my city'. Our home is where we live, where we are the most comfortable. As a wanderer since childhood, I felt as though I didn't belong to only a city. I connected with people from all around the globe. About the theme of my writing, our body serves as the home of our soul. I think that a lot of women face body image issues and thus feel it hard to love themselves. I have dedicated this writing to those women, as I explored my home and how it made me what I am. In a few words, I have tried to sum up the struggle I faced while trying to love myself as a whole.

This Home That I Live In

This home that I live in,
was once just a dot.
A tiny, little blood clot
in the womb of my mother,
so little, that you might not even bother.

This home that I live in,
I wear it as my first skin.
Instead of cracks on the wall,
you would see stretch-marks everywhere,
as if home is full of love,
and all of it doesn't fit inside.

This home that I live in,
has a lot of stories to tell.
But words don't flow in my windpipe,
so, I often keep quiet
and let it be.
But once in a while,
I reminisce,
when I come across a photograph,
a glimpse of what I have been.

This home that I live in,
has two water taps that
over-flow when least expected.
Thus, I keep having
unintentional floods
at the most inappropriate moments.

I often keep my windows open,
I accept all the light and changes that it brings.
But if you ever peek through the glass
you could see me
hiding just beneath the surface.
And I have ceiling-high curtains
around my heart,
that are usually draped gracefully.

But how graceful can a woman be
when she is being herself?

Despite the open windows,
My majestic gates are painted black.

So you know,
Not all guests are welcomed home.

I let in only the few
that know how to behave,
how to be kind,
how to love and respect.
'Cause, honestly that's what we, as humans, need.

This home that I live in,
has a hidden library,
an archive of memories,
of the knowledge I have gathered,
of the lessons I have learned,
of the advice I have been given.
It's where I mostly dwell,
It's where I find myself.

In the living room of my home
rests a fireplace
that keeps me warm
on my coldest days,
when the thunders and snowfalls
don't seem that poetic,
when I open my arms wide
just to wrap them around me.

'Cause, sometimes the comfort a woman needs,
is within her arm's reach.

Shielded by the walls of my home,
I often dance around
in the sanctity of my bedroom.
In my reserved solitude,
I laugh out loud.

You must think that
I love my home
And I do.
But this journey was never that easy,
I didn't always love me.
You haven't yet heard of
the basement,
the roots that make me human.

This home that I live in
has a basement full of thoughts,
some packed, some wired, some irrational and odd.
And there were a whole lot of boxes
that needed to be arranged.
That stench of ugly little thoughts
needed to be changed.
I tried not to dwell there,
but it wasn't like I could resist.

There was once a time
when every time that I descended the stairs,
I could feel the dark thoughts prey.
They made me hate my home,
this body I've been given.
For a long time, I let them haunt
the essence of me
so, one day, I decided
that enough was enough,
that the elephant in the room needed to be addressed.
It wasn't easy,
but I had to do it.

Unconsciously enough,
I was taught to be a girl,
I felt the need to be pretty.
But only is it now, gazing at the departing sun,
that I realise, it's my home
and it forever glows.

I am a warrior, a rising woman.

I may not love certain parts of me,
but I do accept them now.
Because these are the bricks
that have made this home that I live in.

I love who I am
and
Every soul should love its body,
Every woman should love herself.

Wouldn't the world be a better place to live in then?

Manar Toufique Chowdhury, Syhlet, Bangladesh

As the name of the poem indicates, this piece was written to highlight the beauty of a small city that often many people overlook. Moonlight helps us find our way whenever there's a power cut. The terms provided gave me all I needed to know, as I had to talk about how I embraced my hometown despite the lack of many things it is my home and I have embraced it and I had to be the one to tell my story.

Moonlit Sylhet

Home; I had no idea what it meant
Until I set foot on your soil, Sylhet.
Now permanently settled in my heart with your tent
Equal to my mother who I always visit when I need to vent.

High-status rejection and social awkwardness,
Isn't it time we raised awareness?
Do we really need to be a victim of the wealthy's vex?
When we have our motherland all ready to bless us.

So long living like a coward
Plenty dream of leaving this simplicity behind
As that is what they consider moving forward
It is the opinions that are travelling backward.

Men and women cannot tolerate injustice
No one takes the side of the accomplice
Where passion is something no one will compromise
My hometown where nothing is as strong as the Sylhetees
alliance.

Your enchanted starlit night skies that have me hypnotised
Firefly chases on your green soil leaves me tranquilised
Cool of paddy fields on summer nights that beat many
foreign beach breeze
Rather than a stroll between skyscrapers, I'd take a walk in
my home, moonlit Sylhet.

Mandy Khan Sikder, Dhaka, Bangladesh

My grandparents and their unconditional love inspired me.

Home, Are You Still There?

I'd like to believe I'm a resident of the world, for nearly three decades now I've been struggling to find my true niche. The city itself has played an integral role in shaping me into the woman I am today. My early memories of this city were confined to my family home where I lived in pure bliss with my family. Our house still stands strong with its red coloured bricks and the giant mango trees that stand before it. My nanu had planted these trees in 1960, soon after the house was built. My nanu clearly had a premonition of the generations to come and to eat stickily sweet ripe golden mangoes every summer. It has been a staple of my life and it's the most comforting feeling because when we drive onto the old 15 road in Dhanmondi, you can see the massive branches and leaves, it could only mean that I'm home.

Our family business is a hospital that was established in 1992 and is around as old as I am, and I have spent the majority of my life in the private estate tucked away in Rayer Bazaar. It's not a glitzy neighbourhood with kids playing around, I was accustomed to slums and sick people. It's no surprise I have grown up to become a doctor, now able to work in the same space I used to goof around. Once I started kindergarten, my school's campus shifted to Gulshan and then Uttara. As I grew older my horizons expanded, Dhaka seemed to age at my pace. The ever-changing zip codes only added to my story, I grew up watching the seasons transition from the unbearable sticky humid heat of the summer to the heavy monsoon rain. My grandfather, whom I lovingly call Bhaiya, has been imperative to my upbringing. It was his unconditional love and support that gives me the strength and courage to keep going. We are blessed to have visited many countries in our respective lifetimes, but my grandfather had a special bond with the city. He valiantly fought for liberation of the country in 1971 and he worked passionately to improve the lives of thousands.

I was always fascinated with the love he had for this country although, like the majority of the citizens of Bangladesh, I too am guilty of being too harsh on the city I call home. My grandfather made me feel accomplished and worthy. It was with him that I truly felt safe and could laugh my heart out. It's so easy to point out what's missing and how difficult it is to get mundane tasks completed. I owe it to Dhaka that my life was every bit meaningful, and one could never say my life was monotonous.

I've spent a great chunk of my life in airports, going from one end of the world to the other, and for the longest time I used to dread thinking that I have to go back to the dull life that awaited me in Dhaka. That's the funny thing about maturity, you eventually stop caring about shiny new things and high-paced city life, you end up craving for something familiar, for comfort and the reassurance that you will be okay. We've had an ongoing tradition in my household now for over a decade now, every time I'd land in Dhaka my nanu would be sitting on the green couch right across the main entrance door. Sometimes I'd come in while she was praying but she would quicken her speed of reciting all her duas to finish and come and hug me. No matter the time of day, whether it was 7 am or midnight, she'd prepare my favourite meal Murogh polao with extra potatoes just for me. The aroma of the polao rice and ghee would permeate the entire room and I would dig in right away. My nanu would ask me questions about my flight, how I was doing and, of course, most importantly, was I eating enough?

Bangladesh is a beautiful, strong, innovative, and young nation that continuously improves over the years. We lavishly celebrate every occasion in Dhaka. Whether it's Eid, Pooja, NYE, or even Christmas, we go big or we just don't bother at all. I truly feel I inherited my mum's ability to make the most out of any occasion. She is the personification of the colour red, and her kindness is what inspires me to ascertain my life's purpose. My favourite holiday of the year is undeniably Pohela Baishak. It marks the first day of summer in Bangladesh, and people go all out to celebrate. One of the new traditions that is very close to my heart are alponas[1] that are painted all across Manik Mia Avenue in front of the National Parliament building. In a span of just one night, people from all walks of life step out together and paint the streets every colour of the rainbow. It is truly a remarkable sight to see.

Due to the recent COVID-19 pandemic, life has drastically changed all over the world. One thing for certain, it has made me learn to appreciate all that we have in the country and value my loved ones even more. I lost my dear grandfather earlier this year and I'm not sure how I will feel walking back into the house without his booming voice and infectious laughter. I would poke him when he was lost in his train of thoughts or mess his perfectly combed hair. It's hard to believe I won't hear him calling my name or singing his old Bollywood tunes. Things have definitely changed, and I feel like I've become a muted version of the happy child I was. Over the past few decades, new additions of sleek new floors and shiny windows have been added to my beloved home. Despite the sleek new makeover, I'm not sure I can call this house my home anymore.

---

1 alponas - colourful motifs, sacred art, or painting done with hands and paint which is mainly a paste of rice and flour

Anjum Azadi Nakshi, Dhaka, Bangladesh

I always find women living in some kind of limitation, it doesn't matter if she keeps up with the pace of the running world, changing herself into a modern woman or holding onto her traditional values. I agree that everything of this universe has a limitation, but women are unduly limited. Every conscious or unconscious mind forces a woman into an unknown limitation. Even in language, feminine words represent a fragile, weak, and insecure identity. As a woman, and being in a country like Bangladesh, I often find myself in hard situations. Women are victimised in a number of ways in my home, my city.

I just wanted to portray a woman who almost loses herself under the heavy weight of being a woman.

The Darkness of Her Dark Circles

It has been quite normal for Ana to lose herself in bleary thoughts, just thoughts? Or what can be said hiking in the wood of her scattered thoughts? She loves it anyway. Before her marriage, she loved making trips across the wilderness, stepping close to nature, and hearing it breathe is something beyond tranquillity. Nowadays she loves hiking through her thoughts, thoughts that give a touch of warmth in her coldly pleasant life, at least she finds her lost freedom here, her unuttered words and her faded feelings find a shade here. Her sister-in-law Nil gets mad at her; she said beauty sleep is important for girls and sleeping late could make her age fast.

When your soul finds its true colour of happiness in those numb musings why waste it on beauty sleep? Yes, sometimes, for some girls, beauty sleep has no meaning and for Ana the darkness of her dark circles bears more meaning in her life. Both of them are women, but life ties them in a different manner.

175

Today a dark cloud is rolling across Ana's mind. It's all about Rebi. She has known Rebi for two days. It's not like Rebi's situation thrills her, but there is something like a hidden mystery inside her that urges Ana more to know Rebi's world. She found Rebi senseless, lying beside her car. Ana asked her a thousand times why she left her home like this, what's the reason. She looked like a married woman, did her husband torture her or cheat on her? Rebi never answered any and denied all suspicions. She just asked for some money to return to her town. Ana wonders how obscure she is yet holding herself rigidly, *maybe she is not in a state to trust us? But then she could lie, at least give some fake answers, so why this stubbornness?* She wonders, *what is she doing leaving everything behind?*

Ana's Mum had always learned to be a compromising and understanding person in every step of life. It could help her to achieve inner peace. She also believes it. She has a very pleasant family life. She loves cooking; every day she cooks different dishes because everyone has different needs, you can't give rules to children when adults also act naught for a little food. She takes a little time for this cooking mastery, and now she is an expert in everything, even in managing her peace. Her husband is a responsible man, he strictly maintains his duties for family and his privacy even from Ana. Ana respects his privacy issue and also makes her own spaces to hideout. Everything is actually fine, and their sweet home almost looks like a palace. Ana polishes every corner here.

Ana cannot help thinking about why Rebi leaves everything behind. What could be the reasons to push herself to do so? There must be a solution for her, why this decision when she has no serious reason to answer.

The only thing she answered, 'There's no problem, Ana, yet I can't breathe there.'

'Then tell me something, I don't mind helping you out here.'

'You can't help me, you are a happy soul here, happiness veils your eyes of sorrow.' Her rootless talking gets no meaning in Ana's eyes, or maybe somewhere it mirrors a bitter meaning that Ana wants to suppress.

Sometimes it seems like Rebi is more interested in Ana's marital life, as if she wants Ana to violate her husband's privacy. Ana had no idea what to say to her. Ana suppressed all her anxiety; no, she never wants to know about anything of her husband – who texts him at night or with whom he stays at night for business purposes. She is happy with herself and trusts others. In fact, she is happy that Rebi is gone now because her words sound so creepy.

The last thing she says before leaving, 'I left my home because there was a giant and the same giant is living with you, just make an escape, the giant has almost got you.'

What kind of giant? Has she gone insane? How does Rebi know so many things about her husband? her scattered thoughts are rolling around.

Ana holds onto her belief, it is firmly murmuring *everything can be turned into a beautiful ending, I just have to work harder for my peace, I just have to plant some new flowers in the garden and paint my wall into a new colour and cook some new dishes. I'm able to turn my insomnia into my pleasure hour, so how can I give a chance to those weird thoughts to doom my inner peace.*

Ishmam Tasnim, Dhaka, Bangladesh

I believe I have always wanted to write about this magnificent city of Dhaka. As I learned about the local craftsmanship and how it built the city brick by brick, I wanted to capture the beauty, arts, and histories of this city through my writings.

But as I came across the 'My City, My Home' competition, I realised this city is far more connected to me than I could comprehend. Yes, Dhaka is a beautiful yet crowded metropolis, but what makes it 'My City'? How do I find my home here? Then one day I was walking across the city and realised how I have slowly made a home here. This city has shaped me, inspired me, and let me bloom. All of this was done by the people of the city – people I can relate to. This city and its stories are something I have been a part of.

What is art, music, and history but interpretation of different stories at the end of the day? As I indulged deep into the stories of this city, I could realise the unheard stories of this city. I could feel the stories lying within the art, culture, and music within the city.

Most importantly, it's only our home where we can feel safe against all struggles. Home is where we draw our energy from. This city and these people have been an inspiration for me to stand up against all struggles – both internal and external.

The city of Dhaka thus made me stronger. Dhaka enabled me to reach my dreams. The stories of Dhaka surround me, empower me, make me feel alive – just like a home should.

Hence, I wanted to capture this side of Dhaka, where it feels like home. We always have hundreds of memories and stories about our home. This time, I am sharing the stories about my home, my city.

Ode to the Unheard Stories

Returning to my tiny, congested flat after an eight-hour-long shift always feels like a breeze of fresh air.

Home is magical like that – where you're familiar with the smell of the air, you're comfortable with the chair, and you have your favourite snacks stored!

Similarly, we travel and live across different cities in our life, but we have a specific picture of our own city in our mind. This city is where we find a sense of belonging, an identity.

My city is where I know the stories of the people. The city full of people that inspires me to break barriers, the city that lets me outgrow myself.

I find my sense of belonging in a city of nine million people, with people of different cultures, lifestyles, and struggles. I can feel the dreams, heartbreak, and emotions of human relations in this city. This city stands by a riverbank, the river flowing with stories of the ancient land. Here, ancient landmarks stand with the memories of a king's beloved wife. This is also known as the city of mosques – where the mosques are designed as historical architectural sites where passers-by can spend the night. These mosque cultures bear the stories of the nomads of the land. The ancient part of the city still carries the stories of people who stayed and made a change, people who left with their dreams – these stories make me realise who I am. To me, this city is a city of all these stories and dreams.

Then the city developed over time; the stories changed. I found myself in a metropolitan area of diverse people. This diversity inspired my identity, taught me the dynamics of human relations. Nine million people living in a 119 square mile city – making these diverse stories colourful and full of life. Most of the people here are living below the poverty line, living here from some distant village where there is a struggle for survival. The amazing part that inspires me is how these people still make their lives festive out of the little moments of joy. This crowded city is still a city of celebration, a city of dreams. Even the *rickshawala*[1] who barely earns four USD in a day paints his ride in the most festive colours. To me, this is also the city of colours. Women in their colourful sarees and men in their *lungis*[2] celebrate their life, their culture. *Mangal Shovajatra* – the celebration of the Bengali new year is done with colourful vibrant festivities of all sorts. The middle-aged man, who never touched a paintbrush in his life, joins the street painting in the celebration. These spontaneous stories teach me to continuously rediscover myself, celebrate my existence.

This city is the home to many, but home is often just a five square foot wooden room or just a polythene camp for an entire family. Over six lakhs slum dwellers live in this city. Women in these slums provide domestic service worth millions of BDT in order to keep this city running. Our *khala*[3] doesn't know how to read but still manages to do online banking by her sheer willpower to provide for her family living elsewhere. All these *khalas* are breaking new barriers every day and creating their own identity against all odds.

Among all these lights and festivity, this city sometimes feels so frightening. Shadows lurking in the dark want to hold me back. Similar to many other parts of the world, this city is yet to be a safe place for girls. Sometimes, I am scared when I am alone in a dark street and keep wondering if anyone will be able to hear my cries for help. Then I remember how against all these odds, young girls and brave women thrive in this city, making the city thrive as well. Three million women work in the ready-made garments sector in the city, the highest-grossing export industry.

These girls leave their families, their homes, to make their own

---

1   *Rickshawala* – driver for a bicycle-like ride for two persons
2   *Lungis* – men's traditional cloth
3   *Khala* – housekeeper

home, own identity. These fierce women sew through all the fears of harassment and discrimination day in, day out. The stories of the girl who worked regular twelve-hour shifts to buy her family a home, inspire me to reach new heights. The woman who works for the entire day and still attends night school inspires me to break my own boundaries, to take higher education, to do something for people around me, for the people of this city.

My city is the dream city of the girl who found a home, created her identity in this city. Their dreams and hard work contribute to the sustainable economic growth of the entire country. To me, the face of the city is the garment worker girl who stood up against a bus full of men who were harassing her. Against all the shadows and fears, they are the rays of light who teach me to dream higher, to break free.

My city, Dhaka, is the stories of these unbreakable women. Dhaka is the combination of stories of these women who wrap themselves in beautiful sarees after a long day of work and brighten the city with their presence. Their contribution to society inspires girls like me to celebrate my existence, my womanhood, my identity and to be invincible.

Life can be indeed difficult in this metropolitan city, but this city still feels like home because it teaches me to believe in myself. I can dream comfortably about my future in this bright city as these women are tirelessly making this city better every day. As the city gradually develops and improves as a result of our sweat and effort, my dreams surrounding this city also develop. As I grow and rediscover myself, I feel the need to make positive changes to the city. I dream to make this city a safer, sustainable place for the upcoming generations.

I sing, laugh, love, and dream in my Dhaka, wearing my colourful saree. I breathe in the beauty of the city of dreams and stories.

Ayesha Tasnim, Sylhet, Bangladesh

Being a booklover, I always wanted to write something. For an introvert like me, writing is the only way I can express my thoughts. Though I couldn't express myself completely in my work, this initiative has inspired me to write again after a long break, about my city about my dreams, about the light I have found in this very city.

My City, My Home

'Home is the place that, when you leave it, you just miss it.'

Sitting by the window seat, while enjoying a view of the little piece of blue sky and cotton candy like clouds, Tasnim was suddenly reminded of this quote and thinking about her destination, her home, her Sylhet. Sipping her bitter coffee, she tries to control the butterflies in her stomach, but it seems like nothing is going to work today. The clouds look extra fluffy today, even the regular air hostess seems way too friendly and lovely.

Taking a mental glance at her journey of life, Tasnim opened her diary and started to write, 'Look how far you have come, Tasnim. The shy girl who once suffered from an inferiority complex, who used to stutter due to her glossophobia is now teaching thousands of students regularly in medical school. Maybe that's why life is called dynamic and unpredictable.'

'Things have never been easier for me. Growing up in a normal conservative family and studying in a super restricted school in this conservative city for about ten years, I really didn't know if I would be able to achieve my dreams. Things might have been easier if I were a boy, but as a girl I wasn't quite sure about what awaits me in the future. But I have to admit, Sylhet may not have offered varied opportunities as the capital city would have, it allowed me to find my dawn and my shooting star. This city has seen my first steps in my home, my further stumbling steps in my academic life, my self-doubt period during the medical admission test, and my transformation from an ugly duckling into a confident and beautiful swan. I remember being tired of exams and late-night shifts, and then escaping to the nearby tea-garden tranquil place in the midst of greenery with mountains as the backdrop.

As the first-born of my parents, I was given enough liberty to chase my dreams and take risks regarding my career. And probably that's why I could dream of something big in this city. This Sylhet is a city of chaos and echoes, a city where religion is a prime factor of life, but people are still so amicable towards each other, a city which is a heaven for foodies and a city where the dreams meet the final destination, a happy horizon. I could follow my dream of studying in the UK and being a resident doctor there because the people of this city lauded me, appreciated me in every single step of my life. Though current situations regarding rape and molestation deeply hurt, it had been a safe city 5-6 years ago. Once it felt like going out of this city would make my feelings for it fade away. But the roots are still deep inside my heart and that's why I am coming back today, here.'

Tasnim closes her diary hearing the announcement of the flight landing in Dhaka. Thirty minutes more and she will be there in her city, Sylhet. The journey starts again. As it is night-time, all the lights look like little stars from the plane. Tasnim eagerly kept looking through the window and till the journey came to an end, kept humming the song with happiness,

> 'City of stars
> Are you shining just for me?
> City of stars
> There's so much that I can't see
> Who knows?
> Is this the start of something wonderful and new?'

Salwah Chowdhury, Dhaka, Bangladesh

The title reminded me of how, despite having multiple homes in multiple cities, I never got to own mine. I had to share my bedroom growing up, and now that I am married, I still have to share my bedroom with my husband and daughter. The term 'my space' is something I had to find within myself rather than finding it in my city. I wanted to jot down my dilemmas in the short poem, expressing how I am still on the lookout for a home I can call exclusively mine.

Sanctuary

I was reminded by her that it wasn't my home,
I was ensured I will have mine too someday,
If getting married was the only way
I preferred not to.

She understood I was reluctant,
Nonchalant of my room and belongings,
My father's house was the only sanctuary I thought of –
But she, my dear mother, reminded me every time it was not.

My Holy Book reminds me that my grave is the only home,
Knowing that too, I was told how an 'apartment' should be my abode,
I got married and went to live in my husband's home –
But I was told by my friends, it wasn't mine after all.

Months later, I rented an apartment for us,
Just for the three of us –
Us and our daughter,
Again, she reminded me 'paying rent doesn't make the walls my own'.

Tanzia Tasnim Usha, Dhaka, Bangladesh

I have been studying abroad for three years now and every time I come back to Dhaka, I feel welcomed. It feels as if I have returned to the land that has always accepted me. There are so many memories that I had to select only a few to write in the story. I grew up here and I realise that I am what I am because of this city, and I need to write the good it has done for me. It will always be my home, no matter how many times I leave it.

Memories

I lazily walk alongside busy pedestrians, their destiny unknown to me. Wintry air is stabbing my lungs and my nose almost feels violated as it stings every time I breathe in. I ignore this slight pain and enjoy the atmosphere around filled with age-old magic. The fog is making puffs of smoke come out of my mouth while I observe the people around me. Some have adorned woollen shawls with beautiful ethnic designs; kids are wearing sweaters and stylish hoodies. There are teenagers who are giggling amongst each other with their designer bags carrying badminton rackets. A few years ago, I was one of these teenagers loving the winter in Dhaka city: the land of stories, the land of hope and love and dreams. There are so many memories tied to every corner of this city and they always make me smile.

Like that one time I had skipped class with my friends, and we all decided it would be fun to roam around Dhanmondi Lake. We were fifteen and the rush of defying our parents was too much to ignore. I was not wearing a sweater and constantly shivered against the cold wind. My crush had sneaked to my side and decided to help by wrapping his arms around me as I heavily blushed. I was too young and naïve to notice he liked me back then and considered his gesture as being a good friend. For two successful hours, my friends and I enjoyed the wintry air, ate ice cream that had our teeth chattering, and decided to take a boat ride on the lake. I was (and still am) hydrophobic and while I wobbled harshly my crush rushed to my rescue, helping me get on the boat. I was extremely shy that we were going to have an intimate session and scared of making a fool out of myself but the ride, itself, was fun. He had joked with me, asked about my likes and dislikes. We spotted people draped in shawls starting a fire, elderly couples jogging around the lake, and stray dogs wagging their tails as the vendors tossed food at them. At the end of the night, before I travelled home, he had asked me to go out with him some other time. Quickly, I said yes and left the lake with a smile the size of a crescent moon. I had felt like a beautiful goddess blessed by this city and my heart had started to fall in love with it.

Or, maybe that time when the city's magic was ruthless, and heat seeped inside my body while I searched the busy streets of Dhanmondi for my best friend. I was worried about her safety, desperate to find her. People in colourful clothes looked at me, judged me as I breathed heavily asking anyone if they had seen her. After a half-hour search, I found her near Jahaj Bari, a big, monumental building inside the lake, with her eyes red and face sticky with dried-up tears. She had run away from home because of the rumours that circulated in our college and somehow she had been dehumanised by people with bare minimum knowledge about her. I had allowed her to cry on my shoulders while others passed on looks. That day she told me about her newfound addiction to cigarettes, the depression, and that rumours about me circulated as well. With the fresh information, I sunk next to her and listened to all the bad things people had said behind our backs, how people who once were my friends said I was a bad apple because I came from a broken family. That day, until the sunset, my best friend and I had passed our time walking down the alleys and eating street foods. Amongst our journey to support each other I had realised, the city sometimes harboured evil spirits that only wanted to hurt others. This was why it was pushing me to become stronger.

I take turns in Dhanmondi area, crossing road number five and then road number six to finally stop at road number seven. The vendors of Lover's Point – the famous street food stall that garners more attention every day – are selling freshly baked cakes. I stand near the area, ignoring wide-eyed looks and the occasional bumps as people pass me. I never realised Dhaka city as my true home once I left it for higher studies. I constantly compared the air of the foreign land to my home and missed the bitter taste of dust, scorching heat, and icy winds. This city has taught me many things. It has made me the woman I am today, proud of myself for all the beauties and flaws just like it. The beauties that shine from its cold fogs in winter, thunderous skies during the summer, and gentle breeze during the autumn. The flaws of when the cold left others to shiver mercilessly, when the storms destroyed homes, and when the cloudy skies only dampened one's emotion.

In the end, even when this city pushes me away it calls me back. I have realised that Dhaka city has engraved itself in my blood, with a whiff of its wind I remember all the things it has done for me. My identity, my childhood, I owe everything to this city. The times I danced in the streets as traditional Bengali New Year's music blasted through speakers, got chased by a group of eunuchs who demanded a hefty amount of money, journeyed by bus and rickshaws while hawkers took their turns on advertising products, these are all memories I cherish. With memories of this city flooding my mind I walk near the fried food stall where my friends are now loudly laughing with each other, all of them grown and now finishing their bachelor's degree. I join them, creating more memories for the future.

Promila Bittu Safaya-Thomas, Birmingham, UK

For a migrant one never knows where the travelling will end, and which place will ultimately be called Home. Having said that the journey never stops. It's an ongoing pursuit but with age and maturity, one realises what counts in the end is that home is where the heart is!

'Home Is Where the Heart Is'

Where do I belong?
Which city do I call home?
Himalayas are where
My ancestors rose,
Descending to its foothills,
So I am told,
To this place of immense beauty,
Spiritually uplifting,
Where serenity unfolds,
Land of Saints home to
A nomad, the reluctant messiah
Inevitably taking on a soldier's role
Battling to protect his land...

Many many years later
The same blood is shed again
But in Modern times
Only to protect the 'line of control'
Giving birth to
A new entity... Pakistan
From where my parents,
The newlywed, were
Forced to flee in deep distress

Leaving behind a world
And much else.
Hard to comprehend
British rule drawing an end
Saw India divided & hard to mend,
Parting a part of their motherland
As soul-shattering as can be,
My friend!
Seeking refuge across in Srinagar
A stopgap...
To breathe, reflect, reconcile, regenerate
And not in the least, to procreate!

Hard times come knocking again,
Parenthood sees a migrant phase
For a decent family to raise.
Yes for me, the middle of three,
Life full of mischief so free,
A long haul it was this time
In a place of intrigue & food divine
Well suited to spend one's prime.
Hardly surprising if I fell in love
With the 'City of Joy'
Calcutta of my yesteryears
I raise a toast to say... Oh Kolkata!
You were born much later than me.
For I grew up in the shadows of
Your Anglo cousin
Her head forever tossed
With an air of arrogance!
All I reveal here about you is true
Many more memories lurch
in this scanty heap of my silver hue
Only but to mention a few...

Durga pooja's glittering *Pandaal*[1]
Drums beating hard afar...
Diwali, Eid, Holi, Navroz
String of celebrations of course!
Park street's X-mas display
Firpose hotel's Jazz play...
Marbled Victoria memorial
Boasting its grand state,
Horse-carts ready to go
Always waiting at its gates.
World-class Zoo in Alipore
Eaden garden in Cricket downpour,
Birla Planetarium & its silver dome
Felt nothing short of being in Rome!
The Racecourse,
Botanical Park,
Shyam Bazar,
Esplanade...
All set in periods before.
Not mere tram-stations galore,
Buses grinning lopsided,
Weighing heavy at the doors.
Stories about these & many more...

Gauriyahatta, Ballygunge,
My school Shiksha Sadan,
Principal Pushpa Mai Bose
A statuette of disciplined love
Honest & straight as her backbone,
Getting out of there,
Might have taken me a while...

---

1   *Pandall* – marquee

I'm kind of still stuck somewhere
In those Republic Day parades,
Nostalgic National Anthem
Reviving Independence's tantrum
Not to forget a havoc arose
When East Bengal took a pose
As Bangladesh...
Under Pakistan's very nose!
Our shared history, beliefs, and stories told,
Gave us many reasons to hold.
Childhood memories to
My budding adulthood...
All splashed in pure gold!

Sixteen years whizzed-pass
As I was essentially having fun,
Schooling & learning languages
Other than my mother tongue,
Hindi mastered, English in my backpack,
Bengali a bit underdone
Career path had to be chosen
Or even shown.
For me, it came to mean
Not a change in Geography alone
But to learn a new lesson in History
And this time all on my own!
Slaving away ten years or so
Learning Punjabi on the go
Gave me a degree & a chance
To try and explore...

History was to repeat itself,
This time my son's parents were
The migrants...
Sailing to greener pastures ashore,
A long leap it was alright,
Lots of apprehension, a bit of fright
Being tossed up in air thousands of miles
Touching down at Heathrow safely
Did bring about a smile...

Toiling was to be entered again,
As they say, 'No pain, no gain.'
Adjusting, integrating for a while
Made the barren land fertile,
West Midlands it had to be
Where all dreams did come true
Birmingham in particular
Was to be home...
Indefinitely & forevermore
Here I learnt to cook
Something other than my own,
Full English breakfast at times
Or just humble beans on toast,
Fish & chips went down pretty well
As did Sunday roast so swell.

More than food it was the culture,
Many rich heritages mingling Set off my nerves
tingling.
Fusion arts, craft & music
Enriching my senses & soul,
This land, the people, their generous ways
From raising a family to serving NHS
Made everything I did, worthwhile!

Forty years it has been since
I first set foot on this soil,
Coming off the plane at Heathrow
Clinging on to my humble show
It did feel very hard at first
To navigate the professional maze
But once I proved my mettle to them
It helped clear the purple haze.
I remain in awe every bit
Of this city that's given me
So much to gauge,
Known to me now like
The back of my hand.
Home is where the heart is,
And rightly so it is said,
I did fall in love a second time
Where at stake is so much of mine
A true companion for my coming of age
White Christmas, Snowman & Elf
A proud Brummie I call myself!

Jahanara Tariq, Dhaka, Bangladesh

As an aspiring poet and writer based in Dhaka, I continually tend to be inspired and moved by certain happenings in this colourful city. This writing competition was the perfect opportunity to jot down my thoughts. Everything starting from the hours I have spent commuting in this city, to the stories I have heard from my loved ones, to scenes that I love to detest about Dhaka, shows up in this work. The poem is an amalgamation of bliss and misery, revolution and corporation, reunions and heartbreaks because I believe it is the cesspool of these jarring ideas which acts as the defining elements of my home, my city.

Few Notes on Home

Dhaka is drunken serenades of Arnob's *Neelche Tara* and Ahmed's tragic tropes of eighties middle-class anxieties.

Dhaka is a conversation with Buddhadeva about the need for larger horizons, celebration of solitude, and assertions on Art for Art's Sake.

It is Marx-like beards, whips of cream shawls and fuming youth drunk on crafting protests down Kahn's Magnum Opus.

Dhaka is the last condiment needed for romance — Krishna on the flute and a whole lot of empty bellies sprawling through the streets spilling rose petals and spirited profanities.

Rezwana Karim Snigdha, Auckland, New Zealand

This story isn't only a narrative of my life, it is the tale of most women in Bangladesh. 'Me' in this story is not the sole precedent of this entry; rather, it is an account of each untold chronicle of almost all women's lives. Speaking of mine, even after accomplished adequately in academic and professional spheres, I am recurrently advised 'you are a woman, be gratified with what you have effectively achieved; how many young ladies could achieve what you have already accomplished? Be content with that!' As if questioning the triumph of all my achievements, how could it be plausible that I voyaged that far as a woman! Nonetheless, I am constantly reminded that a woman's success is virtually uncelebrated compared to a man's. Yet nobody came to recount the narrative of the lost self of a women's life. Following the pattern, from childhood, I was never given any chances to ask you any questions about stealing my individuality away from me. I have not been given a choice to have you express regrets for the loss of my eccentricity; I have not even been given the opportunity to ask for an explanation when you have snatched myself away from who I am which encouraged me to compose this entry.

My Entirety

If I am asked who I am

On the off chance that I was posed an inquiry... Who am I? What am I? What city do I live in? I was not offered any choice to respond to these questions. I was never asked as to why I resulted in this uncertain world from the womb which was encompassed by security or whether I was keen on being conceived by any means. While most female foetuses are not given a chance to see the light of this Earth, and often get terminated before they get to know and understand the significance of their gender identity or the costs of being female, thankfully my parents were not among those who did not mean to bring me into this world. Therefore, in line with it, I can compose an account of my experience as a woman today. However, at birth, I had no clue about what skin colour, what gender, and what name I would be depicted as. What I should do or what I should not, how I shall behave and how I shall not – all my performance, my role, my duties and responsibilities, even my own name, and the entirety of this is an assortment of orders in your psyche.

After birth, I was told that my name is Snigdha. Even my name has me figured out before I have. The meaning of the name reveals to me that I am a girl. The denotation of men's names is not given in this consideration because this society does not permit men to be delicate, tender, sensitive. Still, my name instructs me to be gentle, to be soft, and it further teaches me that the sole purpose behind my life is to spread the fragrance by dispensing myself. Therefore, I was unceasingly taught I must be delicate, mild, and gentle. I was advised rudeness, sharpness, and laughter aren't for me because I am a female. I was taught that I have the sole responsibility to ensure all the happiness of the family. Eluding all that I am, at the end of the day, I was simply summed up as a woman, leaving me as an empty body. Whether I understand womanhood or not, I was forced to accept that I am not permitted to fly like a winged bird, I am not allowed to loosen up when it is sweltering hot, it is not acceptable to speak loudly, I am not allowed to be ambitious, I am not allowed to speak freely. I am forbidden to have sexual urges, even not allowed to choose the clothes that I wear.

My modesty, the beauty of my face and body, is the first identity that society would esteem. My acceptance is objectively trapped in my adornment, on my decorated body, the social and cultural construction of an ideal woman's chastity. I was frequently reminded that I am a woman, and my responsibility is to dazzle others. I should not commit any errors. I shall not cross my line, not to willingly and truly fall in love. For that, I should be completely controlled by conditioned grownups who haven't had the inner need to question the alleged reality and society. I was trained by the social and religious values that my virginity is only for a man. I have no other choice aside from recognising him as my significant other; my body won't be mine any longer, yet he will entirely claim it. He will consider me to be a premise of his amusement.

In this manner, I never get an opportunity to acknowledge why I should be his entertainment source. Once more, I question why I have no rights over my body, sexuality, or even myself?

Although many women have access to formal education nowadays, they are never appreciated for their knowledge or wisdom, nevertheless. In addition, the knowledge contribution of women is not given any place in the intellectual arena or at the talk of logic and argument stage of scholars.

Along this line, if we close our eyes and look at history in search of wise men, countless names will be revealed, but there is no trace of wise women in our observance in this subcontinent. Therefore, from the page of history, the name of *Khona* from our subcontinent and *Hypatia* from the western world don't get their permeability, and in the long run, these names seem to be lost due to the absence of endorsement. In the same way, women are never applauded for the intelligence, quality of their talent, knowledge, or creativity, never enlightened at any communal affair. The hopelessness of the life of a learned woman reminds me of the account of taking away *Khona's* tongue and consuming *Hypatia* with the label of a living witch.

To you, I am the annihilator since the outset of the creation through the story of Adam and Eve. In the scriptures, my birth is exclusively rooted in the service of men and for the endurance of human progress. The holy books have additionally given me the legitimacy to lay hands on me, and I had to jump into the fire like Sita time and time again to prove my chastity. Disgraced, I have repeatedly taken refuge indoors, and even there I am a 'sex slave' or simply a 'slave'.

Thus, this evening, sitting in tranquillity far away from the county, thinking on the off chance that if I am asked, 'Who am I? Where do I belong?' Would I be able to respond to this? Since I was never allowed to know who I am or what I am. At that point, for what reason is this me again in your male-dominated pride, scorn, and disgrace to know who I am? What am I?

Fazila Nowshin, Dhaka, Bangladesh

My life itself inspired me when writing this piece. I have always liked writing, and this allowed me to write more. Family support is also a reason for me to pursue this passion.

Leaving Behind

Was I leaving behind everything? Or was it a step of going forward? But life was going to change anyways. Did I want this change?

When there were too many questions, the answer was none. Holding the pen, my hand stuck over the piece of paper, eyes looking outside the window and mind elsewhere. It was getting too hard to decide whether to leave or stay. The thought that troubled me the most was of leaving behind this city, my home. But right the next moment, a strange, persistent will was telling me something else.

Everyone dreams. A traveller dreams of wandering, a bird dreams of being free forever, but a commoner dreams of staying onto the ground, gripping tightly to the ground. At a point in time, the fear of losing what we already have overpowers the zeal of what we want. Being an exception is what everyone prefers, spotlight and attention, since for a commoner it's impossible to ever be heard in a crowd of anonymous souls. And sometimes, such a dream comes at a cost of happiness. But I was a commoner, why did I care about this? Why did these thoughts pester me? Countless evenings were spent, distinguishing between wishes and dreams.

The cloudy light, bluish skies, birds chirping around, the still, transparent waters of the river always gave me a sort of calmness. The distant hills, crisp air, and the lovely fragrance of tea leaves would lighten up my mood whenever I felt down. There, I used to spend endless mornings observing everything intently. And with this, a pen and paper would always accompany me. The liveliness in the neighbourhood was warm and genuine. There were countless friends, caring neighbours, and a strong grip among the relations. Sreemangal, a small town in Sylhet, was the best place for leading a life of good health and joy. But suddenly, life changed its course and I soon found myself leaving behind this precious place.

We moved to the megacity, Dhaka, for the sake of good education. I was too small to miss my hometown then, but gradually that feeling came up to the surface. The urbanisation in the lifestyles of Dhaka was far-reaching and at times, really difficult to cope up with. New city and people, new school and all the friends left behind, life had become weary. The monstrous buildings blocked the sun, the skies were cloudy, air was dusty, and neighbourhoods felt lifeless. But back then, I couldn't say what I felt as I myself wouldn't know. The change was big, but life taught me to adjust. But now, I feel surprised how my perspective towards Dhaka drastically changed with the course of time. The neighbourhoods I once found lifeless, dazzled me with the diversity of festival celebrations. Many new friends were made, I found lovely teachers who sharpened my knowledge, and I learnt a lot of things. Hundreds of happy memories of childhood were made right here that made me start loving this city. However, life again put me at the crossroads of choosing ambitions over home, dreams over happiness.

The memories of Sreemangal and Dhaka had occupied me, and I kept looking outside the window. The worry of leaving behind my city, family, and this country was too heavy for my mind to carry. Right then, my mum entered and patted my back as she sat down beside me. She held out a piece of paper to me. It was a child's scribbled handwriting.

'You wrote this when you were only six,' said Mum. She continued, 'we chose to shift to Dhaka when we learnt about your liking of writing, to provide you the best of opportunities.'

I read it. The very first essay that I wrote. I looked at the paper again. Amongst the silly grammar mistakes, one line caught my eyes and I read it aloud. 'I love my home because I am happy.'

Now, it didn't take long for me to sign the paper, as those unanswered questions had left my mind filled with determination. I thought, *if my parents could live against the odds for me, then why can't I? Happiness isn't something to be afraid of losing; there's always a scope of finding more of them.* Though leaving everything behind is difficult, for this, it is fruitful. I finally understood home isn't bound to one city. When truly felt, home is where happiness and freedom lie.

Anushka Hosain, Karachi, Pakistan

Italo Calvino said, 'Cities, like dreams, are made of desires and fears.' The fears and desires of Karachi and its inhabitants are starkly visible. Karachi is one of the hottest, driest, most polluted cities on the planet. This year's monsoon, which should have brought relief, instead caused overwhelming damage to an already broken urban infrastructure, leaving most of the city flooded. The massive inequality, the absence of urban planning, greenery, and sustainable living, are glaring. All these types of factors — gender, environmental, economic — go hand-in-hand. The horrors that Pakistani women face (the Global Gender Gap Index report of 2020 ranked Pakistan 151 out of 153 countries) cannot be underestimated. Yet women of every level continue to fight against their oppression. In writing this piece, I was thinking of the mother goddess (Kali) and the mother as founder (the Mai Kolachi legend), of Indian classical dance (which I learned under Sheema Kermani), and the female power these devotions allow us to claim. It is to the bravery and courage in the survival of Pakistani women that I wish to dedicate this writing.

A Dark Light Stirs

I live in a city that is drowning in light.

We live under open skies, without trees to shelter us. The light is merciless. It beats down, blow upon blow. In summer blinding bars of sunlight strike every surface, forcing us to walk around with eyes half shut. The light breaks through windows and doors, finding a chink, an uncovered corner, forcing its way inside our homes. We carry the weight of light on our heads. We walk with heads bowed.

We live submerged in light and smoke. Our skies are brown

and grey, and our houses are painted to match. House dims into sky, house fades into earth. House dissolves into cloud, house mingles into ground. A dun haze: from heaven to earth, a blended expanse, a muted palette, this vast city unfolding.

I live in a city that shrouds women.

On smoky streets women walk in ones and twos amongst throngs of men, effacing themselves, erasing themselves. Camouflaging to escape predators. Sober faces hiding shining hearts. A woman with a soul of light, a woman with the character of water, a woman shrouded in black.

I live in a city that is drowning in water.

Summer rain and the streets dredge up our shame. Flooding everywhere. Rain falls from the ceiling, water flows through windows, under doors; the courtyard becomes a lake, the street becomes a river. Rickety shacks and one-room homes wash away. The city, ashamed, effaces itself – an urge to return to the primeval. The city dreams of disappearing into the sea.

In the rain and in the sun, women are busy. Burying secrets underground, trampling underfoot what was promised and never given – losing, discarding, forgetting. Shadowed hearts, drowned hopes, submerged dreams.

I live in a city on the frayed edge of the world.

The koel cries, portending rain, flies from its tree, and then! One drop, then another. The parched quench their thirst, swell with gladness, and for a moment it seems we can start over, all shall be mended — but the rain continues. It soon overfills the scanty earth, it takes to the streets, collecting as it goes the scraps and swill that form our lives, the muck and mire that hold up our dwellings, making a wake of remains, scouring the underworld, and spewing the refuse of bodies and minds now clotted and curdled and condensed into something vile and vicious, our rot laid at our feet, this fouled world we have made.

Water used to flow freely here, not long ago. Much of this city was seabed or marshland or mangroves; rivers, canals, and streams ran through it. We pushed back the sea, cleared the mangroves, drained the marshes, stole the land; we covered, clogged, and blocked the rivers and canals. The water swirled in rage at our profanations. Livid, furious, the sea returned to reclaim what once belonged to it.

Women used to walk freely here, not long ago. On the streets, on buses, on bicycles; in skirts or shalwar; shouting, laughing, dancing. We took away their right to move and maunder; we forbade, restrained, shackled; we coerced and compelled them into shrouds. This is a city of silenced, swallowed women, heads bowed with an unnameable grief.

When I was a child, the city was a mass of blocks, houses of modernist white standing stark amidst the brown swirling sand blunting, sharp corners. In those days we had the blazing red, pink, orange, purple, magenta of bougainvillea, its papery delicacy and colourful profusion in counterpoint to the blocky white houses. The colours of dawn and sunset, of fire and sunlight. Amaltas trees with their radiant yellow flowers shaded the streets, lining the roads with their flower carpet: yellow the colour of joy itself. Gulmohar trees with their flame-red flowers stood like glorious sentinels at street corners: red the colour of our gladdening hearts. The flowers feasted on sunshine, softening the light so that it fell on our heads like halos of golden dust.

Against all that white and those brilliant colours was a blue sky: not the clear laundered blue of the new world, not the deep blue of the old sea, nor the temperamental skies of unknown, far-off places. This sky was a worldly, dusty sky, one that had seen history, that had beheld misfortune and misery but had also seen splendour and immensity. This was an ancient sky, one that had witnessed the rise and fall of many peoples, that small portion of a history that contained the rise and fall of mountains and the movement of continents. In this ancient sky, eagles shrilled and soared.

A few hundred years ago or a thousand years ago or never, a woman from a fishing village lost her husband in a storm, and despite the danger, went into the heart of the tempest to rescue him. Or she lost one of her sons to a crocodile, killed the crocodile, and saved her other son. Or she lived in a fishing community in which the men stayed out on the seas, the women were at the centre of village life, she was the head of the village, and the village took on her name, a sign of the respect in which the people held her.

Mai Kolachi: Respected lady, fisherwoman, fighter, leader.
Mai Kolachi: founder, mother. Kolachi, Kurrachee, Karachi.

I live in a city that dreams of a world that once was. I live in a city that dreams of a world that could be.

A dark light stirs. In a shining heart, a thrumming fury grows. Fury swells in the throat — song. Fury swells in the hands — music. Fury swells in the feet — dance. Black fury, whirling with garlanded arms, points of light gleaming above her head. In her black braid, a brilliant, sparkling, blood-red jewel. Song breaks like waves on dark shores, music claps asunder dark air, dance crackles dark earth. Something ancient awakens to reclaim what was once hers.

Shanty Begum, Birmingham, UK

I feel that the terms My City and My Home inspired me by making me think, feel, and ask the question 'Does the city I currently reside in actually feel like home to me?' I guess the next question would be, which is equally as important, 'What would qualify as my home, and do I feel I am at home yet or not?'

My City... My Home?

Gazing intently out of my bedroom window, I look up towards the darkness...

Once again to be reunited with the sparkling jewels of the dark sky...

Hello again stars, my companions, my confidantes, keepers of my innermost thoughts... Let us pick up from where we left off... I have an important question to ask, and I know that you will answer me truthfully while shining your light across the city landscape...

From Manchester to Birmingham, Birmingham to Manchester and now Manchester to Birmingham again... I have settled now in this 'city of thousand trades' but have I accepted this city as my home? Has the city taken me in and accepted me unconditionally?

Friendly faces greet me in the streets, talking and laughter echoing in the parks, music, culture, food, the rich history embedded in the fabric of this magnificent city... So much to see, hear, and feel... yet why, at times, do I feel so disconnected, so lonely, and like my voice, goes unheard?

Can you answer me stars, my companions, my confidantes, keepers of my innermost thoughts?

'You will find the answers to your questions from within, where lies the truth and your light... Only then will you look up towards the dark sky and smile contently in silence...'

Nusrat Tabassum, Dhaka, Bangladesh

The terms 'My City and My Home' brought out a heartfelt complicated confession, an unrequited love for my city's past, fearful hope for the future and much more. Above all, it brought out the truth and a vulnerability, feelings that I never thought I could articulate... Dhaka is my muse, but I hate it sometimes with disappointment and intensity, but I always go back to loving it with a confused heart as cosmopolitan cities tend to play with our conscience. My writing was inspired by recent real incidents, and in the end, the poem became something very close to my heart.

To My Daunting Muse

Dearest Dhaka, I would happily give up
this mortal petty frame,
Dissipate my being into your alleyways and chaotic lanes.
I would restore the mourning Black Buriganga
into its glory days,
With crystal clear water, not a drop of malice,
corruption, or selfishness in its veins.
I wouldn't let them cut down those bloodshot crimson
Krisnochura blooms;
Nor the glorious Radhachuras that reminded me of the
promised Golden Bengal;
Not the violet Oporajita, Jarul, nor the white Kodoms
Of vehement clouds that brought the rains so sound
That it would make everyone gush over the dazzling
Dhaka's beautiful shroud.
Strangers would fall in love with each other in that joyful
ambience of an otherworldly crowd.

But now the dirt of Dhaka is dying with thirst
Because they can't soak the rainwater to clean the rust.
The ground is covered up with concrete
and pitch-black asphalt
By bulldozers of forced development and disgust.
The vast horizon has shrunk so much
That even up above an ugly elevated construction,
you can't see so much.

Dhaka I've seen you through child-like amazement,
I've seen you with teary-eyed teenager's angst,
Through the busy practical business lens,
Through the starving eyes of a street flower vendor,
Through the wrinkled skin of
an old woman bangle attender.
I've enjoyed you, decorated and colourful,
In festivals, in Pahela Baishakh,
Until some hooligans decided to tear apart,
The beautiful red-white saree of a young girl.
I've seen you in revolution, in flood,
in countless other avatars.
You see, I've witnessed it all, the good, the bad,
the mediocre overalls.
A necessary evil, you might be to some,
But to me, you're the forbidden apple of Adam,
And I prefer to gulp down my Hemlock at once,
Drown in dreams of your glorious past,
And hopelessly admire you in whatever state you are
Because I believe,
soon bees will reincarnate you in spring buds.

Faria Rashid, Dhaka, Bangladesh

I got excited about the 'My City and My Home' writing competition from the time I first heard about it from a fellow Bangladeshi woman writer. As an aspiring writer, it inspired me to think about the topic and write a piece on it. It is a great honour and pleasure to share the same platform with women writers from two other different countries along with Bangladesh. I considered this as an incredible opportunity to express my feelings and emotions about my city. I tried a new style of writing for this piece. This writing competition certainly provided me with a platform to express my truth.

Here, I Never Feel at Home

Dhaka - a city that never made me feel home - neither as a little girl nor as a full-grown woman.

It is dangerously unsafe, where I can never freely roam.

Not only for the muggers but also for the strange gazes.

Dhaka is a compact concrete jungle that constantly suffocates me, makes me yearn to go find a space to breathe.

The energy here is so toxic, going inside is your only refuge.

It is a place where my senses are overloaded – not only with the noise, the traffic, the pollution, the beggars, the hawkers proudly occupying the sidewalks, the uncomfortable lighting, the overcrowded spaces, the unplanned urbanisation, the piles of overflowing dirt, the stray dogs, the honking of the vehicles;

but also, with the indiscipline, the crime, the corruption, cruelty, violence, intensity, and the ruthless people.

Dhaka makes me feel *fernweh* – the self in me that wants to feel appreciated, rather feels criticised.

Dhaka will never let you hide to find yourself or to find solace.

It is a space that I have outgrown, certainly not where I belong.

Too much is happening, but I am still not growing.

The feeling of disassociation is always there.

It is not the home where you find your tribe.

In Dhaka, I am alone. I go alone. I do it alone.

I want to go for a long walk home.

Nayeema Nusrat Arora, Dhaka, Bangladesh

I have witnessed so many women around me living such different lives than me. Nothing is common between me and them except the city we live in. I guess we all have built a love-hate relationship with it. We get mad at it, frustrated even but in the end, we don't know any other place to call ours. It is a kind of relationship you have with your loved ones. And sometimes when human bonding is too much to deal with, the city is the only thing that lets you get lost in it.

Belongingness

The smell of freshly applied henna is my favourite. It has a festive vibe as if something very auspicious is about to happen. A very happy beginning. But today the smell means much more to me than just festivity. This henna on my hand is the mark of my womanhood. I am getting married today. Finally, I will have a home of my own. My mother, I think, was not that happy with my birth as she was so sure she was about to have a boy. The light bearer in her darker than a winter's nightlife. But she had me. My father however tolerated me kindlier I would say. I think my mother's harsh comment made him pity me. When I was three years old, I had a sister with whom I shared my misery and my mother's wrath. But she however didn't have to tolerate it for a long time. How lucky! When she was three and I was six years old we welcomed our third sibling and the oldest brother, Badshah. The torchbearer of my mother's life. She wanted a name that suited aptly to her 'rajputra'.[1] Hence, the name. Oh, I so wanted to hate Badshah, but I couldn't. How

---

1 *Rajputra* is a prince or son of a king. Bengali mothers use this word to affectionately describe their sons. In this story, it is used to give an equivalent sense of the English phrase 'apple of my eye'.

could I? Badshah was the humblest, kindest child I have ever seen. Full of love, full of empathy. When my mother used to beat me and then punish me with the 'no food' rule, he would always sneak some in his little pockets and feed them to me when my mother was not looking.

I was ten when we had to evacuate our old house because of river erosion and move to the city, Dhaka – a place larger than life where movie stars and famous cricketers live. We were going to live in the same place as them. But the city had its own cruelty under its glamour. Me, my sister, and Badshah would roam around our new home after eating anything in the house that could be passed as lunch. I had made a new friend, Rahim Chacha. He would let us ride his rickshaw and show us the city life. Somehow, that moving vehicle of a stranger always felt more like home than where I lived. I don't know if it was the absence of my parents' control or the love of Rahim Chacha, or the sweet symphony of my siblings' laughter, but I felt that I existed and that feeling was never of guilt or a burden like I felt when my mother used to scold me for doing something she did not approve of – which was most of the time.

She would say, 'This is not your house where you could do whatever you felt like. Do this when you have your own house, understand? I would not tolerate any of such nonsense.'

I used to get so confused after hearing this. I mean if that was not my home and then what is? But then I learnt, you get a home after you get married. Your husband brings a home along with him. And when you marry him, you marry the house too. Finally, the day has come. Now the happy feeling of existence won't last for just a splitting moment of a rickshaw ride. It will last for eternity.

***

Waiting is exhausting. He always takes such a long time in the shower. The food will get cold and then he will get mad. If he wants to eat hot food, why can't he just come in time? Again, I have to reheat everything, and he will get mad anyhow for the food being late.

'Bring the egg curry.'

'I didn't make any.'

'What do you mean – you didn't make any?'

'There is no egg in the house, so I made a vegetable curry instead.'

'What do you mean there is no egg? Didn't I just buy eggs yesterday? How could you finish them so quickly?'

'The women from downstairs borrowed some and I made a curry yesterday.'

'How dare you distribute my things which I buy from my hard-earned money in the whole neighbourhood? Did you ask for my permission? Look, this sort of things might have been okay in your father's house, but I won't tolerate such stupidity in my house even for a second. Do you get that?'

'Yes.'

'Now go and buy some eggs for me. I want to eat egg curry today. Take this money. And don't you dare waste my money in stupid things.'

I took the money and went out. Called a rickshaw and asked the rickshaw-puller to take me to the furthest shop in the area. I am in no hurry to go back and live in a house that is not mine.

I guess some people are not lucky enough to get a place in this world where they can enjoy their existence and experience a sense of belongingness for eternity. Some just get a fleeting moment in the rickshaw of a stranger in a city they call their own.

Adita Afrose Hasan, Dhaka, Bangladesh

For the many years that I lived abroad, whenever I thought of home (which was often), I thought of my paternal grandparents' house at old Elephant Road in Dhaka, Bangladesh, where I had spent a large portion of my childhood and formative years growing up in a sprawling, joint family property. When I read the brief for My City, My Home, it was the first place that came to mind and that I had the urge to write about. It embodies a golden part of a childhood and time in Dhaka in the 1980s and 1990s that can never be returned to. The house, built in 1960, is now soon to be demolished, its glory days long past, and only my paternal aunt still lives there. Elephant road, once a stretch of land with far-placed bungalows and large residential homes near the sprawling Dhaka University campus, gradually grew into a very busy shopping district quite at odds with the old family homes hidden within its interior 'golis' and bylanes.

Elephant Road er Basha
(The Elephant Road House)

Sometimes I miss home. Childhood. The old house with the forest garden. Untangled, wild, coconut and mango trees; unkempt except for the once a year 'picnic' in winter under the lychee tree, where we made a stove out of mud and cooked khichuri. The three of us, Amita, Anik and I. We never even took a photo. I remember every detail, the sun barely filtering through the thick foliage of the big tree above our heads, mosquitoes occasionally biting our bare legs as we crouched, waiting, sometimes sitting on little *piris*; the smoky smell of the khichuri as it cooked for what felt like hours on the little handmade clay stove built out of the soil, fire burning with dry coconut and banana tree leaves.

214

Banana trees. I had forgotten about those.

The sour mangoes we would climb on the giant roof of the house to pick, using whatever we could find, long sticks, tugging branches to pull them closer to our hands. Edging precariously close to the flat concrete edge with no railing, a free-fall straight down two floors to the garden below. Just close enough for one brief moment to pluck the mango off, and then the branch would swing back, unruly. The smell of those green mangoes, the thrill of our success, anticipating marching down to the kitchen to peel and mix with crushed dried red chillies and salt, mouthwatering. A life-long love of *kacha aam makha*.

I loved that wild garden. I used to like to pretend that garden was a magic forest. Somedays, exasperated, I would wish that the grown-ups would tidy it up, plant some grass or flowers so it would not look so unkempt. I would ask my mother. She would say she had tried; the grass would not grow because there was never enough sunlight. Why not? There were too many trees. They blocked out the sun.

Except on the veranda. Those hours spent on that veranda. The sunlight tracing diamond-patterned shadows over the white mosaic floor; the view of the hammock strung between the mango tree and jackfruit tree right in front. Me sitting cross-legged on the cool white floor, basking in the warmth of that sun. Playing. Singing. Endless hours reading books lying on the bamboo couch in one corner. Eating fresh boiled peas straight out of the pods. Eating juicy pink jambura in bowls. Happy whiling away time alone, yet never really alone in that great, sprawling house full of people. Eating every meal there when we moved the dining table. All the furniture changed around every few years.

The time when we were very little, and a toddler Anik decided to pee through the bars of the upper floor balcony, jetting forth a thin arc of golden streaming water; I watched, fascinated, standing next to him as it made its way down, glittering in the midday sun, where it landed straight on our Dadi's wild head of

215

grey hair, her having chosen that exact moment to step out into the garden from the veranda below. Some shouting about unruly children ensued, and it cannot be said that she was best pleased as realisation gradually dawned. And Anik's mother, who for some reason we all called *Bouma* (daughter-in-law), standing hidden in the shadows behind us, trying half-heartedly to contain her unrestrained guffaws with hastily pressed hands to her mouth, against the rising crescendo of shrieks coming from the garden. A childhood story to be re-told over and over again until it made even Dadi laugh.

But always, the memory of the sunlight filtering through the trees, streaming through the netting and the square grids of the veranda grill, making stretched out, sun-filled diamonds on that cool stone floor. For years, whenever I closed my eyes and thought of home, that was what I saw. To this day, large white mosaic squares with those little dark stones are my favourite type of flooring. Funny, how long it takes you to understand how much childhood influences your choices. Your favourites. Your joys. Your harms.

I miss you, home. So much moving around since; so many places to call home. None that invoke that first confidence imbued within a beloved childhood. Where you felt like you were Boss. That you were important, and you were loved. I wonder, did we all feel that way? Amita, me, Anik?

All those years distilling confidence, slowly eroded – I wonder now if there was a correlation between leaving home and the loss of self-assurance, the beginning of self-doubt. The irony though, for surely somewhere in those memories, childhood is where it all begins. The making of you, the beginning of you. Of who you are, and what you might become.

But for now. I have sun-warmed memories. I was content. I felt loved. And for that, as for those memories, I am eternally thankful.

Zarah Alam, Birmingham, UK

The term 'My City, My Home' raised questions in me which I sought to answer in my poem, for example 'How can I describe my city?', 'What stands out to me in my city?' and 'Does my city feel like my home?' The fact that the words 'city' and 'home' are separated suggested a central tension which encouraged me to also explore some of the negative aspects of my city and to grapple with the question of whether my city truly felt like my home.

Burminum

Birmingham, no, *Burminum* – it tastes salty sweet on my lips –
The rumble of an industrial past held captive in its name.
It tumbles out of my mouth, all frothy and green grey.

I snail through its spindly streets
And marvel at the bus driver's skill,
Not one car hit nor angry beep heard.

I'm all too aware of my dust-glazed eyes,
A symptom of overly familiar sights,
The magic of the minutiae lost in a concrete blur.

I rub my eyes, determined to truly see my city,
When, suddenly, I'm jolted by the tumultuous branches battering
the ceiling.
Trees announce their presence, demand to be seen,

Twist and turn to rebel against their linear formation.
I smile at them, who knew a city could be so green?
It seems I pass a park after every two streets.

217

Colours spring between concrete slabs coming apart,
I used to hopscotch the dried weeds,
Too afraid to stomp out their wild beauty.

As we slither through the city centre
My breathing is stifled,
I feel simultaneously seen and unseen.

A cacophony of claustrophobia and competing voices –
The smooth saxophone – cheerful *a'right bab* – too-loud-to-
understand preachers –
But the chaos of life on full display makes me proud

I imagine what fresh eyes might see: every race, religion, culture,
Every person I pass sings in a new tongue,
I contribute mine and know I'm always welcome.

Only two and a half lifetimes travelling these streets,
My parent's heavy long-haul journeys, leading to *me*.
They tell me home is not where your roots lie, but rather, where
you plant your seeds.

And I know it is my home
Because whenever I hear *Now leaving Birmingham*
A part of me lingers behind, refusing to budge, refusing to leave.

Sana A. Rashid, Walsall, UK

The open-ended questions included in the writing competition brief made me feel relieved. Our stories and our voices deserve to be heard; however, significantly more effort has to be put in, especially for a South Asian to share this voice with the wider world.

When reflecting on the questions, I quickly realised it is best to write with my own voice, rather than that of my mother's. If I did write from her perspective, I felt it would be like stealing her voice and her story, so therefore the best way of expressing my own feelings and emotions as a second-generation child, with the big question of 'home' hanging over me, was to be my own voice. I was able to connect with the question 'Where is home? Where do I belong?' quickly and therefore wrote my initial thoughts on it. When exploring the question, 'Do I love my city? Is it mine? Have I made a home?' I needed to think a lot more. Luckily, through writing several drafts of my competition entry, I unearthed the answers to these bigger questions.

Thank you once again for reading my work and thank you for creating a platform where women's voices are elevated.

I Know From Where

Allama Iqbal had said, *'Beyond the stars, there is another place.'*

Then I think, *What am I? Which place do I belong? From here, or there?*

When I ask my mother, she says, 'I have become a lost country.' What could she mean?

I know

I can see this town. It has rows of semi-detached houses and busy roads and lamp lights which shine bright even under the moonlight. And the rain, its pitter-patter, and the bitter cold air

219

and the warm smell of fish and chips. Salt and vinegar. And the local hot spot where sweets like rasghulleh are tucked in boxes. Sweet. And the array of colourful suits decorate shop windows to celebrate my culture. So it exists. This town, this place, but at the same time, it doesn't.

I know

I am able to sow my seeds in this town. I can breathe out the monsoon of my heritage and grow something new from its soil, but I halt. My attempts to reach my hand out into the mist of somewhere makes me feel like a trespasser. This town stings and doesn't exist as my own anymore. When I walk across the paths, I steal my reflection from the eyes of strangers and see how I'm drifting towards somewhere else. That I'm foreign when I'm not supposed to be.

Ammi said, 'I'm a lost country.'

What do you mean? My eyes glance at her, yet my eyes are met with silence, so I search for the answer within.

Somewhere in the ocean of my mind, something is shifting. Rattling. My history is whispering into my small ears where I am learning. I'm parted by a sea that is filled to the brink with bodies of travellers, who were in search of a better home. I let the tides of distant pain swim through my bloodstream, for their echo exists in ancient stories. Of sacrifice. Of my Abu and Ammijee, who were stripped away from their first home in Pakistan, and then they embraced the arms of this home in England.

I know, I say quietly.

This paradox grows into a strong beam. Where the 'I know' becomes 'I don't know'. When the quiet of the night morphs into nostalgia. I've seen how my long fingers have carried the imprint of Potha village on its skin. I inherit their nostalgia. Across the night's long back, I can sometimes hear the fruits of this motherland say, 'Come! Come!' And when I enter her valleys and streets, every window smells of some unbeknown putrid smell.

'Foreigner, foreigner!' they exclaim. And at times this is what it feels like being a part of two lands and having to choose which one is home.

Mother says I'm a lost country and I nod like a body rooted away from her soul. Like a country floating across space. Like a loud noise that is drifting into silent decibels.

I know

when the light of my local town dims and the space of the night becomes never-ending, I will see. The glittering lights of my town will dance with the drizzle of activity. I live in the English country my body has bathed in. I have stolen her sky's light and she still has let its sun kiss my skin. Am I a thief? No, she calls me her own. I roam the town that has wrapped me with the fabric of its lessons. The kindness of some of its people oozes out from my eyes. The essence of its soul sways. I feel the rhythm of its song making my heartbeat in melodies of reassurance. I can feel this home ripening. This must be my home. Is it?

I may not be over there. And maybe I drift away in thought when I am here. I open my eyes, and in the day, I dream in the scents of these two homes. The ocean of blue swells in the sky and makes me realise what a beautiful place it is to exist in. I open my arms wide to embrace a town in the Midlands and a village in Azad Kashmir. Two identities melt in unison and create a blend. My town's beat chimes in my heart, the blend of a Pakistani village taps in my mind and I take a long loving breath in and say...

'Allama Iqbal had said, *'Beyond the stars, there is another place.'*
I am from here and from there.
From the stars above in the sky,
From this soil. Within that ghazal.
I am everything, my heart understands to be its
I am this moving, travelling home.'

Ishrar Habib, Dhaka, Bangladesh

Being a working woman, stepping on twenty-five, life has never felt so puzzling. Career, marriage, etc., where can she find herself? Where does she truly belong?

Belonging

The wooden bridge across the rushing tributary of the Brahmaputra lay almost broken. The villagers had somehow mended it using a single bamboo and were quite gracefully riding on it to cross the river, some were even carrying small children, some of them were children themselves.

Standing in front of the crumbling bridge, Shoma wondered how the lives of the inhabitants of North Bengal had remained so much unchanged throughout the years, and how they had learned to fearlessly co-exist with intense flood coupled with the lack of proper infrastructure.

With the pair of her shoes in one hand, clutching the dangling lower portion of her kamiz in the other fist, Shoma gathered the courage to cross the river after watching the villagers cross it with smiling faces that showed that they, in fact, were enjoying the ride despite the dangers of it.

She crossed the bridge and reached her grandmother's place, her native home, a small village named Brishtipur. Crossing the dangerously poised bridge felt like a big accomplishment to her. At this stage of her life, while going through a quarter-life crisis, this experience felt like a small proof of her own ability to deal with the uncertainty that life had laid out in front of her.

***

Her grandmother stood at the porch and welcomed her with arms wide open. She had cooked all that Shoma loved to eat. At lunch, Shoma ate with contentment, as a strange comfort began to settle in her mind; away from her own four-wall enclosed flat at Dhaka, here, it felt like home.

It started raining after lunch, Shoma laid herself on a soft, dampened bed and listened to the raindrops pattering on the tin-made roof of the house. The sound soothed her aching heart and slowly she drifted into her childhood memories- how she used to come to visit this place on the occasions of Eid-ul-Fitr and would never want to leave. Yet, after spending only three holidays, she would go back to Dhaka with her parents with teary eyes and a heavy heart that never used to settle in a city of thousands of running and rushing people and cars.

During the Eid holidays in this small village of Brishtipur, she would play with her cousins, and the children from the neighbourhood, who were always available to play with, unlike the children in her neighbourhood at Dhaka who seemed to lack the time or the enthusiasm to even show their faces to their neighbours.

Shoma had always questioned herself about where it was that she belonged. Was it Brishtipur, where her extended family lived, or was it Dhaka, where her parents had settled to build a fortune yet could never set roots?

And now that she had become a woman, she knew that she, like other women, would be pushed towards marriage, which for a woman here, means being transported to another family. Shoma wondered whether the 'shoshurbari' or the house of the in-laws is finally the place to belong as a woman in Bangladesh...

***

223

At night, Shoma was staring at her phone's screen, at the last thread conversation with Rashed who told her 'I know you have other priorities in life, but my priority is getting married and having my own family. Do not rock the boat: get married, and have kids, that way all problems of your life will be settled.'

'Can you give me some time to think about it? You know, Rashed, maybe, I need some more time to discover myself, my abilities, realise my own dreams, first.'

'I do not know what you mean. Cut to the chase, please' had been his cold reply which intended to overlook her feelings.

'Sure, I do not think I want to be with you anymore…' Shoma replied.

There was no use in explaining things to someone who did not intend to understand her or honour her feelings. Rashed's reply crushed her delusion that he was the person who would acknowledge her feelings and who she was meant to be with. And so she quit. That was when Shoma started looking deep inside herself.

***

Shoma, a woman in her late twenties, was having to deal with a lot of questions at once, questions that never arose before, but now they were everywhere, cornering her from every possible direction. The next morning, after a sleepless night, she rose from her bed and walked up to her grandmother's room. As she stood at the door, she found her deeply absorbed in Namaz, praying in a pure white shari. Shoma was about to turn and walk away, as her Nani called out, 'Shoma moni?'

Shoma sat beside her, and her torrid mind blurted out, 'Nani, where do you think I belong?' Shoma asked her grandmother. It startled her a bit, but maybe, she understood what Shoma was going through. She gracefully replied, 'Jonmo hok jotha totha, kormo hok bhalo' (It does not matter where you are born, what matters is your actions.' The age-old Bengali saying seemed to make sense for the first time to Shoma. 'Look, my dear, why can't you think that it is the world you belong to?'

'Then, what about 'shoshur bari,' Nani?' Shoma questioned again, worriedly.

Shoma's grandmother laughed a bit and then answered, 'Nanubhai, the most important thing is to consciously choose your happiness over compulsions. Life: it is like that Brahmaputra that runs wild. Build a strong bridge to cross the wild river of life. Sometimes, that bridge will be shattered by sudden rushes; but what matters, is that you mend it, build it again. Every time it shatters, build it again with whatever you have got. Do not give up. Just like the people of Brishtipur, live courageously. And remember, womanhood is a gift; it itself is sufficient to endow you the courage to withstand the journey of life.'

Sahna Iqbal, Birmingham, UK

The inspiration for my work is my mother. I have written this on behalf of her in first person. After listening to her tell me about how she had to leave everything behind to start a new life in Birmingham, for a better future, has made me think that where we are today is because of them and their parents. So this is just a way of saying thank you.

It bought a tear to my mother's eye whilst I was writing and researching, she connected with the memories again and appreciated me writing this piece.

LHE to BHX

Is there a *Darji* tailor? Just like the ones from Lahore.
Who will stitch my heart together after the migration?
All I remember was the made-to-measure chequered coats
Gifted to us as they said, 'It will be cold.'
We slept in them, as we held onto our Homeland.

No one mentioned anything about Halal,
So we ate like the British, Angel Delights and Bacon crisps.
I recall our daily trips to 'Victoria Wine' corner shop,
Fascinated by the Cadbury's 2p chocolates
As we walked back with them wrapped in our shawls.

We bought cassette tapes with our pennies from Sound & Mag,
Listened to Mahendra's songs to keep us sane.
The smell of samosas that were sneaked into cinemas,
As we watched *'Mera Gaon, Mera Desh'*
We caught a glimpse of our heritage.

We wore crimplene bell-bottoms to our Ladywood School,
And ring belts on weekends too.
Chip butties for lunch and crusty rolls,
It was time we accepted Birmingham, to be our home.

My mother, the seamstress, stitched dresses and gowns,
So we didn't have to eat on loan all the time.
Keeping warm with our paraffin heaters,
We kept change for the electric meters.

Sometimes we'd sit in the dark with a candle flicker,
Sharing our stories of our bygone era,
Of how we escaped the war of 1971,
To have a better life for us and our children.

It has been that long that it feels like a dream,
A memory that has almost faded away,
We have made Birmingham our culture and our home,
But our Motherland will always be what we are made from.

Alishae Abeed, Lahore, Pakistan

The city of Lahore inspired my poem, in all its beauty, history, and pride. My city is my home, but it is also an enigma to me, an ever-shifting canvas of green and gold.

Sunflowers for Lahore

The city parts her lips and whispers to me
'What do you know of me?'
I close my eyes and think deeply
Of a flash of light, a quickening
Heartbeat punctuated by birdsong.
I dip my pen into the ink of the *nehr*[1]
And map out a city of green and gold,
Covered in the dust of a thousand years,
Lahore.

The soul of the city calls out to me,
Peeking through a curtain of moonlit clouds
She asks,
'What do you know of my memories?'
I sing to her of kings and poets,
Of warriors and princesses and mystic hearts.
I hum to the tune of the monuments of the city,
Every curve of marble immortal.
They are the bones of this city,
Remembered not only by its people,
But by the very air itself.

I sit in the sun on a winter afternoon,
A precious few hours of gold in my eyes.

---

1   *Nehr* – canal

Lahore stretches lazily, yawning,
'What do you know of my dreams?'
I know that whoever leaves this city,
Whether for a month or a decade,
Never forgets it, even for a second.
Their hearts yearn, their minds replay
And rewind every moment, honeyed
By hindsight's forgiving sighs.
I know the city dreams of its yesteryear,
Blue skies and a kite on every roof.

I ask Lahore if she speaks to others too.
She smiles and shakes out her hair,
Long and dark and strong,
'Only to those who wish to listen'
I rest my chin in my hand and wonder
Who could ever ignore this city?

I have spent my life to and fro,
Wings yearning to soar high,
The sun of Lahore always guiding me back
When the loneliness of 'abroad' becomes a violent thing,
Folds upon paper folds
Of multitudes within me
Draw me back to the city
Like an infant bird longing to burrow in its home.

One evening I am reading
And the city lays down next to me.
'What do you feel for me?'
And I tell Lahore,
'Even in the winter,
When the air is the deepest blue
My heart is a field of sunflowers for you.'

Mantaha Kishwar, Dhaka, Bangladesh

I was inspired by the loneliness people face in big cities. Especially the immigrant population. Some people feel that they have two homes, but some feel they are a stranger in both places. I tried to figure out if the latter group ever figured out where their city or home was.

Authentic Bengali Chicken Curry

What is 'Authentic Bengali Chicken Curry'? Is there a correct version? Looking at those words plastered in the glass window of the tiny Bengali restaurant she found while roaming mindlessly, Sumi realised she didn't know the answer to that. All she knew was that every single curry that she tasted after moving to England tasted wrong.

Wrong. Yes, that was the word that would pop into her head. They were delicious and one better than the other. But it had tasted wrong to Sumi's tastebuds.

Was it because of the culture? Curries made in England are meant to be different than the ones made by her mum in Bangladesh. But her mother wasn't necessarily a skilled cook.

Sumi never learned to cook. Not properly at least.

It was not that her mother hadn't tried, or Sumi was a rebel. She tried cooking a few times and decided she was so bad that she would rather just eat takeout almost every day.

Bashir never minded because he wasn't a fan of Sumi's cooking either.

'She can't make fried eggs properly without saying every surah she knows. I can't expect Sumi to put herself through so much anxiety every day, can I?' he would say at family gatherings. It would always draw chuckles.

She never told him, but those remarks stung a bit. Sumi was never a homemaker like women in her culture were expected to be. She didn't know how to cook, she was messier than her husband, and couldn't keep a plant alive. Sumi was the opposite of what a proper Bengali woman is supposed to be like.

Uncompromising was the word her mother had used to describe her. She always said that word more than selfish and ill-tempered.

'Uncompromising girls suffer. You must learn to adapt with your future husband and in-laws. Look at me. Did I ever do any of this when I was unmarried? I had to learn everything. Nobody except me would survive with your father's temperamental nature. I compromised.'

'Ma, your rage is just as bad as his,' Sumi would smirkingly reply, *'And no man would've put up with your unsalted food.'*

Her mother would pretend to chastise her, but they always ended up laughing. They used to gossip for hours. Moments like these were where Sumi felt her mother was her best friend.

Then there were those moments. The ones where her mother would actually insult her. Whenever her mum would make a snide remark about her weight, skin colour, or intelligence, Sumi would feel like her mum was her worst enemy.

They had a relationship that was between good and bad. Just like every mother-daughter relationship. Some days they chatted until day's end and Sumi would tell her about the most mundane things. But the bad feelings never left her heart.

She knew her mother was disappointed in her. Disappointed about her career choice, her husband choice, the fact she still isn't becoming a mother even though she's in her 30s. But the thing that she knew her mother absolutely hated about Sumi's life was that she left Bangladesh for England.

'You're leaving your family and you don't even feel bad. Is this really necessary? You can be happy in Dhaka.'

But she couldn't be happy. Sumi never felt like she belonged there. Dhaka was her address, but it wasn't her home, her city. She was rarely allowed to leave the house unsupervised. She never knew the streets properly. She never knew what Dhaka was.

She roamed a lot in London. When she was studying, she used to sit in cafes or visit bookstores. After she met Bashir, they went to see plays or eat at fancy restaurants. Most of the time, they went wherever he chose to go.

London started to feel like home. She found her Bashir here. She thought she found her city. A place without her mother's judgement.

It was also without her warmth as well. When she was anxious, she used to go to her mother and just sit near her. The closeness made her feel safe and secure. Sumi always thought she would receive that love from Bashir. Even more than that love.

Bashir was careless. Some days he loved her so much that she felt all her insecurities burning away. Some days he was cruel. He forgot her and spent his days alone. *'I am an independent and honest person, so are you. That's why we clicked. I don't know why you want me to lie to save your feelings. I am disappointed in you, Sumi. I really am.'*

Those words used to send back Sumi into her childhood. When her mother used to say them to her. But that's how relationships are. With good and bad.

So, Sumi compromised. For Bashir. For London.

'Here is your chicken curry, ma'am,' the young waiter broke her reverie.

'I'm sorry, what?'

'Your curry. The one you asked for? Authentic Bengali chicken curry?'

'Right, yes, thank you so much.'

The curry smelled amazing, and the meat looked tender. The spice combination was just right. It tasted delicious.

However, it tasted wrong. The meat was supposed to be overcooked. There would be no salt. The curry was not watery. It did not taste authentic. Like the way her mother used to make. It didn't taste like home to her.

What would her mother say if she saw this?

'You wasted so much money behind another useless thing. I am disappointed in you. You're always so headstrong and stubborn. Why did you come to this dingy restaurant? Why do you do the things you do? Why did you ask Bashir for a divorce? And now you want to be back in Dhaka?'

Would her mother say that? Or would she understand? Sumi paid the bill and left. She picked up her phone to make that dreaded phone call.

Sumi never felt home anywhere. Not in London or Dhaka. Where was her city? Where was her place of comfort? She was a stranger everywhere.

Roulla Xenides, Birmingham, UK

I was born in Birmingham and have always lived here with the exception of my four years at university in Brighton. Officially British, with a Brummie twang, I nevertheless feel strong ties with Cyprus and particularly Katodrys, the village where my maternal grandparents were born as well as Famagusta, my dad's hometown which we have been unable to visit since the Turkish occupation of the north of the island in 1974. So, although most of my memories and my life story are set in Birmingham, it's all linked to my Cypriot heritage, and I wanted to weave that in.

My grandparents came to Birmingham in the early 1940s following a few years' stay in Glasgow where other fellow villagers had gone in search of a living. I'm fascinated by stories of my gregarious grandfather and the International Restaurant in Birmingham City Centre which he ran for two decades before his premature death at the age of 58 and the restaurant's demolition for the building of the Inner Ring Road and the Queensway tunnel. I think that if he hadn't died when he did and if he'd continue to run a restaurant there's every chance I may have followed him into the business.

There are no surviving photographs of the restaurant (except one exterior shot in one of Carl Chinn's books) so the fact that a significant item like the ornate cash register has remained in the family has always inspired discussion and nostalgia. Thinking of the journey that the cash register made from Birmingham back to my grandfather's homeland, made me think of my grandmother's wedding dress that had remained in Cyprus for decades but which I'd brought back to Birmingham after a holiday in the mid-1990s. The two items crossed the Mediterranean in opposite directions years after their owners' deaths but their survival and the fact that my cousin and I will pass them on to future generations, means that my grandparents' journey for a new life and the link between my hometown and the place of my heritage will always be told.

The Cash Register and the Dress

Birmingham, England.

A 1930s ivory silk wedding dress with its iridescent, tiny-beaded fringe hangs in the wardrobe of a Bournville bedroom. It is hand-sewn and fragile, made from threads gathered from silkworms fed with mulberry leaves by the children of Katodrys village in Cyprus and woven by their mums, aunts, grans, and neighbours.

Nicosia, Cyprus.
An antique cash register, purchased from Stevensons of Digbeth in the early 1940s, takes pride of place in a living room in the district of Ahlanjia. All ornately patterned, polished metal, marble, and glass with red and white keys, it looks as if its true purpose in life is to play you a fairground tune rather than hold the ha'ppenies and half-crowns of pre-1971 Britain.

In 1995, the cash register travelled 2669 miles in a shipping container to its Mediterranean home, having lain in storage since 1964 when the International Restaurant at Horsefair, where it had spent its working life, was demolished to make way for Birmingham's Inner Ring Road. The wedding dress flew economy in my suitcase in the opposite direction around the same time after a holiday to the island of my ancestors.

My cousin, Athos Angelides, born in Birmingham and who moved to Cyprus, is now custodian of the cash register which belonged to our grandfather, Michael Nicholas Angelides, known to his restaurant customers as Nick. The wedding dress was our grandmother's, Fostira, known by the Brummie market traders she visited daily as Mrs Nicholas. The miles of silk thread, the finger-numbing hours, days and weeks of weaving and hand-stitching it took to make it, all coming together for just a few hours of nuptial celebrations in the village surrounded by olive and carob trees before it was left behind by its bride as she joined her husband for a new life abroad.

Born in 1902 and 1906 respectively in the mountain village of Kato Drys, Cyprus, Michael and Fostira Angelides came to Birmingham via Glasgow where many fellow Katodrytes had gone in the mid-1930s in search of an easier, better life than that afforded by the scorched earth of their homeland. My grandad earned a living by selling 'Lefkaritika', intricately embroidered lace linen napkins, tablecloths, and bedcovers brought over from Cyprus to well-heeled Scottish ladies whose doors he knocked.

After several years of door-to-door selling and tenement living, my grandfather was lured to Birmingham in 1942 by his 'koumbaro' and fellow Katodryte, Nicholas Koutsakos. Apparently, with WWII in full flow, Lord Herbert Austin was in need of workers for the factory's munition work.

Somehow, the factory job never transpired. Instead, the two friends ran a fish and chip shop in Balsall Heath, where fights broke out most Friday nights as the locals spilled out of the pubs after closing. After a year of fish-frying and self-defence, my grandfather opened the International Restaurant at Horsefair. More precisely, the restaurant stood on Bristol Street exactly at the spot where a car enters the Queensway Tunnel and every time I drive into the darkness, my mind fills with thoughts of the people that lived, worked, ate, laughed, and argued, right above my head.

The cash register took the hard-earned cash of customers for just over two decades, pinging for the four-shilling (£0.20) three-course lunch or the most expensive item on the menu, steak at seven shillings and sixpence (£0.38). The menu included Moussaka alongside Vienna Schnitzel and Roast of the Day often accompanied by an exotic side dish like koupepia (stuffed vine leaves) which would then be followed by apple pie or jam roll.

During WWII the restaurant drew American soldiers who would bring my mum chewing gum whose flavour she remembers as smoky because of the cigar boxes it was kept in. The International was popular among immigrants, such as Italian hairdresser Bruno, who couldn't get spaghetti in any restaurant at the time and who'd often ask if he could order whatever Greek dish my grandmother had made just for the family.

Within walking distance of both the Alexandra Theatre, Old Rep, and Birmingham Hippodrome, it served pre-theatre diners as well as the artists and crew after curtain down. Although a gregarious host, my granddad, a stickler for timings, turned away Cliff Richard and The Shadows after the first night of their weeklong run at the Hippodrome because they were five minutes past last orders. My teenage mum's consternation was aggravated nightly by the sight of them going to the Chinese restaurant across the road.

The International Restaurant was my first home. My sister was born there, and we lived there in the flat above the restaurant until we moved to Quinton Road. We may have gone suburban, but the city centre and particularly the roads around Bristol Street, Hurst Street, and the Hippodrome remained our stomping ground through our childhood as my grandmother ran a fish and chip shop in Hurst Street (demolished for The Arcadian) and my mum ran the Candy Box on the corner of Hurst Street where we spent all school holidays playing in the streets with friends who still lived in the Back to Backs. I remember the coach station on Inge Street and the theatre tailor Harry Cohen who was our next-door neighbour, a chain-smoking, wise-cracking man. When I went to work at the Hippodrome as Press Officer in the late 1980s it was as if I'd stepped back in time to childhood, finding some of the same staff that had been there twenty years previously.

These memories and more come back whenever I visit my cousin's house and see that beautiful cash register or open my wardrobe and tentatively take out of its plastic wrapping, the nearly transparent and remarkably tiny wedding dress. These two things link all the generations of our family past, present, and future who will hear the story of our grandparents and how they came and made a life in the city that I was born and is still my home.

t. jahan, New York City, USA

To whom it may concern:

Thank you for building 'My City, My Home' to focus on the stories of women writers that have a connection to Bangladesh as well as Pakistan and Birmingham. I have been connected to this opportunity through a mentor who is helping me to find opportunities for emerging Bengali writers.

The piece attached is one of longing for the homeland and the people we leave behind in pursuit of our diasporic dreams. As we progress and evolve, our cities and our homes also seem to grow with or without us. Sometimes, we are unrecognisable to each other. Sometimes, our homes no longer exist. This is the case for my motherland in rural Barisal in Bangladesh. Our time there can only live in our hearts and memories as these locations have been physically erased by the effects of the climate. Our birthplaces, our ancestral homes, our schools, our graves, seem to have been eroded by the rushing tides of time.

I grasp at a sense of permanency; I grasp at a sense of home... through writing. I write to express our migration history to our future loved ones. Because so much of my life, the trauma of war, migration, diaspora, partition, and climate change, has never been spoken of due to the lack of psychological safety. Even now, my life abroad is constantly threatened by the political tug of wars which makes me want to put a blindfold on myself. But I won't. Instead, I write to take the blindfold off of others. And for my fellow migrants, I write to connect with those who feel so, so isolated.

I appreciate you for taking the time to read and honour one of the most vulnerable aspects of my identity and history as I reflect on My City, My Home.

Namaz[1]

The thick, golden slumber of sorrow
Seeps into the delicate folds of her eyes,
Settling into a tattered heart of indigo blue.
As the dark night's wind caresses her freckled face,
She is tucked into old sari turned quilts.

Morning waits patiently for her to pray *fajr*[2]
With inaudible counting and swaying, her eyes quiver,
She prays for those who are rising from *asr*,[3]
Whose sun dips into the waters to greet their sister.

---

1 *Namaz:* prayer
2 *Fajr:* the dawn prayer
3 *Asr:* the afternoon prayer.

Iqra Naseem, Smethwick, UK

I was inspired to write 'Terminal' by the theme both because of Birmingham's rich history as an industrial city and the railway that played a significant role, and the level of community in its diasporas. 'Terminal' was always a story that took root in drawing from how people are willing to share, and the character Noor helped to break the cultural and age barrier, much like what citizens of my city actually do.

Having Noor be a patient in end-of-life care allowed me to explore the quest of uncovering a woman's deep history, her experiences, and how people come together to grant her last wishes – the selflessness I find in ordinary people.

I wrote the story to represent finding common ground and to accentuate that a woman's role in her story does not have to bend to a certain narrative. It can steer away from home-building and adopt a tale of world and life-creation or be both simultaneously. The independence that women can have in a bustling city is thrilling, yet it does not have to be solitary.

A large part of what makes Birmingham special is the amalgamation of culture and how it is certainly not a dividing factor. Rather, it is a diverse experience that makes up the face of the city and this is what I was inspired to exemplify. The community does what the community does best.

Terminal

Before the dying, came the wait.

That first day, I saw Noor fiddle with the hem of her clinical gown and pull thread after thread, the only movement we had seen from her in hours. She watched us lovingly as we took our places around her, palms flat against the faded linen. She wouldn't speak until we had grown comfortable with the chill of plastic chairs and the faded walls covered in stickers of paper moons. I wondered if the inhabitant who had once laid here had people come to warm her feet or listen to her stories or polish her foreign gold.

'She is at rest,' Noor told us, and we did not ask about her again.

On the second day, the people asked Noor to tell them about how she had come to be a city girl, how she had left her faraway land for a gasping city. How we had both expected to find ourselves waiting there. I avoided her eyes, but she knew her tale was mine. Noor said she left for a family. She had found one and more. The day she hopped off onto the pavement in the train station, the city had stopped with gaping mouths at her brown skin (once unearthed) and blinking in the strange, timid sun. They circled like hungry seabirds, and she paused to give them what she had brought with her, a smile, a shake of the head. She had to make do with what she had, and when that fell through, she took their tongue as her second one.

Sometime later, she set up a shop. That was where we had first met, a small off-licence near the station, where customers left with a taste of the east and the earth in the bowels of their mouths, the breadth of the unknown glinting in their oily paper bags. The shop was renowned for its eccentric owner, her stories of old and new. The fish tank she kept was never made to last longer than a few months but sat comfortably in a thick skin of dust and stray cigarette butts. The inhabitants, bulbous with heads like ten pence coins. On the third day, we visited the shop and its new owner. Noor bundled in swathes of silk and linen, a plastic label around her wrist. The fish tank remained. We stood by her, a group of eight, maybe nine of the city's lost souls, patient as she placed her mottling skin near the polished glass and breathed the saline that had never left her clothes.

The fourth and fifth days were spent in her memories, stories of her love for the winter and her friends overwhelming the thin patterned ceiling.

'I was your age,' she gestured towards where I was sitting with her other hand cupped, 'but I still snuck out of my own shop like my mother was standing there, shaking her rolling pin.'

We laughed, each of us imagining Noor and her friends in their twenties, thriving in the winter with chips in newspapers warming their fingers. Once they finished, they fashioned train tickets into floating crowns of gold and watched as they sailed peacefully in the stream up to the old canal line. Noor had known my mother longer than I had and said her boat would sail further than all of theirs. The scramble of limbs and flying headscarves as they would flit between sights was immortalised in memory.

On the sixth day, Noor seemed spirited, bored with the skeletons of our conversations and the pastel walls. Her room was surrounded by greenery as far as the eye could see, exotic pots and houseplants strewn with false care. Noor felt as strange here as she did where she had come from, a starved seal who cared more for chimney smoke and tiny bones of living infrastructure than she did for orchards. The sixth day, she told us to steer her to her first love, the train station. Once demolished more than half a century prior, rebuilt before Noor arrived with her dreams and trinkets.

'Well don't just stand there,' she said with her mouth pursed in a smirk, the lipstick I had applied that morning creased. She was feistier than ever. 'I can't feel them yet.'

It was true, we were too far from the trains themselves to feel the ground's vibrations as they ravaged through the city's insides. So we ventured and took our seats in one, then another and another until we were so far from home, we must have brought whole buildings with us in our pockets. Soon we returned and sat at the nearby benches, its nailed wood growing patches of green like stubble, waiting for her to move.

'My name means light. Illumination, to some.'

We stopped to see where she would take her mind next. This time, eyes drawn to the blinking lights and signs surrounding the station like mechanical fireflies.

'I never liked it, even when I came here. My friends called me Nora.' And she chuckled to herself, as she always would. 'For the first few months, that is.'

We were silent because we knew; she found herself waiting at the platform like all strangers did.

'I like 'Noor' more anyway,' I said to lighten the silence. She held my hand, the two of us close like sinking islands.

Today is the seventh day and she is sleeping with the box of trinkets gathered over the years at her feet, my hand in the other, leaving behind the city she had adopted, smoke trails away from where her life was once born. All that is left of it glints of gold. When I am forced to leave the room, a blur of blue uniforms swarm to her bedside. Once outside, I open my palm and find a crown, black and white, crisp with age and damage—too far gone for the eyes to see.

'This is our last stop,' I say, and I am not sure she hears.

Iqra Naseem, Smethwick, UK

I was inspired to write this poem based on a BBC article on how hospitals were overwhelmed and as my city, Birmingham is severely affected, the grief is all the more personal.

Wrong Number

Excerpts from a BBC article, 'Covid: Royal Glamorgan Hospital staff 'broken' by pandemic deaths'

> *'It's tragic having to do this by telephone or Skype,'*
> *she said, explaining that family members were having to be*
> *at their loved one's death bed via a video call.*

I'm awake when you are not,
fastened in skin. I'm awake when you thumb
the couch's opening and stare at a spot past my head,
palms opening north to sit beside your thighs.
The laminate of your eyes swarming
into the bellies of pools.

> *'We've had to take the place of the family,*
> *hold the patient's hand,*
> *talk to them, and communicate with the family,*
> *and there's been a lot of tears.'*

I'm awake at the brink of dawn
when the slaked cup teeters in your thumbs
and you smile because what are teeth
but a promise that a house will withstand
its burning? Will fling you to a river's bedside
and swallow the mourning whole.

'Everyone's exhausted.'

I was awake the morning you stole the phone off
its counter so close to your chest,
then began digging a shallow ending
and you found yourself trembling
in the warm of earth.

Anam Hussain, Birmingham, UK

This competition was sent to me by a friend. She had said it perfectly matches my cross between two separate countries and cultures – Birmingham and Lahore.

I was born in Lahore, Pakistan, and live in Birmingham. On Instagram, I go by the name Bham To Lahore where I upload photographs of my hybridity – a cultural mix. I often creatively place the two countries into one photograph, either through fashion or literature.

The terms 'My City' and 'My Home' often run through my mind. These words carry a very wide and complicated meaning for me. They create a feeling of bewilderment. I was born in one city and live in another. I have two homes, one in Birmingham and one in Pakistan. So, my city and my home are terms of belonging and acceptance for me, a product of the fusion of two places.

Birmingham to Lahore: Between My Brogues and Peshawari Chappals

Wearing Brogues on one foot and Peshawari Chappals on the other, I stand in-between.

When fashion designers sent models down the runway wearing two artfully different sandals, mismatched shoes became a trend. But for me, it has been a symbol since childhood. I have always walked in an odd pair of shoes, not physically, but mentally.

I am a Lahore-born, Birmingham resident, and just like these shoes, I am unsuitably matched. But I assure you, still stylish.

The footprint from each of my shoes is different, one belonging to Birmingham and the other to Lahore.

Travelling back and forth, living in both countries, I am fortunate to spend a few months each year in my Lahore home, while the rest in my Birmingham home.

Entering and exiting, between cities, one rainy while the other tropical, my set of footprints go in two directions at once.

Through the chaotic, narrow winding streets of the Rang Mahal bazaar with dazzling stalls, and along the vibrant towpath of the Gas Street Basin Canal-side, crossing the footbridge offering delightful views of the Regency Wharf.

Down the old city roads that form the strange intersection between Mughal and British Lahore, and past Broad Street, towards the path of the Birmingham Museum and Art Gallery.

But, I wonder, where do my footprints belong?

Neither in Birmingham nor in Lahore, they are somewhere in-between.

My every step builds a bridge, creating a new track, and connecting the impressions of two different cities and cultures.

As I continue walking down the ramp, with identity as the theme, my shoes leave two blurred footprints, mixing with each other.

Sumera Saleem, Faisalabad, Pakistan

The terms, 'My City' and 'My Home' inspire me to think of memory and amnesia as the embodying experience of 'homing' and 'unhoming' history in ourselves.

My Home, My City: Faisalabad

After the government compels my university to shut down its onsite classes and work, I pack up my bag to travel back to the city, Faisalabad, where I could stay only on weekends for the last eight years due to my professional obligations. I had seen no change in my routine: a life lived in classrooms, offices, libraries, hostels, rickshaws, taxis. I used to have a subconscious murmur in mind that the world is for those who are fond of non-intermittent work, a modern form of love. All of a sudden, Covid-19 has placed the world at a standstill and life is anything but calm. On the way back to my city, I realise how much its landscape has changed, so have our selves, souls, and sense of order. Change is constant and as essential to our existence as death is to our lives. Believe it or not.

I consciously sketch the places I could visit in my teens in the middle of my journey to Faisalabad, filling the belly of time with the leftovers of the past, sweet, sour, sad but not necessarily bitter. It feels how we 'home' and 'unhome' our lives with the notion of memory and amnesia. Alive in my memory is our family visit to Gatwala Wildlife Park, known also as a botanical garden. Playing in swings, throwing tea on each other's frocks just so our faces glowed with our mother's slaps until Chachu (uncle) came to our rescue.

'Baji bacchay hain.' (Sister! Children are always this way).

This is a local way the relatives used to get the children released from the scolding drubbing of parents and elders. I wish he could be here with us in this absurdly changing world to give me the same ruffle of peace. More importantly, how can we really forget our sense of 'homing' life in our bodies, the shapes of ideas flowing through us every nanosecond?

For me, memory is a way of conjuring up the spirits of the past, that keeps us conscious of what 'to home' and cherish in our mindscapes. Sometimes, amnesia wards off the haunting spirits to keep us unmindful of the absurd cycle of the history our lives are wheeling on. Other times, a few chips of history keep our sense of self patched up, tucking our belongingness in the fabric of a larger orientation of nations. It was in my teens when I was surprised to know that the map of my city, Faisalabad, shows the impressions of what can be called, colonial and postcolonial shifts of power.

Every time we visited Jinnah Garden to celebrate the holidays, we wondered why we, the common people, did not have an entry into the spectacular building structure of Chenab Club, standing quite close to the public garden we visited. Spread on an area of 72 Kanals in the heart of the city, Chenab Club still stands as a symbol of high social order for being the hub of relaxation for government officials, diplomats, and the elite class. It was established by Mr Henry Cues (1904–1906), the first deputy commissioner (D.C.) of Lyallpur (now Faisalabad), so that the British officers serving in 'Sandal Bar' could gather at their leisure, barring the contact with 'the lowlanders' in Jhumpa Lahiri's words. It seemed to be rather an attempt to 'home' Englishness in an alien place, tamed as the controlled territory. Still, a norm preserved though not as strictly by the local elite now as was by the British. Boundaries are there as the remnants of history and colonial rule. Believe it or not.

Before every Eid and festival, it was almost a ritual for my parents to take us to the City Clock Tower, a distinguished architectural example of the colonial era that entails the history of the industrial city Faisalabad is. I remember how I observed in the bazars (markets) the women of every kind, wearing dresses along with dopattas, burqas, and even without these headpieces. The same can be said about men with the exception of their wearing burqas though traditionally turban, cap, saafa (a short piece of fabric used as headpiece) are also the types of clothes men wear to cover their head, not out of a religious attachment but for various other reasons like weather, prayer, habit, comfort. As soon as we get into a bazar, grabbing the purse in her hand, my mother started scanning through the lanes of items, ordered and piled in shops, on the vendor's baskets and trays. The eyes dazzle with the flashing of a vast range of goods available in eight bazars in the centre of which stands the clock tower. From books, pottery, clothes to 'Khussa' (hand-crafted shoes), furniture, electronics, and whatnot. Everything is available easily only if you do not get lost, the characteristic of the labyrinth of the eight bazars.

'Why eight? Why not nine or ten or more or less than eight?'

And my mother read for me the words carved on Qaisery Gate, the central gate for the eight markets and she tells me about its construction by Sir Charles Pewaz completed in 1903, under the commission of the British Raj. It was a gift for the commemoration of the long reign of Queen Victoria of England. The history is as quizzical as the visit to the bazars of this clock tower, surrounded by the hustle and bustle of urban life, especially when grand stories of the colonial empire flash before our eyes to the extent of dazzling them to see the truth. We home the history just the way we home the city in us. Believe it or not.

Jane Flint Bridgewater, Stourbridge, UK

Inspired by the workshop with Polly Wright in which I reflected upon my acquired home from my student/junior doctor days in the 1970s/1980s and my final destination.

Birmingham: My Home City

Wondering medical student of 1969,
I wandered from vale site Wyddrington Hall
to a first damp terraced house in Harborne,
an intercalation within my degree
before a more tarted up townhouse
near a psychedelic-fuelled corner boutique,
long disappeared from North Road.
Returning from my American elective
To Obs and Gynae in the beginning of final year,
dreaming on the rebound,
I stayed in bonny Bournville with friends.
After my Paeds exam, I rushed to help turn
Selly Oak red, ferrying folks to the polls,
it was 1974.
Acute medicine at The General Hospital was
marked by the impact of the Birmingham Pub bomb.
Psychiatry residence at John Connolly Hospital,
where a court case followed diminished responsibility,
one patient having set fire to another's bed with him in it,
he knew what he was doing.

Surgery finished my training,
with a plastic surgeon like a Chicago gangster (called me 'Toots'),
who, a decade later, blew his brains out.
Amid the drama, I sang at the Town Hall
and listened to Ravi Shankar once.
My junior years around the city's hospitals fixed
my loyalty, labelled me as a Midlander.
Representing my region, Consultant on the national stage,
Birmingham stated after my name,
I questioned health resource decisions
for our people, my house in a satellite
of Symphony Hall City,
Library City,
Repertory City, my home.

Refa Begum, Birmingham, UK

Memories of when I was little. How I grew up.

My Childhood Memories

Birmingham is my home and my city. To say I am a born and bred Brummie is an understatement, I have lived here for the past forty years. Throughout this time, there have been many changes to the city, many of which are memories, some good, some bad. Growing up in Aston, a deprived and disadvantaged area, my family and I grew up in a council estate, but it is there that I had the best years of my childhood. My parents provided us with the best they could, even though they had no English and no work, they did their utmost best for us.

I have very fond memories of what has gone past, like the time when Prince Charles visited Birmingham and came to my Primary School, Aston Tower, this was between 1986-1989. I do not remember the exact date as I am going back quite some time. Throughout the years we have lost many known buildings, such as the HP Sauce factory in Aston, it was a memorable building and takes me back to when we visited the factory with my primary school. When the building was demolished, it felt a part of Aston was also gone. As I entered my college days, we took a lot of time out in the city centre, the famous Pallasades shopping centre was a great meeting point with friends. The Pallasades was fantastic, great for shopping, you would enter and go all the way through to the Bullring and finally end up at Mark One retail store. Outside you had the old Rag market, where inside you could get loads of bargains from clothes to threads to household items. Another well-known shop that I remember going to regularly with my mum was Big Deal in Newtown shopping centre, it was amazing on price and goods. We would buy our household essentials from this shop which my mum was in love with. It isn't there anymore, even though there is a shop with the same name, the owner is different.

We grew up playing outside with friends, pegs, and rounders and we did so until sunset. It was very safe for us back then, outside my mum's house we had a massive playing field where all our neighbours would come out and the kids would just play, play, play.

Even though I am now a parent myself, I take a look back in my rear-view mirror and when I close my eyes, I can still hear the sound of us playing as kids, I can still hear the ice cream van driving up. To sum it up, if I were asked if I would ever leave Birmingham, the answer would be no. I have too many ties here which I would not change: my family, friends, work, and my children have their connections. Overall, Birmingham has had a great deal of impact on my life, it is where it all started, and it will be hopefully where it ends. Birmingham is my city, my home.

Anadil Shabana, Karachi, Pakistan

As someone who wasn't born in the city I call home, Karachi, the city presented interesting discourses on identity and ownership. Part of these debates always came from the point of view of your ethnicity. Despite my ethnicity not having roots in the city, I still connected to the city's past and communities.

When I moved to America to study. I saw Karachiites based in the US missing Karachi through expensive lifestyles, wanting to see the city develop in unsustainable ways so they can match with the elites, and the TV shows constantly representing the city in black and white.

There is a part of me that wants to talk about the city in very realistic terms, talk about the non-elite, the non-desirable places where breathing humans live. I loved the city, but I spent most of my time being upset about not having enough respect. I don't want other girls to think that they don't belong to the city if they lack the 'high standard', or that their voices are not significant enough. In other words, I wished someone had told me these things when I was growing up in that city. I wish I could go back and fix those discourses and fix my broken teen self. After all, for many Karachi residents, ownership and identity are important aspects of life.

I worked as a journalist in Karachi, but I really want to be a creative writer. I would have written this prose in Urdu but due to lack of Urdu typing speed, I chose English.

A Letter to My Beloved City

Dear Karachi, my beloved city,

I have been missing you lately. Being away from you has let me reflect on our relationship. I wonder, why did I associate with you through your depiction and presentation by the elites in the city? I wanted to seem to be respectable by knowing the expensive neighbourhoods, the places that elites considered worthy, and markets that catered to rich people trying to save money.

Calling you home despite not being born in you was sometimes difficult. I commonly hear that I don't have my roots in you, but I still cared for you. I learned of your history, your diversity, but I still had to look for other people's way of loving you, which made me hate you in the end. When I moved to live in you at the age of eleven, I was so excited. All my life in the Middle East, I consoled myself that I was one day going to my home, Karachi, you. I loved the first year I spent with you. I liked the less modern aspects of life, the rickshaw rides, going to markets, having a big family here, having more fun activities to do than in Saudi Arabia. But then finally, as I entered my second year, I realised how unappealing my neighbourhood was in the larger imagination of the city. I learned that even the neighbouring town where my school was based was made fun of by the rest of the city.

I started reading an English newspaper whose story of art and culture always made sure that my *mohalla*[1] was invisible. I just lived with those complexes somewhere in the back of my mind. I started realising that maybe I was of low status. Over the next few years, I managed to live with the complexes of your richer neighbourhoods, but I did wish desperately to leave my own area and the uncool life. When I went for my A-levels to a school in Saddar area, that is when major complexes began to surface. Now spaces in Saddar are a nice mix of people from very rich to lower-middle-class families. So I, being deprived of all cultural capital, was faced with a loss of identity and association with you.

---

1 *mohalla* – immediate neighbourhood

Now see, Karachi, when people are of low status, they have to make up for that by having talents and skills. I had nothing, so I slid into the shadows. My time was spent mostly daydreaming about escapes. Escape from my *mohalla*, from the city, from the family, and sometimes even from the country. It all had to do with trying to earn a respectable status.

My relationship with you was wanting to escape, even if only temporarily. One day finally, to my own surprise, I was able to escape. I moved to another country. But I wasn't sure what I escaped from. Was it you, was it my family, was it the societal judgements, or was it my own perceptions of my status?

As I happily left you, for months I never missed you. I did try to show off my new life in America to those back in Pakistan via Facebook. A part of me felt like I was finally able to secure status among all those people who made me feel so low about myself back in you. Now I could look them in the eye with my raised status. After all, I was on American soil.

Within two years, I started forgetting the names of your roundabouts, streets, and areas. Why should I remember them? But then why should I forget them? I still visit the city. My knowledge of the city makes the non-elites like me. A lot of Pakistanis assume that I am from the elite area in Karachi. I used to take that as a compliment but now it just comes off as an insult, to you, to me. Why should people who love you and look successful be only associated with a particular class of people or neighbourhood? Don't you ever felt insulted at how the people who exploit you for their personal gains also claim ownership of you?

When I lived in America, I realised that cities are best explored on foot. I never explored you alone on foot but when I did so with others, I always connected so well with the people and their problems. Why did the rich people get to decide what my city could be when they couldn't even be bothered to walk casually on streets even within their areas of residences. They sit in their car, go to fancy places, and step inside the fancy places, cordoned off from the general public. That is how they see and own you, and that is how they developed their control of you to benefit themselves. The Karachi that elites represented through the media, through popular events, through their imagination, through the imposition of consumer cultures was not one that suited me or a majority of residents of the city.

As time passed, I gained more respect in America, and that built my self-esteem. That made me realise how much I had wrongly blamed you for problems I created myself. Why did I hang out with the elites who tore me down? Why did I not protect myself from them? I had watched how the others created the perception of loving you through the ridiculous constructions of malls, shopping centres, places aesthetically pleasing, places that needed to remove poor people to feel safe, clothing not suited to local culture. I did argue with some aspects but still felt my status never added any weight to my voice.

Maybe home isn't just the city where you live, but also the city that loves you back and embraces you. You never embraced me but maybe I should have protected you. I think I have found new places to call home, but you will forever be where I trace my real home back to.

Love,
Your hopeless beloved

Sidra Aslam, Birmingham, UK

In a unique year of sitting with my feelings and discomfort, I have started journaling a lot more. It is a practice that I find very healing, and this is what inspired me to contribute to this piece, as I believe healing and activism go hand in hand. Moving from a narrative of 'Why is this happening to me?' to 'What is this teaching me?' We are all interconnected, irrespective of race, religion, ethnicity, and all the beautiful intersections that make us unique.

For me, the 'My City, My Home' writing competition made me think about how I have come to find myself in a position of social mobility and how I need to use this to continue to do the work. I look at Birmingham and see how privilege and power can oppress marginalised communities. We must advocate for one another, use the arts, use social media, integrate with others, venture out into new experiences, and to do all that we must to feel emotionally safe and look a little deeper into our souls. In a year where physical safety has been prioritised, I believe similarly our emotional safety needs to be something we continue to honour. I feel so safe in Birmingham and yet this year has taught me that loss can happen instantly. This is what ultimately inspired me to write this piece.

Unapologetically Me

Now this an untold story all about how I am honouring my multiple identities as a Brummie Pakistani Muslim woman. A story that isn't easy to tell but one that is part of my healing journey because it is when stories are told that shame dies.

Born in 1985 in Sparkhill, into a large family, I am one of nine with six sisters and two brothers. With two younger brothers,

I always had the privilege of finally being able to sneakily ride their bikes, play football, and challenge the 'good girl' narrative. My mum and dad came here in the 1970s from Pakistan. They didn't speak much English; my dad was a taxi driver and my mum – well she had her hands full nurturing us!

I knew I wanted to work in a field that amplified the voices that have been continually silenced, it is on me to be a good ancestor. Being in a primary school where 98% of pupils were Pakistani and all the teachers were white, I began to become astute to noticing inequalities based on privilege and power and always challenged things so as to do what was right and just. I remember being nearly permanently excluded for challenging a teacher, something she was not used to. I remember being labelled as having 'ADHD' when in fact I was bubbly and energetic, and this wasn't something that was embraced by others.

'Pakistani girls are quiet,' they said.

It was these types of examples that shaped my intrinsic motivation to becoming a psychologist. I have always strived to remain unapologetically and authentically myself and, in the process, inspire others to do the same.

Yet, I grew up watching and learning in this sea of white faces – at times resisting the temptation to emulate them. Choosing myself has meant rejecting oppressive systems in society. Growing up in Birmingham, studying here to become a psychologist, and then deciding I wanted to work for Birmingham City Council. I have worked here for nearly a decade, and in that time I continuously ensure that as a minority in a white middle-class profession, I represent and advocate for the multicultural and diverse communities within my city. I have had to have courageous conversations, moving away from 'people pleasing' and feeling like an imposter. It is growing up in Birmingham that has led me to see how I can be curious in challenging systems that are oppressive at a strategic level.

I am courageous in raising issues at a strategic level as I did when this year unconscious racial bias took place in a team meeting through a case allocation process whereby Psychologists volunteered to select a case from a list of names. Just that – a name. The only non-white-sounding name was not picked. A child that was vulnerable, marginalised, and required a psychological assessment was not selected – that could have been me, that could have been my daughter. For this to happen two weeks after the murder of George Floyd and a time when people were not willing to sit with discomfort – I called them out. My healing and my activism can happen at the same time. Why are we picking and choosing who to assess based on a name? Does a doctor look around waiting room and decide who to see and not to see? So why are we allowing this at a governance level? I raised the unconscious racial bias, and it was at that moment I felt liberated, I was being a good ancestor, encouraging the leading and learning for all. I am proud that now there are stronger governance practices in place for this allocation process.

In my city, we are all capable of learning and unlearning. We do that by venturing out of our comfort zones and honouring our worth and boundaries as Pakistani women. Not only in our professional roles but also our personal identities as sisters, daughters, mothers. Breaking intergenerational cycles of trauma is something we need to do and reclaim our multiple identities. They can co-exist. Use that sadness, use that rage, for anytime you have been made to feel uncomfortable to be seen, heard, and connect with all parts of yourself. We can be vulnerable and strong at the same time.

Dina Choudhury, Birmingham, UK

I understand the importance of the culture and religion I come from which has been given and passed on to me by Mum and Dad. The home I come from and the family I come from. And how it is a real part of who I am. As it passes from generation to generation. And I love seeing it in my home city, Birmingham. My mother country is Bangladesh, my faith is Islam, and my destined birth is Birmingham.

Home is where the heart is.

My City, My Home

Sitting serenely, as white clouds float and gently pass in the sky,

I am composed.

Contrasting the vivid green grass.

Birmingham has plenty of quiet,
Reflective seats to be introspective.

As authentic thoughts trail through my mind,
And sail out of my mouth to smile at a stranger.

A friendly chat,
A friendly heart.
A friendly city.

I meet people as if by a divine plan,
Human speech the invisible gift,
Connecting the various facial features and skin colours of people,
Co-existing with a rainbow of love.

262

Women in black veils greet one another and look into the eyes.
To understand the soul,
A mysterious covering protecting a pure beauty.
A hidden femininity stored with flowery dresses, gold bangles,
and a proud handbag.

Hijab sisters covered in cloth and non-hijab sisters co-exist
wisely from the same community, sharing the same faith and
bowing to the same God. With a bilingual tongue.
As generational differences exist to discuss and harmonise.

British born South Asians wear western clothes,
Transforming on Eid.
Saluting the mother country,
And hugging one another with an impressive table of dishes,
On our sacred merry day.
Relishing the blessed banquet,
In homes all over the city of Birmingham.

Bengali and Pakistani women attentively shop for melons,
mangoes, jack fruit, and lychees,
Bringing the sweetness of South Asia to Stratford Road.
Okra, aubergine, tomatoes, onions to be cooked with
confidence,
And heated up with red chillies awakening the senses to a
flaming alertness.

The spectacular shalwar kameez is displayed elegantly on
mannequins promising a beautiful feeling –
Dazzling, shimmering, finery,
Refreshing the eyes to rays of colour and mirrored glassed
patterns.
The textiles of the East dress a woman's heart as the trader calls
the customer 'sister'.

The halal butchers trading the sacredness of sacrifice to feed
life itself.
The chopping thud on the wooden board echoes in the air,
integrating the Muslim men inviting the public to the light of
Islam, With nearby historical churches in praise of God, too.

Friday congregation begins with the azaan, calling the believers
to a merciful God,
To enter the mosque,
As the soul of the city comes alive.
People from diverse areas pray in an organised, unified manner.
Encircling the ummah and anchoring a spiritually dynamic
feeling.

The Birmingham mosques are sanctified spaces contrasting
with the secular cosmopolitanism.

The azaan becoming distant,
As the buses of Birmingham take over,
A collection of people heading to the city centre.
As passengers gush out the door to speed past each other
And step into the city centre. A world within a world.

The city aspiration soars high,
With glossy structures,
And manicured advert women
Selling an illusion of perfection,

Retail therapy.

As crowds swarm by,
Heading where?
Is the city centre the heart of Birmingham?

Or a transaction?

Food is where the heart is,
A universal love.

Birmingham brims with many meals,
Healing a hunger for more,
Diverse languages are spoken and eaten on a plate.
Feasting on flavours,
Cultural conversing on the palette of the tongue.

The city centre with its travelling trains
Coming from everywhere,

To the heart of England.

A pulsating heartbeat,
To the Birmingham blood of life.

My love, my city, my home.

Maliha Khan, Dhaka, Bangladesh

This is a fiction piece but is loosely based on some experiences my mother had on moving back to Dhaka in the early 2000s with two teenagers. It reflects some common experiences single women still have in renting a place in the city, encountering awkward personal questions, and moral policing.

The House on Rd. 2

On the first call, she was hung up on with a brusque 'We want a family.'

She sighed, going to the next number scribbled under *rd 2, 2 bd + 2 bth* from her rickshaw ride around the neighbourhood an hour ago.

As she dialled, she tried to remember what this one was like. Right, the whitewashed three-storied house with the large balconies and the front-facing first floor to be let.

It was the nicest place she had seen that day which was also affordable.

The children were too old to share anymore. That would mean she'd have to share with her daughter, her 11-year-old already pulling away from her.

Hello?

I'm calling about the flat to rent on road 2.

You know how much it is?

Yes, that's fine. But I would like to see inside, no one was there when I visited earlier today.

He would be at home the next morning, he lived on the top floor.

She replied, *I'll be there at 11.*

Who's coming with you?

Just me.

Uh, what does your husband do?

He works in Dubai, she says, hoping he didn't ask more.
In a stronger voice, she added, *it'll be me and my two children.*
Okay, he said laconically, *come see it tomorrow.*

***

On the rickshaw ride over from her sister's house, she took in the neighbourhood.

She had never seen streets like these in Dhaka— moving to the Gulf in the early 90s, the Dhaka she had left behind had still been bustling, but not like this. Now it was just more – more people, more cars, more horns, those blasted horns.

This neighbourhood, however, was secluded and quiet. The streets were modern, clean, and orderly, not a pothole in sight.

The children could walk the beautiful tree-lined streets to their school, it wouldn't even take five minutes.

Getting off at the house, she dismissed the rickshaw wallah, who offered to wait. *No, it'll take a while.*

The house was as nice as she remembered it, with pink bougainvillea overflowing from the roof down both sides of the top balcony.

Her own parents' house was a sprawling one-storied house, with a rudimentary second floor just being added when she left.

It was partly to escape her parents' house that she had settled on the other end of the city. It was so she could run away again, *being this close to the airport,* she liked to joke.

She had had enough of the conversations that stopped when she entered a room and the smug looks her brothers-in-law exchanged when they visited. Her mother and sisters had all thought the worst when she came back on a month's notice, saying she and the children were here for good.

A collective *I told you so* seemed to hang over her head for the month she stayed there while looking for a good English school for the children. Instead of helping, all five of her sisters kept

267

individually taking her aside and asking why she didn't stick it out, *what about the children? Why did she have to divorce him and not just move back here in a genteel separation? Why had she married him in the first place?*

There was a reason she had dropped out in her second year and ran away from that house, even if it was at twenty-one to marry a senior in engineering who, on graduating, had them both on a plane to Dubai. Too many people in that house, too many voices ready to drop an opinion on her life choices.

***

So, how old are your children?

He's trying to guess how old I am. *I have a 13-year-old son and an 11-year-old daughter.*

And their father doesn't live here?

No, we just moved from Dubai where they were both born.

What does he do?

He's an engineer at a construction company there.

You don't have family here?

I do, her own parents' house was in –

Why aren't you living there?

Oh, my children have been admitted to the school here.

The one by the park?

Yes, it's a good school.

Still, don't you want to live near your family? Since you'll be all alone here?

Well, the children's schooling comes first.

He changes tack.

What about your in-laws? You don't live with them?

It's like you don't want a tenant, she says.

He doesn't crack a smile.

No jokes.

No, they don't have a home here.

That was only partially true, they did live in the city, however, with their eldest son.

They wouldn't take in their daughter-in-law?

She resented that question. Even if all that had happened hadn't, she still wouldn't have gone there.

It's not that. I just want to live in this area, is all.

Well, this building is very tightly knit. It's my family upstairs, my mother lives with us. And the rest four are all families.

Great, we'll fit right in, she smiles encouragingly.

We're very careful about who we rent to.

She could see it coming.

So, I'll need to speak to your husband on the phone.

For what? She asks, gearing up for the inevitable fight.

Well, since you're renting on his behalf and he's paying, I'll need to speak to him.

Yes, he is paying, but I'll be the one dealing with everything.

He says nothing.

We're divorced, she says.

He sits back and says after a while, *then I'll need to speak to your father.*

He's dead, she says, trying to hold in her seething.

Then, I'll need to speak to someone who can vouch for you.

A man, you mean.

I can bring my sister, the next time. She lives over in –

Please have her husband call me then, he says, without looking at her.

I see, she says, standing up. *I'll let you know.*

You can keep your flat.

Downstairs, the rickshaw wallah was still there waiting, chatting with the darwan.[1]

Want to go back?

Yes, please. Back to where we came from.

---

1 *darwan* is a doorman

Afshan Mehmood, Islamabad, Pakistan

My love for mother nature and passion to preserve and conserve it particularly with regards to my own city and conservation of its greenery and scenic beauty inspired me to write this true story.

From Inspiration to Pursuing Passion

Every place has its aroma and a special feel to it. While not every place is welcoming yet some leave heavy footprints on the heart. You feel a sort of connection with them. That is the special connection I used to feel with my city Islamabad whenever I used to visit it in my childhood. Having spent my early childhood years in Lahore, I used to come to Islamabad in summer vacations every year and the magnanimous mountains used to fascinate me. I felt that the mountains were calling me... little did I know that they actually were! At the age of eight, my family shifted business and we ended up moving to Islamabad.

AHHH... The lush green beauty of Margala Hills and the pure pollution-free air; living away from the hustle-bustle of a pollution-hit city like Lahore to experience the serene magnificence of Islamabad was like a dream come true for a nature lover like me. I remember my science teacher telling me in one class that plants too are living beings; they too can feel and breathe and – gosh, I was fascinated! From that day on, I vouched never to pluck leaves or flowers but to admire their beauty from a distance while taking care of them. As they say, when you love someone, you let them live! That expression stuck to my mind and later I understood its actual meaning. Trees and greenery are the real assets bestowed by God as the free oxygen providers. What they ask in return, just a little care and preservation.

Since the essence of Islamabad is its grand mountains, hiking on different trails is a common practice. People mostly go from trail 3 or 5 up to Monal restaurant, at a height of about 1173 meters above sea level, which is the right point from where the exquisite beauty of Islamabad can be enjoyed. The view in itself is just breath-taking! You see greenery and mountains everywhere. Even the waters of Rawal Dam and the grandeur of Faisal Masjid, the epitome of grace, are visible from the top. Not just the view but even the journey itself – whether through hike or car – is worth it. Even while going via road, it has its own twists and turns. The first entry point is near Islamabad Zoo which in itself is a remarkable place to visit. After the zoo, there is a long road of about 9 km, that, although marked with splendid Margalla hills on both sides, makes you remember God with its twirls and curls. However, the journey is worth it when you reach the top where the visitors enjoy traditional cuisines at restaurants along with fresh air and exquisite views.

As I was growing up… little did I know that love for trees and nature and conservation of trees and environment was something in-built in me as I started working on it voluntarily. I took a degree in electrical engineering and wondered how to make it useful to follow my love and passion for mother nature. I heard about sustainable development goals from a university teacher, and I remember coming back home and searching for the term, and then it was like a whole new chapter waiting to be opened. I studied SDGs and learnt that climate action and the provision of affordable and clean energy are part of these goals. Finally, I got the loose end I was waiting for. However, things were still not crystal clear; one has to find one's way through life…

At university, as a starter, I began working on tree plantation drives with my university friends. Hiking was my hobby since childhood, so I said to myself 'why not hike with a purpose?' So I started gathering my friends and cleaning trails as we hiked over them. But the plantation drives and cleaning were never enough – it still isn't. Something needed to be done for environment conservation as Islamabad, being a metropolitan, has been becoming a victim of commercialisation for the past few years. The so-called 'master plans', in the name of development, have ruined the real beauty of

Islamabad; its trees are being demolished and green belts are turning into concrete, the temperatures are rising while the society has been watching this eradication dumb-founded.

Realising the role of community in climate change, energy conservation, saving of trees, and waste management, I decided to raise awareness among society and peers. I had to save my city, my home. This led me to initiate my platform 'The Rising World' with the purpose to help in the implementation of sustainable development goals. I conducted seminars in schools of twin cities (Rawalpindi and Islamabad) and conducted various activities to indulge civil society, especially with the youth, to fight for climate change. Climate March Islamabad was organised last year in collaboration with people from all walks of life – the local community, students, engineers, and professionals came out to raise demands for safer environment and cleaner city. The March in itself was a huge success as many new initiatives were taken on governmental level for the said cause. The Government of Pakistan recently launched the 'Green stimulus plan' to encourage green businesses and nature-based solutions to fight poverty and nature degradation. Since climate change is a global issue, the marches were conducted all over the world, not just in Islamabad.

Yes, my city is my home, but my planet is also my home, and we need to save it because it's now or never. Realising my purpose and passion, I aligned my career as an engineer with my passion and now I am working as a solar engineer and a trainer-academician as well as an activist – collaborating with different platforms like Women in Renewable Energy Pakistan, Rastay, GIZ, and more to promote women participation in the energy sector, to develop innovative solutions and to create awareness in masses regarding environment conservation, climate action, clean energy, and green entrepreneurship via activities like seminars, trainings, webinars, etc.

As they say, do what you love, and you won't have to work a single day.

Saman Mehmood, Rawalpindi, Pakistan

I lost my dad. I saw him in my dreams in our old house in Lahore. It is more about sharing my memories.

My Memories

I was born in Lahore, Ganga Ram hospital. It is said, 'One who has not seen Lahore has never been born yet.' This statement is by Lahoris. I have seen every nook and cranny of Lahore. Being Lahori, I am a foodie. We used to live in the factory area, Jail Road Lahore. It consisted of twelve kilometres of land. We had three big playgrounds. My father was a businessman. He was a philosopher too. He used to quote poetry by Allama Iqbal. He used to love history and read books of warriors. When I think about my childhood, it is Lahore, my home, and my dad I think about. But life is tragic. We had to leave Lahore, we had to sell the factory and house and recently we lost dad too.

Visiting the same city again is pain now, it's cold and my heart says that:

> The road to a friend's house
> Is never too long
> But friends are not there now.
> I miss the anchor, I miss the hold,
> Shelter by dad is no more,
> The same house is not warm,
> Seems there is nothing to belong to.
>
> My City, My Home.

Epa Barua, Moulvibazar, Bangladesh

Women's rights inspired me to write.

My Biography

It's me, Epa Barua, telling my own story. My home is in Sreemangal. I belong to Bangladesh from the Chattogram district. Some memories are still fresh in the folds of thousands of memories throughout my life.

I vividly remember the time my first daughter went to Dhaka to take part in the admission test. A tired, horrified mother in a huge city like Dhaka carrying a bag on my shoulder, another bag on my arm, and holding the other child tightly with one hand. It was very difficult for us to get the proper direction of the city by ourselves. But we didn't give up. Dreams must be many times bigger than reality. I was blinking, my eyes were wet. I felt very alone in that huge city. I wiped away the tears so that they couldn't see. Both my daughters were young, I shouldn't make them afraid. Picking up myself again, I continued to move forward, forward, furthermore. Stage plays, recitation, acting, drama, all my dreams with them remain unfulfilled. The way I have left society and my family behind and haven't bowed down in front of anyone, I want my daughters to grow up that way. I want them to be good people with a lot of self-esteem, not a lot of riches. I want them to take part in the welfare of the country.

This city is mine. My shelter of peace my sanctuary. I do care for my city. We need to know how to organise ourselves efficiently in a team. It's our responsibility to build our city better for tomorrow. 'Home' to me means the place in which one's domestic affection is centred. At the end of the day, at the end of work, that is where I go. I get a lot of love, endless peace. Yes, I have made a home.

The question I ask myself each and every day is 'When I am going to change the world?'

To make memories for the future we have to develop our world. First, we need to start from home. I want each and every woman to get their freedom of speech. Regardless of who they are. Let every man and woman both learn to defend their rights as a human being. The soul of the cities lies in their people and their culture. They inform and are encapsulated in how we walk, sit, carry ourselves, and interact with others. Culture also includes how we express identities among others. Culture is composed of the things that we make and use. Without it, we wouldn't have relationships or society. We learn from each other both directly and indirectly. We learn our personal strengths or weakness and able to develop skills in leadership, communication, and working well as a team.

People say, 'Many a little makes a mickle.' We want to celebrate our lives, our successes, our failures. Every day and every moment of our life we want to celebrate.

Bangla Entries

সূচীপত্র

(Bangla Entries)

Mukta Rani Karmakar/ মুক্তা রানি কর্মকার, Moulvibazar, Bangladesh

The discrimination against girls and women around me, in my city as well as in my country, upsets me and incites me to express my protest through my writing. It may be a short poem but originated from the core of my heart.

একটি মেয়ে

বালিকা তুমি বড়ো হয়ো না, বড়ো হলে বুঝবে জীবন কী;

বালিকা তুমি বড়ো হয়ো না, বড়ো হলে বুঝে যাবে কেউ আপন নয়;

বালিকা তুমি বড়ো হয়ো না, বড়ো হলে বুঝে যাবে এক বিন্দু আনন্দের জন্য পেতে হয় পর্বতসম কষ্ট।

বালিকা তুমি ছোটই থাকো, হবে না লড়তে তোমায় বাঁচার জন্য।

বালিকা তুমি বড়ো হয়ো না, বড়ো হলে বুঝবে এককালের বন্ধু হয় পরে শত্রু;

আত্মীয় হয় পর;

প্রেমিক হয় খলনায়ক;

বালিকা তুমি বড়ো হয়ো না, বড়ো হলে বুঝে যাবে অন্যের হাতে পড়ার আগে তোমাকে জীবিকা অর্জন করতে হবে;

দাঁড়াতে হবে তোমায় নিজের পায়ে, পা ভেঙে ফেলার আগেই;

অন্যের কথায় কান দিলে চলবে না, বাঁচতে হবে বাঁচার মতো করে।

বালিকা তুমি বড়ো হয়ো না, বড় হলে বুঝে যাবে তারা তোমায় মুক্তচিন্তা করতে দেবে না, হবে তোমার স্বপ্নের মৃত্যু;

285

দুনিয়াটাকে যত ভালো ভাববে, তত ঠকবে, দেখবে মুখোশই মানুষ;

তোমার মতের কোনো মূল্য থাকবে না, কাটাতে হবে অন্যের জীবন।

তাই বালিকা তুমি ছোটই থাকো, করতে হবে না তোমায় কোনো চিন্তা।

বালিকা তুমি বড়ো হয়ো না, বড়ো হলে বুঝে যাবে, তুমি সম্পদ নও, তুমি হলে
প্রতিটি ঘরের বোঝা যা কেউ চায় না নিতে;

বিয়ে না করে চাকরি করলে মানুষ দেবে খোঁটা, তবুও তোমায় করতে হবে উপার্জন,
বোঝা থেকে সম্পদ হতে, মানুষ হতে।

আমি বলব, বালিকা তুমি বড়ো হও, তোমার দিকে ওঠা প্রতিটি আঙুল ভেঙে দিতে;

তুমি বড়ো হও, তোমার উপর প্রভুত্ব করার দুঃসাহস চূর্ণ করে দিতে;

তুমি বড়ো হও, তোমার প্রতি করা অন্যায় অবিচার নিশ্চিহ্ন করে দিতে;

তুমি বড়ো হও, দুঃখের উপর সুখের প্রদীপ জ্বালিয়ে দিতে;

তুমি বড়ো হও, বাঁচতে এবং বাঁচাতে;

তুমি বড়ো হও, হাসতে এবং হাসাতে;

তুমি বড়ো হও, মানুষকে মানুষ বানাতে।

Anika Anjum/ আনিকা আনজুম, Dhaka, Bangladesh

Once in my childhood, I saw my mother ripping up the pages of her diary. There was no one at home except me. She probably was fighting back tears while clenching her teeth. Whenever I try to recall the evening, it makes me wonder what could have been written on those pages, what dreams were falling from her eyes disguised in tears.

In the streets of Dhaka, thousands of lives are seen passing in a rush. Their dreakeep sparkling through the eyes. Despite being a part of this big city, certain lives go unnoticed. Their desires remain suppressed within a defined territory.

In this writing, I endeavoured to sketch the dream of a woman who chose to fly instead of being caged for the rest of her life. Maybe it's not freedom which every mother, sister or wife craves for. But when I try to match their position against the sacrifices they make, it urges me to believe that they should survive on their own terms, at least once in a life.

দৃষ্টিসীমা ছাড়িয়ে

১

নীরু নিজের চোখকে বিশ্বাস করতে পারছে না। এক কাপ কফির দাম কখনো ৫০০ টাকা হতে পারে! পুরো মেন্যুতে চোখ বুলিয়েও এর চেয়ে সস্তা কিছু পাওয়া গেল না।

'ম্যাডাম, অর্ডারটা কি এখনই দিবেন?'

ওয়েটারটির দিকে তাকানোর সাহস হচ্ছে না নীরুর। ছেলেটি প্রায় পাঁচ মিনিট ধরে দাঁড়িয়ে আছে তার সামনে। নীরু ভেবে পাচ্ছে না তার কী করা উচিত। মেন্যুটা ছিঁড়ে ছেলেটার মুখে ছুঁড়ে মারতে পারলে ভালো লাগতো।

ব্যাগের ফিতাটা কাঁধে ঝুলিয়ে আচমকা দাঁড়িয়ে পড়লো নীরু। 'কিছু মনে করবেন না,

287

আজ আমার কফি খেতে ইচ্ছে করছে না।' বলেই গটগট করে রেস্টুরেন্ট থেকে বেরিয়ে পড়লো সে।

কী লজ্জার ব্যাপারই না হলো! মনটাও খচখচ করছে। নীরুর অনেকদিনের শখ খুব বড় একটা রেস্টুরেন্টের কোণার দিকের কোনো এক টেবিলে একা বসে আয়েশ করে কফির কাপে চুমুক দেবে আর পুরোনো দিনের কথা ভাববে। কে জানত এসব জায়গায় কফির এত দাম হয়! এই টাকায় এক সপ্তাহের কাঁচাবাজার কিনে ফেলতে পারে সে। আশার কথা হচ্ছে একটা টাকাও এখনো খরচ হয়নি, ব্যাগে পুরো দশ হাজার টাকা।

স্বস্তির নিশ্বাস ফেলতে ফেলতে এগোলো নীরু। আকাশে মেঘ করেছে। হঠাৎ হঠাৎ ঠান্ডা বাতাস বইছে। এমন আবহাওয়ায় রিক্সায় ঢাকা শহর ঘুরতে বেশ লাগে। নীরু আশেপাশে তাকাচ্ছে। একটা রিক্সাওয়ালাও তার পছন্দ হচ্ছে না। অগত্যা হাঁটতে শুরু করলো সে।

খুব ক্লান্ত লাগছে হাঁটতে। বার্ধক্য তার জানান দেয়া শুরু করেছে, ভাবলো নীরু। চল্লিশ বছরের এই জীবনটাকে হঠাৎই খুব দীর্ঘ মনে হতে লাগলো। নীরু চেষ্টা করছে অন্য চিন্তায় মন ফেরাতে। এসব কথা ভাবা তাকে আর সাজে না। আজ থেকে সে মুক্ত। মাথার ওপরের আকাশ আর পায়ের নিচের মাটিই এখন সীমারেখা। চোখের সামনে যে বিস্তৃত লোকালয় তার যে কোনো প্রান্তে সে হারিয়ে যেতে পারে।

নীরু মাথা উঁচু করে হাঁটছে। আকাশ ভেঙে যে বৃষ্টি নেমেছে সেদিকে তার খেয়াল নেই।

২

মইন সাহেব বসে আছেন ড্রয়িংরুমে। এই মুহূর্তে সামনে বসে থাকা লোকটিকে তাঁর কাছে পৃথিবীর সবচেয়ে কুৎসিত মানুষ মনে হচ্ছে। ছেলেমেয়ের ফোন পেয়ে অবেলায় অফিস থেকে চলে এসেছেন। ৩ টা বাজতে চললো, এখনো দুপুরের খাবার খাওয়া হয়নি।

মইন সাহেব বললেন, 'কিছু মনে করবেন না, আফজাল ভাই, একটা কথা বলি।' আফজাল সাহেব এতক্ষণ নিজের মোবাইল ঘাঁটাঘাঁটি করছিলেন একটা নম্বর উদ্ধারের আশায়। মইন সাহেবের কথায় থানিকটা নড়েচড়ে বসলেন।

'আপনি ভাই প্লিজ নম্বরটা বাসায় গিয়ে খুঁজেন। আমাদের ঘরে আজ রান্নাবান্না নেই বুঝতেই পারছেন। আপনি উঠলে আমি একটু দেখতাম খাবারের কী ব্যবস্থা করা যায়।'

'ওহ হ্যাঁ, নিশ্চয়ই।' আফজাল সাহেব বিব্রত বোধ করলেন। 'নম্বরটা পেলে আমি আপনাকে দিয়ে যাবো।'

বলেই বেরিয়ে গেলেন তিনি। এর প্রায় সাথে সাথেই মইন সাহেবের দুই ছেলেমেয়ে ঘরে ঢুকলো। সায়ান বেশ বিরক্তির সাথে বললো, 'আফজাল আঙ্কেলকে এসব জানানোর কি খুব বেশি দরকার ছিল! মা হয়তো একটু পরেই ফিরে আসবে।'

মইন সাহেবের রাগ এবার চরমে পৌঁছলো। 'যা বোঝো না তা নিয়ে কথা বলতে এসো না। আফজাল ভাইয়ের এক দূরসম্পর্কের বোনের হাসব্যান্ড পুলিশের আইজি। তার মাধ্যমে তোমার মাকে বের করার চেষ্টা করছি যেন লোক-জানাজানি না হয়।'

'ফিরে আসার হলে মা এতক্ষণে এসে পড়তো', সোহানা মুখ খুললো। তার চোখে পানি।

'ফিরে না এসে যাবে কোথায়? এই শহরে চলার মত বুদ্ধি কি তার আছে! স্টুপিড মহিলা!', রূঢ়কণ্ঠে বললেন মইন সাহেব।

সোহানা এবার কান্নায় ভেঙে পড়লো। সায়ান ওকে সামলানোর চেষ্টা করছে।

৩

নীরু রেললাইনের উপর বসে আকাশ দেখছে আর হাতের হাওয়াই-মিঠাইয়ে ছোট ছোট কামড় দিচ্ছে। কী অদ্ভুত! একটু আগে কী বৃষ্টিটাই না হলো, আর এখন ঝকঝকে রোদ। মানুষের জীবনও এমন আলোছায়ার খেলা খেলে। অসময়ের মেঘ এসে কাঁদিয়ে যায়; পরক্ষণেই সূক্ষ্ম আলোকচ্ছটা নিয়ে আসে বেঁচে থাকার অর্থ।

নীরুই কি কখনো ভেবেছিল সে কোনোদিন এভাবে জীবনকে দেখতে পাবে! চার দেয়ালের মধ্যিখানেই হয়তো একদিন তার নিঃশ্বাস ফুরিয়ে যেত। এই শহরের এত কোলাহল সে দেখতে পেত না, মানুষের জীবনের এই বৈচিত্র্য না দেখাই রয়ে যেত।

নীরু তাকালো তার সামনে বসা বৃদ্ধটির দিকে। বয়স ষাটের বেশি হবে। তার রিক্সাতেই নীরু এতক্ষণ শহরের আকাশে বৃষ্টি দেখে বেড়িয়েছে।

বৃদ্ধ খুশিমনে হাওয়াই-মিঠাই খাচ্ছে। মুখে কোনো কষ্ট বা গ্লানির ছাপ নেই। নীরু জিজ্ঞেস করলো, 'রিক্সা চালাতে কষ্ট হয় না, চাচা?'

বৃদ্ধ ফোকলা দাঁতে হেসে বললো, 'কষ্ট পাওনের সময় কই, মা? দিন-রাইত কাম করি, মাইনষের রঙ-তামাশা দেহি। দিনের বেলাত এক রঙ, রাইতে আবার আরেক। হেরপর ঘরো গিয়া মাডিত মাথা লাগাইলেই মনে করেন ঘুম।'

নীরু হাসলো। এমন একটা অসাধারণ জীবনই সে চেয়েছিল। কোনো শাসন-বাঁধা, যন্ত্রণা-অপমান থাকবে না। দুপায়ে ভর দিয়ে রেললাইন ধরে হাঁটা যাবে, যেমনটি সে এখন করবে। নীরু দেখতে চায় এ পথের শেষ কোথায়, জীবন তাকে কোন অজানায় নিয়ে থামাতে চায়।

৪

সোহানা চিঠিটা হাতে নিয়ে বসে আছে। এর আগে সে এটি দুবার পড়েছে এবং পড়তে পড়তে অঝোরে কেঁদেছে। বাবা বা ভাইকে এখনো কিছু বলেনি। ও ঠিক করেছে আর এ ব্যাপারে কাউকে কিছু বলবেও না। আরেকবার পড়ে চিঠিটা পুড়িয়ে ফেলবে।

দীর্ঘশ্বাস ফেলে পড়তে শুরু করলো।

সোহা মা,

যে কথাগুলো এখানে লিখতে যাচ্ছি তার অর্থ হয়তো তুমি কোনোদিন বুঝবে না। আমি আজীবন তোমার চোখে একজন খারাপ মা'র উদাহরণ হিসেবেই রয়ে যাব। তাও লিখছি যেন কেউ অন্তত জানে আমার অভিমানের কথা, আমার প্রত্যাশা ও প্রাপ্তির গল্প।

আমার চরিত্রের এক বড় অংশ জুড়েই ছিল অভিনয়। নিত্যদিন মন্দ কথা শুনে হাসিমুখে সংসার করে যাওয়ার অভিনয়, শত অবহেলা সহ্য করেও সংসারটা টেকানোর চেষ্টা করার অভিনয়। মেট্রিক পাশের পর কলেজে ভর্তি হওয়ার স্বপ্ন দেখেছিলাম। সে মায়া ত্যাগ করতে হলো। বিয়ে করে এলাম তোমাদের বাড়িতে। ঝিঙে-পটল, আনাজপাতিকে সঙ্গী করে চলতে থাকলো আমার দিন। তোমার বাবার কাছে আমার কখনোই কোনো মূল্য ছিল না। তার চোখে আমি বরাবরই একজন স্টুপিড মহিলা। খুব কষ্ট হত জানো! কিন্তু কাউকে বলতে পারতাম না দুঃখের কথাগুলো।

290

এরপর ছোট্ট ছোট্ট দুটি ফুলের মত শিশু এলো আমার কোলে। ওদের সাথে একটু একটু করে সব মনের কথা বলতে লাগলাম। অবুঝগুলো আমার কথা শুনে ফ্যালফ্যাল করে চেয়ে থাকত আর আমি হাসতাম। ওদের পৃথিবীটাও ছিল আমাকে ঘিরে।

আস্তে আস্তে ওরা বড় হতে লাগলো। তাদের ছোট পৃথিবীটাও এবার আকারে-আয়তনে বড় হয়ে গেল। নতুন নতুন বন্ধু হলো। এই পুরনো বন্ধুটাকে আনস্মার্ট, অশিক্ষিত মনে হতে লাগলো। এই আধুনিকতার জাঁকজমকের মাঝে নিজেকে বড্ড বেমানান লাগে। আমি এই অবহেলা টের পেলাম। ফিরে গেলাম আমার পুরনো বন্ধুদের কাছে।

কিন্তু এবার আর ঝিঙে-পটলের সাথে আমার ভাবটা জমলো না। বুঝতে পারলাম তোমাদের জীবনে আমার প্রয়োজন ফুরিয়ে এসেছে। পুরনো আসবাবের মত আমাকেও ছুঁড়ে ফেলে দেয়ার আগে আমিই তোমাদের জীবন থেকে বিদায় নিলাম।

শহরের এই কোলাহলের মাঝে আমি একটু একটু করে হারিয়ে যাব। ঠিক করেছি বাকি জীবন রাস্তার বাচ্চাগুলোর সাথে কোনো ব্যস্ত সড়কে ট্রাফিকে আটকে থাকা গাড়িগুলোর সামনে গিয়ে ফুল বিক্রি করবো। কোনোদিন তোমাদের সামনে এল ভুল করে মা ডেকে ফেল না যেন!

ইতি

নির্জনা আহমেদ।

Alija Jaman Shupti / আলিজা জামান সুষ্মি, Dhaka, Bangladesh

I love my city and my home. It's a great feeling to depict my city through my writing. Writing is my soul, and My Home and My City is the background of my writing.

রোজনামচা

৩ বৈশাখ, ১৪২৭

গত পরশু থেকেই ফোনটা বেসুরো সুরে বার বার বেজেছে। মনটা ভয়ে শিউরে উঠেছে। চলমান লকডাউনের ভেতরেই ঘর থেকে বাইরে বের হতে হবে। কয়েক দফা আলাপ আলোচনার পর সিদ্ধান্ত হয়েছে একটি জরুরি প্রয়োজনে অফিসে যেতেই হবে। অতীব প্রয়োজন। পদার্থ বিদ্যার বিখ্যাত স্থিতি জড়তার সূত্রটি টের পেলাম মরমে মরমে, অঙ্গে অঙ্গে। মন অবশ দুশ্চিন্তায়, মনে হচ্ছিল করোনা ওৎ পেতে বসে আছে শুধু আমাকেই ধরবে বলে। এক নাগাড়ে এক টানা বাইশ দিন ঘরে থেকে মনে হলো চার দেয়ালে শ্যাওলার মতো আটকে গেছি। আমি অনন্ত কাল এখানেই আটকে থাকতাম যদি না কেউ আমাকে ঠ্যালা দিয়ে ঘরের বাইরে পাঠাত। যেতে তো হবেই, এ এমন এক ডাক যা উপেক্ষা করার সাধ্য বা সামর্থ্য কোনোটাই আমার নাই। সকাল সকাল উঠলাম, পুরোনো রুটিনে ফিরলাম; রান্না, ঘর মোছা, ছেলেকে খাওয়ানো, টেবিলে দুপুরের থাবার রাখা, তারপর যাত্রার এন্তেজাম করা। আজ আবার বোতলে ক্ষার পানি গুলে নিয়েছি, প্রয়োজন মতো জায়গায় জায়গায় ছিটিয়ে দিতে হবে। মাস্ক ফাস্ক সব ঠিকঠাক পড়ে নিয়ে নেমে এলাম রাস্তায়। কিছুটা পথ হাঁটার পর রিক্সা পেয়ে গেলাম। ব্যাগের থেকে ক্ষার পানি ছিটিয়ে তবেই রিক্সায় উঠে বসলাম। রিক্সা এগিয়ে চলছে, আমি দেখছি চারপাশ, কতদিন পর রিক্সায় চড়লাম। বৈশাখ মাস হলেও রোদের মিঠে মিঠে তাপ, লাগুক না একটু গায়। হুডখোলা রিক্সা, তাপের প্রখরতা না থাকলেও রোদের জৌলুস আছে, কী চকচক ঝকঝক করছে চারপাশ। রাস্তাঘাট বেশ

পরিপাটি, কোথাও আবর্জনার স্তুপ নেই, বোঝা গেল আজ সকালেও রাস্তা ঝাঁট-পাট হয়েছে। পরিচ্ছন্ন কর্মীরা হয়তো কাজ করার সুযোগ এখনো পাচ্ছেন। বাসাবো, খিলগাঁও, সবুজবাগ, নন্দীপাড়া, মাদারটেক, কুসুমবাগ এসব জায়গায় ঢাকার অন্যান্য অংশের চেয়ে গাছপালা কিছুটা বেশি বলেই আমার অনুমান। আমি ১৯৯৭ সাল থেকে ঢাকায় বাস করি, বর্তমানে সবুজবাগ, বাসাবোতে থাকি। বেশি দিন নয় এখানে গত অক্টোবর মাসে এসেছি। এই বছরই আমি বাসাবো বাস স্ট্যান্ড থেকে সামান্য এগিয়ে মূল রাস্তা সংলগ্ন একটি ফুলে ফুলে নমিত শিমুল গাছ দেখে বিস্ময়ে অভিভূত হয়ে থমকে গিয়েছিলাম। একটি পাতাও ছিল না গাছটিতে, কালচে ডাল ভরা লাল ফুল; মুচকি হেসে বললাম, ও এখন তো বসন্তকাল। আমি এর আগে ঢাকা শহরে শিমুল গাছ দেখেছি বলে মনে পড়ে না। মনে হলো, কোন অনন্তলোক হতে সে এসে দাঁড়িয়েছে এই মলিন রাস্তার ধারে।

এমনকি আমার বাসার অদূরেই একটি বউল্লা ফুলের গাছও আছে। আজ এই পোড়া চোখে দেখি এখানে হরেক রকম সবুজের ছড়াছড়ি। একে তো বাস ট্রাক বন্ধ, ধোঁয়া ধুলির মলিনতা নেই, তার উপর গত কয়েকদিনের ঝোড়ো হাওয়ার সাথে হালকা বৃষ্টিপাতে ধুয়ে গেছে বিবর্ণতার শেষ স্মৃতি চিহ্নটুকুও। রাজারবাগ কালিবাড়ি থেকে বৌদ্ধমন্দির পর্যন্ত রাস্তার দুপাশে এখনো চোখে পড়ার মতো গাছপালা ঘিঞ্জি পুরনো ময়লা ক্ষয়ে ক্ষয়ে যাওয়া দালান কোঠার গায়ে গায়ে লেগে আছে, কতগুলো তো মাথা উঁচু করে দালান পেরিয়ে মুখ তুলে আকাশে মেলেছে ডানা। সকাল সাড়ে নটা, পূর্বাহ্নের ভরা যৌবন। এখানে পাকুর গাছের ছড়াছড়ি, পাকুরের নবীন পাতায় বিলোল সবুজ বিচ্ছুরিত হচ্ছে আপন মহিমায়। বসন্ত যেমন ফুল ফোটার সময়, গ্রীষ্ম হলো বৃক্ষের নতুন পাতায় পাতায় সূর্যের লুকোচুরি খেলার সময়। পাতা পিছলে পিছলে আলো গড়িয়ে পড়ছে লোকালয়ে। রিক্সা চলছে হাওয়ায় হাওয়ায়, দুপাশে ভ্যানে দোকানে সজ্জী। সেখানেও সবুজের দাপাদাপি। ঢাউস সব তরমুজ, কালো সবুজ উস্তা, আর টসটসে সবুজ কচি আম, সাথে অন্যান্য শাক পাতা। লোকজনও আছে, বারোটার পরে সব বন্ধ হয়ে যাবে। বাসাবোতে লকডাউন চলছে অনেকদিন থেকে। দেখতে দেখতে রিক্সা বৌদ্ধমন্দির পার হয়ে মূল সড়কে উঠে গেল; সেখানে তিন চার জন পুলিশ কিছুই

বলল না। চওড়া রাস্তা, বাতাস যেন এখানে এসে হাঁফ ছেড়েছে, একটা কভার ভ্যান চলে গেল পাশ দিয়ে, হাতে গোনা কয়েকটা রিক্সা তিড়িং বিড়িং করে চলছে, মতিঝিল অভিমুখে চলছি। হাতের ডানদিকে উঁচু পাঁচিল, ওপাশটা বিস্তৃত কমলাপুর রেল স্টেশন। ঘন বনের মতো নিবিড় বৃক্ষের আচ্ছাদনে ঘেরা। আরেকটু যেতেই দেখি মুগদা আইডিয়াল স্কুলের প্রবেশ পথের কাছে একটি সোনালু গাছ; আরে একি, সোনালু ফুল দুলছে বাতাসে, চনমনে হলুদ ফুলগুলো লাজুক হাসি হাসছে। আমি বাইশ দিনের আটকে থাকা অবস্থা থেকে মুক্তির স্বাদ অনুভব করলাম, শিহরিত হলাম রোদ আর সোনালু ফুলের মাখামাখি দেখে। আহা, জীবন কত সুন্দর! গাছপালা লতাপাতা, ফুল পাখি, নদী, আকাশ, চন্দ্র, তারা এসব এত দেখেও তৃষ্ণা মেটে না। সোনালু ফুলের সোনালি আভা শেষ হতে না হতেই দেখি জারুলের ঘন পত্র পল্লবের ফাঁকে ফাঁকে বেগুনি ফুল ফুটবে কি ফুটবে না করেও কিছু কিছু ফুটেছে, আমার আজন্ম চেনা জারুল, যতবার দেখেছি এই জীবনে ততবারই একটু হলেও থেমেছি। আজ তো রিক্সা সওয়ারী, তাই এক পলকের ক্ষণিক দেখার অতৃপ্তি নিয়েই সামনে তাকালাম। টিটিপাড়া মোড় ঘুরল রিক্সা। যেন হাওয়ায় ভেসে যাচ্ছি, এই মহনগরীর মানুষের মনে ঘোর অমানিশা। অথচ বাইরে আলোর কী উচ্ছাস! দেয়ালে দেয়ালে আলো গা এলিয়ে শুয়ে বসে আরাম করছে। এসে পড়লাম দেওয়ানবাগী হজুরের উটের থামারের কাছে, সুউচ্চ পাঁচিলের ওপাশে নাকি উট আছে; দেখিনি, কিন্তু উটের উটকো গন্ধ বলে দেয় তাঁরা ভিতরে আছেন। অন্যান্য দিন গন্ধটাকে উটকো মনে হলেও আজ কেমন পরিচিত গন্ধটাও ভালো লাগল। একটু এগোতেই ঝম বৃষ্টির মতো এক পসলা বৃষ্টিতে যেন ভিজে গেলাম আমি, আমার চোখের কোণে জল। হিজল গাছ! এ যে হিজল! কিশোরীর চুলের বেনির মতো ঝুলে ঝুলে আছে হিজল ফুলের কলি, এখনও ফুল ফোটার সময় হয়নি, ফুটবে শীঘ্রই। এ পথে কত করেছি আসা-যাওয়া অথচ তোমায় দেখিনি প্রিয়া।

হিজল ফুলের অবিকশিত কলির দিকে চেয়ে মনে পড়ে গেল একদিনের কথা, অনেক দিন পর ঢাকার একটি নামী দামি কনভেনশন সেন্টারে একটি বিয়ের অনুষ্ঠানে আমার বান্ধবী মলির সাথে আমার দেখা হলে আমি বোকার মতো কেঁদে ফেলেছিলাম। ঐ অনুষ্ঠানে ওর সাথে দেখা করার জন্যই গিয়েছিলাম, তারপরও আচমকা আমি বিহ্বল

হয়ে গিয়েছিলাম, ঠিক আজ যেমন হলাম। আর হিজল তো আমার সেই ছোট বেলার সই, কত গেঁথেছি মালা, কতবার পড়েছি গলায়; হিজলের রঙে রূপে বিমোহিত হয়নি এমন বাঙালী কি আছে! অনেকদিন পর দেখলাম কিশোরী হিজল কুসুম কন্যারে, এতদিন পর দেখে আনন্দ উপচে উঠেছিল চোখের সীমানা বেয়ে।

আনন্দাশ্রু শিশির ফোঁটার মতো হীরক-দ্যুতি ছড়ায়, সুখ সুখ লাগে। ভাবালুতা কাটাতে কাটাতে দেখি রিক্সা মতিঝিল শাপলা চত্বরে, রোদ এতক্ষণে আঁচ ধরতে শুরু করেছে। অন্যরকম মতিঝিল, যেন পূর্বজন্মে ফিরে গেছে, হয়তো পঞ্চাশ বা ষাটের দশকে মতিঝিল এমন নিরিবিলি ছিল। তখন মতিঝিল মতিঝিল হয়ে উঠেছিল, নাকি শুধু ঝিল ছিল, মতি ছিল না কোনো। মতিঝিল কবে থেকে ব্যাংকগুলোর রাজধানী হতে শুরু করল সে ইতিহাস বিস্তারিত জানা নাই। শেষ পর্যন্ত বুঝলাম কত কম জেনেই জীবন গড়িয়ে গেল অপরাহ্ণে।

Farah Hasan / ফারাহ হাসান মৌটুসী, Dhaka, Bangladesh

My lovely parents inspired me all the time to do good things in my life. In addition, my beautiful and well decorated home is the source of my positive energy. My home environment gives me peace, love and affection. I think I am largely inspired by great writers and poets. Writing for me is a creative and poetic process. I love being smitten by words when I am not in rush so as to really drive myself in a creative manner. I find inspiration from everyday life. I am fascinated by relationships of all types – happy ones, complicated ones, unusual ones. Inspiration is abundant - one just needs to open his or her eyes, and breathe it in.

আত্মজার দর্পন

মেঘাচ্ছন্ন আকাশে পূর্ণিমার ভরা জোয়ারে ভাসছে ধানমন্ডি বত্রিশের লেকের জল। যেন আমি ম্যানহাটনে স্মৃতিচারণে ব্যস্ত। লিলুয়া বাতাসে আন্দোলিত হয়ে এক কাপ চা নিয়ে বসে আছি আমি ফারাহ হাসান মৌটুসী।

চায়ের চুমুকে মনে পড়ে গেল বাবা'র ভালোবাসা-যুক্ত কপালে চুমু খাওয়া। প্রেরণা বলতে আমি আমার বাবা'র কথাকে বুঝি। সেই স্বপ্ন, আদর্শ কেড়ে নিয়েছে ২০২০ সালের করোনা। করোনার ভয়াল থাবা আমার সকল শক্তি, আশা, বিশ্বাস আর আকাঙ্ক্ষা বিনাশ করেছে। অস্তিত্বের সংকটে নিমজ্জিত হয়েছি সম্পূর্ণ একা আমি।

ধানমন্ডি বত্রিশের লেকের ধারে ছোট একটি অ্যাপার্টমেন্টে আমি, আমার মা ও ছোট বোন নিয়ে আমার সংসার। প্রকৃতির ড্রয়িং রুম সেজে বসে আছে ধানমন্ডি বত্রিশের লেক। সেই লেকের ধারে ছোট একটি অ্যাপার্টমেন্ট; যেখানে দক্ষিণী বারান্দা থেকে কাঠগোলাপের গন্ধ ভেসে আসে।

সেই দক্ষিণের বারান্দা দিয়ে মুক্ত আকাশের নীলিমা দেখা যায়। শরৎ মেঘের ভেলায় আমার পুরোনো স্মৃতিগুলো উঁকি দিচ্ছে বার বার। দরজার পাশে দাঁড়িয়ে

থাকা বাবার আশীবাদ যেন প্রদীপের প্রজ্জ্বলিত আলো হয়ে জ্বলছে।

আমাদের অ্যাপার্টমেন্ট চার ইউনিটে বিভক্ত। অধিকাংশ ফ্ল্যাটে আমার খালারা থাকে। তারা মাঝে মাঝে আমার গান শুনতে চায়। পূর্ণিমায় ছাদে উঠে তাদেরকে আমি গান শোনাই - "চাঁদের হাসি বাঁধ ভেঙেছে"। জ্যোৎস্নায় ভিজে যায় সব ক'টা মানুষ।

বেগুনি রংয়ের অর্কিড আমার বারান্দাকে সুসজ্জিত করে রেখেছে। পূবের বারান্দা দিয়ে জ্যোতির্ময়তা আমার লিভিং রুমে যখন এসে পড়ে, তখন আমার আত্মবিশ্বাসটুকু বেড়ে যায়। স্বপ্ন দেখতে থাকি। আর ভাবতে থাকি আর মনে মনে গাইতে থাকি- "কবে আমি বাহির হলেম তোমারি গান গেয়ে, সেইতো আজকে নয় সে আজকে নয়"।

আমার বাথরুমটাকে স্নানের বাড়ি বলা উচিত! কেননা সেখানে দুইটি আলাদা ঘর রয়েছে। মাঝখানের ঘরে প্রকান্ড এক গোলাকার বাথটব, সেখানে গা ডুবিয়ে বসে একটা সুইচ টিপলেই চারদিক থেকে গরমজলের স্রোত এসে সারা গা ম্যাসাজ করে দেয়। ডানদিকে কাঁচ দিয়ে ঘেরা শাওয়ার রুম। সেখানে নানা রকমের ধারাস্নানের ব্যবস্থা। মাঝখানে আমার সাজসজ্জা করার জায়গা। সেখানে দেওয়ালজোড়া আলোকিত আয়নার সামনে শ্বেতপাথরের লম্বা টেবিল, তার দুই প্রান্তে অতি সুদৃশ্য দুটি পাথরের পাথরের গামলা, সেগুলি আসলে হাত ধোয়ার বেসিন। টেবিলের উপর থরে থরে সাজানো পারফিউম। গরমজলের ধারার মধ্যে দাঁড়িয়ে থাকতে খুব ভালো লাগে। মনের চারদিকে জমে থাকা একঘেয়েমি আর দুশ্চিন্তার ময়লা ধুয়ে যায় কিছুক্ষণের জন্য, টানটান স্নায়ু শিথিল হয়ে যায়।

আধো অন্ধকারে নিখুঁতভাবে সাজানো লিভিংরুমটা অবিকল সেই রূপকথার ঘুমন্ত দেশের মতন দেখাচ্ছে। কাঁচের জানলা দিয়ে চুঁইয়ে পড়ছে জ্যোৎস্নার আলো। বাড়ির সামনে অতন্দ্র প্রহরীর মত দাঁড়িয়ে আছে পাইন গাছ, ঠিক যেন জেলখানার সেন্ট্রিদের মত। জীবনানন্দের সেই কবিতার মতো মাঝরাতের অন্ধকারে একরাশ পাতার পিছনে পুরানো চাঁদটা দাঁড়িয়ে ঠাট্টার হাসি হাসছে।

আমি একটি কর্পোরেট হাউসে চাকরি করি। বাবা বলতেন, ''লেখালেখি করো। তোমার অনুভূতিকে ব্যক্ত করো''। সাফল্য আর উচ্ছ্বাশা বোঝাই নৌকাগুলো জ্যোৎস্নার নদীতে ভেসে যাচ্ছে অর্ধদগ্ধ মৃতদেহের মত। কী যেন নেই আমার এই অ্যাপার্টমেন্টে। বাবার নিঃস্বার্থ ভালোবাসা। হারিয়ে গেছে ভীষণ দামি একটা জিনিস।

ক্লান্ত শরীর নিয়ে যখন অফিস থেকে বের হই তখন বাসায় এসে ড্রয়িংরুমে বিশ্রাম নিই। বিকেলের রোদ্দুরে উজ্জ্বল মসৃণ বাদামি কাঠের মেঝে, তার উপরে সূক্ষ্ম জ্যামিতিক নকশা আঁকা পার্শিয়ান কার্পেটা। সেই কার্পেটে বসে হারমোনিয়াম নিয়ে গান গাই - ''ও যে মানে না মানা''! কখনো কখনো ড্রয়িংরুমে ইয়োগা করি মনকে স্থির করার জন্য। ঈশ্বর প্রার্থনার জন্য আমার এই রুমটা আদর্শ। ভালোবাসা বোধহয় লড়াই শেখায়, মানসিক শক্তি তৈরি করে। আবার কখনো কখনো একা থাকা শেখায়।

হেনরিক ইবসেনের 'An Enemy of the People' নাটকের শেষে একটা বিখ্যাত লাইন আছে – "He fights best when he fights alone"। আমিও একা লড়ছি, নিজেকে একা রাখার জন্য। লড়াই করে অনেকটা পথ অতিক্রম করব বলে। সামনে যে এখনও অনেকটা পথ।

Nasrin Tamanna / নাসরিন তামান্না, Brahmanbaria, Bangladesh

While I travel different places, being a girl, I face different situations. At times I see my father is scolding my mother. All these happenings provoke my thought! I do think about my identity, my place in this society, my abilities, my dreams. Sometimes I want to go somewhere faraway from this unpleasant society where I have to face so many obstacles! Sometimes I get tired! So many scattered Ideas, words are floating in my mind! This "my city, my home" campaign inspired me to gather my thoughts and express my words to the world, to share with those women who are facing the similar issues in a different environment, in another country! It inspired me to make my voice heard internationally!

মায়ের জাদু বাঘিনী

'বারান্দায় দাঁড়ানো বারণ, ছাদে উঠলে ভাইয়ের ধমক।

উঠান পেরুলেই বাবার শাসন।

পাড়ার লোকের নাহ, নাহ, কলরব!

ধামড়ি মেয়ের এত কিসের টইটই?

বড় হয়েছ, জানো তো বিয়ে দেয়া যে ফরজ?'

এই হলো আমার ঘর, আমার শহর।

মাকে বলি, আকাশ আমার ভীষণ পছন্দ! আর যদি থাকে হাজার থানেক তারা, তবে তো সোনায় সোহাগা!

মা বলেছেন, "যাদু আমার, খবরদার! রাতে তোমার বাইরে যাওয়া মানা!"

তবে মা, দিনের বেলাতে তারা দেখা যায় কোন দেশেতে? সেই দেশেতেই যাই।

মা আমার রেগে দিলেন হুংকার!

"যাদু আমার, খবরদার! একা তোমার বাইরে যাওয়া মানা!"

এত বারণ, এত মানা?

মা বুঝালেন, "যাদু আমার! প্রশ্ন তোমার করতে মানা!

যা বলেছেন আমার নানি, তাই করেছেন তোমারও নানি!

সবাই আমরা অবলা জাতি।

চুপটি করে ঘরে বসে, সবার জন্য রান্না করে, পেটের বাচ্চা লালন করে, স্বামীর খুব মন ভরিয়ে, রোজ বিকেলে ব্যালকনিতে এক টুকরো আকাশ দেখে, সন্ধ্যের আগে নীড়ে ফিরে, করতে হবে দায়িত্ব সারা।

এই আমাদের জীবন।

যা বলেছেন তোমার বাবা, যা বলেছেন তোমার দাদা, তাই তোমার সংবিধান, তাই তোমার সীমা।"

বলি, মা, বড্ড সেকেলে তুমি! জানো না বুঝি আজ নারীর অসীম ক্ষমতা! নারী আজ রাস্তায়, মাঠে, ঘাটে, বন্দরে, আকাশে, মহাকাশে!

তুমি বুঝি জানো না মা আজ মেয়েরা কতদূর এগিয়ে?

বোকা মা আমার! হেসে হেসে লুটোপুটি!

বলে কি, "যাদু আমার, খবরদার! ফাঁদে পা দিবিনে। ভোলাভালা থুকি আমার, ফুসলিয়ে ফাসলিয়ে নিয়ে গিয়ে ঐ হায়েনার দল ছিঁড়ে খাবে! গাড়ীতে, অফিসে, রাস্তায়, কোথাও তোর রক্ষা নেই! মর্গেও তোর নিথর দেহে হায়েনারা জ্বালা মেটাবে!

ছিঃ ছিঃ!

জাত গেলে বেঁচে কী লাভ?

কী করবি তখন ঐ ক্ষমতা দিয়ে? ইজ্জত কি আর ফিরে পাবি?

ঘরে থাক যাদু আমার!"

রেগে মেগে আমি আগুন!

তবে কেন লক্ষ্মী ডাকো? দেবী বলে পুজো করো! তাই বুঝি পুজো শেষে পানিতে ফেলো?

যে শহরে আমার স্বাধীনতা নেই, আমার নিরাপত্তা নেই, যেখানে আমার কথা বলা মানা, সে শহর আমার নয়।

আমি কি তবে জলে ভাসা পদ্মাবতী মা?

মা, তোমার যাদুর নাম আছে, পরিচয় আছে, তোমার যাদু অধিকার আদায় করতে জানে।

আমি বিদ্রোহ ঘোষণা করলাম!

আমি প্রতিবাদ করবো।

আমি চিৎকার করবো।

এই শহর আমার!

আমি প্রীতিলতা, আমি জাহানারা!

আমি তারামন বিবি!

আমি এই ঘরের দুর্গা।

দাদি আমার বুড়ি মানুষ। ফোকলা দাঁতে হেসে বলেন, "নাতিনগো? বেডির গুস্যা বেশ্যা, বেডার গুস্যা বাদশা!"

দাদি আমার বড়ই সরল।

সেই যে ৭ বছর বয়সে পিছদুয়ার দিয়ে ঘরে ঢুকলেন, আর কোনোদিন বের হননি। চুলার উত্তাপ, হাঁড়ি পাতিলের পরিসংখ্যান, শাক-সবজি, লবণ আর চিনির পরিমাণ, ওসবেই কৈশোর, যৌবন সব পার করলেন।

শেষ বয়সে ঘরের কোণে বসে খোদার নাম জপেন।

দাদি, তোমার বুঝি দাসত্ব পছন্দ?

তোমার বুঝি শখ আল্লাদ ছিল না?

তোমার বুঝি জগৎ দেখার ইচ্ছা হয়নি?

তোমরা থাকো ঐ চুলো নিয়ে।

চার-দেয়ালের নিয়ম নিয়ে।

আমি নারী!

আমি কালী, আমি সরস্বতী, আমি অন্নপূর্ণা!

আমি আদি মাতা।

আমার গর্ভে এই বিশ্ব ব্রহ্মাণ্ডের জন্ম।

এই ছোট ঘর, ছোট শহর নিয়ে তুমি ভাবছো মা?

গোটা পৃথিবী আমার!

আমি ছাড়া এই ঘর, এই শহর, এই বিশ্ব বিরানভূমি হয়ে যাবে।

আমি ধারণ না করলে পুরুষের ঐ বীর্যের কী দাম বলো দেখি মা?

জ্বালিয়ে দেখাও বংশ প্রদীপ!

আমি নাকি ঘরের লক্ষ্মী, পরের লক্ষ্মী।

আমি রানি মা! আমি স্রষ্টার সৃষ্টি আমার গর্ভে ধারণ করি।

উষ্ণতায়, আদরে, সোহাগে আমি করি তৈরি ভবিষ্যত প্রজন্ম।

যে রাঁধে, সে চুলও বাঁধে।

আমার গুণে, আমার মেধায়, আমার বৃত্তিতে এই বিশ্ব অবাক হয়ে তাকিয়ে রবে।

তরকারিতে লবণ কম হলে বাবা তোমায় আচ্ছা করে দেন বকা। ভাইয়ের যত রাগ, যত দোষ, সব তোমার আর আমার দায়ভার।

ঘরের যত খারাপ সব তোমার ভাগ্যদোষ, যত ভালো সব বাবার কঠোর পরিশ্রম।

বড় সিদ্ধান্ত সব বাবার,

আর বাজারের লিস্টি, ধোপাবাড়ির কাপড়ের হিসাব, দুধওয়ালার দুধের টাকা ঐ সব তোমার।

তোমার বুঝি কর্তা হতে ইচ্ছে করেনা?

তোমার বুঝি আয়েশ করে, পায়ের উপর পা উঠিয়ে, বলতে ইচ্ছা করেনা, "এক কাপ কড়া চা হলে ভালো হয়"?

"আজ অফিস ছুটি, আচ্ছা করে একটা ঘুম দিলে কেমন হয়"?

এই শহরজুড়ে যত গালি, যত তিক্ততা, সব মা তোমার নাম নিয়ে!

এই বুঝি তোমার ঘর, তোমার শহর?

লক্ষ্মী মা আমার, একটা বার এই চুলোর আগুন নিভিয়ে দিয়ে প্রতিবাদ করে বেরিয়ে দেখতে! একবার শুধু শক্ত হয়ে বলতে, আমি মুক্তি চাই!

কেন বললে না তোমার মনের কথাটুকু?

বাবা ঐ লুকিয়ে রাখা ডায়েরির কথা জানেন?

মা বলেন, "যাদু আমার, চুপ কর!

পুরুষ কর্তা, পুরুষ রক্ষক।

দুটো কথা শুনলেই কী হয়? পুরুষের রাগ একটু বেশিই হয়।

তুই ঘরের লক্ষ্মী, ঘরে থাকবি, চুপ থাকবি।

তুই ত্যাগ করবি, বিসর্জন তোর ধর্ম।"

জানো মা, এই দাসত্বের দায় তোমার, আমার, আমাদের!

কেন মাথা পেতে নিয়েছো সব?

বিধাতা তোমায় রানি করে পাঠিয়েছেন।

তোমার পায়ের নিচে জান্নাত লুটিয়ে দিয়েছেন।

তোমায় করে দিয়েছেন উর্বর।

তুমি ছাড়া আদম অসহায়।

এই পৃথিবীর সম্রাজ্ঞী তুমি।

রাজ্যের কর্ত্রী বুঝি কুয়োর ব্যাঙ হয়ে বসে থাকবে?

এই ঘরের, এই শহরের আইন প্রণেতা তুমি।

এই জাতি তোমার কাছে ঋণী।

রাস্তার গলিতে, মাঠে ঘাটে, অফিসে, চত্বরে, কেন আমরা চুপটি করে থাকবো?

বাধা আসবেই। শত্রু থাকবেই।

কষিয়ে একটা চড় মারতে হবে।

'না' করতে হবে।

মাথা উঁচু করে সামনে এগিয়ে যেতে হবে।

নারীর শক্তির উৎস স্বয়ং বিধাতা।

এই ঘর নারীর।

এই শহর নারীর!

কেন তুমি পুরুষকে ভয় পাবে? আমি কেন পুরুষের উপর নির্ভরশীল হবো?

তার শরীরেও রক্ত মাংস, আমার শরীরেও তা।

বিধাতা আমার জন্য তাকে, তার জন্য আমাকে বানিয়েছেন।

আমরা রানি, মা!

রানির কোনো প্রতিযোগী থাকে না।

মা? হাতে একটা অস্ত্র, পরনে থাকি পোশাক, বেশ লাগবে কিন্তু আমায়। তোমার মেয়ে দেশের হয়ে দেশের সেবা করবে। তোমার ভালো লাগবেনা বুঝি?

আর না হয় ঐ আকাশ নিয়ে গবেষণা করে তোমার জন্য এক ফালি তারার রহস্য নিয়ে আসবো।

মা তুমি কি হার্ভার্ডের নাম শুনেছো? অথবা অক্সফোর্ডের?

মা আমি ওখানের ছাত্রী হলে তোমার বুঝি গর্ব হবেনা?

বোকা মা আমার! বলে কি, "যাদু আমার, থাম এইবার! মেয়ে মানুষের এত স্বপ্ন দেখতে মানা। এত পড়ে কী হবে? ভালো একটা বর দেখে তোমার একটা স্থায়ী ঘর হবে। বিসিএস ক্যাডার! এইতো বেশ!

মেয়েরা ওসব কঠিন কাজ পারবে না।

কর্মক্ষেত্র কি নিরাপদ নাকি?

গবেষণা করে লাভ কী যাদু?

বিরিয়ানিটা শেখা ঢের ভালো, রুটিটা যেন গোল হয়।

যাদু আমার তুই মায়ের জাতি। এত যুক্তিতর্কে সংসারে সুখ আসেনা।"

তোমার মেয়ে বাঘিনী, মা!

তোমার মেয়ে বিশ্বজয় করবে।

আর ঐ পুরুষ? আমি তার সম্পূরক।

এই বৈষম্য, এই বিভেদ, এই অসুস্থ প্রতিযোগিতা বন্ধ করো।

এই ঘর, এই শহর আমাদের।

তোমার মেয়ে পুরুষের সাথে কাঁধে কাঁধ মিলিয়ে চলবে।

নারী আর পুরুষের পারস্পরিক শ্রদ্ধায়, সৌহার্দ্যে, আন্তরিকতায় আর ভালোবাসায় আমরা এক হবো।

নারী হবে এই ঘরের রানি, পুরুষ হবে রাজা।

এই শহরজুড়ে বৈষম্য রেখে, নারী পুরুষের বিভেদ ভুলে, মানুষ বলবে চিৎকার করে,

"এই ঘর, এই শহর আমাদের!"

305

Fatima Zerin Prottasha / ফতিমা জারিন প্রত্যাশা, Dhaka, Bangladesh

The belief held by the mass people became a culture and tradition of the society we live in. The notions are taken for granted; so natural that we forget to look and think beyond the apparent boundary. This poem in Bangla is just a search for the truth that connects the inner being of every human soul.

অনুভবে অবিনশ্বর

সুদূর বিস্তৃত আকাশ উপরে,

হয়তো সীমাতীত, হয়তো আবদ্ধ।

দৃষ্টির আড়ালে, নিকষ অন্ধকারে,

স্বীয় শক্তিতে যখন কেউ রুদ্ধ

সংকটের স্থানকালে;

নতুনত্বের নবজন্ম সেখানে!

সেখানেই আবার,

কিঞ্চিত অসমতার যুদ্ধ -

অনির্বাণ স্ফুরণে বিরাট আঘাত হানে কোনো এক

তারই প্রজ্বলিত শিখা, দূর বহুদূর হতে,

ভেসে আসে এখানে, কালস্রোতের প্লাবনে।

অমর অতীতের অক্ষয় আলো স্মৃতি -

পুরনো দিনের কথা বলে।

306

প্রমাণ চোখের সামনে ধরে মেলে।

আমাদের চোখে;

আমাদের কারও কারও চোখে।

আমরা কেউ কেউ যারা,

প্রকৃতির বিশালত্ব জানি, দেখি, প্রতিনিয়ত,

শুনি কেউ বলে, "অন্ধকার ও আলোর উৎপত্তি ঘটিয়েছি"।   [1]

চেষ্টা করি উপলব্ধি করবার,

তাও তাঁকে খুঁজে পাইনা।

আমরা কেউ কেউ যারা,

প্রশ্নাতীত বিশ্বাসে অন্ধ হব না বলে,

অনিরুদ্ধ সত্যের জ্যোতি যদিও বা চোখে পড়ে।

অথচ মস্তিষ্কের অসীম, অসঙ্গায়িত, অনির্ণেয় যুক্তির বেড়াজালে

একমুঠো প্রদীপশিখার জন্য

অন্ধের মতো হাতড়ে বেড়াই!

যখন দেখতে পাই না, বলি, এই অন্ধত্বই তো শ্রেয় সত্য,

"Ruled by mother nature and autonomous by herself!"

আমরা, অবিশ্বাস করি যারা।

অথচ আমাদের মনান্তরালে, আমাদেরই অজান্তে

ব্যর্থতার দীর্ঘশ্বাস, শূন্যতার হাহাকার।

অসীমতার মাঝে সন্তোষজনক যুক্তি খুঁজে ফিরে, ব্যর্থ হই যখন,

তখনও আমাদের মাঝে

অস্বীকারোক্তির অহংকার।

আমরাই সেই প্রাণ হয়েও প্রাণহীন!

কেননা, আমাদের হৃদয়, "পাথরের মতো কঠিন,

বরং তার চেয়েও কঠিন!

কারণ অনেক পাথরের মধ্য দিয়ে প্রবহমান নির্ঝর,

আবার অনেক পাথর ফেটে ফেলে,

ভেতর থেকে পানি গড়িয়ে পড়ে"। [2]

মহাকাশজ্ঞানের অপার বিশালত্বকে ধারণ করতে চেয়েও

হৃদয় আমাদের পাথরের চেয়েও কঠিন।

যদিও আমরাই শ্রেষ্ঠতম, সেটা জানি।

স্বীকার না করলেও, এটাও জানি যে -

কোথায় আমাদের অন্তিম দুর্বলতা,

চিরকালের, চিরজীবনের, চিরপ্রজন্মব্যাপী...!

যদি জন্ম ইতিহাস বিশ্বব্রহ্মাণ্ডের

"Greatest riddle of all times"

তাহলে তার চেয়েও বড় ধাঁধা :

"কী জীবন? কী মৃত্যু?"

"Riddle of the riddles, solved every day."

এর সমাধান পায় যারা একবার,

বলে যেতে নাহি পারে!

আমরা, অবিশ্বাস করি যারা,

আমাদেরই শুনিয়ে বলা হয় যখন,

"তোমার মৃত্যুপথযাত্রী বন্ধুর বিদায়ী প্রাণবায়ু

ফিরিয়ে আনতে পারো না কেন?" [3]

কেন তার চলে যাওয়াকে আমরা রুখতে পারি না?

উত্তরে কেউ বলেন, "তখন আমিই থাকি তার সবচেয়ে নিকটতম।" [3]

আমরা, যারা অস্বীকার করি।

আমাদের শ্রবণানুভূতিতে,

এ সত্যধ্বনির কম্পন বড় দুঃসহ!

কারণ আমরা ঘোষণা করে দিয়েছি :

এ শব্দতরঙ্গের অস্তিত্ব "অসঙ্গায়িত", "অনির্ণেয়",

"unquestioned belief"।

কিন্তু হঠাৎ সব ওলটপালট হয়ে যায়।

যেমনটা মজিদের মনে হয়েছিল,

কেয়ামত নাজিল হবে, "এখনই"!

যেমনটা "Island of despair" এ Robinson Crusoe

ভাগ্যকে বারংবার তিরস্কার করলেও

অশ্রুসংবরণ করতে পারেনি,

যখন অনুভবের কান দিয়ে সে শুনেছিল,

কেউ বলছে তাকে,

"Call on me in the Day of trouble,

& I will deliver,

& thou shalt glorify me." [4]

চিরনির্বাসিত নির্জন কুটিরে চরম হতাশাগ্রস্ত, শুনেছে

একাকিত্বকে সঙ্গী করে নেয়ার দুর্মর বাণী:

"I will never ever leave thee, nor for sake thee."[5]

নির্জনতা, অনুতাপ, হতাশা, দুঃখ থেকে সে

খুঁজে পেয়েছিল বেঁচে থাকার সুখ, অর্থময়তা!

তার অনুভূতিটা ধরতে পেরেছিলাম,

বিশ্বাস করেছিলাম!

কারণ, এমন অনুভূতি একদিন আমারও হয়েছিল;

শুনেছিলাম, "নিশ্চয়ই কষ্টের মাঝে স্বস্তি আছে।"[6]

আমি কিন্তু সেই ঘোর বিরুদ্ধগামী,

তবুও জানি না কেন,

বিরুদ্ধ বাস্তবতায়, নির্মম পরাভবে,

spiritually dead যখন,

অস্থির হয়ে উঠি হঠাৎ এই শব্দঝঙ্কারে,

আশার অমিয় বাণীঃ "মনমরা হয়ো না, হতাশ হয়ো না, দুঃখ করো না,

বিজয়ী তোমরাই হবে।" [7]

Robinson এর মতো আমারও মনে হয়েছিল,

"That these words were to me!

Why else should they be

directed in such a manner,

right at the moment,

when I was mourning over my condition!?" [8]

আচ্ছা, এটাও কি co-incidence?

310

খোলা চোখে কিংবা নির্বাক অনুভবে,
যা কিছু হয়, হচ্ছে, হবে,
সবই কি মায়ার ছলনা, কুহক, প্রহসন?

জানিনা, ভাবতে চাইও না!
বলি, "All those superstitious!"
বলে নিজেদের সান্ত্বনা দিতে থাকি।
আমরা, যারা অবিশ্বাস করি।

কিন্তু কেন এখন হঠাৎ হৃদয়মাঝে এত পূর্ণতা,
এত স্বস্তি, এত প্রশান্তি?
মনে হলো, যেন খুঁজে পেয়েছি কিছু বহুকাল পর।
কিন্তু এটা কী? বলতে পারছি না !
কারণ, এ অনুভূতি এতখানি অনুভব করে ফেলেছি যে,
এর কোনো উপাংশই বাকি নেই আর
যাকে ভাষায় প্রকাশ করা যেতে পারে!

সেই অনুভূতি সদাপ্রবহমান ঝরনার কল্লোলের মত,
সাদা মেঘে বহু উঁচুতে ভেসে বেড়ানো
সোনালী ঠোঁট ঈগলের মত।
এই অব্যক্ত অনুভূতি,
supernova কন্যা, উদ্ভাসিত protostar এর মত।
নবজীবনের আশ্বাসে নবীন।
পূর্ণপ্রাণশক্তিমান হৃদয়ের মত স্বাধীন।

কাছে থেকেও দূরে, কোথায় যেন তাঁর ডাক, অব্যর্থ হাতছানি,
isotropic background radiation এর মত।
তাঁকে দেখতে পারি না কিন্তু,
অনুভূতির মাঝে তাঁকে ধরতে পারি,
মনের মণিকোঠায় বেজে উঠে তাঁর সন্ধানী সংকেত,
Penzias ও Wilson নির্মিত detector এর মত!

হোক অসীম বিশালতা, কিংবা অদৃশ্য ক্ষুদ্রতা,
হোক পরম বা আপেক্ষিক
বাস্তব বা বিমূর্ত পারিপার্শ্বিকতা,
নাই বা দিল ধরা।
নেই আফসোস!
কিন্তু, যেটা সত্য,
তোমার, আমার, সবার প্রাণ, অস্তিত্ব,
অতীত, এখন বা আগামীর স্থানকালে,
নাহি হয় কভু বাঁধনহারা
সেই পরম সত্তার, অবিনশ্বর অস্তিত্ব থেকে।

না চাইতেও খুঁজে পাবে তুমি,
তব হৃদয়ের যাচিত ভাষারই আশ্চর্য আহ্বান।
অবচেতনতার সুপ্ত তরঙ্গগুলো,
তাঁর সাড়ায় উদ্বেলিত হয়ে উঠবে তখন।
একবার না, বারবার!
সেটাকেও কি আগের মতো ভাববে তুমি?

কোনো কুহক, মায়া বা ইন্দ্রজাল??

কতবার ভাববে? নিজেরই সত্তার অংশীদারকে

অস্বীকার করবে? কতবার??

আপত্তি নেই কোনো,

নাইবা আস্বাদন করলে তুমি, হৃদয়ের অমিয় সুধা,

জানবার অধিকার তো তারই আছে, যে জানতে চায়।

নাইবা বিশ্বাস করলে হৃদয়ের পরম সত্য।

জীবন সায়াহ্নে আসবে যখন,

আমার কথাগুলো তখন,

তোমার মনে হলে,

নশ্বর জীবন হতে চিরমুক্তির ক্রান্তিকালে,

কিছু কি খুঁজে পাবে তুমি?

আমাকে কি কিছু বলার থাকবে তোমার?

জানতে চাইব ঠিকই,

কিন্তু তখন অনেক, অনেক দেরি হয়ে যাবে।

শত চেষ্টাতেও, পাব না সন্ধান।

References:

[1] Al Quran: Chapter "Al-An'am" - 6:1

[2] Al Quran: Chapter "Al-Baqara" - 2:74

[3] Al Quran: Chapter "Al-Hadid" - 56: 83~86

[4] Holy Bible (Psalm 50:15)

[5] Holy Bible (Deuteronomy 31:6)

[6] Al Quran: Chapter "Ash-Sharh" - 94:6

[7] Al Quran: Chapter "Al-Imran" - 3:139

[8] "Robinson Crusoe" by Daniel Defoe

Khodeza Akhter Jahan Rume / খোদেজা আখতার জাহান রুমী, Dhaka, Bangladesh

It reminds me myself, my people, my city.

আমার বাড়ি - আমার শহর

স্মৃতির পাতায় স্পষ্ট অক্ষরে লেখা যে কথাগুলো সবসময় আমার মনে ঘুরপাক খায়, তা আমার বাড়ি, আমার শহর। অমিতাভ দাদার গানের কলি, "এক রূপসীর প্রেমে আমার মনবান্ধা - ভালোবাসার স্বপ্নঘাটে নাও বান্ধা , ভালোবেসে লাইলী আমি মজনু আমার গাইবান্ধা"। ১৯৭১ এর যুদ্ধের পরে সেই চার বছর বয়সে চলে এসেছিলাম ছোট্ট শহর গাইবান্ধায়। অসংখ্য গরীব মানুষ, গরুর গাড়ি, আর শীর্ণ রোগা স্যান্ডেল ছাড়া, খালি পায়ে হাঁটা যে জনগোষ্ঠী, তারাই আমার আপনজন, তারাই আমার শহরের মানুষ।

গাইবান্ধায় একটা বিলের মাঝে আমার বাড়ি ছিল। নীরব নিস্তব্ধ এলাকা, আশে-পাশে তখনও কিছু ছিল না, চারদিক খোলা আর হু হু করা মন ভালো করা বাতাস। সকালে শত-শত সাদা শাপলার হাসি আর দিনে বেগুনি সুন্দি ফুলের মায়া। আমাদের বাসার ভিতরে পুকুর, আর তার চারদিক গাছ দিয়ে ঘেরা ছিল।

সেই সময়ে যুদ্ধের পর যে দুর্ভিক্ষ হয়েছিল তার সবকিছু ছিল চোখে পড়ার মতো। পলাশপাড়া স্কুল মাঠে লঙ্গরখানা ছিল। সপ্তাহে দুদিন শীর্ণ, দুর্বল আর ক্লান্ত নারী-পুরুষ, ছেলে-পুলে সহ বাটি গামলা থালা নিয়ে ছুটত। বিলেতি পাউডার দুধ জাল করে তাই দেয়া হত, পাতলা সাদা দুধের রঙটাও ঠিক আসতো না সেই পানিতে। তা নিয়েই হুলুস্থুল, তার জন্যে মারামারি, ঝগড়া আরও কত কী।

আমার স্কুলের নাম ছিল পলাশপাড়া সরকারি ফ্রি প্রাইমারি স্কুল। স্কুলের প্রথম সেই দিন খুব মনে পড়ে, আব্বা আমাকে সঙ্গে নিয়ে গেলেন। আম্মা আমাকে একটা কামিজ আর চুড়িদার পায়জামা আর পায়ে লাল জুতা পরিয়ে দিয়েছিল। আর বই নেয়ার জন্য

সুটকেস। এই বেশভূষায় যখন গেলাম সবাই আমাকে ঘিরে ধরল, আজব গ্রহের কিছু একটা মনে করে হাত দিয়ে ধরে আমার চুল, জুতা, সুটকেস সব পরীক্ষা করে দেখেছিল আমার বন্ধুরা। সেই একদিন স্কুলে জুতা পরে ছিলাম আর তারপর পাঁচ বছর থেকে খালি পায়ে, বই হাতে নিয়ে স্কুল-জীবন পার করেছি। স্কুলে প্রথমে শুধু চাল ছিল, তারপর বাঁশের বেড়া; এরপর টিনের চাল, টিনের বেড়া আর একটা টিউবওয়েলও হলো। দৌড়াদৌড়ি করে ঘেমে-নেয়ে কলের মুখে মুখ লাগিয়ে পানি পান; সেই লোহা মিশ্রিত স্বাদ এখনো রয়ে গেছে। সবচেয়ে সুন্দর ছিল স্কুলের মাঠ আর বিশাল বট গাছ।

স্কুলের একটু দূরে বিলকিস থালাম্মাদের বাড়ি তার সাথেই ফরিদা বুদের বাড়ি। রাস্তার তিন মাথায় আমাদের টিনের বাড়ি। পূর্ব পাশ দিয়ে কলেজ রোড, সেনকাকার দোকান, তার পাশেই নানাভায়ের বাসা। রাস্তা দিয়ে হাঁটার কথা মনেই পড়ে না, জমির মধ্যে দিয়ে এক ছুট দিলেই নানাভায়ের বাসা। ছোটনানি - আমরা ভাবি বলতাম, তার কাছ থেকে আম্মার জরুরি কাজ সেরে আরেক ছুট দিলেই আমাদের বাসা। পলাশপাড়া স্কুলের পিছনে ছিল বাস-স্ট্যান্ড। বিভূতিভূষণের অপু দুর্গার মতো দূরের রাস্তা হেঁটে রেলগাড়ি দেখতে যেতে হতো না; বাসার সামনে দাঁড়িয়েই দেখা যেতো। আমাদের ঘড়ি ছিল না, কিন্তু ছায়ার সাথে সময়ের   হিসাব খুব পাকা ছিল। সময়ের সব হিসাব বুঝে নিতাম আলো-ছায়া আর আঁধারের সাথে সাথে।

আব্বা খুলনায় কাজ করতেন, আমার কাকারা তখন ঢাকায়। তাই চিঠি আর মানিঅর্ডার আসতো ডাকে। আমরা সেই ডাকপিয়নের ডাকের অপেক্ষায় থেকেছি। একটু নাকের তলা দিয়ে ডাকতেন মিঠু উ উ উ, মিঠু উ উ উ তোমার বাবার , কাকা মনজুর চিঠি আর টাকা এসেছে। তোমার মাকে ডাকো। তিনি এসে চেয়ারে বসতেন আর আমরা চারদিক দাঁড়িয়ে দেখতাম। সাদা থামের চারদিক দিয়ে লাল নীল সেই স্বপ্নের রঙগুলো। সেই সময়ে চিঠিতে আব্বা আর কাকাদের দেয়া আদর আর ভালোবাসা শোনার জন্য আম্মার পাশে থাকতাম। মাঝে মাঝে চোখ দিয়ে বেরিয়ে   আসতো আনন্দাশ্রু। আমার দাদি, যিনি সম্পর্কে আমার বাবার চাচি - তিনিই আমাদের সব ছিলেন। তাঁকে ছাড়া আমার সেই জীবনে আলাদা তেমন কিছু মনে পড়েনা। সেই সময়

315

থেকে জেনে এসেছি, আমার আম্মা অসুস্থ। তাঁর কাছে বেশি যাওয়া যাবে না আর তাঁকে যেন আমরা বিরক্ত না করি। আর সেজন্যই নাকি খুলনা থেকে আমাদের গাইবান্ধায় চলে আসা। খুলনায় দোতালা বাড়ির হাফ-ছাদে একটা বেবি সাইকেল চালাতাম; চারপাশে ছিল নারকেল গাছ আর সেই দোয়েল পাখিটা, সে অস্পষ্ট ছবি ছাড়া আর কিছু মনে পড়েনা। কিশোর বেলার সেই দিনগুলোতে সেই বাড়ি আর সেই দোয়েল পাখিটা ছিল আমার স্বপ্নে আর সাধনায়; যা কেমন এক না পাওয়ার অনুভূতি হিসেবে রয়ে গেছে।

গাইবান্ধা আমার নানার বাড়ি; চারপাশে সবাই তাই নানা, নানি, মামা, খালা। দাদার বাড়ি কেতকীর হাট; গাঙের পাড়ে। চরের পাশে তাই নানা বাড়ির লোকজন প্রায়ই বলতো, তোরা তো ভাটিয়া। আহা কী সুন্দর আমার দাদার বাড়ির মানুষগুলো, আদর আর ভালোবাসায় দিলখোলা; তাদের এত অভাব কিন্তু কী যে মায়া আর প্রাণখোলা হাসি। তাদের দরাজ গলায় কথা, হাসি আর একতারা বাজিয়ে গান, গাঙের পানির মুহুর্মুহু আছড়ে পড়ার মতোই হৃদয়ের গভীরে আনচান করা এক অনুভূতি জাগাতো।

বাসায় সুযোগ পেলেই আমরা কলেজের পুকুরে গোসল করে গায়ের কাপড় গায়েই শুকাতাম, সাদা কাদামাটি তাই শুকিয়ে গায়ে ভেসে উঠতো। সারাদিন খেলা আর খেলা। সব কাজও খেলার পর্যায়ে ছিল আমার কাছে। শীতের বিকেলে গমের ক্ষেতে যেতাম বতুয়া শাক তুলতে; তার ফাঁকে ফাঁকে বাদাম গাছ তুলে কাঁচা বাদাম খেতাম। সন্ধ্যায় ধু ধু বালু মাঠে বিশাল চাঁদ। আমরা ছেলে-মেয়ে সবাই মিলে বউচি খেলতাম। খেলার শেষে খোলা উঠানে চাঁদের আলোয় চুলার পাশে বসে মাটির পাতিলে রান্না করা ভাত, তরকারি খেতে বসতাম। শীতের সকালে করকরা ভাত, মুলাশাক, পুঁটিমাছ, লাউয়ের তরকারি - এমন অমৃত মধুর খাবার আর পাইনি এ জীবনে।

মাছ ধরা ছিল আমার নেশা। দাদার বাড়ির পাশে নদীতে গিয়ে মাছ ধরে পাতিলে ভরে এনে দাদিমাকে অবাক করে দিতাম। গ্রামের সবার সাথে গাঙে খড়ি ধরতে যেতাম। তখন মনে হতো না যে ভেসে আসা জিনিসগুলো অন্য কাউকে ভাসিয়ে নিঃস্ব করে এখানে এসেছে। সপ্তাহে নদীর পাড়ে দুদিন হাট বসতো, সেই হাটবার গুলো ছিল খুব

রঙিন। ছোট ছোট দোকানে অনেক ল্যাম্প জ্বলতো, নৌকায় করে অনেক মানুষ আসতো সদাই কিনতে। রঙিন কাগজের ফুল, পাতার বাঁশি আরও কত কী বিক্রি হতো। সে সময় নারীরা হাটে আসতো না ঠিকই, কিন্তু হাটের কাছাকাছি যে কোনো বাড়িতে বসে সব দেখত; তাদের বাড়ির মানুষ হাট করে এসে বউ-ঝিকে সাথে নিয়ে বাড়ি ফিরতো। দাদার বাড়ির ঈদ-গা মাঠের কদম গাছে কত কদম ফুটে থাকত। মাঝে মাঝে সেইসব গাছের তলে সুফি-সাধকরা আসতেন; গ্রামের লোকজন তাঁদের ভক্তি করতো। সন্ধ্যায় গানের আসর বসতো, পালা গান হতো। গ্রামের লোকেরা পালাক্রমে রান্না করে তাদের খাওয়াতো, সম্মান করতো। বছরে একবার সার্কাস আর যাত্রা হতো। আমার শৈশবের সেই রংমাখা দিন আর ভালোবাসার মাটির মানুষদের নিয়ে ছিল ছন্নছাড়া ছোট্ট সেই শহর, আমার ভালোবাসার লাইলী, আমার গাইবান্ধা।

Khodeza Akhter Jahan Rume / খোদেজা আখতার জাহান রুমী, Dhaka, Bangladesh

My pain about my adult life, also women's voice encouraged me to write.

আমার বাড়ি – আমার শহর

ছোট বেলার স্বপ্ন দেখা মন নিয়ে

বিশ্ববিদ্যালয়ের গণ্ডিতে পা রাখতেই

উরু উরু মনের ডানায় ভেসেছিল

রঙিন পাখা, সব সুন্দর সব ভালোলাগার।

পরিচিত গণ্ডির বাইরে এ আরেক জগত,

পায়ে পায়ে বাধার শিকল হয়েছিল অনেক শিথিল।

অপরিচিত ছোট-বড়র সাথে এক কামরায় বাস

রাতের পর রাত জেগে গল্প খেলা সাপ লুডু আর তাস।

মিছিলে মিছিলে রক্ত কাঁপানো স্লোগান।

টিভি নাটকে রঙিন অভিনয়

সাথে গোপন কামরায় কদর্য মাখা প্রস্তাব।

সব নোংরা চোখ ফাঁকি দিয়ে ঘরে ফেরা।

তারপর সে জগতের প্রতি এক রাশ ঘৃণা আর

আগ্রহ হারিয়ে ফেলা। বুকের গভীরে এক

দগ দগে ক্ষত পুষিয়ে রেখে আবার পথ চলা।

কত বার হোঁচট খেয়ে খেয়ে মুখ থুবড়ে পড়েছি

318

আবার দাঁড়িয়েছি, রাজধানী এই শহরের মায়ায়

অলিতে গলিতে দেখেছি অনেক লীলাখেলা।

শ্রীকৃষ্ণ বিচ্ছেদে রক্তাক্ত হৃদয়।

রক্তের আলপনায় সাজিয়ে ছুটে চলেছি

বানিয়েছি নতুন পথ অদম্য শক্তি নিয়ে।

ঘরের মায়ায় বারবার জড়িয়েছি মাকড়সার জালে।

তারপরও পথ চলেছি চলছি, চলবো সামনে।

Aurora Ahmed Psyche / অরোরা আহমেদ সাইকী, Kushtia, Bangladesh

My memories inspired me at the time of my writing.

আমার শহর – আমার বাড়ি

আপন শহর বলতে আমার চোখের সমানে যে এক দৃশ্য চিত্রায়িত হয় তা হলো কুষ্টিয়া নামক ছোট্ট ছিমছাম একটি শহর। এই শহরেই আমার জন্ম, বেড়ে ওঠা। এ শহরের প্রতিটা রাস্তা-ঘাট, আনাচ-কানাচ যেন মায়ের মতোই আপন। এই শহরে আমার হারিয়ে যাওয়ার কোনো ভয় নেই।এ শহরের প্রতিটা মানুষের ভাষা ভীষণ অপরূপ। প্রতিটি মানুষের কথাতে যেন কবিতার ছোঁয়া থাকে, ছোঁয়া থাকে গানেরও। আমার এ শহরটি যে সাংস্কৃতিক শহর! এ শহরে আছে ফকির লালনের স্মৃতি, স্মৃতি আছে রবি ঠাকুরের। ছোট এ শহর ছেড়ে যাওয়ার সময় বড্ড কষ্ট হয় আমার ভিতরে। যেন একটা বোবা কষ্ট! কিন্তু যখন আবার ফিরি এ শহরে, আমার চোখে মুখে আলাদা একটা আনন্দকর চাঞ্চল্য ঝলমল করতে থাকে। শহরের মাটিতে পা রেখে চোখ বন্ধ করে চিৎকার করে যেন বলতে ইচ্ছে করে, "ভালোবাসি তোমায় এ শহর; ভালোবাসি।" এ শহর যেন আমার মায়ের কোল। ছোট বেলায় এ শহরের রাস্তা দিয়ে বাবার হাত ধরে ছোট্ট ছোট্ট পা ফেলে যেতাম স্কুলে, গানের ক্লাসে আর নাচের ক্লাসে। একটা দারুণ ঘটনা আছে। ছোটবেলায় একবার যখন বাবা আমাকে নাচের ক্লাসে রেখে চলে যায়, কোনো একটা কারণে সেদিনকার ক্লাস তাড়াতাড়ি শেষ হয়ে যায়। ছুটির পর আমি বাইরে দাঁড়িয়ে বাবার জন্য অপেক্ষা করতে থাকি। তখন আমার বয়স ছিল পাঁচ বছর। বেশ খানিকক্ষণ অপেক্ষার প্রহর গুনতে গুনতে দেখি বাবার আসার নাম নেই। তখন সিদ্ধান্ত নিই যে একাই যাবো আজ আমি। যেমন

ভাবা তেমন কাজ। শুরু করলাম পথ চলতে। পুরোটা পথ পায়ে হেঁটে তবেই আমি বাসায় ফিরলাম। বাসায় ফেরার পর মামণি আমাকে একা দেখে বাবার কথা জিজ্ঞাসা করে। উত্তরে আমি বলি, বাবার দেরি হচ্ছিল, তাই একাই চলে এসেছি। যেন আমি এক বিশাল কার্য-সিদ্ধি করে ফেলেছি। আর অপরদিকে আমাকে আনতে গিয়ে আমাকে না দেখে বাবা তো চিন্তায় অস্থির হয়ে গিয়েছিল। পরে মামণি বাবাকে ফোন করে বলে আমি বাসায় একাই চলে এসেছি। বাবা তো ভীষণ অবাক হয়েছিল যে ছোউ আমি এলাম কীভাবে এতটা পথ। অবশ্য আমার সাহসেরও তারিফ করেছিলেন বাবা। থাকগে সেসব পুরোনো কথা। আচ্ছা, এবারে আমি আমার বাড়ির কথা বলি এ শহরের শেষ প্রান্তের দিকেই আমার বাড়ি। দোতলা এই বাড়িটি আমার মায়ের ভীষণ যত্নের, ভীষণ সাধনার। বাড়ির প্রতিটি বারান্দার টবে তার নিজের হাতের লাগানো ফুল গাছ। বাড়ির সামনে আছে বিশাল বড় এক খেলার মাঠ। এই বাড়ির ছাদ থেকে দেখা যায় অপরূপ সুন্দর গোধূলি বেলা। তবে এই বাড়ির মধ্যে আমার সবচেয়ে প্রিয় জায়গাটি আমার ঘর; একান্তই আমার। যে ঘরে আমি সাজাই আমার এক আলাদা জগৎ; যে জগতে প্রবেশের অনুমতি আর কারো নেই। আমার সুখ-দুঃখ সব রকমের স্মৃতি রয়েছে এ ঘর জুড়ে। এ ঘরে রয়েছে আমার রাতের পর রাত জুড়ে কান্নার স্মৃতি। সুখের সাগরে ডুব দিতে গিয়ে পেয়েছিলাম অজস্র দুঃখ। এ ঘরে রয়েছে আমার ব্যর্থতার গল্প। এ ঘর আমার রাত জাগার সাক্ষী; কতো রাত যে পার করেছি তারা খচিত রাতের আকাশ দেখে তার নেই কোনো হিসাব। আবার এ ঘরেই আমি আমার কিছু সাফল্যের খুশিতে আত্মহারা হয়েছি। শুধু তাই নয় এ ঘর জুড়ে রয়েছে আমার কল্পনার জাল বুনা। এ ঘর, এ বাড়ি, এ শহর আমার একান্তই আপন, একান্তই ভালোবাসার।

Rima Das / রীমা দাস, Sylhet, Bangladesh

সিলেটের প্রকৃতি আমাকে সব থেকে বেশি আকর্ষণ করে। এখানে ঋতুবৈচিত্র্যের খেলা আকাশ, প্রকৃতি, নদী ও গাছে ধরা পড়ে। এই ঋতুবৈচিত্র্য মানুষের আচরণেও দেখা যায়। মেঘালয়ের পাদদেশের উঁচু উঁচু টিলাগুলো আরও মোহনীয় করে তুলেছে আমার শহরকে; টিলার গায়ে গায়ে সাজানো চা বাগান যেন প্রকৃতির এক অপরূপ দান। শীতের রুক্ষতায় এখানে যেমন সব রুক্ষ রূপ ধারণ করে, তেমনি যৌবনবতী বর্ষায় দুকূল ছাপিয়ে উপছে পড়ে সৌন্দর্য। এই রুক্ষতা ও সৌন্দর্যকে মনে লালন করে আমাদের আচরণের বহিঃপ্রকাশ হয় আমার লেখায়। শহরের বুক চিরে বয়ে চলছে সুদূর পথের যাত্রী কিশোরী সুরমা। শীতের একহারা গড়নের শীর্ণ কিশোরীটি বর্ষায় হয়ে ওঠে পূর্ণ যৌবনবতী। শীতে সে আমাদের আসন পেতে দেয় তার জেগে ওঠা চড়ে, সেই বুকের কচি ঘাসে নেচে বেড়ায় খঞ্জন পাখি। আবার বর্ষায় সেই যৌবনবতী কিশোরী কোলে করে বয়ে নিয়ে যায় আমাদের দূর দূরান্তে। প্রকৃতি ও মানবের এই অপরূপ রূপ আমাকে বার বার উদ্বুদ্ধ করে। প্রকৃতির বৈচিত্র্যের মত আমাদের মাঝেও আছে বিভিন্ন জনগোষ্ঠী, তাদের ঐতিহ্য, সংস্কৃতি, জীবনধারাও উল্লেখ করার মত। মনিপুরী নৃত্য খুবই দৃষ্টিনন্দন, যা আমাদের বিশ্বকবিকেও আকর্ষণ করেছিল। কৃষ্ণচূড়া, রাধাচূড়া, পলাশ, শিমুলের এই সিলেট বর্ষায় সবুজে সবুজে ছেয়ে যায়, কচি কচি সবুজ পাতায় রোদের খেলা অনেকটা ছোট্ট শিশুর তুলতুলে গালের মত দেখায়। এসবই আমার লেখার অনুপ্রেরণা।

রূপান্তর

আজ ঘুম ভাঙতেই আকাশের মেঘগুলোর দিকে তাকিয়ে রুদ্রর মন খারাপ হয়ে গেল। নীল আকাশে কালো মেঘের আনাগোনা। আকাশ থমথম করছে সেদিনের মত, যেদিন রুদ্র মিথিলাকে দেখেছিল। সেদিনও ছিল আকাশে মেঘের ঘনঘটা।জিন্দাবাজারের চৌরাস্তায় রুদ্র দাঁড়িয়ে রুদ্র বেশে, হাতে তার চাপাতি। দুপক্ষের মধ্যে তুমুল মারামারি। সেখানে রুদ্র তার হাতের চাপাতি তুলে ভয় দেখাচ্ছে প্রতিপক্ষকে। মুহূর্তের মধ্যে এলাকার সব দোকান বন্ধ, রাস্তা জনশূন্য, শুধু দু'দলের উচ্ছৃঙ্খল কিছু যুবক রাস্তায়। এরকম এক সংকটময় মুহূর্তে হঠাৎ রুদ্র তার হাতে অন্যের ছোঁয়া পেলো সেদিকে তাকাতেই দেখলো একজোড়া ভেজা চোখ, ফ্যাকাশে ঠোঁটের একটি মেয়ে তার হাত ধরে দাঁড়িয়ে কাঁপছে। রুদ্র মেয়েটির দিকে ঘুরে দাঁড়াতেই সে বললো –

বাড়ি দিয়ে আসবেন? বিস্ময়ে রুদ্র তার শরীরে অন্য ধরণের হরমোনের উপস্থিতি টের পেলো। মেয়েটি রুদ্রকে তার নিজের দিকে তাকিয়ে থাকতে দেখে আবার জানতে চাইল - বাড়ি দিয়ে আসবেন? রুদ্রর একা একলা পৃথিবীতে এর আগে কেউ এভাবে আকুতি জানায়নি। তাই তার মেরুদন্ড বেয়ে শীতল স্রোত বয়ে তাকে কাঁপিয়ে দিয়ে গেল, ভাবিয়ে দিয়ে গেল, নাড়িয়ে দিয়ে গেল। এক কথায় রুদ্রর পৃথিবীতে তখন সুনামির ঝড়। সে কোনো মতে আড়ষ্ট ঠোঁট নাড়িয়ে বললো - দেবো। মেয়েটার চোখে নির্ভরতার ঝিলিক দেখে রুদ্রর চোখে জল এলো। তার মত ছেলেকে অচেনা কেউ নির্ভর করতে পারে সেটা রুদ্রর কাছে অবিশ্বাস্য। রুদ্র ত্রাতা হয়ে মেয়েটার হাত শক্ত করে ধরে নিরাপদ দূরত্বে এসে দাঁড়ালো, জানতে চাইলো অচেনা মেয়ের নাম, সে কোথায় যাবে। মেয়েটি জানালো সে মিথিলা। যাবে আখালিয়া। শুরু হলো অচেনা দুজনের পথ চলা। মিথিলা হাঁটছে আর কথা বলছে। অবাক হয়ে রুদ্র দেখছে বিবর্ণ মুখের যে মেয়েটা কিছুক্ষণ আগে কেঁদে অস্থির ছিল, সেই মেয়েই পরম নির্ভরতায় আপনজনের মত বকবক করে যাচ্ছে রুদ্রর সাথে। রুদ্র তার হারানো সময় খুঁজে ফেরে। সে মনে করতে পারে না তার সাথে কবে কে গল্প করেছিল। তৃষার্তের মত তাই সে মুগ্ধ হয়ে মিথিলার দিকে তাকিয়ে তার চোখের, ঠোঁটের, হাতের নাচন দেখতে লাগল। মিথিলার কথার ঝরনাধারায় রুদ্র অবগাহন করতে লাগলো। তার মনে হতে লাগল মিথিলার কথাগুলো পাহাড়ি ঝরনার মত কুলকুল শব্দে বয়ে যাচ্ছে রুদ্রর নির্জন পাহাড়ি বনাঞ্চলে স্বপ্নের ঘোর লাগা সময়ের রেশ দ্রুতই কেটে গেল মিথিলার কথার বাঁকে বাঁকে এক সময় মিথিলা জানায় - বাড়ির রাস্তায় সে এসে গেছে। রুদ্রর পৃথিবীর তাপমাত্রা তখন এক নিমেষে হিমাঙ্কের নিচে নেমে গেল, তার পথ থমকে গেল, রুদ্ধ হয়ে গেল। অবাধ্য পা দুটো ঐ রাস্তার বাঁকে পাথরের মত নিশ্চল হয়ে দাঁড়িয়ে থাকলো, ঝাপসা চোখ দেখলো ছোট প্রজাপতির মত মিথিলা বড় রাস্তা ছেড়ে গলির ভেতর নেচে নেচে যাচ্ছে। হঠাৎ কুড়িয়ে পাওয়া সুখ রুদ্রর কপালে সইলো না বেশিক্ষণ। এমন সময় প্রকৃতি পাশে এসে দাঁড়ালো তার। আকাশ কাঁপিয়ে বৃষ্টি এলো। বৃষ্টির ধারায় রুদ্র লুকালো তার তপ্ত চোখের ধারা।

রুদ্র তার এলাকায় ত্রাসের অপর নাম। সবাই এক নামে চেনে তাকে, ভয় পায় তার নাম শুনে। তার কাছে খুব প্রয়োজন ছাড়া কেউ আসে না। সেখানে আদর-ভালোবাসা তো দূর গ্রহের কিছু। রুদ্র মনে করতে পারে না শেষ কবে তার বাবা-মাকে এক সাথে গল্প করতে দেখেছে। শেষ কবে সে তার বাবার কোলে উঠেছে, শেষ কবে সে তার মায়ের গলা জড়িয়ে আবদার করেছে। কোনো স্মৃতি নেই সে সবের। বাড়ির কাজের মাসির কাছেও অনাহূত সে। সেই ছোট্ট রুদ্র পত্র-পল্লবহীন অবস্থায়, ভালোবাসাহীন অবস্থায় রুক্ষভাবে কখন যে বড় হয়ে গেল তা কেউ টের পায়নি। শীতের রুক্ষতা নিয়ে রুদ্র নম্রভাবে বড় হলো। সে নিজে জ্বলতে লাগলো আর জ্বালাতে লাগলো চারপাশের অনুভূতিহীন মানুষগুলোকে। যে বয়সে রুদ্রর বয়সী ছেলেরা প্রেমিকা নিয়ে ঘুরে বেড়ায়, সে বয়সে রুদ্রর হাতে কখনো চাপাতি, কখনো দা, কখনো বা ক্ষুর। যে বয়সে রুদ্র মত ছেলেরা কামনা করে প্রেয়সীর উষ্ণ আলিঙ্গন, সে বয়সে রুদ্র আলিঙ্গন করেছে অন্ধকার আর শীতলতা। সেই অন্ধকার শীতল জীবনে আলোর ঝলকানির মত মিথিলার আগমন। রুদ্রর জীবন মরুভূমির মত শুষ্ক। সে বৃষ্টি চায়নি কখনও। তবুও মিথিলার ভেজা চোখ রুদ্রর মরুভূমিতে বৃষ্টি দিয়ে গেল। সে নিজের কাছে জানতে চাইছে বার বার কী আছে সেই দৃষ্টিতে? খুব সাধারণ একটি ঘটনা, দুটো ভেজা চোখ, একটু নির্ভরতা কী করে একটা মানুষকে আমূল বদলে দেয় তা রুদ্র ছাড়া আর কেউ হয়ত জানে না। সেই হেমন্তের মেঘলা বিকেল রুদ্রকে নাড়িয়ে গেল বসন্তের বাতাসের মত। এরপর থেকে রুদ্র নিজেকে আরো গুটিয়ে নিলো। সে সাধনা করতে লাগলো মিথিলার। এভাবে বছর ঘুরে আবার হেমন্ত এলো। আকাশে মেঘের ঘনঘটা দেখে রুদ্র তার ঘর অন্ধকার করে শুনতে লাগলো –

আমার প্রাণের পরে চলে গেল কে

বসন্তের বাতাসটুকুর মতো

সে যে ছুঁয়ে গেল, নুয়ে গেল রে

ফুল ফুটিয়ে গেল শত শত....

সারাদিন বন্ধ ঘরে একা সে। রুদ্র একাকী জীবনের সর্বক্ষণের সঙ্গী একজোড়া ভেজা চোখ। ভালোবাসাহীন, প্রেমহীন, আদরহীন রুক্ষ যুবক অনুভব করছে এক প্রচণ্ড সম্মোহনী শক্তির যা তাকে টেনে নিচ্ছে দূরে, বহুদূরের অজানায়। সেই সম্মোহনী শক্তির প্রভাবে সে সিলেটের আনাচে কানাচে, অলিতে গলিতে খোঁজে সেই দুটো ভেজা চোখ। যে রুদ্র কোনো অনুষ্ঠান দেখতে যেত না, সেই রুদ্র শিশু একাডেমি, শিল্পকলা, শহিদ মিনারের সব অনুষ্ঠানে হাজির থাকত। এই মেঘলা হেমন্তের সকালে রুদ্র প্রচণ্ড মন খারাপে ডুবে যাচ্ছে। সে অনুভব করছে নদীর পাড় ভেঙে যাচ্ছে। আর সেই সাথে সে ডুবে যেতে চাইছে কারো চোখের নির্ভরতায়। সময়ের প্রবহমানতায় হেমন্ত শেষে পরিচিত শহরে রঙের মিছিল নিয়ে আবারও হাজির হয় বসন্ত। বসন্তের ঘোরলাগা এক মায়াবী বিকেলে রুদ্র হাঁটছে তার প্রিয় সুরমায় জেগে ওঠা চরের সবুজ গালিচায়। এই জায়গা রুদ্রর খুব প্রিয়। হাঁটতে হাঁটতে সে অনুভব করছে তার সাথে আছে মিথিলা। নৈঃশব্দে তারা কথা বলছে আর হাঁটছে। এক সময় রুদ্র শুনতে পেলো মিথিলা বলছে - চলো ঐ গাছের নিচে বসি। রুদ্র তাকিয়ে দেখলো তার মত পত্র-পল্লবহীন গাছ বেছে নিয়েছে মিথিলা। রুদ্রর পছন্দের গাছেরা পত্র-পল্লবহীন কংকালের মত হয়। এই গাছগুলোতে সে নিজের প্রতিবিম্ব দেখতে পায়। সেই মুহূর্তে রুদ্র অনুভব করে মিথিলা তার হাত শক্ত করে ধরে রেখেছে। রুদ্রর সামনের প্রকৃতি সব ঝাপসা হয়ে যাচ্ছে। সাহসী, কখনও কখনও হিংস্র পুরুষের দুকূল বেয়ে প্লাবন। সে আর নিজেকে ধরে রাখতে না পেরে ঘাসের বুকের আলিঙ্গনে মুখ লুকালো। হঠাৎ রুদ্রর মনে হলো ভোর হয়েছে, চারিদিকে নতুন আলো। সে ছোট শিশুর মত চোখ মেলে তাকায় আকাশে। আকাশের বুকে গুচ্ছ গুচ্ছ রক্ত দেখে রুদ্রর হৃদস্পন্দন থেমে গেল এক মুহূর্তের জন্য। সে সেই গুচ্ছ রং এ দেখলো মিথিলার ভেজা চোখ আর মিথিলা বাতাস হয়ে লাল রং দিল রুদ্রর বুকে। রুদ্র ভালো করে চোখ মেলে দেখলো, যে গাছকে সে এতদিন শুধু কঙ্কাল বলে ভেবেছে সেই গাছ আজ ফুলে ফুলে সেজেছে। সেখানে বসন্তবাউরির উড়াউড়ি, অন্যান্য পাখির কলতান। রুদ্র অনুভব করল তার ভেতরে পরিযায়ী ভালোবাসা। সে শুনতে পেলো তার নিজের অন্তরের ডাক, সে দেখতে পায় তার চোখের সামনের সবকিছুতে মিথিলার প্রতিবিম্ব। ভালোবাসার কুসুম চন্দন চোখে নিয়ে রুদ্র রূপান্তরিত হয় অন্য মানুষে।

Farjana Yeasmin / ফারজানা ইয়াসমিন, Dhaka, Bangladesh

My inspiration for writing My City My Home is to talk about women's right and all the unsaid things women feel but can't say because of social compulsion. I thank My City My Home from the bottom of my heart for giving me the opportunity to do so.

মাই হোম – মাই সিটি

আমি ফারজানা ইয়াসমিন, একজন গৃহিণী। আমি ঢাকার বংশালে দুই মেয়ে এবং স্বামী নিয়ে বসবাস করি। ভাবছিলাম, আমার বাড়ি আর আমার শহর নিয়ে এখানে কিছু বলবো। আসলে সত্যিই কি আমার বলবার মতো কিছু আছে? আমার মনে হয় না।

আমাদের সমাজে মেয়েদের বোঝা মনে করা হয়, মা-বাবা মেয়েদের নিয়ে সব সময় উদ্বিগ্ন থাকে। আমরা যত পড়াশুনাই করি না কেন আমাদেরকে অন্যরকম চোখেই দেখা হয়, যেটা ছেলেদের বেলায় হয় না। আজ নিজের বাড়িতে আমি কতটা নিরাপদ, এটা নিয়ে আমার নিজেরই সংশয় আছে, আর শহর তো পরের কথা। আমার নিজের বলতে হয়তো কিছুই নেই, এমন কী আমি নিজেই হয়তো নিজের না। মাঝে মাঝে যখন মনে হয়, এই জীবনে কিছুই পাওয়া হয়নি আর করা হয়নি, তখন আমি হারিয়ে যাওয়া নিজেকে খুঁজি বার বার। আমাকে এই বাড়ি বা শহর অনেক কিছুই দিয়েছে, আবার কেড়েও নিয়েছে অনেক। শহরের জীবন বড়ই বিচিত্র, হাসি-কান্না, পাওয়া না-পাওয়া নিয়েই এই জীবন। প্রতিটি মেয়ে ছোট থেকে হাজারো সংগ্রাম করে। কেউ সামনে এগিয়ে যায় আবার কেউ মাঝ পথে ঝরে পরে। এই সমাজ বা দেশ এখনো নারী-বান্ধব শহর গড়ে তুলতে পারেনি বলে আমি মনে করি। কারণ আমি যখন কোনো কাজে বের হই তখন হাজারো খারাপ চিন্তা আমার মাথায় ভর করে, আমি কি নিরাপদে বাড়ি ফিরতে পারবো! আমার নিরাপত্তার কথা ভেবে আমি কোথাও কি মানসিক শান্তি পাই! আমাদের দেশের কিছু কিছু পরিবারে ছেলেদের পাশাপাশি মেয়েরাও অর্থ উপার্জন করে পরিবারের পাশে দাঁড়িয়েছে। তারপরও এখানে নারীর নিরাপত্তা নিয়ে আমরা অনেক

পিছিয়ে আছি। আমি বা আমার মেয়ে বাইরে থেকে দরকারি ওষুধ বা অন্য কিছু আনতে যেতে পারবো না কারণ এই শহর আমাদের জন্য, রাত বা দিন, কখনোই নিরাপদ না। তারপরও আমকে এই শহরে সকলের সাথে পায়ে পা মিলিয়ে চলতে হয়। কারণ আমি এই শহরেরই একজন। আমার বাড়ি বা ঘর, যাই বলি না কেন সেখানেও আমাদের একই অবস্থা। সব শেষে কিন্তু আমরা বাড়িকেই নিরাপদ ও শান্তির জায়গা মনে করি এবং এখানেই ফিরে আসি। আমরা নারীরা চাইলেই সব অসম্ভবকে সম্ভব করতে পারি আমাদের মনের প্রবল ইচ্ছা শক্তিকে কাজে লাগিয়ে। যুগে যুগে এমন দৃষ্টান্ত স্থাপন করে গেছে অনেকে কর্মঠ নারী, যাদের কথা না বললেই নয়। যেমন, বেগম রকেয়া হাজারো বাধা পেরিয়ে সামনের দিকে এগিয়ে গেছেন, আর ইতিহাসে তাঁর নাম স্বর্ণাক্ষরে লেখা রয়েছে। আমাদের দেশের প্রধানমন্ত্রী নারী, তার পরেও আমাদের সমাজ নারী-বান্ধব নয়; এটা খুবই লজ্জাজনক। সবশেষে আমি মনে করি আমরা সবাই ঐক্যবদ্ধ ভাবে কাজ করলে সব অসম্ভবকে সম্ভব করা আমাদের পক্ষে সম্ভব। আমাদের সকলের একটাই চাওয়া, একটা নারী-বান্ধব সমাজ, একটা নিরাপদ শহর আর একটা নিরাপদ বাড়ি, যেখানে আমরা সকলেই ভাল থাকবো এবং অন্যকেও ভাল রাখবো। আমার জীবনের প্রথম লেখা, তাই ভুলগুলি ক্ষমাসুন্দর দৃষ্টিতে দেখার জন্য অনুরোধ করা হোল।

Jisrat Alam Mumu / জিসরাত আলম মুমু, Chittagong, Bangladesh

My city is not just a mere city to me, but a part of my dream, which always inspires me and reminds me that in this world I have a home. When I have got the opportunity to write something about my city, I become very interested. I am a Bangladeshi. I have written it in Bengali language as in my opinion mother language is the best to express my internal emotions. My city is the name of this emotion to me. I love my city Chittagong very much.

আমার শহর আমার বাড়ি

আমার শহর!!! সেটা তো আমার কাছে শুধু একটি শহর নয়.....আমার শুরু.... আমার বেড়ে ওঠা.... আমার শিকড়। এই শহরেই বাবার হাত ধরে প্রথম স্কুলে যাওয়া, বেণী দুলিয়ে অবাক চোখে ব্যাটারি চালিত রিকশা দেখা, বড় বড় ভাব করে কিশোরী বেলায় প্রথম কলেজে যাওয়া....আরো কত স্মৃতি। শব্দ দিয়ে আটকানো যায় না, বুকের মাঝে চিনচিন ব্যথা করে জানান দেয় এমন ভালোবাসা আমার কাছে এই শহর। আচ্ছা বোকা তো আমি.... শহরটার নামই তো বলিনি.... আমার শহরের নাম হলো চট্টগ্রাম। আমাদের চট্টগ্রামের মানুষদের আপ্যায়ন সব জেলা থেকে ভিন্ন.... চট্টগ্রামের মানুষদের খাওয়া আর খাওয়ানোর কলিজা বিশাল!!! এখানকার বিয়ে-সহ মেজবান আর অন্যান্য অনুষ্ঠানের পরিসর আর আয়োজন অনেক বড় হয়। চট্টগ্রামের মানুষেরা কিছুটা সহজ সরল.... আমরা অল্পতেই আপন করে নিই কাউকে, কাউকে আপন করতে বেশি জটিলতার হিসাব নিকাশ করি না। আমি এই শহরটিকে এই সরলতার কারণে বেশি ভালোবেসেছি বলে আমার মনে হয়। শহর তো মানুষকে নিয়েই, তাই না?

আমার জীবনটা যদি একটা নকশী কাঁথার সাথে তুলনা করে থাকি, তাহলে সেই নকশী কাঁথার অপরূপ নকশাগুলো হলো চট্টগ্রাম। আমার জীবনে বেশিরভাগ সুখস্মৃতি এই চট্টগ্রামে, আমার বুকের কত বিশাল অংশ জুড়ে যে আমার শহর চট্টগ্রামের বসবাস

আমি তা বুঝতে পারি যখন কোনো কারণে এই শহর থেকে বাইরে যাই। এমনটি হয়েছিল যখন জীবনে প্রথমবারের মত বিদেশে গিয়েছিলাম। কী যেন নেই, কী যেন নেই, কী যে হাহাকার আমার ভেতর এই শহরের জন্য! যেন আমার শরীরের কোনো গুরুত্বপূর্ণ অঙ্গ আমি ফেলে এসেছি! ফিরে আসার সময় যখন বিমানে চউগ্রামের নাম বলছিল আমার চোখ ভিজে উঠেছিল! যেন মায়ের কোলে ফিরে এসেছি বহুবছর পর, এমন অনুভূতি! মা দরিদ্র হোক, শতছিন্ন পোশাকে থাকুক, হাজারো ক্রটি থাকুক, সন্তানের কাছে সে সবসময়ই রাজরানি, আমার শহরও আমার কাছে তেমন, সব সুবিধা অসুবিধা ভালো খারাপ ক্রটি মেনে নিয়েই সে আমার আপন। কারো কাছে ছেলেমানুষি মনে হতে পারে, কিন্তু আমার কাছে আমার শহরই আসলে আমার ঘর, আমার বাড়ি, আমার নিজের জিনিস, আমার আপনালয়!!!!

কোনো রূপবতী নারীর শরীরে অলংকার পরিয়ে দিলে যেমন তার রূপ বেড়ে যায় হাজার গুন, চউগ্রামেরও তেমনি রয়েছে অলংকাররূপী কিছু স্থান, যেগুলো বাড়িয়ে দিয়েছে এই শহরের আভিজাত্য। কিছু স্থান প্রাকৃতিকভাবে সুন্দর আর কিছু মানুষের কোলাহলে সুন্দর। পতেংগা সমুদ্র সৈকতে আছড়ে পড়া ঢেউ এর সামনে দাঁড়িয়ে জীবনের হিসাবনিকাশ নিয়ে চিন্তা করার সময় আশেপাশে দেখা যায় কত মানুষের কত হরেক রকমের আনন্দ! হয়ত কোনো বাচ্চা তার বাবার সাথে অপার বিস্ময়ে সমুদ্র দেখছে, কোনো নব-দম্পতি এসেছে বেড়াতে, যুবক-যুবতীদের উচ্ছসিত আনাগোনা.... সব মিলিয়েই সমুদ্রকে বিশাল মনে হয়! যেন জীবনের বিশালতা সমুদ্রে মিশে যায়, জীবনের জোয়ার ভাটা সমুদ্রে মিল খায়! প্রাচ্যের রাণী বলে খ্যাত এই চউগ্রামে আরো আছে - ওয়ার সিমেট্রি যেখানে নির্জনতার সাথে আছে ইতিহাসের যোগাযোগ, ভাটিয়ারী লেকের টলমল সৌন্দর্য, ডিসি হিল প্রকৃতির ছায়ায় শরীরচর্চায় ব্যস্ত মানুষদের আনাগোনা,ফয়'স লেক, বাটালি হিল, বায়েজিদ বোস্তামীর মাজার, চন্দ্রনাথ পাহাড়, জাতিতাত্ত্বিক যাদুঘর, বাঁশখালী চা বাগান, মহামায়া লেক, পারকি সমুদ্র সৈকত, বাঁশখালী ইকোপার্ক, খৈইয়াছড়া ঝরনা, বাঁশবাড়িয়া সমুদ্র সৈকত, গুলিয়াখালী সমুদ্র সৈকত, সন্দ্বীপ ইত্যাদিকে চউগ্রামের উল্লেখযোগ্য বিশেষ স্থানগুলোর মাঝে ধরা যায়।

আমার অনেক চাওয়া আছে চট্টগ্রামকে নিয়ে। যেমন একুশে বইমেলা যত বড় পরিসরে বাংলাদেশের রাজধানী ঢাকায় হয়, তত বড় পরিসরে চট্টগ্রামে হয় না। এই ব্যাপারটা নিয়ে আক্ষেপ আছে। চট্টগ্রামের একক ঐতিহ্যগুলো নিয়ে একটা বিশেষ জাদুঘরের স্বপ্ন দেখি আমি, যেখানে একবার ঘুরে আসলেই পুরো চট্টগ্রামকে অনুভব করা যাবে।

আমার শহর বিশ্বের সেরা শহর হোক, প্রগতিতে, উন্নতিতে আভিজাত্যে, গতিতে – এটা আমার আজন্ম চাওয়া। সব মানুষের নিরাপত্তা এই শহরে নিশ্চিত হোক।

কারণ, আমার শহর আমার কাছে শুধু একটি শহর নয়, আমার বাড়ি....।

Sajeda Sharmin / সাজেদা শারমিন, Noakhali, Bangladesh

In today's world everything has a touch of urbanization. I my country life very much. I wrote this piece to reminisce my past life.

আমার বাড়ি

আমার বাড়ি ছোট্ট গাঁও

বাহন আমার পানসি নাও

বসত করি মাটির ঘরে,

ঘুরে বেড়াই বালির চরে

মাথার উপর নীল আকাশ

মন যে আমার হয় উদাস

Sajeda Sharmin / সাজেদা শারমিন, Noakhali, Bangladesh

I am astonished to see the development of my city. To make life comfortable we are gradually sacrificing our nature. I am dreaming of a city with full of happiness.

আমার শহর

এই শহরে আমার বাড়ি

বন্ধু রইলো নিমন্ত্রণ

খুঁজবো কোথায় তোমার বাড়ি

নাম ঠিকানা ছাড়া?

লাগবে কত ভাড়া?

বন্ধু একটু দাঁড়া

দিলাম না হয় ভাড়া

ক্যামনে দিব নাম ঠিকানা

কাগজ কলম ছাড়া?

Sara Pauline / **সারা পওলীন**, Dhaka, Bangladesh

In my writing I get inspiration from to those brave girls, who are struggling in their everyday life not to discriminate between male and female gender. Above all we all are human, we should treat each other as human being. We should not treat anyone by his/her gender. I love to writing. My city and My Home gives me an opportunity to expresse my thought and its really a great inspiration for me.

মেয়ে মানুষ

সমাজ বলে মানুষ হওয়ার আগেও আমার বড় পরিচয় আমি নাকি মেয়ে মানুষ।

আমি চিৎকার করে বলি ভুল বুঝছো তোমরা

আমার প্রথম ও সবচেয়ে বড় পরিচয় হলো আমি এক জন মানুষ

তারপর আমি মেয়ে মানুষ

সমাজ আমাকে ধমক দিয়ে চুপ করিয়ে

বলে তুমি কী বুঝো হে?

তুমি তো মেয়ে মানুষ

মেয়ে মানুষ মেয়ে মানুষের মতই থাকো না

এত বেশি কথা বলো কেন

জানো না তুমি তোমার বুদ্ধি কম

শারীরিক ভাবেও তুমি পুরুষের থেকে দুর্বল

দুর্বল মেয়ে মানুষ কোথাকার কিছুই বোঝে না

মস্তিষ্কহীন এক প্রাণী বটে

বোঝো না তো কিছুই, বলছি তাহলে শোন

পুরুষ মানুষের বীরত্বের কথা

পুরুষ সে তো মহান!

যা খুশি তাই করার সে তো এক মাত্র ক্ষমতাবান

ধর্ষণ, পরকীয়া, নোংরামি এ সব কিছুই করে

দেয় সে তার বীরত্বের প্রমাণ।

যদি করে সে ধর্ষণ চারদিক থেকে বয়ে যায়

হাজারো 'বাহ্ বাহ্' বর্ষণ,

যদি করেও সে পরকীয়া

তবুও হবে না তার চরিত্রের অন্ত্যেষ্টিক্রিয়া

যদিও বা যায় সে হাজারো বেশ্যালয়ে

পুরুষ বেশ্যার আখ্যাটা কখনো কেউ দিবে না তাকে

সব কিছুর ঊর্ধ্বে সে পুরুষ তো বটে

মহাপুরুষের চেয়ে কম কিসে?

তুমি তো মেয়ে মানুষ তবে মানুষ ও বলা চলে

তোমার সাথে কি পুরুষের তুলনা সাজে।

বুঝি না বাবা কী আক্কেল তোমাদের

পুরুষের সমান অধিকার পেতে চাও কী করে,

আরে বুঝে নিও মেয়ে নিজের ভালো তো পাগলেও বুঝে

সব সময় বুকে ও মাথায় ওড়নাটা রাখতে শিখে নিও।

সম্পূর্ণ শরীর তোমার কালো কাপড় দিয়ে আবৃত করে দাও

জানোই তো পুরুষ মানুষের দৃষ্টি সীমাহীন,

বেচারারা নিজেদের দৃষ্টি সংযত রাখতে পারে না

তাই বলতে পারো একটু চরিত্রহীন।

বোঝোই তো পুরুষ মানুষ নিজের বশে বশ্যতা

সহজে স্বীকার করে না,

এতে দোষ কী আর তার তাতে?

দোষ তো দেখি সব তোমাদের মেয়ে মানুষের

মডার্ন ড্রেস পড়ে বুক উঁচু করে ঘুরবে

আর ওমনি পুরুষ ঝাঁপিয়ে পড়লে দোষ তার হবে?

দোষ তো তোমার মেয়ে বুদ্ধি-সুদ্ধি একেবারেই কম তোমাদের

ঢেকে ঢুকে চলো দেখি।

এর পরও যদি পুরুষ আক্রমণ করে

চুপটি করে ঘরে বসে থাকো দেখি।

মেয়ে মানুষের এত বাইরে যাওয়ার দরকারটা কী?

আরে মেয়ে মানুষ তুমি এবার তো একটু বুঝতে শিখো দেখি

মহাপুরুষ বলে কথা, বশ্যতা স্বীকার করে নিলে ভেঙে যাবে তো তাদের

হাজার বছর ধরে চলা সেই পৌরুষের গরিমাটা।

তাই ও মেয়ে মানুষ শোন নিজেকে যতটা পারো সংযত করে চলো

এরপরও যদি পুরুষ মানুষ তোমার উপর ঝাঁপিয়ে পড়ে তার দোষ হবে না কোনো।

Zerin Jannat / জেরিন জান্নাত, Dhaka, Bangladesh

Dhaka is a city of dust, chaos and love. I was born and raised here and am living a life full of comfort and love. This city is my home. Yet, there are those to whom the city offers no sanctuary. They are the less fortunate - born into destitution. They are the vulnerables and unwanted. I was reminded of them when I came across the term My City and My Home. Does this city really become home for all? The poem that I have written (in Bangla) is about a girl born into destitution and to a society that doesn't respect women. She lives in a city that offers neither shelter nor acceptance. This is a poem about her life in Dhaka and of her salvation from a world where she is unwanted. She is a product of my imagination but imagination is, at times, the true reflection of reality.

পরিত্রাণ

অট্টালিকার ঢাকা শহরে, জন্ম তার কুঁড়েঘরে।
ভয় তার জন্মের সাথী
জন্মের সময় ভয়, প্রাণে বাঁচতে দিবে তো তাকে?
মেয়ে হয়ে জন্মেছে, সে তো পুত্রসন্তান নয়।

ধুলোর এই ঢাকা শহরে, অযত্নে মেয়েশিশুটি বেড়ে ওঠে
কেবল ভাবে, আজ সে দুবেলা দুমুঠো খেতে পারবে তো?
মনের জ্বালা চোখের পানিতে মেটায় সে
কিন্তু পেটের জ্বালা কেবল অন্নে মেটে।
মায়ের স্তন ছাড়বার পর তার পেটে যে কেবল ক্ষুধার জ্বালা,
প্রতিদিন সে ভয়ে থাকে, আজও কি মিলবে না অন্ন?

শিক্ষার আলো পাবার সাহস সে করে না,
স্বপ্ন দেখে না সে স্বপ্ন ভাঙার ভয়ে।
এই শহর তার নীড়,

336

তবুও এই শহর তাকে মানে না আপন।

নারীতে রূপান্তরিত হবার আগেই লাল বেনারসি পরে,
ভয়ে কাঁপে, পাশের মানুষটা যে অচেনা!

স্বামীর সংসারে অন্নের নেই অভাব, তবুও তার পাতে জোটে না খাবার
যতদিন না মিলবে যৌতুক, ততদিন রবে সে উচ্ছিষ্ট।

মুক্তি মেলে তার সহসা! আঁতুড়ঘরের রক্তাক্ত বিছানায়।
কৃতজ্ঞতায় চোখ বুজে মেয়েটি,
তার সন্তান জীবন বিলিয়ে দিয়েছে মায়ের মুক্তির জন্য।
মাকে নিয়ে যাবে সে অজানার দেশে,
চলে যাবে সে নতুন শহরে, যেথায় মিলবে পরিত্রাণ।
প্রহার থেকে পরিত্রাণ, ক্ষুধা থেকে পরিত্রাণ,
ভয় থেকে পরিত্রাণ।

Atia Rahman Konica / আতিয়া রহমান কণিকা, Dhaka, Bangladesh

যখন একজন মানুষের কোনো সম্মান বা মূল্যায়ন থাকে না তখন তার নিজের ঘর, নিজের শহরও পর হয়ে যায়। একজন নারীর জন্য ঘর কিংবা শহরকে নিজের করে পাওয়াটা আরও কঠিন। অনেক সময় নারীর কাজও নারীকে মুক্তি দিতে পারে না। কর্মহীনতা তো সেখানে অভিশাপ হয়ে দাঁড়ায়। ঘরে বাইরে যেখানেই হোক মূল্যায়ন ছাড়া প্রতিটা মানুষের জীবনই অর্থহীন। যদি সে নিজের অধিকারের ব্যাপারে সচেতন না হয়, সর্বোপরি নিজেকে না জানে তাহলে মুক্তি সম্ভব নয়। নিজের অনুভূতি প্রকাশের ইচ্ছাই আমার লেখার অনুপ্রেরণা। আমি এই শহরে, আমার ঘরগুলোতে নিজেকে খুঁজেছি, নিজেকে বুঝতে শিখেছি। শহরের কাছে, ঘরের কাছে আমি কী? এসবই এদের থেকে পাওয়া অনুপ্রেরণা।

আমার শহরে বসন্ত আসুক

অন্য কোনো ভুবন কিংবা অন্য কোনো সময়রেখা থেকে একটা শহর আজ শোনাবে এক নারীর গল্প, আমার গল্প, যে ছোট্ট একটা শহরের বড় বাড়ি ফেলে এসেছিল এই বড় শহরের ছোট ছোট ছাউনিগুলোতে। একটা থেকে অন্যটায়। ব্যবসায়ীরা এই বাক্সতুল্য ছাউনির নাম দিয়েছে কখনো   ফ্ল্যাট, কখনো অ্যাপার্টমেন্ট। সময়ের সাথে সাথে নারীটার বয়স বেড়েছে, তার জীবনে মানুষ বেড়েছে, তার জীবনে এসেছে পুরুষ, এসেছে শিশু। এইসব ছাউনিরও আয়তনের পরিবর্তন হয়েছে নারীটির পরিবর্তনের সাথে সাথে। সে-ও স্বপ্ন দেখেছিল নয়তলা বাড়ির নকশা করবে, ছোট ছোট ছাউনির আলপনা আঁকবে, অনেকগুলো স্বপ্নের মধ্যে এটা ছিল তার শেষ স্বপ্ন। ছবি আর কবিতার স্বপ্নগুলোর মতো বাড়ি নির্মাণের এই স্বপ্নটাও হারিয়ে যায়। সেই নারী আমার পথ চিরে কখনো আমারই মতো জ্বলতে জ্বলতে ছুটে চলেছে বুকে নিয়ে তার ব্যর্থতার চিতা। আবার কখনো উৎসবের আলোর সাথে মিশে সে-ও হতে চেয়েছে আলোর কণিকা। আমি পড়েছি সেই নারীর অনুভূতি, তার আনন্দ-বেদনার গাথা। আমি যেমন পুড়েছি প্রতিনিয়ত যন্ত্র-মন্ত্র-তন্ত্রের কলঙ্কের হার গলায় পরে, সেও তেমনি পুড়েছে আমারই মতো। চায়ের কোনো ছোট দোকানে চায়ের ধোঁয়ার সাথে সাথে তার দীর্ঘশ্বাসও উবে যেতে দেখেছি আমি। পুড়তে পুড়তে আমার আকাশ কালো হয় বিষাক্ত ধোঁয়ায়, বিষাক্ত নিঃশ্বাসে। তবু এই নারী তার বাঁকা চোখখানি রাখে আকাশের দিকে তার ভেতরের

দহন নিয়ে। এই দহনের শেষ নেই! এই দহন মিশে যায় শহর থেকে ঘরে, আকাশ থেকে মনে।

ঘর? সে কী বলে? এই শহরে প্রাণের স্পন্দন জাগায় কে, এইসব ঘর নাকি মানুষ?

ঢাকা শহরের ফ্ল্যাটগুলোতে চলতে থাকে স্থায়ী-অস্থায়ী পরিবারের অদলবদল। চলে ঘর ভাঙা-গড়ার খেলা। নিঃসঙ্গ মানুষ ঘর বেঁধে পরিবার গড়ছে আবার ঘর ভেঙ্গে মানুষ নিঃসঙ্গ হয়ে পথে নামছে। এদের কেউ পুরোপুরি শহরের, কেউ পুরোপুরি ঘরের আবার কেউ অর্ধেক ঘরের অর্ধেক শহরের।

একটা ঘরের গল্প, বাঁকাচোখের সেই নারীর গল্প শোনায় একটা ঘর। যে নারী পুরো শহরটাকে নিয়ে এই ঘরে বাস করে। রাজনীতি, অর্থনীতি, আবহাওয়া, মহামারীর সাথে সাথে এই ঘরেও পরিবর্তন আসে। পরিবর্তন আসে সম্পর্কে, প্রেম-অপ্রেমে। পরিবর্তন আসে পুরো ভবনে, এর ছোট ছোট ছাউনিগুলোতে। আমার ঘরের দেয়াল জুড়ে রয়েছে সেই নারীর সময়, স্মৃতি, বিস্মৃতি, স্বপ্ন। এসবের প্রকাশ হয়েছে তেলে-জলে আঁকা ছবির মাধ্যমে। অথবা প্রকাশ পেয়েছে কোনো   কবিতায়। এই ঘরে বসতি গড়েছিল যেসব নারী তারা প্রত্যেকেই আলাদা, আবার একই রকম। এই বাঁকা চোখা নারী ভাগ্যের হাতে বন্দী। বন্দী সম্পর্কের হাতে। বন্দী সময়ের হাতে। তার বেঁচে থাকা এইসব স্মৃতি, বিস্মৃতি নিয়ে। সময়-অসময়ে, স্বপ্নে। সে সেখানেই তার চিন্তা যেখানে। তাকে পরিচয় করিয়ে দেবার মতো কোনো পদবি তার নেই, তাই এই বাঁকাচোখা সম্বোধন।

কখনো মনে হয় সেও আমার মতোই ঘর

কিংবা ঘরের কোনো অংশ,

কোনো রক্তমাংসের মানুষ নয় যেন।

কখনো সে আমার দেয়ালের মতো,

কখনো কৃত্রিম আলোয় স্নাত বেলোয়ারি ঝাড়।

কখনো খোলা জানালা। কখনো রুদ্ধদ্বার।

তার আঙুল ধরে বেড়ে ওঠে শিশুরা, কিছু গুল্ম-বৃক্ষরাও। এসবের ভেতরেও কাজ থেমে থাকে না তার, থেমে থাকে না বেঁচে থাকার আয়োজন। এই আয়োজন, এই খেলনা শহর এবং এই খেলনা ঘর চলে টাকার ব্যাটারিতে, ঘরে থাকা বাচ্চাদের খেলনাগুলোর মতো।

টাকা ছাড়া দেয়ালের ঘড়িটাও থেমে যায়। ঘরের নারীটি বিশ্বাস করে টাকাকে কখনো বন্দী করা যায় না, টাকা মানুষকে বন্দী করে। টাকা মুক্তি দিতে পারে না বরং বিক্ষিপ্ত করে। টাকা শুধু বেঁচে থাকতে সাহায্য করে। তারও টাকার প্রয়োজন আছে, টাকা ছাড়া রঙও মেলে না, কলমও মেলে না। প্রয়োজন আর প্রেম এক বস্তু নয়।

বিক্ষিপ্ত এই নারী নিজের মুখোমুখি হলেই কেবল সংহত হয়। নিজের প্রতিবিম্বের মুখোমুখি। এই আমি তার ঘর সেই বক্রনয়নাকে দেখি যখন সে আয়নার সামনে দাঁড়ায়, আয়নার সামনের জন এবং আয়নার ভেতরের জন কতই না আলাদা! তারা দুজন কি দুজনকে চেনে, নারী তার ছায়াকে অথবা ছায়া নারীকে?

চোখ বন্ধ করেই সে নিজেকে দেখতে পায়। আয়না যেন শুধুই ভরসা।

তার গল্প সে শোনে কখনো তার বর্তমান শহরের কাছে, কখনো তার বর্তমান ঘরের কাছে। কখনো আবার শোনায় আয়নার প্রতিবিম্বটি। সে অনেক শহর বদলালেও এই শহরেই কেটেছে জীবনের অর্ধেকটা সময়। বদলেছে অনেক ঘর। তার নিজের পুরোনো বাড়িটি যে কোনো সময় ভেঙে যেতে পারে, ভেঙে নতুন হতে পারে। একটা জিনিস লিখিত হলেই কি নিজের হতে পারে, যদি সেখানে কোনো স্মৃতি না থাকে? আমার ঘর সেখানেই যেখানে আমি আছি এবং আমি স্মৃতি তৈরি করি। আমাকে বাঁচিয়ে রাখে আমার কাজ - ঘরে, শহরে, প্রেমে। আমাকে বাঁচিয়ে রাখে আমার চিন্তা, আমার স্বপ্ন। রঙ কিংবা কলম নিছক বাহানা। চিন্তা আর স্বপ্নগুলিকে এখনো আঁকতে পারিনি, লিখতে পারিনি। নিজেকে আরও যোগ্য হতে হবে, বিন্যস্ত হতে হবে নিজের অনুভূতিগুলোকে মূর্ত করে তুলতে।

এখন শুধু ভালোবাসতে জানি, আগলে রাখতে জানি। আপন করে নিই এই শহরের নিরাপত্তাগুলো, এই শহরের শুদ্ধতাগুলো, এই শহরের মায়াগুলো। তেমনি ঘরেরও। তেমনি আমার আম্মারও।

ঘরের মায়াগুলো, শুদ্ধতাগুলো আর যা কিছু ভালো সব আমার, বাকি সব অস্বীকার করি। আম্মার ভেতরও যা কিছু শুদ্ধ সবই আমার, অন্ধকার তাকে স্পর্শ করে না। অস্বীকার করি।

এই শহরের রোদে পোড়ে ছাদ, পোড়ে নারী। পোড়ে মানুষ। পোড়ে নিয়ম। পুড়ে পুড়ে রঙ হয়। এই শহরের বৃষ্টিতেও ভিজে যায় কোনো রমনীর ছাদ, ভেজে রমনী। ভেজে মানুষ। ভিজতে ভিজতে অনেকেই আবার মানুষ হয়। মানুষ ছবি আঁকে। ছবি আঁকে রিক্সার

পেছনে, ছবি আঁকে রিক্সায় বসে থাকা কোনো যুগলের পোশাকে। ছবি আঁকে রাস্তায়। শিল্পকলায়। ছবি আঁকে দ্রোহে অথবা প্রেমে।

মানুষ কবিতা লেখে। গান গায়। অনুভূতি বুঝতে পারাতে, বলতে পারাতেই বেঁচে থাকার সার্থকতা। এইসব অনুভূতি কবিতায়, গানে, ছবিতে, কথায়। এই অনুভূতি ভাগ করে নেওয়া এবং পারস্পরিক মূল্যায়নই মনুষ্যত্ব। তা-না হলে পৃথিবী বাসযোগ্য হবে না। বাসযোগ্য হবে না কোনো শহর, কোনো ঘর।

ছাদে বসন্ত আসুক। কোকিলের সাথে সাথে নারীটিও গেয়ে উঠুক-

"নিশা লাগিলো রে,
বাঁকা দু'নয়নে নিশা লাগিলো রে..."

Khursheda Akhtar / খুর্শেদা আখতার, Dhaka, Bangladesh

My experience and surrounding observation inspire me to write. Each day passes in the city with a little joy, a little sorrow. Some get absolute comfort, some face obstacles. Some overcome difficulties, some cannot. Consummation of all these inspires me to write 'My City My Home'.

শহরের পথ চলা

শহরের চোরা গলিতে

একটু থেমে, চমকে পিছন ফিরে

চলতে থাকি, আপন গতিতে

নিজের মাঝে হারিয়ে,

নিজেকে খুঁজে ফিরি

আবিষ্কারের নেশাতে।

একটু হাসি, ভালোবাসি

ঝরনার কলকল ধ্বনিতে

সাত সাগর আর তেরো নদীর পাড়েতে

জ্যোৎস্নার স্নানেতো।

হোঁচট খেয়ে থমকে দাঁড়াই

বেদনার গ্লানিতে

কাকের কা কা ধ্বনিতে।

ঘুরে দাঁড়াই সবুজ আভায়

মুক্তির মিছিলে

বাবার প্রতিচ্ছবি আয়নাতে।

এক চিলতে চাঁদের আলোয়

চলি এই শহরে

স্বপ্ন জাল বুনতে বুনতে।

বটের ছায়ায়

মাটির ফোকরে বেড়ে ওঠা বট গাছে

অথবা বনসাইতে।

Ruma Modak / **রুমা মোদক,** Habiganj, Bangladesh

The struggle of the lady, who helps my household chores as a maid servant, against the odds in the society inspires me to write 'My City My Home'.

রাক্ষস কিংবা মানবের ইতিবৃত্ত

সুবলা তেতে আছে গরম করা কড়াইয়ের মতো, গৌরির মুখ নেই সেখানে দুফোঁটা আম্মপক্ষ সমর্থনের জল দেয়। শুরু থেকেই সুবলা গৌরির দ্বিতীয় বিয়ের তীব্র বিরোধী। সুবলা নিজের দ্বিতীয় বিয়ের নাকে খত দেয়া নানা বিরূপ অভিজ্ঞতা সারাদিন বয়ান করে বিভীষিকা জাগাতে চেয়েছিল গৌরির অভিপ্রায়ে। গৌরি তখন সিদ্ধান্তে নিরুপায় স্থির, ভুল হলে ভুল। ঠিক হলে ঠিক। পঁচিশ কি আর শরীরের ডাক অস্বীকার করার মতো সন্ন্যাসী বয়স?

সুবলার কাছে জীবনের একটাই হিসাব, রাক্ষুসে ক্ষুধা। আমি তো দুইবার সাঙ্গা বইছিলাম দুইডা পেট চালাইবার লাইগ্যা, তর তো হেই চিন্তা নাই! ক্যান আপদ ঘাড়ে নেছ! আহা, নিজেকে আপদ ভাবার দিন বুঝি মুড়িয়েছে নটে গাছটির মতো। মেয়েমানুষ নয়, কোনো কোনো পুরুষমানুষই আপদ এখন। অযাচিত উৎপাত থেকে আপন মাংস রক্ষার ঢাল আর জৈবিকতার প্রয়োজন শুধু। নইলে এই যে মন্টু, দ্বিতীয়বার যার গলায় মালা দিয়ে জৈবিক চাহিদাকে সামাজিক বৈধতা দিয়েছে গৌরি, নিজে থেকে না গেলে তাকে তো ঠেলেও বের করা যায়না ঘর থেকে। দুই দুইটি পরিবার জীবনে জড়িয়ে থাকলেও জীবিকা তার কাছে দায়ও নয়, দায়িত্বও নয়, বরং ইচ্ছা অনিচ্ছার ছেলেখেলা। বসিয়ে বসিয়ে দুবেলা থোরাকি যোগানো ছাড়া উপায় থাকেনা গৌরির।

তিনদিন আগে ম্যাডামকে টাকাটা ফেরত দেয়ার কথা। এই কথামতো ফেরত দিতে না পারা ভবিষ্যতে সাহায্য পাবার সব সম্ভাবনার দরজায় খিল দিয়েছে। গত তিনদিন ধরে গৌরি সময় নিয়েছে, আজ না কাল। আজ আর কোনো অজুহাত নেই দেখানোর মতো। জীবনের খরস্রোতে কত খেয়াই পাড়ি দিয়েছে, কত অচেনা পানিপথ, দুই মেয়ে সহ যেদিন বিষ্ণু বাড়ির উঠান থেকে তাড়িয়ে দিয়েছিল, অতর্কিত আশ্রয় হারিয়ে সেদিনও

হুঁশ হারায় নি সে। ঠাণ্ডা মাথায় সম্মুখের পরিস্থিতি পাড়ি দেবার উপায় ভেবেছে, খুঁজে বের করেছে। আজও পারবে এমনই বিশ্বাস।

ম্যাডামের কাছ থেকে মাসের প্রথমে দশ হাজার টাকা চেয়ে এনেছিল গৌরি। এন জি ও'র শেষ কিস্তি দেবার জন্য। আবার নিজের বালাজোড়া সুধীর বণিকের ঘরে বন্ধক দিয়ে টাকাটা এনেছিল ম্যাডামকে ফেরত দেবে বলে। তিনবাড়ির ছুটা রান্নার বেতন পেয়ে সুধীর বণিককে দেবে। দিন, তারিখ, নির্ধারিত সময়ের তিন চারটা জটিল সমীকরণ মেলানোর চেষ্টায় গৌরি যখন ব্যতিব্যস্ত তখন তিনদিন আগে সকাল সকাল বের হওয়ার মুখে গৌরি দেখে চাটাইয়ের নিচে ব্যাগে টাকাটা নেই, নেই তার দ্বিতীয় স্বামী মন্টুও।

নানারকম সম্ভাব্যতা নিয়ে ভাবে সে। নিজেকে থই-হীন লাগে, তবু পথ খোঁজার লগি-বৈঠা শক্ত হাতে ধরে রাখে। এন জি ও'র কিস্তি শেষ হয়ে গেলে সেলাই মেশিনটা তার। ঘরে বসে জীবিকা। প্রতিদিন আঁধার ভোরে বের হবার তাড়া ফুরাবে। আর আজ ভোর না হতেই সেই পরিকল্পনার আনন্দ গিলে খেয়েছে অপ্রত্যাশিত উৎকন্ঠা!

গভীররাতে মন্টু ঘরে না ফেরাতে নিশ্চিন্ত ছিল, নিশ্চিত গীতারাণীর বাড়ি গেছে সে। ঠিকানা তো দুইটাই। মতি, হরি, লিটনের মতো এ বাড়ি ও বাড়ি উঁকিঝুঁকি দেয়ার বাতিক নাই লোকটার।

এই কথাটা কেন জানি সুবলার গায়ে আগুন ধরায়। তার স্পষ্ট যুক্তি দুটি। এমন বসাইয়া বসাইয়া জামাই আদর করলে অন্য ঘরে উঁকি দিবো কী করতে? পাগলেও নিজের বুঝ বুঝে। আর হে তো সেয়ানা পাগল। সাথে দ্বিতীয় যুক্তিটা দিতেও বিন্দুমাত্র দেরি করে না সুবলা। এ তো ভালা হইলে তরে বিয়া করতে গেল ক্যান।

এটা অকাট্য। দুজনের দুইবার দেখা হতো দিনে। যাবার পথে একবার আর আসবার পথে একবার। ইচ্ছাকৃত নয় আবার অনিচ্ছাকৃত কি না, এ ব্যাপারে নিশ্চিত নয় গৌরি। ম্যাডামের ফ্ল্যাটের গেট সাতটায় খোলে আর নয়টা বাজার আগে রান্না সারতে হয়, তাই গৌরি শীত গ্রীষ্ম বসন্ত ভোর ছয়টাতেই ঘর থেকে বের হয়। আর মন্টুর বাস ছাড়ে সকাল সাড়ে ছয়টায়। হাইওয়ে পার হয়ে ঢাকা পৌঁছাতে ছয়/সাত ঘন্টা। আবার ফিরতি বাসে আসতে আসতে সন্ধ্যা। সময়টা যেন কী করে মিলে যায়। নদীর বাঁধের উপর দিয়ে

পরস্পরকে অতিক্রম করার সময় চার চোখের বিনিময়ে উঁচুতে লাল বাতি জ্বলতে থাকা মোবাইল টাওয়ারের মতো শক্তিশালী রশ্মির মতো শরীরে শরীরে চুম্বকের উত্তর দক্ষিনের বিপরীত মেরুর আকর্ষণ ঘটে!

মন্টু টিনের ছাউনি ছেড়ে বাঁশের ঘরে চলে আসে। সেটা মেস ঘর আর এটা সংসার। সেখানে বুয়া তিনবেলা নিয়মের ভাত তরকারি রাঁধে, লবণ-মরিচ কম হোক বা বেশি, খেয়ে নিতে হয়। আর এখানে একটু শুটকির ভর্তায়ও অধিকার থাকে, আরেকটু দাও, বলার আধিপত্য থাকে। কাল ধনেপাতা দিয়ে রসুন ভর্তা থাওয়ার ইচ্ছা ব্যক্ত করা যায়। আরেকটা অধিকারও থাকে। যখন ইচ্ছে শরীরে উপগত হওয়ার অধিকার।

এর জন্য অবশ্য নিজেকেও অস্বীকার করে না গৌরি। পারস্পরিকই বটে। দুই কন্যাসন্তান নিয়ে মায়ের কাছে আসা অবধি দুই চারজনের উঁকি দেয়া অব্যাহত ছিল। লুকিয়ে চাপিয়ে দুয়েকজনের সাথে বিনিময়ও হয়েছে চাওয়া পাওয়া। কিন্তু বিয়ে করে নিলে আর লোকের পাঁচকথার তোয়াক্কা থাকেনা। যদি এটাকেই পেশা করে নেয়ার ধান্দা থাকত তো অন্য কথা। পারুল, নীহার যেমন নিয়েছে। দুই কন্যার দিকে তাকিয়ে গৌরি ও পথ মাড়াতে চায়না। কত বিচার সালিশ বৈঠক করেও আগের ব্যাটা ঘরে নিলোনা। মেয়েদের ভাগ্যকে এই ব্যাটাছেলেদের ইচ্ছা অনিচ্ছার খেলার মাঠ করতে চায় না সে।

কন্যা দুটোকে লেখাপড়া শিখিয়ে চাকরিতে দিতে চায়। যেন ওর মতো বের করে দিলেও চোখে সর্ষে ফুল না দেখে। সুবলার মতো পেটের চিন্তা আর তার মতো সামাজিকতার আতঙ্কে বাড়তি পেট লালনের চিন্তা তাদের পীড়িত না করুক। তাদের পায়ের নিচে মাটি নদীর কূলের আঠালো নরম অবিশ্বস্ত না হোক, বরং ঢাকা যাওয়ার হাইওয়ের মতো শক্ত কিন্তু মসৃণ হোক। কন্যা দুজন ইস্কুলে যায়।

নিজের প্রয়োজন মনে মনে গুরুত্ব দিলেও ব্যাটা কি আর তা দেয়? ঠিকই গৌরির ইচ্ছা অনিচ্ছার তোয়াক্কা না করে যখন তখন ঝাঁপিয়ে পড়ে শরীরে। পুরোনো বউ নিয়তির কাছেও যায়, সব জেনেই নয়াহাটির ইস্কন মন্দিরে গিয়ে মালাবদল করেছে সে। রকিব মিয়ার কলোনীতে ভাড়া থাকা বিশ ঘরের মানুষ যে ছি ছি করেছে, শুধু রকিব মিয়াই মাসের ভাড়া তুলতে এসে বাহবা দিয়েছে। বেশ কইরছস। নাজায়েজ কাম না কইরা একেবারে সাঙ্গা কইরা লইছস।

সুবলা সাথ নেয়, মেয়েকে একা ছাড়তে রাজি নয় সে। পনেরো থেকে আজ চল্লিশ, পঁচিশ বছরের সঙ্গী এ মেয়ে। পথে নেমে হাঁটা দেয় দুজন। রিক্সাভাড়া করে পঞ্চাশ ষাট টাকা খরচের বিলাসিতা এখন মানায় না তাদের। কয়েক প্যাঁচ রাবারে আটকে রাখা ফোনটা বাজতে থাকে অবিরাম বিরক্তিকর রিংটোনে। পাওনাদার ম্যাডামের ফোন।

রাঙাগাঁওয়ের একটাই রাস্তা। এবড়ো থেবড়ো, বর্ষার নরম কাদায় গাড়ির চাকার ছাপ ফেলে যাওয়া প্রত্নতাত্ত্বিক গর্ত সারা রাস্তায়। বাড়িটাও সে চেনে। বিয়ের পর তাকে নিয়ে একবার এসেছিল মন্টু। নেংটা ছেলের দল এক পলক চোখ তুলে তাকায়। মেয়েটা দৌড়ে ঘরে ঢোকে। ও মা বেডি আইছে। ঘরের ভেতর জমাট জমাট একগুঁয়ে অন্ধকার, বাইরের অবাধ আলো ডেকে নেয়ার সুযোগ না পেয়ে ফুঁসছে। সেখানে আধভাঙা তক্তপোশে অস্পষ্ট মন্টু।

নিয়তিরাণী খোঁড়াতে খোঁড়াতে বের হয় ঘর থেকে, রাস্তা পার হতে গিয়ে ট্রাকের নিচে পড়েছিল সে। পুরামাস কচু সেদ্ধ কইরা খাইছি, ব্যাটা মাত্র বাড়িত আইছে এমনেই দৌড়াইয়া আইছস। আমার পোলাপানের দুইডা ভাত খাওয়া সহ্য হয় না তর?

সুবলা গৌরিকে টেনে বের করে বাড়ি থেকে। সুবলা জানে পেটের ক্ষিধার চেয়ে ভয়ংকর রাক্ষস দুনিয়াতে আর কিছু নাই। যুদ্ধংদেহী মনোভাবে আসলেও গৌরিও চুপ করে বের হয়ে আসে। এই বাচ্চাগুলোও তো প্রায় তার কন্যাদের সমবয়সী।

Jannatul Sharmin Nisa / জান্নাতুল শারমিন নিছা,
Moulvibazar, Bangladesh

When I saw the title 'My City My Home' in a paper, first thing that comes to my mind is that I should write about my city.

নারীর চোখে তার শহর

লেখালেখি তেমন একটা পারি না কিন্তু আমার শহর আমার বাড়ি নিয়ে লিখতে হবে তাই একটু কৌতূহলী হয়ে এই বিষয়ে লিখতে বসলাম।

শহর কী? শহর মানেই উঁচু দালান-কোঠা, পাকা রাস্তা, যানবাহন আর জীবিকার সন্ধানে ছুটে চলা ব্যস্ত মানুষ। অবিরাম ছুটে চলা, সময়ের ব্যস্ত চাকায় জীবনকে পিষে ফেলাই শহরে জীবনের স্বরূপ। আপন ভুবন গড়ে তোলা নিয়েই দিনরাত ব্যস্ত শহরের মানুষ। মানবিক সম্পর্কগুলো শহরের মানচিত্রে জটিল এক সমীকরণ। জীবনের ব্যস্ত গোলক-ধাঁধায় পাক খায় মানুষের আবেগ। আর তাই কাউকে দেখা যায় বিলাসী জীবনের ছন্দে আটকে আছে, আর কেউ বা অযত্নে অবহেলায় মানবেতর জীবন যাপন করছে। শহর যাকে দেয় দু'হাত ভরে দেয় আর যাকে দেয় না সে পড়ে থাকে পথের পাশে। শহর যেন অসমতার এক নীরব তটরেখা। এখানে একই আকাশের নিচে কেউ গরীব, কেউ ধনী, কেউ রাজপ্রাসাদে বাস করে আর কেউ ফুটপাতে। রঙিন বিজলীবাতি আর পাকা বাড়ি শহরে জীবনকে নান্দনিক করে দিলেও কেড়ে নিয়েছে মানুষের আবেগ। শহরের চার-দেয়ালে মানুষের জীবন তাই হয়ে গেছে রংহীন আলপনা। ব্যস্ত শহরের দূষিত বাতাসে আটকে পড়া মন তাই ছুটে যেতে চায় দিগন্তের কাছে। এই ব্যস্ত শহরে ছুটে চলছে মানুষ আপন গতিতে কিন্তু নারীদের জীবন আটকে আছে সেই ঘরের কোণে। নারী ছাড়া পুরুষ চলতে পারে না এ একখানা সর্বজনীন সত্য কথা, ঠিক তেমনি নারী ছাড়া কোনো শহরও চলবে না। কিন্তু দুঃখজনক সত্য হলো নারীরা আজ নিজ শহরে নিজ বাড়িতে নিরাপদ নয়। নারীরা নিজের হাতে সাজানো বাড়িতে শারীরিক নির্যাতন আর ধর্ষণের শিকার হচ্ছে, কেউ কেউ এর বিচার পাচ্ছে কিন্তু অধিকাংশই এই অত্যাচারের বিরুদ্ধে রুখে দাঁড়ানোর শাস্তি হিসেবে নিজের প্রাণ হারাচ্ছে। বেগম রোকেয়ার সেই সমাজ এখন আর নেই। নারীরা শিক্ষার সুযোগ পাচ্ছে ঠিকই, কিন্তু নির্যাতিত হচ্ছে জীবনের প্রতি পদে। গৃহিণীরা সারাদিন খেটে বাবা, স্বামী, সন্তানদের

জন্য বাড়িতে থাকার পরিবেশ গড়ে তুলছে কিন্তু দিনশেষে যাদের জন্য এত পরিশ্রম তারাই লাঞ্ছিত করছে নারীদের।

এবার আমার শহর নিয়ে কিছু লিখতে চাই। পৃথিবীর বুকে ছোট একটি দেশ বাংলাদেশ আর এই দেশের সিলেট বিভাগের ছোট একটি শহর মৌলভীবাজার। অনেকেই এই শহরের নাম শোনেনি বা জানেনা। মৌলভীবাজারের মাটিতে জন্ম আমার। এই শহরের আলো বাতাসে বেড়ে উঠা আঠারো বছরের মেয়ে আমি। এথনো বিশ্ব দেখিনি মৌলভীবাজার এর বাইরে পা পড়েনি এথনও তাই আমার কাছে আমার শহর মৌলভীবাজার সব চেয়ে সুন্দর। এই আধুনিক যুগে মানুষ যখন কোলাহলে ব্যস্ত ট্রাফিক জ্যাম এ আটকে আছে আমি তখন চষে বেড়াচ্ছি এই শান্ত নিরিবিলি শহরে। বিশ্ব যখন বড়ো বড়ো মার্ডারার ক্রিমিনালদের পিছনে দৌড়াচ্ছে আমরা তখন কোনো এক বাড়িতে চোর ঢুকলে ডাকাত পড়লে সবাই মিলে ওর পিছনে ধাওয়া করছি তাই বলে এই না যে আমরা আধুনিকতায় পিছিয়ে আছি।

এই শহরের মানুষ বিশ্বের সাথে তাল মিলিয়ে ঠিকই চলছে কিন্তু তা একটা নির্দিষ্ট পর্যায় পর্যন্ত সীমাবদ্ধ। এই ছোট শহরই কিন্তু আমার বাড়ি, এই শহরের পথে ঘাটে বের হলে আপনজনের অভাব হয় না। নারীদের জীবন সব সময় একটি সীমারেখার মধ্যে আবদ্ধ থাকে, আমার ক্ষেত্রেও এর ব্যতিক্রম নয় কিন্তু আমি নারী কোনো এক অদৃশ্য কারণে নারীদের সব সময় ঘরেই থাকতে হবে এমন নিয়ম শুনে এসেছি ছোট থেকে। নারীরা সবকিছুকে আপন করে নিলেও আসলে তাদের নিজের বলে কিছুথাকে না।

আমি নারী, আমি এইসব আলোচ্ছায়া থেকে বেরিয়ে শান্তিতে নিঃশ্বাস নিতে চাই, একটু শান্তির জায়গা চাই যা শুধুই আমার, একান্তই আমার।

গ্রামীণ জনপদ পেরিয়ে শহরের দ্বারপ্রান্তে দাঁড়ালেই মনে হয় প্রকৃতি যেন পিছনে হাঁটছে। শহরের ব্যস্ততম রাস্তায় বাতাস থমকে যায়। সবুজ মাঠ, অবারিত ফসলের ক্ষেত আর বহতা নদীর বড় অভাব ইট, কাঠের শহরে। নান্দনিক স্থাপত্য, আকাশচুম্বী সব অট্টালিকা শহরকে একদিকে যেমন দৃষ্টিনন্দন করে তুলেছে অপরদিকে করে তুলেছে বিষাদময়। বিশ্বায়নের এই যুগে বিলীন হচ্ছে গ্রাম আর বাড়ছে শহর। জীবনের তাগিদে মানুষ পাড়ি জমাচ্ছে গ্রাম ছেড়ে শহরে। মানুষের শহরমুখী হওয়ার প্রবণতা বাড়াচ্ছে শহরের পরিধি। যান্ত্রিকতায় আটকে যাচ্ছে গ্রামীণ জীবনও। শহর যেমন জেগে থাকে নিশিদিন তেমনি শহরের মানুষও জেগে থাকে নিয়ন আলোর শহরে। অফুরন্ত কাজ আর

ব্যস্ততা এই নিয়েই শহরের জীবন। যে জীবনে সম্পর্কগুলোও ইট-পাথরের মতো জড় হয়ে গেছে। তবুও জীবনকে গতিময় করতে, সময়ের সাথে তাল মিলিয়ে চলতে গেলে শহরে আসতে হয়, হতে হয় শহরে। অনেক সুবিধার পাশাপাশি অসুবিধা শহরে জীবনকে যেন বিষিয়ে তুলে। এইসব নেতিবাচক দিকের প্রভাবে শহরে মানুষের মনের আবেগ, ভালোবাসা, আন্তরিকতা ক্রমেই অনুভূতিহীন হয়ে পড়ছে। নিরাপত্তাহীনতা শহরে জীবনের আরেক বিরূপ দিক। আমি নিজেও আমার শহরের মানুষের হাতে নির্যাতিত একজন নারী। কিন্তু আমার অভিযুগ, প্রতিবাদ, ঘৃণা এই শহরের এই পৃথিবীর বিরুদ্ধে না, বরং শতাব্দী ধরে গড়ে উঠা হাজার হাজার চিন্তার ফলে তৈরি হওয়া পাশবিক মানসিকতার বিরুদ্ধে। আমি স্বপ্ন দেখি এক শান্তির শহরের। আমার শহর আমার স্বপ্নকে ধারণ করে। এমনকি এই শহরের আনাচে কানাচে এমন অনেক নারী রয়েছে যারা চার দেয়ালের বন্ধ কারাগার থেকে বেরিয়ে এসে এই শহরকে নিয়ে স্বপ্ন দেখতে চায়। একরাতে বিপ্লব হয় না। এটি সেই শহর নয় যার স্বপ্ন আমি দেখি, আমরা দেখি। কিন্তু বিপ্লব এক মুহূর্তে হয় আমি চাই সেই বিপ্লবের শুরু আমাকে দিয়ে হোক আমি আমাকে দিয়ে গড়ে তুলবো আমার এবং আমাদের স্বপ্নের শহর।

Ummay Honey / উম্মে হানি, Dhaka, Bangladesh

I live in Dhaka city since 2013. When I first met with the city of Dhaka and the people, I was overwhelmed. But gradually when I went through deeper inside the context of this city, I think there is a purpose for every individual here. Their energy, enthusiasm, and hard work show me the inner meaning of life. The sincerity and hard work of a rickshaw puller sometimes amaze me to do my work properly. So I want to tell the story of people whose stories are untold and unseen. The diversity of life of people helps me to make this city my own home and for this reason, I am writing about my city and my home. And preferably the stories of women inspire me to write about their lifestyle. In my surroundings, I have seen a lot of women who do an extremely difficult job with smiling faces. Their sacrifices, joy and sorrow inspire me all the time.

মানুষের শহর

আমার শহর, আমার বাড়ি। আমার শব্দটির আধিক্য থাকলেও বলতে চাই আমাদের গল্প। একটা শহর, একটা বাড়ি কোনো কিছুরই অস্তিত্ব কল্পনা করা যায় না নারীদের ছাড়া। আমি বাংলাদেশের ২৫ বছর বয়সী একজন নারী, আমার শহর ঢাকা। এই শহরের আজন্ম বাসিন্দা না হলেও এই শহর ঘিরে আশা আকাঙ্ক্ষার শেষ নেই আমার। প্রতিদিনের বাস্তবতায় জীবন অতিবাহিত হচ্ছে আমার আশেপাশের মানুষের কোলাহল আর হাসি-কান্নার সঙ্গী হয়ে। এখানকার অধিকাংশ মানুষ অন্য শহরতলী অথবা গ্রাম থেকে এসেছে একটি সম্ভাবনাময় ভবিষ্যতের আশায়। তাই আমার মত ভাড়া বাড়িই তাদের আপন ঠিকানা। বছর বছর নতুন ঠিকানায় আমাদের আবাস বদলায় কিন্তু বদলায়না ভালো থাকার প্রচেষ্টা। ভাড়া বাড়ির এক চিলতে বারান্দা সারাদিনের পরিশ্রম শেষে মায়ের স্বস্তির জায়গা। জানলার ফাঁক গলে একটুখানি আকাশের দেখা পাওয়া অন্যরকম প্রশান্তি দেয়। ছাদে গেলে পাখিদের উড়াউড়ি ভুলিয়ে দেয় ক্লান্তি আর অবসাদ। শিশুদের কোলাহলে মুখরিত চারপাশ যেন আনন্দের বার্তা বয়ে নিয়ে

আসে সবার কাছে। এই শহরের এককজন নারীর জীবন এককরকম, কিন্তু এক অদ্ভুত সুতোয় গাঁথা। কারো একবেলার খাবার জোটাতে অনেকখানি ইচ্ছা বিসর্জন দিতে হয় পরিস্থিতির কারণে, গ্রহণ করতে হয় নিদারুন পরিশ্রমের কাজ। অন্যদিকে এটাও বাস্তব যে, অনেক নারীই পারিবারিকভাবে এসব সুবিধা–প্রাপ্ত – তাঁরা চেষ্টা করছেন ওই অসহায় নারী ও তাঁদের শিশুদের সাহায্য করতে। এই ব্যাপারটাই এই দুই দল নারীদের এক সুত্রে বেঁধেছে। আমি হয়ত এই দুই দলের কোনো সক্রিয় সদস্য নই, তবে আমিও আছি শহরের নিজস্ব অস্তিত্ব হয়ে; কারণ আমার শহরের প্রাণ হলো মানুষ। শহরের আয়তনের তুলনায় অনেক বেশি মানুষ বাস করে এখানে। নারীদের সংখ্যা পুরুষের কাছাকাছি। সাংস্কৃতিক এবং ধর্মীয় উৎসব গুলো নারীদের কাছ থেকেই পূর্ণতা পায় অধিকাংশ ক্ষেত্রে। একসাথে ঈদ, পূজা, বড়দিন আর বুদ্ধ-পূর্ণিমার মত অনুষ্ঠানে নারীদের সরব উপস্থিতিই যেন সামাজিক মেলবন্ধনের ইঙ্গিত দেয়। এই নারীরা হয়তো খুব সাধারণ একটি বাড়ির প্রতিনিধি কিন্তু তাদের আন্তরিকতা আর ভালোবাসায় উৎসব রঙিন হয়ে উঠে। তাঁরা জানেন কীভাবে প্রতিকূলতা ও সীমাবদ্ধতাকে সহজাত ভাবেই অতিক্রম করতে হয়। ঈদের মায়ের হাতের পায়েস আর মিষ্টির ভালোবাসা মাখা আর পূজা পার্বণের প্রদীপের আলোয় আলোকিত পুরো পরিবারের মানুষ গুলোই আমরা। আমার শহরের নারীদের প্রতিদিনের সহজ জীবনযাপন আমাকে শিখিয়েছে যতটুকু আছে ততটুকু দিয়েই জীবনকে পুরোপুরি উপভোগ করা যায় এবং সবার সাথে আনন্দ ভাগ করে নেওয়া যায়। আমাদের শহরেই দেশের সর্বোচ্চ ক্ষমতার অধিকারী আমাদের প্রধানমন্ত্রী থাকেন এবং তিনিও একজন নারী। প্রতিনিয়ত দেশকে বিশ্বের কাছে তুলে ধরার মাধ্যমে নারীদেরকে শক্তি আর প্রেরণা যোগাচ্ছেন। প্রত্যেকেই নিজ নিজ জায়গা থেকে এই শহরকে ভালোবাসছেন তাঁদের কাজের মাধ্যমে। রাস্তায় যে নারী তাঁর সন্তানের জন্য ভিক্ষা করছেন, তিনিও সন্তানকে সুনাগরিক করার ইচ্ছা পোষণ করেন। যাঁরা শিক্ষিকা, তাঁরা ছাত্রছাত্রীদের দেশপ্রেম বিষয়ে শিক্ষা দিচ্ছেন। যাঁরা ডাক্তার তাঁরা রোগীদের পরম মমতায় সেবা দিচ্ছেন। আইন পেশা, কর্পোরেট অফিস, গার্মেন্টস সেক্টরসহ প্রত্যেকটি অর্থনৈতিক ক্ষেত্রে নিজেকে তুলে ধরছেন। যাঁরা বাসায় থাকছেন সেই নারীরাও থাকার পরিবেশকে সুন্দর করার চেষ্টা করছেন

নিয়মিত। আমার বাসার ছোট্ট ব্যালকনির কিছু ফুলগাছ যেমন পরিবারের প্রত্যেক সদস্যের ভালোবাসায় বেড়ে উঠছে তেমনি মানুষের ভালোবাসায় এই শহর নতুন করে আলোকিত হচ্ছে প্রতিদিন। সন্ধ্যার রাস্তায় জ্বলতে থাকা নিয়ন বাতি গুলোর মত হাজারো স্বপ্ন শহরের নারীদের মনে থাকে। কিছু পূরণ হয়, কিছু হয়না কিন্তু স্বপ্ন দেখা থেমে নেই। আমার শহরের মানুষের সরলতা জীবনের অন্যসব জটিলতা ভুলতে সাহায্য করে। সময়ের সাথে অনেক কিছু বদলাচ্ছে কিন্তু যেটা বদলাচ্ছেনা সেটা হলো মানুষের প্রাণশক্তি। ঢাকা শহরের বাতাসে ধূলিকণা ওড়ে, এছাড়াও অনেক ক্ষতিকর পদার্থ ভেসে বেড়ায়; কিন্তু এই পরিবেশের মাঝেও কীভাবে সুন্দর ভাবে বাঁচা যায় সেই পদ্ধতি যেন নারীদের থেকে ভালো আর কেউ জানেন না। তাইতো শহরের মানুষগুলো ভালোমন্দ সময় পার করে আবারো নতুন ভাবে বাঁচার অনুপ্রেরণা পায়। পুরনো ঢাকার ঘুপচি গলিপথ, রিকশা, মানুষের কোলাহল আর নতুন ঢাকার অত্যাধুনিক বিল্ডিং আর ঝলমলে আলোকচ্ছটা সব নিয়েই আমাদের এই প্রিয় শহর। এখানেই আমি স্বপ্ন দেখি, বিফল হই কিন্তু হাল ছেড়ে দিই না। আমার বয়সী নারীদের সংখ্যা বাড়ছে প্রতিনিয়ত এই শহরে। এবং এই সকল নারীরাই জেদ, পরিশ্রম আর আত্মবিশ্বাস দিয়েই টিকিয়ে রেখেছে শহরের কলকাঠি। এই শহরের নারীদের ভবিষ্যত পরিকল্পনা তাঁদের জীবনের মতই খুবই সাধারণ। বেশিরভাগ নারীই তাদের সন্তান-সন্ততিদের নিয়েই ভাবেন। আমি আমার মাকে দেখি তাঁর সমস্ত পরিকল্পনা যেন আমাদের ঘিরেই এবং এতে তিনি অত্যন্ত সন্তুষ্ট আর আনন্দিত। একটি সীমিত আর ক্ষুদ্র গন্ডির মধ্যেই তাঁদের পরিকল্পনা গুলো বাঁধা থাকে। সীমিত আয়ের নারীদের সংখ্যাই বেশি এখানে। সেরকম ভাবে তাঁদের কর্মক্ষেত্র বিস্তৃত হয়নি। কিন্তু সব পেশায়ই নারীরা সগৌরবে প্রতিনিধিত্ব করছেন। যে পেশাতেই থাকুন না কেন এই শহরের অধিকাংশ নারীরা তাঁদের মাতৃ পরিচয় নিয়ে খুবই গর্বিত। তাঁদের কাছে পরিবার এবং বাড়ি দুটোই খুব গুরুত্ব বহন করে। এমনকি যাঁদের নিশ্চিত আশ্রয় নেই তাঁরাও এই শহরের অস্থায়ী বাড়িটিকে আপন করে নেন পরম যত্নে। এজন্যই নারীদের সাথে এই শহর এবং বাড়ির নিবিড় যোগাযোগ। প্রত্যেকদিনের কাজ এবং বিশ্বাসের মাধ্যমে তাঁরা তা জানান দিচ্ছেন। শহরের একপ্রান্তে রেলস্টেশনে অপেক্ষায় থাকা ভিন্ন ভিন্ন যাত্রীদের গন্তব্য

যেমন ভিন্ন এই শহরের নারীদের জীবনও তেমনি বৈচিত্র্যে পূর্ণ। রেললাইনের পাশে বস্তিতে শীতের রাতে একসাথে বসে আগুনের উষ্ণতা নেওয়া মানুষের কাছে জীবন মানে একটুখানি আরাম আর স্বস্তি। আর এই শহরের নারীরা প্রতিনিয়ত পরিবারের মানুষ গুলোকে সেই স্বস্তি আর ভালোবাসা দিয়ে যান। তাঁদের অক্লান্ত পরিশ্রম আর আন্তরিকতায় শিশুরা বেড়ে উঠছে আর এভাবেই পরবর্তী প্রজন্ম এগিয়ে যাচ্ছে।

Papia Talukder / পাপিয়া তালুকদার, Sylhet, Bangladesh

My write up talks about the horrific situation a lady, who was unfortunately raped. It is composed of society's treatment towards such loathsome work, and the discrimination that the lady faces in her lives. All of these inspired me to write about my city.

ডিগনিটি বাই স্যাক্রিফাইস

একটি স্বচ্ছ বোতল। বিপরীত ভাবে এফোঁড়, ওফোঁড় করে দুটি ছিদ্র করা হয়েছে। এটা দিয়ে চোখ পেতে আকাশ দেখতে ভালোই লাগছে। নীলাকাশ, মাঝেমধ্যে একটি চিল উড়ে যাচ্ছে। হয়তো অনেক চিল উড়ে যাচ্ছে। কিন্তু নীলুর চোখে একটি চিলই পড়ছে। দুটি ডানা দিয়ে সাম্যাবস্থা বজায় রেখে ধী-ধী করে উড়েই যাচ্ছে। এই পাখিটি কি ইচ্ছেমতো বিভিন্ন জায়গায় উড়তে পছন্দ করে? হয়তো করে। আবার না'ও করতে পারে। নীলুর আবার পায়ের তলায় খড়ম অবস্থা। এক জায়গায় বসে থাকতে ভালো লাগে না।

আহা! মানুষের যদি ডানা থাকত। এমনটা হলে নীলু প্রতিদিন পুরো পৃথিবীটাকে ঘুরে দেখতা। তবে কাদের ঘুরে দেখতো, তা নিয়ে কিছুটা সন্দিহান। হয়তো মেয়েদেরই দেখতো। হম! রাস্তা দিয়ে হাঁটার সময় যে মেয়ে গুলো মাথা নিচু করে কেবল রাস্তার ধুলো দেখে হাঁটে, তাদের? নাকি, কফি শপের সামনে মুখে সিগারেটের ধোঁয়া ছাড়ে, তাদের? বুঝতে পারছে না। নাকি, বিশ্ববিদ্যালয়ের আশেপাশে ছোট খাটো টিলার পাদদেশে বসে তাস খেলায় মগ্ন মেয়েগুলোকে? অনেকে আবার গাঁজা, ইয়াবার ঘ্রাণে মগ্ন হয়ে থাকে। হয়তো তাদেরকেই। নাকি, সাদা চামড়ার ওই মেয়েটা, যে থিসিস করতে বিশ্ববিদ্যালয়ে এসেছে? শাড়ি, জামা পরা হলুদ চুলগুলোকে বিন্যস্ত করে বাঙালি সাজার ভান করা মেয়েটি? যে সংস্কৃতি মানতে গিয়ে পুরো শিখে ফেলেছে! থাক, এদের গল্প বাদ। একটু ভাবি অন্যদের নিয়ে।

বিশ্ববিদ্যালয়ে পড়া পবন নামের মেয়েটার কী অবস্থা কে জানে। তার কাজই হলো ঘুরে ঘুরে অবাঞ্ছিত বিষয়বস্তু দেখা। কোথায় কোথায় ঘোরে বলা মুশকিল। আসলে যায় কোথায়? মজার কথা হলো, যায় না কোথায়! সিনেমা হল, হাট-বাজার, ব্যস্ত রাস্তা, সেই

ক্লিনিক যেখানে হাজার হাজার অসুস্থ মানুষের আনাগোনা। কে কাকে দেখছে কোন ইয়ত্তা নেই। প্রতিটি মানুষ নিজেদের সুস্থতার অপেক্ষায় অধীর। কেন জানি মনে হয়, এখানেই এক গভীর সত্য কাজ করে। একাত্মবাদের এক বিশাল সমাহার এখানে। মেয়েটি ক্লিনিকের সব বুয়াদের চেনে। তারাও ওকে চেনে। এদের দেখলে 'বিল্ডাংশ্রোম্যান' এর ক্যারেক্টারগুলার কথা মনে পড়ে। জাস্ট ফর লিভ, মোরালিটির সাথে যুদ্ধ। কোন বুয়া কার হয়ে কাজ করে সব জানে সে। তাকিয়ে থাকে প্রস্রাব টেস্ট করার জন্য টিউব হাতে দাঁড়িয়ে থাকা নারীদের দিকে। আবার মাঝে মাঝে ঘুরে আসে ব্লিচিং ফেলা পাবলিক টয়লেটগুলোতে। একফোঁটা লাল ভালবাসার চিহ্ন দেখতে চায়। বা ভুল করে কেউ মাশুল শুধতে গিয়ে বড় কোনো অংশ বিনে ফেলে গেল কি না! তার কেবল একটা অসম্পৃক্ত অবয়ব চোখে ভাসছে। হয়তো ছড়িয়ে থাকা কিছু পেজো তুলো ছিল। সেটাতে একটা অস্তিত্ব মুড়ে বিনে ফেলে দেওয়া হয়েছিল। তারপর এক মেয়ে শূন্যে ঝোলা রশিতে ধরে এক নিবৃত কান্না দিয়েছিল। পাশে তার বিক্রি হয়ে যাওয়া সোনার লভ্যাংশ দানকারী এক আত্মগোপনকারী নারী বসে বসে সব দেখছে। কিন্তু সকালের আকাশ-মামার রশ্মি দুজনেই দেখেছে। এ এক নতুন জীবনাধ্যায়।

মাইকে ডেকে সবাইকে ক্লিনিক ছাড়ার জন্য বলা হয়েছে। একে একে সব গুলো বাতি নিভে গেল। সিঁড়িগুলোও অন্ধকারে ডুবে গেল। ক্লিনিকের এধারে ওধারে ফুটপাতে একটা রহস্যময় ঘোর অন্ধকার নেমে এসেছে। বয়সের শ্রেণিভেদ ভুলে সবাই স্থান দখল করে নিচ্ছে। ক্লিনিকের ওধারেই মেয়েটির বাসা। হেঁটে রাস্তা পেরিয়ে নিজের বাসার দিকে চলে যাচ্ছে।

একটা সরু গলির মুখেই বাড়িটা। দেখতে পরিত্যক্ত। শ্যাওলা ধরা বিল্ডিং-এ টিনে জং ধরা চাল। ইংরেজ আমলের ইস্পাতে বানানো ভারি একটা দরজা। অনেকের ধারণা এখানে এক ইংরেজ অফিসার থাকতেন। অগণিত মেয়ের সম্ভ্রম লুষ্ঠিত হয়েছে, তাতে সন্দেহ নেই। এখন এখানে কয়েকটি মেয়ে থাকে। কেউ বিশ্ববিদ্যালয় আর কেউ কলেজে পড়ে। এখানে যে যার মতো স্বতন্ত্র প্রার্থী। 'না' বলে কোনো বিরোধিতা আসে না, বরং পদ্ধতি বলে দেওয়া হয়। যাই হোক, মেয়েটি রাস্তায় কাউকে দাঁড়িয়ে থাকতে দেখেছে অন্ধকার থেকে এক স্বর ভেসে এলো - ও নিশি দি! ওপাশে কিন্তু অনেকে দাঁড়িয়ে আছে। এদিক দিয়ে যান, নাহলে আপনার সম্ভ্রম নিয়েও খেলবে মানুষরূপী পশুগুলো।

ওদের শরীরের দূষিত শুক্রাণুগুলো আপনার শরীরের অংশ হবে।

নিশি দিঃ টুম্পা!

টুম্পাঃ হ্যাঁ দিদি। আপনি এ পথে কেন? এটা অভিশপ্ত। তাড়াতাড়ি অন্য পথে যান।

নিশির মাথায় ধাক্কা এলো। টুম্পা! কিন্তু কীভাবে। সে তো কবেই! না, এটা মনে করতে চাই না। ঠিক তখনই নিশির চোখ খুলে গেল। কক্ষটি অন্ধকার। পাশেই টুম্পার বেডটি পরে আছে। একপাশে মাধু শুয়ে আছে। তার মানে এটা দুঃস্বপ্ন। খানিক পরেই ফজরের আযান শোনা গেল। নিশি, মাধু কে জাগিয়ে তুললো। আজ তাদের সাক্ষ্য দেবার দিন। টুম্পা কলেজ ছাত্রী ছিল। বয়সের তুলনায় সুন্দরী, স্ফীত বুক, সুডৌল বাহু। এক কথায়, বাহ! তরুণী মেয়ের রূপ আর মায়া সব কিছুকে ছাড়িয়ে যায়। এক মধ্যবয়স্ক ড্রাইভার তার পিছু নিয়েছে। সব সময় তাকে বিরক্ত করে।

ড্রাইভারঃ ওগো মেয়ে! দেবো নাকি চুমু!

বুকে, পিঠে আর নিচে। গায়ে কি ফুলের গন্ধ? গোলাপ নাকি রজনীগন্ধা! তারপর জিভ বাঁকিয়ে ইঙ্গিত। মাঝেমধ্যে বুকে থাবা দিয়ে পালায়। তারপর এক সন্ধ্যায় ঘটে করুণ এক ঘটনা। কয়েকজন লোক তাদের লালসাকে তৃপ্তি দিয়েছে। টুম্পার সম্ভ্রম কেড়ে নেওয়ার নৃশংস ঘটনার ভিডিও সামাজিক যোগাযোগ-মাধ্যমে ছেড়ে দেয়। রাজনৈতিক ব্যক্তি আর আম-জনতা দুইই নীরব। আন্দোলন করতে বেরিয়ে পড়ে শিক্ষার্থীরা। সামাজিক মাধ্যমে ছড়িয়ে পড়া ভিডিও তে দেখা যাচ্ছে পশুগুলো কীভাবে মেয়েটিকে অত্যাচার করছে। অত্যাচারীদের মেয়েটি বাবাও ডেকেছে, পিপাসায় পানিও চেয়েছে। কিন্তু মৃত্যু ছাড়া কেউ ওর ডাক শুনে নি। তারপর শিক্ষার্থীরা প্ল্যাকার্ড নিয়ে কালো রং-এ মুখ ঢেকে মশাল হাতে প্রতিবাদ করেছে। '৭১ এর পাক-সেনা নয়, কিছু জারজই এদেশে মেয়েদের ভোগ করার পদক্ষেপ নিয়েছে। বাদ যাচ্ছে না কেউই। অসংখ্য শিশুদের যোনি কেটে বড়ো করে অত্যাচার করেছে। বৃদ্ধাও বাদ যায় না। আর যুবতীরা তো বলির পাঁঠা। অসংখ্য যোনি অপবিত্র হয়েছে, এর বিনিময়ে পশুগুলোর মৃত্যুর আইন জারি করতে পেরেছে এই অবহেলিত বীরাঙ্গনারা। যে সম্মান কেড়ে নেবে, তার ঘাড় থেকে মাথা নেওয়া হবে। সেলাম সে নারীদের, যারা ২০২০ তে এসে সতীত্ব হারিয়ে

সোনার বাংলায় ৯(১) ধারায় জোর করে বলাৎকারীদের মৃত্যুর আইন বানিয়েছেন। এই আইন সতীত্ব রক্ষার আইন।

সবার কথা চিন্তা করে নীলুর মাথা ভারি হয়ে গেল। আকাশের চিলটার মাথাও ভারি হয়ে গেল। ডানা দিয়ে কেবল ঝাপটে যাচ্ছে। হয়তো সেও নীলুর মতো, কিছু মেয়ে নিয়ে ভাবছে। কিন্তু পাখিটি কি নীলুকে নিয়ে ভাবে! তার গায়ে যে দাঁত আর নখের দাগ তা কি পাখিটি দেখে! হয়তো না। এত উপর থেকে এ সামান্য ক্ষত চোখে পড়ার মত নয়। হ্যাঁ, হয়তো নয়। তবে এটা সত্যি, যখন থেকে নীলু বোতল দিয়ে আকাশ দেখা শুরু করেছে, তখন থেকেই চিলটা উড়তে শুরু করেছে। এই চিলটা বন্ধু না শত্রু, বুঝতে পারেনা। নীলাকাশে ঝাপসা সোনালি রঙ এসেছে। এসবই দেখে নীলু। এদিকে নীলুর মা ফল আর ভারি খাবার নিয়ে দাঁড়িয়ে আছেন। নীলুর এখন শক্তির প্রয়োজন। নীলুও অনেক ধকল সয়েছে। অনেক গুলো দাঁত তার শরীরটাকে ফালি ফালি করে দিয়েছিল। তার দাগ এখনো শুকায়নি। সপ্তাহখানেক পরে সেও ব্লিচিং ফেলা টয়লেটে একদলা রক্ত ফেলে এসেছিল। নীলুর চোখের নিচে কালো দাগ আরও বেড়ে গেছে। তাহলে টুম্পারও এমন হয়েছিল। হঠাৎ করে সবার মুখ ভুলে গেছে নীলু। মনে পড়ে না এরা কারা। অদৃশ্য ছায়ার মতো মাথায় ঘুরপাক খাচ্ছে। সাথে চিলটার পাখা ঝাপটানোর শব্দ। সব কিছু মিলিয়ে নীলুর তন্দ্রা এসে গেল। গাঢ়, গভীর তন্দ্রা। এই তন্দ্রায় সব কিছু নিরাকার। কেবল কিছু কান্না আর চিলটার করুণ সুর ভেসে যাচ্ছে।

Sushipta Das / সুশিপ্তা দাশ, Moulvibazar, Bangladesh

Our Liberation war in 1971 inspired me a lot.

একটি বিস্ফোরণ ও কিছু স্বপ্নের মৃত্যু

কিছু বুঝে ওঠার আগেই প্রচণ্ড বিস্ফোরণে ছিন্ন ভিন্ন হয়ে গেল একদল সাহসী যোদ্ধার স্বাধীন দেশে নতুনভাবে বাঁচার সোনালী স্বপ্নটুকু।

দাউ দাউ করে পুড়ছে সব। মাথা গোঁজার আশ্রয়, রক্ত জল করা ক্ষেতের ফসল, গ্রামের শেষ মাথায় সুনিবিড় ছায়াতলে গড়ে ওঠা একমাত্র গ্রামীণ হাট, সবকিছুই পুড়ছে। পরাধীনতার শিকলে বাঁধা জীবন বয়ে বেড়ানো আর সম্ভব নয়। মুক্তি চাই! তাইতো সকলের সাথে দেশ রক্ষার লড়াইয়ে সামিল হলো পঁচিশ বছরের টগবগে যুবক মতি।

আজ সকাল থেকেই আকাশে কালো মেঘের আনাগোনা। সাথে নলিনের মুখেও বেদনার স্পষ্ট ছাপ। মনে পড়ছে সহধর্মিণীর সেই মায়া ভরা চাহনি। শেষবার যখন কৃষ্ণাকে দেখেছিল নলিন, সেই মায়াভরা চোখ দিয়ে গড়িয়ে পড়েছিল কয়েক ফোঁটা অশ্রু। মুখটা আকাশের মতই মেঘাচ্ছন্ন। সেই দৃষ্টি নলিনের সারা শরীর জুড়ে যেন এক ঝড় তুলে দিল। তার মনে হলো কৃষ্ণাকে দু'বাহতে আষ্টেপৃষ্ঠে জড়িয়ে রাখে, পালিয়ে যায় দূরে কোথাও। যেখানে গেলে নাগাল পাবেনা এই বর্বরতা, কেউ ছিনিয়ে নেবে না বাঁচার সম্বলটুকু, ভালোবাসার আলিঙ্গনে জড়ানো মানুষ দুটোকে আলাদা করবেনা কোনো নরপিশাচের দল। আকাশ হেসে উঠবে প্রেমের নীলাভ রঙে, বাতাসে ভাসবে প্রেমের মিষ্টি সুবাস। এমন জীবন কখনও আসবে কি? নাহ বিদায় নিতেই হলো নলিনকে। প্রেয়সীর উষ্ণ আলিঙ্গন, ভালোবাসামাখা টলটলে চোখ দুটো উপেক্ষা করে এগিয়ে গেল নলিন। চোখের সামনে ঝাপসা হতে লাগলো কৃষ্ণা। আবার হবে তো দেখা??

আজ মতির চোখে ঘুম নেই। নিদ্রাহীন চোখ দুটো রক্তবর্ণ। যুদ্ধক্ষেত্রে চোখের সামনে প্রিয় সহযোদ্ধা নলিনকে চিরতরে শেষ হতে দেখে বুকের ভেতরটা দুমড়ে মুচড়ে গেছে তার। শত্রুপক্ষের গুলির আঘাতে ঝাঁঝরা হয়ে যায় নলিনের বুক, গগনবিহারী

আর্তচিৎকারে মুহূর্তেই যেন চারপাশটা কেঁপে ওঠে। এ যেন গুলির চেয়েও আরো ভয়ংকর। কিছু বুঝে ওঠার আগেই নিভে গেল নলিনের জীবনপ্রদীপ। একটু আগেই বীরদর্পে বুক চিতিয়ে শত্রুর প্রাণনাশে ব্যস্ত নলিন হট করেই কেমন যেন শান্ত হয়ে গেল। চোখ দুটো তাকিয়ে আছে মতির দিকে। ইশ কী বিভৎস লাগছে, কী অদ্ভুত মৃত্যু। পাহাড়ি ঝরনার মত কুলকুল শব্দে রক্তের বন্যা বয়ে চলেছে নলিনের শরীর জুড়ে। মতির মনে হলো তার হৃদস্পন্দন বন্ধ হয়ে যাচ্ছে। চারদিকে গুচ্ছ গুচ্ছ রক্তের ছোপ। সেও হয়ত মারা যাবে এখন। মাথা ঘুরছে মতির। একেই কি মৃত্যু বলে? নাহ্ মতি দিব্যি বেঁচে আছে। মৃত্যু স্পর্শ করেনি তাকে। শুধু শেষনিঃশ্বাস অব্দি নলিনের তেজোদীপ্ত চোখ দুটো ভাসছে। ভয়হীন চোখদুটো যেন বলছে যতক্ষণ শ্বাস ততক্ষণই লড়াই। আচ্ছা তার কি মনে পড়ছিল কৃষ্ণা বৌদির কথা? নাকি মুক্তির এই সংগ্রাম তাকে করে তুলেছিল হিংস্র পুরুষ, যার হৃদয়ে ভালোবাসা নেই শুধুই মুক্তির নেশা। নাহ্ আর ভাববেনা মতি। এমনই কত শত নলিন প্রান হারাচ্ছে রোজ। বুক চিতিয়ে দাড়াচ্ছে শত্রুর বুলেটের সামনে। রক্তে রক্তে ভিজে উঠছে চিরসবুজ মাটি। নাহ, চিরসবুজ বলা ভুল। এ মাটিতে এখন শুধু রক্তের দাগ। মাটিতে মিশে আছে টকটকে লাল রক্ত। মেটে রঙের সাথে পচে যাওয়া সবুজ আর টকটকে রক্ত মিলে এক নতুন রঙের সৃষ্টি হয়েছে। সাথে গুমোট গন্ধ। নিহাস ভারি হয়ে আসে।

মতি পকেট থেকে শেফালির চিঠিটা বের করে গন্ধ নেয়। রক্তপচা মাটির মত গুমোট গন্ধ নয়, মিষ্টি মেয়েলি গন্ধ। ভালোবাসার কামনা মিশ্রিত মিষ্টি সুবাস। বুক ভরে ওঠে মতির। গোটা গোটা অক্ষরে ভালোবাসার এক রচনা। "অপেক্ষায় থাকব তোমার। আসবে তো তুমি?"

শেফালির লেখার ভাষা আরো দুর্বল করে দেয় মতিকে। তার কি ফেরা হবে কখনও শেফালির কাছে? এই যুদ্ধ শেষ হবে কখনও?

ধ্বংসের শেষ হয় একদিন। মুক্তির নেশায় পাগল দামাল ছেলেদের বহুমুখী লড়াই, ভারত থেকে মুক্তিবাহিনীর ক্রমশ ক্যাম্প অভিমুখে আসার খবরে ভীত হয়ে পড়ে পাকবাহিনী। অবস্থা বেগতিক দেখে ৮ ডিসেম্বর ভোরেই মনু ব্রিজসহ বিভিন্ন স্থাপনা ধ্বংস করে পালিয়ে যায়। মুক্ত হয় মৌলভীবাজার শহর। ওড়ে মুক্তির পতাকা। ১৬ই

ডিসেম্বর চিরতরে গোলামি জীবনের অবসান ঘটিয়ে চূড়ান্ত বিজয় অর্জিত হয়। পূর্ণ হয় মতি নলিনদের যত্নে বোনা স্বাধীনতার স্বপ্ন। মতি বেঁচে আছে দিব্যি। কিন্তু শেফালী কেমন আছে? আজও মতির অপেক্ষায় আছে তো? যুদ্ধের এই কটা মাসে তো একবারও খোঁজ নেওয়া হয়নি। ভালো আছে তো? নাহ, আর তর সইছে না। লজ্জাবনত গোলাপের পাপড়ির মত শুভ্র মুখখানা যেন টানছে মতিকে।

২০ ডিসেম্বর। স্বাধীন দেশ। বাড়ি ফিরবে ওরা। অপেক্ষারত পরিবারের কাছে। আর কেউ জ্বালাবে না বাসস্থান, কেড়ে নেবে না অন্ন, পোড়াবে না স্বপ্ন। ধ্বংসস্তূপ থেকে হেসে ওঠে প্রাণের প্রিয় জন্মভূমি মা। বাড়ি ফেরার আগে সকলে জড়ো হলো স্কুল ঘরে।

বিদায়বেলা। পাকবাহিনীর ফেলে যাওয়া গোলা বারুদ গ্রেনেড সহ জীবননাশী সরঞ্জাম লোকালয় থেকে কুড়িয়ে স্কুল কক্ষে জমা করা হচ্ছে। যানবাহনে চেড়ে আসছে নানান অস্ত্র। লক্ষ লক্ষ প্রাণ কেড়ে নেয়া এই অস্ত্রগুলো দেখে বড্ড হাসি পায় মতির। একটা অস্ত্র যদি দেখাতে পারত শেফালীকে। শেফালী। ভালোবাসা-মাখা এক নাম।

কিছু বুঝে ওঠার আগেই বিকট শব্দে ধুম। কেঁপে উঠলো স্কুল প্রাঙ্গন। শহর জুড়ে তীব্র ভয়। এখন আবার কিসের অশনি সংকেত। বিস্ফোরণ। স্বাধীন দেশের লড়াকু একদল সৈনিক তাদের স্বাধীন করা দেশেই প্রাণ হারালো। হারিয়ে গেল শেফালী মতির অসমাপ্ত প্রেম গাথা। পাকবাহিনীর ফেলে যাওয়া গোলাবারুদ থেকেই ভয়ংকর মাইন বিস্ফোরণ। স্বাধীন দেশে বিস্ফোরিত হলো একমুঠো সোনালী স্বপ্ন।

(১৯৭১ সালের মহান মুক্তিযুদ্ধ ও মৌলভীবাজার জেলায় ঘটে যাওয়া ঐতিহাসিক মাইন বিস্ফোরণের ঘটনা অবলম্বনে রচিত এক কল্পিত কাহিনী)

Bandhana Sinha / বন্দনা সিনহা, Moulvibazar, Bangladesh

Village Women life

অভিশপ্ত জীবন

ঘরের কাজ শেষ করতে করতে এত দেরি হয়ে গেল। কলেজের অ্যাসাইনমেন্টও শেষ হয়নি। মায়ের মৃত্যুর পর যেন জীবনটা বদলে গেল। সারাদিন ঘরের কাজ, কাজ শেষে পড়তে হয়। কোনো কোনো দিন নতুন মায়ের পায়ে মালিশ করতে করতে সেখানেই ঘুমিয়ে পড়ি। আর কপালে জোটে লাথ।

বাবা থেকেও নেই, আমাকে অপয়া বলে গালি দেয় বাবা। কিন্তু বাবা, আমার দোষ কোথায় বলতে পারবে তুমি? মায়ের মৃত্যুর জন্য তুমি আমায় দোষারোপ করে আসছো এত বছর ধরে, কিন্তু আমি তো মাকে মারিনি। তবে আমি দোষী কী করে হলাম? সেদিন কী হয়েছিল কখনো জানতে চাওনি তুমি। আমি কি সত্যি তোমার মেয়ে?

আমি প্রত্যাশা। ইন্টার সেকেন্ড ইয়ারে পড়ি। মা নেই, বাবা আছে। তবে বাবা থেকেও নেই আমার। আমার বয়স যখন ৭ বছর তখন আমার মা মারা যায়। বাবা আর বাকি পরিবারের সবাই আমাকে মায়ের মৃত্যুর জন্য দায়ী মনে করেন। সত্যি বলতে আমি জানি না, কেন। সেদিন বৃষ্টির দিন ছিল। স্কুল থেকে ফিরে বাসায় ঢুকবো, দেখি মা ছাদের রেলিঙের উপর দাঁড়িয়ে আছে। হয়তো কিছু খুঁজছে বা বৃষ্টিতে ভিজছে। আমার মা বৃষ্টিতে ভিজতে খুব ভালোবাসে। তাই আমিও ব্যাগ রেখে ছাদে গেলাম মায়ের কাছে। বৃষ্টি শুরু হয়ে গিয়েছিল ততক্ষণে, তাই দৌড় লাগালাম। ছাদে গিয়ে মাকে দৌড়ে জড়িয়ে ধরতে যাবো ততক্ষণে মা নিচে পড়ে গেলেন।

আর আমিও দৌড়ে গিয়ে নিচের দিকে তাকালাম। মায়ের শরীর পড়ে আছে মাটিতে, চারদিকে রক্তের বন্যা। বৃষ্টির পানিতে রক্ত ধুয়ে যাচ্ছে। বাবা গেটে সিএনজি থেকে চিৎকার করলেন। মাকে ধরে হাসপাতালে নিয়ে যাওয়া হলো কিন্তু ততক্ষণে মা আর এ পৃথিবীতে নেই। এত সময় কারো ধ্যান আমার দিকে যায়নি। আমি চুপচাপ দাদুর কোলে বসে আছি। কী হচ্ছে এসব? মা কি তাহলে মরে গেল? হঠাৎ বাবা এসে আমাকে থাপ্পড় দিয়ে বললেন মায়ের মৃত্যুর জন্য

তুমি দায়ী। সবাই বাবাকে আটকানোর চেষ্টা করছে আর বাবা সবাইকে ছাড়িয়ে আমাকে মেরেই যাচ্ছে। বাবা মার বিয়ে ভালোবেসে হয়েছিল। তারা একে অপরকে অনেক ভালোবাসে। কিন্তু আমি! আমিও তো মাকে ভালোবাসি।

মায়ের মৃতদেহ বাড়িতে আনা হলো দাহ-সংস্কার এর জন্য। আমি মাকে শেষ বারের মতো দেখতে চেয়েছি বলে বাবা সবার সামনে আমাকে দূরে ঠেলে দিয়েছিলেন। সেদিন বাবাকে একটা কথা জিজ্ঞেস করতে ইচ্ছে হয়েছিল "ও বাবা, মাকে তুমি ভালোবাসো তবে কি আমি বাসি না? আমি আমার মাকে কেন মারবো?" কিন্তু জিজ্ঞেস করার সাহস হয়নি আমার। আজও সাহস নেই কিছু বলার। বছর দুয়েক পর সবার জোড়াজুড়িতে বাবা নতুন মা আনলেন। নতুন মা আমাকে অনেক মারে, সব কাজ করায়। বাবাকে বলতে চেয়েও পারি না। কারণ, যখন বলেছিলাম নতুন মা কেঁদে বাবাকে বলেছিল, আমি নাকি ওঁর সাথে গালিগালাজ করে কথা বলেছি। সেদিন বাবা আমাকে কোমরের বেল্ট খুলে অনেক মারেন। সারারাত ব্যথায় ঘুমাতে পারিনি, জ্বর এসেছিল। কিন্তু বাবা একবারও জিজ্ঞেস করেনি আমায়। অথচ যদি মা তুমি থাকতে তাহলে সারারাত না ঘুমিয়ে মাথায় রুমাল দিয়ে দিতে পানিতে ভিজিয়ে।

মা, আজ আমার জন্মদিন। আজ আমি ১৮ বছরের হলাম। কিন্তু দেখো মা আমার পাশে কেউ নেই। কেউ না মা, তুমিও না আর বাবাও না। মাগো, সেদিন তুমি কেন এমন করে চলে গেলে মা? তুমি রাতে গল্প শুনিয়ে বলতে মৃত্যুর পর নাকি সবাই আকাশের তারা হয়ে যায়। মা, তুমিও কি এই আকাশের তারা হয়ে আছো? আমাকে দেখতে পাচ্ছো তুমি মা? মা একবার ফিরে এসে দেখো তোমার পুতুল আর পুতুল নেই মা। নাম তো ঠিক প্রত্যাশা রেখেছো মা, কিন্তু জীবনে আশা রাখার মতো কিছুই যে নেই।

মা, সেদিন তো তুমি পা পিছলে পড়ে গিয়েছিলে, তাই না? আমি তো তোমাকো ধাক্কা দিইনি মা। তবু বাবা বলে আমি তোমাকে ধাক্কা দিয়েছি। কেন মা? ফিরে এসো মা, নাহলে আমাকেই তোমার কাছে ডেকে নাও। সেদিন রেলিঙে তোমাকে দাঁড়িয়ে থাকতে দেখে আমি দৌড়ে আসছিলাম মা, কিন্তু তুমি আমি আসার আগে পড়ে গেলে। মা, তুমি রেলিঙের উপর দাঁড়িয়ে ছিলে সেটা কেউ দেখেনি আমি ছাড়া। কাউকে বলতেও পারিনি মা আমি। কেউ আমার কথা শোনে না। তুমি চলে যাবার পর সবাই আমাকে ঘৃণা করে মা। জানো মা, ঘরে কোনো কিছু ভাঙলে এখন আমাকে দোষী বলে। বলে নাকি সব আমার জন্য হয়েছে।

আচ্ছা মা, তুমি কেন রেলিঙে দাঁড়িয়েছিলে? উওরটা সবার অজানা রয়ে যাবে কি? জানো মা, তুমি আর আমি গ্রামের যে খোলা মাঠে গান গাইতাম সেখানে অনেক দিন যাওয়া হয় না। আমি গেলে সবাই আমাকে অনেক খারাপ কথা বলে। আমার ভালো লাগে না মা। রাতের আকাশের চাঁদের মতো আমার জীবন একাকিত্বে ভরা মা। অভিশপ্ত হয়ে গেছে জীবনটা। তুমি ছাড়া আমি অভিশপ্ত, মা। আমার জীবন অভিশপ্ত।

বৃষ্টির দিনে শত বাধা পেরিয়ে তোমাকে নিয়ে হাসপাতালে ছুটেছিলাম আমরা সবাই। বাবা তো উন্মাদ ছিল। কিন্তু হাসপাতালে পৌঁছে জানতে পারি বৃষ্টির জন্য অধিকাংশ ডাক্তার হাসপাতালে উপস্থিত নেই। তৎকালীন চিকিৎসা না পেয়ে তুমি শেষ নিঃশ্বাস ফেলো।

মা তুমি দেখে নিও তোমার প্রত্যাশা, তোমার পুতুল তোমার দেখা স্বপ্ন অবশ্য পূরণ করবে। ইন্টার পাশ করে আমি মেডিক্যালে ভর্তি হবো মা। ডাক্তার হয়ে দেখাবো মা আমি। আমি ডাক্তার হয়ে এখানেই থাকবো মা, কোথাও যাবো না। টাকার জন্য নয়, গরীবদের সেবার জন্য ডাক্তার হয়ে নিজের জীবন উৎসর্গ করবো। যাতে করে আর কোনো নতুন প্রত্যাশা জন্ম না নেয়। আমাকে ডাক্তারের অ্যাপ্রনে দেখলে তুমি নিশ্চয় অনেক খুশি হবে, তাই না মা? সেদিন কি তুমি নামক তারাটা সবচেয়ে বেশি আলোকিত হবে? এমনটা হলে আমি বুঝে যাবো তুমি অনেক খুশি হয়েছো মা।

তোমার কথা অনেক মনে পরে মা। তোমার কোলে মাথা রেখে ঘুমাতে ইচ্ছে করে মা। তুমি কি একটি বারের জন্য ফিরবে মা? শুধু একটি বার মা..............

Gita Das / গীতা দাস, Dhaka, Bangladesh

আমার শহর আমার বাড়ি শব্দগুলো পড়ে আমার মনে হলো 'আমার' শব্দটি কি আসলে আমার! ব্যক্তি নারী হিসেবে আমি, আমার, আমারই , আমারও শব্দগুলো নিয়ে ভাবনা থেকেই এ কবিতা।

আমার শব্দটি আমার নয়

শৈশবে প্রথম শ্রেণীর বাংলা বইয়ের নাম ছিল আমার বই

ওই বইটি আক্ষরিক অর্থেই আমার বই ছিল।

বিনামূল্যে পাওয়া।

তবে এর ভিতরের সব কথা আমার কথা ছিল না।

আমার ভাইয়ের মনের কথা ছিল।

ছিল ছেলেরা বল খেলে। আমার জন্য ছিল পুতুল খেলা।

এটা পড়ার পর আমার বইটি আর আমার মনে হয়নি।

আমার সোনার বাংলা আমি তোমায় ভালবাসি --- জাতীয় সঙ্গীত গাই

যেখানেই শুনি শ্রদ্ধায় ভাস্কর্য হয়ে যাই।

কিন্তু আমার দেশ দূরে থাকুক, দেশটা যে আমারও তাই কিছু ধর্মান্ধ স্বীকার করে না।

শহরটা যে আমারও তা নগর পরিকল্পনাবিদদের মগজে কাজ করে না।

আমার এবং অথবা আমারই বাড়ি। দূর-দূরান্ত।

আমারও বাড়িই তো কখনো নয়।

দেশ আমারও বলা গেলেও

বাড়ির বেলায় আমার কখনো নয়।

এদিক থেকে পরিবারের চেয়ে রাষ্ট্র উদার।

তাই আমার এবং আমারই শব্দদ্বয় নিয়ে আমি বড়ো নিঃস্ব, ত্যক্ত ও বিরত।

এ শব্দদুটোকে নিজের করতে কত আন্দোলন করছি অসভ্য যুগ থেকে।

এখনো কি সভ্যতার সিঁড়িতে পা দিতে পেরেছি?

যতদিন পর্যন্ত আমার এবং আমারই শব্দদ্বয় আমার নিজস্ব হবে না

ততদিন সভ্যতার সিঁড়ি অদৃশ্যমানই থাকবে।

Gita Das / গীতা দাস, Dhaka, Bangladesh

আমার শহর আমার বাড়ি মানে ভৌগোলিক অবয়ব, বিভিন্ন অবকাঠামো , সম্পর্ক, যাপিত সময়ের সাংস্কৃতিক ও সামাজিক বলয়, এবং ভাষাও এর অবিচ্ছেদ্য অংশ বলে আমি মনে করি। আমি, আমার শহর, আমার বাড়ির সাথে আমার শৈশবে উচ্চারিত ভাষা ও শব্দগুচ্ছের অভাবও অনুভব করি, যা আমায় এ লেখা লিখতে উদ্বুদ্ধ করেছে।

আমার শহরের ভাষা

আমি ষাট বছর বয়সী এক নারী। মধ্য-বয়স অতিক্রান্ত। এ বয়সের চেতনায় মহাকালে বিলীন হওয়ার ভয়, অদৃশ্য শক্তির প্রতি নমিত ভাব থাকার কথা। অলৌকিক শক্তির প্রতি একাত্মতার জন্য আকুলতা ব্যাকুলতা বাড়ার কথা।

কিন্তু আমার চিন্তা চেতনায় আলোড়ন তোলে আমার শৈশব ও কৈশোরের বিহ্বলতায় ভরপুর আমার এলাকা, আমার ছোট্ট মফস্বল শহর, আমার শহরের পাশের নদীটি, পথঘাট, কিছু মানুষ, কিছু সম্পর্ক, মফস্বলীয় বিকেল, দুপুর ও সন্ধ্যা। যাপিত সময়ের সাংস্কৃতিক ও সামাজিক বলয়।

আমার শহরের লোকের ভাষা। উচ্চারণ।

চাকরিসূত্রে ও বৈবাহিকসূত্রে আমি শহরান্তরিত হয়েছি। কিন্তু আমার নরসিংদীর ভাষা আমাকে আপ্লুত করে। আমাকে টেনে নিয়ে যায় অর্ধ-শতক বছর আগের রিকসার টুংটাং মাখা এক শহরে।

অনেক শব্দ আমার মননে গেঁথে আছে। এসব শব্দগুচ্ছ যেন আমার শৈশব ও কৈশোরকালীন যাপিত জীবনের প্রিয় কবিতা। আমার মগ্ন চৈতন্য শিস দেয়। আমাকে বিমোহিত করে। বিভোর করে। বিহ্বল করে।

এখন এসব শব্দ বললে এর অর্থ বলতে হয়। ব্যাখ্যা দিতে হয়। শব্দ প্রয়োগের কারণ বলতে হয়। আমার স্বতঃস্ফূর্ততায় বাধা পড়ে। সেন্সর নামক বিধিবদ্ধ সতর্কীকরণে আমি আষ্টেপৃষ্ঠে বাঁধা। এ সেন্সর আমার মফস্বল শহরের পরিচয়ে পরিচিত হবার আশঙ্কায় নয়। এত আমার অহংকার যে আমার এলাকার নিজস্ব শব্দ ভান্ডার আছে। মাতৃভাষার শব্দ ভান্ডারের মধ্যে - নিজস্ব কিছু সম্পদ। আঞ্চলিকতার প্রলেপ লাগিয়ে একে সংজ্ঞায়িত করার পক্ষে আমি নই। সৌদাগন্ধ জড়ানো শব্দগুচ্ছ আমার! কিন্তু এ

সেন্সর হলো অন্যকে বুঝিয়ে বলার জন্য নিজের আবেগের ছাড়।

নরসিংদীর কিছু স্পেশাল শব্দ আছে। মনে হচ্ছে বিশেষ শব্দটি বললে স্পেশালিটি কম মনে হবে। যেমন, ওঙ্গা তেঙ্গা আমার নরসিংদী এলাকার একটি শব্দ। শরীরটা ওঙ্গা তেঙ্গা লাগছে। তাল পাচ্ছি না। মানে শরীরটার আরামবোধ হচ্ছে না।

অফিসে কখনো খারাপ লাগলে স্বতঃস্ফূর্ত এ শব্দ বলার উপায় নেই। প্রথমত কেউ বুঝবে না এবং এ শব্দ যারা বুঝবে না এটা তাদের সমস্যা নয়। সমস্যা আমি বোঝাতে পারছি না এবং শুদ্ধ বাংলা বলতে পারছি না। প্রমিত বাংলা বলছি না। এর চেয়ে ইংরেজিতে একটা কঠিন শব্দ বলে শারিরীক অবস্থা বুঝালে আমার কৃতিত্ব বেশি। যদিও সবাই বাংলা ভাষাভাষি। কিন্তু প্রমিত বাক্যে আঞ্চলিক শব্দ বসিয়ে কথা বলার মজাই তো আলাদা। অথবা ইংরেজি বাক্যে আঞ্চলিক শব্দ। I am feeling Wonga Tenga.

ছোটবেলা রাতে হারিকেনের আলোয় পড়তে বসতাম। পড়তে পড়তে ঝিমুনি আসলে চিমনিতে কাগজের ঢাকনি দিতাম। জিজ্ঞেস করলে বলতাম আলো চোখে লাগে। বড়রা (একান্নবর্তী পরিবারে বড় হয়েছি বলে মা বাবা ছাড়াও কাকারা, ঠাকুমা, দাদু, ঠাকুমার বাল্য বিধবা বোন ওবোনের ছেলে আরেক কাকা মিলে আমাদের অনেক বড়রা ছিলেন) ঠিকই বুঝতেন যে আমি ঘুমে ঝিমাচ্ছি।

বলতেন, ওঙ্গাবি না। সারাদিন টই টই করে ঘুরে বেড়ায় আর সন্ধ্যাবেলা পড়তে বসলেই ওঙ্গায়। পই পই করে বলেও কথা শুনাতে পারি না।

ওঙ্গাবি না। মানে ঝিমুবি না।

ওঙ্গানোর এমন জীবন্ত চিত্রায়ন কি ঝিমানো শব্দে হয়!

আমার ঠাকুমা বলতেন ঢলক নামছে। মানে মুষলধারে বৃষ্টি পড়ছে। তোড়ে বৃষ্টি নামা। cats and dogs. এখানে আমার ঠাকুমার ব্যবহৃত ঢলক শব্দটি অতুলনীয়। এ ভাষা আমার ঘরের ভাষা। আমার পূর্ব প্রজন্মের ভাষা। আমার পিতামহীর ভাষা। আমার বড় হয়ে ওঠা পরিবেশের ভাষা। আমার শহরের ভাষা। যার অভাব আমি বোধ করি। ঢলক বললে আমার উত্তর প্রজন্ম বুঝে না। কাজেই আমার মন প্রাণ খুলে কথা বলা হয় না।

আরেকটি শব্দ – টিন্দিশ। না, আর কিছু খাওয়া যাবে না। আমি খেয়ে দেয়ে টিন্দিশ। এক শব্দে ভরা পেটের কী চমৎকার অবস্থা। ঠাকুরমা আরেকটা শব্দ ব্যবহার করতেন – থাইয়া দাইয়া শ্যাম হইয়া আছে।

বাচ্চাটা টাব্বুর করে জলে পড়ে গেল। টুপ করে জলে পড়ে যাওয়ার চেয়ে টাব্বুরটা বেশি অর্থবোধক আমার কাছে। পাকা আম   টুপ করে জলে পড়তে পারে, কিন্তু শিশু টাব্বুর করে জলে পড়ে গেছে।

আমার শহরে একটা গালি আছে। বকা আছে। বাপজড়া। বাপের মতো জড়া। দুষ্ট। খারাপ। বদ। এ শব্দ চয়ন আমারে ছোট মফস্বল শহরের। এ সব শব্দ আমার শহরের আদি বাসিন্দা প্রত্যেকে বুঝবে। বাংলাদেশের লৌকিক প্রায় সব গালি গালাজে নারীর সমাহার। যাকেই বকুক – বকাটি জলের মতো গড়িয়ে গড়িয়ে মা বোনদের উপরে গিয়ে স্থিত হয়। কিন্তু বাপজড়া নারী বিবর্জিত। আমার বড়বেলায় এ বকাটি খুব প্রিয় প্রিয় লাগছে।

আমার শহরের এমনই অজস্র শব্দ আমি হারিয়ে ফেলেছি। বড় বেলায় – প্রৌঢ়ত্বে এসে এ সব শব্দ খুঁজি। সামাজিক যোগাযোগ মাধ্যম ফেসবুকের বদৌলতে আমার শহরের অনেককে খুঁজে পেয়েছি। দেশে বিদেশে ছড়িয়ে ছিটিয়ে থাকা আমার পরিবেশের পরিজনদের সাথে অন লাইনে কথা বলি আমার শহরের ভাষায়।

কথোপকথনে   বলি – নাড়া গোড়া করবি না। মানে ঢং করবি না।

কখনো শুনি – তোর তো টিলকি বেশি। মানে উছলিয়া উঠা শখ বেশি – শুধু শখ নয়।

শৈশবের চারিত্রিক বৈশিষ্ট্য মনে করিয়ে দিই – তুই তো দেংশালনি ছিলি। মানে কোনো কিছু পরোয়া না করা।

 আমাকে বলে – তুই তো এখন ঢাকালনি। মানে ঢাকায় থাকি।

এ আবেগ মাখা শব্দগুচ্ছ আমার পিতামহী বুঝতো। আমার মা কম কম বুঝতো। কারণ উনি আমার শহরে বড় হননি। আমার বোন বুঝে। আমার নারী বন্ধুরা বোঝে। কিন্তু আমার ভাই বা এলাকার পুরুষ বন্ধুরা প্রথম উচ্চারণে বোঝে না। তারা একান্ত কিছু বোঝে না। একান্ত কিছু বোঝাবুঝি মানেই নারী। নিজস্ব ভাষা মানেই নারীর কর্ষ! তাই তো আমি আমার ঐকান্তিকতা –– নিজস্বতা খুঁজে ফিরি।

আমার শৈশব ও কৈশোরের শহরের বর্তমান মানুষেরাও আমার এ ভাষা – শব্দগুচ্ছ বোঝে না। আমার প্রিয়তম শহরের ভৌগোলিক অবয়ব, অবকাঠামো, ভাষা ও কথায় শব্দ ব্যবহার পালটে গেছে।   আমার শৈশব স্মৃতির শহর এখন বিশ্বজনীন ভাবনায় আন্দোলিত।

আমি হারিয়ে ফেলেছি আমার আবেগ জাগানিয়া সামগ্রিক শহরটিকে।

Nargis Sultana Nadi / নার্গিস সুলতানা নদী, Dhaka, Bangladesh

আমি লেখার শুরুতেই মনে পাকাপোক্ত ভাবে স্থান দিয়েছি যে, 'আমার শহর-ই আমার বাড়ি' তাই নিজের বাড়ি মনে করেই নিজের শহর কে উপস্থাপন করতে অনুপ্রাণিত হয়েছি আমি, তাই লিখতে গিয়ে মাঝে মধ্যেই এই ভেবে আনমনা হয়ে গেছি বা বলা যায় দোদুল্যমনতায় ভুগেছি যেটা নিয়ে লিখছি সেটা আদৌ কি আমার শহর না মনের অজান্তেই আমার বাড়িতে রূপ নিয়েছে?

আমার শহর আমার বাড়ি

ইংরেজিতে একটি প্রবাদ আছে "God made the Village, man made the town" অর্থাৎ বিধাতা গ্রাম সৃষ্টি করেছে আর মানুষ তৈরি করেছে নগর বা শহর। মানুষ আদিম গুহার অন্ধকার থেকে সভ্যতার পথ পরিক্রমায় তৈরি করেছে অগণিত শহর। রাজ্য-শাসন, ব্যবসা, শিক্ষাকেন্দ্র এই সকল বিষয়কে কেন্দ্র করে গড়ে উঠত প্রাচীন শহরে জনপদ। বিজ্ঞানের অগ্রগতি, চাকা এবং বিদ্যুতের আবিষ্কার পৃথিবীর মানচিত্রে নগর গড়ে তোলার ক্ষেত্রে উৎসাহ যুগিয়েছে। রেললাইনের কল্যাণে এক হয়ে গেছে দূর-দূরান্তের বহু শহর। আধুনিকতা আর শিল্পের ছোঁয়ায় শহরে জীবন পেয়েছে নান্দনিকতা।

সাধারণত শহর বলতে আমরা বুঝি আধুনিক সভ্যতার সকল উপকরণ সমৃদ্ধ লোকালয়কে। যেখানে শিল্প কারখানা থেকে শুরু করে সব ধরণের নাগরিক ব্যবস্থাপনা রয়েছে। শহরের জীবনযাত্রার মান গ্রামীণ জনপদ থেকে অনেক উন্নত। শহর মানেই উঁচু দালান-কোঠা, পাকা রাস্তা, যানবাহন আর জীবিকার সন্ধানে ছুটে চলা ব্যস্ত মানুষ। সভ্যতার ইতিহাসের দিকে তাকালে আমরা দেখতে পাই পৃথিবীর প্রাচীন শহর সমূহকে কেন্দ্র করে গড়ে উঠে বহু সভ্যতা। খ্রিষ্টপূর্ব ৩৬৫০ সালে তুর্কির "গজনিয়াতেপ" ছিল অফিসিয়ালি পৃথিবীর প্রথম প্রতির্ষ্ঠিত শহর। এছাড়া মিশরের আলেকজান্ড্রিয়া, ফিলিস্তিনের জেরুজালেম, ইরাকের কিরকুক এবং চীনের সাঙজি প্রদেশের জিয়ান রয়েছে পৃথিবীর প্রাচীনতম শহরের মধ্যে। বর্তমানেও যত শহর পৃথিবী জুড়ে রয়েছে তার সবগুলোই আধুনিক এবং উন্নত সব প্রযুক্তি সংবলিত। শহর মানেই সময়ের সর্বোচ্চ প্রযুক্তি এবং উন্নত জীবন যাপনের প্রাণকেন্দ্র।

অবিরাম ছুটে চলা, সময়ের ব্যস্ত চাকায় জীবনকে পিষে ফেলাই শহরে জীবনের স্বরূপ। আপন ভুবন গড়ে তোলাকে নিয়েই দিনরাত ব্যস্ত শহরের মানুষ। মানবিক সম্পর্কগুলো শহরের মানচিত্রে জটিল এক সমীকরণ। জীবনের ব্যস্ত গোলক ধাঁধাঁয় পাক খায় মানুষের আবেগ। আর তাই কাউকে দেখা যায় বিলাসী জীবনের ছন্দে আটকে আছে আর কেউবা অযত্নে অবহেলায় মানবেতর জীবন যাপন করছে। শহর যাকে দেয় দু হাত ভরে দেয় আর যাকে দেয় না সে পড়ে থাকে পথের পাশে। শহর যেন অসমতার এক নীরব তটরেখা। এখানে একই আকাশের নিচে কেউ গরীব, কেউ ধনী, কেউ রাজপ্রাসাদে বাস করে আর কেউ ফুটপাতে। রঙিন বিজলী বাতি আর পাকা বাড়ি শহরে জীবনকে নান্দনিক করে দিলেও কেড়ে নিয়েছে মানুষের আবেগ। শহরের চারদেয়ালে মানুষের জীবন তাই হয়ে গেছে রংহীন আলপনা। ব্যস্ত শহরের দূষিত বাতাসে আটকে পড়া মন তাই ছুটে যেতে চায় দিগন্তের কাছে। সবুজ গ্রামের উপর নীল আকাশ যেখানে ছাদ হয়ে ঝুলে আছে।

প্রকৃতি মানেই গ্রাম, যেখানে অবারিত মাঠে খোলা হাওয়া দোল খায় পাকা ধানের শীষে। গ্রামীণ জনপদ পেরিয়ে শহরের দ্বারপ্রান্তে দাঁড়ালেই মনে হয় প্রকৃতি যেন পিছনে হাঁটছে। শহরের ব্যস্ততম রাস্তায় বাতাস থমকে যায়। সবুজ মাঠ, অবারিত ফসলের ক্ষেত আর বহতা নদীর বড় অভাব ইট, কাঠের শহরে। ছয় ঋতুর বাংলাদেশ যেন শহরে এসে অর্ধেক হয়ে গেছে। ঋতু বৈচিত্র্য শহরে নেই বললেই চলে। এখানে ঋতুর পালা বদল মানেই বোশেখের তপ্ত রোদে দগ্ধ হওয়া, কিংবা নাগরিক কোলাহল ছাপিয়ে এক পশলা বৃষ্টির শব্দ। শহরে শীত আসে চুপিসারে, স্বল্প সময়ের ব্যবধানে আবার বিদায়ও নেয়। দালানকোঠার আড়ালে হারিয়ে যায় শরতের কাশফুল। হেমন্তের নবান্ন উৎসব এখানে বড্ড বেমানান। ফসলের মাঠ যেখানে নেই সেখানে নবান্ন আসবেই বা কি করে। এই ছুটে চলা যান্ত্রিক জীবনে বাংলার প্রকৃতি, ছয় ঋতুর পালাবদল কোনো কিছুই চোখে পড়ে না। সবার অলক্ষ্যে নগরের কোনো ছোট উদ্যানে ফুটে থাকে বর্ষার কদম ফুল। শহরে জীবনে প্রকৃতি মানেই সূর্যের উদয়-অস্ত। ব্যস্ত জীবনে এক পশলা বৃষ্টিই সবাইকে প্রকৃতির ছোঁয়া এনে দেয়। শহরে জীবনে প্রকৃতির উপস্থিতি তাই একদমই টের পাওয়া যায় না।

জীবিকার জন্য যেখানে ছুটে বেড়াতে হয় দিন-রাত সেখানে অবকাশ মানে বিলাসিতা। সারা সপ্তাহ কর্মব্যস্ত থাকার পর একদিনের ছুটি জীবনকে যেন উপহাস করে যায়। শহরের বেশিরভাগ মানুষ তাই ছুটির দিনে বিশ্রাম নিতেই বেশি পছন্দ করে। জীবন যেখানে আবদারের ঝুড়ি মেলে রাখে সেখানে ছোট

অবসরটুকুও নানা ব্যস্ততায় কেটে যায়। ছুটির দিনে তাই কেউ কেউ ভিড় জমায় শপিং মলে। দৈনন্দিন জীবনের টুকিটাকি প্রয়োজন মেটাতে ছুটতে হয় শপিংয়ে। কেউবা পরিবার পরিজন নিয়ে ঘুরতে যান চিড়িয়াখানা, জাদুঘর, শিশুপার্ক কিংবা উদ্যানে। শৌখিন থাবার-প্রিয় মানুষ ভিড় জমান পছন্দের রেস্তোরাঁয়। কেউবা চলে যান সিনেমা দেখতে কিংবা শিল্পকলায় নাটক উপভোগ করতে। ছুটির দিনে তারুণ্যের আড্ডায় মুখরিত হয় টি,এস,সি, ব্যস্ত শহরে সন্ধ্যা নেমে আসে। স্বল্প পরিসরের অবকাশ শেষে আবার গন্তব্যে ফিরে যায় মানুষ। শুরু হয় কর্মমুখর, ব্যস্ত শহরে জীবন।

সভ্যতা গড়ে উঠেছিল শহরকেন্দ্রিক হয়ে, আর তাই শহরে সংযোজিত ছিল মানুষের জন্য সর্বোচ্চ সুবিধা। শহরে উন্নত জীবন যাপনের জন্য সব ধরণের সুযোগ সুবিধা রয়েছে। শিক্ষার জন্য রয়েছে নামি দামি সব স্কুল, কলেজ, বিশ্ববিদ্যালয়। চিকিৎসার জন্য শহরে রয়েছে অগণিত হাসপাতাল, ক্লিনিক যা মানুষকে সর্বোচ্চ মানের চিকিৎসা সেবা দিয়ে থাকে। প্রাচীনকাল থেকেই ব্যবসার প্রাণকেন্দ্র হিসেবে বিবেচিত শহর। গ্রাম থেকে বহু মানুষ এখনো শহরে আসে জীবিকার সন্ধানে। কর্মব্যস্ততার কারণে মানুষ এখানে ছোট ছোট কাজের জন্য অপরের শরণাপন্ন হচ্ছে। ফলে তৈরি হচ্ছে নতুন নতুন কর্মক্ষেত্র। অফিস, আদালত, কলকারখানাগুলো শহরে অবস্থিত হওয়াতে চাকুরির অন্যতম স্থান হিসেবেও বিবেচিত হয় শহর। গ্রামীণ কৃষির বাজার বলা হয় শহরকে। গ্রাম থেকে কৃষকরা ভালো দামের আশায় তাদের পণ্য নিয়ে আসেন শহরে। শহরে রয়েছে বিদ্যুৎ, যা সভ্যতাকে আলোকিত করেছে। দ্রুত যাতায়াতের জন্য রয়েছে মোটরযান, রেলগাড়ি এবং উড়োজাহাজ। পাকা দালানকোঠা, রাস্তাঘাট এবং রঙ-বেরঙের বিজলী বাতি শহরে জীবনকে করেছে দৃষ্টিনন্দন। শহরের সবচেয়ে বড় সুবিধা হলো এখানে হাতের নাগালেই সব কিছু পাওয়া যায়।

নান্দনিক স্থাপত্য, আকাশচুম্বী সব অট্টালিকা শহরকে একদিকে যেমন দৃষ্টিনন্দন করে তুলেছে অপরদিকে করে তুলেছে বিষাদময়। শহরের কলকারখানার বিষাক্ত ধোঁয়া বাতাসকে করে দিচ্ছে শ্বাসের অনুপযুক্ত, এর বর্জ্য নদীর পানিকে নষ্ট করছে ক্রমান্বয়ে। জনসংখ্যার সাথে সাথে পাল্লা দিয়ে বাড়ছে যানবাহন। ক্রমবর্ধমান গাড়ির কারণে বেড়ে চলছে যানজট আর শব্দদূষণের মাত্রা। সেই সাথে বাড়ছে দুর্ঘটনা এবং দুর্ঘটনায় মৃত্যুর হার। অনিয়ন্ত্রিত ট্রাফিক ব্যবস্থার কারণে ঘণ্টাব্যাপী আটকে থাকতে হয় রাস্তায়। নিরাপত্তাহীনতা শহরে জীবনের আরেক বিরূপ দিক। অনবরত ছিনতাই, ডাকাতি এবং খুনের ঘটনা জীবনকে

দুর্বিষহ করে তুলে। মাঝে মাঝে লোডশেডিংয়ে শহরের চিত্র বদলে যায়। ঘুটঘুটে অন্ধকারকে তখন মনে হয় বিভীষিকাময় রাত। কর্মব্যস্ততার আড়ালে মানুষের সাথে সম্পর্কগুলো কেমন যেন ঠুনকো মনে হয়। অনেক সুবিধার পাশাপাশি অসুবিধা শহরে জীবনকে যেন বিষিয়ে তুলে। এইসব নেতিবাচক দিকের প্রভাবে শহরে মানুষের মনের আবেগ, ভালোবাসা, আন্তরিকতা ক্রমেই অনুভূতিহীন হয়ে পড়ছে।

বিশ্বায়নের এই যুগে বিলীন হচ্ছে গ্রাম আর বাড়ছে শহর। জীবনের তাগিদে মানুষ পাড়ি জমাচ্ছে গ্রাম ছেড়ে শহরে। মানুষের শহরমুখী হওয়ার প্রবণতা বাড়াচ্ছে শহরের পরিধি। যান্ত্রিকতায় আটকে যাচ্ছে গ্রামীণ জীবনও। শহর যেমন জেগে থাকে নিশিদিন তেমনি শহরের মানুষও জেগে থাকে নিয়ন আলোর শহরে। অফুরন্ত কাজ আর ব্যস্ততা এই নিয়েই শহরের জীবন। যে জীবনে সম্পর্কগুলোও ইট-পাথরের মতো জড় হয়ে গেছে। তবুও জীবনকে গতিময় করতে, সময়ের সাথে তাল মিলিয়ে চলতে গেলে শহরে আসতে হয়, হতে হয় শহরে আর শহর টাই হয়ে উঠে একসময় নিজের বাড়ি।

Zahura Yasmin Elina / শ্রীমতী জহুরা ইয়াসমিন এলিনা, Buffalo, New York, USA

I get inspiration from my surroundings. The term 'My City My Home' inspired me to put my memories in words. Whatever I left behind always recalls me, and my sweetest memories in my life are connected with my city and my home. When I was writing on this topic it brought tears to my eyes. I miss my city, my home. I miss all of them.

স্মৃতির হাতছানি

'প্রয়োজন', জীবনে চলার পথে সবচেয়ে বড় ব্যাপার হয়ে সামনে এসে দাঁড়ায়। 'আমি কখনো এটা চাইনা, এটা করবোনা', এভাবে বলে পুরো জীবন কাটে না। প্রয়োজনের সময় যেটা করার কথা, সেটা করতে মন না চাইলেও দরকার হলে সেটাই করতে হয়। যেমন, আমি জীবনের প্রয়োজনে আজ শত-সহস্র মাইল দূরে আমার প্রিয় জন্মভূমি ছেড়ে। চিরজনমের বাঁধন ফেলে যাওয়ার কী যে নিদারুণ কষ্ট! বুকের ভিতর নিঃশব্দে পাঁজর ভাঙার শব্দ কেউ শোনে না, শুধু আমি জানি দিনরাত আমার কলিজাটা পুড়ে যাচ্ছে, নিশ্চুপ হাহাকারে কাঁদি সারাক্ষণ।

আমার বাড়ি ঢাকা জেলার কেরানিগঞ্জ উপজেলার রুহিতপুর গ্রামে, আর আমার শহরের নাম হচ্ছে ঢাকা। স্মৃতির মায়ায় জড়ানো তিলোত্তমা নগরী, প্রাণের নদী বুড়িগঙ্গা যার পাশ দিয়ে বয়ে যাচ্ছে।

কলেজে যাওয়ার জন্য বা অন্য কোনো কাজে ঢাকা যেতে হলে যখন বুড়িগঙ্গা ব্রীজে উঠতো গাড়ি, আমি নদীর দুইপাশে দেখতাম আর মনে মনে বলতাম এই যে আমার নদী, আমার প্রিয় বুড়িগঙ্গা। দুইপাশে নৌকা, লঞ্চ, স্টীমার যাচ্ছে তার বুক চিরে, দুই ধারে বড় বড় বিল্ডিঙের সারি, কতদিন তোমাদের দেখি না! এই শহরের বুকে প্রতিদিন কত-শত মানুষজন জীবন ও জীবিকার টানে ছুটে চলে অবিরত। পুরো শহরটা জুড়ে থাকে তাদের প্রাণচাঞ্চল্য। মনে পরে রিকশার টুং টাং শব্দ, রিকশায় চড়ার আনন্দ, রাস্তার মোড়ে দাঁড়িয়ে চা, ফুচকা, ভেল্পুরি, ঝালমুড়ি খাওয়া বন্ধুরা মিলে। লোকাল বাসে করে কত জায়গায় যাওয়া। আর রাতের ঢাকা, সেতো অতুলনীয়। রঙিন বাতির বর্ণিল সাজে ঝলমলিয়ে নিজেকে সাজিয়ে

নেয়, আলো আঁধারের খেলায় রহস্যময়ী হয়ে ওঠে। রাতের বুড়িগঙ্গা, সে'ও অসাধারণ। লঞ্চ, স্টিমারে আলোর শিখা, দূরে দুইপাশের বিল্ডিং গুলোতে আলোর খেলা, চোখ জুড়িয়ে যায়। কতদিন দেখি না, জানি না আবার কবে দেখবো, দুচোখ ভরে আমার প্রিয় শহর, তোমাকে। চোখ দুটো জ্বলে যায়, নোনা পানিতে ভেসে যায়।

আমার অস্তিত্ব জুড়ে আমার বাড়ি, পুরো দুনিয়াতে সবচেয়ে আপন, সবচেয়ে ভালো জায়গা আমার কাছে। আমার বাড়ির যে দৃশ্য আমার চোখে সবচাইতে সুন্দর, তা হলো আমাদের উঠানের মাঝখানে অনেকগুলো বড় বড় নারিকেল গাছ। যেদিন জ্যোৎস্না হয়, নারিকেল পাতার ফাঁকে ফাঁকে সেই জ্যোৎস্নার আলো খেলা করে, পাতার সাথে মিতালি করে লুকোচুরি খেলে যায়। আমি দুয়ারে বা ছাদে বসে দুই চোখ ভরে দেখতাম আর মনে মনে বলতাম নিয়তি, আমাকে কোনোদিন এই অপূর্ব দৃশ্য দেখা থেকে বঞ্চিত কোরো না। আমি সারাজীবন তোমাদের মাঝেই থাকতে চাই। কিন্তু এখন চাঁদের আলো আর রাস্তার বাতির আলো মিলেমিশে একাকার। এখন চাঁদ দেখলে চাঁদকে বলি , চাঁদমামা, তুমি আমার বাড়ি যাও, ওইখানে গিয়ে আমার বাবা-মা, ভাই-বোন, পাড়া-পড়শি, আমার প্রিয় গ্রামটাকে ছুঁয়ে দাও, ভাসিয়ে দাও তোমার আলোর বন্যায়। যাওয়ার সময় সাথে করে আমার স্পর্শটুকু নিয়ে যাও। সবাইকে তোমার আদর দিয়ে, সাথে আমার ছোঁয়াটুকুও দিও। আর সবাইকে কানে কানে বলে দিয়ো, আমি ঠিকই আছি তোমাদের সাথে মিশে সবসময়। আমি না হয় আরেক জনমে আমার গাঁয়ের ধূলিমাখা পথই হবো। তখন তোমার মমতামাখা হাসি দিয়ে আমায় ছুঁয়ে দিও।

আমার বাড়ির একেক বেলায় একেক রকম গন্ধ আছে, আছে একেক রকম অনুভূতি যেটা আমি টের পেতাম । সকালবেলার স্নিগ্ধ হাওয়ার মন মাতালো সুবাস, দুপুর বেলায় কেমন যেন বুকটা হাহাকার করা অনুভূতি, মনে হয় কী যেন নেই, কী যেন হারিয়ে যাচ্ছে, বিকেলবেলার পড়ন্ত বাতাসের পরশ, আর সন্ধ্যাবেলার মন খারাপের আবির রাঙা আকাশ দেখে কেন জানি না কান্না আসতে চাইতো। আবার শীতের সকালবেলা কুয়াশা মাখা ভোরের আকাশে সূর্যের প্রথম কিরণ, সেই সময়তেও কেমন যেন একটা গন্ধ পেতাম। কুয়াশার গন্ধ। এখনো চোখ বন্ধ করলেই সেইসব টের পাই, একদম আগের মতো।

আমি যেদিন চলে আসবো দেশ থেকে, তার আগের দিন মনে হচ্ছিলো, মরে যাওয়ার আগের রাতে বুঝি মানুষের এমনই লাগে। কোথায় যাবো এই প্রিয় বাড়ি

ছেড়ে, এই আঙিনা ছেড়ে একা একা। যেখানে যাবো সেখানে তো আমার কেউ নেই, সব অপরিচিত। আমি কেমন করে থাকবো? আমার আপনজন তো সব এইখানে। তখন আমি বাইরে গিয়ে প্রাণভরে নিঃশ্বাস নিয়ে নিলাম, আমার বাড়ির ঘ্রাণ মনে গেঁথে নিলাম। একা একা পাশের রাস্তায় গিয়ে তার গন্ধও নিলাম। এখন আমি খুব বুঝতে পারি, এই কথাটার মানে যে, মানুষ থাকে এক জায়গায়, আর তার মন পড়ে থাকে আরেক জায়গায়।আমার মন আমার বাড়িতে সবসময়, সারাক্ষণ পড়ে আছে।আমি চোখ বন্ধ করলেই সেখানে চলে যাই।

আমাদের ঘরের জানলা দিয়ে গাছের পাতার ফাঁক দিয়ে বৃষ্টি পড়া দেখতে আমার খুব ভালো লাগতো। আরো ভালো লাগতো, টিনের চালের প্রতিটা ঢেউয়ের মাঝ দিয়ে একভাবে বৃষ্টির রেখাগুলো পড়ছে, এটা দেখতে। বৃষ্টি আসার আগের মুহূর্তটাও অনেক পছন্দের। চারদিকের আকাশ কালো করে ঠাণ্ডা হাওয়া বয়ে যায়। আর দু-এক ফোঁটা করে বৃষ্টি পড়তে পড়তেই সবাই ছুটাছুটি করে রোদে শুকাতে দেয়া কাপড়গুলো ঘরে নিয়ে যায়। আমার তখন পাগলা হাওয়ার সাথে দৌড়াদৌড়ি করে বাইরের কাজগুলো করতে কী যে ভালো লাগতো! মনে হতো আমিও বাঁধনহারা বাতাসের সাথে মিলে অনেক দূরের আকাশে ছুটে ছুটে বেড়াই। দিনের বেলায় বৃষ্টি শুরু হলে যেভাবেই হোক, আমি ভিজবোই। প্রতিদিন হলে প্রতিদিনই। বৃষ্টির পরে একটা সোঁদাগন্ধ বের হয় চারিদিকের ভেজা গাছের, ভেজা পাতাগুলো কেমন ঝিকমিক করে, সজীব হয়ে ওঠে চারপাশ। আর রাতের বেলা বৃষ্টির ঝমঝম শব্দ যেন ঘুম পাড়ানি গান হয়ে যায় চলে আসে যেন। চোখ বুজলেই সেই দিনগুলো আমার সামনে। তারা শুধু আমায় পিছু ডাকে। আমি সামনের দিকে তাকিয়ে থাকি, কিন্তু তাদের অবিরত ডাকে বারে বারে পিছনে তাকাই।

মনে হয় যদি একটা পাখি হতে পারতাম, আমার ডানায় ভর করে যখন মন চাইতো,সাথে সাথে ফিরে যেতে পারতাম! মন চাইলেই দেখে আসতে পারতাম আমার প্রিয় দেশটাকে, আমার গ্রামটাকে। কী করছে আমার মা একা একা বসে, কী ভাবছে? পেপার পড়তে পড়তে, বাবা কি আমার কথা মনে করছে? আমার বোন কি কোথাও বেড়াতে যাওয়ার সময় আমায় মনে মনে খোঁজে? নিঃশব্দে আমায় জিজ্ঞেস করে, দেখ তো আপু, এই রঙের টিপ কি আমায় মানায়? তোর জন্যেও একই রকম জামা বানাই? দুইবোন একসাথে পরবো। আমার ভাই কি বাইরে থেকে ঘরে আসার সময় ফোন করে আমায় খোঁজে? ভুল করে বলতে চায়, বুবু ফুচকা

খাবে? নিয়ে আসি? পুরি আনবো, চা দিয়ে খাবে?

আহা রে! মন চাইলেই যদি ফিরে যেতে পারতাম! সাথে সাথে সবাইকে দেখে আসতে পারতাম দু'চোখ ভরে! আমি ফিরে যেতে চাই আমার প্রিয় আঙিনায়, বসতে চাই মাঠের সবুজ ঘাসে। হাত বাড়িয়ে ধরতে চাই আমার বাড়ির গাছগুলোকে, ফুলের বাগানের মাঝখানে গিয়ে চুপ করে বসে থাকতে।

নিয়তির কাছে প্রার্থনা, জীবন, তুমি যদি একটা বৃত্ত হও, তবে শুরু করে এসে মাঝপথে থেমে যেও না। বৃত্তটা পুরোপুরি শেষ করে আর একবার শুরুতে গিয়ে তারপর মিশে যেও দিগন্তরেখায়। শেষ রেখাটা বিলীন হয়ে যাবার আগে, আবার আমার শিকড়ের কাছে আমাকে যেতে দিও।

Zahura Yasmin Elina / শ্রীমতী জহরা ইয়াসমিন এলিনা, Buffalo, New York, USA

I get inspiration from my surroundings. The term 'My City My Home' inspired me to put my memories in words. Whatever I left behind always recalls me, and my sweetest memories in my life are connected with my city and my home. When I was writing on this topic it brought tears to my eyes. I miss my city, my home. I miss all of them.

আমার নকশিকাঁথা

শিউলি ফুলের গাছটা যখন,

ফুলে ফুলে ভরে উঠে,

সেই ফুল সে পুরো পথ জুড়ে বিছিয়ে দেয়।

বাড়ির ঠিক সামনে দাঁড়িয়ে।

হয়তো কেউ কুড়িয়ে নেয়, অথবা কেউ মাড়িয়ে যায়।

প্রিয় আমার শিউলি ফুল, তুমি কি চাও, আমি

এসে দাঁড়াই তোমার ছায়াতলে?

আমি খুব করে চাই, বিছিয়ে থাকা ফুলগুলোকে,

তুলে নিতে দু'হাতের মুঠোয় করে।

রাতের আঁধারে জোনাক পোকারা, দল বেঁধে

বাড়ির পাশের বাঁশঝাড়ে, কার খোঁজ করে?

তোমরা কি জানো?

আমি তোমাদের খুঁজে বেড়াই।

তোমাদের নিভে-জ্বলে, আলোর খেলা দেখতে দেখতে,

কী যে অব্যক্ত খুশিতে ভরে উঠতো মন আমার!

যখন উথালপাথাল জ্যোৎস্নায় পুরো বাড়ি ভেসে যায়,

পাগলপারা সেই আলোর বৃষ্টি গায়ে মেখে,

হেঁটে বেড়াই উঠানময়,

অনন্তকাল ধরে যদি হেঁটে যাওয়া যেত !

আমার গাঁয়ের মেঠোপথ ধরে দূরে, বহুদূরে !

আর ছোট্ট তুমি বেলগাছ,

এখন কি অনেক বড় হয়ে, দুয়ারে আলো-ছায়ার খেলা দেখাও?

আমি তোমার ছোট ছোট পাতার ফাঁক দিয়ে,

বিশাল আকাশটাকে দেখতে চাই।

হলুদ রাঙা করবী ফুল, তুমি কী করো?

বাড়িতে কেউ আসলে,

তুমি কি নুয়ে পড়ে অভিবাদন জানাও?

আমি চাই তুমি টুপ করে এসে বসো আমার খোলা চুলে,

যখন বাতাস এসে, তোমার পাতায় কাঁপন ধরায়।

আমের বোল, আমি যে চাই আকুল হয়ে তোমায় ছুঁয়ে দিতে,

প্রাণভরে তোমার কাঁচা সবুজ গন্ধ মেখে,

তোমার মতো সজীব হতে।

ঝড়ো বাতাসে খুব করে চাই,

কালবোশেখি ঝড়ের সাথে আম কুড়াতে।

তোমরা জানো? আমি মিশে আছি তোমাদের সাথে ।

আমার নদী, তোমার কি মনে পড়ে সেই যে–
প্রতিদিন তোমার আমার দেখা হবার কথা?
আমায় কি দেখতে চাও তুমি?
আগের মতো যদি ফিরে পেতাম দিনগুলো !
এই আঙিনায় দোলনা দোলার দিনগুলো কি,
আর একটিবার ফিরে পাওয়া যায় না?
আমি খুব করে চাই, যদি ফিরে পাই
সেই সোনালী দিন, রঙিন ঘুড়ির মতো করে,
আকাশে উড়িবার।

ফেলে আসা দিনগুলো হাতছানি দেয়,
মনের ভিতর অবিরাম বয়ে চলা স্মৃতির নদী,
ডাক দিয়ে যায় অবিরত,
আমিও তাই নিঃশব্দ চিৎকারে বলি,
আমি ফিরবোই, ফিরে আসবোই একদিন,
চিরচেনা এই পথে,
স্মৃতিমাখা রোদ্দুর যেখানে খেলা করে ।

আর আমার শহর, কেমন আছো তুমি?
তুমি কি ভুলে গেছ আমায়?
জানো? আমার মনে পড়ে তোমায়,
কতশত মানুষ, রিকশার টুংটাং, রাস্তার পাশে জারুল,
কৃষ্ণচূড়ার চিরল পাতায় ঝিরিঝিরি বাতাস,

চোখ বুজলেই সেই বাতাসের ছোঁয়ার অনুভবে,
তুমি আমার প্রাণের শহর ঢাকা। যেখানে,
কোলাহলপূর্ণ জীবন ছুটে বেড়ায়
বিরামহীন। জড়তাহীন।
কখনো কখনো করুণাহীন, কঠিন
ইট, পাথরের দালানের ভিড়ে।
আবার জড়িয়ে নেয় ভালোবাসায়, মমতার কোমল ছোঁয়ায়।
প্রাণচাঞ্চল্যে ভরপুর, অবিরাম বয়ে চলা,
যেন জীবনের প্রতিচ্ছবি।

যেখানে আমার নাড়ির টান – প্রাণের নদী,
খেলার মাঠ, বাড়ির উঠান, সবুজ ধান আর
হলুদ সরিষা ক্ষেত আমার পুরো অস্তিত্ব জুড়ে।
তোমরা সবাই ভালো থেকো, সবসময়।

Sultana Rajia Shila / সুলতানা রাজিয়া শীলা, Dhaka, Narsingdi, Bangladesh

My City and My Home inspire me because of my hobby. So I am Inspired to write and work.

আমার শহর

হে ভিন দেশি মানব স্বজন

এসো গো আমার বাড়ি-

তোমায় দেখাবো আমার

ললিত শহর,

কেমন সোনার সাজন ধরি।

এক সবুজ শ্যামল স্বপন পুরী-

যেন ডাকছে তোমায় নিলাম্বরী

বকুল মালা হাতো

ঐ নিলাম্বুধী সৈকত পেরে-

যেথা ঢেউয়ের ছোঁয়ায়

শিশির পড়ে-

তোমায় করিতে বরণ সোহাগ

ডালায়,

আমি ঘর বেঁধেছি তাতো।

আমার শহর ও বাড়ির মাটি-

সে তো পবিত্র আর বড়ই খাঁটি-

যার ফোঁটায় ফোঁটায় রক্ত ঝরা,

ঐ বঙ্গবীরের গড়া।

যে শিমুল হিজল কদম তলে-

এই জারুল স্বর্ণলতা তলে-

আজ নীরব নিথর সে মুক্তি

শহিদ।

সব ঘুমিয়ে রয়েছে ওরা।

ওগো আমার শহর মুখের হাসি-

বর্ণ বিভেদ ভুলা।

সে তো অতিথির তরে স্বর্গ

খুশির,

যেন পেলো সে নতুন দুলা।

আরো মায়ার দুহাত বাড়িয়ে ডাকে-

সন্তানের আদরে।

সেখা ঘুরবে যেথাই মনের খুশি,

ইচ্ছা যাহা ধরে।

তবে বিনয় আমার বেলা বলি-

এসো গো আমার বাড়ি,

নহে তো শহর পার করিতে,

রাতের প্রহর ধরি।

শুনতে হবে কড়ায় কড়ায়-

আর চোখে পেলে ঘুম-

হয়তো ধড়াস পড়ে ব্যাথার জ্বালায়
পারে আটকে যেতে দম।
ওহে এসো না একবার মোদের বাড়ি-
দেখে যাও শহর ঘুরে,
তোমার দুঃখগুলো সব ভুলিয়ে দেবে,
তাঁর হৃদয় স্নেহ ঘিরে।
হে ভিন দেশি মানব সজন-
আমার যদিও ছোট্টঘর-
তবুও মনের ঘরে রবে সবায়,
কেউ নহে মোর পর।
দেখো আমার শহর ধার ঘেসে-
ঐ নদী গেল বয়ে,
যার পূবাল হাওয়ায় পালের তরী
ছুটছে ভাটির নেয়ো।
উজান দেশে বাইছে কেহ-
মাস্তুলে ডোর বেধে,
নদীর পাড় ঘেঁষে গানে ছুটছে টেনে,
দাঁড় ধরা অন্য জনে।
দিন কি আঁধার রাতের কালো-
নেই ভেদাভেদ শুধুই আলো,
যেন আমার শহর স্বর্ণঝরা,
পূর্ণিমা চাঁদের ফালি ধরা।

384

আরো আকাশ কানন ফুলগুলো সব-

মাথার উপর হাসে।

শুধু একটি কথা বলতে গেলে-

হাতের কলম আর না চলে-

ঐ গাড়ীর চাপায় মরলে মানুষ,

তার চোখ জলে বুক ভাসে।

Kazi Tasmia Tazry / কাজী তাসমিয়া তাজরী, Muradnagar, Comilla, Bangladesh

My city, my parents, my dreams and my rights inspired me.

শহর বনাম স্বপ্ন

ছোট্ট শহরের এক কোণে
মায়ের আদরে ঘেরা
ভাই-বোনের কোলাহলে পূর্ণ
সঙ্গে বাবার মৃদু শাসন।

কী আছে আমার ছোট্ট শহর মুরাদনগরে?
এমন প্রশ্নের জবাব যারা চায়
তাদের আমি বলে দেই, কী নেই বলুন?
গোমতীর তীর থেকে আসা বিশুদ্ধ শীতল বাতাস
আমাদের ভালোবাসতে শেখায়।
আরো আছে আল্লাহ চত্বর, মোহনমার্কেট।
বেড়ে উঠার নিত্য সঙ্গী স্কুল-কলেজ
সেখানে পরিচিত কিছু হাসিমাখা মুখ
ভুলিয়ে দেয় সব কষ্ট।
চেনা রাস্তা, চেনা গলি
যেখানে জেগে থাকে খুপরির মতো ফুচকার দোকান
আড্ডায়-আড্ডায়।

ছোট্ট স্টেডিয়ামে বল নিয়ে ছুটতে ছুটতে
নিজেদের দর্শকের কাছে প্রমাণ করা রাস্তার ছেলেরা

যারা স্বপ্ন দেখে

ছাড়িয়ে যাবে পেলে, ম্যারাডোনা, মেসিকেও

শহরকে নিয়ে যাবে এক অনন্য উচ্চতায়।

আরও আছে শিল্পকলা একাডেমি

যেখানে শিশুরা নেচে বেড়াচ্ছে, গেয়ে বেড়াচ্ছে

হয়তো এরাই হবে বিশ্ববরেণ্য শিল্পী

পরম মমতায় বুকে আগলে নিয়ে

প্রিয় শহরের স্মৃতি।

আমারো বড় ইচ্ছে করে

বুকের মাঝে পুষে রাখা স্বপ্ন পূরণে

ছুটে যেতে বিশ্বদরবারে।

হয়তো দারুণ কিছু অপেক্ষা করছে

বাড়ির চার দেয়ালের বাইরে

শহর থেকে অনেক দূরে।

কিন্তু, তক্ষুনি অনুভব করি শক্ত শেকল

আমার পায়ে বাঁধা।

তবে কি এই শহর আমাকে বড্ড বেশি ভালোবাসে?

নাকি এই শহর মেয়েদের জন্য রক্ষণশীল

ঠিক এখানকার দশটা পরিবারের মতো

যেখানে মেয়েদের লোক দেখানো লেখাপড়া শেখানো হয়

আর উচ্চমাধ্যমিক পেরোবার আগেই,

ধরে-বেঁধে বিয়ে।

স্বপ্ন, লেখাপড়া, ক্যারিয়ার

সব না হয় বিয়ের পর হবে।

সত্যি কি স্বপ্নগুলো পূরন হবে?

আমি সুলতানার মতো জীবন পেতে চাই না
যাকে রোজ মাতাল স্বামীর চড়-থাপ্পড় সহ্য করতে হয়।
কিংবা নিরুপমার মতো,
যৌতুকের টাকার জন্য দীর্ঘদিন নির্যাতিত হবার পর
একদিন সকালে তার লাশ ভেসে উঠেছিল
বাড়ির পাশে পচা ডোবায়।

আমি এভাবে মৃতের মতো বেঁচে থাকতে চাই না।
আমি শুধু নিজের পায়ে দাঁড়াতে চাই।
নিজের স্বপ্নকে আঁকড়ে ধরে বাঁচতে চাই।
তক্ষুনি শুনতে পাই,
চারিদিক থেকে স্বজনেরা চিৎকার করে বলছে,
'দাঁড়াও, বাইরের পৃথিবী তোমার জন্য নয়।
যেখানে স্কুল বাসের জন্য একলা দাঁড়িয়ে থাকা
আট বছরের শিশুকেও
দেখতে হয় নির্ঠুর থাবা,
যেখানে নিষ্পাপ কিশোরীকে
রোজ রাতে আয়নার সামনে দাঁড়িয়ে অশ্রুসজল চোখে
অ্যাসিড ঝলসানো চেহারায়
হাত বুলাতে হয়,
সেই ভয়ঙ্কর পৃথিবীতে

তুমি কখনোই নিরাপদ নয়।
ঘর থেকে বাইরে পা ফেলা মানেই
চরম অনিশ্চয়তায় নিজেকে ঠেলে দেওয়া।'

হয়তো তাদের কথাই ঠিক।
তবু বদ্ধ ঘরে নিজেকে খুব অসহায় মনে হয়
যখন দেখি, পাশের বাড়ির সমবয়সী ছেলেটি
অনেক আগেই পাড়ি জমিয়েছে দূর দেশে
ঘুরে বেড়াচ্ছে, উড়ে বেড়াচ্ছে
নিজের স্বপ্নের পথে।
মেয়েরা কি কখনো পাবেনা উড্ডয়ন-ক্ষমতা?

Halima Khatun / হালিমা খাতুন, Dhaka, Bangladesh

Social discrimination inspired me

আমার বাড়ি

এক সময় ভাবতাম –

যেখায় বেড়েছে মোর আজন্ম শৈশব।

অদৃশ্য মমতায় বাঁধা বন্ধন,

পরিবেশ, পড়শী আর স্বজন,

প্রশান্তি পেতাম দুঃখের দহনে-

নীলাকাশ আর শ্যামলিমা দেখে,

শ্বশুরালয়ে এসব ছেড়ে-

থাকবো কেমন করে।

সব ফেলে এসেছি হাত ধরে অন্যের,

সাজিয়েছি সুখের ঘরকোণের।

এরাই এখন আপন গত হয়েছে পর।

আজ ভাবি, কেমন করে যাব পরপার।

হয়তো এমন করে যাবো চলে,

এদিনকে পাবার বাসনা সেদিনে-

মনকে উদ্বেলিত করবে কিনা,

তা আজ অজানা আর অজানা।

Shahana Yasmin / সাহানা ইয়াসমিন, Dhaka, Bangladesh

In Dhaka, the city I live in, you can see mothers of school children waiting outside the school for 5 to 6 hours every day. This city does not have any public toilet for women. So these mothers cannot go to toilet for a long time, and develop urinary diseases. Their husbands don't find them attractive, so they develop relationships with other women. I wanted to write about the plight of these mothers. My City and My Home inspired me to write this.

এক 'কিছুই করে না' মেয়ের গল্প

ডাক্তার সাহেব জিজ্ঞেস করলেন, আপনি কি করেন?

আমি কিছু বলার আগেই আমার হয়ে উত্তর দিল শাহেদ, কিছুই করে না, হাউস ওয়াইফ!!

'হাউস ওয়াইফ' কথাটা শাহেদ এমনভাবে বলল যেন এর চেয়ে তুচ্ছ কাজ আর নেই, আত্মগ্লানিতে আমি মাথা নিচু করে বসে আঙুলে আঁচল জড়াতে লাগলাম। ডাক্তার সাহেব ঘসঘস করে প্রেসক্রিপসন লিখে আমার হাতেই দিলেন।

- পেসাব চেপে রাখতে রাখতে আপনি রোগ বাঁধিয়েছেন... এই ওষুধগুলোর সাথে সাথে প্রতিদিন প্রচুর পানি খাবেন, আর কখনোই পেসাব চেপে রাখবেন না।

ডাক্তারের ঘর থেকে বেরিয়ে আমি কুণ্ঠিতভাবে শাহেদের দিকে চাইলাম, দেখলাম বিরক্তিতে শাহেদের কপাল কুঁচকে আছে, আমার দিকে একেবারেই তাকাচ্ছে না! বিরক্ত হবারই কথা, অন্যদিন এসময়ে অফিস থেকে ফিরে শাহেদ বিশ্রাম নেয়; টিভি দেখে, ফেসবুক করে। অথচ আজ আমার জন্য প্রায় তিন ঘন্টা গেল ডাক্তার দেখাতে, এখন আবার যানজট ঠেলে বাড়ি পৌঁছাতে লাগবে এক দেড় ঘন্টা! মনে মনে ভাবলাম, বাড়িতে ঢুকে আগে চুলায় চায়ের পানি চাপিয়ে দিয়ে

391

তারপর নিজে ফ্রেশ হতে যাব। গরম এক কাপ চা হয়ত শাহেদের মাথা কিছুটা ঠাণ্ডা করতে পারে!

সব কাজ সেরে শুতে শুতে রোজকার মতোই বারোটা বেজে গেল। শাহেদ ততক্ষণে গভীর ঘুমে; সকালে অফিস আছে বলে ও কোন রাতেই আমার জন্য অপেক্ষা করে থাকে না... একটা দীর্ঘশ্বাস ফেললাম; অনেক চেষ্টা করেও আমি এর চাইতে আগে শুতে আসতে পারি না... তাই কোনদিনই শাহেদের সাথে দুটা কথা বলার সময় হয় না। কিন্তু উপায় কী! আমার দিন শুরু হয় ভোর পাঁচটায়। শাহেদের মতো অফিসে যাই না কিন্তু আমাকেও প্রতিদিন শাহেদের মতোই সকালে বের হতে হয়, তবে আমার বের হওয়াটা শাহেদের মতো কাজে নয়, বরং মেয়ে তৃণাকে স্কুলে নিয়ে যাবার মতো অকাজে। বেরোবার আগে শাহেদের নাস্তা টেবিলে দেয়া, তৃণার টিফিন, দুপুরের একটা তরকারি এসব করতে হয়। দুপুরে কোনমতে এক তরকারি দিয়ে মা-মেয়ে খাই, কিন্তু রাতে ভালোমন্দ রান্না করতেই হয়। খাবার ভালো না হলে শাহেদ রাগ করে বলে, সামান্য রান্নাটাও করতে পারো না!

শুনে মনখারাপ হয়; তাই যতই ক্লান্তি লাগুক, সন্ধ্যা হতেই আমি শাহেদের পছন্দের তরকারি রাঁধতে শুরু করি, রান্না শেষ হতে রাত নয়টা। ফাঁকে ফাঁকে তৃণার পড়া দেখতে হয়। শাহেদ বলে, এমনই এম এ পাশ, যে মেয়েকে পড়াতেও পারে না!

একথা শাহেদ বলতেই পারে। ওর সহকর্মী শায়লা এম এ পাশ করে কেমন সুন্দর চাকরি করছে, অথচ আমি কিছুই করি না। অতএব তৃণাকে পড়ানোর দায়িত্ব আমারই ওপর।

শায়লার কথা ভাবলেই আমার বুকের কোথাও একটা চিনচিনে ব্যথা হয়। শাহেদের মুখে শায়লার প্রশংসা লেগেই থাকে, শায়লা কত স্মার্ট, কী সুন্দর ব্যবহার, কী মার্জিত সাজগোজ, আমার মতো হাউজ ওয়াইফ তো না! শায়লা

তেমন সুন্দরী নয়, কিন্তু সুন্দরভাবে মেকআপ করে সুন্দর শাড়ি পরে মুখে এমন স্মিত হাসি ঝুলিয়ে রাখে যে আমিই মুগ্ধ হই, শাহেদ মুগ্ধ হবে এ আর বেশি কী! শাহেদ যখন অফিসের গাড়িতে ওঠার সময় শায়লার দিকে তাকিয়ে হাসে, তখন ওর চোখ জুড়ে থাকে কী মুগ্ধতা!

প্রতি শনিবার অফিসের গাড়িতে ওঠার সময় শায়লার দিকে তাকিয়ে শাহেদের হাসি দেখি আমি। শনিবারে তৃণার স্কুল বন্ধ তাই আমার সুযোগ হয় জানালার পর্দার পেছনে দাঁড়িয়ে গাড়িতে বসা শায়লাকে দেখার! শায়লা শাহেদের দিকে তাকিয়ে হাসে আর শাহেদও হাসিমুখে গাড়িতে উঠে শায়লার পাশে বসে। আমার খুব মনখারাপ লাগে, কতদিন শাহেদ হাসিমুখে আমার সাথে কথা বলেনি...কতদিন শাহেদের সাথে সুখদুঃখের কথা বলিনি...

আমার সুখদুঃখের কথা বলার সাথী তাহমিনা, রিতা, সাবিহা... এরা আমার বান্ধবী। আমরা বান্ধবী হয়েছি মেয়ের স্কুলে এসে। আমাদের সবার বাসাই আজিমপুরের এই স্কুল থেকে অনেক দূরে। ঢাকার নানা প্রান্ত থেকে দীর্ঘ সময় বাসযাত্রা করে আমরা স্কুলে আসি। ট্রাফিক জ্যামের জন্য বারবার যাতায়াত করা সম্ভব না, তাই আমরা ছুটি হওয়া পর্যন্ত স্কুলের কাছাকাছি ফুটপাতে বসে আড্ডা দিই। আমাদের মতো এমন অনেক মায়েরাই সকালে বাচ্চা নিয়ে এসে ছুটি পর্যন্ত অপেক্ষা করেন ফুটপাতে বসে। ফুটপাতে বসার এই জীবন আমরা বাধ্য হয়ে বেছে নিয়েছি সন্তানের উজ্জ্বল ভবিষ্যৎ দেখবার আশা নিয়ে। এই শহরে যে গুটিকয় ভালো স্কুল আছে তার একটিতে তখন সন্তান পড়ার সুযোগ পায়, তখন আমাদের মতো মধ্যবিত্ত মা-বাবা সেই সুযোগ লুফে নেয়। বাড়ি থেকে স্কুল যত দূরেই হোক, আমরা সেই ভালো স্কুলে ভর্তি করাই। স্কুলে আনা নেওয়ার দায়িত্ব পড়ে 'হাউজ ওয়াইফ' মায়েদের উপরে, এই শহর ছোট মেয়েদের একাকী যাতায়াতের জন্য নিরাপদ নয়।

প্রথমদিকে ভালোই লাগতো, সুন্দর সালোয়ার কামিজ, কখনো শাড়ি পড়ে সাজগোজ করে স্কুলে আসতাম। কয়মাস পরেই সাজগোজ কোথায় উধাও...

আমরা বোরকা পরা ধরলাম কারণ রোদে-ঘামে অল্পদিনেই সব পোশাক মলিন আর বিবর্ণ হয়ে যায়। দীর্ঘ সময় ফুটপাতে বসে থেকেও ঘরে ফিরে ঘরের কাজ করায় আমরা অভ্যস্ত হয়ে পড়লাম। শীতের ধোঁয়াশায় দিনে আমরা ঠান্ডা ফুটপাতে বসে কাঁপি, ঝমঝম বর্ষায় ছাতা মাথায় দিয়ে দোকানের ছাউনির নিচে দাঁড়াই, গ্রীষ্মের চড়া রোদে পুড়ে আমাদের চামড়া কালো হতে থাকে... আমাদের চেহারা ক্রমশ খারাপ হয়...

আমরা বসে কত গল্প করি। একসময় দেখা গেল আমাদের সবার জীবনের গল্প একই - আমাদের সবার স্বামীই এক ছাতের নিচে থেকেও আমাদের থেকে অনেক দূরে থাকে... আত্মীয়- পরিচিত অনেকেই আমাদের করুণার চোখে দেখে, কারণ আমরা দেখতে ঝলমলে না, আমরা তুচ্ছ কাজে ব্যস্ত থাকি! আমাদের স্বামীরা যে আমাদের প্রতি আগ্রহ হারিয়ে প্রত্যেকেই নিজের আগ্রহের জায়গা খুঁজে নিয়েছেন, এসব কথা কাউকে বলার নয়। তাই তাহমিনা, সাবিহা, রিতা আর আমি স্বপ্না, এসব দুঃখের কথা আমরা নিজেদের মধ্যে বলাবলি করে একটু হালকা হই।

ফুটপাতে বসে থাকতে থাকতে আমরা একটা অভ্যাস আয়ত্ত করেছি- সাত আট ঘন্টার জন্য প্রস্রাব চেপে থাকা। প্রতিদিন বাড়ি থেকে বেরিয়ে ফিরতে আমাদের এই সময় লাগে। স্কুলের আশপাশে কোন পাবলিক টয়লেট নেই যে সেখানে যাব, আসলে এই শহরে মেয়েদের জন্য পাবলিক টয়লেট নেই বললেই চলে। এজন্য আমরা সকাল থেকে খুবই অল্প পরিমাণ পানি খাই যাতে প্রস্রাব না পায়। এর ফলে আমাদের প্রত্যেকেরই কোন না কোন শারীরিক জটিলতা দেখা দিয়েছে, যেমন আমার মাঝে মাঝে জ্বর হয় আর সহজে প্রস্রাব হতে চায় না। কিছুদিন ধরে খুব কষ্ট হচ্ছিল দেখে আজ ডাক্তারের কাছে গেছিলাম, কিন্তু ডাক্তার যে বললেন প্রচুর পানি খেতে আর নিয়মিত বাথরুমে যেতে - সেটা কীভাবে করব! নিয়মিত বাথরুমে যাবার জন্য আমাকে তো বাসায় থাকতে হবে; তাহলে তৃণা স্কুল করবে কীভাবে!

ঘুমন্ত শাহেদকে কী নিশ্চিন্ত দেখাচ্ছে। আমার দুশ্চিন্তার ভাগ নেবার মতো কেউ নেই এ বাড়িতে!! দুশ্চিন্তার সাথে যোগ হয়েছে শরীরের কষ্ট, প্রস্রাব করার সময়

পেটে খুব যন্ত্রণা হতে থাকে কিন্তু সহজে প্রস্রাব হয়না। দীর্ঘ সময় বাথরুমের কল ছেড়ে রাখলে পানি পড়ার শব্দে একসময় আমার অল্প প্রস্রাব হয়।

বাথরুমে কলের জলের ধারার সাথে সাথে অঝোর ধারায় আমার গাল বেয়ে জল ঝরতে থাকে; এ জলে মিশে আছে এক মেয়ের যন্ত্রনা, অপমান আর অভিমান। আমার সংগ্রামের কথা ঘরের কেউ বুঝতে পারেনা... কিন্তু এই শহরের রাস্তা আর ফুটপাত কী জানে কতটা কষ্ট করে আমি টিকে আছি!

Sirajam Munira Binte Yusuf / সিরাজাম মুনীরা বিনতে ইউসুফ, Dhaka, Bangladesh

'মাই সিটি মাই হোম' আমাকে নারীদের সম্পর্কে বলার সুযোগ করে দিয়েছে। নারীদের ডানা মেলার সুযোগ নেই। সেই কথাগুলো আমাকে লেখার সময় বারবার মনে করিয়েছে। ধন্যবাদ 'মাই সিটি এন্ড মাই হোম' টিমকে নারীর না পাওয়ার বেদনা তুলে ধরার সুযোগ দেবার জন্য।

মেয়েমানুষ

আমি বিন্দু। গল্পের বিন্দুবাসিনী নই। শাড়ী, গহনা, পান খাওয়া ঠোঁট, হাসিহাসি মুখ সেই বিন্দুবাসিনী নই। ছোট্ট শহর হতে আসা মেয়ে আমি। নরসিংদীর শিবপুরের মেয়ে আমি। আমার ছিল মৃগের মতো এক জোড়া স্বপ্নচারিনী চোখ, যে চোখে আমি স্বপ্ন দেখেছি বড়ো হব বলে। কতটা বড়ো? পরিমাপ করিনি। ছোটবেলা পাইলট হবার স্বপ্ন দেখেছি আকাশে বোঁ বোঁ করে বিমান যেতে দেখে। তারপর বাবা যখন স্কুলে ছেড়ে এল, গুটি গুটি পায়ে নতুন স্বপ্নরা ডানা মেলল। স্কুলের টিচার আপাদের কথা শুনে মনে হত ডাক্তার বা ইঞ্জিনিয়ার হলেই সব স্বপ্ন বোধহয় পূরণ হয়ে যাবে। স্কুলের গন্ডি পেরিয়ে যখন কলেজে এলাম, স্বপ্নগুলো পাল্টে গেল। বাবার হাতে বিবর্ণ বাজারের ব্যাগ, মায়ের ছেড়া আঁচলে মোছা ঘাম, স্বপ্নগুলোকে বাস্তবতায় টেনে হিঁচড়ে নিয়ে এল। তখন স্বপ্ন আমার শুধুই আমাকে পরিচালিত করতে পারে এমন একজন ভাল ছেলে। সব রঙিন স্বপ্ন ডানা ভেঙে দুমড়ে পড়ে মুখ থুবড়ে।

তারপর একদিন আমাকে পরিচালিত করতে পারা ছেলের দেখা মিলে যায়। ততদিনে আমিও কলেজের দেয়াল পেরিয়ে ভার্সিটিতে উড়তে শুরু করেছি। রাফিদ। একটা বিদেশি কোম্পানির হিউম্যান রিসোর্স অফিসার। মাইনে ভাল। ঢাকায় ফ্ল্যাট আছে। একটি গ্রামের মেধাবী মেয়ের জন্য এর চেয়ে বেশি আর কি চাওয়া হতে পারে!

তারপর নতুন শহর। স্বপ্নের শহর। ঢাকা শহর। ইট, কাঠ আর পাথরের সাথে নতুন জীবন। কোথায় পাইলট, কোথায় ডাক্তার, কোথায় ইঞ্জিনিয়ার আর কোথায় স্বাবলম্বী হবার স্বপ্ন! মেয়েদের আকাশে ওড়ার স্বপ্ন আমাদের সমাজে দেখতে নেই। সেটা পাপ বৈকি!

টিপ টিপ শিশির ঝরছে। সবুজ পাতার ওপর শিশিরের বিন্দুগুলো যেন কান্না হয়ে ঝরছে। আমার কান্না। তোমার কান্না। কে জানে, কার কান্না? আজ বিকেলের মন খারাপ করেছে আমার সাথে। সকাল হতেই মন খারাপ। রাফিদ অফিস যাবার আগে খুচরো টাকা ধরিয়ে বলল, সবজি কিনে নিও। আর শুক্রবারে মাছ গোশত (মাংস) কিনবনে। আম্মা দরজায় দাঁড়িয়ে ছিলেন, পোলাগোর কাম মাইয়্যাগরে মানায় না। আজকালকার পোলারা কামচোর।

রাফিদ উপরের আর নিচের পাটির বত্রিশ দাঁত বের করে হাসি দিল। যেন আমার শাশুড়িমা মজার কোনো জোক বলেছেন। আমিও সংকুচিত হয়ে পড়লাম। আম্মা আমার হাতে পয়সা দেওয়াটা কখনই ভালো চোখে দেখেন না। বাড়ির বউদের পয়সা হাতে দিলে তারা নাকি আসমানে ওড়ে। আর কেনাকাটার ভার! সেটা তো গর্হিত কাজ, বাড়ির বউদের জন্য। নেহাত আম্মা বাতের ব্যথায় ভুগছেন, নয়ত এসব কাজ আমার হাতে আসার কোন কারণই ছিল না।

বারান্দায় দাঁড়িয়ে আমি কুমড়োর ফুল আর লাউ কিনছি। বউ ভাল কইরা ওড়না দাও। সবজিওয়ালা বেডা কিমনে চাইয়া আছে!

আমি ওড়না টেনে নিচে ঝুড়ি ফেললাম। সবজিওয়ালার নিরীহ চেহারার সাথে আম্মার বাক্যের কোন মিল পেলাম না। তবে কোথায় যেন মরমে লেগেছে আমার। কত টাকার সবজি কিনলা? টাকা গুইনা রাখছ? দেহি.....দশ....পাঁচ.....বিশ.....চল্লিশ ট্যাহা বাঁচছে। হিসাব রাহ।

চোখ ফেটে জল এল। আমি কি চোর! টাকাটাও গুনে রাখতে হবে ওনার?

সবজি কুটতে গিয়ে খেয়াল করলাম হাতের দিকে। চামড়া উঠছে হাতে।

শীতকালে আমার হাতের চামড়া ওঠে। রাফিদকে বলতে হবে, একটা তিব্বত পমেট এনো। বুকের ভেতর অভিমান জমে ওঠে। কেন বলব? সে কি পারে না, আমি না বললেও আনতে! তিন বছরে এ বাসার অনেক কিছু পাল্টে গেছে। আমি আসার পর বাচ্চা যে বুয়াটা ছিল তাকে আম্মা কাজ থেকে ছাড়িয়ে দিয়েছেন। টাকার অপচয়। আর তাছাড়া বউ বসে বসে করবেটা কী? প্রথম প্রথম আমার হাতের চায়ের বেশ প্রশংসা শুনতাম বিকেলবেলা। এখন সেটা রূপ নিয়েছে বাড়তি খরচে। আর বলেন না ভাবি, বউ আসার পর বাসায় বাড়তি খরচ শুরু হয়েছে।

- কী বলেন ভাবি?

- হুম, প্রতি বিকেলে দুধ চা। দুধ আবার চা পাতা। খরচ কী কম!

চোখ ফেটে জল এসেছিল। আমি বাড়ির বউই রয়ে গেলাম। বাড়তি খরচের বউ। মেয়ে হয়ে উঠতে পারিনি।

কষ্ট হয়। আত্মনির্ভরশীলতা কাকে বলে? দুইটাকার জিনিসও আমি আমার পছন্দে কিনতে পারি না। চাকরি করলে ভাল করতাম। হাতে পয়সা থাকত। সে হবার জো নেই আমার কপালে। বিয়ের আগে যখন দেখতে এসেছিল প্রথম শর্তই ছিল, বউ চাকরি করতে পারবে না। বউ চাকরি করবে না, তবে বউয়ের শখ আহ্লাদ পূরণ করার দায়িত্ব কার! আমার বড়ো পড়ার শখ। বই পড়া আমার নেশার মতন। সময় পেলেই আমি পড়তে বসে যাই।

- বিয়ের পর সংসারে মন দিতে হয়। এসব গল্পর বই পড়লে সংসারের পেট ভরে না।

রাফিদ আসতেই সে কী বকা!

- বলি এসব ছাইপাশ আনিস কেন কিনে? সেজন্যই সংসার হচ্ছে না।

সংসার মানে কী সেটাই এখনো আমি বুঝিনি। বই পড়ার সাথে সংসারের

অনাসৃষ্টি হবার কী সম্পর্ক, আমি তা আজও আবিষ্কার করতে পারিনি। সব করে আমি শুয়ে বা বসেই কাটাই। বই পড়লে কি সমস্যা!

আমি সবজি কুটে রাখতেই মার আগমন।

- বিন্দু?

- জ্বি আম্মা।

- তাহানকে একবার ভাল ড্রেস পরিয়ে দাও।

আমি একবার আকাশ হতে পড়লাম। আজ কি মেহমান আসবে নাকি? আম্মাতো আমাকে কিছু বলেনি।

- আম্মা কেউ আসবে?

- না, আমি তাহানকে নিয়ে রোজীদের বাসায় যাব। ছোটমানুষ। ওর বেড়ানোর দরকার আছে। ওর মন ভাল হবে।

আমার বুক চিরে দীর্ঘশ্বাস বেরিয়ে এল। আমি তবে মানুষ নই। আমি বউ। আমার মন নেই। সে মনকে ভাল করবার জন্য বেড়ানোর কোন প্রয়োজন আমার কেন থাকবে? মনে পড়ে রাফিদের কথা। তুমি মেয়েমানুষ তোমার ঘরেই থাকার কথা। বুকের ভেতর চিনচিন করে বাজে কথাটা, মেয়েমানুষ!

আমি বারান্দায় গিয়ে দাঁড়াই। দূরে বিল্ডিংয়ের কোন ফ্ল্যাটের জানালা দেখা যায়। জানলায় দেখা যায় কারও মুখ। বুকের ভেতর সমুদ্দুরের ঢেউ ভাঙে। শহরের জানলায় মুখ রাখা অচেনা আরেক মেয়েমানুষের জন্য। হয়ত তারও ডানা মেলে আমার মতই ওড়ার স্বপ্ন ছিল কে জানে! আমি চুপ করে শহরের স্বপ্ন ভাঙা মেয়েমানুষগুলোর জন্য বেদনা অনুভব করি। তবু স্বপ্ন দেখি রাফিদের মতন পুরুষরা একদিন আমাদের স্বপ্নগুলোও দেখবে ওদের চোখ দিয়ে। বুঝবে সাইকেল চলতে হলে একচাকা নয় দুই চাকাই সচল হতে হবে। আমরা মেয়েমানুষরাও একসাথে পথ চলব। আমরা এদিন হয়ত একসাথে করব কোন উৎসব! শুধুই প্রত্যাশা!

Sumaiya Santa / সুমাইয়া সান্তা, Dhaka, Bangladesh

A few days ago I learned from the newspaper that a garment worker has been diagnosed with a disease. But she hid her illness from her husband and her family. She knows, in this case, that her husband and his family will not show sympathy and they may leave her. So, she goes to work, hiding her illness. This news hit me hard. The city's going ahead but the attitude towards women has not changed. This incident inspired me to write about `My City, My Home'.

প্রতিটি শহর হতো যদি নারীর প্রিয় বাড়ি

আমার শহরের দিন-দিন উন্নতি ঘটছে। এ শহরে নারীরাও আজ পিছিয়ে নেই। নারীরা এখানে প্রধানমন্ত্রী, সংসদের স্পিকার, বিশ্ববিদ্যলয়ের উপাচার্য হচ্ছেন, উচ্চ-আদালতের বিচারক হচ্ছেন, সশস্ত্র বাহিনীতেও যোগ দিচ্ছেন। শতাধিক বছর আগে বাঙালি নারী জাগরণের অগ্রদূত রোকেয়া সাখাওয়াত হোসেন যে আশাবাদ ব্যক্ত করেছিলেন সে আশা আজ পূর্ণ। শহর সমাজের যে উন্নয়ন হচ্ছে দিকে-দিকে তার অংশীদার আজ নারী, পুরুষের সাথে পায়ে পা মিলিয়ে সেও ভূমিকা রাখছে সার্বিক উন্নয়নে।

যে শহরের উন্নতিতে নারীর অবদান কোন অংশে কম নয় সে শহর নারীকে পুরুষতান্ত্রিক দৃষ্টিভঙ্গি থেকে পরিত্রাণ দিতে পারেনি। যে নারীটি গৃহবধূ সেও যেমন তার স্বামী-পরিবার দ্বারা নির্যাতিত হয়, ঠিক তেমনি চাকুরিজীবি নারীটিও স্বামী-পরিবার দ্বারা নির্যাতিত হয়। অর্থাৎ এ শহর আজ আর্থ-সামাজিক দিক দিয়ে এগিয়ে গেলেও, নারী আজও পুরুষতান্ত্রিক দৃষ্টিতে পদানত।

এ শহরের ফ্ল্যাটগুলো বিলাসবহুল; ফ্ল্যাট গুলোর এত জাঁকজমকের মাঝে পরিবারের কর্ত্রীর ইবাদত করার জায়গাটি হয়তো সুনির্দিষ্ট নয়, বেশিরভাগ ফ্ল্যাটেই নারীর রান্নাঘরগুলো সংকীর্ণ, সেখানে আজও রয়েছে কম ভোল্টেজের আলো। এই বিলাসবহুল ফ্ল্যাটগুলো চকচকে করে রাখতেই হয়তো গৃহকর্ত্রীর

পুরোটা সময় চলে যায়; তাই নিজের যত্ন নেওয়ার হয়তো আর সময় থাকে না।

বিনা পারিশ্রমিকেই যে নারী পরিবারের ঝামেলাগুলো সামলে চলে বছরের পর বছর সে কখনোই পারিশ্রমিক প্রত্যাশা করে না। কিন্তু দিনশেষে হয়তো একটু নির্ভরতাও সে স্বামী-পরিবার থেকে পায় না এ শহরে। এ শহরের পুরুষগুলোর অধিকাংশেরই ধারণা সংসারে কী আর এমন কাজ!!

এ শহরের নারীরা এখন আর গৃহকোণে বন্দী নেই; পুরুষের মতো সেও রোজ যায় অফিস ও কারখানায়। কিন্তু তার যাত্রাপথের নিরাপত্তা নেই এ শহরে। গণপরিবহন গুলোতে নারীর করুণ অবস্থার চিত্র সবারই জানা।

এ শহরের অলি-গলিতে রাত জেগে পুলিশেরা টহল দিলেও দিনের আলো নিভে যাওয়ার সাথে সাথে সে গলিতে নারী আর নিরাপদ থাকে না। শিশু, যুবতী, বৃদ্ধা যে কোন বয়সের নারীই যে কোন জায়গায় হতে পারে ধর্ষণের শিকার।

এ শহরে নারী আজ অনেক স্বাধীন, অনেক আত্মবিশ্বাসী। স্বাধীন! তবু সে হয় ধর্ষণের শিকার। ধর্ষণের শিকার নারীটির অন্তর্জ্বালার সাক্ষী হয়ে থাকে তার ইট-পাথরে ঘেরা বাড়ির দেয়ালগুলো। বেশিরভাগ সময়ই ধর্ষকের বিচার হয় না। নারী কি আজও শুধুমাত্র ভোগের সামগ্রী রয়ে গেল?

শহরের মানুষগুলো একদম যৌতুকের বিপক্ষে! কিন্তু বিয়ের সময় কনের বাবার কাছ থেকে মোটা অঙ্কের টাকা এখনও নেওয়া হয়।

এ শহরের অনেক পুরুষ শুধু ধর্মের দোহাই দিয়ে এটাই প্রমাণ করতে চায় যে, স্বামী সেবা করলেই পরকালে মুক্তি! কিন্তু এ ক্ষেত্রে ধর্মে স্ত্রীর প্রতি স্বামীকে যে কতটা নমনীয় হওয়ার বিধিনিষেধ উল্লেখ আছে তা কি পুরুষদের দৃষ্টি এড়িয়ে যায়? স্বামী-স্ত্রী দুজনেই সহযোগিতায় এ শহরের প্রতিটি বাড়ি হয়ে উঠতে পারে শান্তিময়।

অফিস-সংসার-স্বামী-সন্তান সবকিছু সামলে নেয় পরিবারের স্ত্রীটিই। কিন্তু তার দিকে খেয়াল রাখার মতো কেউ কি আছে ব্যস্ত এ শহরে? মাতৃত্বকালীন সময়ে বা অন্য কোনো অসুস্থতায় কয়টা স্বামী তার স্ত্রীর পাশে থাকে? যত অসুস্থই

হোক পরিবারের দায়িত্ব থেকে তার নিস্তার মেলে না মুহূর্তের জন্য।

অনেক নারী তার শারীরিক অসুস্থতার কথা গোপন করে তার স্বামী ও পরিবার থেকে। সে জানে, অসুস্থতার কথা জানলে সামান্য সহানুভূতি তো দূরে থাক উল্টো তাকে পেতে হবে অবহেলা। নারীর যে সুন্দর একটি মন আছে সে মনের যত্ন নেওয়ার কি কোন অবসর আছে এই ব্যস্ত শহরে?

এ শহরে অনেক সময়ই নারী তার পোশাক নিয়ে সমালোচিত হয়। যে মেয়েটা ওয়েস্টার্ন ড্রেস পরতে অভ্যস্ত তাকে ব্যঙ্গ করা হয় এই বলে যে, 'এদের জন্যই ধর্ষণের ঘটনা ঘটে'। অনুরূপ ভাবে, পর্দানশীল একটি মেয়েকেও তার পোশাক নিয়েও ব্যঙ্গ করা হয়।

বাঙালি নারী জাগরণের অগ্রদূত 'রোকেয়া সাখাওয়াত' বহু বছর আগে আক্ষেপ করে বলেছিলেন, 'স্ত্রী-লোকের কাজের মজুরি কম'। আজও এ শহরে কিছু কিছু ক্ষেত্রে নারীর কাজে কম মজুরি দেওয়া হয়। শহর-দেশের সার্বিক উন্নয়নে গার্মেন্টস শিল্পের অবদান অপরিসীম। সেই শিল্পের চালক যে নারী শ্রমিক, সে কতটা ভালো আছে এ শহরে? ঘন্টার পর ঘন্টা পরিশ্রম করেও যে সামান্য মজুরি সে পায় তাতে ব্যয়-বহুল এ শহরে দিনযাপন করতে হয় তাকে অনেক কষ্টে।

ব্যস্ত শহর আরো ব্যস্ত হচ্ছে দিনে দিনে। কিন্তু এই শহরটা কি কখনও নারীর জন্য শান্তির বাড়ি হয়ে উঠবে না? যেদিন এ শহরে নারী আর হবে না নির্যাতিত, নারীকে শুধুমাত্র তার বাহ্যিক সৌন্দর্য দিয়ে ভোগ্যবস্তু হিসেবে পুরুষতান্ত্রিক দৃষ্টিভঙ্গিতে বিচার করা হবে না, নারীর প্রতি বন্ধ হবে সকল হিংসা, সেদিন এ শহর হয়ে উঠবে নারীর বাড়ি। যে বাড়িতে মা-বোন-স্ত্রী হিসেবে নারী পাবে তার যথাযথ মর্যাদা, যে বাড়িতে নারীর চিন্তা, চেতনা, কাজ যথাযথভাবে মূল্যায়িত হবে। প্রতিটি শহর যদি নারীর নিরাপদ বাড়ি হয়ে উঠতো! কবে আসবে সে শুভ দিন?

Lina Ferdows Khan / লীনা ফেরদৌস খান, Dhaka, Bangladesh

I was inspired by two things. Firstly, I grew up in a woman-unfriendly city. I found myself a voiceless girl to live my own life since my childhood. It is important to highlight the problems and voice our opinions and be part of the discussion to express our needs just to make changes in the society.

Secondly, Bangladeshi women are at a disadvantage as they face barriers in all aspects of their lives. This is a great opportunity to write about the disadvantages & raise my power and voice through writing.

I'm happy to be part My City My Home, this is indeed a great subject to write the untold stories of the women around me. It took me a great deal of strength & power to write about the women who are experiencing or will experience distresses to live their own life. I would like to change our lives and realities through my writing.

শহরের উপাখ্যান

ভোরে ফজরের নামাজ পড়ে চুলায় চা বসিয়ে বারান্দার বাগানের শখের গাছগুলোতে পানি দেয় সুমনা, এই সময়টা তার একান্ত নিজের সময়, চা খেতে খেতে প্রতিদিন নিজের সূক্ষ্ম অনুভূতিগুলো ডায়েরিতে লিখে রাখে সে। এই ঢাকা শহরে এত মানুষ অথচ খুব কাছের এমন কেউ নাই যাকে নিজের একান্ত কথাগুলো বলা যায়, তাই ডায়েরিতে লিখে রাখে সুমনা।

বারান্দায় একটুকরো কমলা-হলুদ রোদ এসে পড়েছে বোগেনভেলিয়া গাছটায়, ম্যাজেন্টা রঙ আর রোদ মিশে কেমন যেন রোমাঞ্চকর লাগছে, গ্রিলে চড়ুই আর শালিক পাখিদের নাচানাচি, স্বচ্ছ নীল আকাশ, মিষ্টি বাতাস – মন ভরে যায় এমন একটা সুন্দর সকালে।

সকাল সকাল রাস্তা পরিষ্কার করছে সিটি কর্পোরেশনের নারী পরিচ্ছন্নতাকর্মীরা। টিফিন বাটি হাতে তড়িঘড়ি বলিষ্ঠ পায়ে হেঁটে যাচ্ছে এক ঝাঁক নারী পোশাক শ্রমিক, এপাশের ফুটপাতে পিঠা আর চা বানাচ্ছে আরেক নারী – তাদের কল-কাকলিতে যেন জেগে উঠেছে এই শহর।

ওদেরকে দেখে মন ভাল হয়ে যায় সুমনার, এই সব খেটে খাওয়া নারীদের একটা নিজস্ব গল্প আছে – সংগ্রামের গল্প, এগিয়ে চলার গল্প। সুমনার কোন এগিয়ে চলার গল্প নেই, একই গল্প প্রতিদিন। ইদানীং খুব নিজের মত করে বাঁচতে ইচ্ছে করে,   সন্তান-সংসারের বাইরে যদি নিজের একটা পরিচয় থাকতো, ছোটখাটো যা হোক তবুও একান্ত নিজের।

লেখা বেশি দুর এগোল না, কলিং বেল বাজলো, দরজা খুলে দেখে গৃহকর্মের সহযোগী শিল্পীর কপালে বেশ লম্বা একটা কালশিটে দাগ, নিশ্চয় কাল রাতে ওর স্বামী আবার মেরেছে।

এসব নিয়ে ভাবার এখন অবকাশ নাই, সকাল বেলা এই শহরের সব বাড়ির গল্প অনেকটা একই রকম।   শিল্পী আটার রুটির থামির করতে করতে তার নির্যাতনের কাহিনী বলছিল, সুমনার চোখ ভরে এলো তবুও দ্রুত হাতে গরম তেলে পিঁয়াজ, মরিচ আর কুচানো আলু ছেড়ে, লবণ-পানি দিয়ে ঢেকে দিল। স্বামীর অফিস, মেয়ের স্কুল তাই তড়িঘড়ি করে রুটি সেঁকা, ডিম পোচ আর আলু ভাজি করে টেবিলে নাস্তা নিয়ে এলো।   এভাবে প্রতিদিন রুটি-সেঁকার মত কত নারীর কষ্টের উপাখ্যান ধোঁয়ায় মিলিয়ে যায়।

মেয়েকে রেডি করতে করতে সুমনা ভাবে – এই শহরে মেয়েদের কোন নিরাপত্তা নাই, নিজের কোন জীবন নাই, মেয়েটা যত বড় হচ্ছে, চিন্তাটা তত মাথা চাড়া দিচ্ছে, প্রতিদিন মেয়েকে স্কুলে আনা-নেওয়া করা আরেক কাজ, এই শহরে কোন মেয়েই তো নিরাপদ নয়! আহা! মেয়েটাকে যদি একটা মুক্ত জীবন দিতে পারতো!

মেয়েকে স্কুলে দিয়ে হেঁটে বাড়ি ফেরে সুমনা, স্কুলের সামনে অনেক মায়েরা সারা দিন বসে রাজ্যের গল্প করে, সুমনার ভাল লাগে না। স্কুল টাইমে ভীষণ ট্রাফিক জ্যাম, তাই হেঁটে বাড়ি ফেরে, তাতে শরীরও ভাল থাকে, এই শহরে মেয়েরা সংসারের ব্যস্ততায় নিজের শরীরের যত্ন নিতে ভুলে যায়। রাস্তার পাশে এক মহিলা একমনে ইট ভাঙছে, পাশেই তার বাচ্চাটি ময়লা একটা আধছেঁড়া কাঁথার উপর শুয়ে হাত পা ছুড়ে অনবরত কেঁদেই চলেছে, কী নির্মম জীবন! সন্তানের জন্য এভাবে কষ্ট করা একমাত্র মায়ের পক্ষেই সম্ভব, ভাবতে ভাবতে আনমনা হয়ে যায় সুমনা, আচমকা একটা লোক পিছন দিক থেকে খারাপভাবে স্পর্শ করার চেষ্টা করে দ্রুত সামনের গলির ভেতর ঢুকে যায়, অপমানে-লজ্জায়-ঘৃণায় গা শিউরে উঠে সুমনার।

বাড়ি ফিরেই অনেকটা সময় ধরে গোসল করে, কিন্তু গা ঘিন ঘিন ভাবটা তবুও যায় না তার। সুমনা চুলায় ভাত-ডাল বসিয়ে দিয়ে ঘরের আসবাবপত্র ঝাড়পোছে লেগে যায়, অনেকটা রোবটের মত, প্রতিটা মুহূর্তের কাজ ছকে বাঁধা, এগিয়ে চলা শহরের সাথে সাথে জীবনও যেন দৌড়ায়, এই শহরের মানুষের কেবল ছুটে চলা। চুলায় গরম তেলে পিয়াজ-রসুন, শুকনা মরিচ-আস্ত জিরে ভেজে ডাল বাগার দিতে দিতে মনে পড়ে যায় এরকম ধোঁয়া ওঠা গরম ডাল-ভাতে ঘি মাখিয়ে মা তাঁকে খাইয়ে দিতেন স্কুলে যাবার আগে। আজ মা-বাবা নেই, তাই আর বাপের বাড়িও নেই, ভাইরা এখন নিজেদের মত সংসার করছে, সেখানে বেশি গেলে তারা ভাবে সম্পত্তির ভাগ চাইতে এসেছে; যে বাড়িতে জন্ম, বেড়ে ওঠা, সেই বাড়িটাতে সে এখন অনাকাঙ্ক্ষিত – ভাবতেই কষ্টে বুকটা ফেটে যায়।

আসলে মেয়েদের নিজের কিছুই থাকে না, ইলিশ মাছের পেটিতে তেল, হলুদ, পেঁয়াজ কুচি, কাঁচামরিচ, সরিষা আর রসুন বাটা মাখাতে মাখাতে মনটা হ হ করে উঠে সুমনার। পাশের চুলায় গরম তেলে কাচকি মাছে একটু চালের গুড়ো, পেঁয়াজ কুচি, মরিচ লবণ মেখে বড়া বানিয়ে গরম তেলে ভাজতে লাগল, সারা বাড়ি রান্নার সুগন্ধে মাতোয়ারা।

প্রতিদিন খাবার টেবিলে স্বামীর পছন্দের খাবার সাজিয়ে একসাথে খাবে বলে অপেক্ষা করে সুমনা, কিন্তু খেতে বসে ভীষণ রকম তড়িঘড়ি করে স্বামী, কোনদিন সে বলে না 'আজ কচুর লতি আর চিংড়িমাছটা অসাধারণ ছিল'। সুমনার চোখের কাজল, পাটভাঙা তাঁতের শাড়ি, কপালের ছোট্ট টিপ কিছুই চোখে পড়ে না তার। পাশাপাশি শুয়ে থাকা মানুষ দুটি যেন দুই শহরের বাসিন্দা। বড় বেশি চাঁদ ছোঁওয়ার প্রতিযোগিতা এই শহরে। জীবন রেসে প্রথম হতে গিয়ে হারিয়ে ফেলেছে কত প্রিয় মুখ, কত আপনজন, সেগুলো ভাবার সময় আছে কারও!

অনেক রাত হয়ে গেল এখনো বাড়ি ফিরছে না সুমনার স্বামী, বাচ্চাটা অপেক্ষা করতে করতে ঘুমিয়ে পড়েছে। খোলা জানালা দিয়ে রাস্তায় জলের মাঝে আলোর প্রতিবিম্ব দেখে মনে হয় মেয়েদের জীবনটা এমনই দেখা যায় কিন্তু ছোঁয়া যায় না। মাঝে মাঝে মনে হয় চারদিকটা রাতের মতই অন্ধকার।

রাতজাগা আলো আঁধারি রুমের নির্জনতা নতুন করে চিনিয়ে দেয় জীবনকে, এই অন্ধকার শহরে স্বামীকে কোথায় খুঁজবে, কার কাছে যাবে কিছুই বুঝতে পারছে না সুমনা, উৎকণ্ঠায় তার গলা শুকিয়ে আসছে, এমন তো কোনোদিন হয় না! সন্ধ্যে থেকে তার মোবাইল ফোনটাও বন্ধ, আজ এত বছরেও এই লোকটাকে ঠিক চিনতে পারলো না, বাড়িতে ফিরে কোন কথাই বলে না। এমন কী কোথায় যায়, কী করে জিজ্ঞেস করলেও বলে না, হয়তো ভাবে ঘরের বউ-এর এত কিছু জানার কী দরকার, ভাত-কাপড় পাচ্ছে এটাই অনেক।

জানলা গলে নিয়নবাতির মায়াবী আলো এসে পড়ে তার ছোট মেয়েটার মুখে, এতটুকু শরীরে কত্তো মায়া, চারপাশের নিকষ অন্ধকারেও যেন বেঁচে থাকার আলো দেখায়। অস্থির ভাবে আবার এসে জানালায় দাঁড়ায়, সামনের লাইট পোস্টের নিচে এক রাত পসারিণী আর দুজন লোকের কথা কাটাকাটি, ধস্তাধস্তি হচ্ছে, মেয়েটিকে চোখের সামনে নির্যাতিত হতে দেখেও কিছু করতে পারলো না সুমনা, কী করবে সে! মাঝে মাঝে খুব কষ্ট হয় তার, কেমন যেন প্রাণহীন পুতুল

মনে হয় নিজেকে, স্বামীর পছন্দে নিজেকেও বদলে ফেলতে হয়েছে, এই শহরে তার দৌড় ওই মেয়ের স্কুল, আশেপাশের ছোটখাটো মার্কেট পর্যন্ত। ঘরকন্না ছাড়া অন্য কিছু করা স্বামী পছন্দ করেন না, সন্তানের ভবিষ্যৎ চিন্তা করে নিজের ব্যক্তিত্ব বিসর্জন দিয়ে এই পোড়া সংসারে পড়ে আছে সুমনা।

যত রাত বাড়ছে ততই উৎকণ্ঠা বাড়ছে, দূরে কোথায় যেন কুকুরের গোঙানি, বুকটা অজানা আশঙ্কায় কেঁপে কেঁপে উঠছে, ঘুমন্ত বাচ্চাটাকে কোলে নিয়ে এই অন্ধকার রাতে স্বামীকে কোথায় খুঁজবে! এত রাতে কেউ জেগে নেই, এই শহরও নিরাপদ নয়। অনবরত পুলিশ স্টেশনে ফোন করছে কিন্তু তারাও ধরছে না, উৎকণ্ঠায় আর্তনাদ করতে ইচ্ছে করছে।

এত বছর থাকার   পরও আজ এই শহরটাকে একেবারেই অচেনা মনে হচ্ছে সুমনার রাতটাও যেন অন্ধকারের চেয়ে আজ বেশি গভীরতর...

হঠাৎ দরজায় কলিংবেল, দৌড়ে গিয়ে দরজা খুলে দিয়ে কান্নায় ভেঙে পড়লো সুমনা।

Lina Ferdows Khan / লীনা ফেরদৌস খান, Dhaka, Bangladesh

I was inspired by two things. Firstly, I grew up in a woman-unfriendly city. I found myself a voiceless girl to live my own life since my childhood. It is important to highlight the problems and voice our opinions and be part of the discussion to express our needs just to make changes in the society.

Secondly, Bangladeshi women are at a disadvantage as they face barriers in all aspects of their lives. This is a great opportunity to write about the disadvantages & raise my power and voice through writing.

I'm happy to be part My City My Home, this is indeed a great subject to write the untold stories of the women around me. It took me a great deal of strength & power to write about the women who are experiencing or will experience distresses to live their own life. I would like to change our lives and realities through my writing.

নিস্তব্ধতা

রাতের নিস্তব্ধতা আমাকে আটপৌরে গল্প শোনায়

নীহারিকা-লোকে হারিয়ে যাওয়া কত প্রিয় মুখ

অন্ধকারে মেঘদের গাল ছুঁয়ে থসে পড়া

তারার শিখণ্ডিত মুণ্ডু, রক্ত জমাট দেহ,

পড়ে থাকে নর্দমায়।

জন্মান্ধ শিশুর ডুকরে কেঁদে ওঠা তমসা এই শহরে

অনন্ত মধ্যরাত নামে

ঘামে ভেজা নোংরা আঁচলে,

লাল-নীল রাতপরীরা ঝলমলে বিষাদের সওদা শেষে

দুমুঠো ভাত রাঁধে, নগর-সরণির নিয়ন জ্যোৎস্নায়।

ইট-শ্যাওলার ভিটে হারিয়ে

কারা যেন অন্ধকারে হারায়

খোলা ছাদে এখনো ভেজে ছেঁড়া শাড়ী, পুরনো আচার।

বৃদ্ধ বাবার কঙ্কালসার হাত

খুঁজতে থাকে শেকড়,

ব্যাধিঘোর জননী চোখ মেলে পথ্যের অপেক্ষায়।

মৌন মুখর রাত্রির নির্মম মায়াবী গল্প সযত্নে তুলে রাখি

মনের নীল নকশায়

সময়ের গন্ধি থেকে হারাবে না অসীমের জনাকীর্ণ নিস্তব্ধতায়।

Raushan Ara Mahmuda / রওশন আরা মাহমুদা, Dhaka, Bangladesh

এই শহরে জন্ম থেকে আমার বসবাস। শহরের ভালো মন্দ আমার কাছে নিজের ভালো মন্দের চেয়ে কোনো অংশে কম নয়। একজন নাগরিক হিসেবে প্রতিদিন চলার পথে নানারকম অসঙ্গতি চোখে পড়ে, যা হয়তো আমার একার পক্ষে নিরসন করা সম্ভব নয়। যদি এই লেখাটি কাউকে উজ্জীবিত করে আর তিনি এই শহরকে বদলাতে বদ্ধপরিকর হোন, তবেই হবে লেখাটির সার্থকতা।

যে শহরে বসত আমার

আমার শহর ঢাকা শহর। এ শহরে পঞ্চাশ বছর ধরে বসবাস করছি আমি। এমন এক ঘনবসতিপূর্ণ শহরে বাস করছি আমি, যেখানে আয়তনের তুলনায় লোকসংখ্যা অনেক বেশি। প্রাণের শহর হলেও এটি পরিকল্পনাহীন, এলোমেলো একটি শহর। হালের নতুন ক্রেজ মেট্রোরেল চালু হলে আরো বেশি মানুষ এ ঢাকায় থাকার জন্য চলে আসবে।

আমি আমার শহরকে ছোট করছি না, দ্রুতই উন্নয়ন হচ্ছে এ শহরে, যা দেখতে ভালো লাগে। পাশাপাশি, প্রদীপের নিচে অন্ধকারের মতোই এখানে লুকিয়ে আছে যানজট, সরু ফুটপাথ, ধারণের অতিরিক্ত জনসংখ্যা, বর্ষাকালের উপচে পড়া ড্রেনেজ ব্যবস্থা, বাড়িঘর বঞ্চিত শিশু, পানির হাহাকার, গ্যাস-বিদ্যুৎ বিভ্রাট ও অপরিকল্পিত বৈদ্যুতিক তারের জট ইত্যাদি।

খুব আশা নিয়ে থাকি আমি, একদিন ঢাকা আদর্শ শহরে পরিণত হবে, হওয়ার মতো সব জিনিসই এর মধ্যে আছে। কিন্তু অপরিকল্পিত ভাবে গড়ে ওঠার কারণে আর সঠিক পরিকল্পনার অভাবে বারবার সংস্কারের পদক্ষেপ নিতে হয়।

গাছপালা বিহীন শহরের অক্সিজেন দিন দিন হ্রাস পাচ্ছে। ঢাকা বিশ্ববিদ্যালয়, বুয়েট আর হাতেগোনা কয়েকটি এলাকা ছাড়া কোথাও সবুজের কোনও রেশ নেই। অথচ সবুজের সমারোহ ছাড়া বেঁচে থাকা কষ্টকর। পরিবেশের জন্য প্রয়োজনীয় গাছপালা এই শহরে নেই বললেই চলে। ভবনগুলোর একটা বড় অংশ অপরিকল্পিতভাবে তৈরি। সেগুলো পরিকল্পিতভাবে তৈরি হলে ভূমিকম্প ক্ষতির ঝুঁকি কমে যেত। বেশিরভাগ

ভবনের সাথে লাগোয়া খালি জায়গা নেই, সেকারণে আগুন লাগলে দমকল বাহিনী সহজে ঢুকতে পারে না, সামান্য আগুনেই প্রাণ ও সম্পদের ব্যাপক ক্ষতি হয়। শিশুদের খেলাধুলার জায়গা নেই, ভবনগুলোর সামনে এমন ফাঁকা জায়গাও নেই, যেখানে খেলাধুলার ব্যবস্থা করা যায়। আমাদের সকাল-বিকাল হাঁটা বা শরীরচর্চার জন্য সামান্যতম জায়গাও পাওয়া যায় না। চারদিকে শুধু ভবন আর ভবন। কংক্রিটের বিল্ডিং এর কারণে একটুখানি ফাঁকা জায়গা নেই যে দুটো গাছ লাগানো যায়। ভূমিকম্পেও তাই কোথাও নিরাপদে সরে যাওয়ার উপায় নেই।

অতিরিক্ত যানবাহন আবহাওয়াকে দূষিত করে তোলে। ব্যক্তিগত গাড়িতে চড়ার সৌভাগ্য আমাদের অনেকের হয় না কিন্তু গণমানুষ হিসেবে বায়ু দূষণের শিকার হচ্ছি প্রতিনিয়ত। অবশ্য যাঁরা ভিআইপি, এতে তাঁদের কোনো সমস্যা হয় না, তাঁরা এসি রুম থেকে বেরিয়ে এসি গাড়িতে ওঠেন, প্রয়োজনে রাস্তাও বন্ধ রাখা হয় তাঁদের যাতায়েতের জন্য। যত সমস্যা হয় সব জনসাধারণের। যানজটের কারণে মানুষের স্বাভাবিক কর্মকান্ড বাধাপ্রাপ্ত হয়, প্রতিদিন হাজার হাজার শ্রমঘন্টার অপচয় হচ্ছে, যার চাপ পড়ছে অর্থনীতিতে। লক্ষ লক্ষ টাকার জ্বালানি পুড়ছে। মুমূর্ষু রোগী বহনকারী অ্যাম্বুল্যান্সকে থামতে হচ্ছে। পত্রিকার পাতা খুললেই আমরা দেখতে পাই দুর্ঘটনার খবর, কোথাও বাসে-ট্রাকে, কোথাও বাসের সাথে বাস, বাস-টেম্পো আবার কোথাও রিকশা বা নিরীহ পথচারীকে চাপা দেয় দ্রুতগামী বাস ট্রাক, কেড়ে নেয় তাজা প্রাণ।

এবার আসি শব্দদূষণের বিষয়ে, কিছু উচ্ছৃঙ্খল গাড়িচালক আর মোটরসাইকেল চালকের যত্রতত্র হাইড্রোলিক হর্ন এর উপদ্রব আর গগনবিদারী শব্দ খুবই বিরক্তিকর। রাজপথে ট্রাক চলাচলের জন্য কোন আলাদা লেন নেই, অথচ ট্রাক হচ্ছে বিপজ্জনক গাড়ি। প্রতি বছর বাস ট্রাক সংঘর্ষে বহু তাজা প্রাণ ঝরে যায়।

শহরের নিম্নবিওদের একটা উল্লেখযোগ্য অংশ গার্মেন্টস শ্রমিক। যত্রতত্র ভাবে গড়ে ওঠা ফ্যাক্টরিগুলো সুনির্দিষ্ট পরিকল্পনার আওতায় আনতে পারলে শহরের কর্মব্যস্ততা ও চাপ লাঘব হবে। প্রতিটি বিভাগীয় শহরের উন্নয়ন করলে ঢাকা শহরের উপর চাপ কমবে, তখন আমার বাড়ি তথা আমার শহর থাকবে আরও সুন্দর। ভালো মন নিয়ে দেখলে সবকিছুই ভালো লাগে। ঢাকা শহরের যে পরিমাণ জনবল, যে পরিমাণ সম্পদ আছে তা বিশ্বের অনেক উন্নয়নশীল দেশে নেই।

দৃষ্টিনন্দন পার্ক ও মাঠের অভাবে আমাদের শহরের তাপমাত্রা কমছে না। ঢাকা শহরের চারপাশে সুন্দর জলপথ নির্মাণ করলে এ শহর আকর্ষণীয় এক শহর হিসেবে গড়ে উঠতো। নবনির্মিত ফ্লাইওভার গুলোতে বিদেশের মতো সুন্দর রং থাকার পরিবর্তে দেখতে পাই পিলারগুলোতে আজেবাজে দৃশ্য সম্বলিত নানা পোস্টারের সমাহার। দেয়াল-লিখন, চিকামারা ইত্যাদিও দৃষ্টিকটু।

বিদ্যুতের প্যাঁচানো তারের জঞ্জাল আমাদের চিরাচরিত ঐতিহ্য। মাটির নিচে তারের সংযোগ স্থাপন হলে দুর্ঘটনা এড়ানো যাবে, রাস্তা ও ঘরবাড়ির সৌন্দর্য বৃদ্ধি পাবে কয়েকগুন। ইন্টারনেট কেবলও কম দৃষ্টিকটু নয়।

আবাসিক এলাকাগুলো থেকে রাসায়নিক গুদাম ও প্লাস্টিক কারখানা স্থানান্তরিত না করলে এ শহর বসবাসের অযোগ্য হয়ে পড়বে। পাদচারী সেতুগুলো উঁচু করার পরিকল্পনা করা যেতে পারে। লেকের পাড়ে বাঁধাই করে ওয়াকওয়ের মত করে তৈরি করলে শহরের সৌন্দর্য বৃদ্ধি পাবে বহুগুন।

নানা ধরনের সামাজিক, রাজনৈতিক ও অর্থনৈতিক সমস্যা এ শহরে বিরাজমান। নারীরা আজ শিক্ষিত ও স্বাবলম্বী হতে চাইছে। কিন্তু কর্মক্ষেত্রে পুরুষের জন্য সুযোগ-সুবিধা ও উদার মানসিকতা যতটুকু আছে নারীর জন্য ততটুকু নেই! নারী শিক্ষায় একটি বিশেষ বাধা হচ্ছে নিরাপত্তাহীনতা। অনেক অভিভাবক তাঁদের কন্যাসন্তানকে শিক্ষা প্রতিষ্ঠান পাঠাতে ভয় পান। এর সাথে রয়েছে চরম দারিদ্র্য। দারিদ্র্যের নিষ্পেষণ থেকে বিপুল জনসাধারণকে মুক্ত করতে না পারলে শুধু শিক্ষাই নয়, শহরের সার্বিক উন্নয়ন পরিকল্পনাও ব্যর্থতায় পর্যবাসিত হবে।

যত্রতত্র ময়লা আবর্জনা ফেলে আমরা শহরের সৌন্দর্য ম্লান করে করে যাচ্ছি প্রতিনিয়তা। দাঁড়িয়ে প্রস্রাব করার দৃশ্যও লজ্জাজনক, যাতে দুর্গন্ধময় হয়ে যাচ্ছে শহরের জীবন।

তবে, যে যাই বলুক, যতই বসবাসের অযোগ্য হোক, এই শহরে আমার বাড়িতে আমার বেড়ে ওঠা। জীবনের প্রতিটি মুহূর্তের সাথেই জড়িয়ে আছে এই শহরের এই বাড়ি। আমার আশা, একদিন ঢাকা শহর হবে সবুজের শহর, গাছ-গাছড়ার শহর, নির্মল বাতাস ও শান্তির শহর।

শহরের পরিবেশ রক্ষায় আমাদের করণীয়ঃ

412

- বিদ্যুৎ ও ইন্টারনেটের তার মাটির নিচে স্থাপন করতে হবে।

- প্রত্যেকটি বাড়ির ছাদে ছাদকৃষি বাধ্যতামূলক করা দরকার। এর জন্য প্রয়োজনে সিটি কর্পোরেশনের সহযোগিতা কাম্য।

- ময়লা ফেলার জন্য কিছুদূর পরপর ডাস্টবিন দেওয়া দরকার।

- রিকশা তুলে দিয়ে ব্যাটারি-চালিত মিনি অটো রিক্সা চালু করা দরকার।

- ফুটপাথগুলো অন্তত পনেরো ফুট চওড়া করা দরকার।

- ফ্লাইওভারগুলোর রক্ষণাবেক্ষণে স্থায়ী রং করা দরকার।

- যত্রতত্র পোস্টারিং, দেয়াল লিখন নিষিদ্ধ করতে হবে। প্রয়োজনে এর বিরুদ্ধে আইনি ব্যবস্থা নিতে হবে।

- ঢাকা শহরের চারদিকে সুন্দর ও নিরাপদ জলপথ করলে জলাবদ্ধতা কমবে, শহরের তাপমাত্রা কমবে।

- মেইন রোডে রিকশা বন্ধ করে দিয়ে শুধু ছোট গলিতে চালু করা।

- স্বাস্থ্য সাথী প্রকল্প এর মতো প্রকল্প চালু করা, যাতে সাধারণ মানুষ সকলেই চিকিৎসাসেবার আওতায় আসে।

- অপ্রয়োজনে গাড়ির হর্ন বন্ধ করতে নো হর্ন জোন বিধিমালা ২০০৬ আইন বাস্তবায়ন করতে হবে।

- আবাসিক এলাকা থেকে রাসায়নিক গুদাম ও প্লাস্টিক কারখানা স্থানান্তরিত করতে হবে।

- সকল আবাসিক ভবন ও প্রতিষ্ঠানে অগ্নিনির্বাপক ব্যবস্থা নিশ্চিত করা।

এ শহরের সাথে জড়িয়ে আছে আমার শৈশব কৈশোরের স্মৃতি। চারপাশে ঘটে যাওয়া সমাজের নানা সমস্যা, জীবনযাপনের সঙ্গতি অসঙ্গতি সহ বিভিন্ন বিষয় নিয়ে শহরের তথা নিজ বাড়ির উন্নয়ন প্রকল্পে বস্তুনির্ঠ যুক্তি ও মতামত জানাতে পেরে আমি গর্ববোধ করছি। এত সমস্যার পরও আমার শহর, আমার বাড়ি আমার ভালো লাগো। খুব ভালোবাসি আমার শহরকে।

Fatema Israt Juthi / ফতেমা ইসরাত যুথী, Dhaka, Bangladesh

To write this story, existing social pattern and inequality between women and men influenced me. By the pace of globalisation, society is changing fast and both village and city are influenced by it.

Especially, women of the city bear the actual brunt of life. The proliferation of the theory of individualism has inspired women to be self-dependent. But still, women are bound to take their husband's title.

নমিতা

রবিবার, ১৩ ই মার্চ ২০১৬

আমি এখন ঢাকায়। গত দুদিন আগে আমি এই নতুন বাসায় উঠেছি। 'আমি' শব্দটা লেখা বোধ হয় ঠিক হচ্ছে না। বরং লেখা উচিত 'আমরা'! কারণ নমিতা এখন বিবাহিত! বিয়ের পর মাত্র একদিন শ্বশুরবাড়ি ছিলাম, তারপরই আবার কাজের শহরে ছুটে এলাম।

গত দুদিন কেটেছে শুধু ঘর গোছগাছ করেই। ডায়েরি লেখার একদমই সময় পাই নি। অথচ ডায়েরির অর্থ – Dear I always remember you! যাই হোক বিয়ের পর এটাই আমার প্রথম ডায়েরি আর আজ প্রথম কিছু লিখলাম। আমার মনের যত কথা, সারাদিনের যত ক্লান্তি, অভিযোগ আর অনুযোগ সব বলি ডায়েরিকে। সে কখনোই বিরক্ত হয় না। এই বিশ্বায়নের যুগে এরকম বন্ধু পাওয়া সত্যিই কঠিন! ডায়েরিতে আমার নতুন প্রেমিক-স্বামী-বন্ধু সম্পর্কে কিছুই লেখা হয়নি।

আমার স্বামী বিয়ের আগে ছিল শুধুই প্রেমিক আর বন্ধু। প্রত্যয়ের সাথে আমার পরিচয় অফিসে। আমরা কলিগ ছিলাম। তবে এখনো আমরা কলিগ! খুব অদ্ভুত-অসাধারণ-আনসোশাল ছিল প্রত্যয়। ভ্যালেন্টাইনস ডে কিংবা নিউ ইয়ারে ওকে কখনো

ইনফরমাল পোশাকে দেখা যায়নি। লিফটে কেউ হাই বললে সে শুধু হ্যালোটুকুই বলতো। আর আমি ছিলাম ওর সম্পূর্ণ বিপরীত। ঠিক কীভাবে যেন ওর সাথেই আমার প্রেমটা হয়ে গেল!

একবার সেন্ট মার্টিনে অফিস টুরে গিয়েছিলাম। সেদিন আমি স্কাই ব্লু গাউন পরে, খোলা চুলে, জীবনানন্দের ধূসর পাণ্ডুলিপি হাতে নিয়ে বিচে হাঁটছিলাম। ওই দিন আমাকে নাকি ওর খুব অদ্ভুত লেগেছিল। তারপর সমুদ্রের পাড়ে নক্ষত্রের তলে অনুভূতি জানাজানি; তারপর প্রেমের কত দিন – রাত পার হলো। দু'বছর পর আমরা বিয়ে করি।

কাল থেকে আবার অফিস শুরু। এতদিন মেসে বুয়া ছিল, সে রান্না-বান্না করতো আর কাল থেকে   হাঁড়ি সামলাতে হবে আবার মাইক্রোসফট ওয়ার্ড আর প্রেজেন্টেশনের কাজও করতে হবে!

সোমবার, ১৪ ই মার্চ ২০১৬

কাল ছিল আমার বিয়ের পর প্রথম অফিস। আমি আর প্রত্যয় একসাথেই অফিসে গিয়েছিলাম। সহকর্মীরা ছোটখাট একটা সংবর্ধনার আয়োজন করেছিল। সব কিছুই দারুণ উপভোগ্য ছিল। কিন্তু কেকের উপরের মিঃ এন্ড মিসেস হাসান নামটি যেন আমায় অফিস থেকে বিচ্ছিন্ন করে দিচ্ছিল।

কি অদ্ভুত সমাজ আমাদের, বিয়ের আগে একটি মেয়ের পরিচয় হয় তার বাবা, বাবা না থাকলে ভাই কিংবা চাচা অথবা বাড়ির পুরুষদের পরিচয়ে। আর যখন বড় হয় তখন তার পরিচয় হয় স্বামী। অথচ স্বামীকে কখনো স্ত্রীর নামের পদবী ব্যবহার করতে দেখা যায় না। দিনটা খুব খারাপ কেটেছে। আজ আর লিখতে ইচ্ছা করছে না।

রবিবার, ২০শে মার্চ ২০১৬

বহুদিন পর ডায়েরি লিখতে বসলাম। লিখতে ইচ্ছা করে না। কিছুই ভালো লাগে না। সবকিছু সময়ের সাথে সাথে পরিবর্তিত হবে এটাই স্বাভাবিক। তবে একটা পরিবর্তন আমি কিছুতেই মেনে নিতে পারছি না। অফিসের সবাই আমাকে মিসেস হাসান বলে সম্বোধন করছে। অথচ আমি একজন ইনডেপেন্ডেন্ট উইম্যান। সবচেয়ে বড় কথা আমি

একজন ইনডিভিউজুয়াল পারসন আর আমার একটা নাম আছে।

সেদিন রাতে প্রত্যয়কে বলছিলাম, সহকর্মীদের দেয়া নতুন নামটা আমার পছন্দ হয়নি। ও অনেকক্ষণ চুপ করে থেকে বলেছিল, "বেশ তাহলে কানে নিও না, তোমার পছন্দের না এটা সরাসরি বললে হয়ত ওরা তোমাকে দাম্ভিক ভাবতে পারে। সবচেয়ে ভালো হয় গায়ে না লাগানো।"

আমি সবকিছুই বুঝতে পারছি। জানি সমাজটাকে একদিনে পরিবর্তন করতে পারবো না। এও জানি এই সমাজে মেয়েদের ইচ্ছা-অনিচ্ছা, পছন্দ-অপছন্দের কোনো মূল্য নেই।

বুধবার, ৩০শে মার্চ ২০১৬

আজ সকালে রান্না করিনি। প্রত্যয় অনলাইনে অর্ডার করে খাবার আনিয়েছে। কোনো কিছুতেই ইদানিং মন লাগে না। নিজেকে কেন জানি মৃত বাতাসের সাথে তুলনা করতে ইচ্ছা করে। সারাদিন ছুটে চলছি, কিন্তু ভেতরে ভেতরে আমি নিস্তেজ আর প্রাণহীন। ভাবছি আজ রাতের ডিনারটা আমি আর প্রত্যয় বাইরে করবো।

শুক্রবার, ১লা এপ্রিল ২০১৬

আজ বহুদিন পর আমি আর প্রত্যয় পার্কে গিয়েছিলাম। মনে হচ্ছিল কিছুক্ষণের জন্য আমরা পুরানো সেই দিনগুলোতে ফিরে গিয়েছিলাম। ভয়ে ভয়ে সেই স্ট্রিট ফুড খাওয়া, দুজনে চোখে চোখ রেখে ভবিষ্যতের স্বপ্ন দেখা, বসন্তকালের বাতাসে স্নান করা আর চাঁদের আলোতে ভিজে যাওয়া!

সত্যিই বহুদিন পর একটু ভালো সময় কাটালাম। এখন রাত বারোটা বাজে। প্রত্যয় ঘুমাচ্ছে আর আমি ওর পাশে টেবিল ল্যাম্প জ্বালিয়ে দিনটাকে কাগজে বন্দী করছি। ভাবছি কাল কিছু গাছ কিনে বারান্দায় লাগাবো।

বৃহস্পতিবার, ৭ই এপ্রিল ২০১৬

আমার বিয়ের প্রায় একমাস হতে চললো। এই একমাসে অনেক কিছু পরিবর্তিত হয়েছে। আমার বাসা থেকে নাম অবধি চেঞ্জ হয়েছে। কিছু পরিবর্তন আমি মেনে নিইনি কিন্তু

মানিয়ে নিয়েছি। এই একমাসে আমার যোগাযোগের পরিমাণ বেড়েছে। সপ্তাহে একদিন গ্রামের বাড়িতে ফোন করি। শ্বশুর-শাশুড়ি-ননদ সবার সাথে কথা বলি।

তবে প্রত্যয়, প্রত্যয়ই আছে। ওর নাম এখনো প্রত্যয়। আর ওর যোগাযোগের পরিমাণ বাড়েনি। ও কখনো আমার বাবা-মায়ের সাথে যোগাযোগ করে না। ভাবছি একটা নিজের কমফোর্ট জোন তৈরি করবো। একটু নিজেকে সময় দিতে হবে। নাহলে হয়ত নমিতা একদিন ভিড়ের মাঝে হারিয়ে যাবে।

সোমবার, ১০ই এপ্রিল ২০১৬

সকাল থেকে বৃষ্টি হচ্ছে। আজ অফিসে যাইনি। আমি জানালার পাশে বসে ডায়রিতে শব্দ বন্দী করছি আর গত রাতের কথা ভাবছি।

প্রত্যয় এখনো আমার সাথে হানিমুনে যাওয়া নিয়ে কোনো আলোচনা করেনি অথচ গতরাতে ও আমাকে বেবি কনসিভ করার পরামর্শ দিল। ইদানিং ওর আচরণ খুব অদ্ভুত লাগে। কিন্তু বিয়ের আগে ও এরকম ছিল না। আমাকে বহদিন বলেছে বিয়ের পর প্রথম হানিমুন হবে বাংলাদেশের সবচেয়ে সুন্দর গ্রামে। বেবি নিতে আমার কোনো সমস্যা নেই কিন্তু আমার একটু সময় দরকার নিজের জন্য। এত দ্রুত কোনো সিদ্ধান্ত নিতে চাইছি না। আমি এখনো মানসিকভাবে স্থিতিশীল নই। হঠাৎ কেন জানি মনে হচ্ছে আমি অন্য কোনো গ্রহে এসেছি।

বাসার সামনে গাড়ির জ্যাম। স্কুলের ছেলে মেয়েরা ছাতা মাথায় দিয়ে বাড়ি ফিরছে। অবিরাম বৃষ্টির ধারা শুষ্ক পৃথিবী শুষে নিচ্ছে। সবকিছুই চলমান মনে হচ্ছে আমি আর ট্রাফিকজ্যামে পড়া গাড়ীগুলো নিশ্চল।

সোমবার, ১৭ ই এপ্রিল ২০১৬

আজ সন্ধ্যায় অফিস থেকে ফিরে দেখি দোলনচাঁপা গাছে শেতশুভ্র ফুল ফুটেছে। ফুলগুলোকে একটু আদর করে মৌরলা মাছের ঝোল রাঁধলাম। প্রত্যয় এখনো ফেরে নি। এখন মনে হচ্ছে প্রত্যয় আসলে বন্ধু আর কলিগ হিসেবেই ভালো ছিল। স্বামী মানেই সেই ক্ষমতাসীন কেউ। ও এখন আর আগের মত আমার দিকে কাজের ফাঁকে মিষ্টি করে তাকায় না কিংবা কফি খেতে যাওয়ার কথাও বলে না।

নিজেকে কেন জানি মনে হয় মেশিন। সকালে ঘুম থেকে উঠে রান্না-বান্না, এরপর অফিসে যাওয়া, ঢাকার জ্যাম মাড়িয়ে বাসায় এসে আবার রান্না করা, আর তারপর স্বামীর আবদার বেবি কনসিভ করার। তারপর মলিন মুখে ঘুমাতে যাওয়া।

ভাবছি একটু নিজেকে ছুটি দেব। একটু রবীন্দ্রসংগীত শুনবো আর জীবনান্দের কবিতা পড়বো।

শনিবার, ২৩শে এপ্রিল ২০১৬

গতকাল আমার জন্মদিন ছিল। প্রত্যয় ভুলে গিয়েছিল। আমি এখন কক্সবাজারে। হোটেলের জানলা দিয়ে সমুদ্র দেখছি। আসার আগে একটা মেসেজ লিখেছিলাম প্রত্যয়কে। এখনো উত্তর দেয়নি। মেসেজটা ছিল:

প্রিয় প্রত্যয়,

জানো, তুমি অনেক বদলে গেছো। আমি জানি তুমি চাও আমাদের বেবি হোক। আমিও চাই, তবে এটা চাই না যে, আমাকে কেউ অমুক-তমুকের মা বলে সম্বোধন করুক। আমি আমার নামকে ভালবাসি। তবে হ্যাঁ, সমাজকে আমি রাতারাতি পরিবর্তন করতে পারবো না। ফিরে আসবো শীঘ্রই আর মা হবো। নিজের খেয়াল রেখো।

ইতি,

নমিতা।

Nasreen Meghla / নাসরিন মেঘলা, Chattogram, Bangladesh

This competition aims a theme 'My City, My Home', which is very close to my heart. My city has always been a center of my emotion and affection. So, when I get to know about this competition I take the chance as a privilege to share my memories with my cities.

আমার চেনা শহর

আমার শহর চট্টগ্রাম, একটি মনোমুগ্ধকর শহর যাকে ঘিরে রয়েছে আমার অনেক স্মৃতি। হাঁটি হাঁটি পা পা করে বেড়ে ওঠা এই শহরে আমার স্কুলের গণ্ডিতে পদার্পণ পূর্ব নাসিরাবাদ এ. জলিল সরকারী প্রাথমিক বিদ্যালয়ের মাধ্যমে। শুরুতে মায়ের হাত ধরে স্কুলে যেতাম। অল্প সময়েই অবশ্য একা একা স্কুলে যেতে শিখে গিয়েছিলাম। স্কুলের খোলামেলা পরিবেশ, চারিদিকের পরিবেশ সবুজাচ্ছন্ন। নতুন বন্ধুবান্ধব, নতুন শিক্ষক, নতুন জামা পরে স্কুলে যাওয়ার মজাটাই ছিল অনেক আনন্দের। সকলের সাথে খেলাধুলা, দৌড়-ঝাঁপ করে অনেক আনন্দের সাথে সারাবেলা পেরিয়ে যেত। বন্ধুদের মধ্যে হীরা, ঝুমা, মায়া, রনি আর মেহেদীর সাথে প্রতিযোগিতা চলত বেশি। কে প্রথম হবে, কার চেয়ে কে বেশি নম্বর পাবে, এসব নিয়েই আমাদের খুনসুটি লেগে থাকত। স্কুলের শিক্ষকরাও বন্ধুসুলভ স্নেহ ভালবাসা দিয়ে আমাদের আগলে রাখতেন।

আমাদের সময়ে আমরা যতটা আনন্দের সাথে দিনটা পার করতাম, এখন আর আগের মত তা হয় না। পুরনো শিক্ষকরা আর নেই; নেই পাঠদানে সেই আন্তরিকতাও। বাচ্চারাও স্কুলে আসার আগ্রহ হারিয়ে ফেলেছে। এখন আর শিশুদের মাঝে জ্ঞানার্জনের আনন্দময় সেই প্রতিযোগিতা নেই। অট্টালিকার ভিড়ে চাপা পড়ে গেছে ছেলেবেলার খেলার মাঠগুলোও। চারিদিকে শুধু ইটকাঠের জঙ্গল।

শহরের এ জীবনটা আমার কাছে অন্যরকম আনন্দের মনে হয়। এ শহরে কাটানো প্রতিটি দিনই আমার জন্য নিয়ে আসে নতুন নতুন স্মৃতি, ভালো লাগার কিছু অনুভূতি।

সাধারন দিনগুলোও হয়ে ওঠে অনন্য, আর বিশেষ দিনগুলো হয়ে ওঠে স্মৃতিময়। ছোট্ট একটা উদাহরন দেই। কদিন আগেই ছিল মহান বিজয় দিবস। প্রতিবছরই বিজয় দিবসে সকালবেলা আমার খুব প্রিয় দৃশ্য হলো আশেপাশের মানুষজনকে ছাদ কিংবা অলিগলি পতাকা দিয়ে ছেয়ে ফেলতে দেখা। আমি নিজেও সকাল সকাল ঘুম থেকে উঠে লাল সবুজ শাড়ি পড়ে শহিদের প্রতি শ্রদ্ধা নিবেদন করতে যাই। লাল-সবুজের এই দিনটি আমার জন্য হয়ে ওঠে বর্ণিল।

আরও একটি দিন আমি অন্যরকমভাবে পালন করি, তা হলো বিশ্ব ভালবাসা দিবস। এই দিনটি সবাই পালন করে তাদের ভালবাসার মানুষের সাথে, আর আমরা ক'জন দিনটা পালন করি পথশিশুদের সাথে। এই দিনটায় আমরা তাদের জন্য দুইবেলা থাবার আর তাদের সাথে খেলাধুলা করে কাটাই। তাদের হাস্যোজ্জ্বল মুখে যখন মিষ্টি রোদ ঝলমল করে, তখনই মনে হয় সত্যিকারের ভালবাসা সহজ হলেও কতটা দুর্লভ।

শহরের শীতের সকালটা অনেক সুন্দর হয়। সকাল বেলা কুয়াশাচ্ছন্ন অবস্থায় কনকনে কাঁপুনিতে শীতের চাদর গায়ে দিয়ে রোদ পোহানো, কিংবা সন্ধ্যাবেলায় মুরুব্বিদের চায়ের আড্ডা। রাস্তার ধারে ছোট বড় ভ্রাম্যমান পিঠার দোকানে হরেক রকমের পিঠা আর চলতি পথে পিঠার জন্য দাঁড়িয়ে পড়া মানুষের ভিড়। আবার রাতের বেলা আগুন জ্বালিয়ে তাপ পোহানো, ব্যাডমিন্টন খেলা। এই ছোট ছোট আনন্দগুলো নিয়েই শহরে থেকেও শীতের কুয়াশায় ডুবে থাকতে ভালো লাগে।

সাগরপাড়ের শহর আমাদের চট্টলা। সাগরের বিশালতায় আর মনোরম পরিবেশে গেলে মনের জানলা দিয়ে যেন এক ঝলক সতেজ বাতাস ছুটে আসে। সাগরপাড়ে বিশাল বিশাল পাথরের থন্ড দিয়ে বাঁধ দেয়া; সমুদ্রবিলাসিরা পাথরের উপর বসে আড্ডা দেয়, গান করে, সূর্যাস্ত দেখে। সাগরপাড় থেকে একটু পথ হেঁটে গেলেই সামুদ্রিক থাবারের পসরা সাজানো দোকান। সন্ধ্যা নামতেই চারিদিকে আলো ঝলমল করে উঠে, শুরু হয়ে যায় উৎসবের আমেজ। আর দূরে ধীরে ধীরে জ্বলে ওঠা শুরু করে ভেসে থাকা জাহাজের আলো। দূরে জাহাজের মিটমিট আলো, সন্ধ্যা তারা, কনকনে ঠান্ডা বাতাস সাথে মশলাদার কাকড়া, এই পরিবেশটা ভোলার মতো

নয়। খুব খারাপ লাগে যখন দেখি একটু পরপরই ছোট ছোট ছেলেমেয়েরা আইসক্রিম, চা-কফি বিক্রি করতে আসে। ওরা সকালে স্কুলে যায়, আর বিকেলে সন্ধ্যা পর্যন্ত ফুচকা, চটপটি, চা, কফি বিক্রি করে; এটাই ওদের পরিবারের রোজগার। জোয়ারের সময় সাগরপাড়ের সৌন্দর্য দেখলে চোখ জুড়িয়ে যায়, বিশেষ করে গোধূলি লগ্নে যখন সূর্যটা সাগরের বুকে ডুবে যায়, সেই সময়টা অনেক বিশেষ কিছু হয়ে ধরা দেয় আমার চোখে।

এ শহরের মানুষ অনেক অতিথিপরায়ণ। আমার শহরের মেজবানি অনুষ্ঠানের খ্যাতি রয়েছে দেশজুড়ে। সারাদেশের বিভিন্ন অঞ্চল থেকে মানুষ এই মেজবানির দাওয়াতে আসে। এই অনুষ্ঠানের প্রধান আকর্ষণ থাকে ঝাল গরুর গোস্ত আর সাদা ভাত। চট্টগ্রাম পর্যটন নগরী, উঁচুনিচু পাহাড়ী টিলায় সাজানো এই শহরে রয়েছে সবুজের সমারোহ। এ শহরের আনাচেকানাচে ছড়িয়ে ছিটিয়ে আছে আমার অনেক গল্প, যা আমাকে সবসময়ই গর্বিত করে। আর এই ছোট ছোট গল্পগুলোই আমাকে এ শহরের সাথে এক মায়ার বন্ধনে আবদ্ধ করে রেখেছে।

Suborna Akter / সুবর্ণা আক্তার, Netrakona, Bangladesh

I thought that I should write about my surrounding. Because, when I share my feelings, I feel comfortable. So, when I saw a theme of name 'My City My Home', I decided to write something about my city.

বাবার বাড়ি ও স্বামীর বাড়ি আছে, কিন্তু নারীর নিজস্ব কোনো বাড়ি নেই

'আমার শহর, আমার বাড়ি' বলতে খুব ভালো লাগে। কিন্তু আমাদের পুরুষতান্ত্রিক সামাজ ব্যবস্থায় একজন নারী হয়ে বুক ফুলিয়ে আমি এটি বলতে পারছি না। কারণ একজন নারীর যে কোনো নির্দিষ্ট ঠিকানা নেই! বিয়ের আগে বাবার বাড়ি আর বিয়ের পরে স্বামীর বাড়ি। জীবনের একটা অংশ বাবার পরিচয়ে আরেকটা অংশ স্বামীর পরিচয়ে কাটিয়ে দেয় একটা নারী। নিজ পরিচয়ে সে প্রকাশিত হতে পারে না। পরিচয় দেওয়ার জন্য তার দুটো বাড়ি থাকে। এক হলো বাবার বাড়ি আর দুই স্বামীর বাড়ি। কিন্তু তার নিজের কোনো বাড়ি নেই। তাই 'আমার শহর, আমার বাড়ি' নিয়ে আমি কী লিখব? তবে হ্যাঁ, আমি যেখানে থাকি, যে শহরে থাকি তা নিয়ে লিখতে পারি। কাগজ ও কলম আমার সব থেকে ভালো বন্ধু। তাকে আমি নিঃসংকোচে সব বলতে পারি। আমি যা বলি এই সাদা কাগজ যেন   সব কিছুই বুঝতে পারে, বুঝতে পারে আমার অনুভূতিগুলো। তাই আমার যখন খুব মন চায় আমার কষ্টের অনুভূতিগুলো শেয়ার করে হালকা হতে, তখন আমি ডায়েরি আর কলম নিয়ে বসি। তবে এটা খুব কম সময়ই হয়। কারণ আমি খুব চাপা স্বভাবের। নিজের কষ্টের অনুভূতি কেন জানি ডায়েরি ছাড়া কারো সাথে শেয়ার করতে মন চায় না।

আমি জাহাঙ্গীরনগর বিশ্ববিদ্যালয়ে জার্নালিজম & মিডিয়া স্টাডিজ ডিপার্টমেন্টে তৃতীয় বর্ষে পড়ছি। আমার বাবা বি.এ পর্যন্ত পড়েছেন আর মা ষষ্ঠ শ্রেণী পর্যন্ত। আমার দাদা ও নানা দুজনই প্রাথমিক বিদ্যালয়ের শিক্ষক ছিলেন।   কিন্তু তাঁরা

কেউই নিজেদের মেয়েদের প্রাথমিকের গন্ডি থেকে বের করেননি ধর্মের দোহাই দিয়ে।

আমার মায়ের প্রজন্ম বেশি পড়াশোনা করতে পারেননি যদিও তাঁদের বাবা শিক্ষক ছিলেন। এখন আমাদের প্রজন্মে সমাজ ছোটখাটো কিছু পরিবর্তন এনে মেয়েদের কিছু সুবিধা দিলেও মূল কাঠামোতে আজও তেমন পরিবর্তন ঘটেনি। বদলায়নি সমাজের মানুষের মানসিকতা।

আমি যথেষ্ট বড় হয়েছি, উচ্চ শিক্ষা গ্রহণ করেছি, নিজের ভালো মন্দ বোঝার ক্ষমতা আমার হয়েছে। প্রতিদিন যা দেখছি, সব বিষয়েই এখনো মেয়েদের ওপর সামাজিক চাপ একটু বেশিই কঠোর। একা বা অবিবাহিতা, কিংবা বিবাহবিচ্ছিন্না বা বিধবা নারীদের নিয়ন্ত্রণে রাখতে সামাজিক বিধি-নিষেধগুলো দৃষ্টিকটুভাবেই বহাল আছে। তারা এটা ভাবে না যে জীবন যার তারই অধিকার থাকা উচিত সে জীবনে কীভাবে চলবে সে সিদ্ধান্ত নেওয়ার।

আমি সাংবাদিকতা নিয়ে পড়ছি যা আমার পরিবার, সমাজ তথা আপনজনদের পছন্দ না। তাদের মতে এটা ছেলেদের পড়ার বিষয়। পরিবার, সমাজ চায়না যে আমি মিডিয়া বা সাংবাদিকতা রিলেটেড কাজ করি, ব্যাংক কিংবা পুলিশে কাজ করি। কারণ আমি মেয়ে। যদিও নানা বাস্তব প্রয়োজনেই আমরা শিক্ষিত হচ্ছি, উচ্চ শিক্ষা লাভের সুযোগও গ্রহণ করছি, কিন্তু বেশিরভাগ ক্ষেত্রে নিজেদের মতো জীবনযাপন বা জীবিকা নির্বাহ করতে পারছি না। সিদ্ধান্ত গ্রহণ প্রক্রিয়ায় আমরা এখনও সমানভাবে অংশ নিতে পারি না।

আমি মেয়ে, তাই আমাকে দ্রুত পাত্রস্থ করে চিন্তামুক্ত হওয়া পরিবার ও সমাজের অন্যতম দায়িত্ব। যে ছেলের সাথে বিয়ের কথা হয় সে আমার সাথে পারসোনালি কথা বলতে চায়। সে এম.এ পাশা। আমার কথা ছিল যে, এখন যদি আমি বিয়ে করি তাহলে আমার স্বামী আমার স্বপ্নকে তার নিজের স্বপ্ন মনে করে আমার স্বপ্ন পূরণে আমার পাশে থাকবে কি না। আর তার বক্তব্য ছিল এমন, যে আমি পড়াশোনা চাকরি সব করবো এতে তার কোনো আপত্তি নেই, তবে আমাকে সংসার সামলে সব করতে হবে। সে একটি

শিক্ষিত ছেলে হয়েও নারী পুরুষের কাজকে আলাদা করে দিল। এই ছেলের তথা পুরুষদের এই মানসিকতা আকাশ থেকে পড়েনি। এই সমাজই তাদের এই মানসিকতা তৈরি করেছে। যাই হোক, কোনো কারণে বিয়েটা হয়নি। তো এটা যে শুধু আমার সাথে হয়েছে তা নয়। এটিই আমাদের সমাজের নিত্য চিত্র। অর্থাৎ, অর্থনৈতিকভাবে স্বাবলম্বী হলেই নারীর আর কোনো সমস্যা থাকবেনা বলে যে একটি ধারণা চালু আছে তা শতভাগ সঠিক নয়। অর্থনৈতিক মুক্তিই নারী মুক্তি নয়। নারীর কাজ এবং পুরুষের কাজ বলে যে বিভাজন তৈরি করা হয় তা-ও আসলে অধিকারবঞ্চিত করে রাখার একটি কূটকৌশল ছাড়া আর কিছু নয়। যেসব পুরুষেরা নারীবাদী কথা বলেন, নারীদের অধিকার আদায়ে মাঠে নামেন তারাও কি কখনো নিজের স্ত্রীকে রান্নাঘরের কাজে সাহায্য করেছেন? মাছ কাটতে পারেন? ৮-১০ টা রেসিপি বানাতে পারেন? এক মাস স্ত্রীকে রান্না করে থাইয়েছেন? উত্তর আসবে, না। কিন্তু উত্তরটা কেন 'না' আসবে? নারীরা তো বাইরে পুরুষের সাথে সমানতালে কাজ করছে। তাহলে ঘরে এসেও তাকেই কেনো পুরোটা সামলাতে হবে? তাহলে কোথায় সাম্যতা? আমরা শিক্ষিত হচ্ছি, প্রতিষ্ঠিত হচ্ছি, কিন্তু পরিবার, সমাজ আমাদের বেঁধে রেখেছে শক্ত রশি দিয়ে। আসলে আমরা তো যান্ত্রিকশক্তি রূপে ব্যবহৃত হচ্ছি পুরুষতান্ত্রিক সমাজের কল্যাণে; পুরুষের সমান নারীর ন্যায্য অধিকার প্রতিষ্ঠায় নয়।

কাউকে তার মানবিক গুণের বদলে চেহারার মাপকাঠিতে বিচার করা অন্যায় ও অশিক্ষা। সেই ধারাবাহিক লজ্জার ইতিহাসে আত্মগোপন করে আছে অসংখ্য কালো মেয়েদের যন্ত্রণা। মাত্র দু'টি অক্ষরের একটি শব্দ 'কালো' এই শব্দ মিসাইলের মতো কাজ করে। এই একটি শব্দ ছুঁড়ে দিলেই একটি মেয়ে কেমন কুঁকড়ে যায়, অসম্মানিত বোধ করে, অসহায় হয়ে পড়ে। অথচ ছেলেদের কখনো সৌন্দর্যের মাপকাঠিতে মাপা হয়না।

মিডিয়াগুলো পর্যন্ত পুরুষতান্ত্রিক আচরণ করে। মূলধারার চলচ্চিত্রগুলোতে আজীবন দেখেছি শাবানা, রোজিনা, ববিতাকে চোখের পানি স্বামীর পায়ে ফেলে জীবন কাটাতে, কথায় কথায় স্বামীর পায়ে লুটিয়ে পড়তে। মিডিয়াগুলো আমাদের শেখাতে চেয়েছে এই শাবানা-ববিতারাই হলো আদর্শ বাঙালী নারীর রূপ। এখনো পর্যন্ত ইন্ডিয়ান সিরিয়ালগুলোতে আমরা এসব দেখেই তৃপ্ত হচ্ছি। যেখানে প্রধান নায়িকা চরিত্র তারা

হয়, যারা অসীম অন্যায় উৎপীড়নকে অনন্তকাল মুখ-বুজে হাসিমুখে মেনে নিয়ে চলতে জানে। গোপনে শোষণের বীজটা ঢালছে এ প্রজন্মের নারীর অন্তরেও। হয়তো বুঝতেও পারছি না কখন সিরিয়ালের নায়িকার জায়গায় নিজেকে বসিয়ে ট্রায়াল দিচ্ছি। আমাদের মা-চাচিদের মনেও ঠিক এভাবেই বোনা হয়েছিল শাবানার বীজ।

একটি নারী ধর্ষণের শিকার হলেও তার দোষ মেয়েটির কাঁধেই এসে পড়ে। পরিবার সমাজ বলবে সে অসময়ে অজায়গায় গিয়েছিল, সে অশালীন পোশাক পড়ে রেপ ইনভাইট করেছিল। হয়তো কখনো কখনো আমি এসবের বিরুদ্ধে ফেসবুকে দু'চার লাইন লিখি। কিন্তু আমার পরিবারের ধারণা কিন্তু ভিন্ন নয়। তারাও এটা গলা উঁচু করে বলে যে মেয়েটারই দোষ। পরিবারের লোকেরাও নারীকে নিজেদের সম্পত্তি মনে করে। নারী নিজের জন্য বিচার চাইবে কি না তা-ও পরিবারের লোকেরাই মূলত সিদ্ধান্ত নেন। প্রকৃতপক্ষে, ধর্ষণ নারীর একার শরীর ও মনের ওপর ঘটলেও সমাজে শরীর ও মনসমেত নারীর নিজস্ব অস্তিত্ব নেই। এমন সমাজ ব্যবস্থার নারী হয়ে আমি বলতে পারিনা 'আমার শহর, আমার বাড়ি।' আমার কিছুই নয়, আমিও তো আমার নই। যে নিজেই তার নয়; তার আবার কী থাকবে?

অ্যালিস ওয়াকারের 'কালার পার্পল' উপন্যাসে ১৪ বছর বয়সী কিশোরী দীর্ঘদিন ধরে বাবার কাছে ধর্ষণের শিকার হতে হতে ভাবে, কেবল বিধাতাকেই অত্যাচারের কথা খুলে বলা যায়। তাই নিয়মিত ঘটনার বর্ণনা লিখে বিধাতার কাছে চিঠি লেখে "প্রিয় বিধাতা..."; বাস্তবে পরিস্থিতি এমনই। আমাদের ওপরে ঘটে যাওয়া পরিবার, সমাজ ও পুরুষতান্ত্রিকতার অন্যায় আচরণ ও বৈষম্যের কথা আমরা স্বতঃস্ফূর্তভাবে বলতে পারিনা। আমরা গুমরে গুমরে কাঁদি কিন্তু বলি না। কেন? বলি না, আমাদের সাজানো সামাজিক, সাংস্কৃতিক, পুরুষতান্ত্রিকতার ঘেরাটোপের কারণে। আমরা জানি আমাদেরকেই হেয় করা হবে, প্রশ্নবাণে জর্জরিত করা হবে।

Israt Jahan Tuna / ইসরাত জাহান তুনা, Dhaka, Bangladesh

To me, writing is a way to express my joy, anxiety and uncertainty. I love to read books and newspaper and try to figure out how a writer or journalist depicts a scenario by creative writing. While reading "Prothom Alo" newspaper, I learnt about the writing competition. The topic seemed very interesting to me. As I have grown up in a city of Bangladesh, I have lots of memories of the city. I am a sixteen plus girl studying in a college. I am living in a culture where most of the time, the voice of girls remains unheard. Writing gives me a freedom to express my feelings without any hesitation. This competition came as an opportunity to prove myself as an emerging writer. When I started to write about my home and my city, I looked behind. I collected the memories of my childhood I passed in my home, in my city. I did not need to struggle to find lines for the write up. After finishing the write up, when I read it thoroughly, it feels like I am seeing my whole journey in the city. The writing is not only a competition but also an effort to recollect my memories and my hope for a better living in the city as a girl through my writing.

আমার শহরের না বলা কথা

আজ প্রায় চার মাস পর বাসা থেকে বের হয়েছি। অনেকদিন পর বাসা থেকে বের হওয়ার কারণে নিজ শহরটাকে কেমন যেন অচেনা মনে হচ্ছে। গত দশ বছর ধরে এই শহরে আছি, কিন্তু এর আগে কখনো এত দীর্ঘ একটা সময় গৃহবন্দী থাকতে হয়নি। তবে করোনার কালে এই দীর্ঘ সময় গৃহবন্দী থাকতে আমার খুব একটা কষ্ট হয়নি, কেননা আমার জীবনের দীর্ঘ একটা সময় ঘরেই কেটেছে। শহরে থাকা মানুষদের জীবন অনেকটাই যান্ত্রিক। এই শহরে কাজ সেরে ঘরে ফেরা আর দশটা মানুষের মতোই কলেজ থেকে ফেরার পর আমার বাকিটা সময় ঘরেই কেটে যায়। আমার ঘরটাও আমার খুব

426

আপন। অনেকের মতে নারীরাই কংক্রিটের চার দেয়ালকে ঘরে এবং সংসারে পরিণত করে। আমিও আমার ঘরটাকে নিজের মত করে এমনভাবে সাজিয়ে রাখার চেষ্টা করি, যাতে সারাদিন পর ফেরার পর মানসিক প্রশান্তি মেলে।

নিজের ঘরের সাথে একটি মেয়ের অনেক গভীর সম্পর্ক থাকে, আমারো তাই। আমার অনেক ভালোমন্দ মুহূর্তের সাক্ষী আমার ঘর। আর ঘরে আমার সবচেয়ে পছন্দের জায়গা আমার বারান্দা। বারান্দায় নিজ হাতে লাগানো গাছগুলোর সাথে অবসর সময় কাটাতে ভালো লাগে। বর্ষাকালে যখন মুষলধারে বৃষ্টি নামে, বারান্দায় হাত বাড়িয়ে বৃষ্টির পানি ধরার যে আনন্দ, তা লিখে প্রকাশ করা মুশকিল।

জন্ম গ্রামে হলেও আমার শৈশব ও কৈশোর কেটেছে এই শহরেই, তাই এই শহরের প্রতি মায়া কোন অংশে কম নয়। সাভার নামের এই ছোট্ট শহরটির সাথে জড়িয়ে আছে আমার অনেক স্মৃতি। আমার শহরের ইতিহাস অনেক পুরোনো না হলেও অনেক সমৃদ্ধ। এই ছোট্ট শহরেও অনেক মানুষের বসবাস। সাভারে আমরা প্রথম যে বাসায় উঠি সেই বাসা ছিল অনেক খোলামেলা আর আমার খুব পছন্দের। ছোট ছিলাম বলে বিকেলে খেলা করতে যেতাম পাশের বাসার মাঠে, কিন্তু ধীরে ধীরে জায়গাগুলো দখল করে নেয় ইটপাথরের দালান। আমাদের এক চিলতে বাসার ভিতরটা ঢাকা পড়ে যায় বড় বড় দালানের আলো-আঁধারিতে। আর আমি হারিয়ে ফেলি আমার ছুটে বেড়ানোর জায়গাটুকু, যেখানে আমি আর আমার বড়বোন মা'র বানিয়ে দেয়া পুতুল নিয়ে খেলা করতাম, হাঁড়ি-পাতিল খেলতাম।

আমাদের শহরের মধ্যে দিয়ে বংশী নদী বয়ে গেছে। ছোটোবেলায় আমি মাঝে মাঝেই মা আর বড় বোনের সাথে নদীর পাড়ে ঘুরতে যেতাম। আগে নদীর দুই পাশে অনেক বড় পাড় ছিল, নদীর তীর জুড়ে বসতো বড় বড় মেলা। কিন্তু এখন নদীকে ঘিরে উন্নয়নের আসর বসেছে, গড়ে উঠেছে অসংখ্য কল-কারখানা। নদীটার মৃত প্রায় চেহারাটা দেখার আশংকায় এখন আর নদীর পাড়ে যেতে ইচ্ছে করে না।

এই শহরে এসেই আমার বন্ধুত্ব হয়েছিল একটি কুকুরের সাথে, ওর নাম চিনু। অবুঝ প্রাণী হলেও আমার সাথে ওর সম্পর্কটা আর পাঁচটা সাধারন বন্ধুদের মতোই ছিল। আমার

স্কুলের যাওয়ার পথে ওর সাথে দেখা হতো, ওকে খাবার খাওয়াতাম। আবার মাঝে মধ্যে কোথায় যেন চলে যেত। আমাদের বন্ধুত্বের গভীরতা গড়ে ওঠার গল্প চলার পথেই থমকে যায়, যখন কে বা কারা চিনুকে মেরে ফেলে রেখে যায়। এ শহরে আমার স্মৃতির খাতায় জমা হয় আরো একটা হারিয়ে ফেলার গল্প।

যদি কেউ আমার কাছে জানতে চায় যে এ শহরের কোন দিকটি আমাকে বেশি আকৃষ্ট করে, আমি বলবো আমার রাতের শহরটাকে দেখতে খুব ভালো লাগে। রাতের বেলায় এই শহরের বুকে এক অদ্ভুত সৌন্দর্য দেখা যায়, আলোয় ঘেরা নিস্তব্ধ শহর। শুধুমাত্র এই সৌন্দর্য উপভোগ করার জন্য আমি মাঝেমধ্যে ছাদে গিয়ে চুপচাপ বসে থাকি। রাতের বেলায় শহরে ঘোরার মধ্যেও রয়েছে এক অন্য রকমের শেকল-ভাঙ্গা আনন্দ। কিন্তু যে শহরে দিনের আলোতেই মেয়েদের নিরাপত্তা দুষ্প্রাপ্য, সেখানে রাতের নরম আলো-আধাঁরে ডানা মেলতে চাওয়ার ইচ্ছাগুলো মনের ভেতরেই বাষ্প হয়ে মিলিয়ে যায়। ছোটোবেলা থেকে এ শহরে বেড়ে ওঠার কারণে এই শহরের রাস্তা, অলি-গলি, হাওয়া-বাতাস সবই আমার আপনজন। ছোট এ শহরেও ভিন্ন ধর্মাবলম্বীদের নিজ নিজ উৎসবে আনন্দগুলো একে অন্যের সাথে ভাগ করে নেয়ার মতো ঘটনাগুলো হঠাৎ করেই মন ভালো করে দেয়ার উপলক্ষ্য হয়ে হাজির হয়।

ইট পাথরে বন্দী হয়েও এই শহরের প্রতিটি ঋতু আমি অনুভব করতে পারি। বৈশাখ মাসে পহেলা বৈশাখ উদযাপন করতে প্রতি বছর জাহাঙ্গীরনগর বিশ্ববিদ্যালয় থেকে মঙ্গল শোভাযাত্রা বের হয়। ক্যাম্পাস বাসা থেকে অনেকটা কাছে, তাই পহেলা বৈশাখে বড় বোনের সাথে ঘুরতে যাওয়া হয় নিয়ম করেই। বৃষ্টি আমার অসম্ভব পছন্দের, রাস্তায় জমে থাকা কাদাজল বৃষ্টি আসার আনন্দে বাধা হয়ে ওঠেনা। শরৎকালে শহরের শেষ প্রান্তে জমে ওঠে কাশফুলের শুভ্র রাজত্ব। শহরে শীতকাল মানেই স্কুল-কলেজে পিঠাপুলির উৎসব, পাড়ার মোড়ে মোড়ে ভাপা আর চিতই পিঠার দোকানে সান্ধ্যকালীন ভিড় আর আড্ডা। আবার বসন্তকাল এলেই বুঝতে পারি, যখন দেখি শহরের ধুলোয় ম্লান হয়ে যাওয়া গাছগুলোর শরীরেও নতুন পাতার শিহরণ, রংবেরঙের ফুলের সাজা। বসন্তবরণের দিন অমরা হলুদ শাড়ি পরে মাথায় কাঁচা ফুল দিয়ে বসন্ত উৎসব পালনে মেতে উঠি। একেক ঋতুতে একেক রূপে আত্মপ্রকাশ এ শহরেরে প্রতি আমার টান আরো বাড়িয়ে তোলে।

কিছু অন্ধকার দিকও রয়েছে মায়ায় ঘেরা এ শহরের। একুশ শতকের আধুনিকতায় বাহ্যিক অনেক পরিবর্তন হয়তো এসেছে, কিন্তু একজন নারী হিসেবে অনেক সময়ই মনে হয় যেন এ শহর আমার নয়। গত বছরের একটা ঘটনা বলি। একদিন আমি আর আমার বড়বোন সাভার থেকে ঢাকা যাচ্ছি মামার বাসায়। মধ্যবিত্তের যাতায়াতের সবচেয়ে সুবিধাজনক নাগরিক পরিবহন বাস। সেদিন বাসে অনেক ভিড় ছিল বলে দাঁড়িয়েই যেতে হচ্ছিলো। কিছুক্ষন পর এক মধ্যবয়স্ক লোক বাসে উঠে আমার পিছনে গিয়ে দাঁড়ায় এবং বারবার আমার গা ঘেঁষে দাঁড়ানোর চেষ্টা করে। পাশে বসে থাকা একজন সহৃদয় ব্যক্তি ব্যাপারটা লক্ষ করে তাঁর সিটটায় আমাকে বসতে দেন। সেদিনের পর থেকে নিজের শহরেই নিজের মতো করে চলাফেরা করা নিয়ে আমাকে ভাবতে হয়।

আমি আমার এই শহরটাকে ভালবাসি, ঠিক যেমন ভালোবাসি আমার নিজের ঘরটাকে। খুব ইচ্ছে করে নিজের ঘরের মতো করে শহরটাকে সাজিয়ে রাখতে। পুরো পৃথিবীকে তুলনা করা হয় একটি গ্রামের সাথে, তেমনি আমি আমার শহরটাকে আমার ঘরের মত করে ভাবার চেষ্টা করি – যেখানে আমি নিজেকে সম্পূর্ণ নিরাপদ ভাবতে পারব, যেখানে চলাফেরার সময় চিন্তা করতে হবে না যে পাশে কেউ বাজে কিছু বলছে কি না বা গায়ে হাত দিতে চাচ্ছে কি না।

খুব করে চাই যান্ত্রিক এই শহরের উন্নয়নর সাথে সাথে মানুষগুলোর চিন্তাভাবনার ও উন্নয়ন হোক। ঘরে যেমন আমি আমার মতামত দিতে পারি, তেমনি শহরের উন্নয়ন পরিকল্পনায় নারীদের মতামত দেওয়ার সুযোগ তৈরি হোক। জেগে থেকেও স্বপ্ন দেখি আমার শহর একদিন নারীদের জন্য কেবলই সুখস্মৃতিময় গল্পের খাতা হয়ে উঠবে।

Khadijatul Kaminy / খাদিজাতুল কামিনী, Dhaka, Bangladesh

I have always been in love with fiction, and also with the real world around me. Writing about my experiences, ideas, and feelings give me solitude. Though I cannot call myself a professional writer, I know that I'm always thinking about writing even when I'm not writing. I came to know about this competition through Facebook. As soon as I saw the theme, I knew that I had a lot of stories in my head. I always wanted to live freely as a human being, and the place I live in has had a great impact on my freedom. From a very young age I knew that my experience of life is extremely different from a man's life. So, the hazards that simply exists in a woman's life have been bothering me since long. I believe, a writer is always influenced by his or her own life, and so am I. The given theme 'My City and My Home' triggered me the moment I came across them. I knew I must write about it because I have stories to tell.

গন্তব্য

- কী যে ভাল লাগে বিকেল বেলাটা ছাদে বসতে আমার! মনে হয় যেন অন্য কোথাও আমি। যেন এই বাড়ি, এই ছাদ, আকাশ, এখানকার মানুষগুলো সবাই অচেনা।

- তুই একটু পাগল আছিস রে। অচেনা হলে ভাল লাগতে যাবে কেন! চেনা মানুষ, চেনা ঘর না হলে বুঝি ভাল লাগে? আমার তো যাদের চিনি না তাদের একদম ভাল লাগে না। কথাই বলতে ইচ্ছে হয় না।

হেসে ফেললো মনিরা, বিন্টিটা এমন বোকা না!

- ধুর, তোকে কী বলছি আর কী বুঝছিস।

430

- তোর যে মাথায় পোকা সেটাই বুঝেছি। আচ্ছা শোন, তোকে একটা কথা বলবো, বলবি না তো কাউকে?

- তোর কোন কথাটা কাকে বলেছি আমি কবে?

একটু তেঁতুলের আচার মুখে দিয়ে তারে ঝুলানো শাড়ী দেখিয়ে উদাস গলায় বলল মনিরা, দ্যাখ কেমন উড়ছে শাড়ীটা – নৌকোর মতন !

- হায় রে কপাল! নৌকো পেলি তুই কোথায়? আর নৌকো উড়তে কে দেখেছে কবে? বলছি একটা কথা আছে, মনিরা-বু, শোন না?

- জ্বালিয়ে মারলি! বল তো দেখি, বল?

- তুই কী বুঝবি! তুই তো পড়াশুনোয় ভাল। আমি মরছি নিজের জ্বালায় বাবা!

- হুম, এই কথা তো? রেসাল্ট নিয়ে ভয় করছে? ও কিছুনা, অমন হয়। দেখিস তুই খুব ভালমত পাশ করে কলেজে উঠে যাবি।

- তুই তো বলবি এসব, নিজে তো সবচেয়ে ভালো কলেজটায় চান্স পেয়ে গেছিস। মুখে সহজেই বলা যায়।

- উফফ! ভারি আমার কলেজ! একদিন ক্লাস হয় তো দশ দিন খবর নেই।

- এই মফস্বলে তুই আর কত ভাল যে চাস! কিন্তু আমি যদি ফেল মারি কী হবে রে আমার, মনিরা-বু?

- কী আর হবে? বেশি হলে চাচা তোর বিয়ে দিয়ে দেবে। তুই তো তাতে খুশি, আমি জানি!

- তা তো ঠিক, খুশি তো হবেই! সেই সুখ কি আর আছে আমার? মা বলেছে রেসাল্ট খারাপ হলে আবুলের মা কে ছাড়িয়ে দেবে, আর বাড়ির সব কাজ নাকি আমার। এটা একটা কথা হলো, বল তো?

- এ আর নতুন কী? ঘরের কাজ মেয়েদের না করে উপায় আছে নাকি!

- আচ্ছা, মনিরা-বু ছেলেদের কি খেতে হয় না? নাকি পরিষ্কার জামা লাগে না, পরিষ্কার ঘর লাগে না?

- তা তো সবার লাগে।

- তবে? আমরাই কেন ঘরের সব কাজ করে মরব? আমার ভাইটাকে দেখেছিস কোনদিন কুটোটাও নাড়তে?

- তোর ভাইটা তো তবু পড়াশুনো করে, আর আমার বড়টা? না করে পড়াশুনো, না করে বাড়ির কোনো কাজ। তাও আম্মার চোখের মণি।

- আর আমার মা? সারাদিন বলছে, মেয়ে পালা মানে হাতি পোষা, পরের বাড়ি গিয়ে কী করে খাব যদি কাজ না করি, উফ্ফ! বিয়ে হয়ে গেলেই বাঁচি।

- কী যে বলছিস না! ঐ বাড়ির আন্নি ভাবির কথা মনে আছে? সবাই বলল গলায় ফাঁস দিয়েছে, আমার তো বিশ্বাস হয়না। কী হাশিখুশি ছিল ভাবি, আর কী মিষ্টি করেই না কথা বলত।

- শ্বশুরবাড়ি কি এমন হয়, মনিরা-বু?

- ধর, একটু এদিক আর ওদিক। মোটের উপর সব এক।

- আমার কী মনে হয় জানিস? মেয়েদের কোথাও শান্তি নেই বু।

- তা তো নেই একেবারেই। দ্যাখ না, ফাতিমার সাথে কী হলো?

- সবাই ওকেই কত বাজে কথা বলছে, কোথায় যেন পাঠিয়েও দিল ওকে।

- ঈশ, ভাবলে গা শিউরে উঠে, স্কুলের স্যার এমনটা করতে পারে!

- ক্যামেরা নিয়ে কত লোক এল কয়েকদিন, তাইনা বু?

- হুম, পুলিশও এসেছে কতবার। কই, এখন তো আর আসে না! সবাই ভুলে গেছে। এখন ফাতিমাকে বাড়ি আনবে কি না কে জানে।

- পুলিশ ভুললে কী হবে ? শহরের লোকেরা ঠিক মনে রেখেছে। আর পারবে না ফাতিমা নিজের বাড়ি ফিরতে। আচ্ছা , আমাদের ছোট শহর বলে এমনটা হয়, তাই না ? বড় শহরে তো মেয়েরা কত কাজ করে, ঘুরে বেরায় , খুশি মত চলতে পারে , তাদের কেউ কিছু বলেনা।

- এজন্যই তো আমি ঠিক করেছি ঢাকায় গিয়ে ইউনিভার্সিটিতে ভর্তি হব। ঢাকা ইউনিভার্সিটি হলে তো কথাই নেই! ভাল করে পড়লে বাবা যেতে দেবে। তাই বলছি তুইও একটু পড়ায় মন দে। আমরা দুজন তাহলে একসাথে ঢাকায় থাকব, ভাবতে পারছিস?

- হুম, তুই ওই স্বপ্নই দেখতে থাক। আমার মাথায় পড়া ঢোকে না।

সন্ধ্যা হয়ে এল, আমি নামলাম আচারের বয়ামগুলো নিয়ে।

মনিরা আর খানিকক্ষণ বসেই রইল। ভাবল, ঢাকা আমায় যেতেই হবে। কত কিছু দেখার বাকি, জানার বাকি। কত ঘুরতে চাই আমি, বড় শহরে না গেলে কিছু হবে না। কেউ চলতে দেবে না ইচ্ছে মতন। এই যে সুন্দর আলো নামে সন্ধ্যায়, কী যে ইচ্ছে করে হাঁটতে রাস্তা দিয়ে। মা দেবে যেতে? ধুর !

নিচে নামতেই বিন্তি দৌড়ে এল।

জানিস কী দেখাচ্ছে টিভি তে? দেখবি আয়।

বিন্তিদের ঘরে ঢুকে টিভির পর্দায় চোখ রাখল মনিরা।

দেখাচ্ছিল, ঢাকা ইউনিভার্সিটির একজন ছাত্রীকে সন্ধ্যায় ইউনিভার্সিটি বাস থেকে নামার পর বাড়ি ফেরার পথে এক মাতাল গাঁজাখোর ধর্ষণ করেছে - তাই নিয়ে প্রতিবেদন।

Sabrina Sazzad / সাবরিনা সাজ্জাদ, Dhaka, Bangladesh

আমার শহরের প্রাণবন্ত নানান উপাদান কবিতাটি রচনায় অনুপ্রেরণা হিসেবে কাজ করে। একজন মানুষ হিসেবে গড়ে ওঠার মাঝে এই উপাদানগুলোই দায়ী। তাই আমি আমার শহরের প্রতি কৃতজ্ঞতা প্রকাশ করার জন্যই কবিতাটি রচনা করেছি।

আমার এ শহর

এই শহর আমার-
মাটি ক্ষুদ্র পরিসর
তবুও অতুলনীয় সেই স্মৃতি।
আমার বুকে যেন খচিত
আকাশের মেঘে আচ্ছন্ন কুয়াশা ভরা সকাল।
মনের এক গভীরতম সম্পদ কাটানো সেই কাল।
স্মৃতি বিজড়িত নববর্ষ হতে নবান্ন
কেটেছে নিমিষেই হারিয়ে
বর্ষার জলে ভেসে নাড়িয়ে।
এবং বাহার নিয়ে এসেছে বসন্ত।

ঠান্ডা এক সকালে, রমনার পথে
হাঁটি এবং ভাবি কোন এক ক্যানভাস যেন-
এই যে চারিদিকের আচ্ছন্ন রোদ,
বাতাসের দোলা দেওয়া গাছের সবুজ পাতা-
ওইযে চলে রিকশা, পাশে মানুষ
যেন এক গভীরতম শিল্পের রং।
যেন এক কল্পনার রাজপথ-
আমার এ শহর।

Amily Mazumder / এমিলি মজুমদার, Chittagong, Bangladesh

I found an intangible connection between the terms My city and My home, which inspired me to write about it.

বাড়ি সাজলেই সাজবে শহর

মা-বাবা , স্বামী সন্তান নিয়ে আমদের পরিবার। পরিবার নিয়েই বসবাস আমাদের বাড়িতে । আর অগণিত পরিবারের বসবাস আমার এই শহরে। আমার শহর, আমার বাড়ি, একটার থেকে অন্যটা কোনভাবেই বিচ্ছিন্ন নয়। আমার জন্ম রংপুরে হলেও বাবা'র জন্মসূত্রে আমার শহর চট্টগ্রাম। তিন বছর বয়সে রংপুর ছেড়েছি, সেই থেকে চট্টগ্রামে। আমার পরিচয়, আমি চট্টগ্রামের মেয়ে, নিম্ন মধ্যবিও পরিবারে আমার জন্ম। কম বয়স থেকেই পরিবারের প্রয়োজনে, প্রথম সন্তান হিসেবে বাবার পাশে দাঁড়াতে হয়েছে। সাধারণত ছেলেরা পরিবারের হাল ধরে থাকে, কিন্তু মেয়ে হলেও পরিবারের হাল ধরতে হয়েছে আমাকে। উচ্চাভিলাষী না হলেও কাজের প্রতি ছিল শ্রদ্ধা, একাগ্রতা, সততা, আর ছিল পরিবারের প্রতি দায়িত্ববোধ। এগুলোই এগিয়ে নিয়ে গেছে আমাকে, সমস্ত বাধা বিপত্তি পার করে আরও দৃঢ় থেকে দৃঢ়তর করেছে আমার অবস্থান। সিদ্ধান্ত নিয়েছিলাম বিয়ে করবো না, কারণ আমার পরিবারের পাশে আমাকে থাকতেই হতো। কিন্তু মা-বাবা কোনভাবে মেনে নিতে পারছিলেন না। ভেবে চিন্তে একটু বেশি বয়সেই রাজি হয়ে যাই, তবে বিয়ের আগেই আমি ছেলের সাথে কথা বলে নিয়েছিলাম যে বাবা-মা, ভাই-বোনদের আমায় দেখতে হবে। সেই থেকে সে আমাকে কোনদিন বাধা দেয়নি। সময় গড়িয়ে আমার ছেলে-মেয়ে হয়। কর্মক্ষেত্রে অনেক বেশি সময় দিতে হতো, ছুটোছুটি করতে হতো দেশ-বিদেশে। তাই বাধ্য হয়ে বাবা'র বাসার সাথে আমি বাসা নিই বড় মেয়ে কোলে আসার পর। ধীরে ধীরে সময় গড়িয়ে যায় , বোনেরা বিয়ে হয়ে চলে যায় স্বামীর ঘরে, ভাইদের পৃথক সংসার হয়, কখন যে মায়ের সংসার আর আমার সংসার মিলে এক হয়ে যায় বুঝতে পারিনি। মা-বাবা রয়ে যায় আমার সাথে। ভাই-বোন , শ্বশুড়বাড়ি সবার সাথেই রয়েছে সুসম্পর্ক ।ভাই-বোনেরা গেঁথে রয়েছি এক সুতোয়।

পরিবারের সবার প্রতি সব দায়িত্ব পালনে আমার এতটুকু অসুবিধা হয়নি। আমার মত অনেক মেয়ে ঘরে বাইরে সব ক্ষেত্রে দক্ষতার সাথে সব দায়িত্ব পালন করে চলেছে। প্রথম কথা হচ্ছে পরিবারকে ভালোবাসতে হবে। পরিবারের সদস্যদের পরস্পরের সম্পর্ক হতে হবে শ্রদ্ধার, সম্মানের, আর এগুলো পরিবারের খুঁটি, যা পরিবারের ভিত শক্ত করে।

পরিবারের সাথে যেমন আমার নাড়ির টান রয়েছে, আমার শহরের জন্যও তেমনি নাড়ির টান রয়েছে। দেশের বাইরে ৫-৭ দিন কাটাবার পর পরিবারের সাথে মিলিত হওয়ার জন্য মনটা যেমন ছটফট করতে থাকে, ঠিক তেমনি শহরটাকেও মিস করতে থাকি। পরিবারের সাথে বাইরে গেলেও, দেশের মাটিতে ফ্লাইট ল্যান্ড করার পরই মনে প্রশান্তির ছোঁয়া লাগে। শহরে নেমে বুক ভরে যেন নিঃশ্বাস নিতে পারি, গন্ধটাই যেন আলাদা। 'বন্দর নগরী' অর্থাৎ 'পোর্ট সিটি', 'বাণিজ্যিক রাজধানী' হিসেবে পরিচিত আমাদের চট্টগ্রাম। কথিত আছে বারো-আউলিয়ার জায়গা আমাদের এই চট্টগ্রাম। প্রীতিলতা ওয়াদ্দেদার, নেলী সেনগুপ্ত, সূর্য সেনের মতো বহু বিখ্যাত লোকের জন্মস্থান চট্টগ্রাম। মাস্টারদা সূর্য সেন, যিনি ভারতবর্ষের ব্রিটিশবিরোধী স্বাধীনতা আন্দোলনের অন্যতম নেতা হিসেবে পরিচিত ব্যক্তিত্ব। প্রীতিলতা ওয়াদ্দেদার ব্রিটিশ বিরোধী স্বাধীনতা আন্দোলনের অন্যতম নারী মুক্তিযোদ্ধা ও প্রথম বিপ্লবী মহিলা শহিদ ব্যক্তিত্ব। বিপ্লবী সূর্য সেনের নেতৃত্বে তখনকার ব্রিটিশ বিরোধী সশস্ত্র আন্দোলনে সক্রিয়ভাবে অংশ নেন এবং জীবন বিসর্জন দেন। বিনোদ বিহারী চৌধুরী ব্রিটিশ বিরোধী আন্দোলনের একজন বিপ্লবী কর্মী যিনি বিপ্লবী সূর্য সেনের সহকর্মী ছিলেন। ড. অনুপম সেন একুশে পদকে ভূষিত বাংলাদেশি সমাজবিজ্ঞানী। অধ্যাপক ড. মুহাম্মদ ইউনূস বাংলাদেশি নোবেল পুরস্কার বিজয়ী ব্যাংকার ও অর্থনীতিবিদ। আমরা চট্টগ্রামবাসী আমাদের কৃতি সন্তানদের জন্য গর্বিতা। গারমেন্ট শিল্প বহির্বিশ্বে আমাদের পরিচয়ের অন্যতম মাধ্যম। সেই পোশাক শিল্পের পথ চলা শুরু হয়েছিল এই চট্টগ্রাম থেকেই, যার মাধ্যমে দেশের বৈদেশিক মুদ্রার একটা বড় অংশ অর্জিত হচ্ছে, কাজ করছে ঘরে বসে থাকা লক্ষ লক্ষ মেয়েরা, পরিবারের ভরণপোষণের ব্যবস্থা করার পাশাপাশি পরোক্ষভাবে অংশ নিচ্ছে দেশ গঠনে।

সাগর, নদী, পাহাড়, লেক কী নেই আমাদের এই চট্টগ্রামে যা দেখতে মানুষ ছুটে যায় দেশ-বিদেশে, দূর-দূরান্তে — প্রকৃতি মায়ায় ঘিরে রেখেছে আমাদের এই চট্টগ্রাম, কিন্তু

আমরা তার যত্ন করি না। একটু হাত লাগালেই গড়ে উঠতে পারে খুব সুন্দর সম্পদশালী এক পর্যটন কেন্দ্র, অর্জিত হতে পারে বৃহৎ অঙ্কের বৈদেশিক মুদ্রা। কিন্তু সুন্দর ফলপ্রসূ পরিকল্পনার অভাবে তা আজও হয়নি! পাহাড় কেটে নদী ভরিয়ে প্রাকৃতিক সৌন্দর্যকে খর্ব করার জন্য যেন উঠে পরে লেগেছে প্রভাবশালী মহল। সবকিছু থাকার পর আজও অবহেলিত চট্টগ্রাম। পোর্ট সিটি বা দ্বিতীয় বৃহত্তম শহর হওয়া সত্ত্বেও, প্রকৃতি উজাড় করে সৌন্দর্য দেয়া সত্ত্বেও, রাজধানীর কৃত্রিম সৌন্দর্য বৃদ্ধি করতে যে অর্থ ব্যয় করা হচ্ছে, চট্টগ্রামে তার এক অংশও করা হচ্ছে না। সঠিক প্ল্যানে প্রাকৃতিক এই সৌন্দর্যকে কাজে লাগিয়ে এই শহরটাকে দৃষ্টিনন্দন নগরীতে পরিণত করতে পারলে অন্যতম পর্যটনকেন্দ্র হিসেবে গড়ে তোলা যেত বলে আমার বিশ্বাস। আমার এ শহরের মানুষ যেমন খেতে ভালোবাসে, তেমনি খাওয়াতেও ভালোবাসে। বিয়ে, মেজবানে এরা হাজার হাজার মানুষ খাওয়ায়। মেয়ে বিয়ে দিয়ে ট্রাকে বা ঠেলাগাড়ীতে করে করে পিঠা, ফল, পোলাও, কোরমা, বিরিয়ানি পাঠায় বেয়াই বাড়িতে, কোরবানীর সময় মেয়ের শ্বশুর বাড়িতে বড়সড় একটা গরু না পাঠালে সম্মান থাকে না সাথে মরিচ মশল্লা! খেতে, খাওয়াতে এদের জুড়ি মেলা ভার, কিন্তু নিজেকে পরিষ্কার রাখতে গিয়ে আশপাশ নোংড়া করা, রাস্তা, ফুটপাত, সমুদ্রের পার ইত্যাদি সুন্দর পর্যটনকেন্দ্রগুলোকে আবর্জনার স্তুপে পরিণত করতেও এদের জুড়ি নেই —চট্টগ্রামের মেয়েরা আগের চাইতে প্রাতিষ্ঠানিক শিক্ষায় এগিয়ে গেলেও মানসিকতার তেমন পরিবর্তন হয়নি। লেখাপড়া শেষ করে স্বামী সংসার নিয়ে ব্যস্ত থাকতেই বেশি স্বাচ্ছন্দ্য করে আজও। বাইরে কাজ করে নিজের একটা আলাদা পরিচয় তৈরিতে এদের অনীহা। চোখ থাকতেও এরা অন্ধ। বিশ্বের মেয়েরা আজ কোথায় পৌঁছে যাচ্ছে, আর আমরা কোথায়! আমি গারমেন্ট শিল্পের সাথে জড়িত। খুব কষ্ট হয় যখন বাইরে বিজনেস মিটিং এ্যাটেন্ড করতে গিয়ে দেখা যায় বিদেশে এই শিল্পের ৮০ শতাংশ উচ্চপদস্থ কর্মকর্তা নারী। আর আমাদের দেশে মেয়ে শ্রমিক রয়েছে হয়তো ৮০ শতাংশ কিন্তু উচ্চপদস্থ কর্মকর্তা মহিলাদের সংখ্যা নগণ্য। পারিবারিক সহযোগিতার অভাবে অধিকাংশ মেয়েরা আজও ঘরবন্দী। খেটে খাওয়া পরিবারের মেয়েরা ঠিকই বাইরে বের হয়ে রোজগার করে সংসার চালাচ্ছে। কিন্তু সামর্থ্যবান পরিবারগুলো থেকে খুব কম মেয়েই এ সুযোগ পাচ্ছে। এর জন্য পরিবারের পাশাপাশি

মেয়েরাই অনেকাংশেই দায়ী। আমাদের মেয়েদের মানসিক সংকীর্ণতা দুর করার ক্ষেত্রে পারিবারিক শিক্ষা অত্যন্ত গুরুত্বপূর্ণ। ছোটবেলা থেকেই মেয়েদের শুনতে হয় — এটা করা যাবে না, ওটা করা যাবে না, এটা বলা যাবে না, ওটা বলা যাবে না, ওখানে যাওয়া যাবেনা, এ পোশাক পড়া যাবে না, মেয়েদের কষ্ট সহ্য করতে হয়, সমঝোতা করে চলতে হয় ইত্যাদি ইত্যাদি। আমাদের পরিবারগুলোতে ছেলেমেয়ের মধ্যেকার প্রভেদ কমিয়ে আনতে না পারলে অবস্থার উন্নতি সম্ভব নয়।

আমরা আমাদের বাড়িটাকে ঠিক করতে পারলে শহর ঠিক করতে বেগ পেতে হবে না। বাড়ি তথা পরিবারের মানুষগুলো যদি দৃষ্টিভঙ্গি, মানসিকতা, উদারতা, সহমর্মিতা, সহযোগিতা, সহিষ্ণুতার যথাযথ শিক্ষা পায় তাহলে শহর তাদের শিক্ষায় আপনা আপনিই আলোকিত হবে। এসো আমরা সবাই আমাদের বাড়িটার যত্ন করি, পরিচ্ছন্ন রাখি, সম্পর্কগুলোর যত্ন করি, ছেলেরা যেন মেয়েদের যথার্থ মর্যাদা দেয়ার শিক্ষা পায়, মেয়েদের নিজের পায়ে দাঁড়াতে সাহায্য করি, আর পরিবারের সবাই মিলে আমাদের শহরের যত্ন করে আমাদের বাড়ি আর শহরটাকে আলোকিত করি।

Monira Ahmed / মনিরা আহমেদ, Dhaka, Bangladesh

I am fond of reading poetry and books. I always wanted to write. But the bad effect of globalization and Information Technology means we are becoming mechanical day by day. I have inner turmoil observing the new trend in young generations. I saw the advertisement for the competition in a newspaper and I thought that It could be a great opportunity for me to write.

Your given topic is very is important because people are migrating from Bangladesh to other countries, with very lame excuses. Whereas you can never love another country more than your motherland.

So the topic is very important as we are born in a country and in a specific village or in a town, where lots of memories are gathered. Those memories and experiences guide us, motivate us to lead our lives in a respective manner.

Your word limit is 1000 so I had to think a lot to make it precise.

But I am feeling very happy for the opportunity that you have given to the women of Bangladesh. Thanks from bottom of my heart.

যেথায় চিত্ত প্রশান্ত, সেথায় আমার শহর, আমার ঘর

আমার বাড়ি যাইও ভোমর,
বসতে দেব পিঁড়ে,
জলপান যে করতে দেব
শালি ধানের চিঁড়ে।

আমার লেখাটি পল্লী কবি জসীম উদ্দীনের 'আমার বাড়ি' কবিতাটি দিয়েই শুরু করলাম। কারণ একটু বুদ্ধি হওয়ার পর আমি এই কবিতাটিকে লালন করেই বেড়ে উঠেছি। আমার জন্ম ০৮ই আগস্ট ১৯৮৫ সালে ঢাকার মিরপুরে। আমার নিবিড়-নিশ্চিন্ত নিবাস ছিল ৬/ডি, ৩/২৭ নম্বর বাড়ি। বাবা, মাকে নিয়ে এককভাবে ঢাকায়

থাকতে চেয়েছিলেন, কিন্তু মা চেয়েছিলেন বাবার একান্নবর্তী পরিবারকে আপন করে তাদের সংসারটি সাজাতে, কারণ সম্পর্কে ওঁরা ছিলেন আপন খালাতো ভাই-বোন। বয়সে বাবা ছিলেন মার চাইতে দশ বছরের বড়, তাই ওঁদের সম্পর্কটি ছিল সম্মান ও স্নেহের। আমার নানা মায়ের বিয়ে ঠিক করেছিলেন। আমার মা ভয়ে বাড়ি ছেড়ে আশ্রয় নিয়েছিলেন ওঁর খালার আঁচলের নিচে। আর এত গুণী, সুন্দরী মেয়েকে কি হাত ছাড়া করা যায়?

আমাদের গ্রাম মুন্সীগঞ্জের শ্রীনগরের বাড়েই গ্রামের মুন্সী বাড়ি। আব্দুর রহীম খাঁ আমার দাদাজান। গ্রামের মুরুব্বিদের তত্ত্বাবধানে বাবা-মা'র বিয়েটা সম্পন্ন হয়েছিল। বাবা-মা'র নানি তাঁর আদরের দুই নাতি-নাতনিকে স্থাবর-অস্থাবর সকল সম্পত্তি খুশি মনে লিখে দিয়েছিলেন। যদিও তাঁর আরো নাতি-নাতনি ছিল।

১৯৮৩ থেকে বাবা-মার বৈবাহিক জীবন সংগ্রামের যাত্রা শুরু। বাবার ৫০ টাকা বেতনে গার্মেন্টসের চাকরী দিয়ে ঢাকাতে টিকে থাকার সংগ্রাম তো চলছিলই। আমার দাদা ইস্ট-ইন্ডিয়া কোম্পানিতে কাজ করতেন। ইংরেজরা ভারত ছাড়ার পর তিনি বিভিন্ন ব্যবসায় নিজেকে সম্পৃক্ত করে জীবিকা নির্বাহ করেছিলেন। আমার বাবা ছিলেন দাদার দশ সন্তানের মধ্যে একমাত্র ভরসা।

বাবা-মায়ের পড়াশুনা তেমন ছিল না, কিন্তু তাঁরা দুজনেই ছিলেন ভীষন পরিশ্রমী এবং সৎ: একজন ঘরে আরেকজন বাহিরে। আমার বাবা-মায়ের আচরণে ছিল তীব্র মেধার দ্যুতি। মা তৃতীয় শ্রেণী পর্যন্ত পড়ার সুযোগ পেয়েছিলেন, তাঁর পাঠ্য কবিতাগুলো থাকত তাঁর ঠোঁটের আগায়। আর আমি বার বার 'আমার বাড়ি' কবিতাটি শুনতে চাইতাম। এই কবিতাটি ছিল আমার 'Childhood Lullaby'। কল্পনায় আঁকতাম আমি সেই বাড়ি।

আমাদের ৬/ডি, ৩/২৭ নম্বর বাড়ি: কখনো ভাবিনি বাড়িটি ছিল ভাড়ায়। ছয় কামরার বাড়ি ছিল। দুপাশে তিনটি করে ঘর আর মাঝখানে গলি। বাড়ির সামনে খোলা বাগান। বাড়ির সামনে এবং পেছনে দুটি অত্যন্ত সুস্বাদু পেয়ারা গাছ। একটার ভেতর ছিল সাদা আর অন্যটির ভেতর লাল, এখনো মুখে লেগে আছে সেই স্বাদ!

দাদা-দাদি, চাচা-ফুপিদের সাথে ভেসেছি অজস্র আনন্দে। আমি পড়তে খুবই ভালোবাসি, আর রবিবার ছিল বাবার ছুটির দিন। রবিবার বাবা ছাড়া মন বসতো না কিছুতেই। এখনো মনে পড়ে বাবার কিনে দেয়া সুনীল গঙ্গপাধ্যায়ের 'ছুটির সানাই' বইটার মলাট, রং আর তুলি। তখন মাঝে মাঝেই বিদ্যুৎ চলে গেলে বাড়ির ছাদে পাটি বিছিয়ে গল্প শোনাতেন মেজ চাচা, কী যে অপূর্ব স্মৃতি।

আমার নিজের জিনিসগুলো গুছিয়ে রাখতেন মা, এ ঘর, ও ঘর করেই অমার খুবই ব্যস্ত দিন কাটতো। ক্যাপ্টেন প্ল্যানেট, মোগলী আর ম্যাকগাইভার দেখার অধীর অপেক্ষায় থাকতাম।

ছোটো কাকু ছিলেন স্কুলের ফার্স্ট বয়। ওঁর পড়াশোনার স্পৃহা, আমার অজস্র বই পড়ার অনুপ্রেরণার উৎস। উনি উপন্যাসের জায়গায় ধরিয়ে দিতেন প্রবন্ধ, যাতে মাথাটা খোলে। দাদার সুললিত কণ্ঠের কোরান পাঠ দিয়ে দিন শুরু হতো, তারপর চলতো রবীন্দ্রসংগীত। যে কবির গুণে মুগ্ধ হয়েছিলাম, তিনি কবিগুরু রবীন্দ্রনাথ। 'আহা আজই এই বসন্তে', 'তুমি রবে নীরবে', আরো কত গান!

আহা! মিরপুর আমার প্রাণের এলাকা আর ঢাকা প্রাণের শহর! মিরপুর এলাকাটি ছিল গাছ-গাছালি আর পাখিদের অভয়ারণ্য। উঁচু দালান-কোঠার সংখ্যা ছিল খুবই নগণ্য। আমাদের বাড়ি থেকে খুবই কাছে ছিল বোটানিক্যাল গার্ডেন এবং তুরাগ নদীর বেড়িবাঁধ। নদী আর শুধুই সবুজ। কী যে স্নিগ্ধ, সুন্দর!

১৯৯৫ সালে আমাদের বাড়িওয়ালা ৩/২৭ বাড়িটি ছেড়ে দিতে বললেন। আমার বাবা ছিলেন অপ্রস্তুত, কারণ আদর যত্নে, ফুল-ফলে, আবেগ এবং স্মৃতি-স্মৃতিতে ভরানো ছিল বাড়িটি। তখন আমি আমার অস্তিত্বকে নড়তে অনুভব করলাম। ভেতরটা ছিল দুমড়ানো-মোচড়ানো, কারণ ৫ম শ্রেনীতে পড়ার সময় স্কুলের দেয়াল পত্রিকায় 'আমার শখের বাগান' নামে লেখা বের হওয়ায় বাবা আপ্লুত হয়ে এক ট্রাক ফুল গাছ দিয়ে সাজিয়ে দিয়েছিলেন পুরো বাড়ি। ওখানে আমার সব প্রিয় ফুল গাছগুলো গন্ধরাজ, বেলি, হাসনাহেনা, আরো ছিল কালো গোলাপ সহ নানা পদের ফুল গাছ। ঐ পাষান্ড গন্ডার লোকটা খুন করলো আমার গাছগুলো আর আমার ক্ষুদ্র, কোমলমতি মন! তখন

আমার ভেতরে প্রথম জেগে উঠলো মেয়ে হিসেবে প্রথম আত্মদর্শন এবং এক অদ্ভুত স্বাধীনচেতা বোধের সাথে আমিত্বের তীব্র সুখবোধের দ্বন্দ্ব।

আমরা নতুন বাড়িতে উঠলাম, একই রোডের ১১ নম্বর বাড়ি। মোজাইক করা দোতলা বাড়ি। পরিবারের সদস্য বেশি হওয়ায় আমার বাবা বিশাল ড্রইং রুমকে তিন ভাগ করে আমাদের তিন ভাই-বোনকে একপাশ সুন্দর করে সাজিয়ে দিলেন। টেবিলে মা গুছিয়ে দিতেন প্রথাগত বই সহ সমসাময়িক লেখকদের বই। আমার দাদা ছিলেন ধর্মপ্রাণ এবং অসাম্প্রদায়িক মানুষ। ওঁর কাছে ছেলে-মেয়েদের মতামতের মূল্য ছিল সমান। আমার দাদি, মা, ফুপিদেরও ছিল নিজস্বতা এবং চিন্তার শৈলী। তবে আমার চিত্ত ছিল অশান্ত, আমি 'Virginia Woolf' এর মতো নিজের ঘর পাওয়ার জন্য যুদ্ধ করলাম। বাবা বারান্দার বাম দিকে থাই গ্লাস দিয়ে খুব সুন্দর একটি ঘর করে দিলেন।

আমার নিজের একটি ঘর, ভাবা যায়! এই পুরুষতান্ত্রিক সমাজে আমার একটি নিজস্ব ঘর, সেখানে আমার ছবি আঁকার ক্যানভাস, হারমোনিয়াম, বেহালা, এ্যকুরিয়াম রঙীন মাছ, টেপ, পড়ার টেবিল আর আমার বই দিয়ে সাজিয়েছিলাম।

ফুপি-চাচাদের বিয়ে হচ্ছিল একে একে, তার ফলশ্রুতিতে আসতে থাকলো আমাদের পরিবারের ভবিষ্যৎ প্রজন্মরা। দাদাজান শিশু ভূমিষ্ট হলে আজান দিতেন শিশুর কানে। তখন বেশির ভাগ শিশুরাই জন্মাতো ধাত্রীর হাতেই। পাত্রে ভেজানো হতো মরিয়ম ফুল, সে এক কুদরতি ব্যাপার! কিন্তু আমাকে এই নিছক জৈবিকতা টানতো না। আমার বিশ্বাস, 'Sexuality is not only sex. Sexuality is always facilitated to connect one language between man and woman and marriage is a constitution and union between two souls with same state of mind.'

ঘটনার আবহে আমার জীবনের সব চাইতে কাছের বন্ধু, দাদাজানকে হারালাম। ওই দিনের মতো এই এলাকা, এই শহরকে এত অচেনা লাগেনি আমার কখনো। কেউ আর আমাকে বলবেনা- 'রঙ্গীলা, রঙ্গীলা, রঙ্গীলারে, আমারে ছাড়িয়া বন্ধু কই গেলারে'।

দশ বছর ঐ বাসায় থেকে ২০০৫ বাসা পাল্টে পাশের সেকশনে ৪/সি, ৭ নম্বর বাড়িতে উঠলাম। সেখানে আমাকে বড় ঘর দেয়া হলো, আর সঙ্গী হলো দাদি। ২০১৪ নিজের

সিদ্ধান্তে বিয়ে করলাম। আমার স্বামী উচ্চ শিক্ষিত, অত্যন্ত বিনয়ী এবং স্থির চিত্তের মানুষ। ওঁর সাথে এই শহরে অনেক অনেক স্মৃতি। উনি আমাকে নিয়ে উঠলেন ওঁর ১৬৮/সি, গ্রীন রোডের বাসায়। আমি আমার মতো সাজিয়েছি আমার ঘর। যেখান থেকে আকাশ দেখা যায়, নিজের মতো নিশ্বাস নিতে পারি, মন খারাপ হলে কাঁদতে পারি। আমার নিজের একটা জগৎ।

নারী-পুরুষ বলে কথা না, সবারই একটা ঘর প্রয়োজন, যেখানে সে নিজেকেই আবিষ্কার করতে পারে। যেমনটি আমি পেরেছি। সদা বর্তমানে থাকার কী যে আনন্দ। আমার আজন্মের সাধ ভালো মানুষ হবো, চিন্তা করবো আর শিখবো স্রষ্টার ভাষা। তাঁর প্রেমেই একমাত্র আকাঙ্ক্ষা।

সেখায় আমার শহর, আমার ঘর, যেখায় আমি আমার স্রষ্টাকে উপলব্ধি করতে পারি, যেখায় চিত্ত প্রশান্ত!

Monira Ahmed / মনিরা আহমেদ, Dhaka, Bangladesh

In my poem I tried to reflect my short story. And I think I can express my feeling by my poetry too. Please do comment and criticize me. I want to write more. Excited to listen from you. Thanks from bottom of my heart. Receive lots of respect and love.

আমার ঢাকা, আমার মীরপুর

আমার প্রাণের ঢাকা, আমার প্রাণের মিরপুর
জন্মেছি তোমারই বুকে
তোমারই রোদ, বৃষ্টি, শ্যামল ছায়াতলে
কাটাই অজস্র রাত, দিন আর দুপুর।

তোমার ধুলাতে প্রথম গড়াগড়ি

প্রথম শব্দ শিখা,
যাবো কি ভুলে? কাদা মাটি জলে
শুধু তোমারই নামটি লিখা।

২৬ শে মার্চ, ১৬ ই ডিসেম্বর আর ২১ শে ফেব্রুয়ারী
ভাই হারানো, বোন হারানোর
দুঃখ সইতে না পারি;
চেতনাতে থাকে বঙ্গবন্ধু, শেরে বাংলা আর ভাসানী
শুনি তবু কেনো দেশটা নাকি কিছুই দিতে পারেনি?

যে যা বলুক কি যায় আমার তাতে
দেশকে আমি দিতেই পারি, দিবোই বা না কেন?
যেমন নীরবে দেশ মা দিয়েছে
উর্বর মাটি, পানি আর ষড়ঋতু।
দিয়েছে ভাষা, রক্ত তাজা

444

মায়ের স্নেহ, শহিদের প্রেম,
রণাঙ্গনে বিসর্জন।

আমার প্রাণের ঢাকা, আমার প্রাণের মিরপুর
দাদার বক্ষে, দাদির স্নেহে
আমি দুলি দুল-দুল;
গল্প শুনি, কবিতা পড়ি
জীবনানন্দ, রবীন্দ্র আর নজরুল।

আমার প্রাণের ঢাকা, আমার প্রাণের মিরপুর
পুরান ঢাকার হাজীর বিরিয়ানী
ক্ষুধায় মধ্য দুপুর; জিভে লাগা স্বাদ!
মধ্য রাতের চাঁদ, আলোর ঝলমলানি
দেখে মনে হয় মাত্র সকাল, দেন-দরবার
ওখানে রাতই হয়নি!

আমার প্রাণের ঢাকা, আমার প্রাণের মিরপুর
আমার দাদির চুনের হাঁড়ি,
বুঝি কিছু খাইছো বলা দুপুর।
দাদি নেই আজ তবুও আছে
ঘরের দেয়ালে চুনের দাগ লাগানি।
কে বলেছে দাগ খুব সুখ দেয় না
আমার অনেক সুখ;
সুখে কেঁদেছি, দুঃখে হেসেছি
দাদি-নাতনি মিলে কত
আমার দাদি, আমার বুঝি
শুকতারাটির মতো
দাদির ময়লা-মলিন কাপড়ে মুখ ডলেছি কত!

আমার প্রাণের ঢাকা, আমার প্রাণের মিরপুর

স্কুল থেকে বিশ্ববিদ্যালয়ের পাঠ করেও শেষ,
মেটেনা আশা, পাঠের তৃষা
আমি বড়ই আপসেট!
আছে বাবা-মা, ভাই-বোন আর স্বামী
সময় শিখিয়েছে সম্পর্কগুলোই দামী।
তারপর হায় কি যে ঘটে যায়
চিনিনা আমি কাউকে!
অনেকটা "Van Gogh" আর "The Starry Night" এর মতো।

আমার প্রাণের ঢাকা, আমার প্রাণের মিরপুর
আমার সমগ্র চেতনার উন্মেষ তোমাকে ঘিরে
আমি যেতে চাইনা ছেড়ে তোমায়
যতোই আদিম বলুক লোকে,
যাবো না আমি নিউইয়র্ক, প্যারিস, সানফ্রানসিস্কো।

আমার প্রাণের ঢাকা, আমার প্রাণের মিরপুর
আমি তোমায় ভালোবাসি;
যা পেয়েছি তা স্রষ্টার দান আর যা হারিয়েছি
তা তো ছিল ভুল বোঝাবুঝি।
তুমি আমাকে গ্রহণ করো, বেঁধো আমায় প্রেমে।

আমার প্রাণের ঢাকা, আমার প্রাণের মিরপুর
আমি তোমায় ভালোবাসি;
আমি তোমায় দিবো অমার বিশ্বাস,
আমার জ্ঞান, বিদ্যা, প্রতিটি নিশ্বাস।
আমার প্রতিটি স্মৃতিতে তুমি,
তুমি আমার কাছে পৃথিবীর সব স্থানের চেয়ে দামি।
আমার প্রাণের ঢাকা, আমার প্রিয় মিরপুর
আমার বাংলাদেশ, আমার প্রিয়তম স্বদেশ
আমার মাতৃভূমি।

446

Nipa Rani Das / নিপা রানী দাস, Narayanganj Sadar, Bangladesh

Lifestyle of city people and my surrounding inspire me.

স্বপ্নের শহর, ভালোবাসার শহর

শহর জুড়ে কুয়াশা হয়েছে। চারপাশে স্তব্ধতা শীতের রাতকে আরো শীতল করে দিচ্ছে। এ চরাচর জুড়ে যেন এক বিশাল শূন্যতা। কোথাও কেউ নেই এমন অনুভূতি শীতের রাতকে আরো বিষণ্ণ করে দেয়। নিয়ন আলোয় চেনা শহরটা যেন অচেনা রূপে ধরা দেয়। আমার শহর নারায়ণগঞ্জ, বাংলাদেশের ক্ষুদ্রতম জেলা। এই শহরে আমার বাস ২৭ বছর। আমার নিজস্ব জায়গা, পরিচিত গলি স্বস্তির নিঃশ্বাস সবই এই শহর ঘিরে। যদিও আমার জন্ম গ্রামে। শিকড়ের টানে গ্রামে যাওয়া হয়ে ওঠে না অনেকদিন। বহু বছরের চেনা শহর গ্রামকে ভুলিয়ে দেয় তা নয়। শহরে জীবনের ব্যস্ততাই অবসর দেয় না। বন্দর নগরী হওয়ার কারণে আমার শহর যেন লোকে লোকারণ্য। বছরের দুটি ঈদ ছাড়া এর ফাঁকা রূপ চোখে পড়ে না। শহর মানেই যেন ছুটে চলা। গতিশীলতাই শহরের প্রাণ। গ্রামের শান্ত নিবিড় সৌন্দর্যের পরশ শহরে নেই। শহর গতির কথা বলে। সকালে বাসা থেকে বের হয়ে যখন রাস্তায় নামি, দেখি গার্মেন্টসকর্মী মহিলাদের ঢল নেমেছে রাস্তায়। প্রাণের স্পন্দন যেন তাদের চলার গতিকে দ্রুততা দান করে। স্বচ্ছল জীবনের হাতছানি তাদের চলার ভঙ্গিতে ক্ষিপ্রতা এনে দেয়। তাদের দেখে আমি অতীতে ফিরে যাই। একটা সময় ছিল যখন নারী স্বাধীনতা বলে কোন শব্দ ছিল না। নারী মানেই যেন পরগাছা, যাদের নিজের কোন বাড়ি নেই, শহর নেই। সেই অবস্থার অনেক পরিবর্তন হয়েছে আজ, তবুও কিছু বৈষম্য কি রয়ে যায়নি? মেয়ে হওয়ার কারণে যখন নানা ধরনের সামাজিক বাধা পায়ে শিকল পরিয়ে দিতে চায় তখন মনে হয় আমরা কি সত্যিই স্বাধীন?

এ শহর কি আমার? স্কুলের পড়াকালীন সময় থেকে আমার শহরটাকে আমি একটু একটু করে চিনতে শুরু করেছি। এর ইতিহাস, ঐতিহ্য সম্পর্কে জানতে শুরু করেছি।

শীতলক্ষ্যা নদীর পাড়ের আমার এই শহর ব্যবসা-বাণিজ্যের জন্য বিখ্যাত। তাই এখানকার সকল কর্মকাণ্ডেই নারী-পুরুষের অংশগ্রহণ দেখা যায়। আমি মনে করি শহরে বাস করার কারণেই আমি পড়াশুনা করার সুযোগ পেয়েছি। শহরের অবাসন সুবিধা, যাতায়াত সুবিধা আমাকে এগিয়ে যেতে সাহায্য করেছে। আমার মা বলতেন, আমার জন্মের তিন বছর পর তিনি গ্রাম ছেড়ে শহরে চলে আসার চিন্তা করেন, কারণ গ্রামে মেয়েদের পড়াশুনার, চলাফেরার সেই সুবিধাটুকু নেই যা শহরে আছে। আজ আমি যখন পেছন ফিরে তাকাই তখন বুঝতে পারি আমার মা কতটা ঠিক ছিলেন। আমার সমবয়সী চাচাতো-ফুফাতো বোনেরা অনেকেই গ্রামে থাকার কারণে বাল্যবিবাহের শিকার হয়েছে। ইভটিজিং থেকে রক্ষা পেতে তাদের বাবা- মায়েরা তাদেরকে কৈশোরকালেই সংসার জীবনের দিকে ঠেলে দিয়েছে। গ্রাম বা শহর দুটোই আমার আপনতর হয়ে পড়েছে। এই শহরেও কি বাল্যবিবাহ, ইভটিজিং নানা ধরনের অন্যায় নেই? আছে, এখানেও নারীর প্রতি সহিংসতা আছে। আছে ধর্ষণের মতো ক্যান্সার। আছে নারীদের নির্যাতনের হিংস্ররূপ। তবুও এ শহর যেন ল্যাম্পপোস্টের আলোর মত স্বপ্ন দেখায়। পথ চলতে সাহায্য করে। আমার ২০ বছর বয়সে যখন আমার মা মারা গেল, বাবা দ্বিতীয় বিয়ে করলেন। আমার সৎ মা আমাদের তিন বোনের কোন খরচই বহন করতে চাইলেন না। তখন আমি অথৈ সমুদ্রে হাবুডুবু খাচ্ছিলাম। পড়াশোনাটাও বন্ধ হয়ে যেত যদি সরকারি বিশ্ববিদ্যালয়ে না পড়তাম। সেই সময়ে এই শহর আমাকে বাঁচিয়ে রাখলো। শহর বলতে তো শুধু ইট, কাঠ, ইমারত নয়। এর মানুষ, এর জীবনাচরণ সবকিছু মিলিয়েই তো একটি শহর। সেই কঠিন দিনগুলোতে নিজেই নিজের উপার্জনের পথ খুঁজে নিলাম। বন্ধুরা পাশে এসে দাঁড়ালো, নতুন করে স্বপ্ন দেখতে শুরু করলাম। শহর আমাকে স্বাবলম্বী করেছে। যদিও মেয়ে বলে, এখনও বিয়ে করছি না বলে সমাজের মানুষের কটু কথা বন্ধ হয়ে যায়নি। একটু বেশি রাতে বাসায় ফিরলে প্রতিবেশী সহ পরিবারের মানুষের সন্দেহের চোখ এড়াতে পারিনি। তবু সবকিছু দেখেও থেমে যাওয়ার কথা ভাবতে পারিনি। রেলগাড়ি যেমন একটি নির্দিষ্ট গতিতে এগিয়ে চলে, আমিও এগিয়ে চলি। আমার নিজস্ব কোন বাড়ি নেই, তাই যেখানটায় থাকি সেটাই আমার ঘর। এই শহরের প্রাণশক্তি হচ্ছে মানুষ। মানুষই এই শহরের চাকা সচল রেখেছে।

আর রেখেছে নদী। নদীকেন্দ্রিক শহরে বাস করার দরুন নদীর স্নিগ্ধ পরশ মনকে প্রশান্ত করে। নদী তো নারীরই আরেক রূপ। সে শুধু দিয়েই যায়। সমৃদ্ধ করে চারপাশের জীবন ও জীবিকাকে। নারী যেমন নিজেকে নিংড়ে দেয় পরিবারের জন্য, সমাজের জন্য। ইতিহাস ঘেঁটে জানতে পেরেছি আমার এই শহরে কত সমৃদ্ধ জনপদ ছিল এক সময়। নদীর পানি ছিল স্বচ্ছ। বাতাস ছিল দূষণমুক্ত। আজ দেখি নদীর পানি দূষিত। বাতাসে সীসার পরিমাণ ভয়ংকর রকমের বেশি, শ্বাস নিতে গেলে বিশুদ্ধ বায়ুর অভাবে ফুসফুস আর্তনাদ করে উঠে। নানা ধরনের অন্যায় যখন আমার শহরটাকে ঘিরে ধরে তখন আমার প্রাণে মোচড় দেয়, মনে হয় আমি বা আমার মত আরও যত নারী আছে তারা কতটা নিরাপদ। নারীদের জন্য নিরাপদ কোন জায়গা কি নেই? নেই কি নিশ্চিন্তে হেঁটে চলার মতো কোন পথ? যেখানে কোন পুরুষ বিনা কারণে কোন নারীর অঙ্গে ধাক্কা দেবে না বা দৃষ্টির লেহনে সংকীর্ণ করে দেবে না নারীর চলার পথ। যেখানে বাসে উঠতে গেলে নিজেকে পুরুষের হাত থেকে বাঁচানোর জন্য বুকে চেপে ধরে রাখতে হবে না ব্যাগা। পাশের সিটে যাতে কোন নারীই বসে সেজন্য সৃষ্টিকর্তার কাছে কাতর মিনতি জানাতে হবে না। বেশি রাতে রাস্তায় হাঁটতে গেলে দ্রুত পা চালাতে হবে না এই ভেবে যে হঠাৎ বুঝি কেউ পথ আটকে দাঁড়াল। আমার দেশের শহরগুলো নারীর জন্য আজও এতটা নিরাপদ নয়। তবুও এই ভেবে আনন্দ পাই, ১৯৭১ সালের যুদ্ধে দেশ স্বাধীন হওয়ার পর আমরা নারীরা ধীরে ধীরে জেগে উঠতে পেরেছি। আমার শহরের অনেক অনিশ্চয়তা থাকলেও এই শহর এই মানুষেরাই আবার আমার সবচেয়ে বড় বন্ধু। চলার পথ তো কখনো মসৃণ হয়না। আমার শহরে যদি অন্যায় থেকে থাকে তবে এখানে অন্যায়ের প্রতিবাদও আছে। পাশে দাঁড়িয়ে গলায় গলা মিলিয়ে অন্যায়ের বিরুদ্ধে স্লোগান দেওয়ার মনোভাব আছে। শহর আমাকে একা থাকার সুবিধাও দিয়েছে। কারও পদানত হয়েই থাকতে হবে, বাঁচতে হবে এ শৃঙ্খল থেকে মুক্তি দিয়েছে। এই শহরের কোন এককোণে আমার নিজের ঘর আছে। যেখানে দিন শেষে আমি ফিরে যেতে পারি। আমি স্বপ্ন দেখি আমার শহর একদিন মুক্ত বায়ুতে পরিপূর্ণ হবে। সবুজের ছায়া স্নেহ মায়ায় জড়িয়ে রাখবে শহরের সকল প্রান্ত। নদীর জল হবে স্বচ্ছ। শিল্প-সংস্কৃতি, পেশা-বৃত্তি সকল ক্ষেত্রে নারীর পথ চলা হবে অবাধ, মুক্ত। সমতা শুধু মুখেই নয় সকল মানুষ

মননেও ধারণ করবে। সবাই সবার প্রাণে প্রাণ মিলিয়ে বাঁচবে। প্রাণের আলোয় মনের অন্ধকার ঢেকে যাবে। তারপর যে ভোর আসবে তা হবে আলোকিত ভোর, নতুন সকাল। সেই নতুন সকালের মিষ্টি আলোয় আলোকের ঝরনাধারায় প্রাণের স্পন্দনে শহর স্পন্দিত হবে। এই অবারিত আলোক ধারায় যা কিছু শুভ তা ভেসে যাবে। শুভ্র, সুন্দরের আগমন ঘটবে। সেখানে থাকবে না কোন হিংস্রতা, কোন ভয়। সবাই সুন্দর জীবনের স্বপ্নে নতুন পথে হাঁটবে। সেখানে কে নারী, কে পুরুষ তার বিচার হবে না। বিচার হবে মেধার, মননের। সবাই মানুষ বলে পরিচিত হবে। নারীদের চলার পথে থাকবে না কোন বাধা। কোন বিঘ্ন এসে পায়ে জড়িয়ে ধরবে না। পরিচ্ছন্ন শহর পরিচ্ছন্ন জীবনের হাতছানি দেবে। নারীরা তাদের সন্তানের জন্য সুন্দর স্বপ্ন দেখবে। শিশুরা ছিন্নমূল হয়ে ঘুরে বেড়াবে না এখানে সেখানে। ফুটপাতে শুয়ে থাকা অসংখ্য এতিম শিশুর মলিন মুখগুলোতে হাসি ফুটবে। আমি এমন এক শহরের স্বপ্ন দেখি, আমার শহর সবার জন্য নিরাপদ হবে। শহরের সকল সুবিধা সবার মাঝে সমানভাবেই ছড়িয়ে যাবে। এখানে কন্যা-শিশু হয়ে জন্মানোর কারণে পরিবারের লাঞ্ছনার শিকার হতে হবে না। নারীর নিরাপত্তার জন্য পুরুষকে সঙ্গ দিতে হবে না। বরং সবাই সবার কাঁধে কাঁধ মিলিয়ে বাঁচবে, হাসবে কাঁদবে। আমার স্বপ্নের শহরের এই রূপে কোন মাদক নামের কোন ধোঁয়া থাকবে না। এখানে জীবন শুরু করার আগেই ঝরে যাবেনা কোন নারী। কন্যাসন্তান জন্ম দেওয়ার দায় তাকে মাথা পেতে নিতে হবে না। স্বপ্ন মানুষকে পথ চলতে শেখায়, নতুন জীবনের হাতছানি দেয়। আমি আমার শহরের এই স্বপ্নময় রূপের কথা ভাবি। যা আমার পরবর্তী প্রজন্মের সকল নারীর জন্য আশীর্বাদ হবে। তাদের স্বপ্নগুলো এই শহরে আরও বড় ডানা মেলে সুদূরের পথে উড়ে যাবে।

Rezina Parvin / রেজিনা পারভীন, Dhaka, Bangladesh

I love to read. My reading habit inspired me to write, especially when it's something about women. My City My Home - this inspired me a lot because they give women a very big opportunity to express their feelings about their home and their state of mind.

আমার শহর আমার বাড়ি

আমার শহর আমার বাড়ি, এই বাক্যটা অনেক আঙ্গিকে আলোচনা করা যেতে পারে। সে আলোচনা পরে করা যাবে, আগে দেখে নিই সাধারন ভাবে প্রথমে বাক্যটা মনের ভিতর কোন অনুভূতির সৃষ্টি করে।

'আমার শহর'-এ আমার শব্দটা নিয়ে ব্যাখ্যা করার কিছু নেই, 'আমার' এই শব্দটার অর্থ খুবই পরিষ্কার ভাবে বোধগম্য, নিজস্ব সবকিছুই আমার, যার উপর আমার স্বত্ব আছে। আর শহর বলতে আসলে এমন একটা জায়গা বোঝায় যেখানে জীবনযাপনের আধুনিক সব নাগরিক সুবিধাগুলো বিদ্যমান থাকে এমন একটি জায়গা।

'আমার বাড়ি'-র ব্যাপ্তিটা আসলে অনেক বড়, যার বিস্তৃতি আমার বস্তুজগৎ থেকে মনোজগৎ পর্যন্ত বিদ্যমান, কারণ বাড়ির সাথে মানুষের আবেগকেন্দ্রিক সম্পর্কের যোগ আছে।

এবার আসি আমাদের শহরের গল্পে, আমার জন্ম গাইবান্ধা শহরের অদূরে একটা গ্রামে, যেখানে আমার জন্ম এবং শৈশব কেটেছে। শহরের সাথে প্রথম ঠিক-ঠাক পরিচয় মাধ্যমিক স্কুলে উঠার সুবাদে, কারণ আমার মাধ্যমিক স্কুলটা গাইবান্ধা শহরে ছিল। এই পড়াশুনার সুবাদেই মুলত আমার শহরগুলো পরিবর্তিত হয়েছে একাধিক বার। যাই হোক, মাধ্যমিকের কঠোর বাঁধাধরা নিয়মের মাঝে শহরটাকে ঠিকমত চেনা হয়ে উঠেনি আর। এর পর সময়ের আবর্তে মাধ্যমিকের গন্ডি পেরিয়ে উচ্চ-মাধ্যমিকের পড়াশুনা শুরু, সাথে সাথে আমার শহরটারও

পরিবর্তন ঘটলো, রাজশাহী শহরে শুরু হলো আমার উচ্চ মাধ্যমিক পড়াশুনা। রাজশাহী, পদ্মা নদীর কোল ঘেঁষে গড়ে উঠা এক শান্ত, সুন্দর শান্তির শহর, যে শহরটার প্রেমে পড়ে যাই আমি। কৈশোরের উচ্ছ্বাস পুরোটা যেন বাস্তবতা পেল এ শহরে। কৈশোর পেরিয়ে যখন বিশ্ববিদ্যালয়ে পড়ার জন্য তোড়জোড় শুরু হলো, তখন এ শহরটা ছাড়তে হবে বলে খারাপ লাগতে শুরু করল, কিন্তু অন্যান্য শহরগুলোর কিছু বিশ্ববিদ্যালয়ে ভর্তির সুযোগ পেয়েও তা বাদ দিয়ে রাজশাহী বিশ্ববিদ্যালয়ে ভর্তি হলাম, কারণ রাজশাহী আমার ভালোবাসার শহর। উচ্চতর পড়াশুনা শেষ করে সময়ের প্রয়োজনে এ শহরটা আমার ছাড়তেই হলো একসময়। জীবনের গতিময়তায় ভীষন বিশ্বাস করি আমি, তাই আমার শহরগুলো পরিবর্তিত হতেই থাকবে বলে আমি বিশ্বাস করি। তবে ভবিষ্যতে আমি বিশ্বের যেখানেই থাকি না কেন এ শহরটাকে আমি ভীষনভাবে অনুভব করব সবসময়।

এবার আসি 'আমার বাড়ি' প্রসঙ্গে। বাড়ি বলতে প্রথমেই যে জিনিসটা আমাদের চোখে ভাসে তা হলো পরিবারের সদস্যরা মিলে যেখানে বসবাস করি এমন একটি কাঠামো। বাড়ি আসলে এমন একটি নিরাপদ বাসস্থল যার সাথে মানুষের জন্মের যোগ থাকে, এ জন্য 'বাড়ি' জিনিসটার সাথে মানুষের আবেগের খুব শক্ত একটা সম্পর্ক বিদ্যমান।

কারণ শুধুমাত্র বাসস্থানকেই বাড়ি বললে বাড়িকে খুব ক্ষুদ্রভাবে সংজ্ঞায়িত করা হয়ে যাবে। কারণ বাসাতেও আমরা নিরাপদে বসবাস করি, তা কিন্তু মানুষের বাড়ি নয়। কারণ বাসার সংজ্ঞা পড়তে গিয়ে দেখা যায় বাসা হলো মানুষের অস্থায়ী বসবাসের স্থান, সাধারনত সেটার মালিকানার স্বত্ব তার থাকে না। দীর্ঘদিন কোন বাসায় বসবাস করলেও সেটা মানুষের বাড়ি হয় না। যেখানে মানুষের জন্ম হয় বা তার অতীত বংশধরেরা জন্মেছেন এমন একটি জায়গাই হলো মানুষের নিজের বাড়ি। আমার দৃষ্টিতে বাড়ি জিনিসটা যতটা না বস্তুগত তারচেয়ে বেশি অবস্থগত অর্থাৎ মানসিক একটা বিষয়।

এবার আসি মেয়েদের জীবনে বাড়ি জিনিসটার ব্যাপ্তি প্রসঙ্গে। এই লেখার প্রতিযোগিতায় মেয়েরা অংশগ্রহণ করছে, তাই মেয়েদের জীবনে বাড়ি জিনিসটা কেমন অর্থ বহন করে, বিশেষ করে বাংলাদেশের মেয়েদের প্রেক্ষিতে, তা নিজের ভাবনাতে তুলে ধরতে চাই।

বাংলাদেশের নারীদের চোখে নিজের বাড়ির প্রসঙ্গ আসলে পরিবর্তনশীল। আর মেয়েরা তার নিজের বাড়িকে চেনে কোনো এক পুরুষবাচক শব্দের বিশেষণের মাধ্যমে, যেমন বিয়ের আগে যেটাকে নিজের বাড়ি বলে চেনে তা বিয়ের পর হয়ে যায় 'বাবার বাড়ি', বাবার মৃত্যুর পর বাবার বাড়িটা হয়ে যায় ভাইয়ের বাড়ি। বিয়ের পর মেয়েরা স্বামীর বাড়িটাকে নিজ বাড়ি হিসাবে পরিচয় দেয়, আবার এখানেও দেখা যায় সেই পুরুষবাচক কোন বিশেষণ! মেয়েদের 'আমার বাড়ি' আসলে কোনটা!?

না, এই পুরুষবাচক শব্দ বা ব্যক্তিগুলোর সাথে আমার কোন লড়াই নেই, আমার আপত্তি এই সামাজিক মানসিকতায়, যেখানে আপন বাড়ির স্বত্ব মেয়েদের দেয়া থেকে বঞ্চিত করা হয় বিভিন্ন ভাবে। মেয়েদের আপনত্বকে এ সমাজ মানতেই পারে না, বিশেষ করে বাড়ির ক্ষেত্রে। যে বাড়িটাতে শৈশব, কৈশোরে হেসে খেলে বড় হয় মেয়েরা হঠাৎ করে তাদের জানানো হয় এটা তোমার আপন বাড়ি নয়, শ্বশুর বাড়িটাই তোমার আপন। এ সমাজটা এত কৃপণ কেন মেয়েদের বেলা? হ্যাঁ, এটা অবশ্যই সত্যি শ্বশুর বাড়িটাও মেয়েদের জীবনে অন্যতম গুরুত্বপূর্ণ জায়গা, কিন্তু যে বাড়িতে মেয়েটার জন্ম হয় কেন এ সমাজ মেয়েটার বাড়ি হিসাবে তার স্বত্ব তাকে দিতে চায় না! আমার কথা, বাড়িটা যদি ভাই জালালউদ্দিনের হয়, সে বাড়িটা বোন জান্নাতেরও হবে। মানুষ যদি বাড়িটাকে জালালের বাড়ি হিসাবে চেনে, তাহলে সে বাড়িটা জান্নাতেরও বলে জানবে, বৈবাহিক অবস্থার জন্য যেন তা পরিবর্তিত না হয়। বাড়ির স্বত্ব সমান হবে, শুধুমাত্র বস্তুগত স্বত্ব নয়, মানুষ মানসিক ভাবেও সে স্বত্বকে স্বীকৃতি দেবে সমান ভাবে। বাড়ির ব্যাপারে যে আপনত্বের আবেগটা থাকে সেখানে মেয়েদেরও সমান অধিকার দিতে হবে।

পুরুষ বা নারী সবারই মানসিকতায় পরিবর্তন আনা খুব প্রয়োজন। আমরা যে সমান সমান সমাজের কল্পনা করি তা কখনোই সম্ভব হবে না যদি না আমরা নারী-পুরুষকে সমান মর্যাদার মানুষ মনে না করি।

নারী হিসাবে আমি চাই, অন্য কারও নামের বিশেষণে আমার বাড়িটাকে আমার কাছে যেন পরিচিত না করা হয়। আমার বাড়িটা এ সমাজ যেন আমার নামেই আজীবন পরিচিত করে। জন্মসূত্রে সমান মানুষ হিসাবে জন্মানো মানুষ হিসাবে সমাজের কাছে আমার এ দৃঢ় উচ্চারণ।

আমি চাই মানুষতান্ত্রিক সমাজ, যেখানে সব মানুষের প্রথম পরিচয় 'মানুষ'ই হবে। নারীর আপন বাড়িটা তার নামেই এ সমাজ পরিচয় দেবে এবং এ সত্য সর্বস্তরে স্বীকৃত হবে। নারী-পুরুষের মধ্যে শ্রেষ্ঠত্ব নিয়ে এ অদ্ভুত প্রতিযোগিতা একদিন বন্ধ হবে, সমতায় এ সমাজ এগিয়ে যাবে মেধা, মনন এবং ঐশ্বর্যে। পুরো পৃথিবীটা একদিন সবার জন্য নিরাপদ হবে। তখন পৃথিবীর প্রত্যেকটা শহর সব মানুষের আপন হবে, পুরো পৃথিবীটা মানুষের নিজের বাড়ি হবে।

স্বপ্নময় সমতার এ পৃথিবীটাই 'আমার বাড়ি' হবে।

Tiasha Chakma / শ্রীমতী তিয়াশা চাকমা, Nagasaki, Japan

My City My Home inspired me to express my celebration of Motherhood into words throughout a 30 years of journey from Khagrachari to Nagasaki.

আমার মা হয়ে ওঠা

ছোটবেলা থেকেই শুনতাম বাবা বলত, আমার দুই মেয়েই ডাক্তার হবে। একজন হবে রোগ সারানোর ডাক্তার, আরেকজন হবে জ্ঞানের ডাক্তার, পিএইচডি। আর আমি মনের গভীরে অনুভব করেছি, শিশুর জন্য ভালোবাসা।

একদিন স্কুল থেকে ফিরে আমি ঘরে বসে আছি। হঠাৎ মা বাইরে থেকে ছুটে এসে গম্ভীর হয়ে দুশ্চিন্তা চেপে রাখার চেষ্টা করতে করতে বসার ঘরে বসে রইল। বাবা অফিস থেকে ফিরলে নিজেরা কী সব ফিসফিস করে বলতে লাগলো। আমি শোনার চেষ্টা করেও উদ্ধার করতে পারলাম না। সন্ধ্যায় এক খালাত বোন এর সঙ্গে দেখা হতে জানলাম। মাকে জিজ্ঞেস করলাম, কে মারা গেছেন, মা? একটু চাপাচাপি করতেই বলল বিস্তারিত।

- স্কুলের পাশের ব্রিজে একটা রাজনৈতিক হত্যাকাণও হয়েছে। ঐ সময় কাছাকাছিই ছিলাম।

- কীভাবে, মা?

- গুলি করে। মোটরসাইকেলে করে এসে গুলি করে চলে গেছে।

মা কেন সেই ঘটনা বা ঘটনার উত্তেজনা লুকোতে চেয়েছেন আমার কাছে? অন্য মায়েরা তো বলত!

আজ বুঝি, মায়ের মা হওয়া হলো সন্তানকে সকল ভয়ংকর ঘটনা থেকে দূরে রাখা।

খাগড়াছড়িতে যখন স্কুল-কলেজে পড়তাম, তখন কেবল পড়াশোনা আর বই পড়া, গান শোনা আর নাচ-গান শেখা, এইই ছিল জীবন। বাবা-মায়ের ছায়াতলে কখন যে আঠারোটা বছর কাটিয়ে দিলাম টের পাইনি। মনে আছে, কলেজে ভর্তির সময় আমি

থাগড়াছড়ির গন্ডি ছেড়ে ঢাকায় পড়তে যেতে পারিনি বলে আমার সে কী প্রচন্ড রাগ! আমার সব বন্ধুবান্ধবরা যাচ্ছে, আমি কেন পারলাম না! আমার শৈশবের শহর তখন আর আমাকে নতুন যুগের হাওয়া দিতে পারেনি। তখন বাংলাদেশে কেবল মোবাইল কোম্পানিগুলো চালু হতে শুরু করেছে। অথচ পার্বত্য চট্টগ্রাম সংযোগের বাইরে। এখানকার রাজনৈতিক অস্থিরতার কারণে নাকি সংযোগ দেয়া হবে না। ঢাকা-চট্টগ্রাম থেকে ফিরলে সবাই মোবাইলের গল্প করতো। দেশ যেখানে নতুন ফ্রিকোয়েন্সিতে আলাপ করছে, আমাদের তখন রেডিও টেলিভিশনের সীমিত প্রচারণার যুগ।

আমার কলেজ জীবনে বোনের বিয়ের পর দীর্ঘসময় মা আমার বিয়ের প্রসঙ্গে কথা বলেনি নিজে থেকে। কেউ জিজ্ঞেস করলে বলতো, পড়াশোনা শেষ করে আগে চাকরি করবে। তারপর বিয়ে। অথচ আমার উৎসাহ ছিল গগনচুম্বী। কোনো লাভ হয়নি। মা নিশ্চুপ, সিদ্ধান্তে অটল।

আজ বুঝি, মায়ের মা হওয়া হলো সন্তানকে স্বাবলম্বী করে জীবনযুদ্ধে ছেড়ে দেয়া।

থাগড়াছড়ি পেরিয়ে জাহাঙ্গীরনগরে আসা ছিল জীবনের প্রথম মোড়। এখানে জীবন মানে ছিল অভিনয়, সংগঠন, বিভাগ, অনুষ্ঠান এ সবের চঞ্চল চর্চা। এত ব্যস্ততাও আমার নারী হয়ে ওঠার ভাবনাকে দমায়নি, বরং উদ্বুদ্ধ করেছে প্রতি পদে পদে। যৌন নিপীড়ন কী বুঝেছি, যৌন নিপীড়ন বিরোধী মোস্তফা আন্দোলন কিংবা সানি আন্দোলনে রাস্তায় নেমে স্লোগান দিতে গিয়ে জেনেছি পুরুষের দৃষ্টিভঙ্গি; প্রতি মুহূর্ত ভাবিয়েছে, নারীর নারী হয়ে ওঠা কী!

এসবের মাঝেই একজনের ভাবনা আমাকে প্রচণ্ড নাড়া দিয়েছে। বান্ধবী শায়লা। বাসা ধামরাই। প্রতি সপ্তাহে ধামরাই থেকে এক সপ্তাহের জন্য হল-এ এসে থাকত। সপ্তাহ শেষে বাসায় ফিরত। আমরা থাকতাম ফজিলাতুন্নেসা হলে। বিকেলে চায়ের কাপে ধোঁয়ার সঙ্গ বা রাতের ভাতের প্লেটে অতিরিক্ত তরকারি ছিল আমার সাংসারিক জ্ঞান। প্রায়ই সংসার প্রসঙ্গে বিভিন্ন কথায় সে রসিকতা করতো। দুজনেই খুব উপভোগ করতাম। তবু আমার কানে বাজতো 'সংসার'। এই মেয়েটা কেন এত সংসার সংসার করে? একদিন জিজ্ঞেস করলাম। শুনে আমি আশ্চর্য হয়ে গেলাম, একই সময়ের দুইজন মায়ের দৃষ্টিভঙ্গি কীভাবে এত আলাদা হতে পারে?

-আমি ছোটবেলা থেকে এই শুনে এসেছি যে আমার সংসার হবে, সুন্দর চমৎকার একটা সংসারের স্বপ্ন দেখিয়েছে মা চিরকাল। তাহলে আমি এখন কেন তা লালন করব না, বল?

- তিনি কি কখনও স্বাবলম্বী হওয়ার কথা বলেননি?

- বলেছে, ততটা নয় যতটা সংসার। বলেছে, জীবন চলার জন্য চাকরি হলেই হবে। তাই কেরিয়ার নিয়ে খুব একটা ভাবা হয়নি কখনও।

আমি তখন কেরিয়ার নিয়ে খুব দুশ্চিন্তা করছি। বাংলা বিভাগে পড়ে সবচেয়ে ভাল কেরিয়ার কী হতে পারে আমি তাই মনে মনে খুঁজে বেড়াচ্ছি। বিশ্ববিদ্যালয়ের শিক্ষক হওয়ার স্বপ্ন দেখছি। বিসিএস পরীক্ষা দিয়ে পুলিশ হওয়ার কথা ভাবছি। আর শায়লার জীবনের লক্ষ্য একটা সংসার! নারীর নারী হওয়া মানে তবে কী? কেরিয়ার? সংসার? নাকি দুটোই? আজ বুঝি, মায়ের মা হওয়া মানে হলো, সন্তানের জন্য সুন্দর সুস্থ পরিবারের স্বপ্ন দেখা যেন সে একাকী জীবন না পায়। কন্যা সন্তান হলে তাকে ভাবী জীবনযুদ্ধ ও সঙ্কটের জন্য তৈরি করা।

অনার্স-মাস্টার্স শেষ করে যোগদান করলাম ইসলামী বিশ্ববিদ্যালয়ে। প্রথম রাতের অনুভূতি বড়ো ভয়ংকর। জেমসের গান "জেল থেকে আমি বলছি" হয়ে উঠলো চরম সত্য। স্বাধীন জীবন থেকে হঠাৎ করে যেন কুয়োয় গিয়ে পড়লাম। খুব দ্রুত মানিয়ে নিতে শুরু করলাম। কিন্তু প্রচন্ড একাকিত্ব আমাকে জেঁকে বসলো। নির্জনতা হয়ে উঠল আমার দৈনন্দিন জীবনের পরিচিত চিত্র। একাকিত্ব আমাকে আঁকড়ে ধরলো অক্টোপাসের মতো হাত পা দিয়ে। শূন্যতা কেবল অন্তর নয়, আমার বহির্জগতকেও আষ্টেপৃষ্ঠে জড়িয়ে ধরল। ভিড়েও একাকীত্ব অনুভব করা হয়ে গেল আমার শখ। আমি অভ্যস্ত হয়ে গেলাম। এভাবে বছর দেড়েক যেতে না যেতেই কথার ফুলঝুরি আসতে শুরু করল, তুমি বিয়ে করবে না? কবে বিয়ে করবে? নিজের কমিউনিটির কাউকে বিয়ে করবে? নাকি বাঙালি বিয়ে করবে? বিয়ে করলে দেরি করো না। সন্তান ধারণে অসুবিধা হতে পারে। বিয়েতে আমরা সবাই খাগড়াছড়ি যাব। ইত্যাদি। ইত্যাদি।

আমি আবার অস্তিত্ব সংকটে পড়ে গেলাম। বিয়ে ছাড়া নারীর গতি নেই? কিন্তু বিয়ে করার জন্য তো আমি মানসিকভাবে প্রস্তুত নই। পরিণত, তবু প্রস্তুত নই। নতুন একজন মানুষকে নিজের জীবনে ঠাঁই দেয়ার জন্য মানসিক প্রস্তুতি আমার নেই। অথচ মা হওয়ার তীব্র আকাঙ্ক্ষা থেকে কেন মুক্তি নেই? একাকী জীবনে জীবনসঙ্গীর চেয়েও একজন সন্তান তীব্র আকাঙ্ক্ষিত। এই আকাঙ্ক্ষায় না সমাজ বড় না রাজনীতি, না সংসার না পরিবার। সবচেয়ে বড়ো সত্য আমি মা হতে চাই।আমার নিম্নগামী স্নেহময় ভালবাসা কেবল সন্তানকে দিয়ে তাকেই পরিপূর্ণ করে তুলে পৃথিবীতে চিহ্ন রেখে দিতে চাই।

এরপর বিয়ে, ঢাকা আর কুষ্টিয়া আমার সংসার, অতঃপর মাতৃত্ব।

পাঁচ মাসের ছেলেকে দেশে রেখে চলে এলাম নাগাসাকিতে। নতুন শহর, নতুন মানুষ, ভিন্ন সংস্কৃতি, ভিন্ন ভাষা। অল্প সময়ের ব্যবধানে নাগাসাকিতে শুরু হলো ছেলে স্বামীকে নিয়ে সংসার। ঘন্টার পর ঘন্টা ছেলের দিকে তাকিয়ে থাকা। প্রচণ্ড চঞ্চল ছেলের পেছনে অস্বাভাবিক সময় দেয়া। পড়াশোনা সব শিকেয় তোলা।

হঠাৎ হঠাৎ মনে হয়, জীবন বড় ক্ষণজীবী এক সত্য। কোন এক প্রত্যন্ত অঞ্চলের খাগড়াছড়ি জেলাশহরের পাহাড়ি বাতাবরণে বেড়ে ওঠা এক মেয়ে শিশু রাজধানী, জাহাঙ্গীরনগর, কুষ্টিয়া ছাড়িয়ে আজ জাপানের এক মফস্বল শহরে জানালা দিয়ে চেরি ব্লসম দেখছি।

তবু কোথায় যেন শূন্যতা অনুভব করি। তবু নাগাসাকির বিষন্ন দুপুরগুলোতে ঢাকা-খাগড়াছড়ি রোডের বারেইয়ার হাটের পর দু'পাশের ঘন সবুজ গাছগাছালির দিকে তাকিয়ে দূষণহীন নির্মল বাতাসে শ্বাস নিতে নিতে বাড়ির দিকে যাওয়ার তীব্র ইচ্ছা বারবার মাথাচাড়া দেয়। তবু নাগাসাকির বরফঝরা ভোরগুলোতে মনে হয়, ছেলেকে একবার সেই পথের সন্ধান দিতে না পারলে আমার সমগ্র সত্তা অস্তিত্বহীন হয়ে পড়বে। আমার সেই ছেলেবেলার শেওলা-ধরা উঠোন কিংবা বিয়েবেলার উঠোনের টকপাতা-কামরাঙা-জাম্বুরা-কলাপাতার মেলায় আর জবার ঝোপের আড়ালে ছেলেকে একবার হারিয়ে যেতে না দিলে যেন ব্যর্থ হবে তিলে তিলে অস্তিত্বের গভীরে প্রোথিত চিরন্তন মাতৃত্ব।

Aditi Das / অদিতি দাস, Sylhet, Bangladesh

The attachment between my city and me inspired me much to write up this article. The term 'MY CITY MY HOME' inspired my work greatly, because I love my city, I belong to this city and this is my origin.

প্রিয় শহর আর সর্বনাশা অক্টোবর

আমার শহরটা আমার কাছে আমার ঘরের মতই ছিল। প্রিয় শহরকে নিয়ে যখন লিখছি তখন আমি অদ্ভুত এক আঁধার সময় পার করছি। হ্যাঁ, কোভিড-১৯ এর কারণে পুরো পৃথিবীই এখন দুঃসময় পার করছে। কিন্তু আমার জন্য সময়টা তার চেয়ে কঠিন, তার চেয়েও নির্দয়।

লেখাটা যখন লিখছি তার ঠিক দুই মাস আগে একদিনের ব্যবধানে আমাকে হারাতে হয়েছে মা ও বাবাকে। যে শহরে আমার জন্ম, যেখানে আমার বেড়ে ওঠা, শৈশবের বর্ণিলতা, কৈশোরের দুরন্তপনা আর যৌবনের আনন্দ-বেদনা যে শহরের আলো-বাতাসে মিশে আছে, নিজের হাতের রেখার মত যে শহরটাকে চিনি, সেই শহরটা আজকাল আমার কাছে বড্ড অচেনা লাগে।

সবকিছু রুপালী পর্দার বিচ্ছেদ গল্পের চেয়েও করুণ মনে হয়। বাবার হাত ধরে প্রথম স্কুলে গিয়েছিলাম। সিলেটের স্বনামধন্য বিদ্যাপীঠ ব্লু বার্ড স্কুলেই আমার শিক্ষা জীবনের শুরু হয়েছিল। স্কুলের সময়টা আমার জীবনে সবচেয়ে মধুময় ছিল। আমার বাবা নিকুঞ্জ বিহারী দাস ছিলেন এই স্কুলের গণিতের শিক্ষক। সবার প্রিয় 'নিকুঞ্জ স্যার'। মা ও ছিলেন এই শহরের একটি সরকারী প্রাথমিক বিদ্যালয়ের শিক্ষক।

করোনাভাইরাস মহামারী নানাভাবে ক্ষতিসাধন করেছে পৃথিবীজুড়ে। কিন্তু আমার মত ক্ষতিগ্রস্ত খুব কম মানুষই হয়তো হয়েছেন। আমি হারিয়েছি আমার মা ও বাবাকে। ভাগ্যের কী নির্মম পরিহাস – মাসটা ছিল অক্টোবর। আমার জন্মমাস। অক্টোবর তাই আমার কাছে বরাবরই প্রিয়, আলাদা, আহ্লাদের। কিন্তু আমি কি আর কখনও ভেবেছিলাম – এই অক্টোবরই হবে আমার সব সর্বনাশের নাম?

ঢাকায় সাংবাদিকতা করতাম। মা আর বাবা সিলেটে একা থাকতেন। চলতি বছরের মার্চে বাবার ক্যানসার ধরা পড়ে। চিকিৎসা শুরু হতে না হতেই করোনার বিস্তার ও দেশজুড়ে লকডাউন। মা একা একা সবদিক সামাল দেন। আমি তখন ঢাকায় আটকা পড়ি। পরিচয় ওয়ার্কিং ফ্রম হোম এর সাথে। কাজ করি, কিন্তু বাবা-মা'র জন্য দুশ্চিন্তা হয়। এভাবে কাটে সাড়ে ৩ মাস। ক্যানসার আক্রান্ত বাবাকে নিয়ে একা একা মা পেরে উঠছিলেন না। তাই জুলাই মাসে সিলেট চলে আসি। সিলেটেই 'ওয়ার্কিং ফ্রম হোম' করছিলাম। সেপ্টেম্বরের মাঝামাঝিতে অফিস থেকে জানানো হলো আর হোম অফিস নয়, অফিসে কাজে যোগ দিতে হবে। কিন্তু বাবা-মাকে এ অবস্থায় রেখে যেতে মন কিছুতেই মানছিল না। অবশেষে চাকরি ছেড়ে দিলাম অনেকটা বাধ্য হয়ে।

৭ অক্টোবর ছিল 'দুঃসাল প্রতিরোধে আমরা'র আয়োজনে ধর্ষণবিরোধী আন্দোলনের প্রথম দিন। আমি আর গৌতমদা বেলা ৪টা নাগাদ সিলেট কেন্দ্রীয় শহিদ মিনারে যাই। সন্ধ্যার পর বাসায় ফিরে দেখি মায়ের জ্বর। ৯ তারিখ আন্দোলনে যোগ দিতে আবারও শহিদ মিনারে যাই। সেদিন সন্ধ্যায় বাসায় ফেরার পর আমার জ্বর আসে। বাবার জ্বর কিংবা কাশি কিছুই ছিল না। ১২ তারিখ বাবা-মা ও আমি কোভিড টেস্টের জন্য স্যাম্পল জমা দিই বাসাতেই। তিনজনেরই রেজাল্ট পজিটিভ আসে। ১৬ তারিখ সকালে মার তীব্র শ্বাসকষ্ট দেখা দিলে তাঁকে শহিদ শামসুদ্দিন আহমেদ হাসপাতালের (সদর হাসপাতাল) আইসিইউতে ভর্তি করি। ক্যানসার আক্রান্ত বাবাকে দেখভালের জন্য কেউ নেই বাসায়। মিষ্টি মাসির (মায়ের ছোটবোন) পরামর্শে বাবাকেও হাসপাতালে ভর্তি করাই। গৌতমদা আর আমার মামাতো ভাই শুভম বাবাকে হাসপাতালে নিয়ে আসেন।

সিলেটে আত্মীয়, বন্ধু, শুভাকাঙ্ক্ষীদের সংখ্যা নিতান্ত কম নয়। কিন্তু কোভিডের এই সময়ে কাকে পাই! দুই-একজন বন্ধু-শুভাকাঙ্ক্ষী যে ঝুঁকি নিয়ে পাশে দাঁড়াননি তেমন নয়। তাঁদের কথা আর আলাদা করে বলতে চাই না। নিজে করোনা আক্রান্ত হলেও রোগীর অ্যাটেন্ডেন্ট হিসেবে আমাকেই থাকতে হচ্ছে। বাবা হাসপাতালের এক জায়গায়, মা আরেক জায়গায় আইসিইউতে। একই সঙ্গে দুই জায়গায় রোগীর খেয়াল রাখা তখন আমার জন্য ভীষণ কঠিন হয়ে উঠেছিল। তাছাড়া চিকিৎসক বা নার্স বললেই ফার্মেসিতে ছুটে যাওয়া। দিনের পর দিন, রাতের পর রাত আমি নির্ঘুম কাটিয়েছি।

২৬ অক্টোবর বিজয়া দশমীর দিন পরপারে পাড়ি জমান মা। মারা যাওয়ার আগের সন্ধ্যায় মা'র ব্লাড প্রেশার লো হয়ে গেল, এত লো যে মেশিনও তা রিড করতে পারছিল না। আমাকে ছুটতে হলো মেডিসিন, স্যালাইন কিনতে। রাত সাড়ে ১২টায়ও মেডিসিন এনেছি। আমি তাই শোক করতে পারিনি, মার হাত ধরে একটু বসে থাকতে পারিনি। তখন মাঝরাত হবে। মনিটরে বিপি দেখাচ্ছিল নিচেরটা ২৭, উপরেরটা কিছুই দেখাচ্ছিল না। আমি আতঙ্কে চাদর মুড়ি দিয়ে শুয়ে থাকলাম অনেকটা নিরুপায় হয়ে। ক্লান্ত শরীরে একটু কি তন্দ্রাচ্ছন্ন হয়েছিলাম? হঠাৎ মনে হলো কেউ এসেছে, ধরমড় করে ওঠে বসলাম। দেখলাম একজন ডাক্তার ও নার্স। পরীক্ষা করে দেখছিলেন জীবিত না মৃত। ডাক্তার যখন নিশ্চিত হলেন, আমার দিকে শূন্য দৃষ্টিতে তাকালেন আর মাথা নাড়লেন। আমি সঙ্গে সঙ্গে চোখ নামিয়ে নিলাম। তখন ভোর সাড়ে চারটা থেকে পৌনে ৫টার মাঝামাঝি একটা সময়। মৃত্যুর খবর প্রথম জানিয়েছিলাম গৌতমদাকে মোবাইলে কল দিয়ে। বলেছিলাম মিষ্টি মাসিকে জানাতে। আমার সাহস হচ্ছিল না তাঁকে জানানোর। দাদা জানানোর পর মিষ্টিমাসি আমাকে কল দিয়েছিলেন। স্বান্তনা দিয়ে বলেছিলেন, 'অনেক চেষ্টা করেছিস মা, এর চেয়ে বেশি আর কিছু করার ছিল না।' কথা বলতে বলতে দুজনে কেঁদেছিলাম। ৫টার একটু পরে গৌতমদা এসে কল দিলেন। বের হয়ে দেখলাম দাদা আর কার্তিক কাকু। তখন আমরা ভাবছিলাম এত সকাল, দাহ কীভাবে হবে। আমার একমাত্র ভাই ভারতে থাকে। সে বলেছিল মাকে দেখবে। আইসিইউ থেকে বের করার পর করিডোরে যখন মাকে আনা হয় তখন তাকে ভিডিও কল দিই। মোবাইল স্ক্রিনেই মাকে শেষ দেখা দেখে নেয়। করোনার ভয়াবহতার মধ্যেও ঠিক ভাবেই শেষ হয় সৎকার কাজ। বেলা বাড়তে বাড়তে শ্মশানে পরিচিত মুখগুলোও জড়ো হতে থাকে। সৎকার কাজ শেষে শ্মশান থেকে ফিরলাম হাসপাতালে। বাবাকে ডিসচার্জ করিয়ে বাসায় নিয়ে এলাম। তখন কে জানত পরদিন সকালে বাবাও চিরদিনের মতো চলে যাবেন আমায় ছেড়ে।

যখন সিংগাপুর ছিলাম বা ঢাকায়, তখন পিছুটান বলতে ছিলেন বাবা-মা। সারাক্ষণ তাদের কাছে চলে আসতে মন চাইত। এই ডিসেম্বরেই চাকরি পেয়েছি নিজ শহর সিলেটে। অথচ এখন আর আমার কোনো পিছুটান নেই।

আজকাল শহরটাকে কেমন অন্যরকম লাগে। খুব মন চায়, মায়ের সঙ্গে সবকিছু শেয়ার করি-আগে যেমন করতাম। আমার কত গল্প জমে আছে-আর কখনও বলা হবে না মাকে। শরীর খারাপ হলে কেউ অস্থির হয়ে উঠবে না। জ্বর হলে কেউ মাথায় পানি ঢালবে না। যখন নিউজ লিখব বা অন্য কোনো লেখা, তখন ল্যাপটপের পাশে কেউ এক কাপ চা রেখে যাবে না। মা দুর্গা পূজায় দুর্গা বাড়িতে যেতে চেয়েছিলেন। অথচ দশমীর দিন দুর্গা মায়ের বিসর্জনের দিনেই মা চিরবিদায় নিলেন। আমার মনে শুধুই প্রশ্ন জাগে, কেন আমার জন্ম মাসে, কেন দুর্গা পূজাতেই বাবা-মা চলে গেলেন?

কোভিড আমাদেরকে নতুন করে দেখিয়ে দিল-মানুষ মাত্রই একা। বাসা থেকে অফিসে আসা-যাওয়ার পথে প্রতিদিনই সদর হাসপাতালের সামনে দিয়ে যেতে হয়। মনে পড়ে যায় হাসপাতালের ভয়ংকর দিনগুলোর কথা। করোনা আইসোলেশন ইউনিটে থাকা না লাগলে আইসোলেশন শব্দটার আসল অর্থ হয়তো বুঝতে পারতাম না।

ঢাকায় দেড় বছরের বেশি সময় থেকেও আবার সিলেটে চলে আসেন বাবা-মা। আমার ভাই ভারতে স্থায়ী হলেও তারা কখনও সিলেট ছাড়ার চিন্তাও করেননি।

এই লেখাটা হতে পারত সিলেটের ইতিহাস, ঐতিহ্য, ভাষা, সাহিত্য, সংস্কৃতি, মানুষ, প্রকৃতি নিয়ে। কিন্তু এ বিরাট ধাক্কার পর আর অন্য কোন কিছু নিয়ে লিখতে ইচ্ছা করল না। এই সিলেট আমার যতটা প্রিয় তারচেয়ে ঢের বেশি প্রিয় বাবা-মায়ের।

Khadija Parvin / খাদিজা পারভীন, Jashore, Bangladesh

মানুষই একমাত্র সত্যের নিয়ামক, অন্যথায় সত্যের কোন মূল্য নেই। এই উপলব্ধি থেকেই আমার লেখা।

আমার বাস্তুভিটা

আমি জমিলা।

নিতান্ত দরিদ্র ঘরের মেয়ে একটা আমি। কোন বিশেষত্ব নেই। বড্ড সেকেলে। আমি আজ যুক্ত আছি একটি কারখানার সঙ্গে, সেখানে আমায় নিত্যদিন শ্রম বিনিয়োগ করে জীবন বাঁচাতে হয়। নিয়তি আমাকে নিতান্ত হাত ধরে, চোখে আঙুল দিয়ে এই স্থানটি দেখিয়ে দিয়েছে। আর বলেছে, এই স্থানটি তোমার জন্য যথার্থ। শহর, নগর, সভ্যতা, ইট-পাথরের দালান-কোঠা সবকিছু ছেড়ে এক পড়ন্ত গ্রামের দেহের বুক চিড়ে মেঠোপথ ধরে, দিগন্তের কাছাকাছি একটি ছোট্ট বাড়ি আমার। গ্রামের নাম জীবনতলী। বড্ড ছোট গ্রাম আমার, পৃথিবীর কোন সভ্যতার ছিটেফোঁটাও লাগেনি সেখানে। না ইলেকট্রিসিটি, না টেলিগ্রাম, না লেখাপড়ার সুব্যবস্থা, না বড়-বড় দালানকোঠা। এই ছোট্ট গ্রামের এক ভেতো বাঙালি মেয়ে আমি। এই ইট-পাথরের শহরের চার দেয়ালের মাঝে মেশিনের সাথে নিত্যদিন ওঠাবসা করতে করতে, সেই ভেতো বাঙালি মেয়েটি কবে যে নিজেই মেশিনে পরিনত হয়েছে, সে খবর তার নিজেরই জানা নেই!

যখন সন্ধ্যার আকাশ কালো মেঘে ছেয়ে আসে, সারা শহর ঘুটঘুটে কালো অন্ধকারে ঢেকে যায়, তখন চোখের কোণটা চকচকে হয়ে ওঠে, বাড়ির ভিটেটার জন্য। হু-হু করে মনে পড়ে যায়, অতীতের দিনগুলির কথা। মনের মধ্যে আঁকিবুকি কেটে যায় সেই স্মৃতিগুলো। ছোট্ট একটা বাড়ি ছিল আমাদের। থাকতাম তো আমি, বাবা আর মা। এর জন্য আর কতোটুকুন জায়গা লাগে? গাঁয়ে পথের ধারে বাঁশের খুঁটি দেওয়া পরচালা যুক্ত দিব্যি পরিপাটি একটা বাড়ি। অন্যের কাছে খুবই সামান্য হতে পারে কিন্তু আমার কাছে স্বর্গের মতো। বাড়ির সামনে কাঠা দুয়েক জায়গা ঘিরে চারদিকে ভাঙা-ফাটা প্রাচীর।

ঘরের মধ্যে নানা রকমের আসবাবপত্র ছিল, ঘরের দুই কোণে দুটি ভাঙা খাট, তাতে বেছানো খান দুই ছেঁড়া মাদুর, কানাভাঙা কলসি, দুটো টোল খাওয়া অ্যালুমিনিয়ামের গ্লাস, দুটো পায়া না থাকা সত্ত্বেও পরস্পরের গায়ে সমবায় সমিতির মতো হেলান দেয়া চেয়ার কোনরকমে দাঁড়িয়ে আছে। ঘরের দু'দিকে গচ্ছিত দুটো দামি সম্পদ ছিল, একটা বাবার অপরটি মায়ের। বাবার ছিল পুরাতন আমলের কয়েকটি বই। বাবা বড়ো কম পড়তে জানতো। তবে বইকটা ছিল বাবার বুকের এক-একটা পাঁজরের হাড়। বাবা বই পড়তো আর মাঝে মাঝে বইটা বুকে জড়িয়ে, দেয়ালে হেলান দিয়ে, দুচোখ বন্ধ করে কি যেন ভাবতো। বলতাম, "বাবা কী ভাবছো?" বাবা আমাকে বুকে জড়িয়ে বলতো "জমিলা, লেখাপড়ার যে কত মূল্য মা! এই বইক'টা যে কতো দামি আমার কাছে!" বাবার এই অমূল্য সম্পদের কোনই মূল্য ছিল না, মায়ের কাছে!

আর মায়ের ছিল একটা ছোট্ট মাটির ব্যাংক। সবটুকুন দুঃখ–কষ্ট নিংড়ে যতটুকুন পয়সা পারে, সেখানে জমিয়ে রাখে। সেই ব্যাংকের মালিক, ম্যানেজার, সিকিউরিটি সবই আমার মা ছিলেন। আমিতো দূরের কথা, বাবারও এর ধারে-কাছে ঘেঁষতে মানা!

এই দুই সম্পদের মাঝে আর একটি দামি সম্পদ ছিলাম আমি তাদের। আমাকে যেন দু'জনে চোখে হারায়। দু'জনের চোখের মণি ছিলাম। শিশবকালে বাবার সাথে এক বিছানায় ঘুমিয়ে, অর্ধেকরাতে দুঃস্বপ্ন দেখে ভয়ে, ছোট্ট হাত প্রসারিত করে যখন বাবাকে খুঁজতাম, তখন বাবা বলতো, "এইতো আমি এখানে!" তখন বাবার বুকে মুখটি গুঁজে গুমরে গুমরে কাঁদতাম। বাবা বলতো, "কী স্বপ্ন দেখেছিস? বল আমাকে?" বাবাকে বলতেই পারতামনা। এই ঘরে আমরা চারটি প্রাণী ছিলাম। ওহ! আর একটা প্রাণী, ওতো আমাদের কালু মানে আমাদের পোষা কুকুর। কালু বড্ড ভালো ছিল। সারারাত জেগে আমাদের বাড়ি পাহারা দিত। আমি খেলতে গেল কালুও আমার সাথে পিছুপিছু যেত। খেলা শেষে যখন বাড়ি ফিরতাম, দেখতাম কোথা থেকে সে ঠিক জুটে যেত। বাবা যখন হাট থেকে বাড়ি ফিরতো, দেখতাম বাবার পিছুপিছু আছে ও। কালুর কথা খুব মনে পড়ে এখন। কে জানে, কোথায় থাকে এখন!

আমাদের বাড়ির চারপাশ সবুজ গাছগাছালিতে ঘেরা। একজন আরেকজনকে জড়িয়ে

যেন আত্মীয়ের মতো বেঁচে আছে এরা। আমার বাড়িটাকে যেন আগলে রেখেছে। ঘরের পুবদিকে একটা কৃষ্ণচূড়া গাছ ছিল। বসন্তে কী যে তার রূপের বাহার! যেন সারা বাড়িটাকে সাজিয়ে রাখতো। পাড়ার ছেলে–মেয়েরা কত আসতো আমাদের বাড়িতে। একসাথে খেলতাম, কৃষ্ণচূড়ার ফুল দিয়ে সাজতাম, কত হৈচৈ! মায়ের কান ঝালাপালা হয়ে যেত। কোথায় হারিয়ে গেছে সেই দিনগুলো! এখন সবই অতীত।

বাড়ির সামনে একটু দূরে, গ্রামের পাশ দিয়ে একটি নদী বয়ে গেছে। চৈত্র মাসে নদী যেন শুকিয়ে কাঠ হয়ে যেত। নদীকে দেখে অনেক বুড়ো লাগতো যেন! মনে হতো নদীর যেন অনেক বয়স হলো! কিন্তু, বর্ষাকালে নদী যেন ভরা যৌবন নিয়ে ফিরতো। চৈত্র মাসে নদীতে মধুমেলা বসতো। মা মেলায় যেতে দিত না! বলতো, "মুসলমানদের মেলায় যেতে নেই"।

বাবার জন্য প্রায় যাওয়া হয়ে যেত। বাবার স্বপ্ন ছিল আমাকে নিয়ে অনেক। বাবা বলতো, "জমিলা তোকে আমি লেখাপড়াটা শেখাবো, আইন নিয়ে পড়াবো তোকে"। ঠিক তখনই অপরদিক থেকে একটা তিরস্কার ভেসে আসতো – মা বলতো, "হহ! চাষার বেটির আবার আইন নিয়ে পড়া! ওহ, আমার যদি একটা ছেলে থাকত!" এটা বলে মা চুপ হয়ে যেত। বুঝতাম না মায়ের ছেলের ইচ্ছেটা কেন এত প্রবল ছিল। বাবা বলতো, "জানিস জমিলা, মানুষই একমাত্র সত্যের নিয়ামক। অন্যথায় সত্যের কোন মূল্য নেই"। বাবার কথা আমি কিছুই বুঝতাম না।

এত স্বপ্ন দেখা সত্য চোখগুলো একদিন হঠাৎ বন্ধ হয়ে গেল! এক মহামারী কলেরায়, বাবা-মা দুজনেই আমাকে ছেড়ে চলে গিয়েছিল। গ্রামের অনেকেই সেবার মহামারীতে মারা গেছিল। বাবা-মা দুজনেই খুব অসুস্থ ছিল। সেই রাতে বাবা একটু পানি চেয়েছিল আমার কাছে, পানি নিয়ে ফিরে এসে দেখি, বাবা-মা দুজনেই চুপ। বাবার কাছ থেকে শোনা "বায়েজিদ বোস্তামির" গল্পের মতো আমিও পানি হাতে দাঁড়িয়ে ছিলাম সেই রাতে, বাবা-মার পাশে। হঠাৎ পাশের বাড়ির এক চাচি এসে বললো, "ও জমিলা! জমিলা রে? তোরা কই গেলি? ওদিকে ঝন্টুর মা নাকি মা...রা......"।

আমি বললাম চাচি, "চুপ করো, বাবা-মা ঘুমাচ্ছে"। চাচি আমাকে জড়িয়ে ধরে বললো,

"পোড়ামুখী! তোর মা-বাবা যে ম...রে...ছে..."। দমকা হাওয়ায় আলো নিভে গেলে, অন্ধকার যেমন প্রকট হয়ে উঠে, ঠিক তেমনি ভাবেই সমস্ত ঘর সকল দিক গুম হয়ে উঠলো। কতদিনের চেনা মুখগুলো, আজ অচেনা লাগলো। ঘরের উপর দিয়ে একটা কাক, কা-কা করে চলে গেল। সমস্ত আকাশটা যেন ছেঁড়া চটের মতো চঙ্কর করে ছিঁড়ে গেল! কয়টা কুকুর উঠানে থেকে-থেকে কেঁদে উঠছে। সেই রাতেই চাচি আমাকে নিয়ে পালিয়ে আসে এই শহরে। পরে জানতে পারলাম, আমি ওখানে থাকলে আমার ওয়ারিশগন আমাকে বাঁচতে দিত না!

সেই রাতে পিছু ফেলে এসেছিলাম আমার বাস্তুভিটা, আমার সবকিছু। পিছু ফিরে দেখেছিলাম আমার ঘরটা, দেখলাম কৃষ্ণচূড়া গাছটা থেকে ফুল ঝরছে। কিন্তু মনে হচ্ছিল ফুল নয়, ওর বুক থেকে রক্ত ঝরছে! তারপর আর পিছু তাকাইনি। কিছুদূর গিয়ে দেখি, কালু পিছুপিছু আসছে। রাতের আঁধারে দেখতে অসুবিধা হয়নি, দেখলাম আমার ভাঙা স্কুলটি। সব স্বপ্ন আজ ভেঙে গেছে। পৃথিবীর বুক থেকে আকাশের কোল পর্যন্ত কূলহীন অন্ধকার। সেই অন্ধকারে কালুকে আর দেখতে পেলাম না। তারপর চোখ মেলে প্রথম আলোয় এই শহর দেখা। এখন মনে হয়, আমার নাম নেই, স্থান নেই, আমার গল্পেরা মিথ্যে হয় প্রতিদিন। আমাকে প্রতিদিন লড়াই করে আমার প্রতিটা গল্প জিততে হয়। ভালোবেসে তবু নিজের ভিটে-বাড়ি খুঁজি, খুঁজি নিজের পরিচয়। দুঃখ-সুখে আমার স্থান চাই, আমার নাম চাই! আর চাই আমার গল্পেরা সত্যি হোক।

Nishita Das / নিশিতা দাশ, Moulvibaza, Bangladesh

Beauty of the historical lake Kamalarani in my region is my inspiration to write about it.

দীঘির নাম কমলারাণী

সকল দেশের রানী সে যে আমার জন্মভূমি। অপরূপ সৌন্দর্যের লীলাভূমি এই সবুজ শ্যামল দেশের সৌন্দর্যে আমি মুগ্ধ হই বারবার। আমাকে স্পর্শ করে যায় ঢাকার বুড়িগঙ্গা, কিংবা চট্টগ্রামের সুউচ্চ পাহাড়, দীর্ঘতম সমুদ্র বন্দর কক্সবাজার, রাজশাহীর আমের বাগান, খুলনার সুন্দরবন আরো কত কী। তবু যদি প্রশ্ন করা হয় সবথেকে প্রিয় বলতে কি কিছুই নেই? আমি বলব আছে। দুটি পাতা একটি কুঁড়ির দেশ, উঁচু উঁচু পাহাড় টিলা, নদী, নালা, খাল, বিল, হাওড়, বাওড় ত্রিমাত্রিক জেলা মৌলভীবাজার। আমি শতবার সহস্রবার এই অঞ্চলের প্রেমে পড়ি।

কবি শামসুল হক তাঁর কবিতায় বলেছেন, আমি তো এসেছি কমলার দীঘি মহুয়ার পালা থেকে। কবির লেখনীতে উঠে আসা সেই কমলার দীঘিকে নিয়ে লোকমুখে শোনা সেই ঐতিহাসিক কাহিনী নিয়েই এই লেখা।

এ দীঘিকে নিয়ে রয়েছে এক কিংবদন্তি। এ দীঘিটি রাজনগর উপজেলা সদর থেকে ১৪ কি.মি. দূরে রাজনগর ইউনিয়নের ঘরগাঁও গ্রামে অবস্থিত।

ইটা রাজ্যের রাজা সুবিদ নারায়ণ ছিলেন খুবই প্রজাবৎসল, সাহসী ও সংস্কারপন্থী। তাঁর ছিল অপরূপ সুন্দরী রানী – নাম কমলারানী, যাঁর রূপে মুগ্ধ ছিলেন রাজা সুবিদ নারায়ণ। রাজার ছিল ৫ পুত্র ও ৩ কন্যা। সুখে-আনন্দে কেটে যাচ্ছিলো রাজা-রানীর সংসার। তবে একটা বিপত্তি ঘটলো। রাজ্যে দেখা দিল জলের অভাব। প্রজাবৎসল রাজা সুবিদ নারায়ণ পড়লেন মহা দুশ্চিন্তায়। কী করে বাঁচাবেন প্রজাদের?

এক রাতে রাজা স্বপ্নাদেশ পেলেন যে তাঁকে একটা দীঘি খনন করতে হবে, যাতে প্রজাগণ সুপেয় জল পান করতে পারেন।

রাজা তাঁর এই স্বপ্নের কথা প্রাণপ্রিয় স্ত্রীকে জানান। কমলারানী উৎসাহ যোগালেন। মহাধুমধামে শুরু হলে দীঘি থননের কাজ। কথিত আছে – দীঘি থননের প্রথম কোদালের কোপ-দাতাকে রানী তাঁর গলার হার উপহার দেন।

একসময় শেষ হলো প্রত্যাশিত দীঘি থননের কাজ। কিন্তু একি আশ্চর্য কান্ড! দীঘিতে একফোঁটা জলও নেই। চারিদিকে ছড়িয়ে গেল এই খবর। অপমানে দুঃখে দিশেহারা রাজা সুবিদ নারায়ণ। কমলারানীও চিন্তায় পড়লেন। কী করবেন এবার?

আবারও স্বপ্নাদেশ এলো রাজার কাছে, "যতক্ষণ সুন্দরী প্রিয়তমা স্ত্রী কমলারানী দীঘিতে নেমে গঙ্গা দেবীর উদ্দেশ্যে পূজা না দিচ্ছেন, ততক্ষণ জলশূন্য থাকবে এ দীঘি"। রাজা তাঁর প্রাণের রানীকে জানালেন স্বপ্নাদেশের কথা। রাজার সম্মানার্থে, প্রজার প্রয়োজনে রানী রাজি হলেন। শোনা যায় রানীর কোলে তখন ৩ মাসের ফুটফুটে শিশু। রাজা রাজ্যের বিজ্ঞ পন্ডিতদের সাথে পরামর্শ করে দিনক্ষণ ঠিক করলেন।

অবশেষে এলো সেই দিন। ভোরের আলোয় আলোকিত দিন। লোকে লোকারণ্য চারিদিক। ঢাক, ঢোল, কাঁসর বাজছে। কমলারানী চললেন দীঘিতে জল আনার উদ্দেশ্যে। স্বস্তিতে আহ্বান করলেন মা গঙ্গার। রানীর প্রার্থনায় দীঘি পূর্ণ হতে লাগলো জলে। এ'যেন এক স্বর্গীয় দৃশ্য। রানী যখন দীঘির মাঝখানে পৌঁছলেন, অমনি কলকল শব্দে ভরে উঠতে লাগলো দীঘি। জলের স্রোতে ভেসে গেলেন রাজা সুবিদ নারায়নের প্রাণপ্রিয় সহধর্মিণী অনিন্দ্য সুন্দরী কমলারানী।

শোকে মুহ্যমান হলো পুরো রাজ্য। রানীর শোকে কাতর হলেন পিতামাতা। পত্নীশোকে রাজা সুবিদ নারায়ণ নাওয়া খাওয়া ভুলে গেলেন। মনস্থির করলেন তিনি বনবাসী হবেন। রাগে ক্ষোভে নিজের বোন ধপাস রানীকে হত্যা করে বসলেন। রাজ্যে নেমে এলো মহা বিশৃঙ্খলা।

এমনই দিনে রাজার স্বপ্নে এলেন রানী। বললেন "আপনি আমাকে প্রতিদিন দেখতে পাবেন। দীঘির পাড়ে ছোট্ট কুড়েঁঘর নির্মাণ করে আমার ছোট্ট সন্তানটিকে সূর্য উদয়ের আগে রাখলে আমি তাকে দুধপান করিয়ে যাব। সাবধান, ১২ বছর আপনি আমায় স্পর্শ করতে পারবেন না। যদি অপেক্ষা করতে পারেন তবেই আমি আবার ফিরে

আসব। রানীর কথামত কুঁড়েঘর নির্মিত হলো। যথারীতি রানী এলেন। রাজা সুবিদ নারায়ণ দূর থেকে দেখলেন প্রিয় রানীকে। বুকটা হাহাকার করে উঠলো তার। এভাবে অতিবাহিত হলো কিছুদিন। রাজা অধৈর্য্য হয়ে উঠলেন। একদিন রানীর কথা অমান্য করে রাজা ছুঁয়ে দিলেন রানীকে। কিন্তু একি হলো। পলকেই রানী মিলিয়ে গেলেন।

দীঘিতে ভেসে উঠলো এক সোনার নৌকো। রানী সেই নৌকায় চড়ে মনের দুঃখে রাজাকে বললেন "আমি আর এই দীঘিতে থাকবনা। চিরদিনের জন্য হারিয়ে যাচ্ছি। আর আমাকে পাবেন না।"

সোনার নৌকো মিলিয়ে গেল দীঘির জলে। রানীকে আর দেখা গেল না। কমলারানী মিলিয়ে গেলেন দীঘির জলে। দীঘির নাম হলো কমলারানীর দীঘি। আজও সেই দীঘি দাঁড়িয়ে আছে কালের সাক্ষী হয়ে।

(তথ্য সূত্রঃ জাতীয় গ্রন্থবর্ষ ২০০২ উপলক্ষে প্রকাশিত "সঙ্কলন", মৌলভীবাজার জেলার ইতিহাস ও ঐতিহ্য, প্রকাশকাল জুন ২০০১)

Ishmam Tasnim / ইশমাম তসনিম, Dhaka, Bangladesh

নানা দেশের নানা জনপদের মানুষের জীবনযাত্রার মিশ্রণে এই শহরের সাংস্কৃতিক পরিচয় গড়ে উঠেছে। সংস্কৃতি আসলে কী? যে গান শুনলে আপনা হতে ঠোঁট মিলিয়ে উঠি, যে খাবারের স্বাদ চিরচেনা হলেও পুরোনো হয়না, জীবনের এরকম টুকরো টুকরো ছবিগুলোই তো সংস্কৃতি। আমার জীবনযাত্রার এই টুকরো ছবিগুলোর পরিপূর্ণ রূপ দেয় আমার শহর। এই শহরে বর্ণিল মঙ্গল শোভাযাত্রায় যখন বরণ করে নেয়া হয় নতুন বাংলা বছরকে, তখন আমরা গলা মিলিয়ে বর্ষবরণের গান গেয়ে উঠি। এটিই সংস্কৃতি। ভাষাকে উদযাপন করার, বর্ষবরণকে উদযাপন করার, নানা উৎসবকে উদযাপন করার আনন্দের মধ্যে আমি আমার শহরকে খুঁজে পাই। একই রকম শাড়ি পরে মা-মেয়ের বিজয় দিবস উদযাপন, কিংবা একই ফুলের মালা খোঁপায় গুঁজে বর্ষবরণ - এই সব উদযাপনেও সম্পর্কের একটি গল্প থাকে - এই গল্পগুলোই আমার শহর। আমাদের চোখে এই শহরের গল্পগুলো আজ সুখকর - কারণ আমাদের জীবনযাত্রা ক্রমেই সুন্দর হয়ে উঠছে। এই সুন্দর আর আরামদায়ক জীবনযাত্রার জন্যে যে মানুষগুলোর কৃতিত্ব, সেই মানুষগুলোর চোখে তাদের শহরের গল্প কেমন? এটিই আমার লেখায় তুলে ধরতে চেয়েছি। আমার লেখার অনুপ্রেরণার চরিত্র বাস্তব। তৈরি পোশাকশিল্পের এক কর্মীর সাথে পথচলার আড্ডার টুকরো অংশই প্রতিফলিত হয়েছে লেখায়। ওঁকে জিজ্ঞেস করেছিলাম, "বাড়ি ফিরতে ইচ্ছা করে না?" ওঁর চমৎকার উত্তর, "আপা, ঢাকাই তো আমাদের বাড়ি। যেইখানে শান্তিতে দুইবেলা খাওন পাওয়া যায়, নিজের আয়ে নিজের মত থাকা যায় - তার চেয়ে আরামের বাড়ি কি আর হয়?" ওঁর চোখের আলোর রোশনাই এ আমি সেদিন স্বাধীনতার স্বাদ দেখেছিলাম। এদেশের মানুষের আজন্ম যে স্বাধীনতার আকাঙ্ক্ষা - সেই আকাঙ্ক্ষার পরিপূর্ণ চিত্র ফুটে ওঠে ওঁর মাঝে। নিজের অর্থনৈতিক, সামাজিক স্বাধীনতার মাধ্যমে পুরো দেশের অর্থনৈতিক স্বাধীনতার ভিত গড়ে দিচ্ছেন এই মানুষগুলো - তাদের চোখে ঢাকার আলোর রোশনাইকে তুলে ধরেছি।

আলোর রোশনাই

ছট করে এককটা দিন গ্রামের কথা এত বেশি মনে পড়ে! আব্বা-আম্মা, মিনু, আরিফ, শরীফ, জমানো টাকা দিয়ে কেনা ছাগলটা - সবাই না জানি কেমন আছে। আব্বাকে এইবার একটা ফোন কিনে দিতে হবে, বাজারে ফোন করে আব্বাকে পাওয়া যায় না সময়মত - বারোদিন হলো কথা হয়নি।

না, এগুলো ভাবতে থাকলে দেরি হয়ে যাবে - তাড়াতাড়ি টিফিন নিয়ে দৌড়াতে হবে কাজে। দেরি হলেই কিছু টাকা কম - স্যান্ডেলটা পায়ে গলিয়ে বের হয়ে যেতে যেতে ভাবে রিনা। গ্রাম থেকে বেশ কয়েকবছর হয় ঢাকায় আসা, এখন ঢাকাকেই আপন মনে হয়, নিজের শহর মনে হয়।

ঢাকায় এসে দিনরাত সেলাই মেশিন চালিয়ে যেতে হচ্ছে - রাতে এইটুকু ঘরে সোমা, শারমিন, আমিনার সাথে থাকতে হয় - গ্রামের মত খোলা বাতাসে নিঃশ্বাস নেয়া যায় না। তবু যেন মনে হয় এখানেই বুক ভরে নিঃশ্বাস নেয়া যায় - এখানে নিজের পায়ে দাঁড়ানো যায়। মনে হবে নাই বা কেন? এই ঢাকায় কাজ পাবার পরেই তো আব্বার ওষুধ কেনা যাচ্ছে, নিজের একটা মোবাইল হয়েছে, মিনুর জন্য জামা আর আরিফ-শরীফের জন্য নতুন খেলনা কিনে দু'বছরে একবার বাড়ি যাওয়া যায়।

আম্মা প্রত্যেকবার কিছু নিতে নিষেধ করেন – কিন্তু এইবার গেলে আম্মাকে একটা শাড়ি কিনে দেয়া যাবে – কী খুশিই না হবেন! এই ঢাকা শহরে এসেই তো মনে হয়, রিনা নামের ১৮ বছরের একটি মেয়ের অস্তিত্ব আছে এই দুনিয়ায় – যে নিজের পরিবারের দায়িত্ব নিয়েছে।

আর ঢাকা শহরটাও কী যে সুন্দর! মাঝে মধ্যে রুমের সবাই মিলে ওরা ঘুরতে যায়। একবার গিয়েছিল – একুশে ফেব্রুয়ারিতে শহিদ মিনারে। এত মানুষ, আর এত ফুল! আর শহিদ মিনারটা কী লম্বা! ফুল কেনার টাকা ছিলনা, তাই একেবারে বেদির সামনে থেকে চারটা ফুল তুলে ওরা চারজন বেণিতে গুঁজে নিয়েছিল - এক ক্যামেরাওয়ালা ভাই ছবি নিয়েছিলেন ওদের। এইদিন নাকি সবাই যাতে বাংলা ভাষায় কথা বলতে পারে – এইজন্য কয়েকজন মারা গিয়েছিল। কী জানি, সবাই তো বাংলাতেই কথা বলে – এইজন্য কাউকে মরতে হয় কীভাবে, রিনার বুদ্ধিতে এঁটে ওঠে না।

আর একদিন দেখতে গিয়েছিল মার্কেট – এত বড় দালান – আর কত রকম যে জিনিস। ওরা অবশ্য ঘুরতেই গিয়েছিল – এত দামি জিনিস কেনার সামর্থ্য কী ওদের আছে! একটা আপা ওদের সামনে আট হাজার টাকার গোলাপি পুঁতি পুঁতি একটা জামা কিনলেন। আ-ট হা-জা-র টাকা! ওর এক মাসের বেতন। আল্লাহ এই শহরে মানুষকে টাকাও দিয়েছেন – একদিন কি সে'ও এই মার্কেট থেকে কিছু কিনতে পারবে? ওই দিন অনেক জায়গায় ঘোরা হয়েছিল –

শিশুপার্কে প্লেনে উঠে কী যে ভালো লেগেছিল! ঢাকার রাস্তার মসজিদগুলো সবচেয়ে সুন্দর – গ্রামের মসজিদের চেয়ে কত বড়!

সব মিলিয়ে ঢাকার জীবন ভালোই লাগে - খারাপের মধ্যে শুধু বাড়ি যাওয়ার সময় বাসে উঠতে ভালো লাগে না। খারাপ লোকজন এমন বদনজরে তাকায়, সুযোগ পেলে গায়ে হাত দিতে চায় – ভয়ে গা কুঁকড়ে ওঠে। কিন্তু একবার এক ছোট আপা – রিনার থেকেও ছোট হবে – বাসে এরকম এক লোককে ওর দিকে এভাবে তাকিয়ে থাকতে দেখে এমন ঠাস ঠাস কথা শুনিয়ে দিয়েছিল, ব্যাটা পরে বাস থামতে নারায়ণগঞ্জ আসার আগেই নেমে গেছিল। এইরকম পড়াশোনা জানা আপারা কী সাহসী – দেখলেই ভালো লাগে। ওইদিনের পর রিনার মনে কেমন কেমন সাহস এসে গেছে – আর শারমিন বলে দিয়েছে সবসময় বাসে সেফটিপিন নিয়ে যেতে। আর সাহস তো করাই লাগে, সাহস করেছে বলেই না একা একা ঢাকায় পা দিয়েছিল!

এতকিছু আজকে মাথায় আসার কারণ – আজকে রিনার মন ভালো। গত এক সপ্তাহ ধরে ওরা চারজন ওভারটাইম করেছে – আজকের দিনটা যাতে ছুটি নেয়া যায়, এইজন্য। আজকে পহেলা বৈশাখ এইদিন রাস্তায় কী সুন্দর সুন্দর আপাদের দেখা যায়। আর এইদিন নিজেদের গরীব লাগে না বেশি – সব আপারা ভাইরা ওদের মতই পান্তা খায়! এইদিনেই মাত্র ঢাকায় মেলা বসে – ওদের বাড়িতে তো প্রত্যেক হাটবারে মেলা বসতো! আপাদের সবার রঙিন রঙিন শাড়ি আর ফুলের মালা মাথায় সেইদিন এই শহরটাকে এত রঙিন আর সুন্দর লাগে। এই রঙিন শহরের এক কোণায় যে রিনাও আছে – এইটা ভেবে নিজেকেও রঙিন লাগে।

আজকের জন্য রহিমাবুর কাছে থেকে শাড়ি ধার নিয়েছে রিনা – রহিমাবু যে বাসায় কাজ করে – সেই বাসার আপা খুব ভালো – প্রায়ই ওকে শাড়ি দেয়। মাঝেমধ্যে এইজন্য মন চায় বাসাবাড়িতে কাজ নিতে – একটু কম চাপ পড়তো। কিন্তু আর কারো অধীনে থাকতে মন চায় না; নিজের স্বাধীনতায় একটা চাকরিই ভালো, যেখানে নিজের মত ছুটি নেয়া যাবে। হোক না একটু কম টাকার – ক্ষতি কী!

সে শাড়িটা পরে নিজেকে সামনের দোকানের কাচে দেখে অবাকই হয়ে যায়, কী সুন্দর লাগছে – ঐ আপাদের মতই তো। সোমা, শারমিন, আমিনাকে অপূর্ব লাগছে – সোমার একটা ক্যামেরাওয়ালা ফোন আছে – আজকে ছবি তুলতে হবে অনেক! ওরা ভোরবেলায় বের হয়েছে মিছিল দেখতে। বিশাল বিশাল পুতুল, হাতি আরো কী কী জানি

নিয়ে মিছিল। দেখলেই কেমন মন ভালো হয়ে যায়! আর অনেক বড় বড় মুখোশা আজকে ওরা রমনা পার্কেও যাবে। ঐখানে প্রত্যেকবার গান হয় – মিনুর বইতে লেখা। মিনুটা পড়াশোনা করছে; ও বড় হয়ে ঐ শিক্ষিত আপাদের মত হবে নিশ্চয়ই।

এই গানগুলোর কথা অনেক কঠিন। কতগুলো শব্দ বোঝাই যায়না – তাও সবাই গলা মিলিয়ে গান করছে দেখে ওরাও সুর শুনে গলা মেলায়। 'আবর্জনা দূর হয়ে যাক' কথাটা বেশ মনে ধরে রিনার। আসলেই তো, শহরের আবর্জনাগুলো চলে গেলেই এই শহরটা যেন বেহেশত। ময়লা-আবর্জনা আর ওদের দিকে আবর্জনার মত তাকিয়ে থাকা লোকগুলো। আজকেও একজন আছে, ওদের পিছন পিছন আসছে – সোমা এখন বাড়ি চলে যেতে চাইছে এই ব্যাটার জন্য। আজকে রিনার মনে হয়, আমিও শিক্ষিত আপা হয়ে যাই, ঘুরে দাঁড়াই – একটু প্রতিবাদ করি।

লোকটার অবশ্য একেবারেই সাহস নেই, শিয়ালের মত স্বভাব। পেছনে ফিরে, 'কী লাগবো আপনার ভাই, ধোলাই থাইবেন নি?' বলার সাথে সাথে উলটো ঘুরে হাঁটা দিল! শারমিনের কী খিলখিল হাসি! আজকে নিজেকে অন্যরকম লাগছে; মনে হচ্ছে, একটা আবর্জনা যেন ওদের আশেপাশে থেকে দূরে সরে গেল। বাতাসে নিঃশ্বাস নিতে নিতে রিনার মনে হয়, এই শহরই তো আমার।

এই শহরের বাতাস, জ্যাম, গার্মেন্টসের খুটখুট শব্দ, সবাই মিলে গুড়-মুড়ি খাওয়া, মাসের শেষে দোকানে গিয়ে আব্বাকে টাকা পাঠানো, ওভারটাইম করতে পারলে রাস্তার পাশের দোকানে চুড়ি কেনা – সবই তো আমার! এই ভালো লাগার রেশ থেকে সবাই মিলে একটা গোলাপি হাওয়াই-মিঠাই নেয়! আহা!

এই রিনা, শারমিনের, সোমার শ্রমে, ঘামে, ত্যাগে গড়ে উঠছে স্বপ্নের ঢাকা, উন্নত বাংলাদেশ। দূরের কোন গ্রামে ঘর ফেলে আসা মেয়েগুলোর বাড়ি, পরিচয় আজ ঢাকাই। এই শহরের সব অন্ধকার, সব বাধা পেরিয়ে আলোর রোশনাই যারা ছড়ায় সবার জীবনে – সেই মানুষগুলোর বাড়ি হিসেবে ঢাকার না-শোনা গল্পগুলো তাই ফিরে ফিরে আসে। আজ বিশ্বের বুকে ক্রমশ উন্নয়নশীল দেশে হিসেবে বাংলাদেশের যে পরিচয়, ঢাকার যে ঝাঁ-চকচকে আকাশ ছাড়ানো দালান – এই গার্মেন্টস-কর্মী মেয়েদের তাতে এক বড় অবদান। ঢাকার পরিচয়ে যেমন তাদের নাম, তেমনি তাদেরও নিজের পরিচয়, নিজের নির্ভরশীলতার জায়গা কোটি মানুষের এই ঢাকা।

Tasben Mahmud / তাসবেন মাহমুদ, Dhaka, Bangladesh

লেখালেখি আমার শখ। বাংলা ভাষার মাধুর্য আমাকে লেখায় আকৃষ্ট করে। 'আমার শহর আমার বাড়ি' বিষয়টি আমাকে আমার শহরের ইতিহাস, ঐতিহ্য, শহরের মানুষের জীবনযাত্রা সম্পর্কে ভাবনা কাগজে কলমে ফুটিয়ে তোলার প্রেরণা দিয়েছে।

শহরের গল্প

আকাশ ছোঁয়া অট্টালিকার ভিড়ে,
আজকাল আকাশের দেখা পাওয়া বড্ড কঠিন।
মোটরের শব্দের ভিড়ে হারিয়ে গিয়েছে পাখির ডাক,
ধুলোয় মাখামাখি এক ধূসর শহর ঢাকা
রাতের নিয়নের আলোয় ঝলমলিয়ে উঠে আপন রঙে।

মসজিদের শহর কিংবা রিকশার শহর
কেউ কেউ বলে জাদুর শহর,
নীরবে বহন করে চলেছে চারশো বছরের ইতিহাস।
তারা মসজিদ, আর্মেনিয়া গির্জা   কিংবা   ঢাকেশ্বরী মন্দির
হঠাৎ পথ রোধ করে পথিকের
অবাক চোখে   থমকে দাঁড়ালো,
ইট পাথরের দালানের নিচে পিষ্ট হয়েছে কত ইতিহাস
বেশি ভাবার সময় নেই,
ছুটছে সকলে জীবনের তাগিদে।

বুড়িগঙ্গাও আজকাল বুড়ি হয়েছে,
রুপালি জল আজ ধূসর অতীত।

শহরের বুকে প্রাণ দিয়েছে
মাতৃভাষা, মাতৃভূমির তরে
শহিদ মিনার, বধ্যভূমি
কত শহিদের আত্মদান।

ঈদ-উল-ফিতর, ঈদ-উল-আজহা   কিংবা মহরম
দুর্গাপূজা, জন্মাষ্টমী, বুদ্ধ-পূর্ণিমা কিংবা বড়দিন
যেন সাম্প্রদায়িক সম্প্রীতির এক জীবন্ত প্রতিমা।

পহেলা বৈশাখে রমনার বটমূলে রমনীর উচ্ছ্বাস।
মঙ্গল শোভাযাত্রায় শিশু, তরুণ, প্রবীণের
মঙ্গলময় বার্তা, এ যেন প্রাণের মিলনমেলা।

ছুটে চলেছে এই ব্যস্ত শহর,
ছুটে চলেছে বাসিন্দারা,
জীবন যুদ্ধে ক্লান্ত ভীষণ
থেমে যাওয়া যেন আত্মসমর্পণ।
শহরের বুকে ছোট্ট নীড়,
যেন সকল শান্তির খোরাক।

দেওয়াল লিখনে মুক্তির বার্তা
তুলির আঁচড়ে প্রতিবাদ,
পথের ধারে গানের সুরে
পথ হারায় একলা পথিক।

নারী আজ ছুটছে শহরের বুকে
স্বপ্নিল নয়নে, জীবন সংগ্রামে
পুরুষতান্ত্রিক সমাজের শেকল ভেঙ্গে
দুর্বলতাকে পেছনে ফেলে,
অনুপ্রেরণায় বলীয়ান।

স্বপ্নিল চোখে হাঁটে তরুণ, তরুণী
শহরটা যে তাদের প্রাণ
চঞ্চল চোখে স্বপ্ন বুনে,
বদলে দেওয়ার অঙ্গীকার।

Tasben Mahmud / তাসবেন মাহমুদ, Dhaka, Bangladesh

অনুভূতি প্রকাশের একটি অন্যতম মাধ্যম লেখালেখি। শখের বসে নিজের মনের কথা কাগজে কলমে ফুটিয়ে তোলার ইচ্ছে আমার লেখালেখির অনুপ্রেরণা। 'আমার শহর আমার বাড়ি' বিষয়টি আমাকে শহর নিয়ে গভীরভাবে ভাবিয়েছে। শহরের প্রতি ভালোবাসা এবং শহরের গৃহহীন, পথশিশুদের নিয়ে ভাবনা এই লেখাটি লেখার প্রেরণা।

জাদুর শহর

রাত ৯.৩০ মিনিটে তূর্ণা নিশিতা এক্সপ্রেস কমলাপুর রেলস্টেশন থেকে চট্টগ্রামের উদ্দেশ্যে ছাড়লো। ট্রেনের জানালার ধারে বসে কান্না চেপে সবাইকে বিদায় দিলাম। পিছনে ফেলে আসা মানুষগুলো আর এই শহরটার কথা ভেবে বুক মুচড়ে উঠছে। পাশ থেকে একজন বলে উঠলো, "খুব শীত পড়েছে এবার"। বুঝলাম, জানলা বন্ধ করতে বলছে। জানলার কাচ নামিয়ে বাইরে তাকিয়ে ভাবতে লাগলাম, এই শহরে এইবার শীতের পিঠা খেতে খেতে রাস্তার ধারে গান শোনা হবে না। শহরে শীত গিয়ে বসন্ত আসবে, অলস দুপুরে রাস্তার ধারের শিমুল গাছটায় বসে কোকিল ডাকবে, বর্ষায় কদম হাতে ফুল হাতে শিশুরা ছুটে যাবে, কৃষ্ণচূড়া ফুলে পুরো শহর ছেয়ে যাবে। শুধু আমিই থাকবো না। খুব মন খরাপ হয়েছিল যখন শুনেছিলাম চাকরির পোস্টিং ঢাকার বাইরে। বন্ধুরা বলছিল, "এই যান্ত্রিক শহরটা ছেড়ে তো যেতে পারছিস এতেই খুশি হওয়া উচিত, আর সারাজীবনের জন্য তো যাচ্ছিস না।" সারাজীবনের জন্য যাচ্ছি না ঠিক, তবে আমার কাছে শহরটা কখনোই যান্ত্রিক মনে হয়নি বরং মনে হতো যুগের সাথে তাল মিলাতে গিয়ে মানুষগুলো যান্ত্রিক হয়ে গিয়েছে।

আমার জন্ম, বেড়ে ওঠা ঢাকাতেই। আমাদের বাড়ি ছিল পদ্মার পাড়ে। নদী- ভাঙনে এক রাতে সব গিলে নিয়েছে পদ্মা। তখন নিরুপায় হয়েই বাবা ঢাকা আসে, আশ্রয়ের খোঁজে। এই শহর এখন আমাদের শেষ ঠিকানা। বাবা বলে, "এই শহর কাউকে ফিরিয়ে দেয় না। সবাইকে আপন করে নেয়। যখন আর কোথাও ঠাঁই হয় নাই তখন এই শহরই ঠাঁই দেয়।" ছোট থাকতে বাবার এই কথাগুলোর অর্থ বুঝতাম না। রেশমার সাথে দেখা হওয়ার পর কথাগুলোর মানে বুঝেছিলাম।

এই শহরের এক পথের ধারে একদিন আমার দেখা হয় রেশমার সাথে। বন্ধুরা মিলে আড্ডা দিচ্ছিলাম। হঠাৎ ফুটফুটে এক ছোট মেয়ে এসে বললো, "আপা ফুল নিবা?" ধুলো মাখা শরীর, তবে চোখের তারার উজ্জ্বলতায় চোখ আটকে গেল। এর পর থেকেই রেশমার সাথে আমার সখ্যতা গড়ে ওঠে। প্রায়ই দেখা হতো। অভিমানের সুরে বলতো, "কালকে আসলা না কেন আপা? আমি তোমারে কত খুঁজছি"। তারপর শুরু হতো গল্প। রাস্তার ধারে মা, ভাই-বোন নিয়ে রেশমার সংসার। কত টাকার ফুল বিক্রি হলো, কত টাকা জমলো সব হিসেব আমাকে শোনাতো। বন্ধুরা মিলে যখন গান গাইতাম, রেশমাও আমাদের সাথে গলা মিলিয়ে গাইতো। "এই শহর জাদুর শহর, প্রাণের শহর ঢাকারে.......।" গান শেষে একদিন রেশমা বললো, "এই শহরটাতে আসলেই জাদু আছে আপা। কত বড় বড় দালান। রাত হইলে কত সুন্দর সুন্দর বাতি জ্বলে। তখন মনে হয় এই পুরা শহরটা আমার। বাপে আমগোরে বাড়ি থেইকা বাহির কইরা দিছে, আবার বিয়া করছে। মা নিরুপায় হইয়া আমগোরে নিয়া এই শহরে আসছে। যখন কোথাও থাকার জায়গা হয় নাই তখন এই শহরের রাস্তা আমগোরে আপন কইরা নিসে।" অবাক হয়ে তাকিয়ে দেখলাম রেশমা কেমন বাবার মতো করে বলছে। হেসে বললাম, "খুব তো কথা শিখেছিস রে, এই শহরটা তো তোরই রেশমা।" শুধুই গানেই না একুশে ফেব্রুয়ারিতে শহিদ মিনারে ফুল দিতে অথবা বই মেলার সময় মেলায় ঘোরাঘুরির সঙ্গী হত রেশমা।

গত বছর পহেলা বৈশাখে মঙ্গল শোভাযাত্রার ভিড়ে আচমকা কে যেন হাত চেপে ধরলো। চমকে উঠে ফিরে তাকিয়ে দেখি অন্য হাতে ফুল নিয়ে রেশমা আমার হাত ধরে টানছে। একপাশে এসে বললাম, "কী রে, আজকে কত টাকার ফুল বিক্রি হলো?" উজ্জ্বল চোখে হাসতে হাসতে বললো, "অনেক আপা।" রমনা পার্কে এসে বসলাম বন্ধুদের সঙ্গে। পেছন পেছন রেশমাও এলো। বুঝলাম তার অনেক গল্প জমেছে। হঠাৎ বলে উঠলো, "আপা আজকে এত মানুষ কেন রাস্তায়?" বললাম, "আজকে তো পহেলা বৈশাখ তাই সব মানুষ বের হয়েছে আনন্দ করতে, নতুন বছরকে স্বাগত জানাতে।" রেশমা অবাক হয়ে বললো, "এই মানুষগুলা অন্য সময় কই থাকে?" হেসে বললাম, "এই বড় বড় দালানগুলোতে থাকে।" খুশিতে ঝলমল করে উঠলো রেশমার মুখ। বললো "মা কইছে,

কিছু টাকা জমলে আমরা গ্রামে যামু গা। গ্রামে গিয়া দালান দেওয়ার লাইগা আমি টাকা জমাইতেছি আপা। রাস্তার ধারে থাকতে অনেক কষ্ট আপা। " রেশমার মন থারাপ ভাব দূর করতে হেসে বললাম, "গ্রামে না যেয়ে ঢাকায় বাড়ি করে থাকিছ।" খিলখিল করে হেসে উঠে বললো, "এই শহরটায় তুমি একটা ছোট বাড়ি কইরো আপা। শহরে বেড়াইতে আসলে তোমার কাছে থাকমু আর যে সব পোলাপাইন আমার মতো রাস্তার ধারে থাকে তাগোরে তোমার বাড়িত থাকতে দিও।"

এরপর অনেক দিন পেরিয়ে গেছে। রেশমার সাথে আমার আর দেখা হয়নি। হয়তো রেশমা তার স্বপ্নের দালানে ভালোই আছে। আজ ট্রেনে বসে রেশমার কথা ভেবে চোখে পানি আর ঠোঁটের কোনে হাসি দুটোই অনুভব করলাম। একটা ছোট বাড়ি তবে করতেই হবে। রেশমার মতো পথের বাসিন্দাদের জন্য একটা ঠিকানা যে করতে হবে। এই শহরে ফিরে আমাকে আসতেই হবে।

Tahmina Rahman / তাহমিনা রহমান, Mymensingh, Bangladesh

আমাদের বাড়িতে প্রথম আলো পত্রিকা পড়া হয়। হঠাৎ একদিন চোখে পড়ে নারীদের জন্য লেখালেখির প্রতিযোগিতার আয়োজন করেছে যুক্তরাজ্যের শিল্পকলা উন্নয়ন সংস্থা 'সম্পদ সাউথ এশিয়ান আর্টস এন্ড হেরিটেজ'। বিষয়বস্তু অত্যন্ত চমকপ্রদ 'আমার বাড়ি, আমার শহর'। তৎক্ষণাৎ বিষয়টি আমার মনকে স্পর্শ করে, কারণ আমার জীবনের সাথে মিশে থাকা কষ্ট, দ্বিধাদ্বন্দ্ব, সিদ্ধান্তহীনতা, আবেগ-উচ্ছ্বাস সব কিছু উজাড় করে প্রকাশ করার সুযোগ যেন হাতে পেয়ে গেছি। তাৎক্ষণিকভাবে এমনটাই মনে হয়েছে আমার। একই সাথে আমার ব্যক্তিগত অনুভূতি এবং প্রতিযোগিতার বিষয় 'আমার বাড়ি, আমার শহর' দুটোই আমাকে এ লেখায় উৎসাহ যুগিয়েছে। শুধু তাই না, এর মাধ্যমে আমাদের দেশে সমাজে প্রচলিত নানা অসঙ্গতি এবং ক্ষেত্র বিশেষে প্রথা ভাঙার বিষয়টিও এখন সময়ের দাবী, এ-ব্যাপারে আমি আমার ব্যক্তিগত অভিমত ব্যক্ত করার সুযোগ পেয়েছি।

আমি মনে করি কিছু ধর্মীয় বিধান বা সামাজিক প্রথা দ্বারা নারীরা নিগৃহীত হয়, কিন্তু এই বিশ্বাস আঁকড়ে থাকলে এর থেকে মুক্তি মিলবে না। বরং নারীকে আত্মবিশ্বাসী হতে হবে। যে কোনো বিধি নিষেধ, কর্ম দ্বারা অতিক্রম করা যায়, সে কর্ম যদি হয় যথাযথ। তেমনি দায়িত্বে অবহেলা, ইচ্ছে করে পিছিয়ে থাকা, সস্তা প্রশংসা পাওয়ার লোভে নিজেকে নিষ্ক্রিয় করে রাখা, প্রয়োজনীয় কথাটা প্রয়োজনের সময় না বলে নিজেকে গুটিয়ে রাখার কারণে নারীরা তাদের প্রাপ্য মর্যাদার অধিকার থেকে বঞ্চিত হয়।

কৃষ্ণ গহ্বর

একটা ফাঁদ থেকে বের হতে চাই

তাই ভীষণ একটা অনুশীলনে আছি;

রাতদিন; এমনকি আমার বয়সের চেয়ে কোটি কোটি দীর্ঘ

একটা কৃষ্ণগহ্বর গিলে ফেলেছে আমাদের মস্তিষ্ক

একটা ফাঁদ; নিঃসন্দেহে এই ফাঁদ একটাই

তাই চাই একটা বুলডজার আর একটা খনন যন্ত্র

ওড়িয়ে দিতে চাই সনাতন মুখস্থ বিদ্যা

মুখস্থ ভাষণ; মুখস্থ চোখ; চোখের বিভ্রম।

একটা উদাহরণ দিতে চাই তাই

মুক্তিযোদ্ধার স্ত্রীলিঙ্গ বুঝি বীরাঙ্গনা?

হতে পারে না; যোদ্ধার কোনো লিঙ্গান্তর নাই।

একটা অশুদ্ধ জীবনের তিলক যদি হতে পারে

গল্পের শিরোনাম; তবে তো ভাঙতেই হবে এ-দেয়াল

মাটিতো খুঁড়তেই হবে অবিরাম।

যতদিন ফিরে না আসে শুদ্ধ চিন্তন

যতদিন খেলা না করে বিশুদ্ধ মনন

ততদিন তো চাইবোই।

একটা বুলডজার আর একটা খনন যন্ত্র

খুঁজবোই।

Nahida Akter / নাহিদা আক্তার, Dhaka, Bangladesh

I was really inspired by this programme. Through this writing, I have been able to write about myself and my city. Thanks to all.

আমার শহর, আমার বাড়ি

আমার শহরে জীবনের শুরু হয় ঢাকা বিশ্ববিদ্যালয়ের ভর্তি হওয়ার মাধ্যমে। প্রথম দিনটা শুরু হয়েছিল ভয়, কান্না, অনিশ্চয়তার মধ্য দিয়ে। ২রা জানুয়ারি ২০১৮ সাল, সেদিন ছিল মঙ্গলবার। আমার ভাইয়া আমাকে ঢাকার আজিমপুরে একটি হোস্টেলে দিয়ে এসেছিল। যখন রুমে যাচ্ছিলাম এক একটা সিঁড়ি ধাপ পার হওয়ার সময় মনে হচ্ছিল, এই পৃথিবীতে আমার চেয়ে একা, অসহায় আর কেউ নেই, চোখ থেকে টপটপ করে পানি পড়ছিল। আমি আর আমার সৃষ্টিকর্তা ছাড়া আর কিছুনেই গোটা এই শহরে।

ব্যাগগুলো নিয়ে রুমে যাওয়ার পর একজন আপু পেলাম, তিনি আমাকে যথাসম্ভব অভয় দিলেন এবং সেদিন আমি অনেকটাই শান্ত হয়ে গেলাম। এ যেন নতুন জীবনের সূচনা ঘটলো। নিজের প্রয়োজনীয় জিনিসপত্র গুছানো, রুমমেটদের সাথে মানিয়ে নেওয়ার ব্যাপারটাও ভালোই জমে উঠেছিল। প্রতিদিন সকালে বিশ্ববিদ্যালয়ের যাওয়ার সময় একা পথ চলা রাস্তায় ভয় করত খুবই। দূর থেকে যখন মুক্তি ও গণতন্ত্র তোরণ দেখতে পেতাম, তখন হাঁপ ছেড়ে বাঁচতাম, এই তো ক্লাসের জন্য চলে এসেছি। তবে ধীরে ধীরে রাস্তা, রাস্তার ধারে নিয়মিত দেখতে পাওয়া কিছু অসহায় মানুষ যেন আপন হয়ে উঠছে। হোস্টেলের খাবার মানিয়ে নেওয়ার চ্যালেঞ্জ তখন নিত্যদিনের ব্যাপার। তার সাথে সাথে যেন হিসেব করাও শিখে গেছি, কখন কোথায় কত টাকা খরচ করতে হবে, নিজের সীমাবদ্ধতাও যেন আরও আঁকড়ে ধরেছে। এবার যেন আমার দায়িত্ব পুরোপুরি আমার উপরই এসে পড়েছে। আজিমপুর হোস্টেলে জীর্ণ শীর্ণ ভবনের পুরনো সেই সবুজ শেওলা জমে থাকা ছাদ, পাশাপাশি হোস্টেলের সবার সাথে যেন একটা আত্মিক সম্পর্ক গড়ে ওঠেছিল। বিশেষ করে হোস্টেলের খালা যিনি রান্না করে আমাদের খাবার দিতেন তিনি, তার মধ্যে যেন মাতৃত্বের পরশ পাওয়া যেত। স্কুল বা কলেজে বা অন্য কোথাও যাবার সময় প্রতিদিন বাড়ি থেকে বের হতে হতে আম্মুকে যেমন বলে যেতাম যাচ্ছি, তেমন বিশ্ববিদ্যালয়ে যাওয়া সময় খালাকেও বলে যেতাম, 'খালা যাচ্ছি'।

481

ক্যাম্পাসে গিয়ে দিনগুলো যেন আরও সুন্দর হতে লাগলো, ক্লাসে সবার সাথে বন্ধুত্বপূর্ণ সম্পর্ক করতে না পারলেও আস্তে আস্তে ভালোই চলছিল, ক্যাম্পাসে হাঁটাহাঁটি এবং বিশেষ করে বিশ্ববিদ্যালয়ের কেন্দ্রীয় লাইব্রেরি আমার খুব পছন্দের জায়গা হয়ে ওঠে। সেই সাথে বিভিন্ন ইভেন্টে যোগ দেয়া, টিএসসির বিভিন্ন ধাঁচের প্রোগ্রামগুলো খুব মনে লাগতে শুরু করে। এভাবেই চলছিল সবকিছু। হঠাৎ ফেব্রুয়ারির ২৬ তারিখ চলে এলো, বঙ্গমাতা শেখ ফজিলাতুন্নেছা মুজিব হলে গেস্ট হিসেবে থাকার সুযোগ হলো। এর আগের রাত অর্থাৎ ২৫ ডিসেম্বর রাতেই জিনিসপত্র সব গুছিয়ে নিয়ে চিন্তা ভাবনা করতে করতে সারারাত আর ঘুমাতেই পারি নি। পরদিন এগুলো কীভাবে নিয়ে যাবো তা নিয়ে চিন্তা করছিলাম। আমার রুমমেট ঝুমু এগিয়ে এলো। ও আমার ব্যাচমেট, ইডেন কলেজে পড়ে। সে রাজি হলো আমার জিনিসগুলো নেওয়াতে আমাকে সাহায্য করবে। পরদিন ক্লাস করে দুপুর ২টার দিকে খালাকে সালাম করে জিনিসপত্র নিয়ে আমি আর ঝুমু রওনা দিলাম।

অবশেষে আমরা ভালোভাবেই হলে পৌঁছে যাই। আমার থাকার ব্যবস্থা হয়েছিল গণরুম "মোহনায়"। রুমের দরজাটা আস্তে করে খুলে প্রবেশ করলাম, এত ভয় করেছিল যে কী বলবো! একটু কথা বলেই জানতে পারলাম সবাই আমার ব্যাচমেট। এ যেন আর একটু স্বস্তির নিঃশ্বাস ফেলা। নিচে গিয়ে ঝুমুকে ধন্যবাদ দিয়ে ওকে বিদায় দিলাম। সেদিন মনে হচ্ছিল জীবনের আর একটা ধাপ পেরিয়ে হঠাৎ করে বড় হয়ে গেছি। লনের ছাদের উপর দাঁড়িয়ে আকাশের দিকে তাকিয়ে সৃষ্টিকর্তাকে বারবার ধন্যবাদ দিয়েছি এই কারণে যে, এই তো একা বাঁচাতে শিখে গেছি। এরপর থেকে হলের গাছ, ফুল, পাখি, বিশেষ করে হলের উপরের ছাদে বসে থাকা একঝাঁক কাক যেন আমার পরম বন্ধু হয়ে গেছে, সেই সঙ্গে হলে অনেক বান্ধবী, বড় আপু হতে থাকলো। তাদের সাথে মাঠে বসে গল্প করা, লনে বসে চা খাওয়া, রিডিং রুমে না গিয়ে অডিটোরিয়াম রুমে বসে চিৎকার করে পড়া, হাসাহাসি, মজা, ডাইনিংয়ে একসাথে খেতে যাওয়া, নামাজ রুমে নামাজ পড়তে যাওয়া। এ যেন আমার সেই প্রত্যাশিত জীবনটি। এ যেন আমার শহর। আমি, আমার বান্ধবীরা, আমার আপুরা, হল, সবকিছুই ক্রমশ আমার হয়ে ওঠতে থাকে। হলের হাউজ টিউটর ম্যামদের দেখলেই অন্যরকম ভালো লাগে।

এতগুলো মেয়ের মাঝে ম্যামদের মধ্যে যেন আম্মু আম্মু একটা পরশ পাওয়া যায়। সেই

সাথে ক্যাম্পাসে বিভিন্ন সংগঠনের সাথে যুক্ত হতে থাকি, ক্যাম্পাস যেন আরও আপন হতে থাকো প্রত্যেকটা ঋতু যেন আসে নতুন পরশ নিয়ে। এর আগে এত ঋতু বৈচিত্র্য চোখে পড়েনি। প্রকৃতি যেন আপন সৌন্দর্যে আমার মনে এসে হাতছানি দেয়া। কিছুদিনের মধ্যেই লক্ষ্য করলাম আমার অনেক বান্ধবীর মাঝে আবিদার সাথে আমার মনের মিল অনেক বেশি। তার সাথে প্রথম থেকেই ক্যাম্পাসে, হলে অনেক ভালো সম্পর্ক। তাকে ভালো লাগার কারণ হলো সে ধর্মভীরু, পর্দাশীল। তার সাথে কথা বলে যেন নিশ্চয়তাটুকু পাই। আমাদের হলে অনেক আপু যাদের বিয়ে ঠিক হয়ে গেছে বা বিয়ে করবে তাদের গায়ে হলুদ করা হয় তখন শাড়ি পরে, আপুদের সাথে এত মজা হয়, হলে বিভিন্ন দিবস, পূজা পার্বণ সবকিছুতে মাতোয়ারা হয়ে যাওয়া, যেন মনে হয় এইতো এত সুখ, খুশি অফুরান। আবার হল থেকে বাড়িতে আসার জন্য পাগল হয়ে যেতাম, যখন বাড়ির পথে রওনা দিতাম তখন হল, ক্যাম্পাস রেখে যাওয়ায় এত মন খারাপ হতো, তখন মনে মনে স্নেহের সুরে বলে ওঠতাম এই তো কিছুদিনের জন্যে বাড়িতে যাচ্ছি আবার তোমাদের কাছে ফিরে আসবো! তখন মনে হতো ইট পাথরের শহরটাকে আমি এত ভালোবাসি!

আবার ক্যাম্পাসে যখন একা থাকতাম, একাকিত্ব নিজেকে ঘিরে ধরতো চারদিক থেকে। তখন মনে হতো কংক্রিটের এই শহরটা বড় নির্ঠুর, চারপাশে এত মানুষ কিন্তু কেউ কারোর নয়। একদিন ক্যাম্পাস থেকে আসার সময় খুব মন খারাপ হচ্ছিল চোখ থেকে কয়েক ফোঁটা পানিও ঝরে গেল। তখন চোখ পড়লো একজন বৃদ্ধার প্রতি যিনি রাস্তার ধারে বসে রোজ বকুল ফুলের মালা বানাতেন। তার কাছ থেকে একটা মালা কিনে মন খুশিতে ভরে গেল; যেন মনের আকাশে এই মেঘ জমে বৃষ্টি, আবার মেঘও জমে থাকে কিছুক্ষণ, আবার পরক্ষণেই এত রোদেলা, আনন্দ, এত খুশি! এই তো আমার শহর আর আমি এখানে রক্তের সম্পর্কের ছিটেফোঁটানেই কিন্তু আছে কিছু আত্মিক সম্পর্ক।

কারোর অসুস্থতা, মন খারাপ, কারোর প্রেমে ব্যর্থতা দেখে ওদের সাথে সাথে আমারও ঠিক তেতোটাই মন খারাপ হতো! এদের সাথে পারিবারিক সম্পর্কের চেয়ে কোনো অংশে কম নয় আবার কোনো কোনো সময় এদের সাথে সম্পর্কটা আরও জোরালো।

সারাদিনের ক্লাস, ক্লান্তি, ব্যস্ততা, দৌড়াদৌড়ির পর যখন নিস্তব্ধ রাতে আকাশের চাঁদ, তারার দিকে তাকাতাম তখন মনে হতো নিজের জন্যই বেঁচে আছি, এবার নিজেকে একটু সময় দিচ্ছি। এই তো জীবন! ধীরে ধীরে চারপাশের সবকিছুই নিজের হয়ে গেছে।

Suraiya Islam / সুরাইয়া ইসলাম, Dhaka, Bangladesh

When I write, people and my surroundings inspire me. In my city there are many people. In this pandemic situation, I saw some people who left this city and their lovely home where they lived for long. But why should we leave? Why are we scared of this situation? This is my city and this is my home. These people are also mine. We should care about them. These feelings inspire me and 'My City My Home' gave me a chance to write about some. It inspired me to prove myself, that I can also create a story. And I think our life is a story itself, there is no need to create any. One needs to explore, and stories can be found in every step of life.

বাড়ির নাম সেঁজুতি

খুব সকাল থেকেই মিসেস সেলিনা রান্নাঘরে কাজ করে যাচ্ছেন। আজ তাঁর ভীষণ তাড়া। অফিসে যেতে হবে, সেই সাথে বীমার খোঁজটাও নিতে হবে। স্বামী রহমান সাহেবের মৃত্যুর পর দীর্ঘদিন সিটি ব্যাংকে চাকুরী করেছিলেন। এরপর অবসর নিয়ে নিজ উদ্যোগে একটা ডে-কেয়ার সেন্টার খুলে বসেন। ছোট ছোট বাচ্চাদের নিয়ে তাঁর সময় কেটে যায়। দুই ছেলে এক মেয়ে নিয়ে ছিল তার ছোট্ট সংসার। এক সময় পুরো ঘর জুড়ে কত আনন্দ ছিল, কত শোরগোল। ধীরে ধীরে সময়ের চাকায় তা আজ শূন্য কেবল। ছেলেমেয়েরা প্রত্যেকে দেশের বাইরে। সময়ের অভাবে কেউই আসতে পারেনা। তা নিয়ে মিসেস সেলিনার মাথা ব্যাথা নেই। অল্প বয়সে স্বামীকে হারিয়ে একা থাকার জীবনে তিনি বেশ অভ্যস্তই বলা চলে। দীর্ঘদিন ধরেই ঘরের কাজের সঙ্গী ছিলেন আসমার মা। আসমার মাও আজ ঠিক সময়ে কাজে আসেনি। তিনি একা সব সামলাচ্ছেন। ঘরে কথা বলার একমাত্র সঙ্গী তার মিনি বিড়াল আর যে কত সময় ধরে আসমার মা থাকেন অতটুকু। তিনি থাবার টেবিল গোছাচ্ছেন আর মিনির সাথে কথা বলে যাচ্ছেন।

- জানিস বুড়ি, আজকাল আসমার মা-টা না ভীষন ফাঁকি দিচ্ছে। যেই আমার ছেলেমেয়েরা আমায় রেখে চলে গেল তারপর থেকেই তিনি এমন করছে। ভাবছে

484

একা বুড়ো মানুষ আমি! কী করে ফাঁকি দেয়া যায়। বুড়োদের সবাই ফাঁকি দেয় জানিস! ঠিক একটা ছোট্ট বাচ্চাকে যেমন চকলেটের লোভ দেখিয়ে ফাঁকি দেয়া হয়। তুই ও কি ফাঁকি দিবি?

বিড়াল ছানাটি ড্যাব ড্যাব করে তাকিয়ে। কথা শেষে কেবল মিউ শব্দ করে জানান দেয় সে সমর্থন দিচ্ছে না। মিসেস সালেহা বিড়ালের বাটিতে খাবার রাখতেই মোবাইল ফোন বেজে উঠলো। অফিস কলিগ মিসেস জাহানারা। তারা শুধু অফিস কলিগই না পরম বন্ধুও বলা যায়। দুজন দুই দিকে থাকলেও অফিস যাত্রা পথ এক হওয়াতে একই সাথে যায়।

- হ্যালো জাহানারা, আমি আর পাঁচ মিনিট পরেই বেরুচ্ছি। তুমি বাস স্ট্যান্ডে কি অনেক ক্ষণ দাঁড়িয়ে?

- না গো। গতকাল রাতে তোমাকে ফোনে চেষ্টা করছিলাম, কিন্তু বন্ধ বলছিল।

- ওহ চার্জ ছিল না, দিতে খেয়াল নেই, ছেলে-নাতির সাথে কথা বলতে বলতেই ফুরিয়ে গেছে। তা অফিস কেন যাবে না? শরীর খারাপ!

- এমা তুমি জানো না? পুরো শহর জুড়ে লকডাউন, আজ কোনো অফিস হবে না।

- কী করে জানবো, দু'দিন ধরে ডিশ লাইনটা ঠিক নেই। এই যে বলছি ঠিক করে দিয়ে যাও, কেউ শুনছেই না! বিল নেবার সময় ঠিকই নিয়ে যায়। বুড়ো মানুষ, একা থাকি, তাই এমন করার সাহস করে। তা কতদিন চলবে?

- তা জানি না, অনির্দিষ্টকালের জন্য। বলা যায় না কী হয়। আমেরিকা, ইতালির অবস্থা নাকি অনেক খারাপ।

- হ্যাঁ, ছেলে তো তাই বলল। তবে ওরা তো নেদারল্যান্ড -এ থাকে, ওখানে আপাতত সব ঠিকই আছে। আচ্ছা রাখছি, দরজায় কলিং বেল বাজছে, কে যেন এলো।

- সাবধানে থেকো, কোন সমস্যা হলে ফোন দিও।

- আচ্ছা।

আসমার মা অনেকক্ষণ ধরে কলিং বেল বাজিয়ে যাচ্ছে। তার একটাই সমস্যা, যতক্ষণ না কেউ দরজা খুলছে, বেল চাপতেই থাকে। মিসেস সেলিনা দরজা খুলেই রেগে গেলেন।

- এতক্ষণে এলি! এই আসার সময়। আমার তো কাজই শেষ।

- হ্যাঁ, আর কী করমু কন, আগে যে বাসায় গেছিলাম তারা না করে দিছে। বলছে আর না আসতে, পরিস্থিতি যতক্ষণ না ঠিক হয়।

- হ্যাঁ, কী এক ভাইরাস, সব মানুষকে ভয় পাইয়ে দিয়েছে একেবারে। যা যা আলাদা কাপড় রাখা আছে পরিষ্কার হয়ে নে। আমাকে তো আমার মেয়ে আগে থেকে সাবধান করেছে, তাই সব ব্যবস্থা আগেই নিয়েছি।

- থালাম্মা, আপনি কি আমারে বাহির কইরা দিবেন? আমি অহন কাজ না করলে থামু কী? বাজারে সব জিনিসের দাম বাড়তি!

- একাত্তরে যখন কারফিউ লেগেছিল আমার আবছা খেয়াল আছে, আমাদের মিনির মা কিন্তু আমাদের বাড়িতেই আশ্রয় নেয়। আর এটাতো সামান্য জীবাণু। এর জন্য তোকে ছেড়ে দিবো কেন? দুজনে সাবধানে থাকলেই হবে।

- জানি না থালাম্মা, কী হইবো! মানুষ নাকি দুই তিন মাসের বাজার একদিনে করতাসে। সবাই যদি এমন মজুদ করে পরে তো আমরা কিছুই পামু না। থালাম্মা টাকা দেন আমিও গিয়া কিছু নিয়া আসি আপনার জন্য!

- দরকার নেই, আমাদের যা আছে তাতেই হবে। বরং তুই তোর মেয়েকে নিয়ে আমার বাসায় এসে থাক। বিশাল বাড়ি, ঘর তো খালি। তোরও সুবিধা হলো আমিও স্বস্তিতে থাকলাম।

- আইচ্ছা আম্মা, তয় মাইনসে কয় এইটা বড়লোকের রোগ।

- ধুর, এইটা কাউকেই ছাড়ছে না। এতদিন কি আমরা ছেড়ে কথা বলেছি? প্রকৃতির উপর কী অন্যায়টা করেছি। যাই হোক, আল্লাহ ভরসা দেখা যাক কী হয়। তুই এখন কাজে নেমে পড়।

মিসেস সেলিনা কথা শেষে বারান্দায় গিয়ে দাঁড়ালেন, দোতালার বারান্দায় দখিনা হাওয়া তিনি দারুণ উপভোগ করেন। কিন্তু আজ তাঁর মনের মাঝে সংশয়, এই হাওয়াতে কেন জানি তিনি স্বস্তি খুঁজে পাচ্ছেন না। কেমন করুণ, শোকাবহ আবহাওয়া চারদিক। তিনি আকাশের দিকে তাকিয়ে, মেঘাচ্ছন্ন আকাশ। হয়ত ঝুম বৃষ্টি নামবে; কিন্তু পৃথিবী কি পরিশুদ্ধ হবে?

লকডাউনের তিন মাস হতে চললো, কোন কিছুই ঠিক হচ্ছে না। মিসেস সেলিনা বই পড়ছেন। রাতে থাবারের পর তিনি বই পড়েন। এদিকে আসমার মা কেঁদেই চলেছে। তাদের বস্তিতে একজন মারা গেছে। হাসপাতালে ভর্তি হতে পারে নি। মিসেস সেলিনা তাকে কিছুতেই শান্ত করতে পারছেন না।

- ওহ! আর কাঁদিস না তো! অনেক তো হলো। এখন আমাদের শক্ত থাকতে হবে। জানি তোর খারাপ লাগছে।

- আমার বড় আপন আছিল, এক সাথে আছিলাম সুখে দুঃখে। এ কেমন দিন আইলো?

- জানি না রে, শেষ বয়সে এসে এই দিন দেখবো ভাবিনি। পুরো শহর মৃত্যুর ভয়ে কাতর। ঠিক যেন নতুন একাত্তর। এই সেঁজুতিতে সেদিন অনেকেই আশ্রয় নিয়েছিল। অথচ আজ দেখ, কেউ কারো বাসায় যেতেই ভয় পায়। একাত্তরের পর এই বাড়িটা আর ভাঙা হয়নি, শুধু রঙ করেছিলেন আমার বাবা। এরপর স্বামীর মৃত্যুর পর আমারও ঠাঁই হলো।

জানলার পাশে দাঁড়িয়ে কথাগুলো বলতেই তার চোখ কেমন ছলছল করে উঠলো। পুরোনো স্মৃতি মনের কোণে প্রায়ই ভেসে উঠে। হঠাৎ চোখ পড়লো রাস্তায় কাঁদতে থাকা এক দম্পতি ও তার সন্তানদের উপর। পাশের লেনের রহমান সাহেব, কিন্তু এত রাতে এইভাবে কোথায় যাচ্ছেন! মিসেস সেলিনা ডাক দিলেন, তাদের উপরে আসতে বললেন। আসমার মা গিয়ে নিয়ে এলো।

- কী ব্যাপার এত রাতে এইভাবে কই যাচ্ছেন?

- চলে যাচ্ছি আপা, কয়েক মাসের ভাড়া বাকি। দেবার ক্ষমতা নেই। তাই চুপ করে চলে যাচ্ছি।

রহমান সাহেবের স্ত্রী কাঁদতে কাঁদতে বললেন।

-আপা বুকটা ফেটে যাচ্ছে। দশ বছর এই পাড়ায়, আমার দুই মেয়ে এইখানে হয়েছে। আমার সাজানো সংসার, প্রতিটা দেয়ালে আমার স্পর্শ, কত-শত গল্প এই ঘর জুড়ে; আজ বাধ্য হয়ে চলে যাচ্ছি।

মিসেস সেলিনা কিছুক্ষন চুপ রইলেন। পরে বললেন,

- আমার সেঁজুতিতে আপনারা থাকবেন। পরিস্থিতি স্বাভাবিক হলে তারপর না-হয় চলে যাবেন। এই শহর আমার, এই নগর, রাস্তা সব আমার, এদের ছেড়ে কেন পালাবেন। না হয় দুমুঠো কম খাবো। কিন্তু এক সাথেই রবো। ঠিক একাত্তরের মতো, যেখানে ভালোবাসা আছে, শ্রদ্ধা আছে, সেখানে তো ভয় কখনোই তার জায়গা করে নিতে পারবে না। দেখবেন একদিন সাইরেন বাজবে, পৃথিবী সুস্থ হয়ে গেছে ঘোষণা আসবে। রয়ে যান আমার সেঁজুতিতে।

রহমান সাহেব রাজি হলেন। রাত তখন অনেক, আকাশে তারার ছিটেফোঁটাও নেই। কিন্তু বাড়িটিতে এখন আলো জ্বলছে, গল্প চলছে। যেন পৃথিবী ভীষণ শান্ত এবং স্বাভাবিক হয়ে গিয়েছে।

Shaheen Samad / শাহীন সামাদ, Dhaka, Bangladesh

My writing was inspired by all the working women I am surrounded by in my life. As a former working woman myself, I have experienced the hardships that working women face on a daily basis, and later in life, witnessed my daughters go through the same battles.

আমার ভালোবাসার শহর

কুয়াশায় মোড়া শহরটা এখনো পুরোপুরি জেগে উঠেনি। নাহিদ ব্যালকনিতে এসে দাঁড়ায়, সকালের এ সময়টা তার খুব প্রিয়। ব্যালকিনতে রাখা গাছগুলিতে সে পানি দেয়। গোলাপের গাছে কুঁড়ি এসেছে। স্বামী, সন্তান ও শাশুড়িকে নিয়ে তার ছোট সংসার। সে নিজে একটা বেসরকারী ব্যাংকে কর্মরতা। স্বামী সরকারি চাকুরিজীবি। দুই বেডরুমের আট'শ স্কয়ার ফুটের ফ্ল্যাটে সে তার সুখী সংসার জীবন পেতেছে। অবশ্য শুরুটা এতো সহজ ছিল না। স্বামীর একা আয়ে রাজধানী ঢাকা শহরে সংসার চালানো কষ্টসাধ্য। ঢাকা শহরে বাড়ি ভাড়া সহ সবকিছুর দাম বেশি, ছেলে জয়কে দু'বছর পর স্কুল দিতে হবে। সব কিছু ভেবেই সে চাকরিটা নেয়। প্রথম থেকেই সে অর্থনৈতিকভাবে স্বাবলম্বী হতে চাইছিল, তার বিশ্ববিদ্যালয়ের ডিগ্রীটা সে কাজে লাগাতে চাইছিল। প্রথম দিকে দুই পরিবারের পক্ষ থেকেই বাধা এসেছিল। কিন্তু সে তার যুক্তিতে ছিল অটল।

শাশুড়ি আর বুয়ার ভরসাতেই চাকুরিটা করতে পারছে। এখনো শহরে সে রকম ভাবে ডে কেয়ার সেন্টার গড়ে উঠেনি, যে কয়েকটা আছে তাও হাতে গোনা। সকাল আটটার মধ্যেই ওদের দু'জনকে বেরিয়ে পড়তে হয়। রিক্সায় বাসস্ট্যান্ড পর্যন্ত যেতে দেখা মেলে প্রচুর বিভিন্ন পেশার মেয়েদের। কেউ ছাত্রী কেউ বা চাকুরিজীবি, তবে বেশির ভাগই পোষাক কর্মী। বাস এলে ওরা দু'জন ভিড় ঠেলে বাসে উঠে পড়ে। নাহিদ যাবে মতিঝিলে আর ওর স্বামী মহাখালীতে নেমে যাবে। রাস্তায় প্রচন্ড ট্রাফিক জ্যাম, বাসে বসে নাহিদ ভাবতে থাকে আজকের ঢাকার সাথে ওর ছোট বেলার দেখা ঢাকা শহরের কত তফাৎ। তখন রাস্তাঘাট ছিল

ফাঁকা। এ লোকজনের ভিড় ছিল না। এত উঁচু উঁচু দালান কোঠা, শপিং মল, এগুলো ছিল না। এখন পুরো শহরটা যেন একটা কংক্রিটের জঙ্গলে পরিণত হয়েছে। ছোটো বেলায় ওরা প্রায়ই রমনা পার্কে বেড়াতে যেত। এখন খেলার মাঠ আর পার্কগুলো যেন কোথায় অদৃশ্য হয়ে গেছে।

ঢাকা এখন কসমোপলিটান শহর হওয়াতে প্রচুর দেশি বিদেশি লোকজন আনাগোনা বেড়েছে। সবকিছুর কেন্দ্রবিন্দু এখন ঢাকা। আসলে ঢাকা শহরের প্রাণ হচ্ছে এই শহরের মানুষেরা। ঢাকা শহরের লোকজনই এই শহরকে বাঁচিয়ে রেখেছে। এত কর্মব্যস্ততা, প্রাণ-চাঞ্চল্য সব থেমে যাবে এরা না থাকলে। এ শহরটা তার বুকে সবাইকে আশ্রয় দিয়েছে। বাসে বসে থাকতে থাকতে একটু ঢুলুনির মতো আসে নাহিদের। মনে মনে ভাবে মেট্রোরেল আর এলিভেটেড এক্সপ্রেসওয়েটা হয়ে গেলে শহরের যানজটটা অনেক খানি কমে যাবে। তখন জীবনটা অনেক সহজ হয়ে যাবে। মুহূর্তে বিরক্তি কেটে গিয়ে তার মনটা ভাল হয়ে গেল, এই শহরটার প্রতি তার মায়া ভালবাসা বেড়ে গেল। এই শহরটার প্রতি তার অনেক কর্তব্য রয়েছে। এই শহরটা অনেক সমস্যায় জর্জরিত, তারপরও সে এই শহরটাকে ভালোবাসে, এই শহরের সুখে সে সুখি, দুঃখে দুঃখি। আজকে অফিসে একটু তাড়াতাড়ি যাবার কথা, একজন মহিলা উদ্যোক্তা আসবেন তার হস্তশিল্পের ব্যবসায়িক প্রতিষ্ঠানটি বড় পরিসরে বাড়ানোর জন্য ঋণের আবেদন নিয়ে। সে যথাসাধ্য চেষ্টা করবে মহিলাকে সাহায্য করতে। এসব ভাবতে ভাবতেই বাস তার অফিসের কাছে এসে থামল। বাস থেকে নেমে দ্রুত পায়ে সে এগিয়ে চলে আপন গন্তব্যস্থলে।

Aysha Siddika Mimi / আইশা সিদ্দিকা মিমি, Savar, Bangladesh

'My City, My Home' project gives me such an enormous opportunity to expose my inner writing talent and creativity. This project helps me to think once again about 'How precious I am to be a girl'! And I can assure, that feeling of amusement would be for every girl like me. Obviously, various kind of stories may have been submitted into your inbox by various women. Huge thanks to you for giving us this opportunity. Women of my country possess various norms, rules, values, customs and rituals. A family, a home and a city, all these are constructed by women in a civilized way. The context of my story is built by a woman's real life story which consists of struggling, hardship, a bit of happiness, a journey of all these things. It will let every woman think that this is not only character's story, it is every woman's story. The difference might be the environment, family background and financial position. But, the context is the same for all women. The project 'My City, My Home' plays a great role to collect all great stories of woman from different age-group and different background.

নারী

"এই সোহেল ভাই, ক্যামেরাটা এদিক করে ধরেন। সব রেডি, অল সেট, উনি কোথায়", বললো তানিয়া। তানিয়া পেশায় সাংবাদিক ও উপস্থাপক। তার কাজ সব অচেনা গল্পকে বের করা। আজ গল্পের প্রধান চরিত্র হচ্ছেন রেহনুমা। "তো চলুন, শুরু করা যাক", সব বুঝিয়ে দেওয়া হলো রাহনুমাকে। আপনার পরিচয়টা দিয়ে শুরু করুন।

আমার নাম রেহনুমা। আমি একজন গার্মেন্টস কর্মী ছিলাম। এক বছর আগে এক accident এ আমি আমার এক পা হারাই। আমার জন্ম ঢাকার এক বস্তিতে।

491

আমার মায়ে মাইসের বাড়িত কাম করতো আর বাপে মার কামাইয়ের টাকা উড়াইতো। তাই, মা বাপেরে ছাইড়া আমারে আর ভাইরে নিয়া আলাদা হইয়া যায়। আমার ইচ্ছা ছিল লেখাপড়া করার কিন্তু ক্লাস 5 পর্যন্ত পইড়া আর পড়তে পারি নাই। প্রথমে আমি চা বিক্রি করতাম। ঢাকা বিশ্ববিদ্যালয়ের সামনে আবার সংসদ ভবনের সামনে আবার মাঝে মাঝে মতিঝিলের শাপলা চত্বরে"। তানিয়া জিজ্ঞেস করলো, "এতদূর যেতেন?"

- হ্যাঁ, কী করুম বলেন, ছোট ছিলাম, ভাবতাম কেনাবেচা না হলে কী খামু। তাই বাসে কইরা যাইতাম।

- হারিয়ে যাননি?

- একবার গেছিলাম কিন্তু মাইসোরের জিগাইয়া আবার ফিরতে পারছিলাম। আবার বায়তুল মোকাররম মসজিদের সামনে খেলনা বিক্রি করছি।"

- কত বছর চাকরি করেছেন?

- ১২ বছর।

- আপনার বর্তমান বয়স কত?

- ২৭ বছর"

- তারপর...?

- আমার এক লোকের সাথে পরিচয় হয় গার্মেন্টসে। তার সাথে আমার বিয়ে হয়। 15 বছর বয়সে ঢুকে গার্মেন্টসে আর ১৬ বছর বয়সে বিয়ে হয়। ১৭ বছর বয়সে বাচ্চা হয়।

- Oh My God! মাত্র ১৭ বছর বয়সে আপনার বাচ্চা হয়!

বিস্ময়ের সাথে বলল তানিয়া।

- হ, আমার পিঠাপিঠি দুই বাচ্চা হয়। বিয়ার ৫ বছরের মাথায় আমার সাথে তার

ছাড়াছাড়ি হইয়া যায়। ২১ বছর বয়সে দুই বাচ্চা নিয়া আমার খুব কষ্ট হইতো। একা ছিলাম ,মাও মারা গেছে, এর মাঝখানে ভাই এখানে সেখানে থাকে।

– পুরো ঢাকা চিনেন আপনি?

– পুরা না চিনলেও, অর্ধেক চিনি।

– যেসব যেসব স্থানে গিয়েছেন সেসব স্থানের জায়গা দেখতে কেমন লাগতো?

– ভালো লাগতো, বিশেষ করে ঢাকা বিশ্ববিদ্যালয়, রাজু ভাস্কর্য, টিএসসি চত্বর আবার বিভিন্ন ভবন, কার্জন হল। এগুলো দেখতে ভালো লাগতো। আবার সংসদ ভবন দূর থেকে এত সুন্দর ভেতরে মনে হয় আরো সুন্দর।

– কখনো মনে হয়নি যে বিশ্ববিদ্যালয়ে যদি পড়তে পারতেন?

– মন চাইলেও তা পারা যায় না। যা আমি পারি নাই আমি চেষ্টা করি তা আমার বাচ্চাকে করে দিতে আর চেষ্টা করমু ওদেরকে যেন ওই বিশ্ববিদ্যালয়ে পড়াতে পারি।

এটাই হচ্ছে নারীর মাতৃত্ববোধ। তাইতো নারীকে মায়ের জাতি বলা হয়।

– এরপর...?

– তারপর আমি চিন্তা করি টুকিটাকি ব্যবসা করার। বাসায় কাঁথা সেলাই করতাম অর্ডারে, সংসার ভালই চলত। বাচ্চাগুলারে স্কুলে ভর্তি করি।

– ওদেরকে কখনো ওইসব জায়গায় বেড়াতে নিয়ে গিয়েছেন?

– হ, আমার ছোট বাচ্চা তো দোয়েল চত্বর দেইখা বলে, না এত বড় পাখি। বন্ধ পেলে ওদেরকে চিড়িয়াখানায় ও জাদুঘরে অভিনয় ঘুরতে নিয়ে যাই । নববর্ষ আইলে মেলায় নিয়া যাই, চেষ্টা করি নতুন জামা কিনে দিতে। না পারলে মেলায় ঘুরাই এতেই খুশি। নাগরদোলায় উঠে, গালে আঁকাই, বাতাসা, মুড়ি মুড়কি কিন্না দেই। ওরা সব চেয়ে পছন্দ করে পুতুল নাচ। একবার সাপের খেলা দেইখা ওরা

ভয় পাইছিল। Accident এ সব উল্টাপাল্টা হইয়া যায়।

- বর্তমানে কি করছেন?

- বর্তমানে বাসায় কাঁথা সেলাই আর হাত মেশিন এর অর্ডারে জামা সেলাই করি।

- আপনার নিজস্ব বাসা আছে?

- হ্যাঁ, আমার মনে কষ্ট করে একটা টিনের ঘর করছে। আমি আবার আরো মেরামত কইরা আরো ভালো করছি। আমি চাই এ বাসায় আমার যা স্মৃতি আছে সুখদুঃখের তার সাথে আরো স্মৃতি জমা হোক। চেষ্টা করমু আরও ভালো করতে পারি বাসাডারে যেন বাচ্চাদের ভালো একটা শৈশব কাটে। ওদের ভালো ভালো স্মৃতি জমা হয়। ওদের নিয়েই তো আমার সংসার।

- কেমন লাগে একজন নারী হিসেবে যখন আপনার ঘর বা শহর নিয়ে চিন্তা করেন?

- যখন বলে নারীরা শহরকে উন্নত করছে, গার্মেন্টস কর্মী বিশেষ করে নারীরা যারা পোশাক শিল্পরে সমৃদ্ধ করে অর্থনীতিকে শক্তিশালী করতেছে তখন খুব ভালো লাগে। মনে হয় নারী হইয়া আমি সার্থক।

- তা ঠিক। সভ্যতা গড়ে উঠেছে অর্ধেক নারীর বলেই। প্রত্যক্ষ বা পরোক্ষভাবে নারীর অবদান সর্বক্ষেত্রেই রয়েছে। সন্তানকে গড়ে তোলা থেকে শহরকে গড়া পর্যন্ত সব জায়গাতেই নারী। 'নারী' এই শব্দটা ছোট, খুব ছোট! কিন্তু এর অর্থ খুব শক্তিশালী। আপনাকে খুব ধন্যবাদ আপনার গল্পটি আমাদের সাথে শেয়ার করার জন্য।

"Cut!", সোহেল বলল। "আপু আপনার গল্পটা বলবেন না ?" তানিয়া বললো, "আমার গল্প আর নারীদের মতই। কারণ তাদের ঘর বা শহর ভিন্ন, গল্পও আলাদা, কিন্তু তবুও আমরা এক। কারণ আমরা নারী"।

Fabiha Tonika / ফাবিহা তনিকা, Dhaka, Bangladesh

I was inspired by the concept of belongingness. Because in most of the cases, we cannot predetermine where we will be born, what will be our environment; but I have had a realization, a home can be a feeling, a moment. Something intangible. It is not always a place, or any group of people. Even a calm and fulfilled soul can be a home for some people. It is the peace within ourselves can help us to find the right place. Thus, I intended to write on this topic.

মহল

তীর শীতেও মগ ভর্তি ঠাণ্ডা পানি মাথায় ঢালে নাজমা। অহেতুক ঝগড়ায় জড়াতে চায় না সে। সারাদিন খাটুনির পর শরীর আর মন, দুটোই শান্তি চায়। শুকনো কাপড় গায়ে জড়ানোর পরও কাঁপুনি লাগে শরীরে। বল সাবানে শাড়ি কেচে, শেষ বারের মত ময়লা আয়নায় মুখ তুলে তাকায় সে। কি আশ্চর্য! এই চোখ। আগে দেখিনি সে। কেমন শান্ত, স্থির। দরজায় কড়া নাড়ে কে যেন; নাজমা সম্বিৎ ফিরে পায়। এক হাতে ধোয়া শাড়ি, সাবান আর অন্য হাতে মোবাইলটা ব্লাউজের ভাঁজে জায়গা করে নেয়।

ঘরের পাশেই শাড়িটা মেলে দেয় সে। ভেজা চুল তোয়ালে জড়িয়ে এদিক ওদিকে চোখ বুলায়। না! এখনো রাত ফুরোয়নি এইখানে। তার মতই অনেকে সবে কাজ শেষে ঘরে ফিরেছে। বাচ্চার কান্নার শব্দে মনে পড়ে, জুলেখার একটা মেয়ে হয়েছে। দেখতে যাওয়া হয়নি। কিন্তু খিদেও পেয়েছে বেশ, এদিকে আকাশের অবস্থা ভালো না; এই শীতে যদি বৃষ্টি হয় তবে মরণ!

নাজমা চাবি দিয়ে ঘরের তালা খোলে, জুলেখার মেয়েকে সকালে দেখবে না হয়, কিন্তু আগে নিজ পেটে কিছু চালান করা চাই।

গোগ্রাসে খাওয়া শেষ করে নাজমা। ব্লাউজের ভাজ থেকে মোবাইলটা বের করে সময় দেখে। বাড়ি থেকে আর ফোন আসবে না! অন্তত কয়েকদিন। তারপর? নাজমা আর ভাবতে চায় না। কেউ আর খোঁজ না নিলেই বা কী? কে সে আসলে?

"আমি কইলাম, তুই বাইর হ এই ঘর থেইকা!" নাজমা বুঝতে পারে ফারুক এসেছে, জুলেখার স্বামী। মেয়ে হওয়াতে খুশি নয় সে। তার উপর অসুস্থ শরীরে জুলেখা কাজে যেতে পারে না, তাই রোজগারও কম। নাজমার হাসি পায়, ঘেন্না হয়, কিন্তু কী করবে? তার কী করার আছে? নাজমা শুয়ে পড়ে, কাল তার অনেক কাজ। যে বাড়িতে ঝিয়ের কাজ করে, সে পরিবার চলে যাচ্ছে বিদেশ। কাল গেলে কিছু বকশিশ নিশ্চয়ই পাবে।

আল্লাহ গো! – ধড়ফড়িয়ে ঘুম থেকে উঠে পড়ে নাজমা। না! না! তার কিছু হয়নি, জুলেখা কাঁদছে। অন্যান্য দিনের চেয়ে প্রকট চিৎকার করছে জুলেখা, তারপরও নাজমা ঘুমাতে চেষ্টা করে। কাল তার কাজ আছে।

নাজমা ঘুমিয়েও পড়ে। কিন্তু শেষ রাতে আবারও ঘুম ভেঙে যায় তার। গায়ের মাঝে উম লাগে, কে এটা? অন্ধকারে ভালো করে দেখার চেষ্টা করে সে। ছোউ একটা মানুষের বাচ্চা তার গা ঘেঁষে আসছে। চোর না তো? নাজমা পাশ ফেরে, কী শান্ত একটা মুখ। ভরাট চোখের পাপড়ি। নাজমা অবাক হয়ে দেখে, মাথায় হাত বুলিয়ে দিতে চায়। পাতলা গায়ের কম্বলটা ছোউ মেয়েটার গায়ে টেনে দেয়। টিনের ফুটো দিয়ে আলো ঢুকেছে ঘরে। পরিষ্কার চাঁদের আলোয় নাজমার চোখ আটকে আছে ছোট এক জোড়া চোখে। কী আশ্চর্য পরিচিত গায়ের গন্ধ। নাজমার তন্দ্রাচ্ছন্ন শরীর মনে করতে চায়, বাচ্চাটি কে? কী করে এলো তার ঘরে? খুব চেনা কেউ একজন। কিন্তু মনে পড়ছে না কেন? ক্লান্ত শরীরে নাজমা বুকে টেনে নিতে চায় মেয়েটিকে। ইস! কী ঠাওই না পড়েছে, আর মেয়েটা কিনা দূরে শুয়ে আছে! আবছা হয়ে আসে আশ্চর্য সুন্দর চোখ জোড়া।

এত আদরেও দূরে সরে আছে কেন মেয়েটি? সে কি ঘুমোচ্ছে আসলে, নাকি ঘুমের ভান করছে? নাজমা হাতড়াতে শুরু করে। কোথায় গেল মেয়েটা? ঘুম কেটে যায় নাজমার। উঠে বসে সে, মনে পড়েছে তার। মেয়েটা বকুল! তার বকুল। কিন্তু সে কোথায় এখন?

বাইরে ভোরের আলো ফুটতে শুরু করেছে। বিছানায় বসে হাপুস হয়ে কাঁদছে

নাজমা, আজ কত দিন পড়ে মেয়েটা তার কাছে এসেছে। শেষ বারও তার পাশেই ঘুমাচ্ছিলো সে; কে জানতো চুরি হয়ে যাবে মেয়েটা? হ হ করে কেঁদে উঠে নাজমা। নিশ্চিত বাপের কাজ, নাহয় শাশুড়ির। নাহয় কপাল!

ও নাজমা! দরজা খোলা– বিছানা থেকে নেমে নাজমা দরজা খোলে। পাশের ঘরের সুফিয়া এসেছে তার কাছে।

জুলেখার মাইয়াডা মইরা গেসে।

কেমনে?

রাইতে ফারুক মিয়া মাইরা ফেলতে চাইসিলো। পরে ধস্তাধস্তি কইরা ভাগসে। পরে শেষ রাতে চোখ উলটাইয়া মরসে। মনে হয় ঠাণ্ডায়।

আহারে। জুলেখা কই?

বইসা আছে মাইয়া লইয়া। দেখবি না?

নাজমা কিছুক্ষণ চুপ থেকে উত্তর দেয়, না। আমি রাতে ফিইরা দেখমুনে।

মাইয়াডারে তো কবর দিয়া ফালাইবো।

দিক। বাইচা থাকতে দেখলাম না, এখন আর – সুফিয়াও সায় দেয়। যে মেয়েমানুষ বেঁচে থেকে দাম পায় না, তার আবার মরণের পর কী এমন মূল্য?

সকালের জন্য নাজমা ভাত তুলেই রেখেছিল, কিন্তু আজ মুখে তুলতে পারলো না। হাত মুখ ধুয়ে জুলেখার ঘরে উঁকি দিল। গতরাতে মারও খেয়েছে মেয়েটা। চোখ-মুখ ফুলে কালো হয়ে আছে। নাজমার দিকে অপলক দৃষ্টিতে কিছুক্ষণ তাকিয়ে ছিল জুলেখা। নাজমা আর দাঁড়ালো না। বস্তির শেষ সীমানায় থাকা ছোট খুপরির বাসিন্দা সে, ভাড়া থাকে তাও সই। ঘরে তালা ঝুলিয়ে বেরিয়ে পড়ে সে। আজ কিছু বকশিশ পেলে তুলে রাখবে। আরও কিছু টাকা জমলে ভাইদের কাছ থেকে নগদে কিনবে ভিটার জমি। তখন আর কেউ বের করতে পারবে না তাকে।

আকাশ পরিষ্কার হতে শুরু করেছে, গতকালের সব মন খারাপও এখন আর জেঁকে বসে নেই। নাজমা দ্রুত পা চালায়, আজ নিশ্চয়ই অনেক কাজ থাকবে।

কি গো নাজমা! আইজকা এত সকালে?- দারোয়ানের বাঁকা হাসি নাজমার ভালো লাগে না।

সব সময় তো এমন সময়েই আসি – দেখেও না দেখার ভান করে নাজমা হেঁটে যায়। সিঁড়ি বেয়ে উঠে কলিং বেল চাপতেই ব্যস্ত হয়ে ম্যাডাম দরজা খুলে দিলেন।

ভালো হয়েছে জলদি এসেছ। আজকে বেশি কাজ নেই জাস্ট ঘরটা ঝাট দিয়ে দাও।

বাধ্য বালিকার মত নাজমা ঘর ঝাট দেয়। বকুলের চেয়ে কয়েক বছরের বড় একটা মেয়ে আছে এই দম্পতির। পুষ্প। নাজমাকে প্রতিদিন নতুন আর মজার সব প্রশ্ন করে সে। আজকেও করবে।

- আচ্ছা, বুয়া তোমার বাসার নাম কি?

- নাজমা প্রশ্নের জন্য প্রস্তুত ই ছিল।

- আমার বাসার নাম? নাজমা মহল!

- আচ্ছা! তোমার নামে তাই না?

- জ্বি।

- জানো? আমরা যে নতুন বাসায় যাচ্ছি ওখানে আমার রুমের একটা নাম থাকবে। তারপর যখন বড় হবো তখন আমার নামে একটা বাসা হবে।

- জ্বি। নাজমার মেয়েটাকে বড় ভালো লাগে কিন্তু কেন যেন কথা এগোলো না।

সত্যিই এই বাড়িতে আর কাজ নেই। শুধু আজ নয়, আর কখনো এই বাড়িতে কাজ করা হবে না। হলেও মালিক হবে অন্য কেউ। বের হওয়ার আগে হাজার পাঁচেক টাকাও পেয়েছে বকশিশ। নাজমার খুব একটা আনন্দ হলো না। কেন যেন মনটা মিইয়ে গেল। বেরিয়েই সিদ্ধান্ত নিল আজ আর অন্য কোন বাসায় কাজে যাবে না। ৫০০০ টাকা থেকে

দুটো ৫০০ টাকার নোট বের করে আলাদা রাখলো। ফাস্ট ফুডের দোকান থেকে একটা চিকেন বান কিনলো। পুষ্প আপাকে অনেকবার খেতে দেখেছে সো। নাজমা ফাস্ট ফুডের দোকানে বসতে পারেনি। পার্কের একটি বেঞ্চে বসে খেলো। ঘুরে ঘুরে ঘরের জন্য নতুন চাদর, পাতিল, চামচ, কিনলো। বিরিয়ানির দোকানে বসে বিরিয়ানি খেল, এরপর সন্ধ্যা হওয়া পর্যন্ত শুধুই হেঁটে বেড়ালো। হাতির ঝিলের পাশে থাকা বেঞ্চে বসে মানুষ দেখলো। সন্ধ্যা শেষে ঘরে ফিরে ময়লা আয়নায় আবার নিজেকে দেখে। ভাবে, বস্তির এই নোংরা ঘরটিই তার নাজমা মহল। এ ঘর ছেড়ে আর কোথাও যেতে চায় না সো। আসলেই তো! অধিকার যখন নেই, তবে ফিরবে কেন?

Parisha Maheshareen / পরিশা মহেশারিন, Dhaka, Bangladesh

শহর কিংবা বাড়ি, সবটাই আমার, কিন্তু এই 'আমার' শব্দতেও রয়ে যায় কিছু না বলা 'কিন্তু'! সেই 'কিন্তু' নিয়েই আমার এই গল্পের ভাবনা। আমার কিংবা আমার আশেপাশে ঘটে যাওয়া কিছু সত্য, কিছু অসত্য, কিছু কল্পনা আর কিছু বাস্তবতাকে কেন্দ্র করে এই গল্পে আমার হেঁটেচলা। কোটি প্রাণের এই শহরে সম-অধিকার কিংবা সম-মর্যাদা নিয়ে আলোচনা হয় অনেক, সেই আলোচনায় কখনই ফোটে না আলো। আলো হয়তো আসবে না ততদিন, যতদিন না আমরা নিজেরা নিজেদের আলোকিত করবো। আজ আমি লিখছি খুব উদার মনে, খুব বড় গলায় নিজের জন্যে বলছি কিন্তু এই আমিই হয়তো একটু পর রাতের আঁধারে কিংবা দিনের আলোতে আমার নিজ ঘরে কিংবা আমার শহরের কোনো জায়গায় পীড়িত হবো। তখন হয়তো এই আমিই বলবো..., থাক, বাদ দিই! এই বাদ দেয়াটাই না বলা কথা হয়ে মিশে যায় আমার মতন হাজারো নারীর সাথে মাটির গহ্বরে কিংবা আগুনের লেলিহান শিখার গুঁড়ো হওয়া ছাইয়ে। এই শহরের যান্ত্রিকতার ভিড়ে নিজেকে নিয়ে দেখা দুঃস্বপ্নগুলোই আমার এই লেখার অনুপ্রেরণা। আর প্রত্যয় শুধু এই একটাই, দুঃস্বপ্নগুলো যেন কখনোই হানা না দেয় নিষ্ঠুর বাস্তবতা হয়ে আমার জীবনে কিংবা আমার মতন অন্য কোনো নারীর জীবনে। ভালোবাসার শহর এই ঢাকায় সত্যিকারের ভালোবাসার প্রতিষ্ঠা হোক, নারী কিংবা পুরুষের আগে এই শহরের প্রাণগুলো হয়ে উঠুক সত্যিকারের মানুষ।

মায়া

সন্ধ্যে হবে হবে। গোধূলির আলো প্রায় নিভে গেছে। আমি হাঁটছি ঢাকার সড়ক দিয়ে। একে ঠিক সড়ক বলা চলে না, গলি। বাহান্ন বাজার তেপ্পান্ন গলির এই শহরের এক গলি দিয়ে হাঁটছি এই আমি। যত দূর পর্যন্ত চোখ যাচ্ছে কারও দেখা পাচ্ছি না, তবু বার বার মনে হচ্ছে পেছন থেকে আমার সাথে হাঁটছে আরও কতক পা। পেছন ফিরে তাকালে কিন্তু পা গুলোকে দেখা যায়না। বিশ্ববিদ্যালয়ের বাস থেকে নেমে বাসা পর্যন্ত যেতে রোজ এই গলিটা পার হতে হয়, আর রোজই মনে হয় আমার সাথে হাঁটছে আরও কতক পা। কিন্তু পেছনে তাকালেই কোথাও কেউ নেই। তাই সেটিকে নিছক নিজের ভ্রম মনে করে ভয়কে বিদায় দিয়েছি। নির্ভয়ে হেঁটে চলেছি গলি ধরে। হঠাৎ পেছন থেকে অতর্কিত হামলা। একটা হাত চেপে ধরলো আমার মুখ, আরেক হাত খুলে নিল চোখের

চশমা। হাঁচকা টানে কোথায় যেন চলে গেলাম আমি। মুহূর্তেই আমার রক্ষিত শরীরের আবরণগুলো খুলে গেল এক এক করে। কতগুলো নরপিশাচ ঝাঁপিয়ে পরলো আমার উপরে। আমার নরম হাত-পাগুলো নিস্তেজ হয়ে নেতিয়ে পরতে শুরু করলো।

ভাঙ্গা ইটের স্তূপের পাশে পরে আছে আমার সদ্য কেনা হলুদ পাজামা। কিছুটা ছেড়া, কিছুটা নোংরা। প্রিন্টের কামিজটা গায়ে, তবে সাথে যুক্ত হয়েছে কিছু নতুন ডিজাইন। কিছুটা লাল ছোপ আর কিছুটা থকথকে সাদার মিশ্রণে হয়েছে নতুন রঙের বাটিক।

ঘড়িতে ঢং ঢং করে দুটো আওয়াজ হলো। রাত দুটো বাজে। ঘুম যখন ভাঙ্গলো দেখতে পেলাম সামনের আলনায় ঝুলছে আমার সদ্য কেনা হলুদ পাজামা আর প্রিন্টের কামিজটা। সুন্দর আর সুরক্ষিত। বিছানার পাশে সাইড টেবিলে রাখা গ্লাস থেকে দু'চুমুক পানি খেয়ে পাশ ফিরলাম আবারও।

ঘুমিয়ে ছিলাম। পাশের ঘরের চিৎকারে ঘুম ভাঙ্গলো। চোখ মেলে দেখি আমার ছোট্ট ঘরটা কেমন ধূসর ধোঁয়ায় আবৃত। পাশে থাকা চশমাটা চোখে দিতেই দেখলাম ঘরের অন্য পাশটায় হালকা লাল কিছুটা নীল ফুল ফুটে আবার নিভে যাচ্ছে। কেমন একটা ঝাঁঝালো গন্ধ নাকে আসছে। হঠাৎ ঘরের এক পাশ কমলা আভায় আলোকিত হলো। দেখলাম আমার শখের বইগুলো পুড়ে ছাই হচ্ছে একটা একটা করে। আমি ছুটে বের হতে চাইলাম। কিন্তু কোথাও দরজা খুঁজে পাচ্ছি না। পাশের ঘরের চিৎকার থেমে গেছে। ঘরের জানালা ভাঙ্গা কাচ গলে ছুটে আসলো একটা নামি কোম্পানির সুগন্ধি বোতল। বিকট শব্দে সেটি আগুনের শিখা ঢেলে দিল আমার গায়ে জড়ানো ওড়নায়। সুন্দর মিষ্টি গন্ধ তীর হয়ে আটকে দিচ্ছে আমার জমে থাকা শেষ নিঃশ্বাস। আমি দরজা খুঁজছি, কোথাও দরজা নাই।

আমি ছটফট করে অস্ফুট চিৎকার করে ঘুম ভেঙ্গে উঠে বসলাম। বালিশের পাশে থাকা মোবাইলের আলো জ্বেলে দেখলাম খুব বেশি সময় পার হয় নি। মোবাইলের ঘড়িতে দুটা ছাব্বিশ বাজে। গায়ের ওড়নাটাও ঠিক গায়েই আছে। পুড়ে ছাই হয়নি। বইগুলো এখনো শেলফে সাজানো আছে সারি সারি। আবারও পাশ ফিরে শুয়ে পরলাম।

বাড়ির মূল দরজায় থটখট শব্দ হচ্ছে। বেল ছেড়ে সবসময় বাবা অমন থটখট শব্দ করে। বিরক্তিকর স্বভাব। গেট খুলে হতভম্ব। আমাকে অবাক করে দিয়ে সে দাঁড়িয়ে

আছে। কতগুলো দিন পার হয়ে গেছে প্রিয় এই মানুষটিকে না দেখে, আজ হাসি মুখে সামনে দাঁড়িয়ে আছে! অন্তরের লজ্জা ভুলে ঝাঁপিয়ে পরলাম উষ্ণ আলিঙ্গনে। দরজা আটকাতে আটকাতে জমে থাকা কত কথা। কত ভালোবাসার বহিঃপ্রকাশ। একসাথে বসে দু'কাপ চা আর না বলা কত অপেক্ষা। হঠাৎ কী করে যেন তার শক্ত হাতে পেঁচিয়ে গেল আমার কোমর অবধি লম্বা চুল। কিছু বুঝবার আগেই সেই মুঠি থেকে মুক্তি পেলাম পুরোনো দেয়ালে হড়মুড়িয়ে আছড়ে পড়ে।

ঘুম ভেঙে গেল। নিজেকে আবিষ্কার করলাম বিছানা থেকে নিচে। হড়মুড়িয়ে দেয়ালে আছড়ে পড়িনি, পড়েছি বিছানা থেকে গড়িয়ে নিচে! বিছানায় উঠে মোবাইল খুলে দেখি রাত তিনটা বিশ। আবারও ঘুমিয়ে পড়বার চেষ্টা করতে লাগলাম।

সকালে ক্লাস। বাসা থেকে বের হয়েছি। দেরি হয়ে গেছে। দ্রুত পায়ে হাঁটছি। হঠাৎ পেছন থেকে সজোরে ধাক্কায় ছিটকে পরলাম গলির মুখে। গলির শেষ প্রান্তে চেনা একটা মুখ দেখলাম থমকে দাঁড়িয়েছে। ততক্ষণে কিছু অচেনা শক্ত হাতে রুপোলি ছুড়ি শোভা পাচ্ছে আমার কণ্ঠনালীর মধ্যখানে। আমার আকুল চোখের আকুতি চেনা মুখটা অন্তত কাউকে ডেকে এনে আমাকে বাঁচাক। কিন্তু চেনা সেই মুখ পালিয়ে গেল তার বাড়ির শক্ত কাঠের দরজার আড়ালে আমাকে মৃত্যু মুখে একা ফেলে। অচেনা শক্ত হাতগুলো বার বার উঠে নেমে যাচ্ছে আমার কণ্ঠনালীতে, আমার ডান হাতের কব্জিতে। আর তাদের চিৎকার করে বলা "এই হাত দিয়েই না লিখতি? এই গলা দিয়েই না বের হতো আমাদের বিরুদ্ধে কথা? সব বন্ধ! সব শেষ!" শব্দগুলো আস্তে আস্তে অপরিষ্কার হয়ে যাচ্ছে আমার কানে। পিচঢালা এই ধূসর গলিতে রুপোলি ছুড়ি হাতে কতগুলো অচেনা হাত ক্রমেই দূরে সরে যাচ্ছে। রুপোলি ছুড়ি থেকে টপটপ করে পরছে টাটকা লাল রঙ, আর গলির মুখে আমার অর্ধকাটা গলার লালগুলো গড়িয়ে পরছে নোংরা ড্রেনটায়। কী সুন্দর জীবন্ত ক্যানভাসে আমি পরে আছি নিস্তেজ নিথর।

ঘুম ভাঙলো। মোবাইলের অ্যালার্ম বাজছে, সেই সাথে আমার বাবার চিৎকার। দুই আওয়াজ একসাথে মিশে নতুন কোনো সুর তৈরি হচ্ছে বোধহয়।

বিছানা থেকে নেমে লম্বা চুল পেঁচিয়ে খোঁপা করতে করতে ভাবছি কি অদ্ভুত দুঃস্বপ্নের রাত শেষ হলো। ঘড়িতে প্রায় সাড়ে ন'টা বাজে। দরজা খুলে বের হতেই বাবার নতুন কিন্তু পুরাতন চেনা কিন্তু কিছুটা অচেনা সুর, "নবাবজাদির ঘুম ভাঙসে! এত টাকা খরচ কইরা লেখাপড়া শিখাইসি, সে এখন চাকরি করবে না। কী করবে? ব্যবসা করবে। আরে ব্যবসা যে করবি টাকা পাবি কই? আবার কী সব ঢঙের লেখা লিখে, রাস্তা ঘাটে বাইর হইতে পারি না। মানুষ আমারে হমকি দেয়। আরে তুই মরবি মর। চৌদ্দ গুষ্টি নিয়ে মরতে হবে কেন তোর!"

ভাঙা রেডিও'র মতন চলতে থাকা একঘেয়েমি সুর উপেক্ষা করে ধোঁয়া ওঠা গরম চায়ের কাপ হাতে নিয়ে উঠে গেলাম সাড়ে তিন তলার চিলেকোঠার ছাদে। রোদ উঠে গেছে। হালকা শীতের সকালে রোদ পোহাতে পোহাতে সিমেন্টের ছাদের এক কোনায় বসে চুমুক দিলাম গরম চায়ের কাপে। পাশের ছাদের কৌতূহলী কিন্তু নোংরা চোখগুলো তাকিয়ে আছে আমার দিকে।

আমার আবৃত শরীর আর অনাবৃত পায়ের পাতাই তাদের আনন্দের খোরাক। নিচে নেমে এলাম। আড়াল করে নিলাম আমার আবৃত শরীর আর অনাবৃত পায়ের পাতা আমার ঘরের চলটা ওঠা পুরনো ড্যাম খাওয়া স্যাঁতস্যাঁতে গন্ধের চার দেয়ালের ভিড়ে।

কোটি প্রাণের এ শহরে অনেক জায়গা, কিন্তু আমার জায়গাটা কোথাও নেই! বাড়ির ছাদ, গলির সরু রাস্তা, বিশ্ববিদ্যালয়ের খোলা উদ্যান, রাস্তার মোড় কিংবা ঘরের দেয়াল এসব কিছুই আমার হয়েও হয় না আমার। মায়াময় এই নগরীতে আমি কিংবা আমার মতন অন্য আমি'রা সবসময়তেই একলা। একলা আমার এই আমি, এই আমার শহর আর এই আমার বাড়ি।

Parisha Maheshareen / পরিশা মহেশারিন, Dhaka, Bangladesh

চারশো বছরের পুরনো এই শহর ঢাকার চিরাচরিত রূপ আমার এই প্রবন্ধের অনুপ্রেরণা। এই শহরের প্রতিটি চার দেয়ালে জন্ম নেয় নতুন নতুন গল্পের। সেই গল্পগুলো তৈরি হয় কিছু সুখ কিছু বিষন্নতা, কিংবা কিছু পাওয়া কিছু না পাওয়ার গল্প নিয়ে। ক্লান্ত তরুণ মনের নিজস্ব কিছু বিষন্নতা আর তা থেকে নিজেই উত্তরণের পথ খুঁজে বের করার গল্পের ফসল আমার এই শব্দগুলো। শহরের রূপ আর তার সাথে মিশে যাওয়া নিজের অভিজ্ঞতার সেতুবন্ধন করে দিয়েছে কিছু কাল্পনিক অধ্যায়। নাগরিক জীবন, শেষ না হওয়া ছুটে চলা পথ, স্বপ্ন আর অস্বপ্নের দোলাচাল এই সবকিছু কে কেন্দ্র করে নিজেকে হারিয়ে যেতে না দেয়ার জরুরী খবর প্রকাশই আমার এই লেখার উদ্দেশ্য।

আত্মকথার উপাখ্যান

দেয়ালের পিঠে দেয়াল। তার পিঠে দেয়াল। পুরোনো, অপুরোনো আর আধা পুরোনো ইট-কাঠের এই ঢাকাকে মায়া নগরী বললে হয়তো ভুল হবে না। কালো কার্বনের মায়ায় আটকা পড়েছে নগরের কোটি মানুষ। গভীর রাতে এখানে কিছু দোকানে ওঠে কয়লা পোড়া কাবাবের ধোঁয়া, আবার কোথাও রঙ মেখে খদ্দেরের আশায় ঘুরে বেড়ায় পাথুরে মায়াপরী। যান্ত্রিক ভোরের আলো ফোটে "আসসালাতু থাইরুম মিনান নাওম" শব্দে। আবার গোধূলি বেলায় হয়তো কোথাও শোনা যায় ঢাক আর শঙ্খের মধুর ধ্বনি। দুপুরগুলো কখনো নিয়ে আসে ঝকঝকে রোদে ঘর্মাক্ত ক্লান্ত শরীর, হয়তো কখনো আবার রিকশা কিংবা মোটরযান গুলো আটকা পড়ে অলি-গলির জলাবদ্ধতায়। আপাদমস্তক নোংরা নির্বাসযোগ্য শহরের তালিকায় ওপর দিকে থাকা এই ঢাকাই আমার মতো কোটি প্রাণের ভালোবাসার শহর। অযত্রে অবহেলায় থাকা এই ঢাকার নিদর্শনগুলোও শিখে গেছে নিজেকে নিজে ভালোবাসবার মন্ত্র। চারদিকে ময়লা-জীবাণু-ক্ষুধার তাড়না সব মিলেমিশে প্রতিদিন এখানে জন্ম নেয় কোটি নতুন গল্পের অধ্যায়, আর সমাপ্তি হয় কত শত সমাপ্ত না হওয়া স্বপ্নের। প্রতি চার দেয়ালে জন্ম নেয় নতুন কোনো অভিনয়। রাস্তার পাশে পলিথিনে গড়ে ওঠা সংসার গুলোও দিনশেষের

ভালোবাসায় মত হয়। অপরাধে ভরপুর নোংরা এই শহরের মায়ায় অন্য দশ তরুণ তুকীর মতন আটকা পরেছি আমিও। প্রতিদিনের সূর্য গুলো নতুন করে হাতছানি দিয়ে ডেকে বলে, 'পালিয়ে যাও!' কিন্তু পালাবো পালাবো করে জীবনের বাইশটি বসন্ত পারি দিয়ে ফেললাম আমার এই মায়ার শহরের ইটের চারটে দেয়ালে। আমার এই চার দেয়াল রোজ আমাকে স্বপ্ন দেখায়। কিছু সুখের স্বপ্ন। কিছু ভুলে ভরা ভুল স্বপ্ন। এই শহরের কোনো এক কাক ডাকা ভোরে ধরণীর বুকে আমার প্রথম আগমন। এই শহরেই আমি হেঁটেছিলাম প্রথম। প্রথম গিয়েছিলাম স্কুল, প্রথম কৈশোর, প্রথম ভালোবাসা, প্রথম রাগ, প্রথম অভিমান, প্রথম তারুণ্য। শত শত প্রথমের ভিড়ে আটকে পড়ে প্রথম বাস্তবতাগুলোও। এই শহরে এই চার দেয়ালেই প্রথম অনুভূত হয়েছে স্বপ্ন ও অস্বপ্নের বাস্তবতা। এখানেই প্রথম জেনেছি সম্ভব ও অসম্ভবের মাঝের ফাঁকরটা কোথায় গেল। জেনেছি এর মাঝের অপেক্ষার গল্পটাও। কিছু বিষণ্নতা, কিছু অবাস্তবতাকে ঘিরেই যে এই শহর আমাকে বাঁচিয়ে রেখেছে আরও কিছু নতুন কার্বনে মাখা ভোরের সূর্য দেখবার অপেক্ষায়, এও এখন আর অজানা নয়। বিষণ্নতাগুলো কখনো নিয়ে যায় গভীর কুয়াশায় ঢাকা আচ্ছন্নতায়, আবার এই বিষণ্নতাই শক্তি যোগায় সামনে এগিয়ে যাবার। তবুও ভয় হয়। এই বুঝি হারিয়ে গেলাম। এই বুঝি মিলিয়ে গেলাম কোটি মানুষের এই শহরের ভিড়ে। দেয়াল থেকে ভেসে আসে নি:শব্দ চিৎকারের প্রতিধ্বনি 'পালিয়ে যাও! হারিয়ে যাও!' পরক্ষণেই অন্ধকার ঘরে তীর চিৎকার করে জেগে উঠে দেখি দুঃস্বপ্ন হাতছানি দিয়ে ডাকছে অদূরে। কিন্তু না। কোথাও যাবো না আমি। আমি আছি, আমি থাকবো। হাজারো নোংরা পুরুষের চাহনি, ঘরে ও বাহিরে নির্যাতন ও অনির্যাতনের গল্পগুলোর শেষেও আমি থাকবো। এই শহরের কালোর মায়ায় হারিয়ে গিয়েও ফিরে আসবো বার বার। হয়তো এই ফিরে আসাই আমার মতন আমি ও আমাদের গল্প। কার্বনের কালোর মায়ায় ঢাকা এই 'ঢাকায়' সকল অশুভ'র উর্ধ্বে শেষ হয়ে যাবে না আমার মতন এই আমি'দের গল্প।

Fahmida Afroz KanokSrabon / ফাহমিদা আফরোজ কনক শ্রাবণ, Dhaka, Bangladesh

Thanks to Sampad for allowing such an incredible opportunity where we could be encouraged to write about our city, our home and bring out the unenlightened stories of this city life. This is a chance for me to highlight the hidden faces of the women, how they fall back every time and lack to embrace the best options of their lives.

মনিরাদের ঘর থাকেনা, ওরা ঘর জুড়ে দেয়

যাদিও বাংলায় এর অর্থ দাঁড়ায়, আমার শহর আমার ঘরবাড়ি। আর এই মুহূর্তে, বাংলাদেশের প্রেক্ষাপটে একজন নারী হিসেবে আমার কাছে এর মানে এই, আমার শহর কি আমার ঘর? হতে পারে এই ঘর তাকে বলে দেয়, কী চাও এই শহরের কাছে? অথবা ঘরকে ঘিরে যে মানুষের সম্পর্কের পারিপার্শ্বিকতায় তোমার বাস, তা থেকে তুমি কেমন করে তোমার শহরে নিজেকে পরিচিত করবে? কী হলে তোমার ঘর তোমার কাছে ততটাই গুরুত্বপূর্ণ, শান্তির, সুখের, আশীর্বাদের?

ঘুম ভাঙে প্রায় ষাটোর্ধ মনিরার, তাহাজ্জুদ পড়ার জন্য প্রতি রাতেই। ইদানিং হাঁটুসহ বিভিন্ন জায়গায় ব্যাথাটাও জানান দেয় বিগত ৫০ বছরের পরিশ্রমে ক্লান্ত অবসাদগ্রস্ত শরীর। কিন্তু মনের কাছে বিন্দুমাত্র হারেনি, বেঁচে থাকতে ক্লান্তির কাছে নয় পরাজয়। আবারও মনে পড়লো লুবনা আপার কথাগুলো! 'নারী', তার নাকি আবার নিজের শহর বা ঘর, এমনও হয় নাকি?

মাত্র ১৫ বছর বয়সে গিয়েছিল স্বামীর বাড়িতে, অনেকগুলা ভাইবোনের ঘরে জন্ম নেয়া মনিরার খুব আদরযত্ন না হলেও অনাদর ছিল না মোটেও। যদিও পড়াশুনার প্রতি প্রচুর আগ্রহ ছিল মনিরার, কিছুটা আফসোস সেখানে রয়েই গেল স্কুলটা পার হওয়া হলো না বলে। তবুও সে আজ অন্যের ঘরকে নিজের ঘর বানাবার স্বপ্নেই বিভোরা। সে সন্তানসম্ভবা।

ঝঞ্ঝাট বাঁধলো তখন, যখন সে পুত্র সন্তান কোলে নিয়ে দু'মাস পর বাপের বাড়ি থেকে ফিরলো স্বামীর ঘরে! তখনই সে প্রথম জানলো তার স্বামী কতটা চরিত্রহীন! পরনারীর

প্রতি আসক্ত স্বামীর অসৎ চরিত্রের নমুনার সাক্ষী হয়েই একমাত্র সন্তানের হাত ধরেই বাপেরবাড়ি ফিরে আসে। সে সময় ব্যাপারটা এত সহজ ছিল না মোটেও! বাবার অনুমতি নিয়ে নিজেকে নতুন পথের দিশার সন্ধানে যাবার ইচ্ছায় নামলো সন্তানকে কোলে নিয়েই। বুঝে গেল বাঁচতে হলে তাকে যুদ্ধে নামতেই হবে, এই প্রতিজ্ঞা নিয়েই বদলে যায় শহর-ও-ঘর বদলানোর গল্প।

হারিয়ে গেল তার সংসার, ঘর, পড়াশোনা হয়তো হবেই না! কিন্তু এত ছোট বাচ্চাসহ কী কাজ তার পক্ষে করা সম্ভব? সে তো স্কুলের গন্ডিই অতিক্রম করেনি।

অতঃপর রাজধানী! ছেলেকে নিচে গ্যারেজে খেলতে দিয়ে অন্যের সন্তানের সেবাযত্নের দায়িত্বপালন করে মা গভর্নেস। মাঝেমাঝে শুধু থাবার খাইয়ে আসে, সারাদিনের ক্লান্তির পর মা ও ছেলের দেখা হয় রাত নয়টায়। তখন পড়তে বসলে ছেলেটি প্রচন্ড কান্নাকাটি জুড়ে বসে, মাকে আর বইখাতা ধরতেই দেয় না। অগত্যা মা সারাদিনের সোহাগ অনাদরে ফেলে রাখা সন্তানের বরাদ্দ নিয়ে ছেলেটিকে থাইয়ে দিয়ে ঘুমপাড়াতে গিয়ে নিজেও ঘুমিয়ে পড়ে। তবে কি আর তার পড়াশোনা হবে না?

বাড়ির গৃহকর্তা অমায়িক মানুষ, তাঁর বিশাল সংসারের ঐশ্বর্যের ভিড়ে তিনি আবিষ্কার করেন নির্লিপ্ত, নির্লোভ, দায়িত্বশীল, কর্তব্যপরায়ণ এক ধার্মিক নারীকে! একদিন তাকে ডেকে নিভৃতে প্রশ্ন রাখলেন, তোমার সন্তানের সাথে আরও বেশ কিছু শিশুর দায়িত্ব তোমাকে দেয়া হলে, তুমি কি পারবে তাদের দায়িত্ব নিতে?

নির্বোধ চাহনি, একসমুদ্র জিজ্ঞাসা! এর মানে কী? আবার কোথায়, কোন শহরে, কোন ঘরে তার ঠিকানা হবে! তার ভাগ্যে কি শুধুই ঘর বদলের এই খেলা চলতে থাকবে? কিছুই করার নেই, সন্তান-সহ কেই বা ঠাঁই দেবে? বাঁচতে হলে এই পরীক্ষায় উত্তীর্ণ হতেই হবে তাকে! সেই শুরু। ৮১ সালে খুলনা জেলার অজ পাড়া-গাঁয়ের থেকে বেরিয়ে আসা বছর বিশের এক লাবণ্যময়ী কন্যা হঠাৎ করেই নারীতে রূপান্তরিত!

রাজধানীর একপাশে বর্ধিত নগরীর এক অংশে চারিদিকে জঙ্গল, ঝোপঝাড়, ঝিলের জলে ঘেরা একটি জমিতে টিন শেডের একটি ঘরে আবারও ঘর বাধে!

"এই শহরের একটি ঘরে সে বসত করে যার কেউ নেই, আছে হয়তো অনেক শতেক তারাই এখন তার সব হয়"

শুরু হলো নূতন ঘরের নূতন সদস্যদের সাথে নূতন পথচলা, আর যাদের নিয়ে শুরু তাদের বলা এই হলো- তোমাদের অভিভাবক, 'বাবা-মা'! যে সমাজে প্রায়শই পিতা মানে জন্মদাতা, আর মা মানে? দিন রাত্রি এক করে পরের- সন্তানকেও আপন করে এক লহমায় বুঝিয়ে দেয়া, একথালা ভাত দশ জনকে ভাগ করে খাইয়ে দেয়া, একটি হ্যারিকেন জ্বালিয়ে দশটি বাচ্চাকে পড়াশোনা করানো এবং এদের মা হয়ে ওঠার জন্য যতরকম ত্যাগ, তিতিক্ষা, পরিশ্রম, একাগ্রতার প্রয়োজন। লোকের কাছে এদের জন্য বিনয়ের সাথে অনুনয় উপস্থাপন করে প্রতিষ্ঠানের প্রতি অন্যদের দৃষ্টি আকর্ষণ করে একসময় তিনশো সন্তানের 'মা' হয়ে ওঠার প্রচেষ্টায় নিজেকে এতটাই ইতিবাচক উদাহরণ তৈরি করলো, যা হয়ে মা মনিরা ব্যক্তি মনিরাকে হারিয়ে ফেলে। মুছে যায় তার একমাত্র সন্তানের বেড়ে ওঠায় তার কত কী স্বপ্ন ছিল। নিজেকে শিক্ষিত নামের একটি দুটো কাগজে বন্দী করার অভিলাষের গল্প, বিধাতার ইচ্ছায় তার চেয়ে শতগুন তাদের প্রাপ্তি হয়ে যায়, যা হয়তো তপস্যা থাকে অনেকের।

এই মনিরাকে কোন শহর তৈরি করেছে এই জাহ্নবী রূপে? আজও এই শহরেই সে নিজের একটি ঘরের প্রতীক্ষায়, তার এই আত্মপ্রত্যয়, নিজেকে প্রবঞ্চনা, আত্মসমর্পণ সব কি ছিল ইচ্ছাকৃত, কে জানতে চেয়েছে? যে মা নিজের একটি গৃহকোণের আশায় এই অবধি শুধু আপন মহিমায় তার মাতৃত্বের মাধুরি ঢালছে যে অনাথ এতিম সন্তানদের জন্য। গত চল্লিশেরও বেশি সময়ে কেউ কি জানতে চেয়েছে পরিবর্তনের এই শহরে তার মন কী চায়? তার নিজের ঘর, সে ঘর কেমন হবে, সেখানে কি তার সন্তানকে নিয়েই থাকতে চান? নাকি অন্য কোন চাওয়ায় তার নিজস্ব ভাবনাগুলো লুকানো?

এ শহর তাকে নিয়ে কী ভাবছে, সে কি তাকে বুঝিয়ে দিয়েছে এতদিন কোন আবহে কী ঘর তার জন্য বরাদ্দ ছিল? মুনিরাদের শহর বা ঘর কখনোই বুঝি থাকে না, তারা মানুষের ভালোবাসা আর বিশ্বাসের ঘরে বসত করে। তাদের শহর তাদের কাছে ফাল্গুনে জন্মানো নতুন পাতার মতো যার ছায়ায় কিছুক্ষন দাঁড়ায়, কিন্তু ঘরই তার বৃক্ষের শিকড়! তাই যে ঘরেই তার অস্তিত্বের বসত, সেখানেই সে তার শ্রম ভালোবাসা বিশ্বাসের সবটুকু দিয়েই তার যত্ন নেয়, পানি ঢালে, পরিচর্যা করে। নিজের বিনোদনের সততার পাখা মেলে ওড়ে! নারী

মুনিরার ঘর বাঁধার স্বপ্ন-শখ কখনোই মেটে না, তার সামাজিক সংসার নামক খাঁচায় থাকার স্বপ্ন পূরন না হলেও সে যত্ন করে গড়ে তোলে একটি করে স্বপ্নের ভীত, অন্য কন্যার মনের গভীরে।

আমার শহর আমার ঘর আমাকে কতটা দেবে বা আমি কতটা নেব, বোধ করি তা ব্যক্তির সম্পূর্ণ নিজস্ব ভাবনার প্রতিফলন ঘটে তার কর্ম বা মানসিক ইচ্ছার উপর। নারী জন্মগত ভাবেই শক্তির আধার, তার কর্মক্ষমতা সর্বকালেই তুলনাহীন, যার জঠরে মানব সন্তান ধারণ করে তার স্নায়ু প্রসব যন্ত্রনা সহ্য করে তাকে কর্মে ও দক্ষতায় প্রগতিশীল করে গড়ে তোলার সুযোগ যদি তার ঘর দেয়, তা থেকে এমন হাজার মুনিরার পক্ষে তার নিজেকে চেনার পরিধি তৈরি হয়। আমাদের শহর পারে শিক্ষার বিস্তার লাভে প্রগতিশীল মুক্তির উন্মোচন হয় এমন কিছু প্রতিষ্ঠান তৈরি করতে যেখানে ভিন্ন ভিন্ন প্রতিভার বিকাশ ঘটে এমন নারীকে শিক্ষায় সংস্কৃতির উন্নয়নের নুতন দিগন্তের সাথে পরিচয় করিয়ে দিতে।

রাষ্ট্রের উন্নয়নে দেশের অর্ধেক নারীর শহর যদি তার চিন্তাভাবনার প্রসার ঘটাতে সুবিধা-বঞ্চিত নারীর ঘরের দরজায় গিয়ে দাঁড়ায় তবে বাংলাদেশের মানচিত্র এতটাই আলোকিত হবে, আগামীতে বার্মিংহামে নয় আগামীর নারী বাঙালি রমনীয় গুণে, জ্ঞানে, কর্মদক্ষতায়, শিক্ষায়, প্রজ্ঞায় ছড়াবে আলো, বিশ্বের যে কোন প্রতিযোগিতার শীর্ষে।

চাইলে যে কোনো শহরেই ঘর গড়ে তোলা যায়, কিন্তু সে ঘর আমার কতটা, তা শুধু মুনিরাই ভালো বলতে পারবে। তবুও নারী দিয়ে যায় নিঃশব্দে, নিঃশেষে। তবুও এই শহরে আমার একটা ঘর তো ছিল, যেখানে দিন শেষে আমার অবসন্নতার অবসান ঘটে।

Sania -E- Aferin / সানিয়া-ই-আফেরিন, Noakhali, Bangladesh

এই প্রজেক্টে নিজের স্বপ্নের কথা বলার সুযোগ পেয়ে অনুপ্রাণিত হয়েছি। নিজের মনের কথা বলার এমন পরিসর সহজে মেলে না। কর্তৃপক্ষকে ধন্যবাদ জানাই এমন আয়োজনের জন্য।

নারীদের জন্য নতুন দিগন্তের দেখা দিল এই আয়োজন।

আমার শহর আমার বাড়ি

ছোটবেলা থেকে দেখছি আমার মায়ের কোনো বাড়ি নেই! শ্বশুরবাড়ি কিংবা বাবার বাড়ি কোনটাই তো তাঁর নিজস্ব নয়। একবার মাকে প্রশ্ন করলে দেখি খুব মন খারাপ হলো তাঁর। বললেন, তুই পড়াশোনা করে বড় হয়ে মাকে একটা বাড়ি করে দিস! আমিও তখন থেকে স্বপ্ন দেখি মায়ের একটা বাড়ি হবে। আমার নিজেরও একটা বাড়ি হবে! বয়স আমার তিরিশের কোঠা পেরিয়েছে, এখনও স্বপ্নপূরণ হয়নি। তবু স্বপ্ন দেখে যাচ্ছি। গ্রামে আমার বয়সী একটা অবিবাহিত মেয়ে থাকাটাই সমাজের বোঝা, সকলের মাথাব্যথার কারণ। প্রতিনিয়ত নিত্যনতুন আঘাত আসে। তবুও আমি বিচলিত নই, আমার সময় একদিন আসবেই। স্বপ্ন আমার পূরণ হবেই। আমার বাড়ি হবে আমার নিরাপদ আশ্রয়, যেখানে কোনো উৎকণ্ঠা থাকবে না। আমার বাড়ির সাথে সাথে আমার গ্রামটাও হয়ে উঠবে নারীদের অভয়ারণ্য ,যেখানে নারী শুধু নারী নয়, মানুষ হিসেবে বিবেচিত হবে। প্রতিটি নারী নিজেকে প্রতিষ্ঠিত করে বাস্তবেই নিজের বাড়ি গড়তে পারবে।

বহুবছর আগে আমাদের গ্রামে বেসরকারি উদ্যোগে নারীদের জন্য একটা মার্কেট হয়। কিন্তু সাহস করে নারীরা না আসায় পুরুষরাই চালাচ্ছে এটা। আমি চাই একদিন নারীরা সব বাঁকা চোখ উপেক্ষা করে নিজেদের অধিকার বুঝে নেবে।

আশার কথা এখন বেশ কয়েকজন নারী এই অজপাড়া গ্রামে থেকেই অনলাইনে পণ্য বিক্রি করছে!

তাই স্বপ্ন আজ পাখা মেলে আরো অনেক দূরে। আমরাই গড়ব আমাদের বাড়ি, গ্রাম, শহর, আমাদের দেশ। বিশ্বব্রহ্মাণ্ডও হবে আমাদের বিচরণক্ষেত্র।

Sania -E- Aferin / সানিয়া-ই-আফেরিন, Noakhali, Bangladesh

আমি নারী হিসেবে নিজের অবস্থান নিয়ে সর্বদা যে বিড়ম্বনা নিয়ে থাকি, আর স্বপ্ন যেমন দেখি তা ভেবেই এই আয়োজনে সাড়া দিয়ে এমন লেখা।

নিরাপদ নগরে স্বপ্ন-বাড়ি

আমার হাসিটা আজকাল কান্নার মত হয়ে গেছে,

কিংবা হাসতেই ভুলে গেছি।

প্রতিদিন নতুন পত্রিকায় পুরাতন খবর আসছে,

অথবা একই খবর দেখছি।

প্রতিটি দিন তাই আর আলাদা মনে হয় না।

নারী হবার আজন্ম পাপ যেন পিছু ছাড়েনা।

এ শহরটা আমার হয়েও যেন আমার নয়,

মায়ায় জড়ানো বাড়িটাও অচিন মনে হয়।

নারীদের যেন নিজের কিছু থাকতে নেই!

অথচ, মিশে আছে এসব আমার অস্তিত্বেই।

কে রাখে এই অস্তিত্বের খবর?

কে দাম দেয় সাহসী স্বপ্নের?

জীবনের মূল্য দিয়েও তাই স্বপ্ন ফেরি করে যাই,

দুঃসাহস নিয়ে অনুচিত স্বপ্ন দেখে অপবাদ কুড়াই।

স্বপ্ন দেখি ভয়হীন পদচারণার,

স্বপ্ন দেখি আকাশ ছোঁয়ার!

সময় এখন সব শেকল ভাঙার,

সব বাধা পেরিয়ে নিজের অস্তিত্ব গড়ার।

আমার স্বপ্নে সাজাব নিরাপদ শহরে আমার বাড়ি,
বিশ্বকে জানিয়ে দেবো, 'আমি নারী, আমিও পারি'।
আমি ভালবাসি আমার অস্তিত্ব,আমার দেশ।
নতুন দিনে হারিয়ে যাক সকল না পাওয়ার রেশ।
আগামীর পৃথিবী নারীর হাসিতে ভরে উঠুক,
নিরাপদ নগর সাহসী পদচারণায় মুখরিত হোক।

Sujana Afrin Oishee / সুজানা আফরিন ঐশী, Dhaka, Bangladesh

First of all, my mother inspires me to write in this event. Then the title 'My City My Home' inspires me to think about my own city, to think about my own home, to think about that if I am really happy and safe in this city or not.

পরের জন্মে তুমি আমাদের হবে তো শহর?

ছোটো থেকে বড় হয়ে ওঠা যেখানে তা হচ্ছে এই ঢাকা শহর। আমার প্রিয় আর সবচেয়ে পরিচিত ঢাকা শহর।

আমার জন্ম এখানে নয় যদিও। জন্ম আমার শরীয়তপুরে। সেখানে নানুবাড়িতে এক ছোট্টো ঘরে আমার জন্ম হয়। কাছেই দাদুবাড়ি। এই দুই বাড়ি মিলিয়ে আমার জীবনের প্রথম দেড়টা বছর কেটে যায়। এরপর ১.৫ বছর বয়সে আমার প্রথম শহরে আসা চাচ্চুর হাত ধরে। এবং যখন আমার বয়স ২.৫ বছর তখন একেবারে শহরে চলে আসি।

এ শহরে এসেই আমার সবচেয়ে বড় ধাক্কা ছিল যখন আমার বয়স ৪ এর মতো। প্রচুর দুষ্ট ছিলাম আমি। সারাদিনই প্রায় একটা ডানপিটে বাচ্চার মতো বাইরে খেলতাম, না হয় অন্যদের ঘরে পরে থাকতাম। ওই ৪ বছরের আমার যেন কোনো ক্লান্তিই ছিল না। একদিন সন্ধ্যায় এক আংকেল এর রুমে যাই আমি। খেলতে গিয়েছিলাম! কিন্তু সে আমার সাথে এমন এক খেলাই খেললো যে আমি ওই রুমে আর কোনোদিন যাইনি। ঐ বয়সের সেই ছোট্টো জুলিয়া কিছুই বুঝতো না। কিন্তু সে এতটুকু বুঝেছিল যে সেই খেলাটা ভালো ছিল না। যেই খেলাতে মায়ের সামনে ছাড়াও অন্য কারো সামনে নগ্ন হতে হয়, এ আবার কেমন খেলা? যে খেলা খেলার পর আম্মুকে বলা যাবেনা এমন শর্ত জুড়ে দেয়া হয় এ আবার কেমন খেলা?

নাহ, এ খেলা জুলিয়া আর খেলবে না। না না, একদম ই না।

আর কোনদিন জুলিয়া সেই দুষ্ট আংকেল এর ঘরে যায়নি।

এরপরও আমি নিয়মিত এ রাস্তায় সে রাস্তায় খেলতে যেতাম, এ মহল্লা থেকে সেই মহল্লায় সে ছুটে চলে যেতাম। আর এদিকে মা প্রতিদিন আমাকে খুঁজে হয়রান হতো। আর আমি প্রতিদিন মাকে চিন্তায় ফেলে দিয়ে শৈশবের আনন্দটাকে উপভোগ করতে ছুটে যেতাম যেখানে আমার ইচ্ছা হতো।

কিছুদিন পর আমি অন্য আরেকটা আংকেল এর রুমে যাই। কিন্তু একি! আশ্চর্য! সেই আংকেলও আমাকে কেমন অদ্ভুত এক খেলা দেখালো। আর মাকে বলতে না করলো। না না, এ খেলা তো ছোট্টো জুলিয়া খেলতে চাইত না। সে তো পুতুল খেলবে।

এমনি করে বয়স যখন ৫ এর কাছাকাছি তখন নতুন এক বাসায় যাই, নতুন বাসা ভীষণ বড়ো। খুব খুশি হয়েছিলাম ছোট্টো সেই আমি। কিছুদিন পর স্কুলে ভর্তি হই। জীবন যেন এক গাদা গোলাপের চেয়েও বেশি সুন্দর তখন। তবে সেই গোলাপের কিছু কাঁটা যেন জীবনকে মাঝে মাঝেই অতির্ণ করে দিচ্ছিল। সেই কাঁটার এতই বিষ যে আজ ১৬ বছর বয়সেও তা যেন ভুলতে পারি না। কী করেই বা ভুলবো? জীবনের প্রতিটা ধাপই যে সেই একই, সেই দুষ্ট আংকেলদের মতো আরো এমন হাজারো দুষ্ট আংকেলের দেখা পেয়েছি। কখনো সেই দুষ্ট লোক ছিল নেহাতই অপরিচিত। কখনো বা খুব কাছের কেউ। এ তো ছিল বাইরের কথা। আমার ঘরেই কি আমি নিরাপদ ছিলাম? নিরাপদ ছিল সেই ছোট্টো জুলিয়া? সে কি স্বাচ্ছন্দ্যে তার বাসায় বেড়াতে আসা আংকেলগুলোর কোলে বসতে পারতো? উত্তরটা হলো- নাহ! জুলিয়া পারতো না।

আমার বাসা থেকে অন্য মেয়েদের বাসার মতো এত বাধা ছিল না। আমার সকল শখ পূরণ করতে দেয়া হতো। চাহিদা ছিল না। তবু মনের কথা বুঝে নিয়েই সব কিছু পূরণ করতো আমার বাবা-মা। একটু যখন বড় হলাম তখন আর এসব দুষ্ট লোকেরা খুব বেশি কাছে ভিড়তে পারতো না। তবে অষ্টম শ্রেনীর সেই বিভীষিকাময় ঘটনা আমি আজও ভুলতে পারি না। যা শুধু আমিই জানি। কোনোদিন কাউকে বলতে পারিনি। আজ এই গল্পেই তার প্রথম আভাস প্রকাশ পেলো।

কিন্তু যখন একটু বড় হচ্ছিলাম তখন থেকেই শুরু হলো ভিন্ন এক ধরনের কাঁটার অত্যাচার। কারণ তখন যে আমি একটা ফুটন্ত গোলাপ। তাই চারপাশের কাঁটাগুলোও আর আগের মতো মসৃণ ছিলনা। এখনো সেই সময়টাই চলছে। এখন আর আগের মতো পরিবারের কাছ থেকে সেই স্বাধীনতা পাইনা। কারণ আমি যে এখন ১৬ বছর বয়সী এক ফুটন্ত গোলাপ। আমাকে যে নিজেকে লুকিয়ে রাখতে হবে। বাইরের কাঁটার আঁচড় থেকে রক্ষা করতে হবে। কিন্তু আমি যে অবাধে উড়তে চাই। সারা দুনিয়াটা ঘুরতে চাই। তবে কেন আমার গন্ডি এত ছোট করে দেয়া হচ্ছে? সারা দুনিয়া তো নয়, বরং কেন আমাকে আমার শহরটাও ঘুরতে দেয়া হচ্ছে না? কেন?

ঘুরতে দেয়া হলেও আমি তো এই শহরে আর নিরাপদ বোধ করিনা। কেন? তবে কি এই শহর আমার নয়?

তবে কি আমি এই শহরের এক আগন্তুক মাত্র? নাহ! এ তো হয় না। এই শহরেই যে আমার বেড়ে ওঠা। আমার কথা বলতে শেখা। আমার চলতে শেখা। তবে কেন এত বাধা সেই শহরেই। কেন এত কাঁটার আঁচড়?

আমি এখনো স্বাধীন নই কেন? একা একা মুক্ত পাখির মতো চাইলেই ডানা মেলে উড়তে কেন পারি না আমি? তবে কি ঘর বন্দী হয়ে থাকার জন্যই আমার জন্ম হলো? আর আমার মতো আরো শত শত জুলিয়া যারা নিজেদের কথা গুলো আমাকে মতোই প্রকাশ করতে পারছে না। যারা আমার মতোই মুক্ত পাখির মতো ডানা মেলে উড়তে চায়। কিন্তু বাইরের কাঁটার আঁচড়ের ভয়ে তাদের ডানাগুলোকে অপরিপক্ক অবস্থাতেই কেটে দেয়া হয়। আচ্ছা, তবে কি তাদের বেড়ে ওঠার জায়গা সেই প্রিয় শহর তাদের নিজের না? কেন আমরা আমাদের চির চেনা-পরিচিত জায়গাতেই এতটা অনিরাপদ? কেন পদে পদে দুষ্ট আংকেলের হাতে ধরা পড়তে হয়? কেনই বা কাঁটার আঁচড়ের ভয়ে লুকিয়ে বাঁচতে হয়? কেন একটু বড় হলেই নতুন এক শহরকে আপন করে নিতে হয় নিজের চিরচেনা এই শহরকে ছেড়ে?

প্রিয় শহর তুমি কেন আমাকে চিরদিন তোমার বুকে আগলে রাখতে পারো না? আমি কেন মুক্তমনে চিন্তাবিহীন তোমার বুকে ঘুরে বেড়াতে পারি না? কী দোষ

আমার? আমিও যে তোমার সৌন্দর্য উপভোগ করতে চাই। আমিও যে দুপুরের রোদে তোমার অলিতে-গলিতে ঘুরে ঘুরে তোমাকে চিনতে চাই, দেখতে চাই। আমি যে সেই ছোট্টো জুলিয়ার মতো সবখানে দৌড়ে বেড়াতে চাই। তবে সেই ভয়ংকর খেলার ভয়ে কেন আমাকে লুকিয়ে থাকতে হয়? সেই কাঁটার আঁচড়ের ভয়ে কেন আমাকে পালিয়ে বেড়াতে হয়? তুমি কি আমাকে নিরাপদ রাখতে পারো না? আমার মতো এই শহরের আরো হাজারো ফুটন্ত গোলাপের রক্ষাকারিনী তুমি কি হতে পারো না?

যে শহরে জুলিয়ারা ছোট থেকে বড় আমৃত্যু নিজের মতো করে বাঁচতে পারে, যেখানে আমার মতো ফুটন্ত গোলাপেরা প্রাণ খুলে হাসতে পারে, গাইতে পারে আর এই শহরের অলিগলির মায়ায় পড়ে সারাটা জীবন নির্ভয়ে কাটাতে পারে।

তবে কি এই শহর আমাদের নয়? আমার মতো ফুটন্ত গোলাপ আর জুলিয়ার মতো ছোট্টো শিশুদের জন্য কি এই শহর নয়?

নাকি আমরাই এই শহরের নই?

তবুও শত বাধা আর আমাকে আপন করে না নেয়ার পরও এই শহরটা আমার। আমার বেড়ে ওঠার এই জায়গাটা আমার। হে শহর, তুমি আমাকে আপন করে না নিলেও তুমি আমার। আমি তোমার বুকেই শান্তি খুঁজে পাই।

এই জীবনে তোমার বুকে স্বাচ্ছন্দ্যে ঘুরে বেড়াতে পারিনি। যদি আর কখনো পৃথিবীতে আসি তবে নিশ্চই তখন তুমিও আমাদের হবে। সেই আশা নিয়েই আমি শান্তিতে মরতে চাই, তোমার বুকেই শেষ নিশ্বাস নিতে চাই পরজন্মে তোমাকে আরও আপন করে পাওয়ার আশা নিয়ে।

আমায় তোমার বুকে আমৃত্যু থাকতে দেবে তো প্রিয় শহর, প্রিয় ভালোবাসার জায়গা- আমার ঢাকা?

Tanjila Taraiyan / তানযীলা তারাইয়্যান, Sylhet, Bangladesh

আমি আমার শহরকে নিজে লিখতে পারবো যেখানে আমি বড় হয়েছি বেড়ে উঠেছি, আমার শহর যাকে আমি ভালোবাসি, আমি যাকে নিয়ে গর্বিত এটাই সবচেয়ে বড় অনুপ্রেরণা।

তারার শহর

আমি তারা। না আসমানের তারা নই! আমার শহরের সবুজ ঘাসের উপর, পাহাড়ের ঢালের উপর, চা-বাগানের মেঠো পথের উপর আর সুরমা নদীর তটে হাসন রাজার গান গাইতে গাইতে বেড়ে উঠা মেয়ে তারা। দুটি পাতা একটি কুঁড়ি, শাহজালাল-শাহপরান, ৩৬০ আউলিয়ার শহর যেখানে, সেখানেই আমার বাড়ি। অর্থাৎ সিলেটে।

সিলেটের আবরণ পাহাড়। পাহাড় দিয়ে ঘেরা শিলং আর সিলেটের সীমান্ত। সেই আবরণের স্নিগ্ধ বাতাসে দোল খায় চায়ের ঘ্রাণ। কারণ সিলেটে রয়েছে অজস্র চায়ের বাগান।

আমার শহরে মণিপুরী সম্প্রদায় এবং বাঙালিরা মিলে মিশে তৈরি করেছে আত্মার বন্ধন। বাঙালিরা ভালোবেসে গায়ে তুলে নিয়েছে মণিপুরী শাড়ি। সেই শাড়ি দাপটের সাথে সারা বাংলাদেশ দাপিয়ে চলেছে। এখানকার মাটিতে শায়িত আছে ওলি আউলিয়া শাহজালাল-শাহপরান থেকে শুরু করে গানের রাজা হাসন রাজা। বঙ্গবীর এম এ জি ওসমানীও সিলেটের সন্তান।

মন ভালো থাকলে সিলেটের মানুষ গান ধরে। বাউল গান, হাসন রাজার গান। আর মন খারাপ থাকলে? সিলেটে থাকলে মন খারাপ থাকতেই পারে না। পাহাড়ের কোল ঘেষে ঝনঝন শব্দে বয়ে চলা হামহাম বা মাধবকুন্ডু জলপ্রপাত মন খারাপ ভাসিয়ে নিয়ে যায়। বাংলাদেশের একমাত্র মিঠাপানির সোয়াম্প ফরেস্টও বৃহত্তর সিলেটে। আছে হাকালুকি, টাংগুয়ার মতো হাওর এবং হাওরের তাজা মাছ। আছে জাফলং, বিছানাকান্দি এবং সাদা পাথরের মতো পাথর নির্ভর দর্শনীয় স্থান। যেইসব জায়গায় বাংলার রূপ খুঁজে

পাওয়া যায়। বাংলাদেশকে সৌন্দর্যের রাণী বলা হয়ে তার মাথায় শোভিত তাজের অনেকাংশ জুড়ে আছে সিলেট।

আমার বাড়ির পাশেই রয়েছে টিলা। তাই জায়গাটার নাম টিলাগড়। চা-বাগান যেতে লাগে মিনিট দশেক। ছেলেবেলায় মন থারাপ হলেই আমি টিলায় চলে যেতাম। তারপর চেঁচিয়ে বলতাম "আমি একদিন আকাশের তারা হবো, মুক্ত বিহঙ্গ হবো"। তা প্রতিধ্বনি হতো অন্তত পাঁচবার। আর আমার মন ভালো হয়ে যেত। একটু বড় হতেই যখন চা পাতার মর্ম বুঝতে শিখেছি তখন চা বাগানে গিয়ে তাকিয়ে থাকতাম বিস্তৃত সবুজ বিছানা সদৃশ চা বাগানের দিকে। গল্প করেছি চা বাগানের শ্রমিকদের সাথে। শুনেছি তাদের দুঃখের কথা, কষ্টের কথা। যা মিশে আছে চা পাতায়।

টিলায় বসে বসে পড়েছি জীবনানন্দ। পড়েছি রবীন্দনাথ। রবীন্দনাথ পড়তে পড়তে ভেবেছি বড় হয়ে ফেরিওয়ালা হবো। চুড়ি চাই.. চুড়ি চাই হেঁকে পাহাড়ে পাহাড়ে ঘুরে বেড়াবো। চীনা পুতুলও থাকবে সেই ঝুলিতে। বাচ্চারা এসে এসে ঘিরে ধরবে আর আমি পুতুল দিয়ে তাদের মুখের হাসি আরো প্রসারিত করবো। বড় হতে হতে সেই ঝুলি ভরে উঠেছে গল্পে। এখন মনে হয় গল্প ফেরি করলে মন্দ হয় না। আমার গল্প, আমার শহরের গল্প, শহরের মানুষগুলোর গল্প, তাদের থাবারের স্বাদের গল্প। ওহ থাবারের কথা বলতে তো ভুলেই গেলাম।

আমার শহরের আছে নিজস্ব থাবারের স্বাদ। সিলেটিদের প্রিয় থাবারের মধ্যে অন্যতম হচ্ছে শুটকি ভর্তা আর সাতকড়া দিয়ে গরুর গোস্তের ঝোল। সাথে হাওরের তাজা তাজা মাছের তরকারি। ভোজন রসিকদের হাত চেটে থাওয়ার জন্য যথেষ্ট। ভালো কিছু রান্না হলে তা পাশের বাড়ির লোকদের না দিয়ে থাওয়া যায় নাকি? সিলেটিরা এই কথা মনে প্রাণে বিশ্বাস করে। হোক তা সাতকড়া বা শুটকি, পাশের বাড়ির মানুষদের পাতে তা উঠবেই। আমার শহরের মানুষ একে অন্যের সাথে দেখা হলেই হাসি দিয়ে বলে "বালা নি"। অর্থাৎ সিলেটি ভাষায় জিজ্ঞেস করে ভালো আছেন তো। ঈদ, পূজা, বড়দিন, নববর্ষ সবাই মিলেমিশে একসাথে উদযাপন করে।

কোন দেশের খনিজ সম্পদ সে দেশকে অনেকটা এগিয়ে রাখে। বাংলাদেশের বিপুল খনিজ সম্পদের অনেকটা সিলেট থেকে। সিলেটে আছে বিভিন্ন গ্যাস ক্ষেত্র, যা বাংলাদেশের মানুষের গ্যাসের চাহিদা অনেকাংশে মেটায়।

প্রাকৃতিক সৌন্দর্য হোক বা মানুষের আতিথেয়তা, আমার শহরকে নিয়ে আমি গর্বিত। বাংলাদেশের প্রথম ডিজিটাল নগরী হলো সিলেট, মানে আমার শহর। যেখানে রয়েছে আমার বাড়ি। যদিও বাড়িটা আমার নিজের নয়, শহরটাও হয়তো নয়। কারণ আমার পৈত্রিক নিবাস নোয়াখালী। কিন্তু বাবার চাকরি সূত্রে জন্ম থেকেই আমি সিলেটে থাকি। তাই নোয়াখালীকে যতটা না আমার বলে মনে হয় তারচেয়ে অনেক গুন বেশি আপন বলে মনে হয় সিলেটকে। সিলেটের বাতাসে মিশে আছে আমার নিশ্বাস। সিলেটের আকাশে প্রতিদিন জমা হচ্ছে আমার গল্প, যা জানান দিচ্ছে, হ্যাঁ সিলেট আমার শহর। তাই একটুখানি পাহাড়ের সাথে গল্প করে বা চা পাতার সাথে ফিসফিসিয়ে কথা বলে তৃপ্তির সাথে বাঁচতে চাই এই শহরে।

খারাপ লাগে তখন, যখন দেখি পাহাড়গুলো ধীরে ধীরে কেটে ফেলা হচ্ছে। নদীগুলো ভরাট করা হচ্ছে। সেদিন একটা টিলা কাটার শব্দে দৌড়ে যেতেই শুনতে পেলাম আর্তনাদ। সিলেট আমায় বলছে "জানো আমার সব রঙ বিবর্ণ হয়ে যাচ্ছে। আমি হচ্ছি নিষ্প্রভ, মলিন। আমার দম বন্ধ হয়ে আসছে। আমাকে বাঁচাও, তারা। "

আমি তাকে আশ্বাস দিয়ে বলতে পারিনি আমি তোমায় রক্ষা করবো। আমিই বাঁচাবো তোমায়। বলতে পারিনি আমি ফিরিয়ে আনবো তোমার রঙ। শুধু স্বার্থপরের মতো বলেছি, আমার শহর আমার দিনগুলো রঙিন করার জন্য আমি তোমায় ভালোবাসি।

Rahela Khurshid Zahan / রাহিলা খুরশিদ জাহান, Dhaka, Bangladesh

I am 70 years old and have many experiences in this city in gaining my independence and identity in this city. The two terms made me think that this is an opportunity to share my untold story - my struggle after I lost my life partner, my struggle in raising my 3 children and creating a life of my own, with a new identity. It took me 20 years to find peace. Which is unfortunate but brought a deep learning at the same time.

মাধবীলতার গান

বিকেলে চায়ের টেবিলে নিগার খবরের কাগজে চোখ বুলাচ্ছে। এমন সময় দুই নাতনি দৌড়ে এসে সরবে তাকে বলল,

- দাদুমনি, দেখ তোমার মাধবীলতা ফুল কেমন দুলছে!

- নানুমনি, ফুলগুলো বাতাসে ব্যালকনি সব ঝরে ঝরে পড়ছে!

পঁচিশ বছর আগে ফুলের চারাটা আমি নিজের হাতে লাগিয়েছিলাম। আজ সে গভীর ভালবাসায় বাড়ির তিন তলায় আমার শোবার ঘরের ব্যালকনিতে দুলছে। এর পিছনের গল্প আজ নাতনিদের না বলে পারলাম না।

সেদিন ছিল ৮ই মার্চ ১৯৯৯ সাল। ঢাকা শহরের একটি হাসপাতালে আমি ট্রেনিং ইভালুয়েশানের কাজ করছি। দাদুমনি, সকাল দশটায় তোমার বাবা হসপিটালে ফোন করল, "আম্মু বাসায় আস, আব্বুকে হাসপাতালে নিতে হবে"। "তোমার আব্বুকে এক্ষুনি গাড়িতে ওঠাও"। বলেই আমি রিকশা নিয়ে উদ্ভ্রান্তের মত বাসায় এসে দেখলাম তোমার দাদু গাড়ির পেছনে বসা, আর তোমার বাবা গাড়ী স্টার্ট দিচ্ছে। দিশাহারা হয়ে আমি গাড়ীর সামনের সিটে বসলাম।

"তুমি পেছনে বস, I am dying"। তোমার দাদুর কথা শুনে তখনি তার পাশে গিয়ে বসলাম। তিন মিনিট পর আমার কাঁধে মাথা রেখে চলন্ত গাড়ীতে তিনি মৃত্যু বরণ করলেন।

সেই ১৯৭৩ সালে আমার বিবাহ হয়, যখন আমি রাজশাহী মেডিক্যাল কলেজের চতুর্থ বর্ষের ছাত্রী। তোমার দাদু তখন সেনাবাহিনীতে ক্যাপ্টেন। পোস্টিং ঢাকা ক্যান্টনমেন্টে। থাকেন আর্টিলারি মেসে। ঢাকায় বেড়াতে এসে আমি মেসেই থাকতাম। ঢাকা শহরের সাথে আমি মায়ার বন্ধনে আবদ্ধ হয়ে পড়লাম।

ডাক্তারি পাশ করে আমিও সেনাবাহিনীতে চাকরি করতাম। একসময় স্বেচ্ছায় সেনাবাহিনীর চাকরি ছেড়ে লিবিয়াতে চাকরি নিয়ে গেলাম। কয়েক বছর পর দেশে ফিরলাম, তখন এই প্লটটা আমরা কিনেছিলাম। বাড়ি বানানোর জন্য তোমার দাদু ব্যাংক থেকে লোন নিয়েছিলেন। বাড়িটা তখন নির্মীয়মান ছিল। সে সময় তোমার দাদুর ব্যবসায় বেশ ক্ষতি হওয়ায় লোনের কিস্তি দিতে পারছিলাম না আমরা, তার কারণে ব্যাংক থেকে ঘন ঘন চিঠি আসতে থাকল।

তোমার বড় চাচু মাত্র দু'মাস আগে সেনাবাহিনীর অফিসার হয়ে বের হয়েছেন। তোমার বাবা আমেরিকায় কম্পিউটার সায়েন্স পড়তে যাবে বলে ভিসার জন্য অপেক্ষা করছে। তোমার ফুপি একটা ইংলিশ মিডিয়াম স্কুল স্ট্যান্ডার্ড সিক্সে ভর্তি হয়েছে। তাই সামনের বিশাল দায়িত্বভার নিয়ে মহাকাশটা যেন আমার মাথায় ভেঙে পড়ল।

ঢাকা শহরের মানুষগুলো যারা আমাদের প্রাণপ্রিয় ছিলেন, বিপদ দেখে সবাই যার যার মত সরে পড়লেন। আমি একটা আন্তর্জাতিক সংস্থায় ন্যাশানাল কনসালট্যান্ট হিসাবে কাজ করছিলাম। শোকে মুহ্যমান হয়ে সেই মূল্যবান চাকরিটা ছেড়ে দিলাম। কিন্তু সংসারের জন্য জীবন যুদ্ধে নেমে পড়লাম।

চোখের জলে ভেসে আবার গাড়ি চালাতে শুরু করলাম। তোমার ফুপির স্কুল বাসের জন্য দরখাস্ত করলাম। প্রিন্সিপাল বললেন,"আমার মেয়ে বাসে দাঁড়িয়ে যাওয়া আসা করবে, এই মর্মে দরখাস্ত করলে আমি এটা বরাদ্দ করতে পারব। কারণ বাসে কোন সিট নেই"। এটা লিখতে গিয়ে আমার বুক কেঁপে উঠল।

চলার শুরুতে বাসে সিট খালি থাকলেও তোমার ফুপি বসতে পারত না। তিনজন নির্ঠুর মহিলা টিচার তাকে ধমক দিয়ে সিট থেকে তুলে দিতেন। দাঁড়ালেই পড়ে যায় বলে নিরুপায় হয়ে বাসের পিছনে গিয়ে সে লুকিয়ে হামাগুড়ি দিয়ে যাতায়াত করত। তার

সালোয়ারের হাঁটুতে একদিন কাদা দেখে ব্যাপারটা জানতে পেরে কান্নায় আমার বুক ভেসে গিয়েছিল।

তোমার বাবা তখনই আমেরিকার ভিসা পেল। তাকে আমেরিকায় পাঠানোর জন্য তোমার দাদু দুই লাখ টাকা মতিঝিলে একটা ব্যাংকে রেখেছিলেন। সেই একাউন্টের কোন নমিনি ছিল না বলে দুঃখজনকভাবে টাকাটা সেখানে আটকে গেল।

আইন অনুসারে কোর্টের মাধ্যমে টাকা তোলার চেষ্টা করলাম। কিন্তু সেটা সময়-সাপেক্ষ ব্যাপার বলে তোমার বাবা সেশন ধরতে পারবেন না। তাই সেই ব্যাংকের এমডির সঙ্গে দেখা করে আমি সব ঘটনা তাকে খুলে বললাম। তিনি ব্যাপারটা অনুধাবন করে অফিসারকে ডেকে বললেন,"আমি চাই, সাত দিনের মধ্যে উনি যেন দুই লাখ টাকা তুলতে পারেন"।

মাত্র তিনদিনের মধ্যে এই অসাধ্য সাধন করে তারা বললেন, ব্যাংকের পঞ্চাশ বছরের ইতিহাসে এমন ঘটনা এই প্রথম। তাদেরকে ধন্যবাদ জানিয়ে আমি টিকেট করা থেকে শুরু করে তোমার বাবার সব কাজ সম্পন্ন করলাম। তাকে মে, ১৯৯৯ সালে আমেরিকায় পাঠালাম।

নানুমণি তুমি এবার শোন, বাড়িতে শুধু আমি এবং তোমার কিশোরী মা। প্রায় প্রতিদিনই গভীর রাতে ফোন আসত, "আমরা আপনার মেয়েকে অপহরণ করব"। শুনে তখন সারারাত ঘুমাতে পারিনি নানু।

বাড়ির বিভিন্ন প্রকার বিল, ট্যাক্স, পরচা, সম্পর্কে আমার কোন ধারণাই ছিল না। একসময় সেটার বিশেষ প্রয়োজন হলো, তাই তোমার মাকে নিয়ে সেগুলো বোঝার জন্য তোমার নানার বন্ধুর বাড়িতে গেলাম। কিন্তু তার স্ত্রী সেটা পছন্দ করলেন না, কারণ আমি তখন বিধবা। তোমার মা আড়াল থেকে তাদের কথোপকথন শুনে আমাকে সেখানে যেতে নিষেধ করল।

তাই ফাইল নিয়ে অন্য এক বন্ধুর বাড়িতে গেলাম। সেখানে বন্ধুর মেয়ের তীব্র প্রতিক্রিয়া দেখে আমি তাদের দুয়ার থেকে ফিরে এলাম।

বাসায় এসে দেখি আমার প্রিয় মাধবী লতা গাছটাকে গোড়া থেকে কেটে ফেলেছেন নিচতলার স্কুলের প্রিন্সিপাল। কারণ গাছে অনেক কীটপতঙ্গ হয়েছিল। চারিদিকের নিষ্ঠুর আচরণে আমি তখন কান্নায় আকুল হয়ে পড়লাম।

নানুমণি, একদিন বিধবাদের জন্য আমার মমত্ববোধের সীমা ছিল না। তার পরিবর্তে বিধাতা আমায় কেন মানুষের এই মন ও মানসিকতার পরিচয় দিলেন তা বুঝে পেলাম না!

লোন পরিশোধের জন্য ব্যাংকের চিঠি আসতে থাকল। তাই ভাল বেতনে আমার একটা চাকরি দরকার। তার জন্য পোস্ট গ্রাজুয়েশান করতে হবে। পাবলিক হেলথ এ মাস্টার্স করার জন্য ভর্তি হয় গেলাম। সেখানে স্কলারশিপ পেলাম।

বাসে হামাগুড়ি দিয়ে যাতায়াত অসহনীয় বলে তোমার মাকে অন্য স্কুলে ভর্তি করলাম। গাড়িতে তোমার মাকে স্কুলে আনা-নেয়ার পাশাপাশি নিজের মাস্টার্সের ক্লাস করতে শুরু করলাম।

পাস করার পর আশানুরূপ চাকরি না পাওয়ায় তোমার মা'র স্কুল যাওয়া বন্ধ করে কোচিং ক্লাসে ভর্তি করলাম। আমার অফিসের পাশাপাশি তাকে রাত পর্যন্ত কোচিং করিয়ে প্রাইভেটে মাধ্যমিক ও উচ্চমাধ্যমিক শেষ করলে তাকে ইউনিভার্সিটিতে ভর্তি করা হলো। শহরে প্রতিটা স্থান এতই দূর যে আমার কাছে সবকিছু বিভীষিকাময় হয়ে উঠল।

কিছু কিছু ব্যাংকের লোন শোধ করেও নানু শেষ রক্ষা আর হলো না। এই বাড়িটা ২০০৩ সালে নিলাম হলো। হন্যে হয়ে বেশি বেতনের চাকরি খুঁজতে খুঁজতে দৈবক্রমে একটা প্রজেক্টে কনসালট্যান্টের চাকরি পেলাম। সেদিন মনটা ভাল লাগল বলে অনেকদিন পর মাধবীলতা গাছটাকে পরখ করে দেখলাম। কী অবাক! গাছটা মরেনি। দুইটা নুতন পাতা আমার চরম হতাশার মাঝে আশার আলো জাগাল।

বেতনের সম্পূর্ণ টাকাই প্রতিমাসে লোন অ্যাকাউন্টে দিতে থাকলাম। তবুও বাড়িটা আরও দুইবার নিলাম হলো। আমি তখন এতটাই বিমর্ষ হয়ে পড়লাম যে কিছুদিন ভয়ে চুলা জ্বালাতে পারিনি। শুধু চিরা, মুড়ি, খেয়ে জীবনধারণ করেছি। ব্যাংক বাড়ি বিক্রয় করার পরামর্শ দিল।

নানু, আমি কিন্তু হাল ছাড়িনি। ঢাকার একটা জমি বিক্রয় করে, আর দীর্ঘ ৮ বছর প্রজেক্টে কাজ করে ব্যাংকের লোন পরিশোধ করলাম। এছাড়া বাড়িতে আরও চারটি ফ্ল্যাট তৈরি করলাম।

অসীম সাহস আর আত্মবিশ্বাসের বলে প্রাণপ্রিয় ঢাকা নগরীতে আমার বাড়িটি আজ সগর্বে মাথা উঁচু করে দাঁড়িয়ে রয়েছে। তোমাদের বাবা, মা, চাচুকে সুশিক্ষায় শিক্ষিত করে সমাজে প্রতিষ্ঠিত করার পর তোমাদেরকে পেয়ে আজ আমি গর্বিত এবং ধন্য। এই মাধবীলতা ফুল তারই বহিঃপ্রকাশ।

এবার হঠাৎ ছোট্ট নানুমণিটা একগোছা মাধবীলতা নিয়ে দৌড়ে এসে দুজনেই আমাকে জড়িয়ে ধরল। দাদুমণি সেই ফুলের গোছাটা নিজের হাতে আমাকে দিয়ে বলল "দাদু তুমি তোমার মাধবীলতার মতই অপরাজেয়"।

Ishrar Habib / ইশরার হাবিব, Dhaka, Bangladesh

I have always thought of this city quite as romantic. But my first heartbreak showed me this city has its own way of governing us. Its tough as realities are beyond our grip. Yet, it holds our home, a home, perhaps not so much rooted.

আমার কাছে এ শহর মানে তুমিই ছিলে

আমার কাছে এ শহর মানে তুমিই ছিলে।
আমায় বলেছিলে পুরান ঢাকার আর্মেনিয়ান চার্চে নিয়ে যাবে,
শাঁখারি বাজারের সিঁদুর-শাঁখা পরিয়ে দেবে,
প্রাচীন বুড়িগঙ্গার রহস্য বাতলে দেবে।
আমিও কত বড় পাগল! এ কথা শুনে কেউ কারো প্রেমে পড়ে!

ঠিক কতটা ভালবাসলে তোমাকে আমি এ শহর দেখার সঙ্গী বানাতে পারি, হয়তো তুমি বুঝবে না।
তুমি ছাড়া এ শহরে আমার ফিরবার, কিংবা আবাস গড়বার আর কোনো কারণ নেই।
আমি এ শহরের কেউ নই।
কটা মানুষ চিনি আমি এখানে?
তাইতো এ দালানকোঠার অরণ্যে তুমিই আমার আবাস ছিলে।

খুব সামর্থ্য ছিল না তোমার; তাতে কী? তোমার আদরের কাঙাল ছিলাম।
এই জন-অরণ্যে আমায় তুমি একটু আশ্রয় দেবে, এটুকুই চেয়েছিলাম।
আমি বাঁধন ছাড়াই তোমার ছিলাম, থাকতাম।
কিন্তু তখনো বুঝিনি, কোথাও চক্রান্ত চলছে।

525

আমার বেদুঈন-সংসার, এ শহর চায় না।
টালমাটাল সময়, নগরীর খুব উন্নয়ন হচ্ছে।
পুরনো ভেঙে নতুন দালান উঠছে।
বাস্তবতার করাত খুব নির্মমভাবে সম্পর্ক ছিন্নভিন্ন করে দিচ্ছে।
ক্ষমতা ছাড়া সামান্য নাগরিক সুবিধা যেখানে দুর্লভ, সেখানে ভালবাসা
ডানা মেলতে পারে?
বন্দী যারা, তারা কি কখনো ভালবাসার উন্মুক্ত আকাশে ওড়ার স্বাদ পায়?

আজ তোমার নিজের পরিচয় আছে, ক্ষমতা আছে।
ঢাকা শহরে খুব ভাল করে বেঁচে থাকবার রশদ তুমি পেয়ে গেছো।
তা নিয়ে আমি খুশি।
তবে এর বিনিময়ে আমি আমার শহর দেখার সঙ্গী হারিয়েছি।
আমার লাপাত্তা হওয়ার প্রয়োজন আজ শেষ।
রাস্তার মোড়ে মোড়ে পড়ে আছে আমাদের নষ্টনীড়,
তাদের জায়গায় আজ নতুন ঝকঝকে দালানকোঠা।

Husne Ara Joly / হসনে আরা জলি, Sirajganj, Bangladesh

I got my writing encouragement from my father as I was inspired by him. My writing is also inspired by my surroundings, social system, and various forms of violence against women. When I see the violence against women I can't stop myself and I always try to protest against this in my writing. I myself have endured various hostile environments, various family and social persecution.

Special thanks to My City and My Home for such a creative competition. It also inspired me to write because it's a big initiative, introducing us to a big global platform and giving us (coming from a small town of Bangladesh) the opportunity to show our skills in writing. I think it's a huge inspiration to write.

এ শুধু আমারই সুখ

চোখ বুজলেই সামনে দাঁড়ায়

আমার শৈশব, উচ্ছল কিশোর বেলা

থালি পায়ে শিশিরের সুখ

রঙের খোঁজে শেফালী তলায়

এক আঁচল ফুলে মালা গাঁথা।

এ সবই আমার সুখ

রেডিও বাংলায় ভোরের খবর শোনা

চুলোর লাল আঁচে স্বপ্নিল মায়ের মুখ

ঘিয়ে ভাজা পরোটা সুগন্ধে

টেবিল, কাপ পিরিচ, চায়ের ধোঁয়া

এ সবই আমার সুখ।

পাকুরের নিক্কন, দক্ষিনা বাতাস

নদীর ভাঙন, যুদ্ধের কামান বারুদ

527

ভারী বুট, লুটিয়ে পরা দেহ
আমার স্বাধীনতা, আমার লজ্জা
বিবস্ত্র বোনের লাশ, পচা দুর্গন্ধ
কুকুরের সাথে গলাগলি শব
সে তো আমার দুঃখের দিন।
বুকের মধ্যে শূন্যতা
লেখার সরঞ্জাম, আশা প্রত্যাশা
ধান ক্ষেতের দোলানো ঢেউ
নীলাকাশে সফেদ মেঘরাশি
নিঝুম রাতের বিষণ্ণতা
হারানো দিনের গানে গানে
কাঁদিয়ে যায় আমার বুক।
চোখ খুলতেই লোনা জল
নদী হয়ে যায় আমার বুকে
ঘুমপাড়ানি গানে গানে
ঘুমের অরণ্যে হারিয়ে যাওয়া
শুধু আমারই দুঃখ-সুখ।
মধ্য দুপুরে রান্না ঘরে
আনমনা মন ছুটে যায় দূরে
যেখানে মধ্য বয়স বাঁধনহারা
ঘাস ফড়িং এর খেলায় মাতে
তখন আমি এমন ছিলাম
কোন একদিন কাজের শেষে
অফিস থেকে ফেরার পথে
দেখা হয়েছিল এক পলক

বাসের নির্দয় শাব্দিক অত্যাচারে
নামতে গিয়ে দেখা হয়ে যায়
পলকহীন চোখের চাওয়ায়।
হঠাৎ করে দেখা, কিছু কথা
ভালো লাগা-প্রেম বোলো না একে
কত কাল দুঃখ পুষে রাখা
নিজের কথা থাকনা এখন
সে তো জানে সময় নেই
মারাত্মক এক ঘুন পোকা
কামড়ে আছে দেহ তার
কথা দিলাম লিখবো আমি।
বলেছিল হাসনাহেনা ফুটলে
জোছনা ঝরবেই ঝরবে
আমি হাসনাহেনার গন্ধে
জোছনা দেখবো বলে বসে থাকি
বলেছিলে ফাগুন বেলায়
ফুল ফুটবেই ফুটবে
আমি ফুলের আসন পেতে
তোমায় পাবো বলে বসে ছিলাম
এ সবই আমার কষ্ট গাঁথা
কিশোরী মেয়ে কয়ে উঠে কথা
মা, এই গল্পটা পড়ো-
ঠিক তোমার জীবন গাঁথা
কী বোঝে ও এই তো বয়স!
সে কি বোঝে জীবনের মানে?

কত ঝড় কত ঝঞ্ঝা শেষে
আমি আজ অভয়া-
ও কি সেই কথা কইলো
গল্পের ছলে ছলে?
ক'জন নারী পারে
মনের কথা খুলে বলতে?
ক'জন নারী পায়
সেই শীর্ষ সুখ।
স্বপ্ন যখন লুট হয়ে যায়
অসম্মানে নুয়ে পড়ে মর্যাদা
অসহনীয় আবেগে ঝাঁঝরা করে বুক
কঠিন সময় পাড়ি দিতে দিতে
আমি হয়ে যাই অভয়া আবার
প্রস্তুতি নেই রুখে দাঁড়াবার
অক্ষরে ইতিহাসে কবিতার পাতায়।

Shamim Ara Begum / শামিম আরা বেগম, Dhaka, Bangladesh

I'm a full-time housewife, got married early; my eldest son is 34. I never really got the chance to continue my studies after 12th. I love taking care of my family at the same time writing fulfills me in a way. I believe, I always wanted to be more than just an ordinary housewife which inspires my writings.

আমার যাপিত জীবনের গল্প

আমার জন্ম, বাড়ি এক অজ পাড়াগাঁয়ে। আমরা দাদাবাড়ি বা আদিবাড়ি বলি। দাদা অবস্থাপন্ন কৃষক ছিলেন। সব ধরনের ফসল আবাদ করতেন। আমাদের বিশাল বাড়ির পেছনের যে পুকুর ছিল তাতে শুধু বাসন মাজা আর শাকসবজি ধোয়া হত। আর সামনের দিকের যে পুকুর ছিল তাতে অনেক বড় সুন্দর ঘাট বাঁধা ছিল। সারা পাড়ার বৌদিরা এসে গোসল করতো আর কাপড় কাচতো। বৌদিরা গল্পে মেতে উঠতো, মনে হয় কিছুটা সময় তারা সংসারের ঝামেলা থেকে মুক্তি পেয়েছে। সবার খবর সবাই রাখতো, আহা! কী মধুর সেই দিনগুলি ছিল। আজ সবার বাসায় পানির পাম্প এসেছে, কেউ আর পুকুরে গোসল করে না। পুকুরের পানিও আজ মরে গেছে। বর্তমানে জীবন যাপন হয়তো সহজ হয়েছে, কিন্তু আমরা অনেক কিছু হারিয়েছি। ছোট ছোট আনন্দ, বেদনা, দুঃখ, ভালোবাসা অন্যের সাথে ভাগাভাগি করতে পারি না; সবার মাঝে থেকেও আমরা একা। দাদাবাড়ির বৈঠকখানার সামনে বিরাট বটগাছ ছিল। সেই গাছে হাজার হাজার শালিক পাখির বাসা, এক বিশাল মৌচাক। সকাল-সন্ধ্যায় পাখিদের ডাকাডাকি এখনও কানে বাজে। ইট-ভাটার জন্য সেই গাছ নিধন হয়েছে। বটগাছের ছায়ার বদলে সেই জায়গা শূন্য মরুভূমি। আমার বাড়ি আমি ভুলতে পারি না, দাদা-বাবা বেঁচে নেই, ইচ্ছা থাকলেও যাওয়া হয় না। জীবিকা এবং সময়ের প্রয়োজন বাবা গ্রাম ছেড়ে শহরে চলে আসেন। আমার বাবার বাড়ির জীবন শুধু বড় বড় তিন রুম, লম্বা টানা বারান্দা, বড় টিনশেডের ছাদওয়ালা পাকের ঘর। লাকড়ির চুলায় রান্না করা রান্নার স্বাদ আজ আর খুঁজে পাই না। এটা হয়তো আমার মনের ব্যাপার। বাড়ির সাথে অনেকটা খোলা জায়গা,

বাবা সেখানে বাগান করেন, তারপরেও অনেক ফাঁকা জায়গা থাকে। আমরা ভাই-বোনেরা আশেপাশের বাড়ির অন্য বাচ্চাদের সাথে সন্ধ্যা পর্যন্ত খেলি। সেই স্বাধীনতা এখনো মনে মনে উপভোগ করি। বর্তমানে বাচ্চাদের ঘরবন্দী দেখে অনেক কষ্ট হয়। আমাদের ছেলেবেলায় মোবাইল গেম ছিল না, কিন্তু সীমাহীন আনন্দ নিয়ে শিবুরি, এক্কাদোক্কা, হরেক রকম খেলা খেলতাম। কাপড়ের পুতুল দিয়ে অনেক মজা করে খেলতাম। আজকের বাচ্চারা তো তা থেকে বঞ্চিত। আজ সেই ছোট শহর দিনাজপুর বড় হয়ে যানজটের শহরে পরিণত হয়েছে। আগেকার পুরনো বাড়ির বুকের উপর দশ-তলা ফ্ল্যাট আকাশ ঢেকে দিচ্ছে। এত দ্রুত বদলে যাচ্ছে সবকিছু, যে চেনা শহর কে আর চিনতে পারি না মাঝে মাঝে। এরপর জীবনের নিয়মে শ্বশুরবাড়ি। এটা এল-প্যাটার্নের বাড়ি। ঘরগুলি বড়, টানা লম্বা বারান্দা তিন ধাপ সিঁড়ি বেয়ে উঠতে হয়। উঠানে অনেক ফুল গাছ। বারান্দার সাথেই ডালিম গাছ যেখানে ঝুলতো বড় বড় ডালিম। শাশুড়ি-আম্মা গাছ লাগাতে ভালোবাসতেন। উনি চলে গেছেন আজ কুড়ি বছর। ওঁর লাগানো লেবু গাছে আজও লেবু ধরে। রান্না ঘরের পেছনে গোয়ালঘর, উঠানের একপাশে মুরগির খোপ, শ্বশুরবাড়ি আমার অনেক পছন্দের। টিনের চালে ঝাঁক বেঁধে কবুতরের চলাচল। এরকম বর্তমানে প্রায় দেখাই যায়না। হয়তো একদিন এটাও ভাঙা পড়বে। আমার বর্তমান বাড়ি ছেলের সাথে ঢাকা শহরে পায়রার খোপ ফ্ল্যাটে। আমি ছেলের যত্ন নিই নাকি ছেলে আমার দেখভাল করে, বুঝতে পারিনা। আকাশ দেখে তৃপ্তি পাই না, বুক ভরে নিঃশ্বাস নিতে পারি না, মানুষের হাতের মুঠার যান্ত্রিকতা কি আমাদের সত্যি আনন্দ দিতে পারে? আমি বারবার পিছন ফিরে তাকাই, আমার ফেলে আসা বাড়ির কথা মনে পড়ে। সত্যিই অনেক আনন্দময় শৈশব, কৈশোর জীবন কাটিয়েছি যা ভোলার মতো নয়, ভুলতে চাইনাও না। জীবনে কী পেয়েছি আর কী পাইনি তা নিয়ে আফসোস নেই বরং অনেক পেয়েছি। জীবন সংসারে প্রকৃতির কাছ থেকে নিয়েছি, বাবা মায়ের স্নেহ আদর ভালোবাসা আর ছোটদের সম্মানে আমার অনেক পাওয়া। প্রকৃতি আমাকে বৃষ্টিতে ভিজতে দিয়েছে, জ্যোৎস্না রাতে চাঁদের দিকে তাকিয়ে আনন্দ পেয়েছি। রাতের বেলা গ্রামের জোনাকি পোকার পিছে ছুটতাম, এসব কি কম পাওয়া? আমি জগত সংসারকে কী দিলাম? শুধু কি নিয়েই গেলাম? মনের মধ্যে স্বপ্ন, বড় জায়গা নিয়ে ভালোবাসার বাড়ি করব। তার বাসিন্দা হবে অসহায় বৃদ্ধ মায়ের

পরিবার থেকে বিচ্ছিন্ন এতিম শিশুরা, প্রতিবন্ধী বা বিশেষ বাচ্চাদের দেখার কেউ নেই, যাদের আশ্রয় নেই তারা সবাই থাকবে। সবাই সবার দেখাশুনা করবে। শেষ সময়ে তার জন্য চোখের দু'ফোঁটা পানি পড়বে তার সাথীদের। ভালোবাসার সেই বাড়িতে প্রাচুর্য থাকবে না, কিন্তু স্নেহ-মমতা ভালোবাসায় পরিপূর্ণ থাকবে। খাওয়া ভাগ করে খেতে হবে হয়তো, কিন্তু শান্তির অভাব হবে না। এই আমার স্বপ্ন। আমি পারি কিংবা না পারি, কেউ না কেউ হয়তো পৃথিবীর কোন প্রান্তে পূর্ণ করেছে তার স্বপ্ন। সৃষ্টিকর্তার কাছে প্রার্থনা করি সব মানুষ যেন তার আপন জনের কাছে নিজের বাড়িতে থেকে পৃথিবী থেকে বিদায় নিতে পারে, বেওয়ারিশ হয়ে রাস্তায় যেন পড়ে না থাকে। মানবতার জয় হোক, কেউ যেন গৃহহীন না থাকে।

کے بڑے لوگ اپنے ہتھیاروں کے ساتھ آئے۔ احمد وہیں موجود تھا۔احمد نے زور سے کہا "هني عياشي پيا
ڪن ڪارو ڪري ماريو ٻنهي كي " (دونوں رنگ رلیان منا رہے تھے دونوں کو کالا کرکے مارو) اس
طرح مجمع میں "مارو مارو" کا شور گونجنے لگا۔ رخسانہ کچھ سمجھ نہیں پائی اور کانپنے لگی۔ برادری کے ایک بڑے شخص نے
رخسانہ کو آخری موقع دیتے ہوئے پوچھا" تمہیں اپنی صفائی میں کچھ کہنا ہے؟" جس پر رخسانہ نے کہا" سائیں میں اس
شخص کو نہیں جانتی" یہ سن کر چند بڑے لوگوں نے آپس میں خسر پسر کی اور فیصلہ سنادیا۔ شور میں گولیوں کی آواز
آنے لگی۔ پہلے اس انجان لڑکے کے سینے پر 3 گولیاں چلائی گئیں پھر معصوم بیٹی کے سامنے رخسانہ پر 3 گولیاں چلا دیں۔
دونوں بے گناہ قتل ہوئے اور معاملہ ختم ہوا۔ برادری میں ایک ہفتے کے طویل عرصے بعد کوئی غیرت کے نام پر قتل
ہوا۔

ورثہ پیرزادو

Virsa Pirzado

Karachi, Pakistan

اب پورے گھر اور بچوں کی ذمہ داری اکیلی رخسانہ پر آگئی۔ فراز نے ملکیت میں ایک گھر ہی چھوڑا تھا کیوں کہ وہ کسان تھا اور گھر والدہ سے وراثت میں ملا۔ اب رخسانہ سلائی کڑھائی کر کے گزر بسر کرنے لگی۔ صبح اٹھ کر پورے گھر کی صفائی کرنا پھر آس پڑوس کی عورتوں کے کپڑے سینا۔ یہ اس کا روز گار تھا۔

گاؤں والے ایک دوسرے کی مدد کرنے سے پیچھے نہیں ہٹتے۔ کوئی خالہ دودھ دے کر جاتی کوئی باجی ناشتہ دے کر جاتی لیکر آتی تو کوئی پچھیری بہن رات کا کھانا لیکر آتی۔ اس طرح آپس میں بات چیت رہتی۔ رخسانہ اپنے کردار کی وجہ سے پورے گاؤں میں مشہور تھی۔ مجال جو کسی نامحرم کی طرف آنکھ اٹھا کر بھی دیکھا ہو۔ وہ اپنے سلائی کڑھائی کا سامان بھی خود بازار سے لاتی۔ کبھی کسی سے مدد نہیں مانگی۔ اپنے بچوں میں سے کسی ایک کو ساتھ لے جاتی اور سامان لے آتی۔ اس کے اسی کردار پر لوگ اس پر فدا تھے۔ ان پڑھ ہونے کے باوجود اپنے بچوں کو سرکاری اسکول میں داخلہ دلوایا۔ جس طرح گاؤں کے امیر گھرانوں کے بچے تعلیم حاصل کرتے تو معاشرے میں اپنا اہم کردار ادا کرتے۔ وہ چاہتی تھی اس کی اولاد پڑھ لکھ کر کچھ بن سکے۔

جب گاؤں میں فراز کے انتقال کی خبر پھیلی تھی تو سب مردوں میں رخسانہ کو حاصل کرنے کی خواہش نے جنم لیا تھا۔ سب چاہتے تھے رخسانہ ایک نظر انہیں دیکھے۔ لیکن رخسانہ سنجیدہ اور ذمہ دار ہونے کے ساتھ ساتھ شرافت کے اعلیٰ مقام پر تھی۔

ایک دفعہ دن دہاڑے گاؤں کا ایک لچا لفنگا احمد رخسانہ کے گھر میں داخل ہوا۔ رخسانہ چارپائی پر بیٹھے بنائی کا کام کر رہی تھی۔ اتنے میں وہ مسکراتا ہوا آگے بڑھا تو رخسانہ نے زور زور سے پڑوسیوں کو آواز دی۔ گھر ساتھ ملے ہوئے تھے اس لیے پڑوسی جلدی پہنچے اور احمد کو پیٹنے لگے۔ پھر رخسانہ نے ہی اسے چھڑوایا اور معاف کر دیا۔ آئندہ کے لیے تنبیہہ کرتے ہوئے کہا" آئندہ اس طرح میرے گھر داخل ہونے کی غلطی مت کرنا" اس جملے پر احمد کو شرمندگی کے بجائے غصہ آیا۔ اس وقت تو وہاں سے چلا گیا لیکن بدلہ لینے کی ٹھانی۔

کچھ دنوں کے بعد رخسانہ سلائی کڑھائی کا سامان خریدنے اپنی بچی فرزانہ کے ساتھ بازار گئی۔ بازار میں اچانک سے پولیس آگئی اور سامنے ہوٹل پر بیٹھے لڑکے کو پیٹتے اور گھسیٹتے رخسانہ کے پاس لیکر آئے۔ یہاں ایک مجمع کھڑا ہو گیا اور برادری

رہی۔ تم سو جاؤ" آدھے گھنٹے بعد باہر کھٹ کھٹ کی آواز آئی۔ رخسانہ کی اماں اٹھی اور باہر جانے لگی۔ دیکھا تو فراز نشے میں دھت گھر میں داخل ہو رہا ہے۔ وہ اپنا سر نیچے کرتی ہوئی کونا پکڑ کر چلتی بنی۔ کمرے میں پلنگ پر رخسانہ گہری نیند سو رہی تھی۔ فراز کمرے میں داخل ہوا اور دھڑام سے دروازہ بند کر دیا۔ جس پر رخسانہ جاگ گئی۔ فراز رخسانہ کے قریب گیا۔ رخسانہ نے اپنی گڑیا زور سے پکڑی اور خوفزدہ آنکھوں سے فراز کو تکتی رہی۔ فراز نے زبردستی گڑیا کو کھینچ کر دور پھینک دیا۔ پھر۔۔۔۔۔ کمرے سے بچی کے چیخنے کی آواز آتی رہی اور ویرانے میں گونجتی رہی۔ لیکن یہ آواز کسی نے نہیں سنی۔۔۔ دوسری طرف ماں کی آنکھ کھلی اور منہ سے بے اختیار بیٹی کا نام نکلا "رخسانہ"۔ تھوڑی دیر سہم گئی پھر اللہ سے دعا کے لیے ہاتھ اٹھائے۔۔۔" یا اللہ میری بچی کی حفاظت کرنا"۔۔۔۔۔

صبح ہوئی۔۔۔ رخسانہ خود کو سمیٹتے ہوئے اٹھی اور جا کر نلکے سے منہ دھویا اور پانی پیا۔ وہ سکتے میں تھی کہ اس کے ساتھ کیا ہوا۔۔۔ پھر یاد آیا "میری چٹکی" اس نے اپنے کمرے کا رخ کیا اور ڈرتے ہوئے اپنی گڑیا اٹھائی اور دوڑتی ہوئی باہر آئی۔۔۔ کافی دیر تک وہ باورچی خانے میں بیٹھی رہی ابھی سوچ میں گم تھی کہ اس کی ماں کھانا لے کر پہنچی۔ ماں کو دیکھ کر وہ دوڑتی ہوئی گئی اور ماں سے لپٹ کر رونے لگی۔ ماں نے کہا "بیٹا کیا ہوا؟ روتے نہیں! دیکھو میں آگئی نا" ابھی رخسانہ کچھ کہتی کہ ماں نے خاموش کرواتے ہوئے کہا" بیٹا بس بس۔۔۔ میں سمجھ گئی ہوں۔ ایسا سب کے ساتھ ہوتا ہے۔ میرے ساتھ بھی ہوا تھا۔ اب اپنے آنسو پونچھو جاؤ۔ نہا کر صاف ستھری ہو کر آ جاؤ۔ میں تمہارا پسندیدہ کھانا لائی ہوں۔ چانول کی روٹی اور پلی کا سالن" ۔۔۔

کئی سال گزرے۔ رخسانہ گھریلو اور سگھڑ بنتی گئی اللہ نے اسے اولاد سے نوازا۔۔۔ تین بیٹیاں اور ایک بیٹا۔ اب رخسانہ جوان ہو چکی تھی۔ فراز اب اتنا بوڑھا ہو چکا کہ بستر سے اٹھنا اور بیٹھنا بھی مشکل ہو گیا تھا۔ بچے بھی بڑے ہو رہے تھے۔ ایک دن رخسانہ جھاڑو دے رہی تھی کہ فراز کے کمرے سے زوردار آواز آئی وہ دوڑتی ہوئی گئی اور دیکھا تو فراز زمین پر مردہ حالت میں تھے۔ رخسانہ کی آنکھیں بھیگ گئی اس بار نہ چیخی نہ چلائی۔ ذمہ دارانہ صلاحیتوں کا مظاہرہ کرتے ہوئے۔۔۔ فراز کو بستر پر لٹایا اور اس کے فون سے اس کے دوستوں کو اطلاع دی جو فوراً گاڑی لے کر آئے اور فراز کے جنازے کا انتظام کیا۔

ہوا۔ تمہیں کچھ خبر بھی ہے ؟" وہ وہیں سے برتن دھوتے ہوئے جواب دیتی ہے "ہائے مجھے تو نہیں پتا۔ کیا ہوا ہے ؟" اس طرح آپس میں سب مل جل کر رہتے ہیں۔ رخسانہ کیوں؟ رخسانہ کی اماں کو فکر کھائے جا رہی تھی۔

آج رخسانہ 12 سال کی ہوئی۔ جنم دن تو خوشی کا دن ہوتا ہے لیکن رخسانہ کی ماں کونے میں آنسو بہا رہی تھی۔ رخسانہ نے آ کر پوچھا ماں کیا ہوا؟ تم اداس کیوں ہو؟ آج تو میں ایک سال بڑی ہو گئی۔ کیا خوشی کی بات نہیں۔ ماں نے لمبی سانس لیتے ہوئے کہا" خوشی کی بات؟ ہاں بلکل خوشی کی بات ہے۔ آج تمہارا رشتہ لینے کچھ لوگ آ رہے ہیں۔ جاؤ جا کر اچھے سے کپڑے پہنو اور ہاتھ منہ دھو کر صاف ستھری ہو جاؤ" رخسانہ مسکرائی اور کہا" میرا رشتہ! ابھی پرسوں انیلہ کی شادی ہوئی۔ اسے اتنے اچھے کھلونے ملے اور اتنی پیاری گڑیا۔۔۔ امی مجھے بھی گڑیا ملے گی نا؟" ماں نے مسکرا کر کہا" ہاں بیٹا سب کچھ ملے گا۔ جاؤ اب تیار ہو جاؤ" وہ اچھلتی کودتی تیار ہونے چلی گئی۔

گھر میں مہمان آئے۔ ادھیڑ عمر شخص اور اس کا دوست۔ رخسانہ چائے لے کر آئی اور معصومیت سے پوچھا " آپ میرے لیے کھلونے لائیں گے نا ؟" وہ شخص عجیب سی مسکراہٹ کے ساتھ بولا" جتنے چاہو اتنے کھلونے خرید لیتا" یہ کہتے ہوئے کھانسنے لگا۔ 50 سال کی عمر میں دمے کا مرض تعجب کی بات نہیں۔۔۔

وہ دن آ گیا جب رخسانہ بیاہی۔ وہ بچی خوشی سے جھوم رہی تھی کہ اسے نئی گڑیا مل گئی۔ اس گڑیا کو رخسانہ نے اپنی دوست بنا لیا۔ رخسانہ نے اپنی دوست کا نام "چکی" رکھا۔ شادی کی رات وہ اپنی والدہ اور چکی کے ساتھ نئے گھر میں داخل ہوئی۔ گھر ویران۔۔۔ کوئی انسان ذات نہیں۔ بڑا صحن جس میں نیم کا درخت لگا ہوا تھا۔ برابر میں باورچی خانہ جسے "ردھنڑو" کہا کرتے تھے۔ ماں بچی کے ساتھ کمرے میں گئی۔ جہاں ایک چھوٹا ٹی وی تھا۔ تفریح کا واحد سامان جو رخسانہ نے پہلی بار دیکھا تھا۔ رخسانہ تھی تو کمسن بچی لیکن سمجھدار اور سنجیدہ۔ ماں نے پلنگ پر بیٹھتے ہوئے رخسانہ کو نصیحت کی۔ "بیٹا! تمہاری شادی جس شخص سے ہوئی ہے اس کا نام فراز ہے۔ تم اسے فراز کہہ کر مخاطب کرنا۔ اور جو بھی فراز کہے ویسا کرنا۔ اس کی ہر بات ماننا اور فرمانبرداری کرنا۔ جس طرح ہمارے گھر میں کام کرتی تھی یہاں بھی ویسا کام کرنا۔ ابھی میں چلتی ہوں۔۔۔ فراز آتا ہو گا" رخسانہ نے فوراً ماں کا ہاتھ تھاما اور کہا" ماں ابھی مت جاؤ۔ مجھے ڈر لگ رہا ہے" اس کے معصوم چہرے پر خوف طاری تھا۔ ماں نے گلے لگا کر کہا" میں یہیں ہوں تمہارے پاس کہیں نہیں جا

This story is basically related to a real life incident. This is not the first time a woman has been killed in the name of honour. It has been happening since ages. The idea reflected to a culture of our society. I tried to put this "Karo kaari" culture in my story to highlight this point.

میرا شہر، میرا گھر

Qatal Hoa, Insaaf Hoa

لاڑکانہ سندھ کے بڑے شہروں میں شامل ہے۔ سندھ سیکیولر اور آزاد سر زمین۔ یہاں کے لوگوں کی زبان جتنی میٹھی ہے اتنے ہی دل صاف اور مخلص۔ لاڑکانہ کے قریب بہت سے چھوٹے چھوٹے گاؤں ہیں۔ گاؤں کے لوگ تو سادہ ہوتے ہیں اور اپنی قدیم روایات کو بڑے لگاؤ سے نبھاتے ہیں۔ حالانکہ دور تبدیل ہو چکا ہے۔ کچھ روایات ترک ہو چکی ہیں اور کچھ بدل چکی ہیں

لیکن یہ ان دنوں کی بات ہے جب ترقی کی لہر نئی نئی آئی تھی۔ اب بھی لوگ بچیوں کی تعلیم کو عیب سمجھتے ہیں۔ اس دور میں لڑکی کی 10 سال پار کرے تو والدین کو اس کی شادی کی تشویش ہونے لگتی ہے۔ رخسانہ ایک سیدھی سادی لڑکی جس نے "ا" بھی نہیں پڑھا، گاؤں والے اسے اللہ کی گائے کہتے ہیں۔

صبح کا سورج طلوع ہوتے ہی سب جاگ جاتے ہیں، زیادہ تر لوگوں کا پیشہ زراعت ہوتا ہے۔ اس لیے سویرے سے ہی فصلوں کا رخ کیا جاتا ہے۔ اس معاملے میں جنسی تفریق بلکل بھی نہیں یعنی خواتین بھی مردوں کے برابر فصلوں میں کام کرتی ہیں۔ رخسانہ گھر میں اکلوتی بچی تھی والد صاحب کا سایہ جلد سر سے اٹھ گیا۔ والدہ سوچتی اگر میں بھی مر گئی تو اس کا کون خیال رکھے گا؟ حالانکہ گاؤں میں سب رشتہ دار ہی ہوتے ہیں اور اس دور میں تو سب کے گھر بھی ملے ہوئے ہیں۔ یعنی گھروں کے اندر کوئی دیوار نہیں۔ ایک کے گھر سے آواز آتی ہے "سنو فرزانہ! یہ اللہ رکھے کے گھر اتنا بڑا جھگڑا

542

بلکہ اس کا تو وجود

ہر شہر میں بھکرا ہوا ہے

ہر شہر اس کا گھر ہے۔۔

1 : کوہاٹ

2 : پشتو کا وہ گانا جو کسی جگہ سے کوچ کرنے کو بیان کرتا ہے

3 : لاہور

4 : ڈیرہ اسماعیل

سیدہ زہرہ علی

Syeda Zehra Ali   Dera Ismail Khan,

Pakistan

543

مگر تم کیسے آسکتے ہو

تم سے تو کوئی رشتہ نہیں میرا

تمہارا آنا بنتا نہیں ہے۔

آخری پڑاؤ

میں اقلیت ہوں

جسے تم کافر کہتے ہو

مگر کیا خدا بھی

کہتا ہے کافر مجھ کو؟

نہیں معلوم

میں کافر ہوں یا تم

یا تم بھی نہیں ہو اور میں بھی نہیں

لیکن یہ کون بتائے گا مجھے

کہ جہاں جاؤں

دھتکار و پھٹکار سے سواگت ہوتا ہے

گھر چھن گئے

خاندان چھن گئے

ایک جوگی ایک بنجارہ کیا کرے گا

کسی ایک شہر کو گھر کر کے

جس کے واسیوں کے خون سے ہر شہر آباد ہو

اس کا کوئی گھر نہیں ہوتا

بچے بڑے ہو جائیں تو
مائیں گود سے اتار دیتی ہیں۔۔

تیسرا پڑاؤ

ایک بار پھر گھر گھر چھوٹا
چلتی گاڑی میں دل اسی کیفیت سے دوچار رہا
جس کو بھلاتے
بلکہ کسی خاموش گوشے میں
دفن کرنے کی ناکام کوشش کرتے
خوشی و غم کا
فرق بھی کہیں پس پشت رہ گیا

'پھلاں دا سہرا'[۴] کیسے
میرا گھر ہو سکتا ہے
کہ میں وہ اقلیت ہوں
جس کے لہو سے
سارے سہرے رنگین اور معطر ہیں
سانسیں کسی گولی کی امانت کر کے
شاید تب تک زندہ رہوں
جب تلک
کسی ہسپتال کے بیڈ پہ
کرب و تکلیف کی بابت
بند آنکھیں تمہیں دیکھنے کے لیے چیخیں

بوجھل روح اشکبار آنکھ اور

خالی دل کو بہلانے واسطے

شہرِ باغات[3] بلاوا دے رہا تھا

مارچ کا مہینہ

اور جوبن پہ بہار

مگر جس کا دل کھنڈر ہو چکا ہو

اس کو رنگینئ ماحول سے

بھلا کیا غرض

دن گزرتے، مہینے

اور پھر سال ہوئے

اپنوں کی تصویریں مدھم ہوتے

بس برسیاں یاد رہ گئیں

شہر شہر نہیں گھر بن گیا

خالی پن کم ہوا

آنکھیں ہنسنے لگیں

ماں کی گود جو سکون دے

کچھ ویسا ہی احساس۔۔

مگر کیا خبر تھی

ابھی ایک اور دکھ منتظر ہے

ایک بار پھر کوچ۔۔

زندگی کمانے کی تگ و دو۔۔

کچھ دیر مزید رک جاؤ
بس ایک آخری نظر
تمہیں اپنے ذہن و دل میں اُتار لوں
کہ پھر کوئی نہ ہو گا
قبر پہ شمع جلانے کو
تمہیں تو گھر اگر بیٹیوں کی مہک سے
معطر رکھنے کی عادت تھی
اب کون خوشبو بکھیرنے آئے گا
بارش سے پہلے کون
میرے دو گز کے گھر کو
محفوظ کرے گا

جانے کتنی آوازیں کتنی دہائیاں دی ہوں گی
پیچھے رہ جانے والوں نے
مگر ایک بار جو گاڑی چل پڑی
تو ایسی خاموشی نے آن گھیرا
جیسے دنیا کے آخری سرے کی طرف قدم بڑھاتے
میں واحد ذی روح ہوں
آگے کیا معلوم کیا ہے
ہے بھی کہ نہیں

ایف ایم پہ "بیاہ°° بار؍°ی"[2]
کفن میں آخری کیل ثابت ہوا

547

مضافات سے گھر پہ لگا عَلم دِکھا

تو لگا جیسے دل دھڑکنا بند کر دے گا

وہ چھت جس پر بیٹھ کر کبھی دھوپ سینکتے

نانی اماں کو نوحے لکھتے دیکھا

اب اس خالی گھر کو دیکھنے

اس کی بے جان چیزوں کو چھونے

اور کبھی زندہ رہنے والوں کی یادیں

جینے پر بھی پابندی ہے

جب اپنوں کی قبریں بلاتی ہوں تو

شہر بدر ہونا اذیت کی آخری حد ہے

مگر مجھ پہ اس فرقے کا ٹیگ لگا ہے

جس کو سب کافر کہتے ہیں

اے پہاڑوں کے دل [1] ۔ ۔

تم پر آخری سلام

کہ پیچھے مڑ کر دیکھنا پتھر کر دے گا

تمہاری آغوش میں کچھ اپنے ہیں

ان کا خیال کرنا کہ

اپنی واپسی ناممکنات میں سے ہے ۔ ۔

دوسرا پڑاؤ

مت جاؤ

Brainstorming during the workshop and my personal experiences have played a vital role in my write up. Had I not experienced the circumstances, I might not have related to the topic much.

Parrao

پڑاؤ

پہلا پڑاؤ

"آپ کے مطلوبہ نمبر سے جواب موصول نہیں ہو رہا"

کتنی ہی بار نمبر ڈائل کیا

یہ جانتے ہوئے کہ

جواب دینے والوں نے

قبرستان اپنا گھر کر لیا ہے

کسی کمزور لمحے

اچانک گاڑی آبائی شہر کے رستے ڈالی

اس رستے پر چلتے جانا

جہاں معلوم ہو کہ اختتام یہ منزل نہیں

بلکہ رائیگانی منتظر ہے

کب آسان ہوا ہے

مگر اصل کھینچتا ہے

اپنی مٹی بلاتی ہے

549

شاری! کب تک چلتا رہے گا میرا شہر ویرانوں میں
یا خدا رحم فرما، اور اثر کر بزرگوں کی دعاؤں میں

شاری مراد

Shari Murad

Karachi, Pakistan

The past and present situation of my city inspired me to write positive and
negative things that are going on in my city.

My City My Home

میرا شہر میرا گھر

میرے شہر کی تر و تازہ ہواؤں میں
پھول کھلتے تھے پُر فضاؤں میں

ہر ایک خوش تھا اپنی ماں کی چھاؤں میں
زندگی گزر رہی تھی اُنکی دعاؤں میں

نہ جانے کہاں سے اِک طوفاں برپا ہو گیا گھٹاؤں میں
عصمتیں لُٹ گئیں ماں، بیٹیوں، بہنوں کی شاہراہوں میں

میرا شہر ایسا تو نہ تھا، جیسا اب ہے
نہ جانے کس کی نظر لگ گئی، اسکی دلکش فضاؤں میں

جو ماں باپ کل تک درختِ سایہ دار تھے
آج وہ بے بس پڑے ہیں، دوسروں کی پناہوں میں

یہی میرا شہر ہے اور یہی ہے میرا گھر
جسکو برباد کرکے بھی، خوفِ خدا نہ آیا حکمرانوں میں

Sayyara Nayyer Syed

Birmingham, UK

سیارہ نیر سید

نہ تھا ہمنوا اپنا ، نہ کوئی عزیز کوئی دوست نہ
اتنے بڑے شہر میں نہ کوئی نظر آیا اپنا

3

جو مشکل گھڑی میں ساتھ دینے کو آتا پاس میں
اس اجنبی شہر میں اس طرز کا ماحول تھا اپنا

اب بر منگھم سے بھی ویسی اُنسیت ہو گئی ہے
سیالکوٹ جیسی اس سے بھی محبت ہو گئی ہے
دل کو بھا گئے ہیں اس کے حسین منظر اپنے
ہمیں رغبت ہو گئی ہے ان گلی کوچوں سے بھی
میرے دل کو سکون دیتی ہیں اب اس کی رونقیں
ہمیں یہاں اب رہنے کی عادت ہو گئی ہے
میرے اپنے بہت سارے ہیں اب یہاں آباد،
مہربان ہو گئی ہے ، قدرت مجھ پہ کچھ اس انداز میں
عمر کے قیمتی لمحات بخشتے ہیں اس کو بنانے سنوارنے میں
بہت محنت و لگن سے اس کے خد و خال بدلے ہیں
محال لگتا ہے اب اس سے جدا ہونے کا تصور
ملی جلی تہذیبوں نے اس کے دن رات بدلے ہیں
ہر رنگ و نسل کے باسی نے کی ہے اس کی نقش نگاری
اس کی کو زین سنواری طرح طرح کے پکوانوں سے

4

سنائی دیتی ہے یہاں پر مختلف زبانوں کی گونج
اب کرنی یہاں پر نئی نسلوں کی آبیاری ہے۔ نیر

553

پہلا تھا ہوائی سفر یہ میری زندگی کا

اپنوں سے بچھڑنے کا گہرا یہ سبب ٹھہرا

ہونا پڑا سب عزیزوں اور احباب سے یکدم جدا

دور چلے جانا پڑا ان سے چکے، سے الگ ہو کر،

اپنا گھر، کل اثاثہ اور زندگی کے بہت حسین لمحے

سب سے ہی بچھڑ جانا پڑا ہو کے تہی داماں،

لے کر بڑا خلاء اپنی زندگی میں اک اتنا

شاید کبھی نہ لوٹ کر، آنے کا حوصلہ لے کر

1

دل پہ رکھ کے پتھر، سات سمندر پار کئے تھے

نئی امیدیں، لے کر کی اک نئی، انجانی منزل،

غم و خوشی کے جذبات کا گھیر اتھا

اک نئے باب کا آغاز کیا تھا ہم نے

اپنے ماضی کے اوراق کو طاق میں رکھ کر

پاٹ لیا تھا اک صحرا، وسیع ہم نے،

ہیں، وہ سب باتیں وہ سب یادیں آج بھی تازہ

نہ ماند پڑتی ہیں وہ سب باتیں نہ دھندلاتی ہیں،

میرے احساسات میں اک ہلچل مچاتی رہتی ہیں

اکثر وہ سب یادیں ان گزرے ہوئے برسوں کی

نئے شہر میں آ کر دنیا، نئی تہذیب اک نئی،

انوکھے خواب سجا کر مستقبل کے دل میں،

بدلنے کو میں ڈھلنے کو، نئے انداز نئے روپ

کیسے کیسے ارماں مٹا کر نہ جانے خود کے،

The place you live in has a very big role to play in your life .Your family,

relatives, loved ones and the place you live in create that safe environment for

you to nourish and grow You make friends, you do various activities to enjoy

what it has to offer for you. When you grow older you take part in shaping and

making it therefore it inspired me to write about the place I have been born and

brought up and reflect my feelings of those past memories.

Having lived in Birmingham for 50 years I have witnessed it change

tremendously over the years.

Having education in Birmingham and then working here gave me an

opportunity to serve the community of Birmingham in many ways.

Those positive experiences have shaped me as a result as much as I have played

a part in its development.

That was my city and this is my city too   وہ شہر بھی میرا تھا یہ شہر بھی میرا ہے

میں نے اُس شہر میں اپنی آنکھ کھولی تھی

میں کھیلی تھی کی مٹی میں جی بھر کے اس

گڈے گڑیاکے بہت سارے کھیل کھیلے تھے

آشنائی تھی اپنی زبان، اپنی تہذیب سے ہوئی

رخ بدلا پھر اک روز تقدیر نے کچھ ایسا

سفر باندھا کوُچ ہم نے کیا اور عزم

I am a big die hard patriot when it comes to my country or my city yet the Nature has made the air flow in a different direction and circumstances are pushing me to move to another country and city in a few months. Hence, as soon as this came to my notice, I knew this was for me and since I already had cluttered ideas in my mind. I was just waiting for a reason to organize them.

جہد روح   **Juhd Rooh**

کھوئی ہوئی میری ذات زندگی کے نشیب و فراز میں

میں ڈھونڈ ڈھونڈ ہاری اپنی شناخت کو

بھٹکی ہوئی روح ہوں چین و قرار سے دور

جو مل جاؤں کہیں تو با خبر رکھنا

جان مسلسل محو سفر لیکن

سفر وہ جس کی منزل لا حاصل، جہد بے سود

اک شور سا برپا ہے کون ہوں میں؟

بے نام و نشاں جس کی منزل بھی لا مکاں

صندل اسلام

Sandal Islam

Rawalpindi, Pakistan

556

چھٹی کے دن وہ ضد کر کے بابا کے ساتھ "گاندھی گارڈن" وقت بہت کم رہ گیا تھا۔ سارا نے اب اپنی لسٹ پر نظر ڈالی۔ یہاں آتی تھی۔ اُس کی صرف تین خواہشات ہوا کرتی تھیں۔ بڑا سا غبارہ، پشاوری آئس کریم اور ہاتھی کی سواری۔ اُس کے خیال میں اُس کا گھر ہی مکمل جنت تھا، جہاں بابا اور ممی کے پیار کی ہوائیں ہر وقت چلتی تھیں۔ یہاں کم سے کم درخت یہاں "تو اب بھی سایہ دار ہیں۔ لیکن سب جانور کہاں گئے؟ پاس سے گزرتے چنے بیچنے والے لڑکے سے اُس نے پوچھا یہ کیا ہوتے ہیں؟ "اور مور، شیر، ہرن، بارہ سنگھا؟ "وہ جانے لگا۔ "مر گیا، "کب کے "ہاتھی ہوا کرتا تھا؟ کہاں گیا؟، میرے کو نہیں معلوم کدھر سے آئی ہو تم؟ آسمان سے؟ بھاگو یہاں سے۔ میرا کراچی تو بس اب ایسا ہی ہے۔ اچانک ایک ہجوم کسی کمزور سے شخص کو جوتوں اور لاتوں سے مار تا ہوا، وہاں سے گزرنے لگا۔ اُس لڑکے نے بھی ایک پتھر اٹھا !۔ احمدی کافر "سالا قادیانی! بھاگ یہاں سے "کر اُس پٹتے شخص کو کھینچ مارا۔

☆☆☆

سارہ کی تعطیل ختم ہو چکی تھی۔ اپنا سرخ شلوار قمیض اور پرنٹڈ دوپٹہ اتار کر اُس نے سفید لبادہ پہن لیا تھا۔ ملاقات کا وقت ختم ہو چکا تھا۔ ایک پرانے سے اخبار کا ٹکڑا اڑ تا ہوا اُس کے قدموں سے آ کر لپٹ گیا۔ سنہ ۷۵ء کا اخبار تھا شاید۔ کل رات ڈیفنس فیز 2 میں ایک بدنام گھرانہ لوٹ لیا گیا۔ خواتین کو بے عزت کیا گیا۔ باپ کو گولی مار دی گئی۔ سینٹ" جوزف کالج کی طالبہ سارہ شاہ گینگ ریپ کا شکار ہو کر، اُسی وقت فوت ہو گئی۔ ملزمان فرار، تفتیش جاری ہے۔ احمد شاہ کا یہ گھرانہ قادیانی بتایا جا رہا ہے۔

کراچی کے ساحل سے آتی تیز ہوا کا جھونکا، اُس کے ہاتھ سے اُس کا اعمال نامہ جھپٹ کر لے گیا۔ اُسے لگا اوپر عالم ارواح میں وہ اب بھی زندہ ہے۔ جبکہ کراچی اب مردوں کا شہر ہو چکا ہے۔ مردوں کا شہر۔ موئن جو دڑو!!!!

Sameena Nazeer

ثمینہ نذیر

Karachi, Pakistan

درمیان میں صحن، اطراف میں ورانڈہ، تین کمرے اور کونے میں غسل خانہ اور پاخانہ علیحدہ _____ میں غلط مکان پر تو دستک نہیں دے رہی ہے؟ مگر نمبر تو وہی ہے۔ اندر سے بچوں کے ہنسنے اور بلند آواز میں انگریزی میوزک سنائی دینے لگا۔ ہم سب بہن بھائی اُس دن اسی طرح سے لوڈو کھیل رہے تھے۔ جب بابا کو کسی نے باہر دروازے پر بلایا اور پھر وہ کس حال میں لوٹ کر آئے تھے۔ یاد کر کے وہ تھر تھر ہی کانپ گئی۔ اگلے دن ہی وہ وہاں سے نکال دی گئی تھی۔

اُس نے بے چین ہو کر انٹر کام پر ہاتھ رکھ دیا۔ اندر سے کسی اجنبی زبان میں نام پو چھا گیا پھر گیٹ سے ایک چینی مرد باہر یہ اب چینیوں کا محلہ ہے۔ بلکہ سارا شہر ہی ہمارا ہے۔ تم کہاں سے آ گئیں۔ بھاگو" نکل آیا" ٹوٹی پھوٹی انگریزی میں بولا اور گیٹ بند کر لیا۔ اُس کے دماغ میں ٹیسیں اٹھنے لگیں۔ وہ غلط بس میں تو نہیں بیٹھ گئی؟ "یہاں سے اختری خالہ کے گھر محمود آباد تک پہنچنے تک سارا شہر کا بدبو اور تعفن سے برا حال ہو گیا۔ سڑک کے دونوں جانب کوڑے کے ڈھیر نہیں پہاڑ کھڑے تھے۔ زخمی اور بیمار کتے بلیاں اپنے زخم چاٹ رہے تھے۔ بچے اسی کوڑا کرکٹ کے درمیان بیٹھے مزے سے کھیل رہے تھے۔ ہر فٹ پاتھ پر لوگ غلیظ اور چیکٹ لباس پہنے تکے بھنبھوڑ رہے تھے۔ اچانک اُس کا پیر ایک گٹر کے ڈھکن پر پڑا اور نیچے پاتال میں اترنے لگی۔

میں سندھی ہوں۔ تو مہاجر ہے۔ میں پنجابی ہوں۔ تم کون ہو؟ مارو مارو! یہ کافر ہے۔ کی آوازیں وہاں گونج رہی تھیں۔ ڈھانچوں کے انبار لگے تھے۔ اُس نے غور سے دیکھا۔ ایک طرف لڑکیوں کی چھاتیوں کا ڈھیر تھا۔ ایک طرف اُن کی ران وہ چیختی ہوئی وہاں سے دور دوڑنے "باجی! ران کا گوشت لو گی؟ یا سینے کا؟ قیمہ بنا دوں؟" کہ۔ ایک قصائی برہنہ بیٹھا تھا گئی۔ لڑکیوں کی ایک لمبی قطار وہاں لگی تھی۔ عبایہ پہنی، نقاب پوش عورت لڑکیوں سے ڈگری، ٹھنگرو، آرٹ برش، قلم اور گٹار لے کر، اُن کے ہاتھوں میں بیلن، چمٹا، فیڈر، حجاب تھماتی جا رہی تھی۔ تم کیا لو گی کہ ڈائپر؟ سارہ نے وہاں سے بھی رستہ بدل لیا۔

اب اُسے یہاں کئی دروازے نظر آنے لگے۔ ہر کسی پر ایک تختی لگی تھی۔ ٹارگٹ کلنگ، شیعہ سنی فسادات، اغوا برائے تاوان، بچیوں کے ریپ۔ بچوں کے ریپ۔ ڈکیتی۔ لینڈ مافیا۔ اسلحہ فروشی۔ منشیات۔

ایک مرد وہاں کھڑا "کہاں جاؤ گی لڑکی۔۔ فائل دو۔۔ اچھا تمہارا بھی ریپ ہوا تھا۔۔ گینگ ریپ؟ کتنے آدمی تھے؟" سارہ کے منہ سے بمشکل نکلا۔ نہیں۔ وہ سول۔ نہیں "اختری خالہ کی طبیعت کیسی ہے؟ وہ زندہ ہیں؟" مگر وہ ہنسی ہنس رہا تھا۔ ہسپتال میں ڈاکٹروں کی ہڑتال کے باعث سک سک کر مر گئیں۔ بھاگو یہاں سے۔

In the days of world as global village, still everyone connects ones home as a place of comfort, security and growth. City is another home for everyone, and when it's snatched or departed people feel alone. My story is dealing with a similar concept.

موئن جو دڑو

Mohenjo Daro

تعطیلات کا اعلان ہوا۔ تمام لڑکیوں نے سفید لبادوں والا یونیفارم اتارا اور چلیں اپنے اپنے شہروں کی طرف اُن جہاں کے گھر تھے۔ ریتو نے ڈھاکہ جانا تھا کہ اُس نے زرد ساڑھی پہن کر بندیا لگا لی۔ بنتو فری ٹاؤن، افریقہ سے تھی، فٹافٹ بڑے چھاپے والا رنگین بوبو پہن کر، گھنگھریالے بالوں پر ہم رنگ پگڑ باندھ لیا۔ آنچل، ایلس، عبیر، جمیلہ سب ہنستی ہوئی ایک دوسرے کو چھیڑ رہی تھیں۔ کسی نے اپنے منگیتر کو دیکھنا تھا۔ کسی نے اپنے بوڑھے والدین کو۔ سارہ پریشان تھی کہ وہ کراچی جا کر کیا کرے گی۔ بے شک اُس کا مکان اب بھی وہاں تھا مگر ہر مکان گھر تو نہیں ہوتا۔ راستے بھر وہ کراچی کے تمام محلوں کی فہرست بنا رہی تھی جہاں اُسے جانا تھا۔ اختری خالہ محمود آباد میں رہتی تھیں، بیمار تھیں جب اُن سے سارہ کی آخری ملاقات ہوئی تھی۔ بریسٹ کینسر ہو گیا تھا انہیں۔ شاید موت کو شکست دے دی ہو۔ شکیلہ آپا کی شادی ہو گئی ہو گی کیا؟ وہ یاد کرنے لگی کہ اُن کا گھر کہاں تھا۔ سارہ کے ہوسٹل میں کوئی فون، ڈاک یا رابطے کی کوئی بھی صورت نہ تھی۔ کتنے برس ہو گئے مجھے کراچی سے گئے؟ پچاس یا بیس؟ یاد کیوں نہیں آرہا؟ اُس کی تو یاد داشت مثالی ہوا کرتی تھی۔ سینٹ جوزف کی قابل ترین طالبات میں اُس کا شمار ہوتا تھا۔ سپورٹس سے لے کر، بیت بازی، ڈرامہ کلب اور کوئز تمام میں سارہ احمد شاہ پیش پیش رہتی تھی۔ پھر۔۔۔

اچانک اُس کا سفر ختم ہو گیا۔ وہ اپنے مکان کے سامنے تھی۔ کیسے بھول سکتی تھی وہ۔ کونے پر جامع مسجد، پھر وہاں سے دائیں ہاتھ تیسری گلی اور پانچوں مکان۔ مگر یہ کیا۔ میرا گھر ایسا تو نہیں تھا۔ اُس کی تو دوسری کیا پہلی منزل بھی نہ تھی۔

یہ تو ماہ جبین تھی جو کسی بھی راہ چلتے سے متاثر ہو کر اپنے کو اس کی جگہ پر رکھ کر سوچتی تو وہ کانپ جایا کرتی تھی۔ صبح کا وہ وقت اسی لیے اسے پسند تھا کہ اس وقت وہ اپنے شہر کو جگمگاتا دیکھا کرتی تھی۔ ہر منفرد شخص کی زندگی سے متاثر ہو کر چند لمحوں کے لیے خود کو اس منفرد زندگی میں محسوس کیا کرتی تھی۔ اور اپنی اوقات یاد رکھا کرتی تھی۔ اپنے سوالات کے جوابات بھی اسے وہیں سے ملا کرتے تھے جہاں سے یہ سوالات جنم لیتے تھے۔ اس لیے کسی جواب کے لیے اسے کھوج نہیں لگانی پڑی۔ ہر انسان کا اپنا مقام ہوتا ہے۔ جو جیسی زندگی جی رہا ہے وہ اس کا مقام ہی تو ہے۔ یہ تو ہم انسانوں کا فیصلہ ہوتا ہے کہ ہم نے اپنے آپ کو کس مقام تک پہنچانا ہے۔

یہ تو کوئی نہیں جانتا کہ اس بچی کی کیا مجبوری تھی جو اتنی چھوٹی سی عمر میں اسے دنیا کی حقیقت کا سامنا کرنا پڑ رہا تھا۔ کون جانتا ہے کہ اس عورت کو کن مسائل کا سامنا تھا جو اسے اپنے بچے کو لے کر یوں لوگوں کے آگے ہاتھ پھیلانے پڑے۔ مگر ماہ جبین اتنا ضرور جانتی تھی کہ کسی پہ انگلی اٹھانے سے پہلے یا کسی کو دھتکارنے سے پہلے ایک بار چند لمحوں کے لیے اس کی زندگی میں جھانکنے کی کوشش کی جائے تو الزام تراشی اس معاشرے سے ختم ہو جائے۔

Roha Ahmed

روحہ احمد

Rawalpindi, Pakistan.

ہر سو پرندوں کی چہچہاہٹ، ہر طرف گہما گہمی، ہر جانب نئے دن کے آغاز کی تیاریوں میں آہستہ آہستہ بڑھتا ہوا شور، ہر شخص ان سب سے لاپروا اپنی ہی دھن میں مگن دکھائی دے رہا تھا۔ جب ماہ جبین کی آنکھوں میں اچانک ایک چمک سی نمودار ہوئی۔

دھاگے میں پروئے ہوئے موتیے، گلاب اور گیندے کے گجرے اٹھائے ایک ننھی بچی گاڑیوں کے شیشے بجا رہی تھی۔ صبح کے جلد بازی کے اس پہر میں یا تو لوگ اسے دھتکار رہے تھے یا پھر نظر انداز۔

ماہ جبین کو اس پر بہت ترس آیا اور اس کا دل چاہا کہ اس بچی سے سارے گجرے خرید لے۔ مگر وہ بچی اب اس کی نظروں سے بہت دور جا چکی تھی۔ "بہت مرتبہ انسان چاہ کر بھی کوئی نیکی نہیں کر سکتا۔" ماہ جبین کی سوچوں کا تسلسل اور بڑھتا گیا۔ جہاں وہ بچی حلال روزی کمانے کی غرض سے گاڑیوں کے شیشے بجا رہی تھی وہیں سڑک کی دوسری جانب ایک عورت بازو پہ بچی کو اٹھائے لوگوں کے سامنے اپنی چادر پھیلا رہی تھی۔ کچھ فاصلے پر کچی زمین کے ایک ٹکڑے پہ چند جھگیاں بنی دکھائی دیں جن کے باہر خواتین لکڑیوں کے اوپر روٹیاں پکا رہی تھیں۔ جوں جوں وہ اپنی منزل کی جانب بڑھ رہی تھی بہت سے سوالیہ نشان اس کے دماغ کو الجھاتے چلے جا رہے تھے۔

کہیں لڑکیاں کھڑی اپنی اپنی سواری کا انتظار کر رہی تھیں تو کہیں کوئی خاتون اپنے بچوں کی سواری خود بنی دکھائی دیتی۔ کہیں کوئی عورت سڑک پر دوکان کھولنے میں مصروف دکھائی دیتی تو کہیں کوئی ورزش کے گرم لباس میں ملبوس عورت کھلے میدان میں ٹہلتی دکھائی دیتی۔

ان سب کی جگہ خود کو رکھ کر سوچنا بہت مشکل کام ہے کیونکہ ہم ہمیشہ اونچی جگہ پہ خود کو دیکھنے کا تصور کرتے ہیں۔ کون چاہتا ہے کہ وہ نیچے دیکھے، کون چاہتا ہے کہ وہ اپنے سے نچلے درجے کے لوگوں کی جگہ پر اپنا آپ تصور بھی کرے۔ اسی لئے ہم انسان ناشکرے ہیں کیونکہ ہم کسی کی زندگی کے سخت مرحلے کو سمجھنے سے قاصر ہیں۔

I was inspired to write this story by my thoughts and my daily routine of travelling to university as a day scholar.

Travel towards Garden

سفر گلزار

صبح کا اندھیرا اور مدہم روشنی، کھلے آسمان تلے ہلکے بادل اور ان میں موجود شفق کی سرخی، زمین پہ کہرے کی ہلکی سفیدی اور پھولوں پہ موجود شبنم کے قطرے۔۔۔ کھڑکی پر پڑی اوس ان مناظر کو دھندلا رہی تھی۔ یہ سب ماہ جبین کے لیے کچھ نیا نہ تھا۔ مگر چند لمحوں کے گزرتے ہوئے ان مناظر سے لطف اندوز ہونے کے لئے وہ ہر تھوڑی دیر کے بعد اپنے دائیں ہاتھ سے شیشے کو صاف کرتی۔

ماہ جبین ایک ایسی شخصیت کی مالک تھی جسے اس کے مزاج سے پہچاننا آسان نہ تھا۔ انتہائی سادہ، خوش مزاج اور دوسروں کو خوش رکھنے کی کوشش کرنے والی لڑکی، جو لوگوں کی نظر میں تو چلبلی اور خوش اخلاق سہی۔۔۔ مگر اندر سے کتنی سنجیدہ تھی، وہ کیا سوچتی تھی اور اس کا ہر چیز کو دیکھنے اور پرکھنے کا انداز کیسا تھا یہ از کیا نہیں جانتا تھا۔ بس کے چلتے ہی اس نے دائیں طرف لگے پردے کو تھوڑا اور کھسکایا۔ درختوں کے بیچ میں سے جھانکتی سورج کی شعائیں اس کے چہرے پر پڑنے لگیں جو اس کو کافی پر سکون کر رہی تھیں۔ مختلف موڑ مڑنے والی سڑک جتنے راستوں کو آپس میں ملاتی تھی اس سے کہیں زیادہ لوگوں کو اس نے آپس میں جوڑ کر رکھا تھا۔ اس سڑک سے منسلک ہر شخص کی اپنی ہی کہانی تھی اور ہر جگہ ہر شخص کو دیکھ کر ماہ جبین ان سب کی کہانیوں کو اپنی سوچ سے بن رہی تھی۔ وہ سب لوگ اپنی جگہوں پر اپنا مقام بنا چکے تھے۔

"کیا ماہ جبین کا بھی اپنا کوئی مقام ہے؟" یہ خیال اکثر افراد کو دیکھ کر اس کے ذہن میں عیاں ہوا کرتا تھا۔

562

جب بھی واپس لوٹتی تو دل میں ایک خیال ہوتا ہے کہ یہ چیز اپنے شہر کو بھی دے دوں. جتنی بار نئے لوگوں میں اٹھی بیٹھی، محسوس ہوا کہ لوگ تو مجھ سے متاثر ہو رہے ہیں کیونکہ میں ایک چھوٹے سے شہر سے تعلق رکھنے کے ساتھ ساتھ ایک سرمایہ بھی بن گی ہوں اس شہر کی. ایک جھجھری سی محسوس ہوتی تھی کے لوگوں کو بتاؤں گی تو کیسا سمجھیں گے مجھے، ہائے کس کونے سے آئی ہو جہاں لڑکے لڑکیوں کے ساتھ بیٹھنے کی جگہ بھی نہیں. اور پھر لوگوں کا کہنا کہ ہم کیسے آئیں گے وہاں اس چھوٹے سے گاؤں میں. عرصے بعد ایک خیال آیا کہ سخت دھوپ میں جب چھاؤں مل سکتی ہے تو اس چھوٹے شہر کی تنگ گلیوں سے میں باہر کیوں نہیں نکل سکتی؟

اس شہر کی چھوٹی گلیوں میں جب باہر بھاگتی تو لگتا جیسے ٹھنڈی ہوا کی تازگی پورے جسم کو متاثر کر رہی، جب اکیلے گلیوں میں ختم کے میٹھے کی پلیٹیں اٹھائے گھر گھر جاتی تھی تو ایک اپنائیت کی کیفیت محسوس ہوتی تھی، جس نے لوگوں میں گھلنا ملنا سکھایا. چھوٹی چھوٹی تقریبات میں اٹھتے بیٹھتے محسوس ہوتا تھا کہ ہم سب ایک ہی تو ہیں، بس اس پیار کو محسوس کرنے کی دیر ہے.

اب جب دیکھتی ہوں پیچھے مڑ کر تو لگتا ہے کہ ایک لمبا سفر طے کیا ہے مگر اصل میں تو وہ چند لمحات تھے جو اس چھوٹے سے شہر نے سکھائے. جس نے مجھے ایک طاقت ورلڑکی بنایا. جو آج میں اپنے اس چھوٹے سے شہر کی نمائندہ ہوں اور فخر سے کہتی ہوں کہ اسی چھوٹے سے شہر جیکب آباد سے وہ شخص ہوں جس نے ہر مقام پہ مصیبت کا سامنا کرکے سیکھا کہ میری شخصیت میری مرضی ہے اور میری شہر کی نمائندگی میری زمہ داری ہے. آج عہد پورا ہوا، میں اپنے چھوٹے سے شہر سے متاثر ہو گئی

Nameera Fayyaz

نمیرہ فیاض

Islamabad, Pakistan

I was very inspired by the tag line of the project. Actually whenever I used to travel outside my city, I always saw a gap between myself and other more developed cities people. I always made myself comfortable to engage with them, but I experienced that people were not ready to accept me due to me coming from a small city. This particular programme made me recall all the beautiful memories and the working strategies for my city. This has actually helped me in accepting that the small city of Jacobabad has taught me the moral principles of mingling and accepting every single person coming from any background.

My City My   **Home**   میرا شہر، میرا گھر

سخت گرمی کی ٹھنڈی چھاؤں ڈھونڈ کے بیٹھے تو پتا چلا کے ہسپتال سے آواز آئی، مبارک ہو سر، آپکو بیٹی ہوئی ہے. تائی اور تایا دوڑ کے آگے بڑھے اور گود میں لے لیا اور لپک کے اک سیٹی بجائی. اچانک گڑیا نے آنکھیں کھولیں اور دیکھا. شاید ساز اور دھن شروع سے پسند رہے اسے دیکھنے میں اماں کی طرح تھی، گلابی ہونٹ، ہلکی بھنویں، چمکدار گال اور خوبصورت تیلی ناک یہ نہیں جانتے تھے کہ ضد میں بالکل ابا کی طرح ہے، سخت اور اصول پسند. وقت گزرتے ہی میں بڑی ہوگئی، ان تلخ باتوں کو سنتے کہ لڑکی ہے، کیا کر لے گی اس چھوٹے سے شہر میں. جیکب آباد سندھ کا ایک چھوٹا سا شہر ہے جہاں میری تربیت اور رہنمائی ہوئی. اچھے خاندان میں پیدا ہو جانا صرف خوش نصیبی نہیں تھی اس شہر میں بلکہ ایک مضبوط شخصیت کا بننا بھی ضروری تھا. ساتویں جماعت سے جب شہر سے اکیلے باہر نکلی تو پتا لگا کے باہر کی کھلی فضا میں تو بڑا فرق ہے، شاید تھوڑی پر رونق اور تازہ ہیں لیکن اپنے شہر کی مہمان نوازی اور خلوص کو بھول نہیں سکی.

یہ شہر جو میرا ہے،
اس میں مجھے بھی رہنے دو!
کہیں خاک نہ ہو جاؤں اس تلاش میں،
شہرِ زندگی میں مجھے بھی جی لینے دو!

Nadia Umer

نادیہ عمر

Lahore, Pakistan

دل کی آبیاری کو محبت چاہیے،

انصاف کا زینہ چاہیے،

تحفظ کی کھڑکی کھلے گی،

تو آزادی کی ہوائیں اس گھر کو مہکائیں گی۔

یہ دل جی اٹھیں گے،

تو شہر جاگ جائیں گے

اگر دل میں احساس اجاگر ہو گا،

محبت کا، تحفظ کا، انصاف ملنے کا،

تو گھر کیا، شہر کیا، یہ جہان میرا ہے۔

زمین میری ہے، آسمان میرا ہے!

وقت آن پہنچا ہے!

جو غاصب ہیں میرے حق کے،

اب ان کو زمین پر گرا دو!

جو وکیل ہیں اس بے انصافی کے،

اب ان کو بھی دھمکا دو۔

جو کھڑے ہیں راہ میری روک کے،

اب ان کو بھی روند ڈالو!

آگے بڑھو اور تھام لو اس حق کو،

وہ حق جو میرے رب کا عطیہ ہے۔

وہ حق جو نہ اس کا ہے اور نہ تیرا ہے

وہ حق جو ہمیشہ سے بس میرا ہے

اس حق کو جو صرف میرا ہے،

میرے پاس رہنے دو!

دل میں گر خوف ہو لٹنے کا،

عزت کے، مال کے، جان کے!

تو کیسے جی پائیں گے؟

کسی بھی شہر میں، کسی بھی گھر میں!

جس کی زمین میں میری خواہشات کی لاش دفن ہو،

جس کی بنیادوں میں میری آزادی کا لہو ہو،

جس کی دیواروں کی اینٹیں میرے جذبات کی بھٹی میں سلگائی گئی ہوں،

جس کی چھت میری بے بسی کی ستونوں پہ استادہ ہو،

وہ گھر میرا تو نہیں!

مگر کسی کو یہ احساس ہی نہیں۔

کہ یہ دل مر جائیں گے،

یہ آوازیں گھٹ جائیں گی۔

سانس چلتی بھی رہے،

مگر زندگی کہیں کھو جائے گی۔

شہر خموشاں تو کئی ہیں مگر،

اس شہر کو کیا نام دے پائیں گے؟

اس آگ میں اگر میں دھواں ہو جاؤں گی،

تو یہ شہر اور گھر، سب جل جائیں گے۔

مگر اب بہت ہو چکا!

یہ سلسلہ اب بند ہونا چاہیے۔

اس دل کو بھی ہنسنا چاہیے۔

اس شہر کو بھی بسنا چاہیے۔

اس گھر کو بھی آباد ہونا چاہیے۔

belong everywhere. We need to call this world OUR HOME. Our one big, happy city!

Dil Kay Shehar

"دل کے شہر"

ہم بھی کس قدر سادہ ہیں!

جہاں رہتے ہیں اسے گھر مان لیتے ہیں۔

جہاں سانس لیتے ہیں،

اسے ہی اپنا شہر کہتے ہیں۔

اس نام کے گھر،

اور نام کے شہر کو اپنی پہچان سمجھتے ہیں۔

ہم بھی کتنے سادہ ہیں!

کیونکہ ہم یہ بھول جاتے ہیں کہ،

ہم شہروں میں نہیں، شہر ہم میں رہتے ہیں۔

ہم گھروں میں نہیں، گھر ہم میں بسیرا کرتے ہیں۔

ہمارے شہر، ہمارے گھر، ہمارے دل ہیں!

یہ دل گنگنائیں، تو شہر رقص کرتے ہیں۔

یہ دل بولیں، تو گھر باتیں کرتے ہیں۔

یہ دل اجڑ جائیں،

تو شہر اجڑ جایا کرتے ہیں۔

یہ دل ویران ہوں، تو گھر سونے ہو جاتے ہیں۔

I found this topic to be deceptively straightforward. Mere curiosity to delve into its enriching layers made me drown into its complex web, and what I discovered in the end was what makes me as a person. I was able to identify "ME", in the search for the place I can call home. Just like my physical self does not define the whole Me; it cannot sum up my aspirations, longings and fears. Similarly, a physical home is not entirely a HOME unless I connect with it on a deeper, spiritual level. Both the physical and inner selves need to be in sync. with a place to call it our own. One could live in a place for all their lives yet home could be miles away. There are places, cities, communities etc. where you feel connected, appreciated, respected, cherished and emancipated. Those are the places that deserve to be called "Home". We all struggle to find those bases, those homes. That is why the term "feel at home" makes total sense to me now. Moreover, being a woman, why cannot this whole world be my home? Why some places fill us with dread, fear and insecurity? What we seek is the feeling of being welcomed everywhere in this world. A woman does not deserve to feel like a pariah on basis of colour, caste, language, faith, dress code etc. What I wrote is an outrage at crimes against womanhood. It is a tirade against societal oppression, judgement and hypocrisy. This is not solely about women in Pakistan, Bangladesh or UK. This is about every woman wronged or oppressed. This is about "Universal womanhood", because the geographical boundaries divide us but our stories connect us. We share similar fears, dilemmas, struggles, desires and inspirations. We are one. We belong here. This world is ours. We

پھر جب امی نے مجھے لاہور بھیجا لاہور میں زندگی تھی روانی تھی مسکراہٹ تھی ماں جیسی محبت جو ہر کسی کو جوڑ دے۔ پھر مجھے آر کینٹیکچر میں داخلہ ملا تو خوشی اس بات کی تھی کہ یہاں لائبریری ہے خوب کتابیں پڑھوں گی۔ مگر لاہور سے ملاقات ہوتی آر کینٹیکچر نے مجھے زندگی اور لاہور دونوں سے ملوادیا جب شروع میں موسیقی سے ملاقات ہوئی رہی پھر منٹو، فیض احمد فیض، ناصر کاظمی، انتظار احمد، بانو قدسیہ اشفاق احمد سے ملاقات ہوتی گئی لاہور وہ شہر ہے جس نے مجھے آپ سے بنا ڈرے ملاقات کرنا سکھایا آر کینٹیکچر کی ڈگری کے تیسرے سال میں جب میرے سال ڈر ختم ہوئے تو ہر وہ چیز جو میں چاہتی تھی۔ میں نے یونیورسٹی میں ریڈیو پہ لوگوں سے بات کر نا شروع کی۔ مشاعرے میں جاتی تھی۔ لاہور نے مجھ پر اپنی محبت کے دروازے واکر دیے یہ پہلی دفعہ تھا میں نے مرد کو عورت کے لئے کھڑے ہوتے بھی دیکھا اور عورت کی بات کچھ حد تک سنی بھی جاتی تھی۔۔ یہاں میلے ہوتے ہیں محبت کی بات تھی۔ لاہور نے مجھے ادبی میلوں میں کبھی بطور اداکار دکھایا اور کبھی بطور مصنفہ۔۔ یوں کہیئے مجھے انسان بنایا

اسلام آباد سے میر ا پہلا تعارف نوکری کی تلاش کے سلسلے میں ہوا مگر لاہور کے بعد اس کی خاموشی سے ڈر کے میں نے واپس لاہور ہی چنا مگر دوبارہ میری اسلام آباد سے ملاقات اسلام آباد لٹریچر فیسٹول میں ہوئی اس بار بھی اس کی خاموشی مجھے ڈرانے لگی پھر میں نے اسلام آباد سے ہر ہفتے ملاقات کا سلسلہ بنالیا یہ سوچ کہ آخر ایسا کیا ہے جو مجھے اس دورے ہے یہ شہر اور دو سال ماسٹرز کی ڈگری کے لئے جانے جاتی رہی جسے میں نے سمجھ آئی تو اپنی نظم میں لکھا۔

Ishrat Shaheen

Pakistan ,Lahore

عشرت شاہین

دوست کوئی نہیں بنایا۔ راستے میں چھوٹے سے تالاب اور بڑے پیپل کے درخت کے نیچے بیٹھ کر گاؤں کے لوگ آتے جاتے دیکھا کرتے۔ سب میرے آنسوؤں میں شریک تھے۔ اگلی طرف اسکول کا خالی گراؤنڈ تھا۔ گھر میں کھڑی بھینس اور بکریاں میری دوست رہی۔

اسکول سے واپس آکے گھر ان سے باتیں کرنا عام معمول تھا۔۔ جب گھر میں لڑائی اور مار پیٹ شروع ہوتی تو میں امی کو بچانے جاتی تو مجھے بھی مار پڑ جاتی۔ میرے دوست مجھے زندگی بھر سنتے رہے۔ اسکول جانے سے دو لفظ لکھنا آئے۔

امی کی ایک دوست ماسی حلیمہ جس کی بھٹی تھی اس کے پاس کبھی کبھی دانے بھنوانے جاتی۔ گھروں کے دروازے دوسری گلی میں کھلتے تھے تو آس پاس کے گھروں سے گزر ہوتا۔۔ مگر رسمی سلام دعا کے بعد کوئی زیادہ بات کبھی نہیں کی یا کبھی امی گھر کا سودا دلانے بھیجتیں تو چچا خلیل جس کے کریانے کی دکان تھی جو کبھی سودا کے ساتھ کچھ ٹافیاں دیتا تو میرے چہرے پہ مسکراہٹ آجاتی۔

۔۔ پانچویں کلاس میں لگا کہ امی کو نہیں بچا سکتی، پیٹتے ہوئے بھی نہیں دیکھ بھی نہیں سکتی تو سب چھوڑا اور گاؤں اور زندگی سے تعارف بے بسی اور محرومیوں کے سوا کچھ نہ تھا۔۔ پھر میں ناناکے گھر ضلع بھکر کی ایک تحصیل جہاں میرے نانا ابو رہتے مشہور اور تلوک چند تھے۔ یہ شہر کوئی عام شہر نہیں تھا اسی شہر سے پاکستان کے مشہور لکھاری منو بھائی کا تعلق بھی تھا یہاں مقیم رہے یہ شہر سحر ایں آباد تھا جسے تھل کہا جاتا۔ دریائے سندھ کے کنارے شاعر پاکستان بننے سے پہلے یہاں کے لوگ دین اسلام پہ اتنا عمل کرتے تھے کہ عورتیں ٹوٹی پھوٹی برقع پہن کے باہر نکلتیں اور گلی کے نکڑے پہ کھڑے لڑکے اور بزرگ پاؤں سے پہچان لیتے کہ یہ کون جا رہی۔

عجیب تضاد تھا گرمیوں میں درجہ حرارت 48 ڈگری تک جاتا اور رات کو دریا کی مٹی کی خوشبو پانی کی آواز راحت جاں بن جاتے۔ نانا کے گھر کے ساتھ ہی ایک کچا راستہ جس کو نانا ابو نے آم کے درخت لگائے کھے تھے دریا کی طرف جاتا اور اس کے نیچے دریائے سندھ بہتا ہے اور بالکل قریب ہی ایک ریت کا ٹیلہ دکھتا جسے 50 فٹ کی دورہ دریا پار کر کے دیکھا جا سکتا تھا مجھے وہ کسی کہانی کا شہر لگتا تھا۔ جہاں نئی مخلوق بستی ہو۔ یہ شہر عورت کا شہر نہیں تھا یہ مکمل طور پر مرد کا شہر تھا پاکستان کے کئی شہروں کی طرح جہاں عورت بات کرے تو لوگ کہتے بی بی کوئی مرد ہے تو اس کو بھیجو۔ اس شہر میں عورت محبت بھی کرتی تھی تو برقع کی اوٹ میں۔۔

سویا تو کوئی لمحہ چھوٹ جائے گا۔ اس کی مسکراہٹ اور زندہ دلی کا شور اس میں مقیم لوگوں کو اداس نہیں ہونے دیتا۔۔ یہاں ڈھول کی تھاپ، محبت اور عقیدت اس کے ہیں۔ کسی افسانے کا شہر جس میں ہر لمحہ کردار بدل رہے ہیں کہانی بدل رہی ہے مگر یہ کہانی ایک ایسے کردار کی کہانی ہے جو مضبوط، باکمال، اور ہر لحظہ کسی نہ کسی سٹر میں ڈھل کر بھی انفرادی سی حیثیت رکھتا ہے۔

یہ ایک انسان جو واقعی انسان بن کر جیتا ہے اور کسی مسلک سے دور پر امن اور انسان کا ہمدرد دوست ہوتا۔

وقت کی دھوپ اور گزرے زمانے کی روشنی میں لاہور آج ایک ایسی ماں ہے جس کے بچے جوان ہو گئے ہیں اور وہ ایک جدید زندگی گزار رہے ہیں اور وہ چاہتے ہیں ان کی ماں بھی جدید طرز کے رموز و او قاف اپنا لے۔ وہ چاہتے ہیں کہ ان کی ماں بھی یہ چادر اتار دے اور پرانی روایات کو بگاڑ دے۔۔ شلوار قمیض کی جگہ تنگ پاجامہ پہن لے بال کٹوا دے۔ اور وہ ویسا بن جائے جیسے اس کے اپنے بچے چاہتے ہیں اور آس پاس کے لوگ چاہتے ہیں۔ کیونکہ ان کو اب پرانی ماں کو اپنے نئے زمانے کے دوستوں سے ملواتے ہوئے شرم آتی ہے۔

میں نے زندگی میں کئی ہجرتیں کیں۔ اور ان ہجرتوں کے درمیان ہر پڑاؤ نے میری شخصیت میں اپنا حصہ ڈالا۔

"Khana Badoshi"   خانہ بدوشی

زندگی میری زندگی کی شروعات ایک گاؤں سے ہوئی۔ جہاں محرومیوں کے سوا کچھ نہیں تھا۔ جہاں مخالف جنس کو ظالم اور بے حس پایا۔۔ جہاں بہن اور امی کو اکثر مار پڑتی۔ اسکول جانے بھائی کوئی نہیں تھے۔

لاہور سے والہانہ محبت، یہ وہ شہر ہے جس نے مجھے بطور انسان جینے کے حقوق بھی دیئے اور سلیقہ بھی۔۔ مگر پچھلے کچھ عرصے میں میٹرو ٹرین چلانے کے لئے کئی پرانی تاریخی عمارتیں گرا دی گئیں۔۔ تو میں نے تحریر لکھی۔

لاہور اگر انسان ہو تو کیسا ہو تا — If Lahore was a Person

میں نے ایک شاعر سے پوچھا کہ لاہور اگر انسان ہو تا تو کیسا ہو تا تو انہوں نے کہا ناصر کاظمی جیسا ہو تا۔ پھر میں نے ایک ماہر تعمیرات سے پوچھا تو انہوں نے کہا میرے لیئے لاہور اب ایک ایسی محبوبہ کی طرح ہے جو بہت خوب صورت ہو جوان ہو مگر اب وہ موٹی بھدی ہو چکی ہو اور جس کے تین بچے ہوں اور تینوں ہی بد تمیز۔

مجھے لگتا ہے انسان اگر لاہور ہو تا تو تو بہت ہی لمبا تڑنگا سا انسان ہو تا مگر اس کا خوب صورت چہرہ کسی افسانے کی محبوبہ کی طرح ہو تا۔ اس کے بھی کئی مخفی کر ادر ہوتے ہیں جیسے اس کے بارہ کے بارے میں کہا۔ عورت کے دل میں بہت سارے خانے ہوتے ہیں جس میں وہ مختلف محبتیں سنبھال رکھتی ہے۔۔ یہ لاہور کے دروازے بھی تاریخ کے کئی صفحوں پہ جاکھلتے ہیں مگر آپ نو آباد شہر میں رہیں آپ یہ اندازہ بھی نہیں لگا سکتے یہ کتنا گہرا ہے۔ مگر یہ شہر وہ انسان ہے جو وقت گزرنے کے ساتھ بوڑھا ہونے کی بجائے نئے تجربات کی نذر ہو رہا ہے۔ جیسے انسان کے بال سفید ہونے لگے تو وہ انہیں رنگنے لگے۔۔ وقت کے گہرے نشان نظر آتے ہیں مگر اس شہر کے عاشق جوانی سے لے کے اب تک ویسے ہی ہیں۔ جیسے لکھاری ٹھنڈی سڑک، چیرنگ کراس، مال روڈ کا ذکر کرتے ہیں۔۔ یوں لگتا ہے محبوب کی زلف کا تذکرہ سر عام کیا جا رہا ہے۔۔ یہ میلوں، ادبی لوگوں، ٹر ساز، سنگیت، اور محبت کا شہر ہے۔۔ میں نے اس شہر کا نام محبت رکھا۔ یہ ایک انسان جو اپنے مساکین کے ہر رویے پہ محبت بانٹ رہا ہے۔۔ جیسے صابر شفیق باپ اپنی ذات سے عاری اور ماں کی ممتا کو سموئے ہوئے ہے۔۔۔ وقت تو گزر رہا ہے اس پہ مگر نحیف نہ ہوا یہ آج بھی رات کو جاگتا ہے اپنی پوری سچائی لیئے۔۔ جو واقعی میں اس سے ملنا چاہیں وہ رات کی روشنی میں آ ملیں۔۔ لاہور تو یوں جاگتا ہے جیسے

اسلام آباد میرا شہر ہے اور مجھے اپنے شہر سے محبت ہے ۔ محبت کا ثبوت متفکر ہو کر دیتے ہیں تو ایسا کیسے ہو سکتا ہے میں محبت کا دعوٰی کروں لیکن اپنے شہر کی پرواہ نہ کروں؟ مجھے اسلام آباد کا شہری ہونے پر فخر ہے۔ اللہ میرے شہر کو ہمیشہ سلامت اور شاداب رکھے (آمین) ۔

حبیبہ رحمان

Habiba Rehman

Islamabad, Pakistan

میں کچھ ان لوگوں کی بھی ہیں جو اسلام آباد کے تصور میں آنے سے پہلے چھوٹے چھوٹے گاؤں اور قصبوں میں آباد تھے۔ میں نے شاید اسلام آباد کو ان لوگوں کی طرح شہر میں تبدیل ہوتے نہیں دیکھا، لیکن میں نے اس کی تزئین و آرائش کو ہوتے دیکھا، مثلاً اس کی طویل سڑک 'کشمیر ہائیوے' کو وجود میں آتے دیکھا، اس کی اونچی ترین عمارت کو بنتے دیکھا، بازار نما بازاروں سے خریداری کے لئے شاپنگ سینٹر بنتے دیکھے۔

اسلام آباد کو لوگ اس کی قدرتی مناظر اور ہریالی کے لئے جانتے ہیں مگر اسلام آباد مذہبی اور صوفی لحاظ سے بہت جانا جاتا ہے، یہاں ایشیا کی بڑی مسجد یعنی فیصل مسجد محل وقوع ہے۔ اس کے علاوہ یہاں پہاڑیوں میں دربار اور مزار موجود ہیں جہاں ملک بھر سے لوگ آتے ہیں۔ اسلام آباد کی پہاڑیاں یعنی 'مارگلہ ہلز' سیاحت کے لئے بہت مشہور ہیں، ان پہاڑیوں میں ریسٹوران ہیں اور پتھریلی گزرگاہ ہے، جسے مقامی لوگ کوہ پیما کی طرح تفریح کے لئے طے کرتے ہیں۔ اس کے علاوہ اسلام آباد میں میوزیم، پارک، چڑیا گھر جیسے مقامات ہیں جہاں لوگ آتے ہیں اور یادیں سمیٹتے ہیں۔ اسلام آباد کی سب سے دلفریب چیز اس کی مسحور کن شامیں ہیں۔ جب لمبی سرمئی قالین نما سڑکوں پر پیلی روشنیاں چمکنے لگتی ہیں (یعنی کہ بجلی کے کھمبے سے سڑک کو روشن کرنے والے چراغ) اور آفتاب غروب ہو کر افق کو پہنچ جاتا ہے تو اسلام آباد اپنے ہونے کا احساس دلاتا ہے۔ مون سون میں اسلام آباد کو چار چاند لگ جاتے ہیں۔ ہر سبز چیز کو نیا سبز رنگ لپیٹ میں لے لیتا ہے اور ہر چیز مزید خوبصورت لگنے لگتی ہے۔ اسلام آباد کی شامیں ہمیشہ میرے لئے ایک خوبصورت یاد رہیں گی۔

اسلام آباد کی خوبصورتی اس کے گھنے پیڑوں اور قدرتی مناظر میں ہے۔ تو مستقبل میں ہمیں ان باتوں کا خیال رکھنا چاہیے اور مزید درخت لگانے کے لئے جدوجہد کرنی چاہیے۔ میرے اپنے شہر کے لئے یہی خواب، آرزو اور تمنا ہے کہ یہ ہمیشہ یوں ہی پر رونق اور شاداب رہے اور مزید لوگ اس کے نام سے واقفیت رکھیں۔

ہر شہر کی اپنی رونق اور روح جیسا جذبہ ہوتا ہے۔ کچھ شہروں کی قدیم عمارتوں میں، کچھ کی موسیقی کی دھنوں میں، تو کچھ کی اس کی ثقافتوں میں لیکن میری رائے ہے کہ لوگ ہی ویرانوں کو آبادیوں میں بدلتے ہیں تو اسی لئے لوگوں سے اور شہریوں کے برتاؤ سے ہی شہر یاد کیے جاتے ہیں کیونکہ اگر شہری ہوں گے تو ہی موسیقی کی دھنیں شہر میں سنائی دیں گی، شہری ہوں گے تو عمارتیں کھڑی ہوں گی، شہری ہوں گے تو ہی فن کے کرتے نظر آئیں گے۔

I have always wanted to express my thoughts about my city so this was a great opportunity

My City My Home

میرا شہر میرا آشیانہ

یہ الفاظ ایک لڑکی کے نظریات کے نام جس نے سولہ سال ایسے شہر میں گزارے جو کسی آشیانے کے مانند ہے۔ چڑیا تنکا تنکا اپنی چونچ میں دبا کر آشیانے کو شاخ پر کھڑا کرتی ہے جیسے سوئی والی سلائیاں ایک ایک کر کے کپڑے پر گل کو تشکیل دیتی ہیں۔

گھر کے لغوی معنی تو پناہ گاہ ہیں لیکن اگر اس دو الفاظ پر مبنی لفظ پر غور کیا جائے تو اس کی تشریح اتنی محدود نہیں کیونکہ ہم انگریزی میں ان لوگوں کیلئے بھی تو لفظ گھر کا ہی استعمال کرتے ہیں جن سے محبت کرتے ہیں۔ تو گھر کہاں ہے؟ آئیے میں آپ کو اپنے تجربات سے سیکھے گئے مطلب سے روشناس کراتی ہوں۔

بچپن میں جماعت میں ہر طرح کا کھلونا موجود تھا لیکن پھر بھی میرا اسکول میں دل نہیں لگتا تھا حالانکہ اسکول کی ہر در و دیوار رنگ برنگی تھی تا کہ بچے اس طرح کی چیزوں کو دیکھ کر دل بہلا لیں لیکن پھر بھی گھر کی طرح کا سکون نہ تھا۔ اب گھر بھی اینٹوں کا اسکول بھی مگر ایسا کیا تھا؟ گھر جیسا محفوظ احساس نہ تھا۔

'تعلق' ایک جذبات سے بھر لفظ ہے۔ پھول کو توڑ کے کسی بھی گل دستے میں لگا دیں، پیداوار تو وہ اسی پودے کی رہے گی جس سے اس پھول کو پتیاں، رنگ اور پتیوں میں رچی بسی خوشبو ملی۔ تو میرا تعلق بھی وہیں سے ہے جہاں کے لوگوں میں، میں رہتی اور کھلتی ہوں۔

میرا شہر اسلام آباد ہے اور اس شہر نے مجھے خزانے کی تجوری دی ہے جس میں میری بہت سی یادیں ہیں جو کسی جواہر سے کم نہیں۔ اسلام آباد پاکستان کا دارالحکومت ہے اور دنیا کے خوبصورت ترین دارالحکومتوں میں ہونے کا اعزاز رکھتا ہے۔ اسلام آباد سیر و تفریح کے لئے بہترین شہر ہے اور سہولیات سے لبریز شہر بھی۔ اس شہر میں بہت سی کہانیاں ہیں جن

ریلوے اسٹیشن تک جاتے جاتے میں نے اس شہر کے ہر منظر کو بڑے غور سے دیکھا۔ جن گلیوں میں 'میں اپنے آبائی شہر سے زیادہ اپنائی گئی تھی۔

یہاں سے جاتے جاتے میرے لئے یہ طے کرنا بہت مشکل ہو گیا تھا کہ میں واپس اپنے شہر اپنے گھر 'اپنے شہر اپنے گھر' جا رہی ہوں یا 'اپنے شہر اپنے گھر سے 'جا رہی ہوں۔

Aisha Hassan   عائشہ حسن

Lahore, Pakistan

باتوں باتوں میں ہم نے کافی بھی ختم کر لی تھی۔ اتنے میں کمرے میں کچھ گرنے کی آواز آئی۔ آنا ایک دم سے بو
'لی۔'!او سنو کی

میں ہنسنے لگی اور اپنے کمرے کی طرف چل پڑی۔ یہ سنو کی تھی (آنا کی پالتو بلّی)۔

میں بھی اپنے کمرے کا دروازہ تھوڑا سا بھی کھلا چھوڑ دیتی۔ سنو کی محتر مہ جھٹ سے میرے بستر پر براجمان ہو جاتی
اور تب تک چلاتی رہتی جب تک اسُ کی اس شرارت اور کھیل کا حصہ نہ بنتی۔

میں نے جب پہلی مرتبہ سنو کی کو دیکھا تو مجھے بڑی حیرت ہوئی۔ کیونکہ ہمارے ہاں تو لوگ ایسی بلّی کو دیکھ کر راستہ بدل
لیتے ہیں۔

مگر کچھ ہی دنوں میں 'میں جان گئی کہ میں آنا کے نہیں 'سنو کی کے اپار ٹمنٹ میں رہنے آئی ہوں۔
وقت گزرنے کے ساتھ ساتھ میں بھی سنو کی سے مانوس ہونے لگی۔

میں یہ بات اچھی طرح سمجھ گئی تھی کہ مجھ میں اور اس میں صرف جنس کا فرق ہے۔ اپنی کھیل مکمل کرنے کے بعد
سنو کی باہر چلی گئی۔

میں اپنے بستر پر لیٹے لیٹے اپنے کمرے کی کھڑکی سے اندر آتی ہوئی مدھم سی روشنی میں کھڑے دیو مالائی درختوں کو دیکھتے
دیکھتے کب سوئی اور کب جاگی پتا ہی نہیں چلا۔

ہم نے ہلسنگ بوائے سینٹرل اسٹیشن کے لیے ٹیکسی منگوائی۔ آنا اور میں 'میر اسامان اپار ٹمنٹ سے باہر لے جانے
لگے۔ میں نے پیچھے مڑ کر ایک نظر پھر اپار ٹمنٹ کو دیکھا۔ میرے کمرے کا دروازہ کھلا ہوا تھا اور سنو کی اس کے باہر
بیٹھی ہوئی تھی۔

میرے آبائی شہر میں پٹھان عورت کو 'بو بو جی'

کہہ کر پکارا جاتا تھے۔ جس کے معنی پردہ دار عورت کے ہیں۔ مطلب یہ کہ میں نے پیدا ہوتے ہی اپنے جسم پر اپنا اختیار

کھو دیا۔

سو میں نے برسوں سے اوڑھی ہوئی جھجک اتاری اور سوئمنگ کا سٹیوم پہن لیا۔ سمندر میں سورج غروب ہو رہا تھا۔ اور میں

میں طلوع ہو رہی تھی۔

آج میں ان تمام محرکات کو اور اچھے سے سمجھ پائی، جن کی وجہ سے ہم اپنے ہی وجود کو برداشت نہیں کر پاتے۔

انیسویں صدی میں سامراجیت اور استعمار گری کے جسمانی خدوخال کے حوالے سے پھیلائے جانے والے احساس

کمتری کے نظریے نے دنیا کی کسی ثقافت کو نہیں بخشا۔ مگر در حقیقت آزادی اور خوشی محسوس کرنے کا حق ہر جسم کو

یکساں حاصل ہے۔

سمندر کی لہروں کو میں اپنی ٹانگوں پر آتے جاتے دیکھ رہی تھی۔ میں ان گزرے ہوئے پلوں میں ڈوبی ہوئی اپنے

موبائل پر تصاویر دیکھ رہی تھی کہ میرے کمرے کے دروازے پر دستک ہوئی۔

وہ آنا تھی (میری ہاؤس میٹ۔) اور ہم دونوں باورچی خانے میں کافی پینے چلے گئے۔ اس اپارٹمنٹ میں میرا آنا کے

ساتھ سب سے زیادہ وقت باورچی خانے میں ہی گزرا۔

ہر بار کی طرح آنا نے کافی بناتے ہوئے سگریٹ سلگالی جسے وہ پیار سے 'سگی' کہا کرتی تھی۔ مجھے باورچی خانے کی صفائی کو

لے کر آنا پر بہت غصہ آیا کرتا تھا۔

ہفتے کی شام اکثر اوقات ہمارے اپارٹمنٹ میں پارٹی ہوا کرتی تھی۔ جس میں آنا کئی لیٹر وائن پینے کے بعد گھر کو اسٹور

روم میں تبدیل کر دیا کرتی ۔

مگر اگلے دن میرے ڈر سے پورے ہفتے کی لانڈری اور ٹریش کی ذمہ داری بڑی ایمانداری سے نبھایا کرتی تھی۔

کافی بنانے کے بعد اس نے ایک کپ میرے سامنے رکھ دیا اور اپنی کافی کا کپ لے کر میرے پاس بیٹھ گئی۔

وہ اکثر مجھ سے کہا کرتی تھی کہ سوچ کے اعتبار سے میری وابستگی اس کے علاقے سے زیادہ ظاہر ہوتی ہے۔

مگر میری رائے میں ہر انسان کی جگہ وہی ہے جہاں وہ کھل کر سانس لے سکے۔ پھر خواہ اسے اس بات کا ادراک ہو یا نہ ہو

۔

My composition is inspired by the suffocation of the tribal culture, which I have experienced myself.

Therefore when I gave thought to the term 'My City My Home', I started looking upon my town where my self esteem was hurt many times and about the other places where I got healed. I penned down what I went through.

My City My Home　　　　　　　　　　میرا شہر ، میرا گھر

آج میرا اس اپارٹمنٹ میں آخری دن تھا۔ میں بار بار فلائٹ انکوائری کر رہی تھی کہ شائد جیسے پہلے کووڈ کے چلتے میری دو فلائٹس کینسل ہو گئیں تھیں . یہ بھی ہو جائے'اور میں کچھ اور وقت ہلسنگ بوائے میں گزار سکوں۔ میں یہاں فروری کے مہینے میں آئی تھی جب یہ شہر سرمئی آسمان 'غیر متوقع بارش اور ناقابل برداشت ہوا کی وجہ سے کانٹے کو دوڑتا ہے۔ مگر میں نے اس شہر کو بیوہ سے سہاگن ہوتے دیکھا۔ جب میں پہلی مرتبہ جون کے ابتدائی ہفتے میں ساحل سمندر پر گئی تو میں نے لوگوں کو وہاں کافی حد تک جسمانی خد و خال سے بے پرواہ پایا۔

نیدرلینائی علاقوں میں ظاہری زیبائش کا خط مغربی یورپ کی نسبت کم پایا جاتا ہے۔ یہاں ماضی میں نسوانی حقوق کی آزادی کے لئے بہت سی تحریکیں چلائی گئیں۔ جن میں ریڈ سٹاکنگ قابل ذکر ہے۔ اسی تحریک کی وجہ سے آگے چل کر یہاں کی عورتوں کو قانونی طور پر آزادانہ طریقے سے اسقاط حمل، زچگی کے لئے چھٹی، اور تنخواہ میں برابری کے حقوق حاصل ہوئے۔

سوئمنگ کو سٹیوم پہننے سے پہلے میں نے اپنے اندر ایک جھجک محسوس کی۔ ایک پل کو 'میں اپنے آبائی شہر پہنچ گئی۔ جہاں مجھے پندرہ سال کی عمر میں بڑی سی چادر میں لپیٹ دیا گیا تھا۔ یہ کہہ کر کہ پشتون عورتیں پردے میں رہتی ہیں۔

Urdu Entries

Contents

(Urdu Entries)

Contents

(Urdu Entries)

Urdu Entries

My City, My Home

میرا شہر میرا گھر